# The
# Shadow
# of What
# Was Lost

# The
# Shadow
# of What
# Was Lost

## The Licanius Trilogy: Book One

## JAMES ISLINGTON

www.orbitbooks.net

Copyright © 2015 by James Islington

Cover design by Lauren Panepinto
Cover illustration by Dominick Saponaro
Cover copyright © 2016 by Hachette Book Group, Inc.

Orbit
Hachette Book Group
1290 Avenue of the Americas
New York, NY 10104
orbitbooks.net

Previously self-published in 2015
First eBook Edition: July 2016
First U.S. Hardcover Edition: November 2016

Orbit is an imprint of Hachette Book Group.
The Orbit name and logo are trademarks of Little, Brown Book Group Limited.

The publisher is not responsible for websites (or their content) that are not owned by the publisher.

The Hachette Speakers Bureau provides a wide range of authors for speaking events. To find out more, go to www.hachettespeakersbureau.com or call (866) 376-6591.

Map copyright © 2016 Tim Paul

ISBNs: 978-0-316-27409-8 (hardcover), 978-0-316-55274-5 (ebook)

Printed in the United States of America

LSC-C

10  9  8  7  6  5  4  3  2  1

*For Sonja.*

*Without your enthusiasm, love, and support,*
*this would never have been possible.*

Tacin Rada

Ildora

ISLES
OF
CALANDRA

SEA OF
STORMS

Narutav

NARUT

Deilannis

Lantarche

DESRIEL

Menaath
Mountains

Thrindar

Tasidel

Devliss

Malacar

Talmiel

ANDARRA

Variden

Caladel

VASHIAN OCEAN

N

W        E

S

Shal
Terom

N        E        S        K

Ilshan Gathdel Teth

Tawwas

Eryth Mmorg

TALAN GOL

The Boundary

Gahille

Menaath
Mountains

Ilin Illan

Alsir

ANDARRA

Naminar

Lake
Tyria

Prythe

ARYTH OCEAN

Mountains of Alai

Jais

Caldiarre

Ishai

NESK

OTHYNNE

# Prologue

Lightning.

For a moment the waters of Eryth Mmorg were lit, roiling and churning as though a great knife had plunged deep into the pool's murky heart. A dark wave shattered against a barely discernible outcrop of black rocks, hissing, spitting spray a hundred feet into the air before subsiding. The world flickered back into darkness, but the waves, if anything, increased their intensity. Another roared, hissed, sighed, even louder than the peals of thunder that followed. Another.

Tal watched impassively from his rocky perch, high above even the spray. Only his cloak moved as it flowed out behind him, billowing and snapping in the gusting wind. Old eyes set against youthful features stared unblinking into the night, fixed upon the point where he knew the gaping maw of Eryth Mmorg lay. Another flash illuminated the oval of jagged rocks; the waves licked at them hungrily, waiting to devour any who ventured close.

Behind him lay the flat, barren rock that was Taag's Peak. No life grew there, not even the hard, poisonous foliage that survived elsewhere in the wilderness. The obsidian surface was worn smooth by the constant buffeting wind; twenty paces from Tal it ended in another precipice, almost as sheer as the one he currently overlooked. Few men could gain Taag's Peak, and fewer still desired to.

To the north, on the horizon beyond the pool, the darkness was suddenly broken by a dull red glow. Tal's eyes cleared after

1

a moment, flicked toward the light. The beacon seemed about to fade before blossoming into a ball of brilliant orange flame, searing light across the wastelands and burning into Tal's head. He gasped, shutting his eyes for a moment, steadying.

How long had he gazed into the depths? Too long; the alarm had been raised and his flight discovered. A cold, sharp pain clawed at his chest, something he had not felt in some time. Fear.

"Hold," he murmured to himself, fixing his gaze once again upon the angry waters. "Hold." It was very nearly done, despite his lapse in concentration.

"You are running, Tal'kamar. I warned you against running." The sound rumbled around the peak, a presence rather than a voice.

Tal's stomach twisted and he turned, searching for his pursuer.

"I know the truth," he said quietly. He could see it now, at the far end of the peak but crawling toward him. A shadow, darker than the rest. A being not quite there. His master.

The creature chuckled, a sickening sound. "You do not know what truth is anymore. He was one man, Tal'kamar. He lied; you said it yourself. You slew him for his falsehood. You took his head and set it on a pike. You placed it at the Door of Iladriel as a reminder, for all to see! Do you not remember?" The shadow stopped, watching Tal. Waiting.

Tal hesitated, staring for a long moment into the gloom.

"Yes," he whispered hoarsely. His master's presence was overpowering; for a moment Tal wanted only to grovel before his lord, beg that all be forgiven.

Then the moment passed, and he sensed a feeling of anticipation from the shadow—and something more, barely discernible. Something he had never felt before from his master.

Nervousness.

He continued, growing more confident with each word. "Yes," he repeated slowly, "but I was mistaken. I followed the path he set me upon. I found proof." He paused, his voice stronger now. "I went to Res Kartha. I asked the Lyth." Stronger again. "I went to the Wells of Mor Aruil and spoke with the Keeper. I found Nethgalla at the Crossroads and tortured her until she told me all she knew." Now he shouted, the rage of so many years finally released, a mighty roar that seemed to echo across all of Talan Gol and beyond. "I went deep beneath the mountains, beneath Ilin Tora itself. I found the Mirrors. I gazed into them and found one thing!" He stopped, panting, face twisted in grim triumph. "One truth above all others."

The shadow crept closer, menacing now, the silver gone from its voice. "What did you find, Tal'kamar?" it hissed mockingly.

Tal drew a deep breath. "You are false." He said it calmly, staring defiantly at the dark mass. "Completely, utterly false."

He turned, gesturing downward toward the waters. A bright-blue circle began to glow just above the waves, spinning ever faster. When he turned back the shadow was at his face, filling his vision, its breath a foul stench on the air. It laughed, a filthy sound that contained only contempt.

"You cannot escape this place," it snarled. "You cannot escape me."

For the first time in years, Tal smiled.

"You are wrong. This time I go where Aarkein Devaed cannot follow," he said softly.

He stepped backward, over the edge. Fell.

The shadow slithered forward, watching as Tal passed through the Gate and beyond reach. The whirling ring of blue fire flickered white for but a moment; then it was gone, leaving no trace of its ever having existed.

The creature stared at where it had been. The waves below were quieter now, as if appeased.

Suddenly it understood.

"The Waters of Renewal," it hissed.

Its screams filled the world.

# Chapter 1

*The blade traced a slow line of fire down his face.*

*He desperately tried to cry out, to jerk away, but the hand over his mouth prevented both. Steel filled his vision, gray and dirty. Warm blood trickled down the left side of his face, onto his neck, under his shirt.*

*There were only fragments after that.*

*Laughter. The hot stink of wine on his attacker's breath.*

*A lessening of the pain, and screams—not his own.*

*Voices, high-pitched with fear, begging.*

*Then silence. Darkness.*

Davian's eyes snapped open.

The young man sat there for some time, heart pounding, breathing deeply to calm himself. Eventually he stirred from where he'd dozed off at his desk and rubbed at his face, absently tracing the raised scar that ran from the corner of his left eye down to his chin. It was pinkish white now, had healed years earlier. It still ached whenever the old memories threatened to surface, though.

He stood, stretching muscles stiff from disuse and grimacing as he looked outside. His small room high in the North Tower overlooked most of the school, and the windows below had all fallen dark. The courtyard torches flared and sputtered in their sockets, too, only barely clinging to life.

Another evening gone, then. He was running out of those much faster than he would like.

Davian sighed, then adjusted his lamp and began sifting through the myriad books that were scattered haphazardly in front of him. He'd read them all, of course, most several times. None had provided him with any answers—but even so he took a seat, selected a tome at random, and tiredly began to thumb through it.

It was some time later that a sharp knock cut through the heavy silence of the night.

Davian flinched, then brushed a stray strand of curly black hair from his eyes and crossed to the door, opening it a sliver.

"Wirr," he said in vague surprise, swinging the door wide enough to let his blond-haired friend's athletic frame through. "What are you doing here?"

Wirr didn't move to enter, his usually cheerful expression uneasy, and Davian's stomach churned as he suddenly understood why the other boy had come.

Wirr gave a rueful nod when he saw Davian's reaction. "They found him, Dav. He's downstairs. They're waiting for us."

Davian swallowed. "They want to do it now?"

Wirr just nodded again.

Davian hesitated, but he knew that there was no point delaying. He took a deep breath, then extinguished his lamp and trailed after Wirr down the spiral staircase.

He shivered in the cool night air as they exited the tower and began crossing the dimly lit cobblestone courtyard. The school was housed in an enormous Darecian-era castle, though the original grandeur of the structure had been lost somewhat to the various motley additions and repairs of the past two thousand years. Davian had lived here all his life and knew every inch of the grounds—from the servants' quarters near the kitchen, to the squat keep where the Elders kept their rooms, to every well-worn step of the four distinctively hexagonal towers that jutted far into the sky.

Tonight that familiarity brought him little comfort. The high outer walls loomed ominously in the darkness.

"Do you know how they caught him?" he asked.

"He used Essence to light his campfire." Wirr shook his head, the motion barely visible against the dying torches on the wall. "Probably wasn't much more than a trickle, but there were

Administrators on the road nearby. Their Finders went off, and..." He shrugged. "They turned him over to Talean a couple of hours ago, and Talean didn't want this drawn out any longer than it had to be. For everyone's sake."

"Won't make it any easier to watch," muttered Davian.

Wirr slowed his stride for a moment, glancing across at his friend. "There's still time to take Asha up on her offer to replace you," he observed quietly. "I know it's your turn, but...let's be honest, Administration only forces students to do this because it's a reminder that the same thing could happen to us. And it's not as if anyone thinks that's something you need right now. Nobody would blame you."

"No." Davian shook his head firmly. "I can handle it. And anyway, Leehim's the same age as her—she knows him better than we do. She shouldn't have to go through that."

"None of us should," murmured Wirr, but he nodded his acceptance and picked up the pace again.

They made their way through the eastern wing of the castle and finally came to Administrator Talean's office; the door was already open, lamplight spilling out into the hallway. Davian gave a cautious knock on the door frame as he peered in, and he and Wirr were beckoned inside by a somber-looking Elder Olin.

"Shut the door, boys," said the gray-haired man, forcing what he probably thought was a reassuring smile at them. "Everyone's here now."

Davian glanced around as Wirr closed the door behind them, examining the occupants of the small room. Elder Seandra was there, her diminutive form folded into a chair in the corner; the youngest of the school's teachers was normally all smiles but tonight her expression was weary, resigned.

Administrator Talean was present, too, of course, his blue cloak drawn tightly around his shoulders against the cold. He nodded to the boys in silent acknowledgment, looking grim. Davian nodded back, even after three years still vaguely surprised to see that the Administrator was taking no pleasure in these proceedings. It was sometimes hard to remember that Talean truly didn't hate the Gifted, unlike so many of his counterparts around Andarra.

Last of all, secured to a chair in the center of the room, was Leehim.

The boy was only one year behind Davian at fifteen, but the vulnerability of his position made him look much younger. Leehim's dark-brown hair hung limply over his eyes, and his head was bowed and motionless. At first Davian thought he must be unconscious.

Then he noticed Leehim's hands. Even tied firmly behind his back, they were trembling.

Talean sighed as the door clicked shut. "It seems we're ready, then," he said quietly. He exchanged glances with Elder Olin, then stepped in front of Leehim so that the boy could see him.

Everyone silently turned their attention to Leehim; the boy's gaze was now focused on Talean and though he was doing his best to hide it, Davian could see the abject fear in his eyes.

The Administrator took a deep breath.

"Leehim Perethar. Three nights ago you left the school without a Shackle and unbound by the Fourth Tenet. You violated the Treaty." He said the words formally, but there was compassion in his tone. "As a result, before these witnesses here, you are to be lawfully stripped of your ability to use Essence. After tonight you will not be welcome amongst the Gifted in Andarra—here, or anywhere else—without special dispensation from one of the Tols. Do you understand?"

Leehim nodded, and for a split second Davian thought this might go more easily than it usually did.

Then Leehim spoke, as everyone in his position did eventually.

"Please," he said, his gaze sweeping around the room, eyes pleading. "Please, don't do this. Don't make me a Shadow. I made a mistake. It won't happen again."

Elder Olin looked at him sadly as he stepped forward, a small black disc in his hand. "It's too late, lad."

Leehim stared at him for a moment as if not comprehending, then shook his head. "No. Wait. Just wait." The tears began to trickle down his cheeks, and he bucked helplessly at his restraints. Davian looked away as he continued imploringly. "Please. Elder Olin. I won't survive as a Shadow. Elder Seandra. Just wait. I—"

From the corner of his eye, Davian saw Elder Olin reach down and press the black disc against the skin on Leehim's neck.

He forced himself to turn back and watch as the boy stopped in midsentence. Only Leehim's eyes moved now; everything else was motionless. Paralyzed.

Elder Olin let go of the disc for a moment; it stuck to Leehim's neck as if affixed with glue. The Elder straightened, then looked over to Talean, who reluctantly nodded his confirmation.

The Elder leaned down again, this time touching a single finger to the disc.

"I'm sorry, Leehim," he murmured, closing his eyes.

A nimbus of light coalesced around Elder Olin's hand; after a moment the glow started inching along his extended finger and draining into the disc.

Leehim's entire body began to shake.

It was just a little at first, barely noticeable, but then suddenly became violent as his muscles started to spasm. Talean gently put his hand on Leehim's shoulder, steadying the boy so his chair didn't topple.

Elder Olin removed his finger from the disc after a few more seconds, but Leehim continued to convulse. Bile rose in Davian's throat as dark lines began to creep outward from Leehim's eyes, ugly black veins crawling across his face and leaching the color from his skin. A disfigurement that would be with Leehim for the rest of his life.

Then the boy went limp, and it was over.

Talean made sure Leehim was breathing, then helped Elder Olin untie him. "Poor lad probably won't even remember getting caught," he said softly. He hesitated, then glanced over at Elder Seandra, who was still staring hollowly at Leehim's slumped form. "I'm sorry it came to this—I know you liked the lad. When he wakes up I'll give him some food and a few coins before I send him on his way."

Seandra was silent for a moment, then nodded. "Thank you, Administrator," she said quietly. "I appreciate that."

Davian looked up as Elder Olin finished what he was doing and came to stand in front of the boys.

"Are you all right?" he asked, the question clearly aimed at Davian more than Wirr.

Davian swallowed, emotions churning, but nodded. "Yes," he lied.

The Elder gave his shoulder a reassuring squeeze. "Thank you for being here tonight. I know it can't have been easy." He nodded to the door. "Now. Both of you should go and get some rest."

Davian and Wirr inclined their heads in assent, giving Leehim's limp form one last glance before exiting the Administrator's office.

Wirr rubbed his forehead tiredly as they walked. "Want some company for a few minutes? There's no chance I'm going straight to sleep after that."

Davian nodded. "You and me both."

They made their way back to the North Tower in thoughtful, troubled silence.

❦

Once back in Davian's room both boys sat, neither speaking for a time.

Finally Wirr stirred, expression sympathetic as he looked across at his friend. "Are you really all right?"

Davian hesitated for a moment, still trying to sort through the maelstrom of emotions he'd been struggling with for the past several minutes. Eventually he just shrugged.

"At least I know what I have to look forward to," he said wryly, doing his best not to let his voice shake.

Wirr grimaced, then gave him a hard look. "Don't say that, Dav. There's still time."

"Still time?" Normally Davian would have forced a smile and taken the encouragement, but tonight it rang too false for him to let it go. "The Festival of Ravens is in three weeks, Wirr. Three weeks until the Trials, and if I can't use Essence before then, I end up the same way as Leehim. A Shadow." He shook his head, despair thick in his voice. "It's been three *years* since I got the El-cursed Mark, and I haven't been able to do so much as touch Essence since then. I'm not sure there's even anything left for me to try."

"That doesn't mean you should just give up," observed Wirr.

Davian hesitated, then looked at his friend in frustration. "Can you honestly tell me that you think I'm going to pass the Trials?"

Wirr stiffened. "Dav, that's hardly fair."

"Then you don't think I will?" pressed Davian.

Wirr scowled. "Fine." He composed himself, leaning forward and looking Davian in the eye. "I think you're going to pass the Trials."

His tone was full of conviction, but it didn't stop Davian from seeing the dark, smoke-like tendrils escaping Wirr's mouth.

"Told you," Davian said quietly.

Wirr glared at him, then sighed. "Fates, I hate that ability of yours sometimes," he said, shaking his head. "Look—I *do* believe there's a chance. And while there's a chance, you'd be foolish not to try everything you can. You know that."

Wirr wasn't lying this time, and Davian felt a stab of guilt at having put his friend in such an awkward position. He rubbed his forehead, exhaling heavily.

"Sorry. You're right. That wasn't fair," he admitted, taking a deep breath and forcing his swirling emotions to settle a little. "I know you're only trying to help. And I'm not giving up...I'm just running out of ideas. I've read every book on the Gift that we have, tried every mental technique. The Elders all say my academic understanding is flawless. I don't know what else I can do."

Wirr inclined his head. "Nothing to be sorry for, Dav. We'll think of something."

There was silence for a few moments, and Davian hesitated. "I know we've talked about this before...but maybe if I just told one of the Elders what I can see when someone's lying, they could help." He swallowed, unable to look Wirr in the eye. "Maybe we're wrong about how they would react. Maybe they know something we don't. It *is* different from being able to Read someone, you know."

Wirr considered the statement for a few seconds, then shook his head. "It's not different enough. Not to the Elders, and certainly not to Administration if they ever found out." He stared at his friend sympathetically. "Fates know I don't want to see you become a Shadow, Dav, but that's nothing compared to what would happen if anyone heard even a whisper of what you can do. If it even crosses their minds that you can Read someone, they'll call you an Augur—and the Treaty's pretty clear on what happens next. The Elders may love you, but in that scenario, they'd still turn you in to Administration in a heartbeat."

Davian scowled, but eventually nodded. They'd had this conversation many times, and it always ended the same way. Wirr was right, and they both knew it.

"Back to studying, then, I suppose," said Davian, glancing over at the jumble of books on his desk.

Wirr frowned as he followed Davian's gaze. "Did it ever occur to you that you're just pushing yourself too hard, Dav? I know you're worried, but exhaustion isn't going to help."

"I need to make use of what time I have," Davian observed, his tone dry.

"But if you ever want to use Essence, you need to sleep more than an hour or two each night, too. It's no wonder you can't do so much as light a candle; you're probably draining your Reserve just by staying awake for so long."

Davian gestured tiredly. He'd heard this theory from plenty of concerned people over the past few weeks, but it was the first time Wirr had brought it up. The trouble was, he knew it was true—when a Gifted pushed their body past its limits they instinctively drew Essence from their Reserve, using it to fuel their body in place of sleep. And if he was draining his Reserve to stay awake, his efforts to access the Essence contained within were doomed to failure.

Still, three years of keeping sensible hours had done nothing to solve his problem. Whatever prevented him from using the Gift, it ran deeper than a lack of sleep.

Wirr watched him for a few moments, then sighed, getting slowly to his feet. "Anyway—regardless of whether you plan to sleep, *I* certainly do. Elder Caen expects me to be able to identify the major motivations of at least half the Assembly, and I have a session with her tomorrow." He glanced out the window. "In a few hours, actually."

"You don't sleep *during* those extra lessons on politics? I just assumed that was why you took them." Davian summoned a weary smile to show he was joking. "You're right, though. Thanks for the company, Wirr. I'll see you at lunch."

Davian waited until Wirr had left, then reluctantly considered the title of the next book he had laid aside for study. *Principles of Draw and Regeneration*. He'd read it a few weeks earlier, but maybe he'd missed something. There had to be *some* reason he couldn't access Essence, something he hadn't understood.

The Elders thought it was a block, that he was subconsciously resisting his power because of his first experience with it, the day he'd received his scar. Davian was doubtful, though; that pain had long since faded. And he knew that if he really was an Augur, that fact in itself could well be causing the issue… but information on Andarra's former leaders was so hard to find, nowadays, that there was little point even thinking about the possibility.

Besides—perhaps it was simply technique. Perhaps if he read enough about the nature of the Gift, he could still gain sufficient insight to overcome the problem.

Despite his resolve, now that he was alone again he found the words on the cover blurring in front of him, and his jaws cracking open unbidden for a yawn. Perhaps Wirr was right about one thing. Exhaustion wasn't going to help.

Reluctantly he stood up, leaned over, and extinguished the lamp.

He settled into his bed, staring up into the darkness. His mind still churned. Despite his tiredness, despite the late hour, it was some time before he slept.

# Chapter 2

Davian awoke with a start.

There was a moment of silence, then the sound that had woken him—an insistent knocking at the door—came again. He looked around blearily, the fog of sleep not yet departed. What time was it? The distant chatter of voices from the courtyard below indicated that lessons had already begun for the day. Motes of dust drifted lazily through the light that streamed in through the still-open window; from the angle he realized it must be at least midmorning, if not later.

Muttering a curse under his breath, Davian flung himself to his feet. He usually woke at dawn and had trusted his body to keep to that schedule, but apparently he had deprived it of sleep for one too many nights in a row. The knocking came again; hurriedly throwing on some clothes, he stumbled over to the door and opened it.

The girl waiting outside had blond hair hanging loose around her shoulders, and the recent good weather had left her with the faintest smattering of freckles high on her cheeks. She smiled at him, a guileless expression, and amusement danced in her sea-green eyes.

"Hello, Ash," Davian said awkwardly, suddenly aware of his disheveled appearance.

"Morning, Dav. You look…"

"I know." He raked through his thick, unruly black hair with his fingers, but he knew it would make little difference. "Apparently I overslept."

"Apparently you did. Quite a bit," said Asha, with a brief, meaningful glance toward the window. Then, after a careful examination of the hallway to make sure they were truly alone, she lowered her voice. "Mistress Alita's been keeping me on the run this morning, but I came as soon as I had an excuse." Her smile faded. "I heard about Leehim."

The memory of the previous night came crashing back into Davian; it must have shown in his expression because Asha stepped forward, eyes suddenly soft with sympathy and concern. "Are you all right?"

"I am." It was a lie; he actually felt a renewed flood of fear as he remembered Leehim's convulsing form, the black veins crawling their way across the other boy's face. Still, he wasn't about to admit any of that to Asha. "It was nothing I hadn't seen before. It just...reminded me how close the Trials are, I suppose."

Asha grimaced at that but nodded, saying nothing.

Davian's chest tightened a little as he watched her. As the last few months had flown by, he'd faced plenty of fears about becoming a Shadow. It had been only recently, though, that he'd realized that never being able to see Asha again was far and away the worst of them. That their friendship of the past couple of years had developed into something more, at least for him.

But he couldn't say anything. Not now. It would only make the next few weeks harder on both of them, regardless of whether Asha felt the same way.

There was silence for a few moments; Davian glanced at the angle of the sun, which was high enough now that it barely came through his east-facing window. "I'll tell you the full story later," he promised, suddenly remembering that he had other responsibilities. He forced a smile as he spoke, trying to sound cheerful. "I'm supposed to be getting supplies from Caladel today."

"You were supposed to be getting supplies from Caladel two or three hours ago," corrected Asha. "Actually—I don't want to make your day any worse, but that's why I'm here. Mistress Alita's realized that you haven't been by to get the list of things she needs bought."

Davian groaned. "What did she say?" Mistress Alita took students' shirking of their responsibilities more seriously than any of the Elders. Worse, since she'd all but raised Davian, any sign of his avoiding his tasks was considered by the head cook to be a personal affront.

Asha shrugged. "You know—the usual. Something about you, boiling water, and that large knife she keeps hanging by the bench. It was too detailed to remember all of it." She gave him a rueful smile. "I'm sure she'll be happy to repeat it for you, though."

"Wonderful." Davian paused. "I don't suppose you could... omit...that I overslept, when you speak to her?"

"She's going to ask."

"Lie." Davian raised an eyebrow. "I meant lie."

Asha gave him a look of mock surprise. "You of all people..."

Davian sighed, repressing a smile. "I'd owe you one."

"Another one," Asha corrected him.

Davian narrowed his eyes, but this time couldn't help grinning. "Thanks, Ash."

Once Asha had vanished down the stairs he shut the door again, his mood improved. As little as he was looking forward to a tongue-lashing from Mistress Alita—and as heavily as the memory of last night was beginning to weigh on him again—waking up to a visit from Asha was far from a bad start to the day.

He stood in front of the mirror, taking a few minutes to rub the sleep from his eyes, straighten his clothes, and rake his fingers through his hair until it sat in a vaguely respectable state. The Elders insisted upon anyone going outside the school walls appearing presentable. He was already late, so there was no point worsening his lecture by rushing off and looking disheveled into the bargain.

Finally satisfied with his appearance, Davian hurried down the spiral staircase of the North Tower and into the inner courtyard of the castle. A group of younger students were gathered around Elder Jarras at the far wall, some of them giggling at a story he was telling them. Davian watched as the thick-bearded man made a deliberately overdramatic sweeping gesture with his deep red Gifted's cloak, his eyes widening comically, sending the children into more peals of laughter. Davian smiled. Everyone liked Jarras.

He moved on, hurrying through a narrow breezeway to the back entrance of the kitchen. Most of the students used the main door from the dining area, but he'd been a serving boy here long before becoming a student, and a lifetime of habit was hard to break.

He slipped inside as quietly as possible, taking in the familiar sensations. The heat from the fireplace as a pot boiled busily above crackling flames. The smells of various spices mingling together. The cheerful chatter from Tori and Gunder, a cook and her apprentice, their backs facing him as they chopped away at some vegetables. Even after three years, this felt more like home than his room in the tower ever had.

He hesitated; Mistress Alita was nowhere to be seen. Tori, a middle-aged, dowdy woman who had always spoiled him before he had discovered he was Gifted, finally noticed that someone had entered. She glanced away again when she realized who it was. Her conversation with Gunder died within seconds as the teenage boy saw, too.

Davian flushed, as always feeling as if he were intruding. Gunder and Davian had been apprentices together, had shared a room until Davian's abilities were uncovered. Now they were strangers. The servants here might work for the Gifted, but the war had left too many scars for them to look past what their employers were. What *he* was.

Sometimes he caught the familiar faces looking at him, a kind of sad accusation in their eyes. As if he had betrayed them, chosen this path rather than been pushed down it.

Davian forced himself to ignore the stares today, eyes darting around the room for the slip of paper that would tell him what was needed from town. If he could just find that list and leave before Mistress Alita returned...

"Is this what you're looking for?"

The familiar voice came from behind him. His heart sank as he turned to see the head cook standing with a frown plastered across her face, waving the list at him.

Davian winced. "Sorry," he said, abashed.

The portly woman shook her head in irritation. "Don't apologize to me. The Elders are the ones whose plates will be empty at lunch. I'll be sure to let them know who to speak to when they ask why."

Mistress Alita appeared set to launch into one of her tirades when she suddenly stopped, eyes narrowing as she examined his appearance. "You look tired." She was clearly still displeased with him, but there was a question in her voice now. "I haven't laid eyes on you in days."

Davian glanced over toward Tori and Gunder, but they had both returned to their task and were talking between themselves. Students were not supposed to speak to non-Gifted about their training, but he and Mistress Alita regularly flouted that rule. She had looked after him for years after he'd been left to the school's care as an infant. She had a right to know at least a little of what was going on in his life.

"The Trials are soon," he said quietly by way of explanation.

The head cook's brow furrowed, and she lowered her voice so that it would not carry to the others. "No progress?" Her frown deepened as she studied his face. "You're still not sure if you can pass?"

Davian bit his lip. He didn't want to give Mistress Alita cause for concern. "It's...still a risk," he said, keeping his tone carefully neutral.

"But you're worried." It was a statement rather than a question. She knew him too well.

Davian hesitated. "Terrified," he admitted softly.

Mistress Alita gave him a sympathetic smile, placing a hand on his shoulder in a maternal manner and giving it a light squeeze. "El doesn't give us burdens we can't carry, Davian. Always remember that."

"I will." Davian nodded, but the words didn't make him feel any better. Mistress Alita had tried raising him as an adherent of the Old Religion, but everyone knew that all confidence in El and his Grand Design had died along with the Augurs twenty years earlier. Davian—like most people in Andarra now—couldn't bring himself to believe in something that had been so clearly disproven. Still, Mistress Alita was devout, and he had always respected that.

The head cook pressed the slip of paper and a few heavy coins into his palm, then gave him a light but firm cuff to the back of the head with her other hand, her usual grumpy exterior reasserting itself. "Now get moving; Administrator Talean is expecting you. And if this happens again, I'll be thinking up a proper punishment, Trials or no." She leaned forward, lowering her voice conspiratorially. "And it won't involve Asha waking you up next time, either. I think you'd enjoy that a little too much."

She sent him on his way with a gentle push, leaving him blushing in surprise.

He chewed his lip as he walked. Were his feelings becoming so obvious? Asha spent plenty of time around the kitchens; whatever Mistress Alita suspected, he just hoped she would be tactful enough not to say anything.

He headed toward the Administrator's office. The courtyard was quiet now; Jarras and his class had vanished. A couple of younger students were sparring to the side, overseen by a still-somber-looking Elder Seandra, but otherwise there was no sign of movement.

Davian paused for a moment to watch the bout. Despite his best efforts, jealousy stabbed at him as whip-thin tongues of light periodically lashed out from the students' hands, flicking toward the other before being met by bright, rippling shields of Essence, energy crackling as the two forces collided.

He examined the contest analytically. The children—they could not have been older than twelve—seemed about equal in strength, but Davian could immediately see the smaller one's shield was better formed, more complete. Even as he watched, a sliver of bright Essence pierced the taller one's shield and touched him on the arm, making the boy yelp in surprised pain. The match would soon be over.

Davian tore his eyes away and kept walking, pushing down the frustration he felt every time he saw the Gift being used. Move on. Get his chores done quickly, then try again. There was nothing more he could do.

His stomach twisted as he approached the Administrator's office, the memory of last night still fresh in his mind. The door to Talean's office was ajar but as Davian moved to knock, he heard low voices coming from inside—one of which he didn't recognize. That was unusual in the small, close-knit school, enough so that it made him pause.

"So you understand our true purpose here?" the unfamiliar voice was asking.

There was silence for a few moments, then, "You've come for the boy." It was Talean.

"We have. The Northwarden thought it was time."

Davian frowned. The Northwarden—the king's brother and head of the Administrators? What were they talking about?

Talean spoke again. "I would hope so. I heard about the school at Arris."

"Dasari was hit, too." A different stranger's voice this time, a woman's, her tone grim. "A hundred or so dead, and no one saw anything."

Talean let out a long breath. "I am sorry to hear that."

There was a grunt, evidently from someone dubious about the Administrator's sincerity. "Tell me. What are your defenses like here?"

"Three guards at the gate at all times. Usually an Elder and two senior students, or three students if need be. The castle walls are warded; if anyone tries to scale them, the Elders know immediately." There was a pause. "You think there should be more?"

"Perhaps," came the first stranger's voice, sounding unimpressed. "It should suffice for now."

"That's good." A pause. "So do you think it's Hunters, then? I heard that—"

There was a scuffling of feet too close for Davian's comfort, right by the door. He darted away. Whatever that conversation had been about, it hadn't been meant for his ears, and it sounded far too serious for him to simply interrupt.

He walked around the hallways for a few minutes, uneasy as he puzzled over what he'd heard. Schools had been attacked? He knew it happened every so often—Hunters usually tracked and killed Gifted alone as they chased their illegal bounties, but would occasionally organize to try larger targets. Sometimes, too, these types of attacks were simply from common townsfolk deciding that they didn't like living so close to anyone who could wield Essence. But Davian hadn't heard of any major attacks in the last few months, and certainly none on the scale the strangers had been suggesting.

21

Eventually he sighed, realizing that he hadn't overheard enough to understand what was really going on. If it was something he and the other students needed to be worried about, he was sure the Elders would let them know.

Soon he decided that enough time had passed to try again; sure enough, when he returned to the Administrator's office the door was wide open. Talean was alone as he pored over some notes, his shirtsleeves rolled up and his blue Administrator's cloak draped over the back of a nearby chair. He removed his reading glasses and stood as Davian came to a halt in front of the desk.

"Ah, so Mistress Alita finally found you. I see you're still in one piece," he said with a hint of amusement.

The corners of Davian's mouth turned upward; he was relieved that Talean was not going to dwell on the events of last night with him. "I'll wait until everyone finds out why there's no midday meal before I celebrate," he said drily.

Talean grinned. "Probably wise." He gestured for Davian to follow him over to a chest of drawers in the corner, the motion revealing the tattoo on his bare right forearm. Davian repressed a shudder, as he did every time he saw an Administrator's Mark. It was the same as his own—a circle surrounding a man, woman and child—but while for the Gifted it was an unwanted inevitability that simply appeared the moment they first used Essence, Administrators actually chose to receive theirs. Administrators' Marks were always colored red, too, not black. It made them look like burns, as if they had been seared into the flesh.

"It's been a while since I've had to put one of these on you," Talean noted as he opened the top drawer.

Davian shrugged. "I don't get sent out as often as everyone else. I can't imagine why," he added, sarcasm thick in his tone.

Talean paused, glancing over his shoulder at Davian. "It is out of a desire to protect you, Davian. In their shoes I might do the same. There's no shame in it." He scratched his beard. "Speaking of which—I know you don't usually go out alone. I could ask Elder Olin to find you a companion, if you'd like."

Davian reddened, shaking his head. "It's been three years. I don't need special treatment anymore. From anyone," he added significantly.

Talean sighed. "True. True enough." His hand emerged from the drawer grasping a torc, the twisted bands of onyx-like metal polished so brightly that Davian could see his own distorted reflection in them. "Hold out your arm. You should sit down first, too."

Davian shrugged. "I've never found it has much effect on me."

Talean grunted. "Still. I've had too many students say exactly that, and then wonder why I can't be bothered catching them when they fall. Not a few Elders, too, though don't tell them I told you so."

Davian grinned. "Fair enough." He sat compliantly in a nearby chair, stretching out his left arm so that the wrist was exposed, along with his own tattoo. He flinched as Talean pressed the two points of the open end of the torc against his Mark, shivering as he felt the device molding itself to his arm, the ice-cold metal slithering forward over his skin and finally joining, completely encasing the forearm. The entire process took only a few seconds.

He looked up at the Administrator, who was watching him closely.

"Take your time," said Talean.

Davian shook his head. "No need." Most Gifted found putting on a Shackle a fairly traumatic experience—it could cause lethargy, dizziness, even nausea for some. All Davian felt, though, was slightly weaker and a little more weary, as if the cold metal had stolen away an hour or two of the previous night's sleep. Even that much could have been his imagination, given how tired he was already.

Before, he'd always considered that good fortune... but today he found himself wondering whether it was something else entirely.

Still—Davian could sense a cold layer of *something* sitting just beneath his skin, encasing him, sapping at his strength. The device was definitely working.

He stood, Talean still watching him intently. Davian rubbed at the Shackle with his finger, tracing the markings etched into the cold steel.

"I'm not even sure why I need to wear this, sometimes," he said, a hint of dejection in his tone. Talean raised an eyebrow at him, and Davian snorted at his expression. "Don't worry, I'm not questioning the Treaty. I only meant that I can't use the Gift anyway. This, the Tenets—none of it really seems relevant to me at the moment."

Talean winced, so briefly that Davian wondered if he'd imagined it. Then the Administrator gave him a sympathetic nod. "Of course. Even so." He placed his hand on Davian's shoulder. "By the Fourth Tenet, return to the school once you have finished."

Davian rolled his eyes, feeling the slight warmth on his left arm as the Tenet took effect. While the Treaty itself was quite complex—a series of alterations and addenda to Andarran law—the Tenets were the rules that truly bound the Gifted. Once the Mark had appeared on their skin, they became literally incapable of breaking the oaths that had been sworn to the Northwarden fifteen years earlier. Talean's invocation of the Fourth Tenet meant that Davian would be compelled to do as he'd commanded.

"Is that necessary?"

Talean raised an eyebrow. "You want me to risk a troublemaker like you running away?"

Davian gave a slight smile, shaking his head in wry amusement. "Fine. I'll see you when I get back."

He felt a sudden stab of nervousness as he walked back out into the courtyard; he hadn't had time to think about it since waking, but this would be the first time in months he'd been outside alone. Despite his bravado to Talean, he really would have felt more comfortable with a companion on the journey.

It was always that way, though. He couldn't let his past—his fears—inconvenience everyone else forever.

He hitched Jeni, the school's mule, to the rickety old cart they used for transporting supplies. She was a placid animal, and as always stood happily until the process was complete. He absently noted that there were three horses tethered in the courtyard, where there would usually be none. They belonged to the mysterious visitors he'd overheard talking to Talean, presumably.

Soon enough he was ready. Taking a deep breath to steel himself, he gave Jeni's reins a gentle tug and set off for Caladel.

# Chapter 3

The road was quiet.

Davian led Jeni at a relaxed pace, kicking loose stones along in front of himself as he walked, enjoying the feel of the sun on his back. This—the solitude—was always his favorite part of the journey. The cliff-side road had been a major highway before the war, but now it was all but abandoned; the cobblestones were cracked and crumbling where nature had taken its course, and weeds sprouted anywhere they could get a foothold. It was still easily the shortest route north for anyone living in town, but it also passed within a hundred feet of the school. Only the Gifted used it anymore.

Soon enough, though, he rounded a curve in the road and the picturesque township of Caladel came into view, nestled between the sparkling coastline and surrounding hills.

He sighed.

Davian was avoided as he made his way down into the streets, Jeni and cart in tow. A few hawkers and merchants were out selling their wares, but none called to him as he passed. They knew he would not have money for them—and, worse, his being seen at their stall or shop would keep other customers away.

For his part Davian kept his eyes lowered, trying not to meet the gaze of the townspeople giving him a wide berth. He'd been to Caladel many times before, but the wary, sometimes disgusted looks in the eyes that followed him still stung. After a while he found himself hunching his shoulders, as if the stares were a physical pressure on his back. He hurried between his destinations as unobtrusively as possible.

His purchases went smoothly today. In the past some merchants had refused to sell to him or had demanded outrageous prices for their goods; whenever that happened he knew to return to the school empty-handed rather than cause a scene. This afternoon, though, much to his relief, the storekeepers were cold but willing to trade. Most people didn't want to be seen dealing with the Gifted, but the school brought in a lot of business—and when earnings were counted at the end of the day, a coin from the Gifted was just as good as one from anyone else.

Even so, it was with some relief that Davian hitched Jeni outside the small, dimly lit butcher's shop that held the last items on his list. He'd dealt with the owner many times before, and didn't anticipate any trouble.

"Afternoon, Master Dael," he said respectfully as he entered.

The butcher was a thin man, no older than forty, with a bushy mustache that dwarfed his narrow face. "Morning, lad," he replied, looking neither happy nor unhappy to see him. He never learned the names of his regular Gifted customers—none of the shopkeepers did—but Master Dael was unfailingly polite, which was an improvement on most.

Davian handed him a slip of paper. "This is everything."

"Shouldn't be a problem," Master Dael said as he read the list.

Behind Davian the bell hanging above the door rang as another customer entered. The butcher glanced up, and immediately his demeanor changed.

"Get out," he growled, looking twice the size he had a moment earlier. "We don't serve the likes of you here."

For a moment Davian thought the order was directed at him; some shopkeepers were willing to sell to the Gifted only when there was nobody else present to see. In those situations, Davian knew to simply take Jeni around to the back of the shop and wait for the shopkeeper to come and find him.

Master Dael's gaze was focused past him, though. Davian turned to see an unfamiliar young man—no more than five years older than Davian himself—frozen in the doorway. Even in the dim light, Davian could see the black spiderweb of veins running jagged lines across his face, outward from his eyes.

The butcher's scowl deepened when the newcomer didn't move. "You heard me," he said angrily.

"I just wanted—"

Before Davian knew what was happening there was a stout oak club in Master Dael's hands, and the thin man was advancing around the counter.

The Shadow turned and fled, leaving only the clanging of the door's bell in his wake.

Immediately Master Dael's expression reverted to its usual businesslike state, as if nothing had transpired. "I apologize for that."

"That's…all right," said Davian, trying not to sound shaken. He glanced again at the shop door, hesitating as he thought of Leehim. He knew he shouldn't say anything more. "So you don't serve Shadows?"

The butcher gave him a withering look. "No self-respecting shopkeep would, and fates take me if I care what they do up in Ilin Illan. I may not like you Gifted, but this is a business and I'd be a poor man if I only traded with those I liked. Shadows, on the other hand…" He looked around as if trying to find somewhere to spit. "I've been hearing plenty about them and this Shadraehin fellow that everyone's talking about. The types of things, the *evil* things that their kind get up to…well, some stories you just can't ignore. A man has to draw the line somewhere."

Davian kept his expression carefully neutral. He'd never heard of this 'Shadraehin' before—not unusual, as the school was too isolated to get many of the rumors that filtered down from the capital—but this just sounded like the usual fearmongering Administration liked to spread.

Still, he could hardly say that to Master Dael's face. All that would earn him was a forceful ejection from the shop, and the distinction of losing the school one of its few reliable suppliers.

"Maybe they're not all like that," he pointed out, trying not to sound argumentative. "Most are only Shadows because they weren't strong enough to pass their Trials—they didn't actually do anything wrong. It's just that the Tols won't let them stay on as Gifted, and the Treaty doesn't allow them to go anywhere else until their ability is completely blocked. They're just...unlucky."

The butcher's face darkened, as if he'd just realized to whom he was talking. His glower was the only response he gave.

Davian kept his mouth shut after that.

Before long he was heading outside again, the butcher having regained his usual cool composure and instructed him to load up his cart around back. Davian looked briefly for the Shadow before leading Jeni into the alleyway beside the shop, but the young man had fled. He felt a brief pang of regret, wondering if he should have said something more in support. It would have been pointless, even foolish to bring down Master Dael's inevitable wrath on himself. Still.

Before long Master Dael had helped him secure the last of his purchases and had disappeared back inside the shop. Davian took Jeni's reins.

A small object flew over his shoulder from behind, missing his face by inches.

He spun, startled, to see a group of boys lounging at the mouth of the alleyway. They looked younger than him by a couple of years—they were perhaps fourteen—and all wore wide smiles as they observed his discomfort. One of the boys was standing, tossing another small rock from hand to hand, eyeing him in the same way Davian had seen cats eye mice.

"Sorry, bleeder. Must have slipped," said the boy, affecting innocence. The others laughed.

Davian gritted his teeth, biting back a retort. *Bleeder*. A common enough slur against the Gifted, he knew, though he'd rarely heard it directed at him.

"What do you want?" he asked uneasily. He was accustomed to hostility and even outright verbal abuse, but there was something about this situation that was...off.

The boy who had called out—clearly the leader of the pack—smiled at him, hefting the stone in his hand.

Davian's anxiety hardened into a sliver of panic; for a moment all he could think about was waking up three years earlier, barely able to move from his myriad injuries. He tensed himself to run, to abandon his purchases in the event of an attack. The boys were all smaller than he, but the Shackle would rob him of some of his strength, and it would be five on one in a straight fight.

Besides, he couldn't risk an altercation. Administration would never listen to his side of the story. He'd be accused of provoking the attack, no matter the facts.

Suddenly there was a flash of blue on the main street.

"Administrator!" yelled Davian, trying to keep the desperation from his voice.

The Administrator paused at the shout, head swiveling toward the alleyway. He was a younger man, perhaps thirty. His eyes absorbed the scene with cool disinterest.

Then he turned and kept walking. Within moments he was lost from view.

The boys had hesitated when Davian cried out, but now their swagger returned.

"Nice try," called one mockingly.

Their leader sauntered closer. "How did you get to be so ugly, bleeder?" The boy grinned, tracing a finger down his cheek to indicate Davian's scar.

Davian turned to run...and the blood drained from his face as he discovered more of the group had cut around the buildings, blocking off the other end of the alley.

The boy continued, "It looks like you got it in a fight. Bleeders aren't supposed to be able to fight, you know." The other boys muttered their agreement.

Davian's mouth went dry. "It was an accident, from a long time ago," he said, trying to keep his voice steady. His hands were shaking, though whether it was from fear or anger he wasn't sure. He did his best to sound deferential. "I apologize, but I really must be going." He moved to step around one of the aggressors, but the boy sidestepped back into his path, staring at him with a smile that never touched his eyes.

"You'll be violating the Treaty if you attack me," Davian said desperately, stepping forward once again. This time the boy shoved him backward, hard enough that Davian landed flat on his back, breath exploding from his lungs. Then the youths' leader was leaning over him, face close to his.

"Do I look like an Administrator?" he whispered, a cold hunger in his eyes.

Davian tensed, expecting to feel the first blow at any moment.

Instead an angry male voice yelled something from the main street; suddenly the boys were scattering, leaving him lying alone, dazed, on the sun-warmed stone.

He sensed rather than saw the approaching figure. Heart still pounding, he stumbled to his feet, hands held out in a defensive posture.

"Easy, lad. I'm not going to hurt you." The man standing before him gestured in a calming manner, his voice gentle with concern. Davian squinted. The voice was vaguely familiar, but the man was a stranger—middle-aged and with a thin, wiry build, probably in his mid- to late forties. The small round glasses he now peered over gave him the appearance of a kindly, absentminded scholar.

More importantly, he wore the crimson cloak of one of the Gifted, and his left arm was exposed to display his Shackle. Davian lowered his hands, finally taking the time to glance around. His assailants had vanished.

He took a deep, steadying breath.

"Thank you," he said, straightening and trying to brush the dust from his clothes.

The man inclined his head in acknowledgment. "Were you harmed at all?"

"Only my pride," replied Davian, a flush of shame running to his cheeks.

The man gave him a sympathetic nod. "Something we can all relate to, these days." He held out his hand. "I am Elder Ilseth Tenvar."

Davian shook the outstretched hand as firmly as he could manage. "Davian." The handshake felt off; glancing down, he noticed that the man's forefinger was missing, only a scarred stump where it had once been.

Ilseth's expression hardened as he gazed toward the street where the boys had vanished. "Do you know who they were?"

Davian shook his head. "I've never seen them before."

Ilseth's scowl deepened. "Opportunists, then. Cowards and

fools. And here I was thinking that things might be different in the borderlands." Sighing, he clapped Davian on the shoulder. "Do you have much more to do here in town?"

Davian gave Jeni a reassuring pat on the neck, though the gesture was more for himself than for the implacable mule. "I was just about to head back to the school."

"Wonderful—I was actually on my way back there myself. Would you terribly mind company?"

Davian glanced at Ilseth sideways, suddenly placing his voice. The man who had been talking with Talean.

He nodded and relaxed a little, secretly relieved that he didn't have to make the return journey alone. "It would be my pleasure, Elder Tenvar."

Ilseth smiled. "Please, call me Ilseth. At least until we reach the school."

They made their way out of Caladel in silence, Davian lost in his own thoughts, still dazed from the attack. He began replaying events over in his mind, a bitter mix of anger and humiliation starting to burn in his stomach. He'd done nothing wrong. Nothing to deserve this.

As if reading his thoughts, Ilseth placed a comforting hand on his shoulder. "You're not to blame, you know."

"I just don't understand why people are like that." Frustration lent an edge to Davian's tone. "Administrators and townsfolk both. Why do they hate us so much? The war ended fifteen years ago; I had nothing to do with it. Those boys—I doubt they were even born back then!" He took a deep breath. "I know, we have to accept the Treaty, live with the Tenets. It just doesn't seem *fair*."

Ilseth paused, considering Davian for a moment. "It's not," he said quietly, his tone matter-of-fact. "Not to any of us." He shrugged. "As to the other…well, they hate us so much because they fear us. And they fear us because they know they can never control us. Not completely. Even though the Tenets make them our masters for now, we'll always be stronger than them. *Better* than them. That's a hard thing for people to accept, and it's what drives them to push us down at every opportunity. They broke us once, and now they worry that if they don't keep at it, we will rise up again and exact vengeance." There was no heat to his words, only resignation.

They walked on for a while, the only sounds the gentle breeze in the trees and the creaking of the cart. Davian absently rubbed at his scar as he thought about what Ilseth had said.

"This wasn't the first time, was it?"

Davian turned to see Ilseth watching him. "No," he admitted after a moment.

"What happened?"

Davian hesitated, then gave an awkward shrug. "It was a few years ago. I was just a servant at the school, back then—I've lived there all my life. Mistress Alita had sent me into town, and some of the men there must have known I was working for the Gifted. They were drunk...I don't remember much of it, to be honest." Only the fragments he dreamed about, in fact. Nothing else between leaving the school and waking up—every nerve on fire, his face slashed open and the Mark emblazoned on his forearm.

He stopped. It had been a long time since he'd had to tell this story to anyone. He took a deep breath of the fresh sea air, continuing, "They attacked me, were going to kill me, but there was another Gifted—an Elder—who was passing by, and he...protected me. When he saw what they were doing to me, he killed them." He fell silent.

"Ah," said Ilseth, his expression changing to one of recognition. "You're him. The boy Taeris Sarr saved."

"You've heard about it?" Davian couldn't keep the surprise from his tone.

Ilseth gave a short laugh, though there was no amusement in it. "I doubt there are many Gifted in Ilin Illan who haven't. Administration claimed Sarr found a way to break the Tenets in order to kill those men. He denied it, of course, but it made little difference to the Northwarden. Sarr was executed before Tol Athian could even formally protest."

Davian nodded, a little sadly. He'd never been able to thank the man who had saved him. Sarr's execution had troubled Davian more than his injuries, in some ways. It had shown him exactly how little saving his life had been worth.

"Did you know him?" Davian asked.

Ilseth shook his head. "Not personally. He was at the Tol when the sieges began, and traveled a lot after, so our paths never really crossed."

Davian acknowledged the statement with another nod. Originally there had been five Tols—five different strongholds of the Gifted, each teaching different philosophies and skills in their various schools, filling specific roles for the Augur leadership. The sieges had marked the beginning of the war; three of the Tols, along with every school in Andarra, had been wiped out within months. Only Tol Athian, under whose governance his own school fell, and Tol Shen had endured until the end.

He looked up, suddenly registering what Ilseth had said. "So... you *weren't* at Tol Athian during the war? You fought?"

Ilseth chuckled. "'Fought' would perhaps be overstating things." He saw Davian's blank expression and grimaced. "'Hid' may be a better term," he elaborated, arching an eyebrow.

"Oh—of course. Sorry," said Davian, abashed. Everyone called it "the war," but everyone equally knew that the bloodshed had been mostly one-sided. He gave Ilseth a curious glance. "I've just never met anyone who didn't spend the war inside a Tol."

Ilseth grunted. "That's because there weren't many of us left, by the end. If you weren't lucky enough to be behind the walls of Athian or Shen when it all began, your chances of survival were... slim. Believe me."

"What was it like? If you don't mind me asking," Davian added hurriedly, suddenly realizing he was prying.

Ilseth gave a slight shrug, looking distant. "I don't mind, lad. It was a long time ago." He scratched his beard. "It was... lonely. Most people will tell you the worst thing was the pressure of being hunted, the constant fear, how you always had to be on your guard. They're not wrong, exactly—you slept light and felt lucky if you got to the end of the day. But for me, it's the loneliness I remember the most."

Davian wiped a bead of sweat from his brow; being mostly uphill, the return walk from Caladel always required a little more exertion, and the sun was now beating down with intensity as well. "You didn't try and get back to Tol Athian?"

Ilseth smiled wryly, as if at a poor joke. "Only those of us who couldn't take it anymore did that. It was suicide to be anywhere near the capital, let alone try and get to Athian. The same went for Tol Shen down south—and the other three Tols had all been destroyed by that point."

He shook his head slightly at the memory, continuing, "No—I just went from town to town, trying to stay quiet, always on the lookout for Hunters and Loyalists. And always alone. During those days, if you spotted someone else who was Gifted, you went in the opposite direction. Most of us who survived were like me—smart enough to realize that aside from direct skin contact, the Finders could only detect you while you were using Essence. And if you could sense another Gifted, it was because they were doing exactly that…which usually also meant that the Hunters were on their way."

Davian stayed silent, trying to imagine it. Loyalists—those who had supported the royal family during the rebellion, under the command of the famed general Vardin Shal—suddenly in every town, equipped with Finders and other weapons against the use of Essence. Three entire Tols wiped out, the other two besieged. Every school in the country overrun, everyone who had lived there butchered. A time when things were *worse* for the Gifted, when they had leaped at the chance to sign the Treaty, submit themselves to the Tenets.

He watched Ilseth from the corner of his eye. The Elders at the school were always reticent when it came to the Unseen War, but Ilseth seemed perfectly willing to talk about it.

"Did you ever meet the Augurs? Before it all started, I mean?"

Ilseth shook his head. "I worked at the palace, so they were around, but I never met any personally. I wasn't much past a student myself, back then."

"But you saw them use their powers?" Davian tried to keep his tone casual.

Ilseth raised an eyebrow, looking amused. "The Augurs? I suppose I did—a few times, whenever I went to watch them Read petitioners. Though honestly, there was nothing to actually *see*. Someone would come in with a claim. The Augurs on duty that day would stare at them for a few seconds, discuss, and then pass judgment. It was about as exciting as watching the king and the Assembly do it now, I imagine."

Davian frowned. "So...they didn't use Essence to Read people?"

"No. Of course not."

"You're sure?" Davian held his breath. He'd long suspected this, but had never been able to get a straight answer from either the Elders or any of the school's few Administration-approved texts.

Ilseth snorted. "Lad, what have they been teaching you at that school? Think about it. Essence can only affect things *physically*—pick things up or break them apart. Pull, push. Harm or heal. How could it possibly be used to read someone's mind?"

Davian nodded, too fascinated to feel embarrassed. "But the Augurs could use Essence, too? Like the Gifted?"

Ilseth adjusted his glasses. "Well...yes. I remember one man who tried to lie to them—there were a few who thought it was possible, believe it or not—ran when he realized he'd been caught. The Augurs had him wrapped up in Essence before the guards could even move."

Davian digested this information in silence, a flicker of relief in his chest. His other ability wasn't the problem, then. It didn't solve anything, but it *was* one less factor he had to worry about.

"So they could Read people, and See the future. What else?" he asked eventually.

Ilseth shook his head, smiling. "You're a curious one, aren't you?"

Davian flushed. "Sorry. I've always wondered about what it was like before the Unseen War, but the Elders won't talk about it."

Ilseth scowled, and for a moment Davian thought he was angry at him. "They're fools, then," said the older man, and Davian realized he was talking about the Elders. "I don't care what the Treaty says. The Loyalists burned half our knowledge when they destroyed Tol Thane. We can't let the other half just evaporate through cowardice."

There was silence for a few seconds, then Ilseth sighed, calming. "In answer to your question—nobody really knew what the Augurs could do, except the Augurs. They were nothing if not secretive, and there were only maybe a dozen of them at any one time. The only abilities we know they had for certain are the ones mentioned in the Treaty."

"So Reading and Seeing." Davian knew that part of the Treaty all too well.

Ilseth nodded. "Beyond those, lad, you're into the realm of rumor and speculation. And we have enough of that going around from Administration without me adding to it."

Davian nodded, trying to conceal his disappointment. He kicked a stone along the road idly. "Do you hate them?"

Ilseth frowned, puzzled. "The Augurs? Why would you ask that?"

"The Elders won't talk about it, but I can tell that they blame them for the way things are." Davian shrugged, trying to hide his discomfort. "Administration says the Augurs were tyrants, and I've never really heard anyone claim otherwise."

Ilseth considered for a moment. "Administration will also tell you that we were their willing accomplices—that back then, every single one of us used the Gift to take advantage of those less fortunate," he pointed out. "For the most part it's just rhetoric, taking the exception and presenting it as the rule. The Augurs were far from loved—feared, mostly, to be honest—and sometimes they did things that were unpopular. But until just before the war, people accepted them. Understood the value of having them in charge."

Davian frowned. "So they didn't oppress anyone?"

Ilseth hesitated. "I don't think they ever meant to...but at the end, when they realized their visions were no longer accurate, they panicked. Didn't tell anyone what was happening at first, not even the Gifted. Covered up the worst of their mistakes. Refused to cede any authority once people found out, and instead tried to create stricter laws and harsher penalties for any who opposed them— which they then tasked the Gifted with enforcing." He shrugged. "They were just trying to buy time to find out what had gone wrong with their visions, I think, but...things got messy after that. Fast."

He sighed. "So yes—with the way they acted just before the Unseen War, they *are* at fault. Undoubtedly. But do I hate them? No. I suppose I understand why others might, but I don't."

Davian nodded in fascination. "So what do you think happened to their visions?" Another matter on which the Elders were always tight-lipped.

Ilseth raised an eyebrow. "Perhaps I can tell you the location of Sandin's Emerald? Give you the names of the five Traitors of Kereth? Let you know who the Builders were, how they constructed their wonders, and then explain where they disappeared to while I'm at it?" He laughed. "It's the greatest mystery of my generation, lad. I don't know. Nobody does. There are a lot of theories, but none with enough evidence to give them any merit. They just…stopped getting things right." He sighed. "I was there that night, you know. I was in the palace the night that Vardin Shal and his men attacked. The night the Augurs died."

Davian felt his eyes widen. "What was it like?" he asked before he could stop himself.

"Chaotic," replied Ilseth grimly, apparently not offended by the question. "People running everywhere screaming. The Gifted not knowing that Traps even existed, not knowing that their Essence could be suppressed and dying where they stood as a result. It wasn't the glorious battle the Loyalists would have it be, that's for certain." He shook his head. "I'd been studying late that night, and it saved my life. Those asleep in the Gifted quarters had their throats slit where they lay. Even the children."

Davian blanched. He'd never heard details like that before. "That's awful."

Ilseth shook his head. "That was tragic, despicable even. Walking into the meeting chambers and seeing every Augur in Andarra dead—*that* was awful." His face twisted at the memory. "It's difficult for your generation to understand, but they were more than just our leaders. Their passing meant the end of a way of life." He fell silent, remembering.

Davian burned with other questions—the Elders he'd met were never this open about the Unseen War, and certainly not about the Augurs—but he bit his tongue. He'd learned more in the last few minutes than he had in a year of quietly searching, and he was a little concerned that Ilseth would become suspicious if he continued to press right now. Visiting Elders rarely stayed at the school for less than a week, anyway. There would be time for some more carefully worded questions later.

They walked on. Ilseth looked lost in thought, and the distraction of conversation had already done much to calm Davian after what had happened in Caladel, so he remained quiet.

Eventually Ilseth stirred again. "Speaking of changes," he said with what felt like forced cheerfulness, "are you prepared for tomorrow?"

Davian frowned. "Tomorrow?"

"The Trials," said Ilseth, raising an eyebrow.

Davian barked a nervous laugh. "The Trials are not for three weeks—at the Festival of Ravens," he assured Ilseth.

Ilseth winced, saying nothing for a few seconds. "Ah. They haven't told you yet." He laid a sympathetic hand on Davian's shoulder. "Sorry, lad. For various reasons, we had to move the Trials up this year. That's why I'm here—I've been sent by Tol Athian to oversee them." He bit his lip as he watched Davian's reaction. "I'm truly sorry, Davian. I thought you already knew."

Davian felt the blood drain from his face as he processed the information, and for a moment he thought his knees might buckle. "Tomorrow?" he repeated dazedly.

Ilseth nodded. "At first light."

Davian was too light-headed to respond.

He walked on toward the gates of the school in stunned, disbelieving silence.

# Chapter 4

Davian was numb as he tethered Jeni.

Ilseth had already departed in the direction of the Elders' quarters, murmuring something about finding his traveling companions. Davian finished his task and trudged toward Talean's office, still light-headed, scar throbbing as it always did when stress got the better of him. The tiny hope he'd been clinging to for the last few months had finally faded. Disappeared.

The Administrator stood as Davian entered, grimacing as he saw the expression on the boy's face. "You've heard."

Davian nodded, his chest tight. "I met one of the Elders in Caladel." He recounted the incident in town.

Talean shook his head, looking dismayed. "I am sorry, Davian." He scowled to himself. "And embarrassed. I will speak to Administration in Caladel first thing tomorrow, you have my word."

Davian inclined his head. He knew the Administrator who had ignored his plight would never be identified, but he appreciated the gesture. "Thank you."

Talean was silent for a few moments as he placed his hand on the Shackle around Davian's arm. "I've been thinking about your situation. I am happy to plead your case, if you wish me to," he said suddenly as the cold force that had been sitting beneath Davian's skin slithered back into the torc. Talean removed the device and placed it back in its cupboard, continuing, "For most people, the extra few weeks wouldn't matter. But for you they may have made a difference. There is no reason the Gifted cannot take you along to Tol Athian, put you through the Trials at the proper time."

Davian felt like a drowning man clutching at a piece of driftwood. "Do you think they would agree to that?"

"I don't know," said Talean honestly. "I don't know what these Elders are like." He hesitated. "I cannot use the Fourth Tenet to make them do it, though. I hope you understand that."

Davian nodded; the thought had occurred to him, but Talean was right. "You can't interfere with the affairs of the school. I know," he said. "If you would speak to them on my behalf, though, I would be in your debt." Talean wasn't like the Administrators in Caladel—or anywhere else, if the stories were true. He believed in the Treaty, in protecting the Gifted just as much as protecting everyone else from them. He would do his best to help.

Talean gave him a slight smile, clapping him on the shoulder. "Just remember that we Administrators are not all bad, and that will be payment enough."

Davian nodded, unable to summon a smile in return. "When can you talk to them?"

Talean glanced out the window. Davian followed his gaze to see three red-cloaked figures—one of them Ilseth—striding across the courtyard toward the Elders' quarters.

"No time like the present," noted Talean, pulling his blue cloak across his shoulders. "I'll find you as soon as I have an answer."

Davian swallowed, suddenly nervous again as he watched Talean hurry after the newcomers.

He made his way back to his room, avoiding eye contact with the other students he passed. Word had spread of tomorrow's Trials, and everyone knew what that meant for Davian; with less than a hundred people living within the school walls, his inability to use the Gift was far from a secret.

Some people still stopped him as he passed and wished him luck for the morning, their expressions bidding him a pitying farewell. Those conversations always died out, the well-wishers trailing off awkwardly and eventually retreating. Others glanced away when they saw him, as if they feared that by acknowledging him, they would somehow share his fate.

He'd thought that reaching the relative safety of his quarters would help matters, but he had only to glance at the faces of Wirr and Asha—who were waiting for him—to know he was wrong. The rims of Asha's eyes were red, and Wirr was more subdued than Davian had ever seen his friend. Davian opened the door to let them inside, then slumped onto his bed, the last of his energy leaving him.

Asha and Wirr sat on either side of him, silent for a time. Asha eventually put her arm around his shoulders and pressed him close to her. Her physical proximity would normally have made Davian awkward, but today it made him feel as if his heart were being wrenched from his chest.

Just like everyone else, this was her saying good-bye.

They sat there for what seemed like minutes, Davian letting Asha's soft blond hair press against his cheek. Eventually he took a deep breath and straightened, forcing a smile.

"If you two could stand it one last time," he began in a light tone, careful not to choke on his emotions, "perhaps you could keep me company this evening?"

They both nodded immediately. "Of course," said Wirr. He hesitated. "Do you want to practice at all?"

Davian shook his head. "I just want to spend some time with my friends," he said softly.

Wirr's face twisted for a moment, revealing the depth of his pain. It was gone in an instant. "Then so it shall be," he said with a smile.

After a while longer they wandered back downstairs, taking their dinner and then finding their usual spot atop the tall west-facing wall of the school. The view over Caladel and the ocean beyond was spectacular as always; the setting sun bathed everything in a warm, almost otherworldly orange glow. A few of the returning fishing vessels were silhouetted against the glittering water, making their way tranquilly into harbor at the end of a long day. A great hawk circled above them; the three of them just watched the majestic creature soar for a while, mesmerized, silent but completely comfortable in each other's company.

Davian closed his eyes for a second, capturing the image: sitting with his friends high above everything, his troubles for just a moment held at bay. It was perfect. A perfect farewell to his friends, his life. He would remember this and always think of better times.

They talked of small things. Davian decided not to tell them about Talean's efforts to help; as more time passed, he became increasingly sure that a reprieve would not come. He would face his Trials tomorrow, the same as everyone else of age. And he would face the consequences of failure as stoically as he could.

Finally the sun dipped below the horizon, and the gentle sea breeze soon became unbearably cold. When they reached the bottom of the wall, Talean was waiting for them. One look at his face told Davian all he needed to know.

"It seems I am saying this a lot today, Davian," said Talean, voice rough with emotion, "but I am sorry. They refused."

Though Davian had been expecting it, the news still felt like a punch to the stomach. "Thank you for trying," he said, doing his best to sound calm.

Talean inclined his head. "El be with you tomorrow," he said, a hint of sadness in his tone. Davian blinked; he'd never heard an Administrator invoke the Old Religion before.

Talean looked as though he was going to say more, then spun on his heel and walked away.

Wirr and Asha both gave Davian a questioning look, but he just shook his head. "It doesn't matter now," he said heavily. His last sliver of hope gone, tiredness came crashing in. "I think perhaps I should get some sleep." He forced a smile at the other two. "It's a big day tomorrow."

His friends smiled back, though he could see the pain in their eyes. Wirr nodded, and Asha gave him a lingering hug. "We will see you in the morning, Dav," she said, looking close to tears.

He gave them one last tight smile, and headed back up to the North Tower. As soon as his door was shut he collapsed into bed, not even bothering to undress.

Oddly enough, now his fate was sealed, he had no trouble sleeping.

The soft, insistent tapping at the door pricked at Davian's
consciousness.

He lay there for a few seconds as the events of the day came flooding back, settling like a physical weight on his chest. He rolled onto his side, staring out the window into the darkness beyond. It was still pitch-black night—he wasn't sure how late, exactly, but there was dead silence from the courtyard below, a sure indicator that it was at least past midnight.

The gentle knocking at the door came a second time, finally rousing him. He frowned as he sat up. It didn't sound like Wirr's usual confident rap, but perhaps his friend was just exercising some extra caution. Being caught out this late, the night before the Trials, would undoubtedly bring down the wrath of the Elders.

He crossed the room and opened the door, blinking in the sudden torchlight. Ilseth Tenvar stood in the hallway, looking nervous.

"Elder Tenvar!" Davian said bemusedly. There was an awkward pause. The Elders conducting the Trials normally stayed overnight in Caladel, making Ilseth's presence doubly surprising. "How can I help you?"

Ilseth glanced around, clearly uneasy. "May I come in?" He clutched something small in his left hand, but it was covered in cloth, concealed from view.

Davian shrugged. "Very well," he said, trying not to sound too reluctant.

Ilseth entered, shutting the door behind him. Noting the open window, he crossed the room and shut that, too. Looking around and apparently satisfied, he took the chair at Davian's desk; Davian perched opposite him on the bed, still trying to deduce what was happening.

Ilseth paused for a moment, composing himself. Then he made a few gestures in the air; streams of energy flowed from his fingertips, settling into the walls around them.

Davian frowned; he'd seen this done before. Ilseth was Silencing the room.

Once he had finished, Ilseth stared at the cloth-covered bundle in his hands. "Before we begin," he said, tone grave, "you need to know that I am sorry to put this burden on you." He scratched his beard, then took a deep breath. "There is no easy way to say this. I know you're an Augur, Davian." He paused for a moment to let that sink in.

Davian felt the blood drain from his face; he leaned back, as if physical distance from Ilseth would somehow help. "I don't know what you're talking about."

Ilseth held out his hands in a calming motion. "I am not going to turn you in," he said quickly. "But I do need you to be honest with me. It's true?"

Davian stared at the floor for several seconds, heart thudding as he struggled to sort through a wild tangle of emotions. Finally he took a deep, steadying breath, squaring his shoulders. There had been no black smoke from Ilseth's mouth. The Elder was telling the truth—he wasn't going to turn him in.

"It...might be," he admitted reluctantly. "I've never had visions of the future, if that's what you mean. But I've always been able to tell when someone is lying to me...it *could* be a form of Reading, I suppose. I've never really been sure." He frowned. "How did you know?"

"We've been watching you. Your inability to use Essence is an indicator, and..." Ilseth shook his head. "The details are not important, Davian, and there isn't enough time to explain everything. What *is* important is that you trust me. I need you to use your ability now. I need you to Read me, to believe what I'm about to tell you." He looked Davian in the eye. "Will you do that?"

Davian nodded. He was concentrating on what Ilseth was saying; his ability would do the rest. "Go ahead. I'll know if you're lying."

Ilseth gave him a relieved smile, then began unwrapping the package in his hands. The white cloth fell away to reveal a small box made of bronze, with intricate details etched into each face. Ilseth held the box carefully, almost gingerly.

"Our meeting in town today was no accident. I came looking for you," the Elder admitted. He hesitated. "What do you know of the Boundary?"

Davian frowned. "The barrier of Essence in the north? It's... old. Impassable." He rubbed his forehead, trying to remember. "It's from the time of the Eternity War, I think. From the golden age of the Gifted. So it was created...a thousand years ago? Two?"

"Closer to two." Ilseth didn't take his eyes from the box in his hands, its burnished surface seeming to glow in the dim light. "And do you know why it was built? How it came into being?"

"Only what the stories from the Old Religion say." Davian scratched his head, trying to recall what little he'd been taught of the Eternity War, drowsiness still slowing his mental processes a little. "It was to seal off Aarkein Devaed and his creatures...to trap him before he completed his invasion. Before he wiped out everyone in Andarra, if you believe that sort of thing."

"That's right." Ilseth's tone was serious. "It's not a myth, though. Devaed was very much real—not the embodiment of evil the Old Religion would have you think, perhaps, but he was certainly a very powerful, very dangerous man. And the creatures he commanded were real, too. Truly terrible things that even the Darecians, at the height of their powers, couldn't kill."

Davian frowned. "How can you be sure?"

"There were once entire books devoted to that period of history. Accounts from people living during the Eternity War." Ilseth gave a rueful shake of his head. "Like everything else, though, we kept them at the library at Tol Thane. I'm one of maybe five or six people still alive who once took an interest in that era."

Davian nodded slowly. He'd often heard the Elders lamenting just how much had been lost the day Tol Thane had burned to the ground.

"I believe you," he said eventually. "But what does all this have to do with me?"

Ilseth gazed at Davian for a long moment, assessing him. He took a deep breath. "The Boundary is weakening, Davian. Failing. We know how to fix it, but it was created by the Augurs... and without the Augurs' powers, we can't do anything about it." He rubbed his hands together, a nervous motion. "Devaed is long dead, of course, but there have been...incidents in the north. People disappearing, or dying in the most violent ways imaginable. Sightings of creatures that match the description of dar'gaithin, eletai, shar'kath—horrors that haven't been seen since the Eternity War." He shook his head. "We think some have already made it through—things that no one alive today is equipped to deal with. There's no telling what else is waiting beyond if that barrier fails completely."

Davian looked at Ilseth in disbelief. Dar'gaithin? Eletai? They were supposed to have been among the most terrifying of Devaed's monsters, twisted fusions of men and animals that left only death in their wake. "And you want *me* to help? But...I have no training. No *idea* how to—"

"That's fine." Ilseth made a calming gesture. "Have you heard of the sig'nari?"

"Of course. The Prefects—the Gifted who served directly under the Augurs."

Ilseth nodded. "I was one, before the Unseen War. A few of us survived, and we've been watching for the return of the Augurs. For you, and others like you." He held out the cube toward Davian. "We're gathering the Augurs again, Davian. Trying to fix this before a terrible evil is unleashed upon Andarra, and hopefully help the new generation of Augurs in the process. If you are willing, this will lead you to somewhere you can be trained. To people who can help you understand and use your abilities."

Davian rubbed his temples; his head had begun to ache. He sat in stunned silence for a few seconds. "Do the other Elders from the Tol know about this? About...me?"

"No." Ilseth grimaced. "The truth is, Davian, very few of the Gifted can be trusted with your secret. The Tol has been split for years on what to do should an Augur ever be found. Regardless of what is happening at the Boundary, people like me see the Augurs as our way back to restoring balance in Andarra, to stopping the oppression of the Gifted."

Davian gave a slow nod. "And the others?"

"Would see everyone with those abilities dead." Ilseth said the words flatly. "And they are in the majority. You said it yourself—many Gifted still hate the Augurs for what happened, for what they seemingly threw away. And like it or not, people will think of you as one of them, no matter how you differ from what they eventually became."

Davian was silent for several seconds. Ilseth hadn't lied.

He leaned forward, taking the bronze box from the Elder.

"You said this will guide me, somehow? How does it work?" Davian turned the box over in his hands. It emitted a slight warmth, more than it should have from simply retaining Ilseth's body heat. It was covered in minute, strange symbols—writing, perhaps, though it was no language that Davian had ever seen.

"I'm . . . not sure," admitted Ilseth. "I think it's a Vessel, though it's older than most I've seen before. But I don't know how to use it." He shrugged uncomfortably. "I'm only told what I need to know. That way, if I'm ever discovered, I can't give away anything important."

Davian frowned. Vessels were devices that stored and used Essence for a particular purpose, usually something that one of the Gifted would be unable to achieve alone. Only the Augurs had known how to make them. They were highly illegal.

"Then what am I supposed to do with it?"

"Just take it north. Do that, and I promise it will take you where you need to go." Ilseth leaned forward. "You see now why I needed you to Read me, Davian? You're going to have to take a lot on faith. You need to leave tonight. *Now.* If you stay, by sunset tomorrow you'll be a Shadow, and all of this will have been for nothing."

Davian gazed at Ilseth for a moment longer, massaging his temples again to ease his aching head. No puffs of black smoke had escaped Ilseth's mouth while he'd been speaking. He *was* telling the truth. Davian felt a little dizzy, trying to take it all in. "I need to talk with Elder Olin."

"*No.*" The force of Ilseth's response surprised Davian. The older man hesitated, then sighed. "I'm sorry, Davian, but if the Elders here find out, they will tell your Administrator. And you may have a good relationship with Talean, but if he finds out you're an Augur, he is bound by the Treaty to turn you in. You know that."

Davian opened his mouth to respond, but Ilseth held up a hand, forestalling his protest. "Even if I'm wrong, and you can trust the Elders not to say anything—do you really think Elder Olin would just let you go? Leave the school without a Shackle, unbound by the Fourth Tenet, with no explanation, on your word? Even on mine? You can trust me because you *know* I'm not lying. No one else has that advantage."

Davian hesitated. Ilseth was right; none of the Elders would just let him leave, no matter how much trust there was between them.

He acknowledged the statement with a terse nod. He was trapped, underwater with nowhere to surface. The entire conversation felt surreal.

Ilseth watched him closely. "I know this is a lot to take in," he said, "but I have to know. Will you go?"

Davian shook his head, not wanting to have to make the decision. "What of the people here? What will you tell them?"

"Nothing." Ilseth's tone was firm. "They will think you've simply run away for fear of becoming a Shadow—we both know it's common enough. They'll send people to look for you, but Tol Athian doesn't have the resources to waste on runaways for long. At worst they will tell Administration... but you'd need to be avoiding run-ins with them anyway."

Davian's stomach twisted. Asha. Wirr. What would they think? He couldn't go and explain what was happening now; even if there was time, he had no doubt that they would try to stop him.

He hesitated, then looked Ilseth in the eye. "If I go, you need to promise me you will tell my friends why I left. They can keep a secret."

"The two I saw you with earlier, I assume." Ilseth sighed. "They know of your ability?"

"Yes."

There was silence as Ilseth thought for a moment, adjusting his glasses absently as he did so. "Very well. I'd advise against it, but if it will make your decision easier, I will speak to them after the Trials tomorrow. You have my word."

Davian nodded. It did make the decision easier—not palatable, not comfortable, but it *did* help.

And, he realized with surprise, he'd made that decision. Ilseth hadn't lied once. The chance to finally confront this strange ability he had, the chance to be around people who could tell him *something* about the Augurs—he had longed for it for some time. And compared to what would happen if he stayed...

"So. North," he said quietly, hefting the cube in his hand.

"Yes," said Ilseth with a visible flash of relief. He obviously hadn't been certain that Davian would go. "I was told only that you need to head northward for as long as it takes, and that you will know exactly where to go when the time comes." He spread his hands in an apologetic gesture. "I hate to be so cryptic, but that is all the information I have."

Davian just nodded. He was accepting so much else on faith, the vagueness of the directions felt hardly surprising. He looked around his room, mind clearer now that he knew his course. "It will take me a few minutes to gather my things." He paused. "Someone will be on duty at the gate."

"Leave that to me." Ilseth drew a small pouch from beneath his robe. It clinked as he tossed it to Davian. "For your journey. Stay away from towns where you can, but you'll need to buy food, and there will be some nights where it's too cold or wet to sleep out in the open."

Davian peered inside. A number of gold coins glittered in the heavy pouch—enough to feed him indefinitely, and more. A small fortune.

"Fates," he breathed, a little stunned. "Thank you."

Ilseth stood, laying a hand on Davian's shoulder. "If you can learn to become a true Augur, lad, then it's worth it a hundred times over." He headed for the door. "Give me a quarter hour to take care of the guards, then leave. No later, mind you. I won't be able to distract them for long." He paused. "And be very careful over the next few weeks, Davian. Stay out of sight where you can. People will be looking for you."

He opened the door and slipped through, shutting it again behind him.

Davian sat for a few minutes, just holding the bronze box Ilseth had given him, trying to gather his scattered thoughts. Was this really happening? Dazedly he recalled what he'd overheard earlier that day. Could he be "the boy" Talean and Ilseth had been talking about, that the Northwarden himself was so interested in? He dismissed the idea immediately. If the other Elders had no knowledge of his ability, there was no way the Northwarden would.

He stood mechanically, fetching a bag from beneath his bed and throwing his scant belongings into it. A couple of plain woolen tunics, a pair of trousers, the cloak Mistress Alita had given him for his last birthday. He had not bothered to undress for bed; he tucked the pouch of coins safely into his belt, hidden from view. Bandits would be an issue on the road anyway, but there was no benefit to tempting them.

The box Ilseth had given him he wrapped in its cloth and then slipped into a pocket. It was bulky, but if it was as important as Ilseth said, the discomfort was worth having it on his person.

Just as he finished, another soft knock from the hallway—this one familiar—made him curse silently. Wirr's timing couldn't have been worse.

He hesitated, considering just waiting until his friend left. The room was unlocked, though, and locking it would give away that he was there; Wirr was just as likely to come in uninvited as he was to give up.

Moving quietly, Davian stuffed the bag beneath his bed.

Wirr looked up as the door swung open, a solemn expression in place of his usual grin. Davian gestured for him to enter, mind racing. There were only minutes before he had to leave, and Wirr would want to stay for longer than that.

He came to a decision before the door was shut. Ilseth had warned him not to talk to anyone, but this was Wirr. Besides, he needed to tell *someone*.

"I'm leaving, Wirr. Tonight." He said the words softly but firmly.

Wirr blinked. "*What?*" He had begun to sit, but now stood again, shaking his head. "Dav, no! That's a *bad* idea. I know becoming a Shadow is a terrifying thought, but—"

"I'm not running away," Davian interrupted. "Elder Tenvar, from Tol Athian, was just here. He asked me to go." He hurriedly related the conversation, finishing by reaching into his pocket and pulling out the bronze Vessel. He unwrapped the cloth cover and held it up for Wirr's inspection. "The Elder doesn't know what this is, only that it will guide me to where I need to go— somewhere to the north. Once I get there, I'll start my training. Learn how to become an Augur. Hopefully help seal up the Boundary again, before it's too late."

Wirr, who had listened to the entire story in silence, frowned. "You're sure he was telling the truth?"

"Yes. Completely. I wouldn't be doing this otherwise."

Wirr's expression didn't change; if anything his frown deepened as he thought. " 'North' is a little vague, don't you think?"

Davian shrugged, turning the box over in his hands. "Apparently this will lead me the rest of the way."

"Perhaps." Wirr still did not sound convinced. "And you can't mention this to anyone here?"

"I know how it sounds, but it *does* make sense. There's a reason we haven't told the Elders what I can do." Davian glanced at the door. "I have to go in a couple of minutes, Wirr. Ilseth is distracting the guards; it's my only opportunity. I'm sorry to leave you like this. Truly."

Wirr considered his friend, looking conflicted. Then he straightened. "I'm going with you."

Davian shook his head fiercely. "No. I appreciate the offer, but I have nothing to lose. You do. You'll do well at Tol Athian, probably end up an Elder in ten years or so. You can do something meaningful with your life. I can't let you give that up."

"I know exactly what I'm giving up, and it's my decision to make." Wirr's voice was calm, his words measured. "You're my friend, Dav, and this thing that you've been asked to do—it sounds dangerous. Fates, if the Boundary is really about to collapse, it *is* dangerous. I'd regret it forever if I let you go without someone there to watch out for you." Gone was the customary lightness to Wirr's tone.

"You can't come," Davian said, lacing the sentence with as much authoritative finality as he could muster.

"Then I'll have to go and wake Elder Olin," responded Wirr.

Davian ran his hands through his hair in frustration. Wirr had the upper hand, and both of them knew it. "There's no time. You don't even have any clothing."

"I have about as many things as you do, Dav. It will take me all of two minutes." Wirr stood, heading toward the door. Davian instinctively stepped into his path, but Wirr just raised an eyebrow in amusement at him, looming over his much smaller friend. "Really?"

Davian flushed, then stepped aside. "I'm not happy about this, Wirr."

"Strangely enough, I'm fine with that." Wirr paused as he opened the door. "I'll meet you in the courtyard. And Dav"—he held up a finger in warning—"if you leave without me, I'll raise the entire school to come after you."

Davian rolled his eyes but nodded a grudging acknowledgment, releasing a breath he hadn't realized he was holding as Wirr vanished down the hallway. Beneath his reluctance he felt a flood of relief. Davian truly hadn't wanted his friend to make such a sacrifice for him... but he hadn't wanted to do this alone, either.

He waited for a few more minutes, each seeming an eternity in the silence of the evening. Eventually he snatched up his bag and slipped outside as quietly as possible. There was little chance of running into anyone at this hour, but he nonetheless kept to the shadows where he could, heart pounding. The night was cloudy, with only a few stars providing any natural light. That was good—it meant that once they were outside, there was little chance of being spotted on the road.

Wirr was already waiting when he reached the courtyard, clutching a bag similar to Davian's. "No sign of Jarras and the others," he whispered as Davian approached. "Your Elder seems to have kept his word."

Davian nodded, a jolt of anxiety running through him. This was it, then. "We shouldn't waste any time," he whispered.

Without speaking further they crept toward the gate. Every muscle in Davian's body was taut, and he expected someone to shout out a warning at any moment. Nothing stirred, though. Within seconds they were beneath the portcullis, and then past the edges of the torchlight and into the night.

They jogged silently along the road until they were at the tree line, then stopped as if at some unspoken signal, turning and looking back at the school. There were no cries of discovery; the looming structure was quiet. Peaceful.

"So. This is the last time we'll be here," Wirr said softly.

Davian nodded; he felt it, too. Regardless of how their journey went, he did not expect to see the school again.

"It's not too late for you to turn back," he observed.

The corners of Wirr's mouth curled upward. "You won't get rid of me that easily."

Davian just inclined his head in response. Tearing their gazes from the familiar lines of the castle, they continued along the derelict road and into the shadowy forest.

Neither looked back.

# Chapter 5

Asha stared dully at the ceiling.

She'd been doing that for the past few minutes now, ever since she'd woken and remembered what was happening today. She knew she should be leaping from her bed and finding Davian before the Trials began, even if it was only to spend just a few extra seconds with him. Her body, though, refused to move. Today would be the last she would see of him for a long time— probably ever. Getting out of bed felt as if it would just bring his leaving a little bit closer.

Finally she gritted her teeth and found the energy to throw back the blanket; she rose, shivering in the morning chill, and quickly dressed. The first true rays of dawn were brightening the horizon outside her window, and Asha grimaced at the sight. The Athian Elders would have already departed their inn in Caladel. When they arrived, the Trials would officially begin.

Suddenly she paused, puzzled.

She'd seen several Trials during her time at the school; from her experience there should be a cacophony of sound from the court-yard outside—certainly *something* to indicate students and Elders were preparing for such a big event. The silence was decidedly odd.

The more she thought about it, the more she realized that the entire feel of the morning was...*off*. From the corner of her eye she could see that her roommate, Quira, was still fast asleep in her bed. That wasn't unusual, though; the younger girl tended to sleep well past dawn. Asha turned and was about to slip outside when something made her hesitate.

The room was *quiet*. More so than normal. Now that Asha thought about it, Quira hadn't stirred once. The girl was a restless sleeper at best, as well as a terrible snorer.

Asha crept over to the bed, frowning. Quira was lying on her side, facing the wall. Gently, Asha placed a hand on her shoulder. The slight pressure caused Quira to roll onto her back.

Asha's breath caught in her throat. She just stared for a moment, paralyzed.

There was blood everywhere. *So* much blood. It was pooled mainly around Quira's head and chest, staining the mattress a dark, violent red where it had poured from the gaping wound in her neck. Dark smears were streaked across her face; Asha realized numbly that they were where Quira's attacker had covered her mouth to muffle any screams. The young girl's soft brown eyes, wide with shock and fear, stared into Asha's. Pleading.

Suddenly there was a voice, screaming for help, desperate and afraid. It took a few moments for Asha to register it was her own. She slumped to the ground beside the bunk, dazed, waiting for someone—anyone—to come to her aid. She sat there for what seemed like hours.

Nobody came.

Finally gathering her wits, Asha forced her body to move, trying to shake off the shock that was rapidly setting in. The female students' quarters were adjacent to the courtyard; even at this early hour, someone should have been awake to hear her cries.

In the hallway the school again felt unnaturally quiet. Limbs heavy with dread, Asha moved to the next room, where Taranne and Jadan slept. The door was ajar. Somehow, she knew what she would find before she entered.

There had been no attempt to hide the slaughter in this room. The blood had spilled out onto the gray stone; the girls' heads were twisted at odd angles, with Jadan's body hanging in grisly fashion halfway out of her bed. Unlike Quira's, their throats had not been cleanly slit, but had rather been torn out so completely that the sharp white of the spine was visible through the pulpy red tissue.

Asha fled.

She stumbled along the hallway, too numb to cry, to scream,

to do anything but keep moving, look for someone else who had survived. She couldn't be the only one. She *couldn't*.

Room after room of people she had grown up with passed in a blur. Tessia, the sweet girl who had shown more promise in her first two years than even Wirr. Danin and Shass, who had arrived only a few months earlier and couldn't have been older than ten. She had comforted them during their first night as they had wept, helped them accept the difficult truth that their family had abandoned them. They had made her a daisy necklace to thank her, which she still kept pressed in one of her books. Now they just stared after her with horrified, vacant eyes. In each room there were more.

It only got worse.

Outside, the courtyard was littered with corpses. She almost collapsed when she saw Jarras. The Elder's head had been torn completely off, a trail of blood between it and his torso glistening wetly in the early-morning light. Jarras's expression, usually full of warmth and mirth, was frozen in a contortion of pure, wide-eyed fear.

Fenred and Blaine—the two boys who had evidently been on guard duty with him—lay a few feet away. Like the others, their throats had been ripped away, leaving only slivers of torn flesh and bone between their shoulders and heads.

She moved on, wandering almost mindlessly now; each room had more bodies, some of them barely identifiable with so much blood covering their features. Mistress Alita's plump figure and long dark locks lay near the entrance to the kitchens, her face blessedly turned away from Asha. Elder Olin was still in his bed. Administrator Talean lay just outside his office.

Then something registered through the haze of panic and grief. The boys. Davian.

She was sprinting toward the North Tower in a moment, all other fears suddenly pushed aside. He *had* to be alive. She ran up the steps and burst into his small room in the tower, breathing heavily from both exertion and anxiety.

A quick scan gave her a sliver of hope. The bed was empty, the room devoid of any signs of violence. Her heart began beating again. Maybe he'd escaped. Maybe he'd been miraculously left alone, the same as she.

Her fears far from allayed, Asha made her way back out of the tower and toward Wirr's quarters at a determined run. She didn't stop to look in the other boys' rooms as she passed, but most of their doors were ajar, and the splashes of red she saw from the corners of her eyes told her all she needed to know.

Asha skidded headlong into Wirr's room, having only a moment to register the three surprised faces turning toward her before a massive weight slammed into her, forcing her to the ground with her face hard against the cold stone floor.

Her first reaction was blind panic, and she thrashed wildly against the pressure. Then she stopped, breath coming in ragged bursts, too emotionally exhausted and grief-stricken to do anything more.

After a few seconds, she felt herself being lifted up. She glanced down to see coils of Essence wrapped around her body, raising her smoothly into a standing position.

She looked up again to see three people watching her grimly. She recognized them now. The Elders from Tol Athian, the ones there for the Trials. They weren't responsible for this, weren't going to kill her.

Every muscle in her body went limp with relief, only the bindings preventing her from collapsing to the floor. It took her a moment to realize that one of the men was talking to her.

"Fates, girl, *who are you*?" the dark-skinned man asked her again, his tone urgent. His face was drawn, haggard, and he kept glancing nervously toward the door as if he expected an attack at any second. "You're obviously Gifted, else the First Tenet would have stopped us from binding you. What do you know?"

Asha forced herself to breathe slowly and evenly. She was far from calm, but the mania that had threatened to take over a few seconds earlier was receding. She was safe with the Elders.

"Ashalia," she said as steadily as she could manage. "My name is Ashalia. I woke up...I don't know how long ago." She glanced out the window. The sun was now well above the horizon. Had she been stumbling around the school for an hour? Hours? "Quira was dead...everyone in the girls' quarters, too. They're all dead." Saying the words made it sink in and she choked back a sob, trailing off into silence.

The Elders exchanged meaningful glances.

"She's the first one, Ilseth," said the woman.

The one called Ilseth nodded thoughtfully. "I'll find out if she knows anything more. You two should go and look for any other survivors."

The other man raised an eyebrow. "You don't think we should stick together?"

Ilseth shook his head. "Whatever did this, Kasperan, it's long gone. The danger has passed."

Kasperan nodded his acknowledgment, and he and the woman left Wirr's room. As they did, the cords of energy holding Asha vanished; Ilseth put a supporting arm around her shoulders, guiding her to sit on Wirr's bed. "Now. I know this has been traumatic, but we need to know everything you can tell us. Are there any other survivors? We were in Caladel overnight; we only arrived a few minutes ago."

Asha swallowed. "I think…I think my friends might still be alive. Wirr—this is his room—and Davian. Davian's room was empty, and neither of them were in the courtyard. I checked." She shivered. "They must have gotten away. But I don't know about anyone else."

Ilseth drew a slip of paper from his pocket, the wax seal on it already broken. He handed it silently to Asha. It was addressed to Elder Olin.

She opened it with still-trembling fingers.

*Elder Olin,*

*Davian and I have had to leave at short notice, on a matter of some importance, and one I believe needs my oversight. Send no one after us—Davian is under my protection. Please tell my father that if we are caught, I will use the name I used here. He can retrieve us both at his earliest convenience, and I will explain matters to him then.*

*Torin*

"I don't understand," she said, looking up at Ilseth in confusion. "Who's Torin?"

Ilseth just nodded to himself, glancing toward the doorway. Then he gently removed his arm from around Asha, standing.

"It can never be easy," he sighed, drawing a small black disc from his pocket. In a sudden movement he leaned forward and pressed it against Asha's neck.

Asha tried to jerk away, but the second the disc touched her skin it stuck like glue; she found herself paralyzed, able to move only her eyes. She stared at Ilseth as he crouched down on his haunches in front of her, calm as he observed her for a few moments. She tried to talk, to ask him what he was doing, but no sound came from her throat.

"Becoming a Shadow is not so bad," Ilseth said quietly. "It is quick, and you won't remember the pain. In fact, you won't remember anything since you woke up this morning. Almost a blessing, given what you've seen today." He stared into her eyes. "Regardless, I can't risk anyone realizing that Davian got away. I would ask you whether he foresaw what I was planning, or whether he saved your friend through sheer dumb luck—but I doubt you know. And if you don't know about that, I doubt you understand why the escherii spared you, either. But still...if it saw fit to let you live, then I suppose I should do the same. There are always reasons for these things."

Asha tried desperately to move, to call for help, but it was no use. She watched in terror as Ilseth reached forward, pressing his finger against the disc on her neck and closing his eyes. For a few seconds a gentle warmth flowed through her body, relaxing every muscle.

Then the heat inside her became a raging fire, searing through her blood as if she were being burned alive from the inside. Every nerve shrieked in agony; her back arched of its own accord as muscles spasmed and convulsed. The tiny corner of her mind not screaming in pain watched as Ilseth nodded in quiet satisfaction, then turned and left.

Eventually the room, and then the pain, faded. She knew no more.

# Chapter 6

Davian held his breath as another group of blue-cloaked Administrators walked by, Finders glinting on their wrists as they observed the preparations for the evening's festivities.

"They're everywhere," he muttered to Wirr, keeping his eyes firmly on the road ahead as he walked.

"Just ignore them. And try not to scratch your arm," said Wirr without looking at his friend.

Davian scowled, snatching his hand away from his left forearm. The makeup they had bought a few days earlier hid their tattoos from all but the closest inspection, but it itched constantly. At the time it had seemed unnecessary—the vials of thick paint-like substance had cost more than Davian would have credited, and taken hours to mix to the right skin tones—but the last half hour had proven otherwise. The fashion in Talmiel, it appeared, was to keep the forearms bare. A way for people to show that they were not Gifted.

"My nerves cannot take much more of this," he said.

Wirr snorted. " 'We need to go *north*, Wirr. Talmiel can't be *that* dangerous, Wirr. You don't know what you're *talking* about, Wirr.' "

Davian grunted. "I know, I know. You warned me." He checked in both directions as they emerged into a new street, but there was no sign of any blue cloaks here, only the general bustle of people hanging decorations. "I just didn't think there would be so many, even with the festival tonight."

Wirr sighed. "This is the only border crossing into Desriel, Dav. *Desriel.* The one country that hates the Gifted *more* than

Andarra." He shook his head. "The Administrators do a lot of their recruiting here. The only reason we haven't been caught so far is because people like us aren't stupid enough to come here anymore, so nobody's really looking." He glanced around, unable to hide his apprehension. "Our luck will run out sooner or later, though. Are you sure we need to be here?"

Davian hesitated, unconsciously touching the pocket where he kept the Vessel. It had been nearly three weeks since they had left Caladel, and the farther they traveled north, the more he had expected it to do...something. Something to show him what came next. But though he examined it at least once each day, the bronze box never changed.

"Ilseth said to travel north until I knew where to go next," he said eventually. He gave his friend an apologetic look. "I just don't know what else to do."

Wirr nodded ruefully. "I know." He shook his head. "I cannot believe I thought that sounded like a plan back at Caladel."

"Thinking you should have stayed behind?"

"Thinking I should have tried harder to stop you from leaving." Wirr shot him a crooked smile, then nodded toward an inn a little farther down the street. "We should at least get inside. As many Administrators as there are now, there will be twice as many out tonight. It will be safer indoors, and it's late anyway."

Davian nodded his agreement. Talmiel was bustling with activity as it prepared for the Festival of Ravens; people hurried about everywhere in brightly colored clothing, and officials had begun lighting the traditional blue lanterns that lined each street of the city. Natural light was fading fast, and Davian had even seen a few children in ill-fitting Loyalist uniforms, the costume of choice for the feast that celebrated the overthrow of the Augurs. Davian had always found it odd that Tol Athian normally held its Trials to coincide with the festival. He could only assume that it must have held a nice irony for someone.

They made their way over to the inn, which the sign out front proclaimed to be the King's Repose. If a king had ever stayed there it must have been generations earlier; the facade was dirty and cracked, and the picture on the sign had faded almost entirely. Exchanging dubious looks, Davian and Wirr headed inside.

The interior of the King's Repose was as uninviting as the outside: the common room smelled of stale beer, and the tables and chairs looked rickety at best. Still, there were already plenty of people laughing and drinking, and the rotund innkeeper was friendly enough once he saw their coin. Before long he was showing them to a small but clean room upstairs.

Once the innkeeper had left, Davian locked the door behind him and collapsed onto one of the beds with a deep sigh.

Wirr sat on the bed opposite. "So. What now, Dav?"

Davian drew the Vessel from his pocket, staring at it intently. As always, it was warm to the touch. Was it his imagination, or was it emanating more heat than previously? After a moment he replaced it with a shrug. "We keep heading north, I suppose."

Wirr frowned. "Into Desriel?" He began chewing at a fingernail, a sure sign he was nervous. "You do know that any Gifted that the Gil'shar capture are executed as heretics, don't you?"

Davian nodded. He'd read about the Gil'shar: part government, part religious body, they had absolute authority in Desriel. "I think they call us abominations rather than heretics, actually. They say only the gods are supposed to wield the Gift," he said absently.

Wirr massaged his forehead. "You might be missing the point, Dav."

"I know. But the Boundary's a long way north; we were always going to have to go further. And if the sig'nari are in Desriel, that's where I need to go." He hadn't come this far to turn back. "If you don't want to come, though, I will understand."

Wirr hesitated, for a moment looking as though he was considering the offer before shaking his head irritably. "You can stop staying things like that. Given where we are, I think I've proven that I'm with you the rest of the way." He sighed. "Can I safely assume you have absolutely no plan to get over the border?"

"Elder Olin always said you were very astute."

"He always said you were the sensible one, too," pointed out Wirr, his tone dry. He thought for a moment. "The bridge over the Devliss is like a fortress; people get stopped and checked with Finders on both shores, even on a night as busy as tonight. Not to mention that this makeup on our arms won't stand up to close inspection—we wouldn't even make it past the Administrators on this side. So the first thing will be to find another way across the river."

Davian raised an eyebrow. "You've been here before?"

Wirr was silent for a few moments, then nodded. "I have. Briefly. Let's leave it at that."

Davian inclined his head. The two of them had an unspoken agreement never to discuss Wirr's life before the school; whatever had happened to him, it was clearly too painful to talk about. Wirr had simply lied about it to the other students, but he hadn't had that luxury with Davian.

"So we find a boat," said Davian.

Wirr shook his head. "The Devliss is all rapids and waterfalls. Wide, too. There's a reason that Talmiel is the only crossing."

There was silence as they both thought for a few seconds, then Wirr blinked in surprise as his stomach emitted a low growl. "Perhaps we can think on it further over dinner?"

Davian hesitated. "What if there are Administrators in the common room?"

"In a place like this? Unlikely. They'll be out there, soaking up the attention." Wirr gestured at the window as he spoke, through which the faint sounds of music and laughter were drifting up to them. "Besides, it would be suspicious if we stayed holed up in this room tonight. That innkeeper may be friendly, but I doubt he'd be shy about mentioning unusual behavior to a passing Administrator."

Davian conceded the point, and they made their way back downstairs. The common room was crowded; a few tables here and there were unoccupied, but for the most part everything looked just as one would expect on the night of a festival.

Wirr nodded toward an empty table against the wall, slightly apart from the rest of the room. They gave their orders to a pretty serving girl with a put-upon expression on her face, then sat in companionable silence for a few minutes, watching the proceedings, each lost in his own thoughts.

They ate with gusto when their food came; with their careful shunning of built-up areas over the past few weeks, hot meals had been a rarity. The stringy mutton and vegetables were plain fare but filling, and it wasn't until Davian was settling back with a sigh of contentment that he noticed the strange warmth emanating from his pocket.

Frowning, he surreptitiously reached down and took out the Vessel, still wrapped in its cloth. A gentle but palpable heat pulsed through the fabric.

"What are you doing?" murmured Wirr, noticing what was in Davian's hand.

Davian hesitated, not taking his eyes from the cloth-covered bundle. "Something's happening, Wirr," he said softly. "It's getting warmer."

His friend looked at him uncertainly. Wirr had examined the Vessel on their first day out of the school and on several occasions since; each time he had denied being able to feel any unusual heat. "Give it to me," he said eventually, holding out his hand. Davian passed it across; Wirr held it for a few seconds, brow furrowing in concentration. Then he shook his head.

"Still nothing. I believe you, Dav, but I don't feel anything. You're certain?"

Davian nodded. "I wouldn't bring it up otherwise."

Wirr looked at the cloth-covered lump in his hand, his expression troubled. "Then it's specific to you somehow. I don't know how that's possible, but…fates, I can't say I like it." Sighing, he handed the box back to Davian.

As he did so, a flap of the cloth slipped and the skin on Davian's palm made contact with the bare metal beneath. The touch wasn't hot enough to burn, but sharp and unexpected enough that Davian flinched. The cube slipped from his grasp, its covering falling away as it tumbled to the timber floor with a dull thud.

Davian moved swiftly to pick it up again, then froze as he looked at the now-exposed Vessel.

The faint outline of a symbol had appeared on one face of the box, superimposed over the writing. It was *glowing*—not brightly, but enough to be distinct. A wolf, he thought from his brief glimpse.

Opposite him, Wirr leaned down and collected the Vessel himself, grimacing in Davian's direction before grabbing the cloth and calmly concealing it from view again. Davian recovered himself enough to glance around at the other patrons. None appeared to be taking any notice of them.

Wirr thrust the now-covered cube back into Davian's hands. "Best put it in your pocket and leave it there, Dav," he said after looking around too, exhaling. "The only thing I know about that box is that it's valuable, regardless of what it actually does. Administration has a massive bounty out on Vessels. Flashing it around a place like this is just asking for trouble."

Davian nodded and was about to say more when he caught movement from the corner of his eye. He looked up as a man he had never seen before stopped at their table and proceeded to sit, his smile friendly.

"Act like you know me, understand?" said the man, slapping a bemused-looking Wirr on the shoulder. "My name is Anaar. That Hunter in the corner has been staring at you two like a hawk at rabbits for the last few minutes. I hope you had not planned for a quiet evening." He watched them, waiting for a response.

Davian's mind raced. He had noted the woman in question earlier—an attractive girl, alone, but none of the men had gone anywhere near her. He'd thought it odd at the time.

Then he remembered the cloth-covered box, still in his hand. Was that why Anaar had come over? Davian slipped it back into his pocket. For a moment he thought Anaar's eyes flicked toward him, but it was so fast it could have been his imagination.

Wirr gave a sudden laugh, leaning back in his chair. He waved over one of the serving girls. "A drink for my friend Anaar here," he said, loud enough to be audible to anyone listening.

Davian forced himself to lean back, too, though he doubted his effort to look relaxed would be convincing. He studied Anaar in silence. Approaching middle age, the swarthy, strongly built man had a neatly trimmed beard and close-cropped, thick black hair. His voice was gravelly, and had the confident sound of a man who was accustomed to giving orders and having them obeyed.

"So you think she's a Hunter," said Wirr, still smiling, though his tone was flat.

"I know she's a Hunter," replied the older man smoothly. "And she can't stop staring at you two. There is usually a reason for that."

"We're handsome men," said Wirr with a shrug.

Anaar chuckled. "No doubt. But even if it's just because you're easy on the eyes, I'd still suggest leaving Talmiel soon. Tonight, if you can; the festival should provide you with ample cover. People that Breshada takes an interest in have a tendency to...disappear...after a few days." He shrugged. "And usually reappear on the other side of the river with a noose around their neck."

"She's working for the Gil'shar? On Andarran soil?" Wirr's tone was dark. "I thought they were steering clear of that sort of thing."

Anaar's eyebrows lifted. "Oh, they are, of course—officially," he said with amusement. He looked at Wirr consideringly. "But Breshada and her ilk don't have much opposition here. Half of Talmiel is full of Loyalists, the other half Administrators. It's basically a province of Desriel."

Wirr scowled; that notion clearly irked him. "And you? Why help us?" he asked in a low voice.

The man shrugged. "I'm a businessman, and Administrators and Hunters are good enough to deal with when they're comfortable. A couple of Gifted caught trying to travel through their city, though...and on the Night of the Ravens, no less...well, suddenly they are less comfortable. Increased patrols and more questions in the days to come. Generally bad for business, if you get my drift." Anaar pushed his chair back, giving them a brief nod. "Still, heed my warning or not. It's your choice."

"Wait." Wirr wore a thoughtful expression. "You seem like a man who...understands how things work around here." He bit at a fingernail. "How would one go about getting across the river—quietly?"

Anaar paused in the act of rising, then sat again with a frown. "*Into* Desriel? Without using the bridge?" He stared at Wirr as if reevaluating him. "I can't say as that's a request I've heard before."

Wirr shrugged. "Is it possible?"

Anaar rubbed his beard thoughtfully. "I can safely say that it *could* be done. It is a little more expensive than using the bridge, though."

Wirr dug into the pouch on his belt, bringing out a couple of gold coins and surreptitiously showing them to Anaar.

The dark-skinned man smiled, revealing a row of perfect white teeth. "Perhaps I misspoke. A *lot* more expensive than using the bridge."

Sighing, Wirr fished a few more coins out of the pouch. It was more than half of what they had left, enough to feed and house a family for a year. Davian was about to protest, but a quick glance from Wirr made him snap his mouth shut.

Finally Anaar nodded. He leaned forward, keeping his voice low. "You have rooms here?"

Wirr hesitated. "Up the stairs, third on the right." He held up a hand. "Before we agree to anything, though, I need your word that you'll not harm us or turn us in."

Anaar gave him a wide, vaguely incredulous smile. "My word? If it will ease your mind, then you have it," he said with a chuckle. "As I said, I'm a businessman. So long as I get paid, you'll be in no danger from me."

Wirr glanced at Davian, who gave him the slightest of nods in response. Anaar wasn't lying.

"Good enough," said Wirr.

Anaar rubbed his chin, still looking amused. "Go back to your rooms for now, and wait there for me until late this evening. Do not leave for any reason, and do not open the door for anyone except me. Be prepared to depart as soon as I arrive." He plucked a couple of the coins from Wirr's palm. "I will collect the rest once you are in Desriel," he concluded.

Wirr inclined his head. "Agreed."

Anaar rose and walked away without another word.

Davian and Wirr sat in silence for a few moments. Then Davian turned to his friend.

"What was that?"

Wirr stood, stretching. "He's a smuggler, Dav."

"I guessed as much," said Davian drily. "But why are we trusting him?"

"Did he lie to us?"

Davian frowned. "No, but that is hardly the same thing as being trustworthy. He could change his mind in the next few hours, and we wouldn't know until the moment he's stabbed us in the back."

Wirr shook his head. "He already knows what we are; if he'd

been able to profit from turning us in to Administration, he would have done so already. This way he gets to keep the streets of Talmiel quiet and earns some coin at the same time. We get into Desriel. Everyone wins." He paused, considering the last part of his statement. "Well. As far as these things go."

"I think he saw the Vessel," said Davian, unable to keep the worry from his voice.

Wirr grimaced. "I wondered about that, too, given the timing, but what's done is done. If he did see it, we can only hope he doesn't know what it is."

They made their way back through the common room. From the corner of his eye Davian could see the woman Anaar had pointed out watching them thoughtfully, but she made no move to stop or pursue them as they left.

He breathed a sigh of relief once they were out of sight. She was so young, barely older than he and Wirr. Could she *really* be someone who tracked and killed the Gifted for profit?

"I haven't used Essence since we left Caladel," murmured Wirr, his thoughts obviously running along similar lines. "And she never got close enough for skin contact. She can't have noticed us with a Finder."

That hadn't occurred to Davian. "Then how..."

"Exactly."

They walked the rest of the way to their room in uneasy silence, Wirr latching the door as soon as they were inside.

Davian gathered his belongings—which had barely been unpacked—and lay back on the bed, determined to get some rest before they had to leave. He was uncomfortable placing so much trust in Anaar, but he knew it was a chance they'd had to take. If the bridge was as heavily guarded as Wirr believed, the smuggler was probably their best chance of getting across the border.

Still, he touched the Vessel in his pocket again, unable to shake the impression that Anaar had seen it. He could only hope the man hadn't recognized it for what it was.

Suddenly remembering what had happened in the common room, Davian took the Vessel out, removing its cloth and studying it closely. The glow he'd seen earlier had vanished, and its metallic surface wasn't even particularly warm anymore.

"What are you looking for, Dav?" asked Wirr.

Davian hesitated. "There was...some kind of symbol on it, when I dropped it downstairs. A wolf, I think. You didn't see it when you picked it up?"

Wirr shook his head.

Davian sighed but nodded, unsurprised. "It's gone now, anyway." He stared at the cube intently for a few more seconds, then wrapped it again and slipped it back into his pocket.

Wirr watched him with a worried frown. "Let me know if it comes back," he said eventually.

Davian just inclined his head in acknowledgment, and they lapsed into a companionable silence.

He puzzled over what he'd seen for a few more minutes before deciding to put the issue from his mind, at least for now. Worrying about it, or the impending journey into Desriel, for that matter, gained him nothing. He had to trust that Ilseth and the sig'nari had known what they were doing when they'd sent him here.

He closed his eyes with a deep sigh and settled down to wait.

# Chapter 7

Less than an hour had passed when someone knocked at their door.

Wirr and Davian looked at each other, expressions uncertain. "It's hardly 'late evening,'" said Wirr. He kept his voice low, though whoever was outside was unlikely to be able to hear them over the cheerful commotion of the crowd in the street.

"Maybe he had to come early," said Davian, his words lacking conviction.

The knock came again, this time more insistent. "Open up. Anaar sent us," a voice called quietly from the other side.

Wirr hesitated. "He said not to open the door for anyone but him," he called back.

"Plan's changed," came the voice again, soft but urgent. "A Hunter got wind of what was happening."

Davian ran his hands through his hair, wavering. Finally he nodded to Wirr. "It's a risk either way. And if they're here to turn us in, they'll just end up breaking down the door anyway."

Wirr grimaced. "True." He unlocked the door, opening it to admit two rough-looking men. One was thin with long, stringy hair and a mustache, while the other was square-faced and almost bald. They bustled in, looking around before turning their attention back to the boys.

"You ready to go?" the long-haired man asked.

Davian and Wirr both nodded, watching the men closely. The balding man stared back at them for a second, then gave a curt gesture toward the hallway. Relaxing a little, Davian grabbed his pack and headed toward the door.

Suddenly Wirr gave a startled shout; before Davian could turn, his left arm was being twisted behind him and had something hard touched to it. The Shackle was sealed before he realized what was happening.

Davian spun, only to be met with a fist crashing into his nose. He collapsed, too stunned to cry out in pain. Dazed, he saw Wirr on the floor farther back in the room, holding the side of his head, where he had evidently been punched. The cold black of a Shackle glinted on his arm, too.

"Bleeders," spat one of the men. "You'd think they'd be smart enough not to come here anymore."

Davian tried to get to his feet, only to have a heavy boot crash down between his shoulder blades, pressing him back to the hard wooden floor.

"More gold for us, Ren," said the long-haired man cheerfully. "We don't even need to lose half the profits getting across the bridge this time. No cloaks and no Shackles, so they're runaways. We can march them straight over and it'll be completely legal."

Rough hands searched Davian for any hidden weapons, after which he was hauled to his feet and his wrists bound. He shook his head to try to clear it, wincing as he wrinkled his nose. He didn't think it was broken, but there was definitely blood trickling from his nostrils. He glanced dazedly across at Wirr, who looked as if he was having trouble focusing. Whether it was from the blow to the head or the effects of the Shackle, Davian wasn't sure.

Suddenly there was movement at the door, and Davian turned to see the young woman from the common room standing there, watching what was happening with an odd expression on her face. She looked...regretful. Almost sad.

The long-haired man grinned at her. "Sorry, Breshada, not this time. These ones are ours," he said, tone cheerful. "Saw you had your eye on them downstairs. I'm surprised you didn't move sooner." He spoke casually, as if to an old acquaintance.

Breshada grimaced, her waist-length blond hair swinging from side to side. She gazed at Wirr and Davian for a long moment, then turned her attention to the other two men. "Renmar. Gawn.

Please know that I am truly sorry it was you." She took a couple of steps inside the room, flicking the door shut behind her with her heel.

Both men froze. "What are you doing?" asked the one called Renmar, a confused look spreading across his face.

Features set in a grim expression, Breshada reached over her shoulder, drawing her longsword. It gleamed darkly in the candle-light, and suddenly the room was . . . quieter, as if the sounds from outside were now coming from far away. An odd sensation ran through Davian as he watched the blade; there was something not quite right about the sword, but he couldn't put his finger on exactly what.

Rasping steel filled the sudden silence as Renmar and Gawn drew their own swords. "Breshada," said Gawn, tone a mixture of fear, warning, and query. "We got them first, fair and square. I don't understand why you're doing this."

"I know," said Breshada softly.

It was over in seconds. Breshada was quick and elegant despite the size of her sword and the confined space; even with Renmar and Gawn trying to use the boys as shields, they stood no chance. There were no cries of pain, no lingering deaths. When Breshada's sword touched their flesh, they simply crumpled to the ground, eyes glassy. Davian and Wirr just watched in mute, horrified shock.

Once Gawn's lifeless form had joined Renmar's on the floor, Breshada stood for a moment in front of the boys, examining them through narrowed eyes. She was barely breathing hard, though the exertion had brought a slight flush to her cheeks.

She shook her head. "I don't see it," she muttered, disgust thick in her voice. She grabbed Davian by the shoulder; at first he was sure she was going to strike him, but instead she simply steadied him before slicing through the cords binding his hands. Then she did the same for Wirr.

Davian felt a loosening around his arm, and suddenly his Shackle was clattering to the floor. A few moments later, Wirr's was doing the same. Davian stared at the open metal torcs in confusion.

"Death breaks the bond," an impatient-sounding Breshada

said by way of explanation, seeing Davian's expression. She looked at them warily. "Do not attack me. And do not use your powers, else there will be an army of Administrators here within minutes. My saving you will have been for naught."

Wirr inclined his head. "I wasn't going to," he said cautiously. "And thank you."

Breshada scowled, and Wirr and Davian both took an involuntary step back. The look of hatred and disgust that suddenly raged in her eyes was unmistakable. "Do not *thank* me," she hissed. "I have killed my brethren here to save your worthless lives. Two skilled Hunters for two stupid *gaa'vesh*. Tell Tal'kamar that the debt is repaid, a thousand times over." She paused, looking as if she was going to be sick. "If I see you again, I *will* kill you." She spun, flung open the door, and stormed out of the room, not looking back.

Wirr moved slowly over to the door and shut it again. He looked at Davian with a dazed expression. "Are you all right?"

"I'll live," Davian said shakily. "You?" He rubbed his wrists to restore the circulation, then grabbed a cloth, dabbing at his nose and grimacing when the material came away soaked a dark red.

"The same." Wirr touched his head where he'd been struck, looking pale, though he appeared to be suffering no serious ill effects from the blow. "I wonder what that was about."

Davian stared at the door. "A Hunter *saving* Gifted. That must be a first."

"Not that she was particularly happy about it," pointed out Wirr. He paused. "And who in fates is Tal'kamar?"

Davian shook his head, grunting as it exacerbated the pounding inside his skull. "No idea. But I think we owe him a drink if we ever meet him."

"I won't argue with that." Wirr glanced down at the two corpses lying on their floor, his brief smile fading and his tone sobering, as if what had just transpired was finally sinking in. "I won't argue with that at all."

A soft knock at the door made Davian start fully awake.

He hadn't really been asleep but rather lying drowsily, his concerns mixing together in his head to create a disquieting sense of unease. He sat bolt upright and took a quick glance out the window. It was late night; there was still noise from outside, but less than there had been earlier. The blue lanterns had burned down to a dull glow, and the streets looked almost empty.

Wirr was moving before Davian could stand, cocking his head as he listened for anything suspicious outside the door. "Who is it?"

"Anaar," came the reply. The smuggler's gravelly voice was unmistakable.

Wirr unlatched the door, opening it a crack and peering through before swinging it wide. Anaar and an impressively muscular man stood in the hallway, both looking as calm as if they were about to retire for the evening. Anaar's eyes widened when he looked through the doorway and took in the corpses lying on the floor, though. He examined the boys' faces, taking particular note of Davian's bloodied nose.

"Trouble?" he asked.

Wirr looked the smuggler in the eye. "Nothing we couldn't handle."

Anaar nodded, his expression thoughtful, gazing at the two boys with a touch more respect than previously. Then he gestured toward the hallway; Davian leaped to his feet, stomach fluttering as he snatched up his small bag and followed Wirr out of the room.

Nothing was said as they left the inn and walked through the streets of Talmiel, steering clear of the remaining revelers, most of whom were convincingly drunk by this stage of the night. They followed a distinctly circuitous route; after ten minutes of walking without incident, Davian realized that Anaar must know the Administrators' scheduled patrols and be deftly avoiding them.

Soon they were out of the town and into the nearby forest that lined the Devliss, gradually leaving the sounds of the festival behind. Still no one spoke. There was little light beneath the trees, but the almost-full moon provided enough illumination to navigate. They walked at a brisk pace for another twenty minutes before Anaar held up a hand, bringing them to a halt.

"Just through here," he said softly, indicating an almost indistinguishable break in the thick shrubbery.

They pushed through what appeared to be an impenetrable wall of foliage; suddenly Davian found himself stumbling onto the beach of a tiny natural cove, protected on all sides by either stone or forest. The Devliss rushed past just beyond the mouth of the inlet, quicksilver in the moonlight. The water was moving uncomfortably fast, but it at least appeared smooth here, with no jagged rocks to create the white-tipped rapids for which the river was famous.

A little way down the beach was a small boat, pulled out of the reach of the water. Davian stared at it dubiously. He'd never been in a boat before, but this one looked small to be making such a dangerous crossing; it would barely fit all four of them, particularly as Anaar's companion counted for almost two.

Anaar saw Davian's expression and grinned, slapping him on the back. "It's perfectly safe, my friend. Not comfortable, perhaps, but it will get the job done."

Wirr examined the boat with a concerned look. "Surely it will just be swept away by the current?"

Anaar shook his head. "That's why I brought Olsar along," he said, gesturing at the burly man, who was now dragging the boat toward the water. "With the two of us rowing, we can make it to the other side without any problems."

"We'll have to take your word on that," said Wirr, nervousness making his tone strained.

"Indeed," said Anaar absently, his attention focused across the Devliss. Water stretched almost as far as the eye could see, but as Davian followed the smuggler's gaze a darker mound resolved itself on the horizon, barely visible in the darkness. Suddenly a tiny orange light, little more than a dot, bobbed into view. Soon it was joined by several more, all in a line.

"Patrol," Anaar explained to Wirr and Davian, not taking his eyes from the lights. "They pass by every few hours. It takes close to an hour to reach the other side, which gives you a little more than two to get well clear of the border." He nodded to Olsar as the lights winked out again, the distant patrol moving on. The large man gave the boat a final shove, leaving it bobbing in the river. "No talking once we're away—sounds carry over the water, especially at night. Once we touch the shore, we conclude our business and have nothing more to do with one another. If you're caught, you never met me. Understood?"

Davian and Wirr both nodded mutely. Anaar gestured for them to get into the boat, then hesitated.

"One more thing," he said. "Every border soldier in Desriel has a Finder, so if you use your powers to so much as blow your nose once you're over there, they'll know. And believe me, once they know, they won't stop hunting you until you're dead." He gave them a serious look. "Which would be terribly inconvenient if Olsar and myself were still nearby. So I want your word—nothing until at least an hour after we've parted ways. Agreed?"

"Agreed," said Wirr, sticking out his hand. Anaar shook it, then offered his hand to Davian, who grasped it firmly.

As he did, Anaar's eyes strayed downward, toward Davian's pocket.

Davian stiffened. The other man knew.

A flash of anxiety ran through him, followed by . . . something else. A surge, rippling through his body and coalescing in his palm before draining away—straight into Anaar. Davian pulled his hand back sharply, fingertips tingling.

Anaar gave him a confused look, then shook his head as if to clear it. The smuggler turned away, and Davian released a breath he hadn't realized he'd been holding. Whatever had just happened—*if* something had just happened, and it hadn't been Davian's imagination—Anaar was unaware of it.

Soon they were in the tiny craft, Anaar and Olsar pulling with long, practiced strokes toward the opposite shore. Davian's fear that the vessel would be taken by the currents proved unfounded. Both smugglers rowed with power and precision as they angled against the flow of the river, their progress gradual but steady. For a while Davian wondered if they would be able to keep up such a hard pace, but eventually he began to relax. Neither man appeared close to tiring.

The shore on the Desriel side of the river grew slowly larger. The only sounds were the slight splashes of oars dipping beneath the Devliss's surface, the gentle creaking of the timbers, and the occasional warbling of waterfowl singing softly into the night.

Davian felt every muscle tense as individual trees resolved

themselves out of the shadowy mass ahead. Whatever the danger had been over the past three weeks, the moment they stepped onto that shore it would be increased tenfold.

The boat finally ground into the soft, muddy bank; Olsar slipped out, barely making a splash, and dragged the craft out of the water with the others still sitting in it. Davian marveled at the man's strength. Anaar was at least short of breath from the constant rowing, but Olsar was to all appearances unaffected.

Unlike the sand of the Andarran shore, there was only a muddy embankment where they had landed. Wincing as his feet sank into the soft mud—the shoes he wore were his only pair—Davian scrambled up the riverbank and into the long grass, exchanging relieved glances with Wirr. It seemed that their arrival had gone undetected.

Anaar soon joined them. He stood for a few seconds, listening to the sounds of the forest. Apparently satisfied, he put his fingers to his mouth and gave a low, musical whistle.

Shadows stirred from deeper in the trees and two burly men emerged from the darkness, silently taking up positions behind the boys, their swords held at the ready.

Davian's stomach twisted as he realized they had been betrayed.

"What is this?" hissed Wirr, rounding on Anaar.

"Business," replied Anaar, spreading his hands apologetically. "I am in a position to renegotiate our deal, and as such, I have decided that the price is a little higher than was originally discussed."

There was a long silence. "You mean all of it," said Wirr eventually, resignation in his tone.

"I am afraid so," said Anaar with a nod. He held up a cautionary finger. "And I know the First Tenet means you cannot hurt us, but please also remember what I said about the soldiers around here. They are *very* enthusiastic about their work. Try and escape us using your powers, and you will bring down a hundred times worse on your heads. You doubtless feel like you are getting the raw end of this bargain, but I am sure a few extra coins are not worth your lives."

Davian scowled at the smuggler. "How do we know you won't

just kill us once you have the gold?" he asked, trying to keep his voice low.

Anaar smiled. "I *did* give you my word. Besides, if that were my intention, would I not just kill you and take the gold from your bodies? No," he chided. "Too much mess to clean up. My men will take your payment by force if need be—but if you cooperate, you have my word that there will be no violence."

Davian considered Anaar for a moment. The man wasn't lying, exactly, and yet...something didn't ring true.

"But you don't want us to use Essence, either," he said slowly. "If we do, it won't give you enough time to get out of crossbow range before the patrol gets here. That's why you haven't tried to kill us. It isn't worth the risk of our retaliating."

Anaar shook his head, still relaxed. "Nonsense. Even if the patrol runs here, we have plenty of time to get away."

Again Anaar was telling the truth and yet Davian saw the man standing behind Wirr shift, looking uneasy. It was all the encouragement he needed.

Taking a deep breath he plowed on, ignoring Wirr's warning glance. "But you won't have time to cover your tracks. This has to be the only place to cross the Devliss by boat in, what...a hundred miles?" He crossed his arms. "The Gil'shar are obviously already aware it's possible, seeing as they have a patrol passing so close by. If they found any sign the crossing was being used— especially if they thought *Gifted* were using it—well, I imagine that would make undertaking your *business* far more difficult. Impossible, one might say."

Anaar's face darkened. "Use Essence, and I will kill you," he promised.

"Try to kill us, and we'll use Essence," responded Davian. "Look, we're going to need to eat. Just let us keep a few of the coins. It's not worth risking the profits of your entire operation here, is it?"

Anaar stared at Davian stonily for a few moments, then barked a low laugh.

"Clever boy," he murmured, a touch of reluctant admiration in his voice. "You have nerve, I will give you that. Very well. Take three coins for yourself, then toss me the rest."

Davian nodded; he wasn't willing to push the issue further. He drew the small leather pouch from his pocket, drew three coins out, and tossed it to Anaar. The smuggler caught it neatly and opened it to look inside. There were a tense few moments as he examined the contents, and Davian felt sure he was about to ask for the bronze box as well.

Then Anaar drew the strings on the pouch, giving a satisfied nod. "It seems our business here is complete."

The smuggler gave an absent wave to the two men behind Wirr and Davian, who moved toward the boat without a word. One of them was carrying a crate of something heavy, which he placed gently in the stern—no doubt whatever goods Anaar was illegally transporting back to Andarra—and soon they were dragging the boat back into the water.

Anaar hesitated as the boat bobbed away, then dug into the pouch he'd taken and flicked another coin toward them. Davian caught it before it disappeared into the long grass. It was gold.

He stared at the coin in surprise, then looked up at the smuggler again. Anaar gave him a brief, impish grin, then turned back to face the Andarran shore before Davian could respond.

"That was quick thinking, Dav," Wirr said after a few seconds, watching the boat pull away from the shore. "Risky, but quick."

"Thanks." Davian exhaled heavily, finally feeling able to breathe again.

"We should get moving. The further we get from here in the next hour or two, the better."

"Agreed."

Wirr turned and headed into the forest, Davian trailing after him. In seconds the thick foliage had hidden the boat, river, and distant shore of Andarra from view.

They walked as fast as they dared, careful not to leave too obvious a trail behind them. It was unlikely a Desrielite patrol would notice their passing, but there was no reason to take the chance.

They moved with silent determination for the first hour or so, neither willing to make more sound than the snapping of twigs and rustling of leaves underfoot, which alone were still thunderous in the hush of the night. After a while Wirr slowed to a stop in a copse of tall trees, looked around cautiously, and then indicated a fallen log.

"We should rest," he said, a little out of breath.

Davian nodded his acquiescence; he was not as fit as Wirr, and was feeling the fast pace. Wirr was doubtless tapping his Reserve for extra energy, too. His friend had assured him that it was safe to do so—that so long as the Essence remained within his own body, it could not be detected by Finders. More than ever, Davian hoped Wirr knew what he was talking about.

Wirr sat on the log, then began unlacing his boot.

"What are you doing?" asked Davian, sitting beside him.

Wirr upended the boot, holding out his hand. There was a jingling sound, and then five silver coins slid into his palm, glinting in the moonlight.

Davian stared at them for a few moments. "You thought something like this might happen," he said eventually, not knowing whether to be impressed or irritated.

Wirr shrugged. "He was a smuggler, Dav. Not exactly an honest line of work." He sighed. "Part of me wishes I'd taken gold instead of silver, but there would have been trouble if the purse had been too light. At least between the two of us, we've saved enough to keep us going for now."

They sat in contemplative silence for a time. "It looks like he didn't know about the Vessel after all," Wirr remarked suddenly.

"Maybe." Davian wasn't convinced. He'd had a chance to think during their walk through the forest—to ponder that moment on the Andarran shore of the Devliss, when he had shaken hands with Anaar. He hadn't imagined that fleeting look the smuggler had cast toward his pocket.

Wirr picked up on his doubt. "He wouldn't have left it with us if he'd known," he said. "It's probably worth ten times what he took. I think he would have risked killing us for it, to be honest."

Davian hesitated. "On the beach, just before we cast off. I think, maybe..." He shook his head. "I don't know. I think I did something to him. Maybe made him forget, somehow."

Wirr raised an eyebrow. "I see." From his tone he clearly didn't.

Davian scrunched up his face, trying to think of how best to explain. "It felt a little like when I see someone lying."

Wirr frowned, looking only a little less skeptical. "I imagine it's possible," he said after a while. "The Augurs were supposed to

79

be able to do all sorts of things. But if you're not sure that's what happened...well, I wouldn't get too excited about it." He clapped Davian on the back.

Davian nodded, letting the matter drop. Wirr was probably right. Still...*something* had happened. He was sure of it.

After a few minutes they stood, brushing away the scraps of bark that still clung to their clothing.

Without further conversation they continued northward into Desriel.

# Chapter 8

Asha rode in silence.

She stared around listlessly as they made their way along Fedris Idri. The sole pass into Andarra's capital cut through the mountain in a narrow, surgically straight line; sheer cliffs towered hundreds of feet on either side, their dark-brown rock flat and smooth, polished to an almost glass-like sheen by the ancient power of the Builders.

The famous sight should have filled her with wonder, but instead she felt nothing except the stares of people passing by. Most looked away if she turned to face them, though some met her gaze, openly disgusted or fascinated. And how could she blame them? She had seen her own reflection many times in the past few weeks since leaving Caladel, and the black lines across her face, radiating like burst veins from her eyes, would give anyone pause.

She was a Shadow now, a broken Gifted. A rare, harmless, ugly curiosity.

Ignoring the stares as best she could, Asha unconsciously touched her left forearm again as she moved forward, the feeling of smooth skin there still alien even after three weeks. Her Mark had begun fading that first day on the road, and now had all but disappeared.

She hadn't known that would happen, but in retrospect she supposed it made sense. If she was no longer able to use the Gift, then she was no longer bound by the Tenets, either.

"We're almost there, Ashalia."

The voice cut through her thoughts, and she turned to face Elder Tenvar.

"And then you'll explain? Tell me why I'm here? Why I'm... like *this*?" She gestured to her face. Even after three weeks of asking the same questions, she couldn't keep the ice from her tone.

"Everything." Ilseth gave her a sympathetic look. "I know... I can't imagine how hard this has been for you. How frustrating. But you'll understand when we reach Tol Athian. You have my word."

Asha nodded curtly; she'd heard the same promise a hundred times since waking up on a horse outside Caladel, but even now she wasn't sure she believed it. Elder Tenvar, Elder Kien, Elder Kasperan—none had been willing to part with even a hint as to what had happened. She'd pleaded with them...railed at them... none of it had made a difference. She still didn't know whether to be eager or terrified to find out the truth.

She blinked in the sudden sunlight as they passed through the final of the three Fedris Idri gates; the narrow road came to an abrupt end, and then Asha was staring down into Ilin Illan itself.

In stark contrast to Fedris Idri's cool, enclosed dimness, the city was bright, cheerful, *alive*. It spread away from their position outward and downward; the incline was steep enough to show everything at a glance, but not so steep as to give Asha even a hint of vertigo. The elegant white-stone buildings stretched far into the distance, beyond which she could make out the sails of ships as they came and left the massive harbor. Past even those, the crystalline blue waters of the Naminar River glittered in the afternoon sun.

To Asha's right and left, the massive brown-black cliffs of Ilin Tora extended away like two outstretched arms, enveloping the entire city in their embrace. From what she could see, she suspected that nowhere did the tops of the sheer rock walls come closer than a hundred feet to the tops of the buildings.

Even through her turbulent emotions, Asha couldn't help but be impressed.

Elder Kien murmured something to Ilseth and then was off down a side street, evidently about some other business. The two remaining Elders left Asha little time for taking in the view, moving quickly along a wide road to the right, parallel to the looming cliffs.

They rode for only a few minutes before the crowds began to thin, soon reaching a massive iron gate set into the cliff face. At least twenty feet high and wide enough to fit ten men walking side by side, it was closed, guarded by two men whose red cloaks stood in stark relief against the gray metal.

One of them nodded in recognition to Ilseth before pressing his palm against the shining metal surface. Slowly and soundlessly the gate swung open.

Ilseth turned to Asha, gesturing for her to dismount.

"Welcome to Tol Athian, Ashalia," he said quietly.

The Tol was darker than Asha had envisaged.

Carved into the bedrock of Ilin Tora, the enormous central tunnel was lit by several lines of pure Essence pulsing along the roof, which sat at least fifty feet above the floor. Other, smaller tunnels branched off at regular intervals; these were illuminated by only a single line of Essence each, but their smaller sizes meant that they were better lit.

Gifted hurried to and from those tunnels in a flurry of red. Under normal circumstances Asha would have been astonished at the scene—there were more Gifted in front of her than she had ever seen before in one place—but today she barely noticed. Her sense of anticipation was growing stronger with every step. After three long weeks, she was finally going to find out what was going on.

She trailed after Ilseth and Kasperan, a mixture of excitement and nervousness building in her stomach. Soon they were heading down one of the smaller passageways, eventually coming to a door manned by two bored-looking guards.

"The Council have been waiting for you, Elder Tenvar," said one of them when he spotted the group, opening the door and gesturing for them to enter. Asha caught the other one staring at her; she held his gaze steadily until he dropped his eyes, looking slightly abashed. She walked past him without saying anything.

Through the door another short passageway led out onto a

large circular floor. Two long rows of seats overlooked it; in those seats about a dozen red-cloaked Gifted—members of the Athian Council, presumably—paused in their conversations and peered down at her and her escorts.

"We should begin," announced a wiry older man with commanding hazel eyes. He hadn't shouted but the acoustics amplified his voice, carrying it clearly to everyone present. Once he was sure he had the attention of the room, he leaned forward in his chair, staring down at them intently.

"Finally. You have some explaining to do, Ilseth."

Ilseth inclined his head in deference. "Nashrel. You received my message?"

"The pigeon arrived two weeks ago," replied Nashrel. "Though I cannot say it explained much." His tone was reproachful.

"I apologize for that," said Ilseth respectfully. "I thought it best to be...discreet."

Nashrel nodded. "Of course," he said, though from his tone he was still clearly displeased. "So. You were unable to find him?"

"That's correct," confirmed Ilseth, casting an uncertain glance in Asha's direction. She immediately got the impression that this was not a conversation meant for her ears.

The Elder nodded, as if he had expected the answer. "Fortunately that does not matter a great deal. We have a Trace."

Ilseth's attention snapped back to the Council members. "A Trace? Surely it would be wiser to—"

"It is already done, Ilseth." Nashrel waved away Ilseth's obvious alarm. "No need for concern. They have been instructed not to harm anyone."

The other Council members had thus far remained silent, but now a woman to Nashrel's left spoke up. "Perhaps there are some other matters that should be discussed first?" she suggested to Nashrel politely. "So that our young guest can...get some rest?"

Nashrel nodded, for the first time seeming to register that Asha was in the room. "Ah. Yes, you're right," he said, shaking his head as if surprised at his own absentmindedness. He studied Asha's features. "What is your name, girl?"

Asha started, for some reason surprised at being addressed

directly. "Ashalia," she replied, trying to sound duly respectful. Despite her efforts, her tone held a sharp edge.

Nashrel appeared to take no offense. "What do you remember of the attack, Ashalia?"

Asha frowned in confusion, silent for a few moments. "Attack? All I know is that I went to sleep one night, and the next thing I remember, I was sitting in front of Elder Kasperan on a horse, halfway to Jereth and like this." She gestured coldly to her face.

"We thought it best to hold off telling her, Nashrel," interjected Ilseth.

"She was made a Shadow the morning after the attack," supplied Kasperan, who had been standing to one side, allowing Ilseth to do the talking.

Nashrel rubbed his forehead. "And why was that, exactly?"

Ilseth looked uncomfortable. "That's another matter we need to discuss, actually. It's my fault, I'm afraid." He grimaced. "She ... forced me to do it."

"*What?*" Asha found herself speaking before anyone else in the room had a chance to react. She took a furious half step toward Ilseth before being bodily restrained by Kasperan. She'd *made* him do it? It was a lie. It had to be.

Nashrel looked between Asha and Ilseth, expression darkening. "Why in El's name would she *ask* for this, Ilseth?"

Ilseth sighed, turning to speak directly to Asha. His tone was gentle, full of regret. "The school at Caladel was attacked, Ashalia. Everyone died—everyone but you." He paused to let that sink in. "That morning, you woke and saw exactly what we saw: bodies everywhere, murdered in some of the most gruesome ways imaginable. Except unlike us, you didn't see strangers. They were your friends, your teachers ... people you had grown up with. By the time you found us, you were near incoherent with grief and fear."

Still firmly in Kasperan's grasp, Asha could feel the other Elder nodding his agreement. She stared at Ilseth, heart pounding, sick to her stomach. It couldn't be true.

Ilseth continued, "You told me that before running into us, you had gone to your friend's room, to see if he was alive. A boy who lived in the North Tower."

Asha's blood went cold. The Elders had been avoiding telling her what had happened, and this was why. Before Ilseth spoke again, she knew what he was going to say.

"He had died, Ashalia," said Ilseth softly. "He had died just like the others, and you couldn't take the memory of seeing it. You...went wild, when I refused to help. You attacked me." He rolled up his sleeve, revealing a half-healed burn.

"I felt the blast," confirmed Kasperan.

"I begged you to wait, but you insisted," continued Ilseth. "You said you'd just keep attacking me until I did it...and that if I left it too late, if you were stuck with the memories, you'd... well, that you'd kill yourself instead. Without any Shackles available, I didn't know what else to do." He was visibly upset at the remembrance. "After that, we thought it best not to tell you until we were here. With only the three of us to watch you, we just... well, we didn't know how you might react."

Asha felt tears forming in her eyes. Her knees buckled, and only Kasperan's grip kept her from collapsing to the floor. A part of her still wanted to protest, to say that she would *never* have asked to be a Shadow, would *never* have done the things Ilseth was saying.

Yet Davian was dead. Her friends were *dead*. She couldn't imagine that, either.

There was an awkward silence for some time, everyone watching Asha as she struggled to keep her emotions in check. Finally Nashrel cleared his throat.

"A difficult situation to be in, Ilseth," he said quietly. "And your actions under those circumstances are...understandable, I suppose. Still, the girl was not of age and had not failed her Trials; this is not something we can overlook entirely. We shall discuss the appropriate punishment later."

Ilseth nodded, looking chastised. "I understand."

Nashrel steepled his fingers together. "The question remains, though: how did Ashalia here survive? You've seen all three attack sites, Ilseth. There were no others left alive. Have you any idea as to what made Caladel different?"

Ilseth shook his head. "All I know is that it seems unlikely to be a mistake. Whoever, or whatever, has been carrying out these attacks has been thorough. There must be a reason." He bit his lip. "I would recommend Ashalia stay at the Tol, for now. Not just because we need to understand why she survived. I feel...I feel like I owe her that much."

Asha just stared at him, understanding the words but unable to process them. All she could think about was Davian. What it must have been like to find him like that.

"Agreed," said Nashrel, glancing across at Asha sympathetically. "Ashalia, I'll have someone show you to your new rooms; one of the Elders will be along later to help you settle in. Ilseth, if you could stay a little longer. There is more we need to discuss."

"Of course." Ilseth inclined his head deferentially. A few moments later a man Asha didn't recognize was taking her by the arm and leading her from the room.

She didn't resist, didn't say anything.

All she felt was numbness.

Asha's room was far from luxurious, but it was certainly not the cramped stone cell that she had expected.

The walls were carved from the same bleak stone as the hallway outside, but the floor was mostly covered by two large, plain brown rugs. The bed in the corner was small but looked comfortable enough. A desk and chair sat neatly against the far wall; a single Essence-infused bulb hung from the wall, providing a low but steady light. A smaller room to the side contained a basin and other amenities. In all—with the exception of the lack of windows—it could have passed for an Elder's quarters in Caladel.

"Elder Eilinar has requested that you stay here until you are asked for," the Gifted who had accompanied her said politely.

Asha just stared at him, not responding. She knew she was being rude, that none of it was this man's fault, but she didn't care anymore. After a few moments of awkward silence, the Gifted ducked his head and left, closing the door behind him.

The slight mechanical click of a lock followed seconds later. So she *was* a prisoner, then. She'd had that impression, but no one had said anything specifically, and she was still too dazed—too heartbroken—to ask.

A mirror hung on the wall, and she flinched as she caught a glimpse of herself in it. Jagged black lines spread out like a spiderweb from her eyes, which themselves were sunken, as if she had spent many days without sleep. Her skin, never conducive to tanning at the best of times, was a sickly, pallid hue, as if the color—the life—had been leached out of it.

She looked away. No point dwelling on what could not be changed. Even being a Shadow seemed meaningless now.

She moved over to inspect the desk, surprised to find it well stocked with paper and writing equipment. The pencils here were not made for it, but she would be able to pass the time sketching if she so chose, something she'd often enjoyed back at the school. For some reason the thought reassured her. At the very least, she would not lose her mind to boredom in here.

There was a Decay Clock, too, the Essence within it indicating late afternoon. She couldn't replenish it once it was depleted, of course; she'd need one of the Gifted to do that for her. But if it was anything like Elder Olin's Decay Clock back at the school...

Suddenly she couldn't finish the thought, the wall in her mind that had been holding her emotions in check finally crumbling. Elder Olin was dead. They were *dead*. Gone, all of them. She would never see them again.

She collapsed on the bed and wept into the pillow. She screamed in pain, in anger, until her throat hurt. Still the ache in her chest was too great, had nowhere to go.

Some time after, exhausted, she slept.

She wasn't sure how long had passed before a soft knock came at the door. She sat up warily, fully awake, hurriedly wiping her tear-streaked face as the door opened a second later.

She scowled as Ilseth Tenvar walked in.

"What do you want?" she snapped.

The Elder held up his hands. "I have come to apologize."

Asha blinked. There was silence for a few moments, then she gestured tiredly, her fury draining away to be replaced by a despondent numbness. "Come in."

Ilseth walked in, looking awkward. He stood in the middle of the room for a few moments, staring at the ground, then cleared his throat.

"I really am sorry," he said eventually, regret thick in his voice. "I know you don't remember, but it was madness, that morning. Everyone was terrified, shocked...not thinking straight. I'm not trying to justify what I did," he added, "but at the time, I felt like I had no choice." He indicated his burned arm apologetically.

Asha said nothing for a time. A part of her was furious beyond belief at the Elder, didn't want to believe a word he said. But then, she couldn't imagine what her reaction would have been...seeing Wirr, Davian...

"Why did you wait until we were in front of the Council to tell me about..." A sudden spurt of emotion choked her words, and she looked away.

Ilseth moved forward, laying his hand on her shoulder. "It wasn't an easy decision," he said softly. "But if I had told you on the road, what would you have done?"

Asha paused, considering. "I would have wanted to go back," she admitted.

Ilseth nodded. "I think you would have *tried* to go back. Or... worse. The three of us by ourselves weren't equipped to deal with that. And as you can imagine, the Council needed to hear my report as soon as possible. We couldn't afford any delays." He rubbed his forehead. "What happened to you was not fair, Ashalia, and I don't expect your forgiveness. But—please, just know how sorry I am."

Asha looked away for a moment. She was still angry, still hurting, but sleep had dulled the pain and brought some clarity back to her. She hated what Ilseth had done, and part of her wasn't sure she could ever forgive him, but the nagging knowledge remained: it was unfair to place the blame entirely at his feet. Not given the circumstances.

"I...accept your apology," she said stiffly. It hurt to say the words when all she wanted to do was lash out, but venting at Ilseth would only make her position here worse. She needed *someone* on her side.

Ilseth gave her an appreciative smile. "Thank you."

"And I want to help." Asha crossed her arms. "You said that there was a reason I was left alive. That I might be a...clue, in what's been happening. Anything I can do..."

"Of course." Ilseth nodded. "I'm sure the Council will be seeking your cooperation soon. Until then, though, the smart course of action is to stay here in the Tol. Blend in, keep your head down. The last thing we want is to draw attention."

Asha frowned. "There's nothing I can do now? Straight away?"

Ilseth shook his head. "I know it must be hard, but being patient is the best way you can contribute at the moment. Don't worry, though. You'll get your opportunity."

Asha sighed. She didn't like the answer—but for now, at least, there didn't seem to be any alternative. "Elder Eilinar said there were other schools that were attacked?" she asked eventually.

Ilseth nodded. "Arris and Dasari. The same as Caladel. But no survivors."

Asha swallowed. After the war Tol Athian had managed to reestablish only eight schools—one for each region of Andarra—and now, suddenly, the three southernmost ones were completely gone. The thought that someone out there was strong enough to attack, to *obliterate* well-fortified groups of Gifted was frightening, to say the least. "Do you know if it's Hunters? Or is it someone else?"

"I have no idea. I wish I did," said the Elder, sincere regret in his tone. "We will find out who is responsible, though, I promise you that much. And I'll make sure that if we learn anything new, you are the first to know."

"What about Administration?" Asha frowned. "Shouldn't they be looking into it, too? Isn't their protection of the Gifted supposed to be part of the Treaty?"

"Administration is...conducting its own investigation." Ilseth's expression was wry. "The Northwarden himself is heading it up, and our relationship with him is even worse than usual right now. They probably know more than we do—their resources are considerable, and Administrators being killed concerns them greatly, even if protecting the Gifted does not. But if they do find anything, they are not likely to share it with us."

Asha bit her lip, suddenly hit by a wave of sadness as she thought of Talean. For some reason, when she'd heard about the attack, she had assumed the Administrator would have been spared. "Surely if we offered to work with them, though...I mean, I would be happy to talk to—"

"No." Ilseth shook his head. "If Administration finds out about you, they will assume the worst—that you're a conspirator, allowed to live because you had some role in the attack. You're not protected by the Tenets anymore, Ashalia. If they get hold of you, there will be nothing stopping them from trying to extract information any way they see fit."

Asha paled. "Surely they wouldn't—"

"They would. Believe me." Ilseth's expression was serious. "We've gone to great lengths to protect you, to make sure they don't know there was a survivor. Your name is on Administration's records as a student from Caladel, so we'll be organizing a new identity for you. You may have noticed that there was no Administrator present when we spoke to the Council—not even a Scrivener to record the session? As far as Administration or anyone outside the Council is concerned, you will simply be another Shadow who failed her Trials and has come to work at the Tol. If you want to stay safe, make sure you keep it that way."

Asha frowned, but gave a reluctant nod.

Ilseth took a deep breath. "Speaking of your safety, Elder Eilinar has made you my responsibility. I've organized a position for you amongst the other Shadows here, so that you'll blend in— their work is mostly related to copying out the Tol's rarer texts, from what I understand. I assume you know how to read and write well enough?"

"Of course."

"Then I'll be by tomorrow morning to take you to the library." He gestured toward the door. "When you're not working, you will have free rein of the Tol, though I think—and the Council has agreed—that it is best if you don't go into Ilin Illan itself. If you were left alive for a reason, then whoever carried out the attack may want you for another purpose. May even have followed us, and know you are here."

Asha felt a chill run through her. "I won't go anywhere."

"Good." Ilseth glanced at the Decay Clock, then stood. "Now. There are other matters to which I need to attend, but I'll return in the morning—take you to the library, introduce you, get you settled in."

"Thank you."

Ilseth shook his head. "Not at all. I can't imagine how hard this all must be to take in." He leaned over and gave her a light, reassuring squeeze on the arm. "The next few days are going to be a bit of an adjustment, so if you need anything—anything at all— please let me know. I want to do everything I can to help."

He gave Asha a comforting smile and then headed out, closing the door quietly behind him.

She was alone once again.

# Chapter 9

Asha rubbed her forehead, trying to focus on the text in front of her.

The library was quiet today, for which she was grateful. She wasn't sure she could handle another Gifted staring at her with thinly veiled discomfort, or another Administrator treating her like so much dirt.

It had been only a week since she'd arrived at the Tol, and already her life felt...less. Every day was the same. Repetitive, meaningless transcription work in the library. Being ignored by everyone around her. Assurances from Ilseth that the Tol's investigation was ongoing, but no answers, nor any way for her to help get them.

And above all, the reality of what had happened at the school—the reality of Davian's death—settling in just a little deeper.

Asha's vision blurred for a second, and she shook her head, taking a deep breath. She was always tired now; she'd had difficulty sleeping almost every night since being made a Shadow, and arriving at the Tol hadn't changed that. If anything, it had made things worse. The need to do something—*anything*—to find out what had happened at Caladel sat in the pit of her stomach, always there, but worse at nights when there was no work to distract her. And it was a need she had no idea how to fulfill.

She looked up as voices approached, cutting through the relative silence of the library.

"I apologize, Administrator Gil. I just don't know where it is."

It was Raden, one of the dozen or so other Shadows who lived at the Tol. He sounded frightened.

"Look harder." Gil's tone was curt, bordering on angry. Only a few rows of shelves separated Asha from Raden and Gil now; she could hear everything they were saying clearly.

"Perhaps if you waited until Haliden returned," Raden said, a note of panic in his voice. "We're only in here for transcription, but he's the librarian—"

"I don't have time to waste waiting on that El-cursed bleeder," said Gil coldly. "Fates, I'm not even supposed to be in this El-cursed situation to begin with. So find me the El-cursed book before I lose my temper."

"But—"

Asha leaped to her feet as there was a crashing sound. She darted along the aisle to see an entire bookshelf had been toppled, with Raden lying helplessly on top, a look of shock on his black-scarred face. The short, squat man in the blue Administrator's cloak loomed above him.

"What are you doing?" she exclaimed.

The Administrator didn't take his eyes off Raden. "Nothing that concerns you, girl. Best you stay out of it."

A flash of anger washed through Asha. "I certainly will not," she said, stepping closer.

Gil turned and there was a blur of motion; the next thing Asha knew she was on the floor, shaking her head dazedly, tasting blood.

She twisted to stare up at Gil in shock, not quite believing what had just happened.

"You can't do that," she said, running her tongue over her split lip. Her astonishment turned quickly to anger. "You can't just hit—"

"Of course I can. Who's going to stop me?" Gil replied, tugging his cloak as if to prove the point. His weaselly eyes gazed at her in amusement.

A wave of fury swept over Asha, and she scrambled to her feet.

"Lissa. It's all right." Raden was only a little older than Asha, but he spoke with the resigned, dolorous heaviness that many of the Shadows she'd met had taken on. As if any life, any joy had been sucked out of him. "It was my fault. Administrator Gil was right to chastise me."

Asha hesitated, as she still did every time someone used her new name. Then she gaped at Raden, gesturing at the books scattered across the floor. "He attacked you because you couldn't find the book he wanted. That's not even *your job.*"

"It was my fault," Raden insisted.

"You should listen to him, girl," said Gil, not even looking in her direction. "You're fairly new here, so I won't give you the beating you deserve. Next time, though…"

Asha's anger flared again; she made to move toward Gil, but a hand on her shoulder restrained her. She turned to see Jin standing behind her, the unofficial leader of the Shadows at the Tol shaking his head in silent warning.

Asha hesitated a moment, then with an effort let her taut muscles relax.

Gil looked up a second later, nodding to himself when he saw she wasn't protesting. "Good. You're learning," he said cheerfully.

Then he noticed Jin, and his face paled a little.

"Administrator Gil," said Jin with cold politeness.

The blue-cloaked man looked uncertain for a moment, then his face hardened. "You need to get your people into line, Jin," he snarled.

Jin looked unconcerned. "Did you do this?" He gestured to the fallen bookshelf, then at Asha. "Did you strike Lissa?"

"She tried to interfere—"

"You're overstepping." Jin said the words softly, but there was a definite menace to them.

Gil scowled. "I don't think—"

Jin stepped close to the Administrator, right up to his face so that the height difference between the two was accentuated. Then he leaned down, whispering something in the other man's ear.

When he'd finished, Gil had gone white as a sheet. He turned back to Raden, looking more sick than angry now. "You'd better make sure Haliden finds me that book as soon as he returns, or… there will be consequences." His tone was unconvincing this time.

"Of course," said Raden obsequiously, bobbing his head.

Still looking shaken, Gil left without another word.

Nobody moved until Gil had exited the room. As soon as he was gone, Raden scrambled to his feet and rounded on Asha.

"You're lucky you didn't make him angrier," he said furiously, brushing himself off. "What were you thinking? Acting like that only puts us all in danger, you know." He turned to Jin. "And you. I know what you said to him, and I want nothing to do with that. I'm not going to—"

"Enough, Raden." Jin held up his hand. "Lissa has only been here a few days; I did it for her sake, not yours. If he harasses you again, I won't intervene. You have my word." He sighed. "You should get cleaned up, and then get back to work."

Raden muttered something under his breath, but gave a brusque nod and walked away.

Asha stared after him in astonishment. She touched her lip gingerly; it was swollen, but would heal soon enough. "I was just trying to help."

Jin gave her a rueful look. "I know. A lot of Shadows are just convinced that they're not worth helping, unfortunately."

She turned to him. "Isn't there...something we can do about Gil? Can't we report him?"

Jin smiled, though there wasn't much amusement in the expression. He was perhaps thirty, though the black lines across his face made telling his age difficult. Asha thought he would have been handsome before becoming a Shadow; his curly black hair framed strong features and piercing hazel eyes. "To whom? Administration?"

Asha hesitated. Administration wouldn't lift a finger to even investigate the accusations of a few Shadows. "The Council?"

Jin shook his head. "They'd be sympathetic, of course. To an extent. But they have about as much control over the Administrators as we do."

Asha gritted her teeth in frustration. This wasn't the first time she'd seen Shadows being treated poorly since she'd started working here—mostly by Administrators, occasionally by the Gifted. It was the first time it had been anything worse than verbal abuse, though. She hadn't thought that sort of thing would be allowed to happen within the walls of the Tol.

"What did you say to him, to make him leave?" she asked eventually.

Jin hesitated, giving her a considering look.

"I told him you were under the Shadraehin's protection," he said. "Have you heard of him?"

Asha shook her head at the unfamiliar name. "No."

Jin watched her for a long moment, then nodded to himself, gesturing for her to follow him. "There's something I want to show you. Something I think you will appreciate." He held up a hand as he saw her questioning glance. "I can't explain here. Just trust me on this."

Asha frowned. "Very well," she said, trying not to sound skeptical.

They left the library and were soon winding their way down several unfamiliar passageways, the flow of red cloaks around them steadily decreasing as they walked farther into the Tol. Finally they entered a short hallway that was entirely abandoned, with only one door at its end. Jin stopped in front of the sturdy-looking oak and, after making sure that there was no one else around, produced a key.

The lock clicked and the door swung open on well-oiled hinges, revealing a dimly lit staircase spiraling downward.

Asha stared at it. "Where exactly are we going?"

Jin glanced over his shoulder again. "It's something only a few of us Shadows know about. And we'll be in trouble if we're caught going down here, so we should get inside," he said quickly. He grimaced as he saw the uncertainty on her face. "You want to know why Gil backed off? The answer is down here."

Asha paused a second longer, then nodded.

Once they were inside the stairwell and the door was locked again behind them, Jin visibly relaxed.

"The lower level has been sealed off, all but abandoned since the war began," he explained as they started downward. "With so many fewer Gifted around, the Council decided the upkeep was impractical, not to mention unnecessary."

"So why are we down here?" asked Asha.

"Because this is where the Shadraehin is." Jin smiled at her dubious expression. "Sorry to be so mysterious, but it's easier if I just show you."

Asha shivered as Jin used his key again and they emerged from the first landing of the stairwell. The tunnels on this level were still lit with lines of Essence, but the illumination was dimmer, colder. Closed doors lined the way ahead; there was no dust or grime—the power of the Builders had evidently seen to that—but the corridors still fairly reeked of abandonment. The grim silence was broken only by the echo of their footsteps as they started forward.

They walked for several minutes through a series of dimly lit tunnels; though Jin navigated the twisting passageways with confidence, Asha knew she probably wouldn't be able to find her way back to the stairwell if she needed to. She had no reason to think Jin meant her ill, but the realization still made her uneasy.

Finally they came to a halt, the way ahead blocked by a large door. Unlike the other doors they'd passed, this one was made from smooth gray steel and looked as if it would be impossibly heavy to open.

Asha squinted. There was something engraved on it in elegant, flowing script:

*All that I wanted, I received*
*All that I dreamed, I achieved*
*All that I feared, I conquered*
*All that I hated, I destroyed*
*All that I loved, I saved*
*And so I lay down my head, weary with despair*
*For all that I needed, I lost.*

"We call it the Victor's Lament," said Jin quietly, following her gaze. "Nobody knows who wrote it or why it's here, but I always thought it was appropriate."

He stepped up to the shining metal and placed his hand against its surface. Nothing happened for a few moments, and then there was a sharp click. The door swung open soundlessly.

Asha gazed in astonishment into the hallway beyond. The
walls were darker than those in the Tol, closer to black, though

still displaying the effortless smoothness that typified the work of the Builders. There were no lines of Essence here; rather torches lit the passageway at regular intervals, stretching out into the distance for as far as she could see.

Two burly men sitting just inside the door, both Shadows, sprang to attention as it opened. They relaxed only partially when they saw Jin.

"Who's this?" one of them asked Jin in a suspicious tone, jerking his head toward Asha. "We weren't expecting anyone new."

"This is Lissa. I'll vouch for her," said Jin.

The two men exchanged a look, then the first one shrugged, stepping aside. "She's your responsibility until the Shadraehin clears her."

"That's fine." Jin ushered her inside, past the men and down the long passageway. Asha flinched as she heard the steel door boom shut behind her, her sense of unease growing. Wherever they were going, there was no easy way back now.

Finally the tunnel ended, opening out onto a large balcony. Asha stopped short as she emerged into the light, gaping at the scene before her.

The cavern was enormous. The wide stone ledge she was standing on was at least fifty feet above the floor; she could see distant walls to her left and right, but the space stretched back farther than she could make out. The smooth black expanse below was dotted with sturdy-looking structures and people moving between them; everything was illuminated by a warm yellow-white light, bright after the torch-lit passageway.

The men and women below were all Shadows, Asha realized after a moment; the cavern echoed with the sounds of their conversation, their laughter, and the general hubbub of life. There was a row of simple houses off to one side, with several more evidently under construction. Fires dotted the vast floor.

Despite the strangeness of it all, it was the source of the light that held her attention—a massive cylinder that lit the entire space with its gently pulsing glow. As she focused on it, she realized it was a sort of pipeline; the energy within it was rushing upward, an unending torrent of power flowing from floor to ceiling.

"Beautiful, isn't it?" murmured Jin, following her gaze.

She turned to him. "*What* is it?" She gazed around again, barely believing what she was seeing. "What is this place?"

"This is the Sanctuary," said Jin, a note of pride in his voice. "Somewhere Shadows can come and be free to go about their lives in peace, away from those who would abuse us. Here people can live without having to be subservient, without fear of Administration or the Gifted. Without having to be *less*." He gestured to the pillar of light. "As for that—from what I understand, it powers Tol Athian. The lights, the defenses, all the things the Builders designed. It's also deadly to anyone who isn't a Shadow, which is why the Shadraehin chose this place to make a home."

Asha stared out over the bustling scene below. "It's remarkable," she said softly.

Jin gave her a wide, approving smile. "Administration doesn't think much of it, of course—they think the Shadraehin is gathering a militia of some kind, planning to strike at them somehow. They're wrong, obviously, but people like Gil don't know that. Which can be useful, on occasion." He grinned, then headed for the stairs, beckoning for her to follow. "I'll make some introductions, show you around. You'll like the people down here. They're the ones who still have some spirit left in them...or, in other words, are nothing like the Radens of this world," he added with a roll of his eyes.

Asha raised an eyebrow, thinking of the conversation back in the Tol. "So Raden knows about the Shadraehin, and wants nothing to do with him? With any of this?"

"He's not alone, either," said Jin with a regretful nod. "When people become Shadows...a lot of them just give up, to be honest. Raden and his ilk live miserable lives, and yet they act as if it's nothing more than they deserve. As if because they get treated like they're worthless, they really are." His shrug was resigned. "So rather than seeing the Sanctuary as something positive, they just worry that the Shadraehin is going to stir up the Administrators against us, draw attention, make things harder. And maybe that's even true—but fates, in my opinion, it's well worth it."

They reached the bottom of the stairs, and Asha gazed around in astonishment. Appearances from above hadn't been deceiving; 100 disregarding the odd setting, there was little to distinguish the scene before her from any other small village in Andarra. Somewhere out of sight, the sound of hammering indicated that construction of some kind was under way. Not all the structures were houses; one appeared to be a school, with several young children listening attentively to a man in threadbare clothes. There was even a building serving as a makeshift tavern.

They were closer to the torrent of Essence now, and Asha craned her neck to look up at it, trying to see where it disappeared into the cavern roof. She could make out the swirling threads of energy distinctly now, crashing together and ripping apart again as they hurtled upward. She felt as though there should have been a thunderous roar emanating from the column, but it was completely silent.

Her gaze traveled downward, and she frowned. Sitting what looked to be only a few feet away from the base of the cylinder was a man, cross-legged, his face hidden by a deep black hood. He was motionless as he stared into the streams of power rushing by.

"What is he doing?" she asked, indicating the man.

Jin's cheerful expression slipped a little.

"He is...not one of us," he said slowly. "We don't know who he is. Sometimes he's here for days, just staring into the light. Then he'll be gone for a few days, or a week, or a month. No one ever sees him arrive, and no one sees him leave." He frowned as he gazed at the motionless man. "The Shadraehin calls him the Watcher. I get the impression the Shadraehin knows more about him than the rest of us, but..." He shrugged.

Asha frowned. "I take it nobody talks to him?"

Jin shook his head. "Nobody can get that close to the light and live. Not even Shadows." He shuffled his feet. "Whoever—whatever—he is, Lissa, I would stay clear of him."

Asha nodded, shivering slightly as she tore her gaze from the black-cloaked figure.

They started walking again, and soon the unsettling sight was blocked by a row of well-made houses, all built from stone.

"Got a new one, Jin?"

Asha turned to see a man smiling genially at them. He looked slightly older than Jin—was one of the oldest Shadows she'd ever encountered, then, and probably among the first to fail his Trials after the Treaty was signed. He stuck out his hand. "I'm Parth."

Asha shook Parth's hand. "I'm . . . Lissa," she said, stumbling over the name only a little this time.

"I had to stop Lissa from attacking an Administrator with her bare hands today," Jin told Parth with a grin. "I figured she could probably handle seeing this place."

Parth grinned back as Asha blushed. "Good for you," he said approvingly. Then he laughed. "Though it's probably for the best that Jin stopped you. You're new to being a Shadow, I take it?"

Asha nodded. "It's been about a month."

Parth gave her a sympathetic smile. "It gets easier." He gestured at their surroundings. "Especially when there are those who are willing to help, and somewhere to get away from it all."

Asha nodded. "I can see that," she said. "So you decided to live down here?"

Parth shook his head, sobering a little. "Wasn't really much of a decision. See the boy in the green top, third row from the front?" He pointed toward the group of children in the school. Asha quickly located the child, a curly-haired boy who couldn't have been older than four. She nodded.

"That's my son, Sed."

Asha's brow furrowed as she studied Sed, along with all the other children. None of them had marks on their faces. "Being a Shadow isn't inherited?" she asked eventually.

"Our children are able to survive down here, so we think *something* must be passed on," conceded Parth. "Otherwise? Not as far as we, or anyone else, can tell. That's why we're here. Administration doesn't want non-Shadows being raised by Shadows."

Asha stared at him in disbelief. "But he's your son."

Parth gave a resigned shrug. "If you're a Shadow, and someone—*anyone*—else isn't, Administration will do what they believe is in the best interests of the person who isn't," he said quietly. "Remember that, and you shouldn't be surprised by much."

He sighed, glancing over his shoulder and then turning to Jin. "I have to go and help Feseith, but if you've got time before you leave, drop by and see Shana. Maybe you can stay for dinner." He clapped the other man on the back. "But if not, it was good to see you again. And it was very nice to meet you, Lissa." He nodded to them both, and then was on his way.

Jin appeared to be on good terms with most of the Sanctuary's occupants, and they were stopped for several other friendly conversations after that. As Asha heard more stories, she began to understand why these Shadows had taken refuge underground. Many had children in the same situation as Sed. There was a woman who had been working at House Tel'Shan, and had left to escape the too-close attentions of Lord Tel'Shan's younger son. One man had lost fingers after being attacked on the street by a drunken soldier; he'd been immediately thrown out by his employer, and now could not find work anywhere. A few others were simply looking for relief from the constant hatred of those in the city above, searching for a sense of community.

And yet all of them seemed happy now. Free. Asha watched them as they talked, and found herself more than a little envious.

Time passed; it was hard to tell exactly how much, but Asha suspected it was at least a few hours later when she and Jin found their way to Parth's house. Parth was still elsewhere, but Shana, his wife, turned out to be a bubbly young woman who immediately insisted they stay for dinner. Soon they were seated in the kitchen, chatting amiably as they waited for Parth to arrive.

Asha smiled as she leaned back, enjoying both the conversation and the coziness of the room, which had old but comfortable furniture and a fire crackling in the hearth. It felt like an eternity since she'd been able to sit down somewhere safe and warm and just enjoy other people's company. To *relax*.

"Lord si'Bandin wasn't too happy about our being together," Shana was saying, her back to them as she started preparing dinner. "That made it tricky for us, especially back then. He tried getting Administration involved at first, but they weren't too interested at that stage. And then we—"

She turned to face them.

Her eyes went wide, focusing over Asha's shoulder. The pot she'd been holding clattered to the floor, and a second later she let out an ear-piercing shriek.

Asha and Jin both leaped to their feet, spinning to see what Shana was so afraid of.

A man stood in the doorway; Asha's stomach lurched as she took in the black cloak and the deep, face-concealing hood.

The man she'd seen before. The Watcher.

There was a scuffling sound as Shana fled through the back entrance. Jin's face had gone deathly white, and he started to edge in the same direction, indicating Asha should as well. She started to move around the table.

"Halt." The man's voice sent a chill down Asha's spine. It was deep, whispery. Old.

Not quite human.

Then it turned to Jin. "Leave us. I must talk with this one."

Jin swallowed, looking for all the world as though he wanted to do as the stranger had said, but he shook his head. "I'm not leaving Lissa alone."

"As you wish."

It happened in an instant. The figure glided forward, faster than Asha would have believed possible. Its hand flicked out, and suddenly it was holding something dark and insubstantial. Little more than a shadow, but elongated and shaped. An ethereal blade.

It sliced silently across Jin's neck.

Jin stared at the man in disbelief, hands frantically trying to seal up the gaping wound in his throat. Blood, red and bright, seeped out between his fingers.

Then he collapsed, a bubbling gasp the only sound he could make as he died.

Asha watched in mute horror, her limbs leaden as fear paralyzed her. The black-cloaked man—if it truly was a man—turned to her, ignoring the corpse at his feet.

"Do not run, Ashalia Chaedris," he said, his voice raising the hairs on the back of Asha's neck.

Asha gritted her teeth and nodded, sinking back into her seat, trying not to look at the growing pool of crimson on the floor. "What do you want with me?" she whispered, fear making her voice catch.

"I wish to know if you are here to kill me."

Asha blinked, then forced her gaze up. She couldn't see beneath the man's hood, but she could feel his eyes on her.

"No." She shook her head slowly, clenching her hands into fists to stop them from shaking. "No, of course not. Why would you think that?"

"Because your presence marks the beginning. It means death is coming, for all of us. It has been Seen," said the man quietly.

Asha swallowed. "What…what do you mean, 'all of us'?"

"For myself, and my siblings. Four hunt. One hides, cognizant of what he is. A true traitor. An escherii." The man gazed at her. "And I Watch."

Suddenly shouts echoed from outside, and the hooded figure rose.

"I must go." He leaned forward. "I ask only one thing of you. When the time comes, do not let Vhalire suffer."

Before Asha could respond, he was gliding out the door.

Once she was certain she was alone, the crushing fear that she'd been holding at bay finally came crashing down on her. Trembling, she leaned forward and tried to steady herself against the table, light-headed. From the corner of her eye she could see Jin's body lying motionless, the pool of red still slowly spreading outward.

She stayed that way, motionless, until the Shadows found her.

# Chapter 10

Wirr flipped one of their few remaining coins from hand to hand.

"I think I have an idea about how we can make more of these," he announced, gazing down through the trees at the township below.

Davian glanced sideways at his friend. "Safely?"

Wirr caught the coin and turned, giving Davian an injured stare. "Of course." He hesitated. "Relatively."

Davian sighed. "I suppose that's the best we can hope for, right now. Let's have it."

Wirr explained his reasoning. Davian listened intently; when his friend was finished he sat back, considering for a few moments.

"That's a terrible plan, Wirr," he said eventually. "It's going to take them two seconds to realize something's amiss."

Wirr raised an eyebrow, hearing the hesitation in Davian's tone. "But?"

Davian gave him a reluctant nod. "But you're right. We're out of supplies; we need the coin." He stood, brushing bits of dead leaves from his clothing. "Let's go and meet the locals."

Davian tried to look inconspicuous.

The tavern, like much in Desriel so far, surprised him by how normal it seemed. It was well lit and cheerful, full of men who were taking their ease after a long day of farming or selling their wares. The proprietor circulated through the room continuously, laughing with regulars and trying to ingratiate himself with new customers. A young man with a flute played a merry tune in the corner, and occasionally would get the crowd clapping along to a favorite verse. Davian and Wirr had been to a few Andarran taverns on their journey, and they were almost indistinguishable from here.

There *were* differences, of course. The serving girls were more modestly clad than their Andarran counterparts; men flirted, but did not take the same liberties they might have done back home. The tables were made from white oak, an extremely hardy wood unique to northern Desriel and a commodity the Gil'shar refused to export.

Then there was the plate by the doorway, above which loomed the sigil of the god Talkanar. Wirr had insisted that they drop one of their few remaining coins into it; according to him, each tavern in Desriel was aligned with one of the nine gods, and it was good form—if not law—to make an offering if you intended to partake of anything. He'd apparently been right, because the barkeep had given them an approving nod as they sat down.

Davian stared back at the offering plate in fascination. It was nearly overflowing with silver; in Andarra the entire thing would have vanished within minutes, gone in the hands of some enterprising thief. Here, however—despite many of the tavern's occupants looking less than reputable—nobody was giving it a second glance.

"There are a lot of coins on that plate," he murmured to Wirr.

"The Gil'shar torture and execute people who steal from the gods," Wirr whispered.

"Good to know," Davian whispered back.

They fell silent for a few moments, observing everyone in the large room. Davian fiddled absently with the sleeve of his shirt. Its tight fit had made it uncomfortable to wear on the road, which meant that it was in a better state than most of the other clothes he'd bought after leaving Caladel. He'd taken the time to bathe in a nearby river before coming into town, too. He needed to look at least vaguely respectable for this.

Finally Wirr nodded toward a small group of men gathered around a table.

"Them," he said, keeping his voice low.

Davian followed Wirr's gaze to a booth in the corner of the room. The three heavily muscled men sitting there were better dressed than most of the people in the tavern; there were empty seats around them, as if the other patrons were wary of getting too close. Each of the men held a fistful of cards and wore an expression of intense concentration.

"They look important. And much bigger than us," said Davian doubtfully.

"They look wealthy," Wirr corrected. "More likely to take it on the chin if they lose a few pieces of gold here and there."

Davian shrugged. "If you say so."

They stood. Wirr hesitated, biting a fingernail, then laid a hand on Davian's shoulder. "Whatever happens, just stay calm."

Davian frowned, a little irritated that Wirr thought he would crumble under the pressure, but nodded. They walked over to the table, which fell silent as they approached. One of the finely dressed men glanced up from his cards, giving them a disdainful look. He had jet-black hair, and sported the same neatly trimmed beard as the other two.

"Can we help you?" he asked, his expression indicating he had no desire to do any such thing.

Wirr gestured to one of the empty seats. "Looks like you could use a fourth."

The man raised an eyebrow, obviously taking note of Wirr's age. "I don't know who you think you are, boy, but this is a private game. So run along."

Wirr sighed, turning. "Figures. You look to be the type who can't take a little competition."

The whisper of steel being unsheathed filled the room, and suddenly conversation in the tavern stopped, every eye turning toward them. All three of the men were standing, though none of their drawn blades—as yet—were actually pointing at Wirr.

"Perhaps I should have mentioned from the start. We're playing Geshett. This game is for blooded Seekers only." The man leaned closer, smiling to reveal a row of perfectly white teeth. "So. You ever faced an abomination, boy? Put it down so it can't get back up?"

Davian used every ounce of his will to keep still, to not turn and flee. *Seeker* was the word they used in Desriel. In Andarra these men would be known as Hunters.

109

Wirr, however, barely twitched. "I haven't," he said, "but my friend here has."

Davian tried to look neither shocked nor terrified as the men turned to him as one, inspecting him skeptically. Finally the man who had first spoken gave a derisive laugh. "I don't believe you. He looks like someone's carved into him, rather than the other way around. He doesn't even have a blade. He couldn't kill a cockroach." The others chuckled in agreement.

Wirr scowled, then reached into his bag, tossing something onto the table with a metallic clank. Davian started as he realized it was the two Shackles they had taken from the Hunters back in Talmiel. "That scar is not from a cockroach," said Wirr.

The man's smile faded as his gaze went from the Shackles to Davian, then back again. Eventually he gave a slight nod, pushing the torcs back toward Wirr and turning to Davian. "Who taught you?"

"Breshada." Davian regretted it as soon as it left his mouth, but it was too late; the question had caught him by surprise and it had been the only thing he could think to say. Still, it had an effect on those around the table, and a low murmur went around the tavern as the name was repeated to others who hadn't been near enough to overhear. Everyone was still watching, Davian realized, fascinated by the exchange. He just hoped they wouldn't be spectators to his and Wirr's sudden and untimely deaths.

"*The* Breshada?" asked the man, more surprised than dubious now.

Davian inclined his head, trying to look confident. "I was in Talmiel with her just last week. We cut these off a couple of abominations that were stupid enough to come into town."

The man just stared at Davian for a few seconds, then nodded, gesturing to the empty chair. "A student of Breshada the Red is welcome at our game anytime," he said, only a little reluctantly.

Davian gave him a tight smile, hoping it made him look arrogant rather than relieved, and sat. Seeing that nothing else interesting was going to happen, the rest of the patrons went back to their conversations, though Davian could see a few of them still casting sidelong glances in his direction.

Inwardly he cursed Wirr. His friend hadn't batted an eyelid.

He'd *known* they were Hunters, and had kept Davian in the dark for fear he wouldn't go along with the plan.

He would *kill* him if they made it through this in one piece.

The man who had been doing the talking stuck out his hand. "I am Kelosh," he said, all traces of surliness gone now that he had made the decision to believe them. "This is Altesh and Gorron." The other two men nodded to him as Kelosh said their names.

"Shadat," said Davian, a common name from Desriel that he'd decided upon earlier.

"Keth," supplied Wirr, who was still standing.

Kelosh glanced up at him. "You want to play?"

Wirr shook his head as he took a seat to the side. "Rounds are too short with five. Besides, Shadat already took all my money," he added with a grin.

Kelosh chuckled, though he and the others gave Davian an appraising look. "Very well," he said, shuffling and starting the deal.

Davian took a deep breath, concentrating. Geshett was fairly simple; Wirr had taught him the game over the past few hours. How Wirr had known these men here were playing it, though, Davian had no idea.

"So you've come from Talmiel," said Kelosh, his tone conversational. "You wouldn't have heard about the trouble up north?" Davian shook his head and Kelosh paused, evidently excited to find someone new to tell. "A boy in one of the villages up there found out he had the sickness a couple of weeks ago. First abomination in Desriel in ten years." Kelosh's lip curled. "He went mad. Killed his entire family, half the rest of the villagers, too."

Davian didn't have to fake his reaction. "That's awful." Then he frowned. "Wait. How?" The First Tenet should have stopped one of the Gifted from hurting anyone, regardless of where he had been born.

Kelosh nodded solemnly, clearly having anticipated the question. "That's what has everyone talking."

"They say he doesn't have the Mark," interjected Altesh.

Kelosh shot him a look of irritation, then turned back to Davian. "I heard that, too, but unlike my idiot friend here, I don't believe *every* whisper in Squaremarket. The Gil'shar are taking    111 him to Thrindar for a public execution—making an example of him and all that—so they have it under control. They'll let us know if we need to start looking for something new." He rubbed his hands together apprehensively. "Still, word's out that he was from here, so everyone's understandably a little nervous. I had three people today ask me if we were thinking of setting up posts in Thrindar again."

Davian set his face into as grim a mask as he could muster. "Meldier forbid that's needed," he said, invoking the name of the Desrielite god of knowledge.

"I'll drink to that," replied Kelosh, and the others muttered their agreement.

Davian breathed a sigh of relief as the conversation died out, the others focusing on their cards. He mentally ran through the rules of Geshett again. Everyone started with ten cards. Players either passed—eliminating themselves from the round—or lay one, two, or three cards facedown on the table, called their combined value, and made a bet of any amount. The card value called had to be higher than any previously played.

Once a bet had been made, another player could claim "Gesh"—becoming the Accuser—indicating that they thought the cards laid down were not of the value called. If Gesh was invoked, the cards were turned faceup. If the call had been honest, the Accuser paid the player double their bet. If it had been false, though, the player not only honored their bet, but gave the same amount to the Accuser.

Whoever finished the round having played the highest cards—either honestly or without being caught—collected everything that had been bet during that round.

Davian settled in, focusing. It was meant to be a game of skill, in which a person's ability to bluff was key. He wasn't sure how successful his own bluffing abilities would be, but as for the others, he knew they had no chance.

For a split second, he almost pitied them.

Kelosh slapped Davian on the back as Gorron continued to glare at the overturned cards.

"Do you ever bluff, my friend?" he asked as Gorron reluctantly slid two silver pieces in Davian's direction.

Davian took them and added them to his pile, which had grown large in the last hour. "Only when I know you won't call me on it," he replied with a grin.

Kelosh roared with laughter. The drinks had been flowing, and the big man's demeanor had loosened considerably since Davian had first sat down. Davian was grateful for that. He'd been careful in his play, as Wirr had advised—losing occasionally, letting the smaller bluffs go uncalled—but he had still won enough coin to last a couple of months, maybe more. And Wirr had been right. While the men had not enjoyed losing, Kelosh and Altesh had taken it in stride, almost seeming amused that they were being beaten by a boy.

Gorron had been less amiable. To be fair, his pile had dwindled the most of the three, and now consisted of little more than a few copper pieces. Once those disappeared, the game would likely finish for the evening. To that end, Davian intended to call Gesh the very next time he saw a puff of shadows coming from Gorron's mouth. Despite feeling a little more comfortable than at the beginning, he still itched to be far, far away from these men.

"Breshada must be as good a teacher as she is a Seeker," Gorron said with a growl as he watched his coins disappear into Davian's pile.

"One eight. Three coppers," said Altesh, laying a single card on the table. He looked across at Davian. "Tell us more about Breshada, Shadat. Is what they say about Whisper true?"

Davian tried not to panic. There had been only gentle banter around the table thus far; the game generally required too much concentration for small talk. This was the first time he had been asked a question that he didn't know the answer to. What was Whisper?

"I don't know. What do they say?" he asked, trying to sound casual. He laid two cards facedown. "Two twos. One silver." It was his standard bet, now he had the money. Small enough not to matter if he didn't win the round, large enough to be worthwhile if someone called Gesh on him. Kelosh had been right—he *always* played it true, and folded if he couldn't. He had a guaranteed way of making money. There was no point in gambling.

Kelosh snorted. "You know the stories. Whoever holds it cannot be touched, by abominations or the gods themselves. One cut from Whisper steals your very soul and makes the blade stronger. That sort of thing." He stared at his hand for a moment. "Two sevens. Six coppers."

Davian hesitated. Kelosh was lying about his cards, but Davian ignored it, instead thinking back to that night in Talmiel when the young woman had rescued them. He thought about the way their captors had died. "I don't know about stealing souls," he said quietly, "but all it takes is a nick, and you're dead. Instantly. I've seen it with my own eyes."

There was an impressed silence for a few seconds, then Gorron snorted. "Likely story," he said, shaking his head in derision. "Three eights."

Davian prepared himself. Gorron had lied. It was finally over.

However, Gorron paused before making his bid, then stood, unbuckling the leather-sheathed sword from around his waist. He drew it out, laying both sword and sheath on the table. The blade itself was beautiful, elegantly curved with delicately worked silver inlay on the hilt. It looked more than ornate, though. Like the sword of a master craftsman.

"The workmanship alone is worth twice what any of you have in front of you," he said. "But the blade? The killer of a thousand heretics and abominations? It is priceless."

Kelosh gave Gorron a look of open surprise. "You're betting Slayer? Why?" He scratched his head. "This is just a friendly game, Gorron."

Gorron was silent for a moment, then scowled. "I'm not going to lose to *him*, Kelosh," he said, jerking his head in Davian's direction. "I don't care who he's trained with, how many abominations he's killed. Look at him! He's a child!" He glared at Davian. "I find it hard to believe he's ever even seen a real sword except from the wrong end. Let's see him try and win one."

Kelosh shrugged. "It's your decision, Gorron," he said, shooting Davian an apologetic look. He looked around. "Anyone want to call him on it?"

Davian saw Wirr shaking his head from the corner of his eye.

Gorron obviously loved the blade. *The killer of a thousand her-*

*etics and abominations.* The fear that had been with him all evening was suddenly gone, replaced with a burning anger. These men killed Gifted. They *killed* people like him, Asha, Wirr. And they were proud of it.

"Gesh," he said softly.

Gorron stared at him in shock, a stricken look on his face. Davian had so much in front of him to lose, and only a fool would have assumed Gorron was bluffing with a bet that large. Kelosh saw the expression on his friend's face and groaned.

"Perhaps we can figure out an alternate means of—"

Kelosh was cut short by a cry of anger from Gorron. Before Davian could react the Hunter had drawn a dagger from his belt and was lunging at him.

Time slowed.

From the rage on Gorron's face, Davian had no doubt the man was going for a killing blow. Still seated, he snatched Slayer from the table, desperately putting it between himself and the leaping Gorron.

The tip of the sword caught Gorron in the chest.

It slid in smoothly, more easily than Davian had imagined a blade would go through flesh. Gorron froze, the dagger clattering from his hand to the floor, then stumbled back. He looked uncomprehendingly at Davian; he gave a racking cough and blood sprayed from his mouth.

Then his eyes rolled upward and he collapsed. Altesh rushed to his side, but Davian knew what he would say before he got there.

"He's dead," said Altesh, stunned.

The entire tavern was silent, everyone looking alternately at the corpse on the floor and at Davian, who was still holding the bloodstained sword. He lowered the blade.

Kelosh stared at him solemnly for a few moments.

"I have never seen *anyone* move that fast," said the Hunter eventually, his voice soft with awe. "You do Breshada credit, Shadat." He sighed, shaking his head as he looked at Gorron's motionless body, then gestured to the table. "You and your friend should go. Take your winnings; I will deal with the watch. I'll tell them it was between Seekers, and it will be fine. If they see how young you are, though, it will only hold things up."

Davian just nodded, too numb to respond otherwise. He and Wirr quickly swept the pile of coins into their satchel.

Before anyone could move to block their exit, they were outside and hurrying into the night.

They ran for a quarter hour before Wirr held up his hand, breathing hard, and came to a gradual stop.

"I don't think anyone is following us," he said between gulps of air. "We can probably—"

He cut off with a cry of pain as Davian's fist crashed into his nose.

"What in *fates* were you thinking?" Davian hissed, putting as much venom into the words as possible without making too much noise. "You knew! You knew they were Hunters, and you sent me right to them. Worse. You didn't even tell me!" His friend had struggled back to his feet, but Davian stepped forward and drove his fist squarely into his nose again, eliciting another moan of pain. "This is not a game, Wirr! We could *die* out here!"

Wirr stayed on the ground this time, looking up at Davian with pure shock on his face. "Dav!" He scrambled backward in the dirt as Davian took a menacing step forward. "I'm sorry!"

Davian looked at his friend—stunned, upset, *scared*—and the anger drained from him, exposing the emotion it had tried to cover.

Shame.

He sunk to his knees next to his friend, suddenly realizing his entire body was shaking.

"I killed him, Wirr," he whispered after a few seconds. "I just picked up the sword, and..."

Wirr hesitated, but seeing his friend's rage had subsided, shifted over to sit next to him. He tested his nose gently with a finger. "It wasn't your fault, Dav," he said. "He was going to kill you—just like he killed all those other Gifted. Remember what he was."

Davian stared at the ground, unable to concentrate with all the emotions swirling in his head. "And that makes it right?"

Wirr bit his lip, silent for a few seconds. "It couldn't be avoided, Dav. Same as Talmiel," he noted eventually.

Davian screwed up his face. "Except I wasn't holding the sword in Talmiel."

"So it's all right for someone else to save your life, but not if you do it yourself?"

Davian ran his hands through his hair. "I don't know, Wirr," he admitted. "I just feel…dirty. Sick to my very core. Like I just made the biggest mistake of my life, and there is no way I can ever take it back."

Wirr just nodded, obviously not sure what to say. They sat in silence for a while, then Wirr cleared his throat. "I should have told you. But I knew you'd never go along with it."

Davian took a deep breath. The silence had given him time to order his thoughts, push the shock of what he'd just done to the background. "How did you know who they were? And, fates— why, *why* did you choose them in the first place?"

Wirr winced. "Geshett is a Hunter's game," he admitted. "They say it helps hone their ability to tell when people are lying, and to conceal things themselves. It's the *only* game they play, Dav, and no one else is allowed to play it." He shrugged. "Your ability doesn't set off Finders and isn't covered by the Tenets. It was the only way I could think of to get enough money."

Davian gritted his teeth. It made sense, though they had been beyond fortunate that none of the Hunters had been suspicious enough to check them with Finders. "Just…tell me everything next time. It was all I could do not to run when I realized who they were."

Wirr gave a slight smile and hefted the satchel, which made a jingling sound as he shook it. "All things considered, Dav, you did very well."

Despite everything, Davian laughed softly. "All I could think of half the time was what Breshada's face would look like, if she ever found out I was using her name to dupe her 'brethren.'"

Wirr smirked. "Angry. Angry is how I picture her."

Davian smiled, and a tiny part of the pain—the worst part— faded just a little. He stood, sticking out his hand. Wirr hesitated for a moment, then grasped it firmly, allowing Davian to pull him back to his feet.

"I think you broke my nose," Wirr grumbled, pulling a kerchief from his pocket. He dabbed at his nose and grimaced as the cloth came away soaked in blood.

"Nothing you didn't deserve," noted Davian.

Wirr grunted. "I suppose that's true." He looked at Davian, expression thoughtful. "Dav...I have to ask. How did you do it?"

Davian stared at his friend in confusion. "Do what?"

"How in all fates did you move so fast? One second you were sitting there, and the next that sword was sticking clean through Gorron. I don't doubt you have fast reactions, but that was..." He shook his head. "Something else."

Davian looked at the sword, still in his hand. He unsheathed it, hefted it, admiring the sense of balance and the clean lines of the blade. "He called it Slayer," he pointed out. "If it has a name..."

Wirr snorted. "A Hunter trying to sound important, nothing more. It's not a Named sword, Dav. It would be easy to tell. Like Breshada's."

Davian nodded, acknowledging the truth of the statement. As soon as he'd seen Whisper, he'd known there was something different about it, even before seeing how effectively it killed. For most Named swords he'd heard of, the names themselves hadn't made sense to him. Having seen Whisper in action, though, he knew it was the perfect word to describe it.

"Slayer," on the other hand, didn't fit. It was a nice sword—a *very* nice sword—but Wirr was right. It had no unusual powers.

Gently he tossed the sword into the long grass at the side of the road. Valuable or not, he wanted nothing more to do with it.

Wirr looked about to protest but then just sighed, nodding.

"If it wasn't the sword, then I don't know," Davian finally admitted. "Everything seemed to move more slowly, I suppose. I grabbed the sword, and..." He trailed off, stomach churning as he remembered the moment. For an instant he thought he was going to vomit, but a few deep breaths settled him again. "I can't explain it, Wirr."

Wirr grunted. "Whatever it was, it saved your life." He grimaced. "Probably both our lives. I was about to try and use Essence to hold him back."

Davian gave a low whistle. "First Tenet or not, that would have made things interesting."

"You have no idea," muttered Wirr, almost to himself. He glanced around. The sky was clear tonight and though it was too early for much moonlight, the stars provided enough illumination to see the road. "We should keep moving. The further we are from here come dawn, the better."

They walked for a while in silence, the quiet of the night calming Davian's jangling nerves somewhat.

Abruptly Wirr cleared his throat. "I meant it, you know," he said hesitantly. "I really am sorry."

"I know, Wirr," said Davian. "It's all right."

There was silence for a while longer, then Davian rubbed his hands together, keeping them warm against the chill of the night air. The motion caused his sleeve to pull upward a little, and he found himself staring at the carefully covered patch on his forearm.

"Strange, what Kelosh said," he said idly. "Do you really think there's a Gifted out there without a Mark? Maybe if we got far enough away from Andarra..."

Wirr shook his head. "No. I've read about Gifted as far away as the Eastern Empire having the Mark—when the Tenets were created, a lot of countries nearly went to war with us over it. They were all outraged that Andarra had unilaterally enforced laws that some of their citizens were bound to... but of course with the Gifted in their armies unable to fight, they were too weak to make an issue of it." He kicked a stone along in front of him. "It's interesting. The Gil'shar were supposedly amongst the most angry when the Treaty was signed; they thought the Loyalists should have pressed their advantage. But in the end, it helped them more than anyone else. Their army never relied on Gifted, so they were unaffected—and now they're stronger than ever."

Davian nodded, though he hadn't really been paying attention after the first sentence. Politics was Wirr's passion, not his.

"It's a shame," he noted. "Even with all the Finders around, being free of the Tenets would have been useful out here."

Wirr frowned. "How so?"

Davian raised an eyebrow. "It would be easier to defend ourselves, for a start. And you could have used the Gift to steal some coin, rather than us having to risk our lives for it. It wouldn't take much Essence to pickpocket a few people—not enough to set off Finders, anyway."

"I suppose," said Wirr, sounding reluctant.

Davian shot him a surprised look. "You disagree?"

Wirr shrugged. "I just don't like the idea of using our powers to steal from people."

Davian stared at his friend, not sure if Wirr was joking. "Isn't that *exactly* what we just did?"

Wirr shook his head. "Those men chose to gamble their money. They wagered you couldn't tell when they were lying, and they lost. It's a fine line, I know, but it *is* different." He sighed. "I'm not disagreeing, Dav, particularly about the part where we could actually protect ourselves. But we need to be careful what we wish for."

Davian frowned. "They're Desrielites," he protested. "They'd string us up from the nearest tree, given the chance. Why should we feel badly about taking their coin? Weren't you just saying my *killing* one of them was justified?"

"That wasn't your fault," pointed out Wirr. "He was a Hunter, a murderer, and it was self-defense. What you're talking about is going out and using the Gift to steal from ordinary people. I know we're in need, but... it would still be an abuse, Dav. Before the war, the Augurs let the Gifted use Essence to take advantage of others when they 'needed' to, too. They said it was to make Andarra a better place. Look at where that got us."

Davian shook his head, surprised at the direction of the conversation. "So... you think the Treaty is justified?" he asked in confusion. Debating the Treaty was forbidden among students; with Talean always around, this was a topic that had never come up between them. It shouldn't have needed to, though. *Every* Gifted wanted the Treaty, and particularly the Tenets, gone.

Wirr shook his head. "Of course not," he said, a little defensively. "But if you had the chance to remove all the Tenets, or just some of them—what would you do?"

"Remove them all," said Davian without hesitation.

Wirr sighed. "Really? You don't think *some* restrictions on how the Gift is used are a good thing?"

"Like what?"

Wirr shrugged. "There's four Tenets. Let's take the first: no use of the Gift with the intent to harm or hinder non-Gifted. Why is that so bad?"

"Because we can't defend ourselves," said Davian. "I know the argument is that it only reduces us to the level of normal people, but the Gifted are *hated*. We never get attacked by just one person; it's always a mob." He unconsciously touched the scar on his face.

"Right." Wirr looked uncomfortable for a moment, realizing how close to the mark he'd come. "So what if that Tenet were changed, allowing the Gifted to use Essence to defend themselves?"

Davian thought for a moment. He wanted to say it still wouldn't be enough, but as he followed the argument through to its conclusion in his head, he knew he had no case. "I suppose that would be fine," he said reluctantly.

Wirr nodded in satisfaction. "The Second Tenet: no use of the Gift to deceive, intimidate, or otherwise work to the detriment of non-Gifted. Problem?"

"We can't steal things."

Wirr rolled his eyes. "Seriously."

Davian sighed, thinking for a moment. "It's the same as the first," he said. "It's too general. I can't use the Gift to hide myself as a thief, and that's fine. But I'd like the ability to hide myself if there are people chasing after me, trying to kill me, just because I'm Gifted."

Wirr nodded in approval. "A problem that would mostly be solved by the exception to the First Tenet."

Davian smiled. "Thought about this a lot, have we?"

Wirr shrugged. "The joys of studying politics."

Davian gazed up at the starlit sky as they walked. "So let's say the Third Tenet stays, for our own protection if nothing else—that Administrators and Gifted can do no harm to one another, physical or otherwise. What would you change about the Fourth Tenet?"

"I think the Fourth could probably be removed," admitted Wirr. "As long as the other three are in place, I see no reason why we should be forced to do what the Administrators tell us all the time. We don't need keepers."

Davian nodded, relieved that his friend mirrored his thoughts on at least that much. "And the Treaty itself? The changes to all the Andarran laws?"

Wirr shrugged. "Some of those would have to be revised, too, of course. But there are some reasonable checks and balances in there."

"You don't think we should rule again?"

Wirr looked at Davian levelly. "I'm stronger and faster than a regular person. I can do the work of several men each day, then tap my Reserve at night to do other things rather than sleeping. All being well, I'll live twenty years longer than most people, maybe more." He paused. "But does that make me wiser? Fairer? Do those qualities automatically make me a good ruler, or even just a better one than someone who doesn't have the Gift?"

Davian remained silent. He knew Wirr had a point but it irked him nonetheless; for some reason he'd never really thought it through before. It had always simply been accepted within the school that the Treaty was wrong, that the Gifted had been usurped from their rightful place.

Eventually he sighed. "You're right. The thought of you in charge of anything is terrifying." He exchanged a brief grin with Wirr, then shrugged. "It's not like it matters, anyway. From what I understand, the Vessel that created the Tenets can only be used to change them if King Andras and one of the Gifted work together. And everyone knows that King Andras won't trust any of the Gifted enough to do that."

Wirr nodded. "True. Still an interesting exercise, though."

Davian inclined his head, suddenly realizing that the conversation had—finally—taken his thoughts away from earlier events.

"That box of yours still glowing?" asked Wirr, changing the subject.

Davian had almost forgotten about the Vessel after the events of the evening. He took it out of his pocket, half-blinded by the sudden light in the darkness. He'd seen the iridescent symbol several times over the past few days, but it had always been inconsistent, often fading even as he examined it. It had been only this morning that the glowing lines had become stronger, more constant, though still emanating from just a single face of the cube.

He turned the box slowly. A different face lit up with the wolf's image. He turned it again, this time back to how he had originally been holding it. The first side lit up once more.

"You still can't see it?" he asked Wirr.

"No," said Wirr, sounding worried. Davian couldn't blame him. The symbol was undoubtedly being generated by Essence; for it to be visible only to Davian should have been impossible.

Davian twisted the box vertically; again the face that had been lit faded, and a new face became illuminated. He ran his fingers over the engravings. Was it a puzzle? An indication of how to open the box, or something else? He shook it gently, but as always, nothing shifted. It was either empty, or it was completely solid, or whatever was inside was securely packed in.

He tapped the side showing the symbol. It was warm to the touch; when his finger made contact with the metal, the tip disappeared into a nimbus of white light. Aside from the heat, though, there were no sensations. Certainly nothing to help him figure out the box's purpose.

Frustrated, he tossed it in the air, spinning it as he did so that the edges blurred together.

He frowned as he caught it. Had he just seen...?

He tossed it again, this time higher, spinning the box so viciously that it appeared more of a cylinder than a cube. He snatched it out of the air with an excited grin, then repeated the action. A thought began to form, small at first but quickly growing until he became certain.

He tossed the cube upward one last time, laughing.

Wirr squinted, watching him with a worried expression. "Are you... all right, Dav?"

Davian came to a stop, then held up the cube in front of Wirr's confused face.

"I'm better than all right," he said triumphantly. "I know where we're supposed to be going."

# Chapter 11

"You're sure about this?" asked Wirr, trying unsuccessfully to keep the doubt from his voice.

"I am." Davian did his best to sound confident, though inwardly the certainty of last night had faded a little. They had walked all morning before reaching the crossroads at which they now stood. If they continued along the road to the north, they would keep heading toward Thrindar. If they accepted Davian's theory, though, they would turn east, heading into the Malacar forest and away from civilization.

The bronze box was actually a Wayfinder. It had to be. Davian had read about them once, years earlier—one object attuned to another, a Vessel that acted as a sort of compass, always pointing to its counterpart.

He rolled the cube in his hands. Currently, no matter which way it was turned, it was the side facing east that lit up with the wolf symbol. It made sense. Ilseth had said that it would guide him to the sig'nari when the time came. It *had* to be the right explanation.

The only problem was, as Wirr had dubiously pointed out, that the art to making Wayfinders had been lost centuries earlier. That—combined with Wirr's continuing inability to see the glow at all—left Davian with more uncertainty than he was entirely comfortable with.

There was a long pause as the two boys contemplated the different roads. Then Wirr gave the slightest of shrugs.

"I trust you," he said. There was no mocking or query in his voice.

Davian shot him a grateful look, and they set off eastward without another word.

The road leading to the Malacar forest was much quieter than the one they had been traveling for the past few days, and as a result the tension that had been sitting constantly between Davian's shoulders began to loosen. The weather was fine but not too warm, and he and Wirr made good time as they traveled in comfortable, companionable silence.

Idly, he wondered again how Asha had reacted to their leaving. It was something that had been on his mind a lot over the past few weeks; every time he tried to put himself in her shoes he felt a stab of guilt, knowing that if their positions were reversed he would feel concern, confusion, maybe even a sense of betrayal. He wondered what she was doing at that very moment—she was probably in a lesson, if everything had returned to normal after the Athian Elders had left.

He sighed to himself. As much as he missed her, it was better that she was at Caladel, safe from the dangers he and Wirr were facing.

He looked around. They had reached the edge of the Malacar; open fields were quickly being replaced by tall, thick-trunked trees. Soon the road was canopied by foliage overhead, with only a few stray rays of sunlight slipping through the cover and reaching the road itself. Still, the forest had a cheerful, airy feel to it, unlike much of the menacing jungle they had been forced to navigate so far on their journey. The trees were spaced far enough apart that visibility was high, and undergrowth was minimal.

Davian and Wirr were chatting amiably, the sun finally threatening to slip below the horizon, when Davian frowned and came to an abrupt stop.

Wirr took a few extra steps before realizing his friend had halted. "Tired already?"

Davian shook his head, reaching into his pocket and almost
jerking his hand back out again when he felt the heat of the Ves-

sel inside. Cautiously he pulled the box out. It was like touching a stone that had sat too long in the sun; it was possible to hold, but only delicately, and even then he had to change his grip every couple of seconds to keep the heat from becoming too much.

He held it away from his body, trying to examine it. The glow was so bright now that the wolf symbol was impossible to make out.

"I think we're close," he said.

Wirr stared at the box, his expression troubled. "If you say so," he said with a sigh. "Is it still pointing east?"

Davian squinted for a moment, then nodded.

"Then I suppose we keep going that way until it says otherwise."

They walked on for a few minutes, the heat from the bronze Vessel becoming uncomfortable even through the rough cloth of Davian's trousers. He was considering asking Wirr to hold it for him when they rounded a curve in the road and came to an abrupt, jarring halt.

Ahead, in a clearing just off the road itself, a group of soldiers in the livery of Desriel were setting up camp. At first glance there looked to be about ten of them, each one with the telltale glint of a Finder on his wrist. A couple of the soldiers looked up, noticing them.

"Keep walking," Wirr said softly. "Worst thing we can do right now is look scared."

Davian forced his legs to move, mechanically putting one foot in front of the other. They had seen Desrielite soldiers before, but not so close and certainly not such a large group of them. Davian's mouth was dry, and he felt a strange combination of chills and sweat. He knew the blood had drained from his face; he tried to keep his breathing even, getting himself slowly back under control. The soldiers were looking at them, but none had moved to stop them. It was fine. Just keep walking.

Wirr gave the soldiers a friendly wave as they passed and a few nodded in polite response, apparently satisfied they were simply travelers and posed no threat. Even in his terrified state, Davian couldn't help but be impressed by Wirr's poise. His friend looked as though nothing were amiss; he strolled, meandered, as if simply enjoying the warmth of the afternoon.

Thankfully, the next bend in the road was only a hundred feet away. Within a minute the soldiers were obscured from view once again.

As soon as the boys were certain they were out of sight, they stopped. Davian bent over with his hands on his knees, releasing a long, slow breath, then almost laughing aloud as relief washed over him. Wirr let out a similarly deep breath, holding out his hands for Davian to see. They were trembling.

"You did well back there, Dav," said Wirr seriously, facade dropping. He now looked as shaken as Davian felt. "You looked almost happy to see them."

Davian laughed. "Me? I would have turned tail and run if you hadn't kept your head," he said, a little giddily. "It took everything I had not to turn around, but you just strolled on past like you owned the El-cursed forest." He rubbed his face, repressing what probably would have come out as a maniacal giggle.

Wirr clapped him on the back. "Well, we're past, at any rate."

After taking sufficient time to recover their wits, they kept moving. Before a minute had gone by, though, Davian stopped again. Something was wrong; the warmth of the Vessel had begun to fade.

Alarmed, he dug into his pocket and pulled it out, examining the bronzed surface with narrowed eyes. Then he groaned, twisting the box in his hand a few times, vainly hoping he was mistaken.

"What is it?" Wirr asked.

Davian bit his lip. "It's pointing back the other way."

"Towards the soldiers?"

Davian hesitated, then nodded. "Towards the soldiers."

Wirr let out a low string of violent curses that Davian had never heard him use before. Then he took a few deep breaths to compose himself.

"Of course it is," he said calmly.

By the time the two boys had made their way back to within view of the soldiers' camp—using the surrounding brush as cover—the sun had vanished below the horizon, leaving only a dull pink glow in its wake.

They were no more than a hundred feet away, but the deepening shadows made for easy concealment so long as they made no sudden movements. From Davian's prone position he could see the entire camp, which appeared neat and orderly. Most of the soldiers sat chatting and laughing around a small fire; a pair of sentries sat halfway between the fire and the road, their backs to the flames.

Closer to the others but still set apart, another man reclined against a small covered wagon. As Davian watched, the man peered through a narrow window at the front of the wagon, saying something in a low voice and then spitting inside. A soldier by the fire who was watching him just laughed.

From the men's demeanor, no one thought an attack was likely. The pair of sentries were dicing, only intermittently glancing toward the road to look for signs of movement. The man by the wagon appeared half-asleep as he listened to his companions' conversation, stirring only to call out an occasional comment to them.

Still, it looked as if someone would be awake the entire night. Whatever the Wayfinder was leading Davian to, it would be difficult to retrieve.

Wirr shifted beside him. "So what exactly are we looking for?" he whispered. "I can't imagine the sig'nari would be keeping company with this lot."

"I'm not sure," admitted Davian. He frowned, scanning the camp. There was little doubt that the Wayfinder was pointing to something here—the heat emanating from his pocket had become uncomfortable again as they had drawn closer. Could one of the sig'nari really be hiding among a group of Desrielite soldiers? Or had the Wayfinder's counterpart object somehow been found, or stolen, by these men? He tried not to think about the implications of the latter.

Wirr shifted position again, peering through the brush. "Perhaps in the wagon?" he suggested.

Davian squinted, trying to better see the wagon. It was solidly built, more so than normal; instead of the traditional canvas roof it had one of sturdy wood, making it look like a large box on wheels. The only window visible was a small slit at the front, crisscrossed with thick steel bars that glinted in the firelight.

After a moment Davian realized that a heavy wooden beam lay across the door, clearly to prevent anyone on the inside from getting out.

"You're right," he said, biting his lip. "Whoever we're looking for must be locked in there."

"Wonderful." Wirr sighed but didn't dispute Davian's statement, evidently having come to the same conclusion himself. "We've come this far. I suppose we're going to try and get them out?"

Davian stared at the armed soldiers for a few seconds.

"I suppose we are," he said reluctantly.

They spent the next few hours waiting, whispering to each other only when necessary.

Eventually the soldiers around the campfire began drifting one by one to their tents, soon followed by the pair of men who had been keeping watch on the road. The fire died down to little more than glowing embers, then was doused entirely by the last soldier to retire. A heavy silence fell over the camp, broken only by the occasional sound of the lone sentry by the wagon muttering to himself.

"They don't seem too worried about being attacked," said Davian, keeping his voice low.

Wirr nodded. "They're Desrielite soldiers. I'd doubt even the bandits around here would be desperate enough to get on the wrong side of the Gil'shar," he whispered back.

Davian rubbed his hands together nervously. "So how do we go about this?"

Wirr bit a fingernail. "I suppose we sneak up on the guard, knock him out, and try and get into that wagon before anyone else wakes up," he said, sounding more uncertain than Davian would have liked. "Then we disappear back into the forest."

Davian grimaced. "There's nothing you can do with the Gift to make it a little less...risky?"

Wirr shook his head. "I thought about that, but there isn't. The First and Second Tenets will stop me from hurting them, or binding them, or putting them all to sleep, or anything useful at all really. Best I can probably do is open that wagon door in a hurry, if we need to."

Davian grunted. "We're in trouble if it comes to that. We're going to need as much of a head start as we can get."

"Malacar's a big forest, and I know how to cover a trail," Wirr reassured him. "Unless they're right on our heels, we should be fine."

Davian acknowledged the statement with a terse nod, though he felt anything but fine as he gazed at the darkened camp. Still, they had come this far. If they could just make contact with the sig'nari, there would surely be a way out.

Without any further discussion, Davian and Wirr made their way around the edge of the clearing, Davian wincing each time his foot found a dry twig. Soon they were positioned as near as they dared come to the wagon, fifty or so feet away. The camp was cloaked in darkness; there was only a sliver of moon tonight, and clouds moved sporadically across even that. In the dim light the wagon, tents, and sentry were little more than vague shapes against the darker backdrop of the forest beyond.

Wirr glanced across at Davian, who nodded grimly, trying to ignore his pounding heart. The men in their tents should be asleep by now. It was as good a time as any to begin.

They stole forward at a slow, crouched jog, approaching the wagon from an oblique angle, out of the guard's eye line. Wirr had located a sturdy tree branch a few minutes earlier; holding it like a club, he slipped around the side of the wagon in front of Davian. There was a dull crunching sound, followed by a heavy thud.

Davian cautiously rejoined his friend and they stood stock-still for a few seconds, holding their breaths as they listened for cries of alarm from the tents. None came.

Nodding to Wirr, Davian crept forward, moving as lightly as he could. He ignored the motionless sentry, examining the door to the wagon.

The latch mechanism was sturdy, but simple enough. He cast another nervous glance back toward the tents. Wirr raised an eyebrow at him, but Davian made a quick motion with his hands, indicating that everything was under control. No need for Wirr to use Essence just yet.

Barely daring to breathe, he undid the latch and slowly raised the thick wooden bar holding the door in place. It was well oiled and slid upward easily, with none of the squeaking Davian had feared. He pulled the small door open and climbed the stairs, peering inside into the gloom.

If it was dim outside, the interior of the wagon was pitch-black. Davian stood at the doorway for a moment, squinting, gagging a little at the smell as he allowed his eyes to adjust to the murk. He had to bend almost double to avoid hitting his head against the roof once inside; he eventually knelt, nearly jerking up again when he discovered there was a pool of moisture on the floor. He wrinkled his nose, praying that it was just water.

He could just make out a figure slumped against the far wall of the wagon. It shifted and he realized that the prisoner was awake, watching him.

Davian crawled toward them.

"I'm here to help," he whispered. "Ilseth Tenvar sent me."

There was a long silence, and then the figure shifted again. The clanking of chains made Davian's heart sink; he spun as fast as he could on his hands and knees, peering out the door. The camp was still silent.

He exited, crept around to where the guard lay, then hastily patted him down until he heard the faint jingle of keys. Davian grabbed them from the soldier's pocket and hurried back into the wagon.

His eyes were able to adjust quickly this time, and he drew up short as he took in the condition of the man he was trying to free. Massive bruises covered his entire face with ugly discolored splotches; one eye was swollen shut, and his lip was split in more than one place. Dried blood was smeared down the left side of his head and neck from an older wound, staining a tunic that had been torn so much that it was now little more than a rag. More bruises were evident through the tears in his clothing, as well as a Shackle gleaming darkly on his left arm; the man's breath was labored, but he was watching Davian closely and at least seemed to be aware of what was going on.

As the two men considered each other, Davian absently touched the Vessel in his pocket, his finger brushing the metallic surface of the box. He paused. Near the manacle on the stranger's right wrist, a glow had appeared—gone again in an instant, but distinctive against the darkness.

Davian put his finger against the Vessel again, frowning, ignoring the uncomfortable heat. The same light flared to life. He leaned forward for a closer look as the glow faded once again, then nodded to himself.

The wolf symbol was tattooed in thin black lines on the prisoner's wrist. This was definitely whom he had been sent to find.

There were only three keys on the ring, and the second one fit the keyhole. The lock fell open with a sharp click, and Davian thought he saw what looked like gratitude sweep over the man's face, though it was replaced instantly by a scowl of pain as he tried to move his weight.

"Can you walk?" Davian whispered.

The man nodded; levering himself up through what looked like sheer force of will, he crawled toward the door. Davian helped him out of the wagon, wincing at the stranger's condition. In the moonlight the man's injuries looked even worse. Davian marveled that he still had the strength to stand.

Suddenly there was a shout from within the cluster of tents. Davian's heart lurched.

Wirr, who was waiting for them outside, blanched when he saw the stranger's poor condition but made no comment. "They know we're here," he said, tone urgent as other shouts answered the first. "We need to go."

Davian looked at him, dismayed. "We're not going to get far."

"We have to try."

Time seemed to slow as Wirr grabbed one of the stranger's arms and Davian the other; they ran awkwardly toward the forest as soldiers burst from their tents, swords at the ready.

Deep down Davian knew it was over. Had they been alone, they might have been able to disappear in the forest. Carrying the prisoner, they wouldn't make it more than fifty feet before they were caught.

The man between them sagged onto Davian as Wirr dropped him, spinning to face the oncoming soldiers. He stretched out his hands; blinding white cords snaked forth from them, speeding outward. Davian steadied the injured man and then turned, too, watching in mute fascination as the Finders on the soldiers' wrists lit up a sharp blue.

Davian wasn't sure what Wirr was attempting to do—the Tenets restricted him from doing much that could help now—but even through his panic, he couldn't help but be impressed. He'd always known Wirr was strong, but had never seen him use all his power at once, which he must surely be doing now. It was more energy in one burst than Davian had ever seen.

And it was for naught. The last of Davian's hope vanished as the threads of light struck an invisible barrier around the soldiers, evaporating before they got within a few feet. At least one of the men had a Trap, then, too—a device that dissipated all Essence within its radius. Whatever Wirr had been trying to do, it had never had a chance of succeeding.

Just as the soldiers were almost upon them, the clearing exploded in white light, the force of the blast knocking Davian to the ground.

The impact stole the breath from his lungs, and for a few moments he just lay there on his stomach, gasping for air and trying to make sense of what was happening. Had Wirr tried something else, something new? However much power he had been using the first time, this was ten times more. A hundred.

His vision cleared. The soldiers were moving again, getting to their feet, dazed but apparently unharmed. It took Davian a few seconds to spot the figure behind them, shrouded in a cloak so black that it actually stood out against the darkness. It paused there for a moment, motionless. Watching.

Then it moved.

It glided rather than walked forward. Davian's blood froze; it made no sound but it had a sinuous menace, imparting a sense of heavy danger that made his legs feel like lead. The soldiers sensed it, too, turning away from the boys. Davian couldn't see their faces, but their sharply drawn breaths were audible even from this distance.

A disconnected part of Davian's mind registered that all other sounds had stopped—everything from the nocturnal animals and birds to the chirping crickets and buzzing mosquitoes. It was as if the world were holding its breath.

The figure flowed forward, difficult to follow in the darkness. It made a grasping motion with its hand as if pulling something from the air, and suddenly there was something coalescing, long and thin, as shadowy and indistinct as the figure itself. A dagger, Davian realized. Fear clenched him so tightly that he couldn't move, couldn't make a sound. Couldn't shout, either in horror or in warning.

The creature—Davian could not believe it was human—continued toward them, reaching the first soldier. Without pausing, it flicked out its arm as it passed. The action was casual, dismissive. Almost disdainful.

The soldier fell silently, dark blood spraying from where his jugular had been opened. His body hit the grass with a soft thud.

The sound finally snapped the other soldiers into motion; two scrambled for their swords while another held out a long, thin Trap with a trembling hand as if it were a ward against evil, the whites of his eyes visible. Still no one shouted, as if everyone feared that doing so would draw the creature's attention.

The scene had a surreal quality to it. Davian still couldn't move. He couldn't tear his eyes away as another soldier fell to the dagger, his bubbling final breath horrible in the hush. The third soldier took a wild swing at the creature, but his sword stopped in midair as if hitting a brick wall. He died like the other two.

The creature's trajectory was clear now. It was deviating slightly to remove the soldiers, but it was coming for the boys.

The last soldier fell. It had all happened within the space of about ten seconds; the shadow was moving so fast that it was almost impossible to comprehend. It turned toward Davian, only a few feet away now. It was human at least in shape, its face hidden by a deep black hood. But its knife was not solid; it pulsed and faded with darkness, ethereal steel one second and translucent black glass the next.

"*Sha nashen tel. Erien des tu nashen tel,*" it hissed. Its voice was deep and whispery, cold and angry. It spoke of something ancient and terrible, and Davian felt himself getting light-headed at the words.

The hairs on the back of his neck rose, and he felt a massive charge of energy from behind him.

Light roared past Davian and crashed into the creature. Not a beam, but a torrent. A river. It did not touch Davian, but he still felt as though he needed to grab on to something to keep from being swept away.

It hit the creature squarely in the chest, and for the briefest of moments its face was illuminated. Its features were humanlike, but twisted almost beyond recognition. Its skin was bruised and sagging, its lips white and horribly scarred.

Its eyes were recognizable, though. They were wide with what was very clearly surprise.

Then the light stopped. When Davian's sight returned, the creature was gone.

Davian stood rooted to the spot for a few more seconds, his body refusing to believe it was over.

Then with a shuddering chill he dropped to his knees, gasping for air. He'd thought he'd been afraid when the Hunters had caught them in Talmiel, and again when it had seemed that there was no escape from the Desrielite soldiers tonight. But this had been something else. It had been abject, crushing terror flowing through his veins. Now that it was gone, every part of his body felt tired, weak.

He finally came to his senses enough to turn around. Wirr was sitting on the ground, too, hugging himself with his arms around his knees. Even in the dim light, Davian could tell his friend was white as a sheet.

"That was amazing, Wirr," said Davian, awe making his tone hushed. "I never imagined you had anywhere *near* that much power! It was like . . . a god! It was—"

"I don't." Wirr cut him off, not bothering to look up. "I didn't do anything. It was him." He nodded toward the prone body lying a few feet away, the Shackle that had been around the stranger's arm now embedded in the dirt next to him.

The man they had rescued.

For a moment Davian thought he was dead, but the slight rise and fall of the man's chest reassured him.

Davian watched a moment longer, then shook his head disbelievingly. "Look at him, Wirr. He's barely breathing. He couldn't have had enough Essence to light—"

"It was him. The Shackle fell off when that last soldier died, and...it was him," said Wirr. There was a finality to his tone that made Davian snap his mouth shut. He still wasn't sure he believed his friend—not entirely—but now was not the time or place to argue. His wits returning, he staggered to his feet and then offered his hand to Wirr, helping him do the same.

"They would have seen that in Thrindar," he said.

"They would have seen that in the Eastern Empire," replied Wirr grimly. "Nothing for it. Let's grab him and get moving."

"What about the soldiers? Shouldn't we...bury them or something?" wondered Davian.

Wirr shook his head. "There's no time." He rubbed his forehead. "Though it means that when they find the bodies, they'll think we did this."

Davian shrugged. "It's not like they can execute us more."

Wirr gave a slightly hysterical giggle at that, and suddenly they were both snorting with fits of nervous laughter, relief and shock finally finding an outlet.

They were still chuckling when, from the darkness behind them, there was yet another flash of light.

Then both Wirr and Davian were on their knees, their hands forced behind their backs. Thin, pulsating cords snaked around their wrists and ankles, binding them where they lay on the ground; another cord coiled around the unconscious man, tying him just as securely. Davian struggled against the bonds, laughter replaced in an instant by fear, but it was of no use.

"I hope you two have a very good explanation for this," a deep voice said behind them. The words were spoken calmly, but there was restrained anger in them.

Davian tried to turn, but all of a sudden he felt exhausted, as though the strain of the last month were crashing down on him all at once. To his left he could hear Wirr yawning, too.

The last thing he remembered was lying on the soft grass, and then a sharp white flash all around him before everything dimmed.

He slept.

# Chapter 12

Asha jerked at the handle once again, despite knowing the door was locked.

She frowned around at the black stone walls of her cell, trying in vain to deduce what was going on. She'd still been reeling from the shock of Jin's murder when she'd fallen asleep—or passed out, as the case may have been—but that had been on a couch in Shana's house, surrounded by concerned Shadows and with no indication that she was in any trouble. Shana herself had already verified the presence of the Watcher; after that, everyone had seemed to accept that she wasn't responsible for what had happened. If anything, they had all appeared concerned for her well-being.

Something had changed in the meantime, though, because when she'd woken she had found herself here. Alone. The solid door locked, with apparently no one in earshot to hear her shouting.

Frustrated, she bashed on the door with the palm of her hand, the sound echoing in the passageway beyond.

"Hello? Is there anyone there?" she called.

As before, there was no response, no indication that there was anyone nearby to hear her. She returned to her bed with a sigh. The room contained only the bed, a couple of chairs, and a table—nothing she could use to get free. There was little else to do but wait.

She tried to distract herself while she lay there. Despite everything that had happened, she'd been impressed with the Sanctuary;

the people living down here seemed like good, honest folk, and the efforts of the Shadraehin in creating the underground community were something she admired.

And yet, as hard as she tried to focus on something positive, she kept drifting back to the moment the Watcher had appeared. Wondering how he'd known her name, puzzling over what he'd said to her. And then, each time, reliving Jin staring at her in terror as his life seeped away between his fingers.

Maybe an hour had passed when there were echoing footsteps in the hallway outside, and a key rattled in the lock.

Asha leaped to her feet as the door opened to admit a wiry-looking Shadow, a man with a thin face and a scruffy-looking beard. She stared at him in surprise. The oldest Shadows she'd ever seen were in their early thirties—those who had been among the first to fail their Trials after the war. The Treaty had a clause that amnestied any Gifted who had taken the tests prior to that...and yet the Shadow who stood opposite her was at least forty.

The man smiled slightly when he saw her expression. "Older than you expected?"

Asha flushed, caught off guard, and the man waved away her embarrassment apologetically. "It's fine. Everybody has that reaction the first time. Please, sit," he added, gesturing to one of the chairs. "We have much to discuss."

Asha remained standing. "Who are you?" She crossed her arms, noting the two men who were taking up positions to stand guard in the hallway. "Why am I a prisoner here?"

The man raised an eyebrow, looking more amused than annoyed. "My name is Scyner, but everyone here calls me the Shadraehin. I suppose you could say I'm in charge of the Sanctuary. I'm the one whose responsibility it is to keep the people here safe." He paused, leaning forward, and suddenly his eyes were hard. "And when someone comes into the Sanctuary and lies about their name, it raises questions about their trustworthiness. Ashalia."

Asha stared at the cool certainty in his eyes for a moment, then slowly moved across to the chair and sat.

"Good. I'm glad we're not wasting time with denials," said
Scyner, his cheerful demeanor returning in an instant.

"How did you find out who I am?" she asked.

The Shadraehin scratched at his beard. "We thought you may have been a spy for Administration, at first," he admitted. "They've tried that before—offering Gifted who are about to become Shadows an opportunity, a 'better' life. But Administration had no record of any Lissa from Nalean at all, which didn't make sense. Why bother to change your name? Why lie about where you're from?"

He reached into his pocket. "And then we put the pieces together. The timing. And we went through Administration's records of the students from Caladel, and found the image of a young Gifted girl. Ashalia Chaedris." He produced a piece of paper and unfolded it, holding it up for her to see. The sketch was a couple of years old now, from the last time one of Administration's artists had come to Caladel, but it was still a good likeness.

Asha gave a brief nod as she took in the image, for a moment feeling a stab of pain as she thought of the school, remembered when she'd sat for that picture. She switched her gaze back to the Shadraehin.

"I was the only survivor," she said quietly, seeing no advantage to concealing the truth. "I don't know anything about what happened, but the Council thought I might be important somehow. They hid me in the Tol and asked me to lie about my name, to make sure Administration couldn't find me." She looked Scyner in the eye. "I didn't mean you or your people any harm."

"And yet one of my good friends is dead." Emotion flashed across the Shadraehin's face, gone in an instant. He took a deep breath. "We will get to your situation shortly. First, though, I would very much like to hear what happened with Aelrith."

"That's...the Watcher? The man who...?" Asha trailed off.

"Yes," said the Shadraehin. "Though whatever else he may be, he's not a man."

Asha shivered a little but nodded, unsurprised by the comment. She related what had happened, stopping a couple of times as the emotion of the memory got the better of her. Once she had finished, the Shadraehin watched her for a few moments, considering.

"I believe you," he said eventually.

Asha inclined her head, relieved; the last thing she needed was someone challenging her version of events. "Did you catch Aelrith?"

"No. We didn't even see him leave," admitted Scyner. "If it hadn't been for Shana's word, I'm not sure we would have believed he was even in her house."

Asha paled. "Then he's gone? He's free?"

The Shadraehin nodded. "He uses the catacombs to come and go—they run for miles, have exits everywhere from in the city to out past the mountains. But we don't know our way around most of them, even if we wanted to go hunting someone as dangerous as Aelrith. We've sent people too deep in there before, and they haven't come back." His tone softened as he saw her expression. "I wouldn't worry. From what you said, I don't think he's a threat to you. If anything, it sounds like we may never see him again."

Asha acknowledged the statement with a nod, though it didn't stop her stomach from churning as she thought of the black-hooded figure still out there.

"What do you think it all meant—what he said to me?"

Scyner shrugged. "It makes as little sense to me as it does to you, Ashalia," he admitted. "In all honesty, I'm not sure it meant anything. Whatever Aelrith may be, I don't think he's entirely sane." He grimaced. "In fact, after what he did to Jin, I'm quite certain of it."

Asha shuddered at the memory. "What *do* you think Aelrith is?"

The Shadraehin sighed. "I don't know for sure. There were rumors after the war ended that Tol Athian had been experimenting on some of their people, trying to create soldiers that were immune to Traps and Shackles...if I had to guess, I'd say maybe he's one of them. Whether the Council knows he's still down here, though, I have no idea."

He rubbed at his chin, gaze growing distant. "When I first discovered this place and realized it could serve as a haven for Shadows, Aelrith was already here, staring into that light. Aside from today, it's the only time I know of that he's stopped to speak to someone. He and I came to an agreement—we wouldn't go near him, and he wouldn't go near us. Today is the first time either of us has broken that accord."

There was silence for a few seconds; finally Asha straightened, taking a deep breath. "So what are you going to do with me now?" she asked, dreading the answer.

Scyner raised an eyebrow. "Do with you? You're free to return to the Tol, Ashalia. Or free to stay if you wish," he said, looking mildly surprised. "You were locked up because I thought you might be a spy. Now I know you're not." He hesitated. "However, before you make any decisions, I *do* have a proposition for you which you may find interesting."

Asha exhaled, tense muscles loosening a little. "Which is?"

"I have...something of an interest in finding out exactly what happened to your school and the others that were attacked," said the Shadraehin. "I suspect you do, too. If you're willing, I think I know how we might work together to find some answers."

Asha stared at Scyner for a moment, barely daring to believe her ears. "How?" she asked eagerly. Then she paused. "Though... why would you be interested?"

The Shadraehin leaned forward. "The thing is, Ashalia— Administration knows about the Sanctuary. Not where it is, exactly, or how to get here. *Yet.* But they know it exists, and they have dedicated people trying to find a way to destroy it."

"But won't any Administrators die if they come down here?" asked Asha.

Scyner nodded. "That's true—we're not worried about a direct attack, at least not yet. At the moment Administration is focused on cutting off our supplies. Water isn't an issue; there's a river a little way into the catacombs that we use. Food, though...we can't produce sufficient crops down here." He sighed. "Up in the city, Shadows are now being told that they need a letter from their employer if they want to purchase large quantities of food. We can get around that for now, but it won't be long before Administration starts making things even harder."

He shrugged. "So as you can imagine, I've been looking for a way to get them to leave us alone. I've reached out a few times, tried to negotiate, but they just aren't willing to listen. So now we're keeping an eye on everyone with power in Administration. Trying to figure out a way to...force the issue."

"To blackmail them, you mean," said Asha, a little darkly.    143

Scyner gave her an apologetic smile. "I know it's not the most pleasant method, but we have already tried the other avenues at our disposal." He shook his head. "Regardless. A few months ago, we noticed that the Northwarden was abandoning some of his duties. A *lot* of his duties, in fact—in order to focus on something else. And as it turns out, that 'something else' was his trying to get to the bottom of the attacks."

Asha frowned. "That doesn't sound terribly strange."

The Shadraehin raised an eyebrow. "We're talking about the Northwarden—head of the Administrators, the man who created the Tenets. A man who hates the Gifted like few others. His looking into the attacks wasn't unusual, but to not attend the formal swearing in of new Administrators? Turning down meetings with the Great Houses, missing entire sessions of the Assembly? It was definitely odd."

Scyner smiled grimly. "And as it turns out, the more we looked into it, the more it became evident that the Northwarden was a little too interested in what was going on. Obsessed, I suppose you'd say. The man doesn't sleep, some nights...from what we can tell he's kept his inquiry from Administration, too. He's been very carefully hiding the fact that he's even interested."

He rubbed his forehead. "What we don't know is why. We have many contacts in the palace, and even some in Administration itself—but none have been able to get the answers we need."

Asha watched him, an uneasy feeling growing in her stomach. "And how do I fit in?"

The Shadraehin looked her in the eye. "I want to tell him who you are, and where you are."

Asha just stared at him for several seconds, trying to decide if the man was making some kind of odd joke. "You cannot think I would agree to that."

Scyner just held up his hand. "Hear me out," he said calmly. "I understand the danger if Administration finds out about you... but the fact is, I don't believe the Northwarden will tell them. He's going to want to question you, maybe even take you back to the palace with him to keep you close. But if he turns you over to Administration then he loses that direct connection to you, has to share any information you might reveal." He shook his head. "No—it's more than likely that he'll keep your secret. And if he wants your cooperation, he's going to have to let you in on his investigation. Which is your best chance of getting answers."

Asha bit her lip. "And maybe after a while he might let slip why it's so important to him, too."

"Exactly. Which you can then relay back to us." The Shadraehin smiled. "Once we know the details, we can hopefully use the information to force the Northwarden's hand, get him to have Administration back off. And we would find a way to do it without implicating you, of course," he quickly assured her.

Asha frowned. "But that's all you would use the information for?"

"That's all," promised the Shadraehin.

Asha shook her head. "It's a huge risk," she observed. "And even if the Northwarden doesn't tell Administration about me, it doesn't mean he won't try to torture information from me himself."

The Shadraehin nodded. "I know. And I won't force you to be a part of this," he said seriously. "But from what you were saying earlier, the Council has no leads. So if you really want to find out what happened at Caladel, this may be a chance you're going to have to take." He paused. "I can give you time to—"

"I'll do it," said Asha.

There had never been a question, really. She was useless sitting at the Tol, and each day that passed was another day the trail of Davian's killer became colder. At least this way there was a possibility she could make a difference.

"Good." The Shadraehin rose, laying a reassuring hand on her shoulder. "We will do everything we can to make sure you're safe, Ashalia—there will always be someone keeping an eye out for you, you have my word. And if everything goes according to plan, I'll make sure we find a way to contact you discreetly once you're inside the palace." He wandered over to the door, whispered something into one of the guards' ears, then turned back to her.

"Shanin here will guide you back to the Tol, and...organize an explanation for why Jin is missing," he said quietly. "Little enough time has passed since you left—your absence shouldn't have been noticed." He gave her a polite nod in farewell. "Fates guide you, Ashalia. I hope we meet again soon."

As abruptly as that the meeting was over, and Asha was left to follow Shanin back into the Tol.

Soon she had found her way back to the familiar confines of her room.

It was late, but after sleeping earlier she wasn't tired. She paced around for a while, then sat pensively on the bed. How long would it be before the Northwarden came to find her? Hours? Days? She glanced at the Decay Clock. Most of the night had gone; it was only a couple of hours until she had to be at the library.

She couldn't sleep, but there was no point in wasting energy. No point in thinking about what was coming, either. She couldn't stop it now, even if she'd wanted to.

Taking a deep, steadying breath, she lay back on the bed and settled down to wait.

# Chapter 13

Davian groaned.

He reluctantly emerged from unconsciousness, head throbbing. Something wasn't right. Groggily he moved to rub his forehead, only to find that his arms were pinned to his sides.

He came fully awake, remembering everything in a rush. Their rescue attempt. The soldiers. The creature.

His eyes snapped open and he struggled again to raise his arms, to move his body much at all. It was to no avail. With a chill he realized he could feel the cold metal of a Shackle sitting snugly around his arm. He thrashed around for several seconds; finally he took a deep breath, twisting his head—which appeared to be the only part of his body that had been left unrestrained—and forcing himself to take stock of the situation.

The room was small, tidy, and fairly plain; there was another bed set against the far wall, and a pallet squeezed in between for good measure. The window was open and the curtains drawn back, but this was clearly an upper floor and he could see little but rooftops from where he lay. The bustle of the street below drifted into the room, the sounds of merchants hawking their wares mingling with the clip-clop of horses on cobbled stone, the creak of carts, and the general chatter of people as they went about their daily business. Clearly a large town, perhaps even a city, though he had no clue as to how he'd gotten there.

Wirr was stretched out on the other bed, Shackle on his arm, lying in an awkward position as a result of his bindings. There was a none too gentle snoring coming from his direction, and much to Davian's relief he did not appear to be injured.

The pallet on the floor was occupied by a slender young man, also fast asleep. His shoulder-length reddish-brown hair fell loosely over his face, but Davian still recognized him. The bruises were gone and his ragged clothes were a little cleaner, but this was the man from the wagon—the man he and Wirr had tried to save. He was younger than Davian had first thought, no more than two or three years older than Davian himself.

Davian noted with chagrin that thick rope encircled the stranger's hands and feet, and a Shackle was closed around his arm, too; it appeared the success of their rescue had been somewhat short-lived. At least, he consoled himself, someone had tended to the man's injuries.

Before Davian could assess the situation further, there was a jangling of keys from just outside. He tensed as the door swung open.

The man who strode into the room was middle-aged; his hair still maintained its sandy-blond color, only a few flecks of gray starting to appear around the sides. It was his face that drew Davian's attention, though. It was a mass of scars—some small and some large, some old and white, others still pink from recent healing. One in particular was puffy and raw, streaking from nose to ear, the red punctuated by black where it had been sewn together again. It gave him a terrifying aspect, and Davian shrank back.

The man's deep-set eyes scanned the room as he entered; seeing that Davian was awake, he stopped short.

"Don't yell," he cautioned, his deep voice quiet but authoritative. In contrast to his face, it was reassuring. "I'm Gifted, too. If you draw attention to us, we are all dead." He rolled up his sleeve to reveal his Mark; seeing that Davian did not seem inclined to start making a commotion, he relaxed a little. "You're awake much earlier than you should be."

Davian took a couple of deep, calming breaths. They hadn't been captured by the Gil'shar. That was a start.

"Who are you?" he asked. "If you're Gifted, why am I tied up?"

"You're tied up because I don't know what to make of you yet. We can talk about the other once I do." The stranger motioned to the man on the floor. "You freed him. Why?"

Davian frowned. "It's...complicated."

"Then simplify it for me." The man sat down on the sole chair in the room. "I have time."

"He's Gifted. It seemed like the right thing to do." Davian barely kept himself from cringing; he could hear the lack of conviction in own voice.

His captor could hear it, too. "We're in the middle of Desriel, lad. You didn't rescue him on a whim. You'll need to do better than that."

Davian shook his head. "I'd prefer not to say."

"What you'd prefer doesn't really come into it," said the stranger, his ruined face impassive. "You can tell your story to me, or you can have the Gil'shar pull it out of you. I know which option I'd choose. But until you've explained your part in this, to my satisfaction, you'll not be untied."

Davian paled. The man was not lying.

The stranger's expression softened, as much as that was possible, as he saw the look on Davian's face. "Look, lad, we're likely all on the same side here. I was tracking this man for a week before you and your friend came along—I may have even tried saving him myself at some point. But that's a risk I would have taken for my own reasons. I need to know what yours are before I can trust you." He hesitated. "If it's any help, I know you're an Augur. So that's one less thing you need to hide."

Davian froze. He opened his mouth to deny it, but he knew from the other man's face that it would serve no purpose. There was certainty in his eyes, cold and still.

He felt his resolve wilt under the stranger's steady, calm stare. "I...I don't know where to start," he said, a little shakily.

The man leaned forward in his chair.

"From the beginning, lad," he said quietly. "Start from the beginning."

Davian's throat was dry by the time he'd finished.

He'd related everything; if the stranger already knew he was an Augur, there was little point in concealing the rest. The scarred man had listened in attentive silence, occasionally nodding, sometimes frowning at one piece of information or another. Now he gazed at Davian and seemed...sad.

"Quite a tale," he said softly. "You've raised more questions than you've answered, but...quite a tale."

Davian released a deep breath. "So you believe me?"

Ignoring the question, the man drew something from his pocket. The bronze Vessel, Davian realized after a moment. The stranger turned it over in his hands, examining it, though Davian could tell from his demeanor that he had already looked it over. "Yes. I believe you," he said. "That isn't the same as me trusting you—not yet—but it is a start." He raised his gaze from the box, looking Davian in the eye. "This box cannot be just a Wayfinder. It's ancient, whatever it is. You truly don't have any idea what it does?"

Davian shook his head. He could see that the part of the box facing the unconscious man was still shining brightly. "It's still active," he supplied. "Whichever side of it is closest to him"—he nodded toward the man on the floor—"lights up with that wolf symbol so brightly that it's hard to look at."

The man grunted, staring at the bronze box as if he could see the same thing if he just looked hard enough. "The symbol you're talking about, the one tattooed on his wrist—it's the symbol of Tar Anan. The symbol found all across the Boundary."

Davian frowned. "What...what does that mean?"

"I'm not sure." Davian's captor glanced at the man on the floor. "When I'm holding this, his tattoo lights up. But I see nothing on the box itself." He screwed up his face in puzzlement. "No, I don't doubt it's a Wayfinder; the symbols are the link. It will probably stay active until the two physically complete the connection, actually touch each other. But what I *don't* understand is how the box could possibly be coupled only to you. Not without your knowledge. Your consent." Sighing, he tucked the Vessel into one of the folds of his cloak.

Davian shifted uncomfortably. "Are you going to untie me now?"

The stranger glanced at Wirr and the young man on the floor, then shook his head. "No. I have the means to verify at least some of your story, so I'll do that first. I *do* believe you...but then I've met some good liars before. Even ones as young as you."

Davian scowled. "Do you at least trust me enough to tell me your name?"

The man nodded. "Taeris Sarr," he said, watching Davian's face for a reaction.

The name took a moment to register. The same name as the man who had saved him three years earlier, who had supposedly broken the First Tenet to kill his attackers.

The man who had been executed by Administration.

"No, you're not," said Davian, his brow furrowing. "Taeris Sarr is dead."

The man smiled. "Is that what they've been saying? I wondered." He shook his head in amusement. "But no. Definitely not dead."

"You're lying." Davian's voice was flat.

"Is that what your ability is telling you?"

Davian went silent. No puffs of black smoke had escaped the man's mouth.

"How?" he asked after a few seconds.

The stranger rubbed his disfigured face absently. "I escaped. Presumably Administration decided to tell everyone I'd been executed as planned, rather than face public embarrassment." He shrugged. "I fled here—one of the few places no one would think to look for me. Though it seems I cannot escape my past entirely," he added in a dry tone.

Davian made to protest, then subsided. Again the man was telling the truth.

This *was* Taeris Sarr.

"It's...it's an honor to meet you, Elder Sarr," said Davian when he'd recovered enough to speak. "I can't tell you how many times I've wished I could thank you for what you did."

"Taeris will do just fine. Anyone overhears you calling me *Elder*, and we're all dead." Taeris cleared his throat, looking awkward. "And you don't need to thank me. Three grown men attacking a thirteen-year-old boy? I'd have been a poor excuse for a man to *not* intervene."

"Still. I'm grateful." Davian shook his head, dazed. "I have so many questions."

Taeris glanced out the window. "There is time, I suppose. We cannot do anything until the other two wake, anyway." He gestured. "Ask away."

Davian thought for a moment. "Did you really break the First Tenet, when you saved me?"

Taeris chuckled, though the sound held little humor. "Ah. So you still don't remember, after all this time?" He sighed. "No, lad. I had a couple of daggers, is all. I told them to stop, and they attacked me. So I defended myself. They were drunk, and I'm faster than I look...but after it was done, all Administration saw was three dead men, and an old Gifted who couldn't have possibly overpowered them."

"And I was useless as a witness," realized Davian, horrified. "I'm so sorry."

Taeris waved away the apology. "You were unconscious for most of it, truth be told—and even if you hadn't been, your word wouldn't have been enough. Administration was set on making an example. I was a nice way to remind people how dangerous the Gifted could be without the Tenets. Without *them*."

"So how did you escape?" asked Davian.

Taeris hesitated, then drew two small stones from his pocket, one black and one white. "These are Travel Stones," he explained. "Vessels that create a portal between each other. They've come in rather handy, over the years. That day was no exception. Nor was last night, actually."

Davian gaped at Taeris for a moment. He'd never heard of a Vessel like that before, but at least it explained how Taeris had managed to quietly transport three unconscious boys from the middle of the forest to an inn. "So why are you in Desriel?" he eventually asked, recovering. "Why were you after him?" He jerked his head toward the young man on the floor. "Are you looking for the sig'nari, too?"

Taeris winced. "I have some bad news for you, lad. The man who sent you here—Tenvar—has misled you. There are no sig'nari in Desriel."

Davian scowled. "That's not possible. He wasn't lying."

"And you're sure about that? You said you haven't been able to learn anything about your ability."

152    "I'm sure," snapped Davian.

Taeris looked at him appraisingly. "Does it work through a Shackle?" Davian nodded. "Then let me show you something. I will tell you three things—two truths and one lie. Let's see if you can tell me which one is false."

Davian shrugged. "Very well."

Taeris closed his eyes for a moment, concentrating. "It is midday. We are currently in a town called Dan'mar. I am forty-five years old."

Davian frowned, his head throbbing a little as he tried to process what was happening. No puffs of darkness had escaped from Taeris's mouth. "They were all true," he said slowly.

Taeris shook his head. "It is midafternoon, we are in a town called Anabir, and I am forty-eight."

Davian stared in disbelief. Again, nothing.

"How did you do that?" he asked, stunned.

Taeris shrugged. "An old trick. Not one many of your generation would know, but common enough knowledge back when the Augurs ruled. It's a mental defense, a shield against invasions of the mind. It takes training to do for any period of time, but most people could hold it for a few minutes effectively enough." He shook his head, seeing the stricken look on Davian's face. "I am sorry, lad. Truly."

"But..." Davian stared at the man on the floor. "Who is he, then? Why did Elder Tenvar send me here?"

"That's what we're going to find out. For what it's worth, I don't believe Tenvar was lying about the Boundary. He probably had to lace his tale with as much truth as possible, to be sure he could fool your ability." Taeris rose. "I have a few inquiries to make in town. If your story checks out, we'll talk some more."

He started walking toward the door, then paused, indicating the man sleeping on the floor. "It's not likely he'll wake before I'm back, but if he does...best to pretend you're still asleep. I don't know why Tenvar lied to you, but if he went to such lengths to send you here, he probably didn't have your best interests at heart. Which means that man probably doesn't, either."

He left. The door closed behind him, leaving Davian pale and shaken.

Tenvar had lied. It had all been for nothing.

# Chapter 14

Daylight was fading outside by the time Wirr finally stirred.

It didn't take Davian long to explain to his disbelieving friend what had transpired. Wirr took the news about Ilseth's deception stoically, for which Davian was grateful. It was Davian's blind trust in his ability that had led them here, placed them in such a perilous situation. He wasn't sure he could have handled anger from Wirr atop his own guilt.

Once Davian was finished, Wirr shifted awkwardly on his bed, evidently trying to stretch out some stiff muscles. "So you're sure it's Taeris Sarr?"

"As sure as I can be."

Wirr bit his lip. "Dav, if it is...I know the man saved you, but...you should know that I've heard things about him. He's supposed to be dangerous. Unbalanced, even. If he—"

He cut off at the sound of a key rattling in the lock on the door.

Taeris bustled in, apparently oblivious to the fact he'd interrupted their conversation, and gave a satisfied nod when he saw the man on the floor was still unconscious.

"Davian's told you who I am?" he asked, turning his attention to Wirr.

Wirr nodded, watching the scarred man with a mixture of trepidation and curiosity. "Yes."

"Good." Taeris went on to ask Wirr a series of questions about the past few weeks; once he was satisfied that Wirr's and Davian's accounts were the same, he strode over to Davian's bed and began untying him. "My contacts in town were able to verify parts of your story. A well-known Hunter killed in a scuffle in Fejett. A man in Talmiel who collapsed under suspicious circumstances, and woke up with the last two years of his life missing. Not much, but enough for now."

Davian massaged his wrists as he sat up straight, stretching muscles stiff from disuse. "What did you say about the man from Talmiel?" he asked suddenly, a chill running through him.

Taeris gave him a considering look. "You wondered whether you had done something to make your smuggler friend 'forget' about the Vessel. From the sounds of it, you were right." He moved on to releasing Wirr.

Davian felt sick. Anaar might have deserved punishment, but that was of little comfort. He was another person Davian had managed to hurt because he'd been too eager, too gullible to see through Tenvar's lies.

Wirr stood as soon as he was able, walking in circles to loosen his muscles. He nodded to the man on the floor. "So what do you know about him?" he asked Taeris, mistrust thick in his voice. "Davian says you were tracking him. Why?"

"Because of what's happening at the Boundary. That part of what Tenvar told Davian, at least, I believe to be true." Taeris sighed. "Except it's more than that. I don't think the decay of the Boundary is happening naturally. I studied it for years, even before the war. The Essence that sustains it has only started to noticeably decay in the last decade."

Wirr frowned. "Why is that significant?"

"Think of it as a physical wall. You build the wall out of good, thick, solid stone, and you leave it for two thousand years. When you come back, it's still standing—crumbling, maybe, and worn by wind and rain, but still strong. Still serving its original purpose." Taeris paused. "Then you come back a decade after that, and it's completely gone. What conclusion do you draw?"

Davian's brow furrowed. "Something knocked it down."

"Or someone," Wirr added quietly.

"Exactly."

There was silence for a moment, then Wirr frowned. "Do the Tols know about your suspicions? You said you began noticing the decay ten years ago, and you've only been in exile here for three."

"I tried to tell both Councils, several times, but..." Taeris shook his head in frustration. "The Tols stopped checking the Boundary regularly more than a thousand years ago, so my old notes were the only real proof that the decay had accelerated. They accepted that the Boundary might be decaying, but not that it was happening rapidly—they didn't believe that it was being caused by anything except the passage of time. Tol Athian told me I was being alarmist, and Tol Shen just laughed in my face."

"But you *are* certain."

"Yes. So for the last few years, I've been keeping watch for anything that might be related. Any sign that the Boundary failing is part of a greater plan, proof that I can take back to the Tols." He walked over and pulled back the man's sleeve, revealing the black wolf tattoo on his wrist. "I found a few clues, but nothing I could use or pursue—until a contact of mine told me about this. This symbol is carved into every Boundary Stone. And our friend here has it tattooed on his wrist."

"So you think he may know something. Be involved, somehow." Davian stared at the sleeping man with new trepidation.

"And by extension, so may Ilseth Tenvar," noted Wirr, his tone grim.

Taeris nodded. "That this particular symbol was used as the link for you to find him...I don't know what it means, yet, but it has to be significant. *Something* is going on." He hesitated. "There's more, though." He drew back the man's left sleeve farther, baring his left forearm.

For a moment Davian didn't understand. Then his eyes widened, and to his left he heard Wirr's sharp intake of breath.

The young man did not have the Mark.

"*Fates*. He's not bound by the Tenets?" Wirr asked softly.

"It seems not," said Taeris.

Davian suddenly made the connection. "*This* is the man the Hunters were talking about—the one who killed all those people?"

Taeris nodded. "At least that's what the Gil'shar are saying. An entire village slain, and they're claiming it was by his hand." He shook his head. "As to the truth of it, I can't say; I know all too well the stories people make up out of fear of the Gifted. Unfortunately, the result is the same."

"That story is everywhere. The entire country will be looking for him. For *us*," breathed Wirr.

Taeris nodded. "Before you intervened, he was being taken to Thrindar for a very public execution—during the Song of Swords, no less. The Gil'shar wanted to show all the countries present that not only are the Gifted evil, but that they are something to always be feared. That the Tenets are no reason for anyone to accept us, to relax their guard."

Davian frowned, taking a small step away from the sleeping man as the new information sank in. He didn't *look* like a murderer, and he was still tied up, but...even so.

Beside him Wirr was becoming increasingly agitated. "If the Gil'shar finds out that he was freed by other Gifted..." He shook his head, a flicker of fear in his eyes. "There will be outrage. Claims it was ordered by the Andarran government, or that we're using him to find a way for *everyone* to break free of the Tenets. A case for war."

Taeris nodded, giving Wirr a respectful look. "One of the many good reasons I hadn't already rescued him," he said, a little drily. "The Gil'shar barely need an excuse for war as it is. The one reason they haven't attacked Andarra over the past fifteen years is that they fear it will cause King Andras to change the Tenets—but if they think we're trying to get around them anyway, there will be nothing holding them back."

Davian paled; the implications of their actions reached further than he could possibly have imagined. "So what can we do?" he asked. "We can't just give him back to the Gil'shar."

"We can if he's guilty," pointed out Wirr. "We *should*. Better to let them have their political posturing in Thrindar than to risk an incident like this."

Davian turned to his friend, aghast. "You cannot be serious."

Taeris held up his hand. "Let's hear his story before we make any decisions. He's healed at a remarkable rate—I think we can wake him now."

Wirr raised an eyebrow. "You didn't heal him?"

Taeris shook his head. "I couldn't risk using Essence; there are too many soldiers around with Finders. But it seems he's instinctively drawing from his own Reserve to heal himself anyway. It's quite remarkable."

Davian eyed the sleeping man nervously. Gifted could accelerate their own healing, but he'd never heard of anyone who was able to do it unconsciously.

Taeris stooped beside the redheaded man, then hesitated. "Davian. I doubt he'll have the awareness to mask any deception, even if he knows how. Tell me if he lies." He gripped the sleeping boy by the shoulder and gave him a gentle shake.

The young man groaned, coming awake.

"Where am I?" he asked, voice rasping slightly.

Taeris, Davian, and Wirr all looked at the stranger in silence for a few seconds. His appearance was markedly different from last night; his skin was pale, showing no sign of the bruising that had covered it only hours earlier. Ice-blue eyes searched the room, trying to evaluate what was happening; his reddish-brown hair hung to his shoulders, framing a face that looked narrower than it would normally due to his sunken cheekbones. His frame was slight, but that was again most likely due to a lack of food and not part of his natural physical appearance.

It was Taeris who finally spoke. "For now you are safe. But if you lie to me, you will be back in Gil'shar custody within the hour. Do you understand?"

The stranger nodded mutely.

Taeris held up the Vessel in front of him. "What is this?"

The stranger squinted at the object. "I don't know."

Taeris flicked a quick glance at Davian, who inclined his head. It was the truth—so far as he could tell, anyway.

"But you can see it glowing?" asked Taeris.

The red-haired man nodded. "The same as my wrist," he said, sounding confused.

Taeris considered for a moment. "Very well," he said. "Who do you work for? What were you to do with this after it was delivered to you?"

The stranger gave Taeris a perplexed, helpless look. "I am sorry. Truly," he said quietly. "I don't know what you're talking about. My memory is..." He shook his head. "Beyond three weeks ago,

I remember nothing. I don't even know if I'm guilty..." He trailed off again, a pained look in his eyes.

There was a moment of silence, then Taeris gave a derisive snort. "You will need to do better than that."

Davian had been watching the stranger, a small frown on his face. He turned to Taeris. "I think he's telling the truth."

Taeris scowled. "Do you at least have a name?"

"Caeden," said the man. "That's what the villagers said, anyway."

Taeris grunted. "Caeden. Like the Darecian fairy tale. How appropriate," he said drily. "Well, Caeden, perhaps you should tell us what you *do* remember, and we can go from there."

"There is not much to tell," Caeden admitted. "A few weeks ago I found myself in the middle of the forest, no recollection of how I got there or who I was. I didn't even know which country I was in. I was holding a sword, and my clothes were soaked in blood. At first I thought the blood was mine, but apart from a couple of scratches, I wasn't injured.

"I found a stream and tried to wash the blood out of my clothes, but most of it had already stained. I wandered for a few hours until I found a road, and eventually a group of men came across me. When I told them I couldn't remember anything, they offered me shelter in their village and food for the evening. One of them thought he recognized me, said I'd probably been attacked and beaten by bandits. They seemed like good people at the time." Caeden grimaced at that.

"The next day word came that my village had been wiped out. Someone had gone through the town and put everyone to death. *Everyone.* The people who'd seen the aftermath said there were women and children lying in the streets, blood everywhere. And that all the faces had been... disfigured. Mutilated beyond recognition." He shuddered. "Many of the people where I was staying had friends and family that had died. There was a lot of grief, a lot of fear.

"It didn't take long for people to make a connection. At first they just locked me up—said not to worry, that I'd probably been a survivor, maybe a witness, and that they were doing it 'just in case.' But I think they'd already made up their minds.

"After a couple of days, there was a farmer whose wife had

been visiting the other village when the attack came. He'd gone and found her body—what he thought was her body, anyway—and then come straight back to find me." He shivered. "He was a big man, so they let him into my cell. The constable just looked the other way. Locked the door with the two of us inside and left. I tried to explain, but he was so *angry*." Caeden's voice wavered as he remembered. "He was going to kill me. I was so afraid, and then I just...reacted. I used the Gift, I suppose. Threw him back against the cell door so hard that he broke his neck." He ran his hands through his hair.

"It was an accident, but no one believed it. The village cleric's Finder went off, so they knew how I'd done it. But I didn't have a tattoo, which made them even more afraid...once they knew I had powers, though, it settled any doubts they'd had.

"They were going to hang me—there were enough people who wanted it to happen—but the Gil'shar sent word that they wanted a public execution in Thrindar. So they put a Shackle on me, and kept me locked up for another week." His hands shook as he remembered; he clasped them together to stop them from trembling.

"They beat you?" interjected Taeris, his tone gentler now.

Caeden nodded. "Every day," he said softly. "And when the soldiers came to take me to Thrindar, they took me out every evening and did the same. Gave me just enough time to heal so that I would be conscious for the next night." He hesitated. "I am grateful we didn't reach Thrindar, though."

Taeris didn't respond. He thought in silence for a few seconds, then turned to Davian. "Well?"

Davian didn't take his eyes from Caeden. "It's all true," he said eventually.

Except it wasn't. On Caeden's last sentence, the tiniest puff of darkness had escaped from the young man's mouth. He'd been lying about not wanting to reach Thrindar.

He'd wanted to be executed.

Taeris inclined his head in acknowledgment and Davian could see the struggle on his face, knew what the Elder was thinking.

"We can't give him to them," Davian observed. Wirr nodded his agreement.

"And he doesn't know an El-cursed thing about the Boundary," growled Taeris, though he didn't argue the statement. "You're sure he wasn't lying?"

"As sure as I can be." Davian tried to keep the bitterness from his tone.

Taeris was silent, then turned to Caeden, still holding the Vessel. "I can't say as I like our choices here, but someone went to an awful lot of trouble to get you this box. You're important, somehow. Too important to turn over to the Gil'shar." He shook his head. "We're going to have to get your memories back."

"How?" asked Caeden.

"There's a device in Tol Athian. A Vessel meant to repair the mind. That's where we need to go, so...we're going to have to trust each other, I suppose." He began untying Caeden's hands. "I'm going to leave the Shackle on, though. If you—"

Without warning the door exploded inward off its hinges, flying past Taeris's head and embedding itself in the far wall.

Everyone froze, stunned, as the figure in the doorway slithered into the room.

Davian quickly took in the black cloak, the shadowy hood, the swirling blade that wasn't quite there. The creature from last night.

Taeris moved with a speed that Davian would not have credited him with had he not seen it. The older man leaped to one side and rolled; as he came up he crossed his wrists in front of himself, closing his eyes. A blinding flash roared through the air and the creature staggered a few steps backward, its disfigured, pallid face briefly illuminated, mouth curled in a silent rictus of pain. Davian's heart dropped as the creature stopped, steadied, and then started forward again. With Shackles on, there was little any of them could do to help.

The creature's blade flashed at Taeris's head; Taeris ducked backward, a shield of blazing white appearing in front of him. The dagger darted forward again, into the shield. Rather than producing the expected clash, the blade sliced straight through Taeris's defense, extinguishing it in an instant.

Dismissing the older man, the creature turned toward the three boys in Shackles, holding its dagger aloft.

*"Sha'teth keloran sa, Aelrith!"* Taeris yelled.

The words stopped the creature. It lowered its blade and turned back to Taeris, staring at him through its unblinking, dead eyes for several long seconds.

*"Sha'teth di sendra an,"* it growled. Taeris's eyes widened with astonishment as it let out a guttural laugh, then swiveled, preparing to deliver the killing blow.

The contents of Wirr's satchel had spilled all over the floor during the initial attack; while the creature's back was turned Caeden had knelt, scrabbling awkwardly for something that he had seen fall under the bed. For one gut-wrenching second, Davian wondered if Taeris had dropped the Vessel in the confusion and almost made to stop him.

Then Caeden found what he was looking for. Another Shackle. By the time the creature turned back, Caeden was ready.

He leaped forward, beneath the swinging blade of shadows, hands plunging deep beneath the creature's hood and pressing the ends of the torc against its neck.

The scream that followed was chilling, a sound filled with pain and torment. The blade vanished from the creature's hand; it stumbled backward, flailing wildly as the shackle began melding to its throat, wailing in a high-pitched screech that forced all four men to cover their ears. Its hood fell back, and Davian recoiled in horror. Even set against ashen skin and disfigured features, the creature's eyes were recognizably human, locked on to him and pleading for mercy.

Then it fell to the floor and, with a final convulsion, lay still.

Taeris stared at Caeden, wide-eyed. "That was…"

"Quick thinking," Davian breathed. He clapped Caeden on the back, as much to stop his hands from shaking as anything else. Caeden inclined his head, still panting from the adrenaline.

"Is it dead?" asked Wirr cautiously.

Suddenly there was a crash downstairs, and the sound of angry voices echoed along the hallway outside. Taeris groaned, then sprung into action, gathering up his scant possessions.

"We need to go. All of us," he said with a meaningful glance at Caeden. The red-haired man hesitated, then gave a single relieved nod of assent.

For a split second Davian looked at Taeris, puzzled, before realizing why there was such urgency in his tone. Taeris had used the Gift. They had minutes, if that, before the inn was swarming with Gil'shar soldiers.

They hurried downstairs and slipped out through a back door, apparently without raising any suspicion. It was past dusk but there were still plenty of people about; Davian risked a glance back as they mingled with the crowd, moving slowly but steadily away. As he watched, a group of about twenty soldiers rushed inside the inn, silent but grim-faced. Even at this distance, he could see their Finders out and a Trap at the ready.

The town was large, but those in the dirty, poorly lit streets paid them little heed as they hurried past, and they made good time. Davian flinched at every glance that came their way, but they were soon through the eastern gate without incident.

"Where do we go now?" asked Wirr, the first any of them had spoken since the inn.

"North," replied Taeris. "I'll explain more when we're well clear of this place."

Wirr grimaced, obviously disliking the answer as much as Davian did, but there was little else either of them could do but nod.

They started down the dark road in silence.

# Chapter 15

They had traveled for only a few minutes before Taeris stopped, signaling the others should do the same.

"Now. Tell me which one of you has given Tol Athian a Trace," he said, expression grim as he stared at the three boys. "And then you might like to tell me why they have decided to use it, too."

Davian frowned. What was a Trace? He glanced across at Wirr, but his friend was just glaring back at Taeris.

"If it was me, I don't remember," pointed out Caeden. "I don't even know what a Trace is."

Taeris examined their faces for a moment, then nodded in Wirr's direction. "He can explain it to you."

Wirr's scowl deepened, eyes still locked with Taeris's. "A Trace is a small sample of your Essence, sealed in a container that keeps it... fresh. Pure. Everyone's Essence is unique, so if Tol Athian needs to find someone, they can use their Trace to help locate them."

Taeris nodded. "It's like a person's scent," he elaborated to Caeden and Davian. "And the sha'teth are the hounds. Except that the Trace can only guide them if the person they are tracking uses the Gift." He rubbed his forehead tiredly. "Which young Wirr here did in the process of rescuing Caeden, I assume."

"But not at the inn," protested Wirr.

"They can use it to track you for up to a day after. Longer, if you've got a deep Reserve." Taeris frowned at Wirr. "When you expend that much power, you're using your body as a focal point, drenching it with energy—and that takes time to fully dissipate. Finders can't pick it up, but a sha'teth's senses can."

"I didn't know that," said Wirr softly.

"You should have asked," growled Taeris. "The question is—why does Tol Athian want to kill you, Wirr? What crimes have you committed that they would go so far as to take a Trace?"

Davian and Caeden had both watched the exchange in open-mouthed silence. Davian stared at his friend in disbelief. *Wirr* had brought that creature down on them?

"It's called a...sha'teth?" Davian had never heard the word before. "What is it?" He looked at Wirr in confusion. "What's going on?"

Wirr frowned, looking almost as puzzled as Davian. "I'm not sure." He turned to Taeris. "If Tol Athian sent the sha'teth after me, it was not to kill me, I promise you that. I don't know why it attacked. They *do* have my Trace, but not because I've committed any crime." He shook his head. "It's complicated, but I cannot say more."

Taeris's face darkened. "The sha'teth are assassins—that is their only purpose. You'll tell me everything, boy, or that Shackle won't be coming off your wrist anytime soon."

"Then that's the way it must be. I'm not lying, though." Wirr met Taeris's gaze flatly, without fear. He'd never been afraid of standing up to the Elders in Caladel when he felt he was in the right, and it seemed he was no more intimidated by Taeris.

"He's not lying," agreed Davian.

Taeris turned to Davian. "And you're not in the slightest bit curious as to why the sha'teth are hunting your friend?"

Davian studied Wirr for a long moment, then took a deep breath. "I am, but...I trust him. If we need to know what's going on, he'll tell us."

Taeris glowered as Wirr gave Davian a grateful nod. "We'll talk more of this later, when we're safely away," the scarred man promised. "The immediate danger has passed, at least—you won't be able to attract the rest of them while you're wearing a Shackle. We should be safe." He grimaced. "As far as these things go."

Caeden shifted. "There are other sha'teth?" he asked, echoing Davian's thoughts.

Taeris nodded. "Four of them. The one you killed was their

best tracker, though. We called him the Watcher. When the other sha'teth would leave the Tol to search for someone, he was never with them. It was as if he'd just wait until he sensed his target and...jump there somehow. None of us knew how he did it, but I'm fairly sure he was the only one of them who had that ability." He glanced back in the direction of Anabir. "Still. Whether Tol Athian still holds their leash or not, the others could be coming, and I doubt they'll be pleased that their brother has been killed. We should keep moving."

Wirr held up his hand. "Before we follow you blindly wherever you're taking us, you need to answer a few of *our* questions."

Taeris inclined his head wearily. "Of course."

"The other sha'teth. Will they come after us?"

"Almost certainly." Taeris sighed. "Once, perhaps not. But if what you say is true and they were not instructed to kill you... well, from what I just saw, they may be operating outside of Tol Athian's purview. The one that attacked us certainly ignored my command easily enough, and that should not have been possible."

"What did it say to you?" asked Davian.

Caeden spoke up. "It said, 'The sha'teth no longer serve.'"

They turned as one to look at Caeden, who shrugged. "I didn't understand it at the time, but just now, remembering...I knew what it meant." He glanced at Taeris. "Am I right?"

"Yes," said Taeris slowly, his expression curious as he stared at Caeden. Then he shrugged. "It could be that the commands have changed since my time, and that the creature was simply mocking me. Still..." He looked troubled.

Wirr gestured to the road ahead. "So along with avoiding the other sha'teth, you said we need to get back to Tol Athian to figure out what's happening with the Boundary. Why are we heading north?"

Taeris sighed. "With Caeden's escape, the Gil'shar will be focused on the borders; it will be all but impossible for us to get across unaided. And we don't have the option of finding a smuggler, as you did to get here—even those types would be unwilling to cross the Gil'shar on this, no matter how much coin we offer."

"True," conceded Wirr, "but heading towards Thrindar is hardly the solution."

"The Song of Swords is being held in Thrindar," corrected Taeris. "As of now, there is still a week of the festival remaining. The royal entourage from Andarra will be there, and Desriel allows visiting royalty to bring a small contingent of Gifted. If we can get into the city, I have contacts who can get us an audience. You may be able to slip over the border with them when they leave."

There was silence for a couple of seconds. "It won't work," said Wirr.

"It's our best chance," countered Taeris. "The Gil'shar will assume Caeden is running straight for the border, and they don't know for certain that anyone else is involved. They certainly won't imagine he has any way of contacting the Andarran delegation."

Wirr shook his head doggedly. "But they'll never let us join them. If they did and we were discovered, it wouldn't just be grounds for war—it would *start* it, then and there. The official Andarran delegation, smuggling Gifted out of Desriel? Including one accused of murder?" He shot an apologetic glance at Caeden. "I'm sorry, Taeris, but you must see how irresponsible that is. Our lives are not worth that sort of a risk."

Davian looked at his friend in surprise. Wirr had not raised his voice, but something about his demeanor had changed. For just a moment, the easygoing boy he knew had vanished. There was heavy concern, genuine intensity behind his words.

Taeris considered Wirr for a second, then sighed. "You're right, Wirr, but think for a moment about what I have told you today. Our lives are not my first concern. If there is some force at work trying to bring down the Boundary, do you imagine there's no threat to Andarra?"

"*If* there is, we don't know *what* it means," said Wirr stubbornly. "Whereas war with Desriel is most certainly a threat."

Taeris bit his lip, then came to a decision. He reached into his satchel, drew out a small metal box, and opened it, shivering as he gingerly picked out the paper-thin object within. It was about the size of his palm and completely black; though at first appearing polished to a mirror finish, it reflected none of the fading light as Taeris held it up. He leaned over, offering it to Wirr. "Be careful. The edges will slice through your fingers if you slip."

Wirr took it cautiously, visibly shivering as his hand touched its surface. He squinted as he examined the irregularly shaped disc. "What is it?" he asked with a look of horrified fascination.

"A scale from a dar'gaithin," replied Taeris.

Wirr dropped the disc as if burned; it fell to the grass beside the road without a sound. He stopped and began rubbing his fingers together as if trying to remove any trace of the object from his skin, though Davian could not see any physical residue. "Of course it is," he said with a shaky laugh, recovering himself somewhat. "Part of a mythical creature that you carry around in your pocket. Naturally." Despite his words he stared at the fallen black disc as if it might leap up and attack him.

Caeden frowned. "A dar'gaithin?"

"A mixture of snake and man. One of the five Banes used against Andarra in the Eternity War," explained Taeris.

"It's part of the Talan Gol myth," continued Wirr to Caeden, sounding dubious. "When Aarkein Devaed invaded, he supposedly led warriors that were almost impossible to kill—mixtures of animals and men. The dar'gaithin were snakes." He shook his head, turning back to Taeris. "I want to believe you, but... I took what Tenvar said about those creatures on faith, because we didn't know he could lie to Davian at the time. To be honest, when we found out he could, it made sense to me. It's hard to believe that they really exist."

Taeris grunted. "Well, the creature I found on the northern border of Narut a few months ago was certainly real enough," he said quietly. "I removed that scale from its carcass myself."

"You actually saw one?" asked Wirr, clearly caught somewhere between astonishment and skepticism.

Taeris nodded, choosing to ignore the doubt in Wirr's tone. "Just this side of the Boundary. The effort of crossing must have killed it." He sighed. "I took the scale and went to the garrison at Shandra, thinking to get help bringing the body back. By the time we returned, it had disappeared."

"So if the Boundary is still killing whatever tries to escape the north... that means someone from *this side* had hidden it?" asked Wirr, doubtful.

"It would appear so."

Davian glanced at Wirr and Caeden, not knowing what to make of Taeris's claim. Wirr still looked reluctant to believe the older man, but Caeden was staring at the scale on the ground in fascination. He walked over next to Wirr and squatted, looking at the thin black plate without touching it. Then he grabbed a stick and shifted the disc.

"I believe you," he said.

Davian stared at the patch of grass where the scale had been lying. The blades, green only a few moments earlier, had turned black and shriveled. Lifeless.

Taeris turned his attention to Caeden. "You remember something?"

Caeden shrugged. "It's difficult," he said slowly. "I get these... flashes. It's not memory, exactly, but it's not like knowing how to talk, either. It's... an instinct, I suppose. You told me what a dar'gaithin was, and suddenly I knew the grass underneath its scale would be dead. But I can't even tell you why I thought that." He rubbed his forehead in frustration. "Sometimes I feel like I'm so close to knowing something, to remembering. And then it just slips away again."

Taeris gave him a sympathetic nod. "It will come." He turned to Davian. "Try picking it up. Careful, though. Avoid touching the edges."

Davian reached down and cautiously plucked the scale from the ground. As he touched it, he shivered. A wave of nausea rolled through him—gone in an instant, but leaving him feeling drained, far more tired than a moment earlier.

Aside from that sensation, the scale had a cool, metallic feel to it. He handed it back to Taeris, who promptly dropped it back in its metal container.

"What *was* that?" asked Davian, suddenly understanding Wirr's reaction to touching the thing. He could still feel its cold surface against his skin.

"Dar'gaithin were supposed to be impervious to attack from the Gifted, and I think that's the reason why," Taeris said, gesturing to the dead patch of grass. "Their scales absorb Essence, draw it in. Maybe even feed off it."

There was silence as everyone stared at the blackened grass.

"For the sake of argument, let's say we believe you," said Wirr, looking shaken. "What are you trying to tell us, in truth? That Alchesh was right all along? That Devaed's been sitting patiently in his prison for two thousand years, just waiting for his chance to wreak havoc upon the world again?"

Taeris stared at the boy for so long that Wirr actually reddened. "For a young man with such a healthy skepticism, you know a great deal about the Eternity War."

Wirr scowled. "I read," he said defensively. His scowl deepened as he saw Davian's eyebrow raised in half-questioning amusement. "I do!"

Taeris smiled slightly. "In answer to your question—I don't have proof of anything like that. I *am* trying to keep an open mind, though. I've seen some astounding things done with Essence; it's unlikely, but if there is even the slightest chance Devaed could still be alive…" He sighed. "Put it this way—the dar'gaithin I saw, along with everything else going on with the Boundary, has certainly made me look at Alchesh a little more seriously."

He turned to Davian and Caeden, seeing their blank expressions. "Alchesh was an Augur from the time of the Eternity War. The stories say he was so immensely powerful, he was driven mad by seeing too much of what was to come," he explained. "After the Boundary was created, he foretold that it would one day fail, that Devaed and his armies would eventually be freed. People took it seriously for a long time. They manned forts, checked the Boundary regularly for any signs of attack.

"After a few centuries without so much as a sighting, though, a lot of people began to think that Alchesh's foretelling must have been a result of his madness—that not even a powerful Gifted like Devaed could still be alive after so many years. The opinion became popular enough that the Old Religion eventually struck Alchesh's visions from their canon and declared the Eternity War over. Soldiers were reassigned, and the Tols gradually stopped taking their readings. People forgot about the north as they focused on more immediate threats—the civil war in Narut, then the constant little skirmishes between Desriel and Andarra, Andarra and Nesk. After that there was the Great War with the Eastern Empire."

He shrugged, turning his attention back to Wirr. "And maybe Alchesh really was mad—but it doesn't change the fact that the Boundary failing right now is a problem. I can't say anything for certain about Devaed, but I *saw* that dar'gaithin corpse, and we can tell from the stories that those are fearsome, malevolent, intelligent creatures. Should they break through in numbers, they're going to attack regardless of whether they have any guiding force behind them."

Wirr thought for a moment, then gave a reluctant nod. "You're right," he admitted. "If those creatures really do exist, then it almost doesn't matter whether Devaed is alive—even by themselves, they're worse than anything the Gil'shar could hit us with. If the Tols aren't prepared, we'll be massacred." His shoulders slumped. "Which I suppose means you're right about what we need to do next, too."

"If you think of a better option, we will take it," said Taeris seriously.

"What about your Travel Stones?" Davian shrugged as everyone turned to look at him. "Couldn't we just send one across the border, then use the other to create a portal?"

Taeris shook his head. "Even if we found someone trustworthy to take one into Andarra, it wouldn't work. Creating a portal uses a vast amount of Essence, which needs to be stored up in the stones before they will work. I keep them on me so they constantly feed from my Reserve, but any more than a trickle and I'd be setting off Finders...it took me two months to charge them, last time. We won't be able to hide here for that long."

"Then it's Thrindar," concluded Wirr unhappily. He looked across at Davian. "I can't say as I like it, but he's right. If we don't get back to Tol Athian, find out what's going on with the Boundary, we could be risking far worse than Desriel's army."

They walked in silence for a while. After a few minutes, Taeris dropped back beside Davian, tugging on his sleeve to indicate that he should slow down. Wirr was talking cheerfully to Caeden—about what Davian wasn't sure, but the two of them were laughing. He smiled. Caeden had looked dazed, lost, ever since he'd woken, but Wirr was always the right person to put someone at ease.

Taeris glanced at the two boys up ahead, frowning. "You and Wirr need to be careful," he said, keeping his voice low.

Davian followed his gaze. "Of Caeden?" he asked. "You think he's hiding something?"

"Oh, I believe him well enough," replied Taeris. "But that doesn't mean he didn't murder those people, or that he isn't complicit in what's happened to you. For all you know, that box could have been meant to restore his memories, after which he may have been meant to kill you." He sighed. "I'm not saying that's what I think. But it *is* a possibility."

Davian looked at Caeden again. Could this young man, laughing and joking with his friend, really be a killer?

"What *do* you think?" he asked.

Taeris didn't reply for a few moments. "I think there are a handful of people *in the world* who could have translated what the sha'teth said to me," he said quietly. "What that means...I don't know. But if he turns out to be an enemy—well, you need to stay on your guard."

Davian swallowed. "And if we discover he really is dangerous, when we restore his memories at the Tol?"

"Then at least we've chosen the battleground," observed Taeris.

Without anything further he increased his pace again, quickly catching up to the other two. Davian soon joined them, but he kept mostly silent as they talked.

Taeris had given him much to think about.

# Chapter 16

Asha leaned back in her chair and glanced around the library for what was probably the hundredth time that day, unable to concentrate on the work laid out in front of her.

It had been almost a week since the Sanctuary and there had been no sign of the Northwarden, nor any indication that the Shadraehin had followed through on his plan. She sighed, shuffling the pages in front of her. She still half expected everything to go horribly wrong when the head of Administration found out about her, but now she just wished it were done either way. The waiting, the uncertainty, was worse by far.

"The book's that exciting, is it?"

She turned to see Tendric watching her with a mildly amused smile. She forced a smile back, hoping that the sudden twisting of her stomach wasn't evident on her face. Tendric was Jin's replacement; she didn't know whether he was one of the Shadraehin's people, but she suspected not. His dolorous outlook on life was much closer to Raden's than those from the Sanctuary.

"I'm just tired," she lied, hoping the man would leave her alone.

Instead Tendric took a seat opposite her. He looked around, then leaned forward a little, lowering his voice.

"I've been wanting to ask. Do you know where Jin went?"

Asha shook her head, unable to look him in the eye. "No idea."

Tendric sighed, looking disappointed but nodding. "Raden said the last time he saw him was with you. I was hoping maybe he'd said something before he disappeared...I can't say his is a job that I'd really hoped to be doing," he admitted.

"He didn't say anything," Asha reiterated, just wanting the conversation to be over.

The curly-haired Shadow was apparently oblivious to her discomfort. "But he didn't seem worried at all that day? Jumpy?" he pressed. "Haliden says he probably just got tired of things here and left, but Raden thinks something else happened to him. Like maybe he got on the wrong side of the crowd he was involved with...if you know what I mean." He shook his head, clearly more interested in spreading gossip than in Asha's opinion. "In which case he brought it on himself, I suppose."

Asha knew she shouldn't say anything, but it was too much.

"Fates, Tendric! I'm sure it had nothing to do with the Shadraehin," she snapped, unable to keep the anger from her voice. "Jin was a good man, and Raden is a slimy little fool if he's spreading lies like that."

Tendric gaped at her a little, taken aback by the outburst.

"I...uh. Sorry," he said after a moment, looking guilty. "You're right. I'm sure Jin's fine."

Asha set her jaw, glancing at the Decay Clock. It wasn't quite the end of the day, but it was close enough.

"I have to go," she said, pushing back her chair and gesturing to the papers on her desk. "I'll finish these up tomorrow."

She walked off, leaving Tendric gaping after her.

Once she reached her room she closed the door behind her and collapsed on the bed, trying to shut out the image of Jin's final moments. She stared up at the ceiling, the frustration and pain of the last few weeks welling up inside her, threatening to break free. She wasn't sure how much more of being here at the Tol, like this, she could take. She emitted a long, deep sigh.

From the corner of her room, there came a polite cough.

"Ashalia, I presume?"

Asha leaped up again to see two men standing at the far end of the room, having apparently appeared from thin air. A man and a boy, she realized on closer inspection. The boy was near her age, short and thin, with a pallid complexion. A servant of some kind, she thought. The man, though...

A rich blue cloak. Tall, and though he looked older, his blond hair had not yet faded. He had a strong jaw and piercing blue eyes, as well as a little beard that on most people would have looked like an affectation, but instead gave him a dignified air.

"Who are you?" she asked shakily, though she already knew the answer.

"Duke Elocien Andras," said the Northwarden. He held up his hands in a calming gesture. "Please, don't be alarmed. I'm only here for information."

Asha nodded, trying to gather her scattered thoughts; though she had been expecting this, she was still dazed—and not a little intimidated—that the head of Administration had actually come to see her. She glanced toward the door, which was still shut. "How did you get in here? Your Grace," she added hurriedly.

"I will explain later." Suddenly the duke frowned, turning to glance at his servant, who leaned over and whispered something in his ear. He faced Asha again, studying her for a long few seconds in silence.

"It seems this was a waste of time," he said. "I am sorry to have bothered you."

Asha gaped at him for a moment, confused. She hadn't known what to expect from her meeting with the Northwarden, but summary dismissal hadn't been one of the possibilities she'd considered.

"Please, don't go," she said quickly, desperation in her voice. She didn't know what she would do if she lost this opportunity. "I want to help you find out what happened to my friends, if I can. I want to know who killed them, and why."

The Northwarden turned, scowling, and looked about to make a retort when his eyes fell upon some of the loose pages on her desk. He closed his mouth, frowning, and stepped closer to examine them.

"You knew these people?"

Asha nodded. She'd been sketching some pictures of her friends at the school in her free time, something she'd wanted to do before their faces became too dim in her memory. There were plenty of images of Davian, and a few of Wirr and the others, too. She'd been told, some time ago, that she had a talent for drawing. It had helped her pass the time, and to deal with her grief.

Asha swallowed the lump in her throat that formed every time    177 she thought of Davian. "They're my friends, Your Grace," she said softly. "The ones who died."

The duke stared at her for a few moments, his expression softening.

"Tell me about them." It was a request rather than a command.

Asha hesitated. A part of her didn't want to share her memories of Davian and Wirr with this man. But it felt good to remember.

"Davian is sweet. A little too quiet, sometimes; he gets wrapped up in his problems and forgets he can share the burden. But he's honest, and smart, and loyal." She smiled as she talked about him. "Wirr is loud and brash. He'll sometimes act before he thinks it through, but then is clever enough to fix whatever he did wrong before he gets in too much trouble. He's funny and good at..." She gestured vaguely. "Well, he's good at everything, truth be told. And he knows it. He's not arrogant, mind you, but he's more confident than anyone has a right to be. It drives the Elders mad, actually." She felt her expression twist as she realized she had been talking about them in the present tense. "Drove them mad, I mean," she amended softly.

She looked up, and was startled to see the Northwarden's expression. He was leaning forward, giving her rapt attention. As soon as he registered her surprise his face became an impassive mask, but she was certain of what she had seen.

The duke didn't say anything, and the long silence began to grow uncomfortable. Just as Asha was about to break it, the duke straightened, looking at his servant.

"You're sure?"

The young man inclined his head, the slightest of motions. "Yes, Your Grace."

The duke shook his head as if surprised at what he was about to do, then sighed, turning to Asha. "You want to help? You want to come to the palace, find out more about what's going on?"

Asha nodded, barely daring to hope, though she didn't understand what had changed the duke's mind. "Of course, Your Grace."

"Then come with me. And call me Elocien, at least when we are not in public. 'Your Grace' becomes tiring after a while." Elocien raised an eyebrow at his servant. "Time to knock on Nashrel's door, I suppose."

He smiled.

❧

The duke paused outside the Council chamber door.

He turned to Asha. "Let me do the talking in here," he said seriously. "I know how to handle the Council. Let them think you're robbing them, then ask them for what you really want." He waited until Asha nodded her assent, then turned to consider the door in front of him. "Now..."

A thunderous crash echoed through the Council chambers as Elocien kicked the door open as hard as he could.

The duke returned Asha's shocked stare with a shrug. "Puts them off balance."

He strode inside, blue cloak flowing majestically behind, leaving Asha gaping after him.

"What is the meaning of this?" cried a startled voice, joined quickly by others. The shouts were silenced, however, as soon as Elocien entered the room.

Asha trailed after the Northwarden, his servant following her. Most of the Elders' seats were full this time; another man in a blue cloak sat to the side of the Elders, and a younger Gifted sat next to him with a pen and paper, scribbling furiously. An official Council meeting, then, from all appearances.

Elder Eilinar paled as his eyes darted from Elocien to Asha, then back again. There was a deathly hush, even the sound of the Scrivener's pen vanishing as the young man stared down at them in shock. The other Administrator looked equally stunned.

"Duke Andras," choked out Nashrel, just as the silence became almost unbearable. "We were not told you were—"

"No. You weren't." The relatively friendly demeanor the duke had shown Asha had vanished. He glared up at the supervising Administrator and the Scrivener. "Out," he growled.

The two men had disappeared before the Northwarden had time to turn back to Nashrel.

"Now, Elder Eilinar. Let us discuss why I am here."

Nashrel looked around desperately, as if searching for an exit. "She had nothing to tell, Your Grace," he said. "We didn't want to bother—"

"You didn't want to share," said Elocien, cutting off Nashrel for the second time in a row. He gave an impatient sigh. "I try not to exercise the Fourth Tenet too much, Elder Eilinar, but sometimes you make me wonder why."

There was silence from the gallery as Nashrel stared at the ground, chastised. Several of the other Council members looked equally abashed. "I apologize, Your Grace," Nashrel eventually said stiffly. "She is the only one to survive an attack, and we wanted to keep her close, observe her so we could find out why. We were mistaken not to inform you, though."

"Keep her close? You made her a Shadow and put her to work," growled Elocien. "If I hadn't found her, she likely would have rotted in here."

Nashrel coughed. "And if I may be so bold as to ask—how *did* you know about the girl?"

Elocien just stared at Nashrel until the other man looked away again.

The head of the Administrators let the silence drag for a few more seconds, then crossed his arms. "If you insist on acting like children, you will be treated like children. The girl will be coming with me."

Nashrel's face reddened. "Why? What possible use could you have for her?"

"That is my business," the duke replied.

"I'm sorry, Northwarden, but you don't have the right," Nashrel spluttered. "You need the Council's permission to take one of us from the Tol. To do otherwise would violate the Treaty!"

"A shame you decided to exempt her from the Treaty, then," said Elocien, staring squarely at Nashrel. "She's not Gifted anymore, in case you hadn't noticed."

"But you have no cause, no charge. You still cannot take her against her will."

"She wants to go."

Everyone's gaze turned to Asha, who reddened under their stares. Nashrel looked at her in disbelief. "Is this true?" He leaned forward. "If you say you do not want to go, he cannot take you, child."

Asha looked back at him steadily. "I want to go."

There was a stunned silence in the chamber as Nashrel just stared at her, openmouthed.

The Elder recovered himself after a few seconds, giving Elocien a hesitant glance before looking away again in obvious frustration. "Take her, Northwarden, and you lose your best chance at finding him."

The assertion meant nothing to Asha, but the room went very quiet, as if everyone was suddenly holding their breath. Elocien stepped forward, his composure threatening to crack for the first time.

"Was that a threat?"

Nashrel swallowed. "No, of course not, Your Grace," he said hurriedly, holding up his hands in a defensive posture. "I meant only that by observing the girl, we may learn something that could help. If you take her, we cannot do that."

Asha studied Elocien, trying to determine what was going on. He looked displeased but seemed to be acknowledging the truth of the statement; he paused for a long few seconds, rubbing his chin thoughtfully.

"What if I were to reconsider my stance on your having a Representative at court?"

Nashrel's eyes lit up at the suggestion, and there was a ripple of excited murmurs from the other Elders in the gallery. "What do you propose, Your Grace?"

"One Gifted Representative from Tol Athian. Ashalia becomes their apprentice," Elocien said. "Athian pays her wages. Your Representative mentors her, and continues to monitor her for any clues as to who attacked the schools, or how she survived."

It took a few moments for Asha to register what the duke was proposing; when she did she stared across at him in shock, certain she must have misheard. Representatives were the Tol's ambassadors to the palace; even as an apprentice to one, she would still be considered an envoy of Tol Athian.

For one of the Gifted, it would be an extraordinarily prestigious position. But for her...

Nashrel looked at Ashalia and then back at Elocien, aghast, evidently thinking the same thing. "But...she's a Shadow!" he exclaimed. "Do you know how many Gifted would kill for that position? How can she possibly represent the Tol? Surely you understand that we need someone who—"

"It's this or nothing, Nashrel," interrupted Elocien. "Such a role requires no ability to use the Gift. Her situation may even be of use—once the Houses know she isn't with the Shadraehin, there are plenty who will feel more comfortable talking to her than one of the Gifted." He paused. "At least, you'll need to explain it to everyone else that way, because you're going to continue to pretend that there were no survivors of Caladel. Her real reason for being at the palace cannot leave this room. Ever. If it does, I'll know it was one of you who released the information, and I'll expel your Representative. Again."

"You seem certain we will accept these terms, Your Grace," said Nashrel roughly.

Elocien sighed. "If you refuse, I will take Ashalia with me and you will continue to have no presence in the palace. So this is a good deal, Nashrel. The best you'll hear from me."

Nashrel glared at Elocien, and Asha imagined she could hear his teeth grinding even from that distance. Eventually he turned to the other Council members. "Any opposed?" There was silence from the gallery, and Nashrel's expression twisted as he turned back to look down on Elocien. "Accepted," he said, bitterness thick in his voice. "We will select a senior Representative before the end of the day."

Elocien nodded. "Send them directly to the palace; Ashalia will be staying with me."

"But—"

Elocien cut off Nashrel with a sharp gesture. "I'm informing, not asking."

Nashrel gritted his teeth, but nodded. "As you say, Your Grace."

Elocien spun and headed for the exit; after a moment a still-stunned Asha realized she was expected to follow him, and she half jogged to catch up.

182    They left. As quickly as that, it was done.

Asha and Duke Andras walked through the sun-drenched streets of Ilin Illan.

Wherever they went people stopped and stared; women bent down and pointed them out to their children, and a small crowd even drifted after them as they moved along at an unhurried pace. At first Asha thought they were gaping at her black-veined face, but before long she overheard some of the whispers as they passed, and she knew that most people weren't even noticing her. They were all focused on Elocien. The Northwarden, the king's brother. The man who had created the Tenets.

She tried to talk only once.

"Do you really mean to make me a Representative?" she asked the duke.

"Yes."

"Why?"

Elocien shook his head slightly, not taking his eyes from the road. "All in good time," he murmured.

They walked the rest of the way in silence.

# Chapter 17

Davian struggled forward through the throng, jostled constantly by the mass of people around him, trying to follow Taeris as closely as possible as he snaked through the crowd.

The late afternoon sun beat down on Thrindar's main street, which was choked with travelers trying to gain entrance to the Great Stadium in the town center. Dust kicked up by hundreds of feet drifted everywhere, combining with the sweat on people's faces to make them look more like coal miners than city folk. Merchants on the side of the road yelled hoarsely at anyone foolish enough to glance their way, well aware that this was the largest crowd they would likely see for many years. The entire scene was dirty, hot, and chaotic. Davian didn't like it at all.

"How long now?" he muttered to Taeris, wiping beads of moisture from his brow and scowling as another stranger shouldered past.

"I said fifteen minutes, and that was ten minutes ago. How long do you think?" replied Taeris, irritation creeping into his tone. Like Davian, he was visibly not enjoying battling through the sweaty crush.

Davian gave a short nod in response, glancing across at his other companions. Wirr wasn't paying attention, looking more excited than anything else, staring at every new sight with genuine fascination. Caeden, on the other hand, plowed forward with the grim determination and characteristic silence he'd shown for most of their journey.

"How are you holding up?" Davian asked Caeden in a low voice as they were pushed together by the press of bodies.

Caeden gave him a nervous smile. "I'll be glad to get indoors."

Davian nodded in understanding. Word of Caeden's escape had arrived in Thrindar well before them, and already there were plenty of posters with his likeness nailed up around the city.

"Shouldn't be long now," he said, trying to sound reassuring despite the churning of his own stomach. Taeris had already made sure to alter Caeden's appearance as much as possible—cut his hair short, made him wear several layers of clothes to give him a more portly appearance—but all it would take was one person who could see through the changes.

Still, they'd made it this far without incident. It had taken them a full six days to reach Desriel's capital. Traveling had been a tense affair, if uneventful; the constant threat of being discovered by Gil'shar soldiers had been surpassed only by the fear of being found by another sha'teth. Still, there had been no sign of pursuit and they had made good time, arriving several days before Taeris expected the royal entourage to leave.

Davian pushed on behind the others. After a couple of minutes he shifted his gaze upward from the crowd, catching his first glimpse of Thrindar's Great Stadium as it began to loom ahead. It was at least fifty feet high and made of solid stone; the tops of the walls were draped with colorful banners, each one emblazoned with a different symbol.

"The insignias of some of those competing," said Wirr, following Davian's gaze.

"There must be a hundred banners up there," murmured Davian, wiping sweat from his brow. "Are all the fighters lords and such?"

Wirr shook his head, face glowing as he took in the atmosphere; despite his oft-mentioned reservations about Taeris's plan, he looked more excited than worried. "Not all, but most. Noblemen learn swordplay younger than most, and then have more time to practice as they grow up. It tends to be an advantage."

"No doubt being able to afford entry is an advantage, too." Davian turned sideways to avoid being run down by a fat woman and the two bawling young children she was dragging behind her.

Wirr laughed. "*No one* can afford entry by themselves," he assured Davian. "The costs are..." He gestured, shaking his head to indicate that he had no words to describe their enormity. "Some very few get invitations. Everyone else has backers— sponsors who share the entry cost, and reap a percentage of any winnings."

Davian raised an eyebrow. "And the winnings are enough to share around, with everyone profiting?"

Wirr gave an emphatic nod. "With gold to spare."

Davian looked up at the banners again as they became slowly larger. "I wonder who they are," he said absently. He vaguely recognized a couple of the designs, but couldn't identify any of them.

"There's only a few Andarran. Plenty of Desrielites and Narutians. A couple from Nesk. Even a few from the Eastern Empire, I suspect."

Davian shot his friend a sidelong glance, partly amused and partly curious. Wirr was enjoying himself more than he had since they had decided to come here. "You really recognize all these banners?"

Wirr shrugged. "Most of them. Jarras's politically minded lessons were fairly thorough."

Davian grinned as he thought of the Elder. "Jarras would have a heart attack if he knew where we were."

Wirr smirked. "Most of the Elders would, I imagine."

The throng thinned a little as they stepped into the shadow of the arena; soldiers and attendants lined the entrance, studiously funneling people into the appropriate sections of the stadium. Taeris hung back, studying the crowd as the other three gathered around him.

"What are you looking for?" asked Wirr.

"We have no chance of getting into the stadium itself. Not so that we could speak to the Andarran delegation, anyway," said Taeris, softly enough that no passersby could overhear. "But there must be Gifted coming and going. If I can make contact with one of them, we might be able to gain an audience."

Caeden frowned. "And if you are refused?"

Taeris shrugged. "We will deal with that problem should it arise."

Davian fanned his face, the heat of the day by now quite intense. "How will you recognize them? Even with their cloaks, they'll be hard to spot in this crowd."

Taeris gave him a slight smile. "You'll see."

They loitered for a while, occasionally moving around and browsing through shops and stalls to avoid looking suspicious. It wasn't difficult to remain anonymous; the crowds were so thick that they probably could have stood still the entire day without anyone noticing.

Eventually Taeris tensed, nudging Davian. "There," he said with a slight nod of his head.

A man in a red cloak was emerging from one of the stadium entrances, shadowed closely by a guard holding a Trap prominently in front of him. The crowd parted wherever the cloaked man went; several people spat on the ground as he passed. The noise of the crowd, which had been a roar only moments earlier, quieted to a low rumble as people stopped their conversations to watch.

"You want to pass a note to *him*?" Wirr said softly, his tone incredulous. He glanced at Taeris, then back at the red-cloaked man, who was still very obviously isolated and had every eye trained on him. "You may as well ask the man with the Trap to pass it on for you."

Taeris gave a thoughtful nod, scratching his beard. "I didn't think it would be this bad," he admitted.

They watched as the Gifted man, looking more amused than intimidated by the attention, purchased something from a very displeased-looking vendor. Davian shifted to get a better view, and was so intent on the red-cloaked man that he walked straight into someone before he realized she was there, causing her to stumble to the ground.

He looked down in horror, reddening, and quickly bent to help his victim to her feet. She was about his age, pretty, with long black hair and green eyes that sparkled as they looked up at him with amusement. Her hands were soft and smooth as he pulled her up, stammering his apologies.

A shift in the crowd distracted him for a moment. The Gifted was meandering back into the stadium, still followed by the vigilant-looking guard; as soon as he had disappeared the crowd's conversations resumed, and the scene returned to normal as if
nothing had happened.

Davian glanced around to see if the girl was uninjured, but she was already gone.

Wirr was watching him with an amused smile.

"Say nothing," Davian warned. "It was an accident."

"Of course it was," said Wirr. "Girls who look like that are easy to miss. Practically invisible, really."

Davian glared at his friend. He'd usually have played along, but this time Wirr's jibe only reminded him of Asha, back at Caladel and probably wondering why they had abandoned her. As always, the accompanying stab of guilt—and fear that she would not forgive him, if he ever saw her again—put him in a bad mood.

Wirr sighed, still smiling, but wisely deciding to let the matter go. He turned to Taeris, who had been ignoring the exchange and was still staring thoughtfully toward the stadium. "So it looks like we should find another way across the border."

Taeris shook his head. "No. There's another chance. A little more direct than I'd like, but it should work."

Without adding anything further, he gestured for them to follow and then set off down the road.

They wound their way through a series of narrow streets until they came to a stop outside a large building. Its facade was ornate, with finely carved designs inscribed onto every available surface, and its architecture gave it gentle curves that were distinct from the houses and stores around it. It wasn't circular, but the entire structure gave the impression of having no corners, and as a result was somewhat dizzying to the eye. After a few moments of consideration, Davian decided he didn't like it.

"Where are we?" he asked Taeris.

"The Temple of Marut Jha Talkanar, God of Balance." It was Caeden, his expression fascinated as he stared up at the structure.

Taeris gave the young man a sidelong glance, then nodded confirmation to Davian.

Wirr gave Taeris a disbelieving look. "You're hoping to get help from *here*?" He looked around to make sure no one was close enough to overhear. "Isn't it a little dangerous? What with the sacredness of Essence, and those who use it being abominations, and all that?"

Taeris started up the stairs. "Just say nothing, do as I tell you, 189 and we will be fine." He vanished inside without waiting to see if his companions were following.

The other three exchanged glances. "We've trusted him this far," noted Caeden.

Davian nodded, and Wirr gave a reluctant shrug of agreement.

They entered the temple cautiously. Once the doors had closed behind them, the bustling sounds from outside vanished and they were left with only a peaceful hush. Somewhere a fountain burbled, and somehow a fresh breeze from one of the high windows was cunningly directed downward by the odd shape of the walls, sighing in the enclosed space. Skylights meant the large room was well lit, but scented candles burned in the corners, too. Aside from the three of them, the room was unoccupied.

Just as Davian had finished taking stock of their surroundings, a side door swung open and Taeris strode through, followed by what appeared to be a very drunk priest. The man staggered over one of the steps, then tripped completely, sliding along the polished marble floor with an odd grace. Taeris snorted, then hurried over to help him up and make sure he was uninjured.

"I present to you the high priest of Talkanar, God of Balance," whispered Wirr to the others.

Davian stifled a giggle that would have echoed quite embarrassingly around the open room, and even Caeden, usually more reserved, hid a smile.

Eventually the priest managed to make his way over to where they stood without falling, though that was mainly due to the assistance of Taeris. Taeris propped him up as they came to a halt, making sure he wasn't going to collapse again before letting him go.

"Boys, this is Nihim Sethi, someone we can trust. Nihim—this is Wirr, Davian, and Caeden."

The man called Nihim looked at them through bleary eyes. "Pleased to meet you," he slurred.

Taeris winced. "Don't blame him. It's the month of debauchery," he explained with a roll of the eyes. "Of all the choices, getting drunk is about the most moral thing you can do and still look pious."

"Seems like it should be more popular," said Wirr, gesturing to the empty space around them.

Nihim snorted. "Popular? No. In fact, these days we only survive through the decree of the Gil'shar." He shook his head groggily. "This month may be all well and good, but there's a month of abstinence, too. A month of gluttony and one of starvation. A month of pleasure and a month of pain."

"So you'd be devout half the year," said Wirr with a grin.

Nihim winced. "I take it you're not from around here. Don't let anyone else hear you talking like that," he slurred. "Here, you choose one of the nine gods, and that's your path. Set in stone, no changing, no slacking off. If you don't follow the precepts, and then get caught..." He made a slicing motion with his finger across his throat.

"They kill you?" said Davian in astonishment.

"We like to think of it as aggressive evangelism," replied Nihim glibly.

"There's a reason the Gifted are so hated here, Davian," Taeris interrupted. "Being devout isn't just a choice in Desriel. It's a way of life, indoctrinated and law." He hesitated. "So you can see what a risk Nihim is taking for us."

Nihim stared at a spot on the ground. "Taeris. I'm in no state to help you and your friends right now, but give me an hour. We have tonics in the back for...clearheadedness." It was obvious he was struggling to concentrate. "The others shouldn't be back for days; I'm basically in charge for the moment. No one wants to be stuck in the temple during Jil'imor. You shouldn't be disturbed if you stay in there." He gestured to the smaller room from which he had just emerged.

Taeris gripped him by the arm. "Thank you, Nihim," he said sincerely.

The four of them filed into the side room, Davian glancing behind him to see Nihim stumbling off to another section of the temple. There were comfortable-looking chairs and couches lining the wall of this room, but none of the finery that was on display in the main chamber. It appeared to be a common room for the priests, rather than for public use.

They talked quietly among themselves. Davian was full of questions about the Song of Swords; to his surprise Wirr was able to answer more of them than Taeris. The last two winners of the Song were fighting in this tournament, apparently, though Selbin Hran—the victor from fourteen years ago—was almost forty now.

Caeden seemed fascinated by the entire concept, but, as always, he kept his thoughts mostly to himself. Davian observed him surreptitiously for a while, as he'd tried to do a few times this past week. He liked Caeden, but he knew he had to be careful about his instincts. It was his credulous nature that had landed them in this mess in the first place. He couldn't just give Caeden the benefit of the doubt—he had to wait until they were safely in Ilin Illan, and their companion's role in all of this had finally been explained, before trusting him.

Eventually the door to the main chamber opened again, and a much more composed-looking Nihim stepped through. His long black hair was now bound, and the redness around his eyes had all but vanished. He was also tall, Davian realized with a start; he must have been slouching considerably before. He moved with a sure step and confident air that were much more befitting a priest.

"I apologize for the wait," he said to them in a strong, clear voice. "Even with the medicines at my disposal, this time of year can be a trial."

"Not your fault," said Taeris amiably. "Do I need to do the introductions again?"

Nihim chuckled. "No, no. Davian, Caeden, Wirr." He pointed to each in turn. Then he sighed, giving them a considering look. "So, Taeris, you've gathered a small group of friends. I never picked you as the type to enjoy company." His tone was casual, but there was definitely a question behind it.

Taeris gave him a slight smile. "You're right about that, but sometimes we don't have a choice in the matter." Wirr rolled his eyes at Davian, who grinned.

Nihim just nodded. "I hear there was some trouble down south. Bad stuff, Gifted involved and everything. A man caught helping someone mixed up in that would probably not end up on the good side of the Gil'shar."

"True. But then, a favor that large would clear a lot of debts, too," said Taeris.

Nihim smiled at that. "I wouldn't go that far, but it will be a start." He clapped Taeris on the back. "So beyond giving you a roof over your heads, what can I do for you?"

"I need to get a message to the king," said Taeris. "Before he leaves Thrindar."

"Ah." Nihim nodded. "Of course. Safe passage across the border. A good thought, I'll give you that." He shrugged apologetically. "One problem. The king isn't here."

Taeris's smile slipped. "What?"

"There's still a delegation," Nihim rushed to assure him, "but it's led by the princess."

Taeris frowned. "Karaliene is being given duties of state? She's just a girl!"

"She's eighteen, Taeris," said Nihim with a grin. "She's old enough to have suitors trailing after her like a pack of wolves."

Taeris shook his head. "Eighteen," he muttered to himself. "Time has flown. Still, I would not have thought King Andras comfortable enough to send her to Desriel. Not in these times."

Nihim shrugged. "From what I hear, one of the tournament favorites is a close friend of hers. She wanted to come."

"Regardless." Taeris turned back to Nihim. "Karaliene may not understand the message, but she will surely have an entourage of Gifted who are old enough. If you can give them this"—he pressed something into Nihim's palm—"and arrange passage for us into the stadium to meet them, that will be more than enough."

Nihim inspected the small metal token in his palm. It was a simple design, like a coin, but steel and with three triangles punched from the middle. "What is it?"

"A symbol from the Unseen War—a request for sanctuary. Any Gifted who lived in Andarra through those times will know what it means." He pointed to the triangular holes. "One triangle meant the person asking was in no danger. Two meant they were in some danger, but not immediate." He shrugged. "Three meant that if sanctuary wasn't granted, the Gifted was most likely going to be captured and killed."

Nihim nodded. "I think you are probably right to use the three triangles, then," he mused.

"As it is, it's the only one I have left."

Nihim inspected it for a few more seconds, then gave a sharp nod, slipping the token into his pocket. "Very well." He glanced at the boys, then back to Taeris. "I would have a word in private first, if it's not too much trouble."

Taeris inclined his head, looking unsurprised by the request. He turned to the boys. "Wait here," he said. "This won't take long."

He followed Nihim out the door. Davian, Wirr, and Caeden exchanged curious glances, but none made any move to follow.

"So who do you think he is?" asked Wirr as soon as the door had closed.

Davian shrugged. "He knows we're Gifted, and isn't trying to kill us. That's good enough for me." Caeden nodded his agreement.

Wirr was having none of it. "He's a Desrielite priest—or posing as one, anyway. Aren't you the least bit curious?" He leaned forward. "My guess is that he's one of Tol Athian's spies. An informer."

Caeden gazed at the closed door. "Dangerous job if he is."

"More so, now we know he's a friend to the Gifted," observed Wirr. "Even if he's not a spy, this is a significant risk he's taking. He must owe Taeris for something big, to not have turned us away."

"Maybe that's what they're talking about," said Davian.

Wirr cast a longing look toward the door, and for a second Davian thought he meant to follow the two men. Then he sighed. "Whatever it is, it's obviously nothing they want us to overhear."

After that there was only the occasional wisp of conversation as they waited; mostly Davian and Wirr talked, though occasionally Caeden would contribute a word or two as well. The young man rarely spoke more than that at one time—he'd sometimes ask about things he'd either forgotten or never known about, but mostly he just listened, apparently fascinated by what others were saying.

For all that, when Caeden did talk he had a friendly if shy manner, and was unfailingly polite. Not for the first time, Davian found himself convinced that—if nothing else—the Gil'shar's charges against him had to be false.

194    A half hour had passed by the time Taeris returned.

"Nihim is taking the message to the Great Stadium," the scarred man said in answer to the boys' questioning looks. "If he is successful, we should be escorted there within a couple of hours."

Davian nodded, allowing himself a glimmer of hope at the news. He flashed a tight smile at Wirr, but his friend was staring concernedly into space and didn't respond, looking more upset than relieved at the news.

"Everything all right?" asked Davian, giving his friend a gentle nudge with his elbow.

Wirr blinked, then shook his head as if to clear it. "As right as it can be, given the circumstances," he said with a shrug. He still looked uncomfortable, though.

"Wishing you hadn't come with me?" asked Davian.

"Fates, yes," said Wirr with a grin. "But you wouldn't have made it a day without me, so maybe it was worth it."

Davian gave a half smile, half grimace back; the words were said in jest, but a pang of guilt stabbed at him anyway. "I'm sorry I got you into this mess," he said softly, so only his friend could hear.

Wirr shook his head. "You've been apologizing all week, Dav. You don't need to anymore," he said, his tone firm. "It's not your fault. You couldn't have known. And anyway—if what Taeris tells us is even close to true, some good may yet come of all this. If we can get Caeden to the Tol, find out whether there really is something dangerous going on with the Boundary, it will all have been worth it."

Davian paused, then inclined his head. "Thanks."

He leaned back, looking around. Caeden was sitting quietly; his eyes were closed, but Davian suspected he was still awake. Taeris had sat himself down at a desk and was thumbing through some papers he'd discovered.

"How do you know Nihim?" Davian asked Taeris. "He didn't seem too concerned about having four of the Gifted in his temple."

Taeris paused in what he was doing. "He's an old friend. Someone we can trust." He gave Davian a hard look. "More than that is not my place to say." There was an air of finality to the statement, a tone that brooked no argument. Davian accepted it with a reluctant nod.

Some time later the door opened and Nihim stepped through, trailed by two uneasy-looking Desrielite soldiers. For a panicked moment Davian thought they had been betrayed, but Taeris rose smoothly from his seat, calm as he gestured for the boys to do the same. Trying to look composed, Davian stood.

"Children of Marut Jha," said Nihim grandly. "These soldiers have been ordered to take you directly to the Great Stadium for your audience with Princess Karaliene Andras." He paused, and though his expression was serious, Davian thought he saw laughter in the priest's eyes. "If they do not carry out this duty swiftly and faithfully, you will let me know."

Taeris bowed. "For the glory of the Last God."

"For His glory alone," responded Nihim.

They followed the soldiers from the temple, with no further good-byes uttered to or by Nihim. Soon they were back within sight of the Great Stadium, the massive walls towering above them. The crowds outside had thinned somewhat; the gates had been shut, and Davian thought he could see more than one disappointed face among the crowd. The stadium must be at capacity.

For a moment he wondered if they would be allowed entry, but as soon as the soldiers at the entrance saw them, they were opening the steel gates a crack and ushering them through.

The stone passageway in the underbelly of the stadium was pleasantly cool compared to the outside. Davian barely had time to marvel at the intricate stone friezes set into the walls before they were ascending a set of winding stairs; at the top a pair of burly guards waved them through into another long passageway, with a narrow window cut out of the side overlooking the arena itself.

Davian couldn't help but gape a little as they walked along. Thousands upon thousands of people were packed into the stands; it was a writhing sea of color such as he had never seen before, could not have imagined. There was the low rumble of countless excited voices in the air, and the atmosphere itself felt alive, buzzing with anticipation.

196     Finally their escorts reached another set of guarded doors, these

ones closed. There was a quick discussion between the two pairs of soldiers, and then they were being guided into a side room, isolated from the crowd and completely empty. A small window gave them a view of the arena, but only when they stood right up to it.

"You will wait here until after the final bout," said one of the soldiers. His tone was firm, but his eyes betrayed his nervousness. He evidently didn't want this delay getting back to Nihim.

Taeris frowned, looking displeased, but he obviously decided it was not worth risking closer examination by forcing the issue. "Very well." There was a pause, and then Taeris added, "You may leave us."

The soldiers, clearly relieved there would be no reprisal for the delay, fled gladly.

Wirr glanced at the window. "While we're here…"

Davian was already moving. "Agreed."

Taeris and Caeden soon joined them, and the four stood in a line along the elongated, paneless window, leaning forward against the ledge it provided. In the center of the arena were two men. One stood relaxed, casual as he sauntered around in small circles, swinging his blade through the air to test its weight and balance. He was slim, lithe, and looked much the same age as Davian.

His opposition was a giant of a man. Muscle rippled along his arms with every movement, and in his hand his sword looked more like a rapier than the broadsword it actually was. His face was crisscrossed with scars; it was difficult to tell, but he looked older, possibly in his early forties. He stood stock-still, staring at the other man as if watching his prey.

"They're not wearing armor," Davian noted in surprise. Both men wore simple pants and loose-fitting shirts that were open at the front; there was no protection to speak of. Their swords glinted in the afternoon light.

"The edges of the swords are blunted," explained Wirr.

"Surely that's still dangerous?" asked Davian.

"It *is* a sword fight," noted Wirr.

"It's very rare anyone gets killed," interjected Taeris. "Broken bones are usually the worst of it."

There was silence as they watched for a few more seconds. The beginning of an announcement had caused the crowd outside to hush, though the voice was too muffled from their position to understand it.

Wirr squinted at two large banners draped from a far balcony, evidently representing the two finalists. "I think one is an Andarran. I recognize the sigil...Shainwiere. I think."

"Which one?" asked Davian.

Wirr studied the two men in the arena. "The younger," he said eventually. "Lord Shainwiere would be too old to be here, and I doubt he'd have the skill anyway. It must be his son."

A trumpet sounded, signaling the beginning of the fight. The crowd roared as the combatants began circling each other warily, each feinting occasionally with his feet but otherwise simply sizing up his opponent.

"Our man's a bit smaller than the other one, then," observed Davian drily.

Wirr shrugged. "Strength is important, but it's usually the quicker, smarter man that wins."

The two men were still circling, but suddenly Shainwiere flew into action. He launched himself forward in a blur of movement; his sword flashed again and again as the other man blocked blow after blow, moving quickly backward as the younger man threatened to come in under his guard. When the swords touched there were sparks of light, and the large man's eyes were wide as he desperately tried to follow the arc of Shainwiere's blade. Some in the crowd leaped to their feet, and a rousing cheer echoed thunderously around the stadium.

Shainwiere had broken off the attack; Davian could tell even from this distance that both men were breathing heavily. The larger man did not wait long before responding, though. He came forward in a rush, swinging his enormous sword as if it were light as a feather.

It was Shainwiere's turn to move backward, though when he retreated he did so smoothly, catlike, as if it had been his intention to do so all along. Despite the blaze of sparks he appeared to be blocking his opponent's blows almost lazily at times, though Davian had no doubt that it was taking every ounce of his
strength and concentration to do so.

Without warning, Shainwiere stopped retreating and dove forward, evidently picking up on some flaw in the other man's footwork. Even from this distance Davian could see the surprise in the big man's eyes as Shainwiere's sword slashed across both his legs; Shainwiere rolled and came to his feet behind the massive man, watching as he slumped to his knees, mouth open in a bellow of pain that was lost beneath the roar of the crowd.

For a second Davian thought the fight was over, but the big man forced himself to his feet and began circling again, his smooth motion showing no sign of his injury.

Swords clashed again and again; minutes passed as the two combatants fought. With each engagement the crowd roared louder, with more fervor, and before long Davian realized that the cheers were heavily favoring the larger man.

"They don't want an Andarran to win," murmured Taeris to no one in particular, as if reading his thoughts. "The Song's not supposed to be about politics, but there's a lot of bad blood between the two countries right now. It would be a slap in the face to Desriel if Shainwiere got the victory here."

As he spoke, there appeared to be a slight shift in the battle. The muscular man pressed forward at a furious pace; rather than breaking off as he had done previously, he kept up the offensive, his sword a blur as Shainwiere backed away desperately. Just as it seemed he could attack no more, the man gave one last, heavy blow, the force of it knocking Shainwiere's sword from his grip and sending it sailing out of reach. The younger man's shoulders sagged, but he clenched his fist and held it over his heart, a sign of both surrender and respect. The crowd screamed its approval, and then it was over.

Davian looked at Wirr with a disappointed expression, but his friend seemed relieved, as did Taeris. Caeden just looked thoughtful.

"Good," Taeris muttered to himself, turning away from the window. "Time to get out of this place."

If he had been expecting an immediate audience, though, he was to be disappointed. It was at least another hour, well after the presentation to the winner had been completed, before the door to the hallway outside finally opened again.

Taeris groaned under his breath as a tall, thin man in a red cloak swept into the room. "He's from Tol Shen. This may be more difficult than I first thought," he muttered to Davian.

The Elder stopped when he saw Taeris, staring hard into his scarred face for several seconds. Then he gave a sneering laugh. "Taeris Sarr," he said with a smile that held a complete lack of warmth. "I almost didn't recognize you. So you're still alive. I always thought we got rid of you a little too easily." He examined Taeris disdainfully. "What happened to your face?"

Taeris stiffened, but ignored the insult. "Administration was… not kind, before I escaped," he said quietly. "We've had our differences, Dras, but I hope we can look past them today. I need your aid. We have nowhere else to turn."

Davian watched Taeris silently. None of them had asked their companion how he had come by his myriad scars, but Davian had wondered—and now he knew. Another on the list of sacrifices Taeris had made for him.

Dras sighed. "I've already distracted a Gil'shar escort *and* Karaliene's two Administrators just to come and see you. I'm not sure what more I want to do for a criminal like yourself."

Taeris kept his face smooth. "These boys need safe passage out of Desriel."

Dras stared at Taeris for a moment, then roared with laughter. "Is that all?" he chuckled. He turned from Taeris, shaking his head in disbelief as he inspected Davian, Wirr, and Caeden. It was only a cursory glance, but then his smile faded and he looked at them again, this time through narrowed eyes.

"You are keeping worse company than usual, Taeris," he said, all traces of amusement gone from his tone. He pointed to Caeden. "His disguise may have fooled the savages thus far, but I wouldn't trust to it doing so for much longer. Those likenesses around the place are surprisingly accurate."

"He was falsely accused, Dras," said Taeris. "You know what the Gil'shar are like."

"Even if I believed you and was inclined to help, did you really think the princess would allow this man to travel with her? Did you think she would vouch for him at the border?" Dras shook
200    his head, not taking his eyes from Caeden, who had shrunk back

under the thin man's gaze. "Even *you* are smarter than that, Taeris. Why would she take the risk? If the Gil'shar found out, it would likely start a war."

"Who's starting a war?" a female voice came from the doorway.

As one, everyone in the room turned. The young woman who had spoken swept into the room, followed closely by several others; from the way everyone moved, Davian had no doubt that this was the princess.

He felt himself gaping a little at her entrance. She was magnificent. Her long flaxen hair was delicately arranged so that not a strand was out of place. Her elegant deep-blue dress was simple but stylishly cut, and sparkling jewels glittered on her ears and at her neck. She was pretty, with green eyes and high, delicate cheekbones. But beyond all that, she had an air of authority, an indefinable presence that made him stand up a little straighter. To Davian's left even Caeden, normally all but unreadable, wore a captivated expression as he looked at her.

Behind her trailed two men and a woman who immediately faded into the background; bodyguards, unless Davian missed his guess. After them came a couple of older attendants, then a younger man and woman, who looked around as if uncertain as to whether they should even be present.

With a start Davian realized that the young man was the fighter they had seen out in the stadium. He had changed clothes and bore no signs of the bout he had lost, though his demeanor seemed odd. He stood in the corner of the room, and if Davian had not just seen him put up such a brave fight in front of thousands of people, he would have said he looked sulky.

Taeris stepped forward, ignoring Dras and bowing to the woman. "Your Royal Highness," he said formally. "I hope that no one will be starting anything. My companions and I are in grave danger, and..." He trailed off, realizing the princess was no longer paying attention to him.

Davian turned, following her gaze.

At the back of the room, Wirr was cringing under the princess's increasingly outraged glare. Taeris and Dras both looked from Karaliene to Wirr, and then back again in complete confusion.

201

"You," Princess Karaliene said imperiously, pointing directly at Wirr. "Walk with me."

Wirr winced, shuffling forward, avoiding everyone's stares. As Karaliene's entourage began to follow her from the room, she turned, shaking her head at them. "You will stay here and attend to these men until I return," she said firmly.

"Princess!" The cry of protest came from Dras. "I must insist that someone accompany you. This boy is traveling in the company of a murderer. Two murderers! There is no telling what danger he might pose!"

"Are you refusing to follow my express command, and thus the command of my father, Representative Lothlar?" snapped Karaliene. She had the exasperated sound of someone who had had this conversation before.

Dras hesitated, then subsided, confusion still plastered on his face. "No. No, of course not, Your Highness," he said, giving her an obsequious bow.

Karaliene responded with a curt nod, then spun on her heel and left, Wirr trailing behind. The door shut, and everyone in the room was left gaping at each other in open astonishment.

Taeris turned to Davian. "That," he said with a mixture of puzzlement and concern, "was unexpected."

Finally recovering his wits, Dras rounded on Taeris, fire in his eyes. "Sarr," he spat venomously, "what game are you playing at here?"

Taeris couldn't keep the bafflement from his features. "For perhaps the first time, Dras, I am as ignorant as you." He shot a questioning glance at Davian, who shook his head. He was as stunned as everyone else at the turn of events.

Having little other recourse, they settled down to wait for Wirr and the princess to return.

❦

Wirr followed Karaliene, silently cursing his bad luck. He'd known this moment would come eventually, but he'd wanted it to be on his terms, not like this.

They reached another small room, not too far from the one they had just left, but empty. They entered, and Karaliene closed the door behind them with a cold anger that made Wirr even more certain of the trouble he had caused. He braced himself.

Karaliene turned to him, arms crossed, assessing him with those calculating green eyes he remembered from so many years earlier.

"Hello, Cousin," she said darkly.

# Chapter 18

Wirr gave an embarrassed smile.

"Hello, Kara," he said, trying to keep his tone light. "Fancy seeing you here."

Karaliene scowled at him. "Don't do that. Don't act like this is all a joke." She shook her head. "Fates, Torin, where have you been? How are you here, of all places? Do you have any idea how sick with worry both our fathers are?"

Wirr made what he hoped was a calming gesture. "I'm sorry," he said softly, putting as much penitence in his tone as he could muster. His shoulders slumped, and the last of his bravado left him. "I never meant for things to get so out of hand."

Karaliene continued to glare at him for a moment. Then she sighed, and the hint of a smile crept onto her lips. " 'Kara.' No one except my father and yours calls me that anymore." She stepped forward to give him a sudden and tight hug. "It's been weeks… we didn't know what to think, Tor. It's good to see you."

Wirr returned the embrace. "Torin. I'm going to have to get used to that again." After so many years he couldn't help but think of himself as Wirrander now, even though it was the second of his given names. He ran his hands through his hair. "So, I take it your father told you the truth about me? About where I've been?"

Karaliene nodded. "He told me as soon as we heard the news about the school; he was panicking and there was no way to hide it from me. I'm the only one, though. To everyone else you've just been delayed in returning from Calandra. You probably have another month or so before anybody becomes too suspicious."

Wirr nodded. The court had been told that he'd gone to the Isles of Calandra, to serve at the Andarran outpost there. It was unusual but not unheard of, sending a prince to one of Andarra's outlying colonies to learn warfare and tactics, to experience some "real danger." The Isles were so remote that only someone who had served at the actual outpost would be able to confirm he hadn't been there—and those men had all sworn oaths not to reveal that information.

Then he frowned. Something Karaliene had said…

"What did you hear about the school?" He shook his head. "All things considered, I'd have thought they'd want to keep our running away fairly quiet."

"Running away?" repeated Karaliene, nonplussed. "Torin…" She hesitated. A range of emotions flashed across her face, from confusion to understanding to pity. "Oh, Tor. You haven't heard. Something terrible happened. Someone…" She trailed off, suddenly flustered. She stepped closer, giving his arm a comforting squeeze. "The night you left, someone, or something, attacked. Everyone who was still there…they died."

Wirr stared at Karaliene. "That's a poor joke, Kara."

Karaliene just looked at him sadly.

His body recognized the truth before his mind could; his knees went weak and he slumped into a nearby chair, hands suddenly shaking. "All of them?"

Karaliene nodded. "I'm so sorry, Tor. There were no survivors."

The next few minutes passed in a blur. At first he was simply dazed, unable to comprehend the idea that everyone he had known for the last few years was dead. Once the reality set in, though, he felt only emptiness inside. It had surely been his fault. Whoever had attacked had been looking for him. It was *his fault*.

There were no tears, for which he was grateful; a disconnected part of his mind thought he would have been embarrassed to cry in front of his cousin. At one point an Andarran guard opened the door to fetch the princess for some event or other, but Karaliene waved him away silently. Eventually Wirr's initial dizziness at the news passed and he took some deep breaths, focusing again on the present.

They sat in silence for a little while, then Karaliene said gently,

"We assumed either you'd escaped and were in hiding, or had been taken. But if you didn't know—why leave?"

"It was important. We heard a rumor that the Boundary was weakening, maybe about to collapse. The sig'nari were gathering Augurs, and my friend was...he had a way to find them. He needed my help, and I needed to find out how much of it was true. And to make sure the sig'nari weren't planning some kind of rebellion. It...seemed like the right choice at the time." The words came out heavily. He gave a hollow laugh when he saw the expression on Karaliene's face. "Don't worry—they're not. Though I think the Boundary side of it might be true. It's...a long story."

"I have time."

Wirr hesitated, taking a deep breath. "I can explain, but first I need your word—you won't act on anything I tell you, and what I say doesn't go beyond this room. There are some things you're not going to like. Some things I'm not sure I like, to be honest."

Karaliene's look was far from approving, but she nodded.

Wirr told her the whole story, leaving nothing out. A part of him wondered at the wisdom of it, but it all seemed so insignificant in light of the news. Even as he spoke, names and faces flashed through his head. Asha. Elder Jarras, Elder Olin, Alita. Talean. Absently, he wondered if he was lucky to have left with Davian when he did, and then immediately hated himself for the thought. With a flood of nausea, he realized he would have to be the one to tell his friend the news.

Karaliene listened to his story in silence, her expression changing only once—when he admitted to having helped rescue Caeden from the Desrielite soldiers. Wirr saw the dismay on her face, and she opened her mouth to interject, but quickly closed it again to let him continue. He was grateful for that. If he'd had to stop, he didn't know if he could have started again.

He finished, and Karaliene watched him for a few moments before speaking.

"Tor," she said softly. "What have you done?"

Wirr tensed. "Don't discount what Taeris says, Karaliene. I don't know if he's right, but clearly *something* is going on. If there's some threat waiting for us beyond the Boundary, we need to be prepared. And getting Caeden back to Andarra, restoring his memories—it's the only way I can think of to find out more."

Karaliene held up her hand. "Taeris Sarr is a murderer, Torin. Administration was within its mandate to cover up his escape, but now I know...I should be taking him back to Andarra to complete his sentence, not helping him."

Wirr frowned. "I told you there would be things you didn't like. You haven't even spoken to him." He crossed his arms. "I was dubious at first, too, but he killed those men to save Davian's life."

Karaliene shook her head. "I was at his trial, Tor. He didn't just kill them. He *mutilated* them. Carved marks into their faces while they were still alive. And he never revealed how he got around the First Tenet."

"Taeris tells a different story. And he explained about the First Tenet."

"Tell that to the twenty or so who heard the screams of the men he was killing, some from several streets away." Karaliene looked troubled. "The evidence was overwhelming...your father passed his sentence, you know."

"I know." Wirr hesitated. He also knew that Davian remembered nothing of that day, or at least had forced the memories so far into the recesses of his mind that they were no longer easily accessed. And if Taeris had lied, he apparently could have hidden it from Davian's ability.

What Karaliene said was possible, he supposed.

Still, he had met Taeris. He was capable of violence, certainly—but was he the kind of man to delight in it? Wirr thought not.

"So you're telling me that there have been no reports from the north of anything unusual." Wirr gave her a querying look.

Karaliene scowled. "There are *always* reports from the north, Torin! Every year they come in. Hoaxes played by children who were weaned on stories of Talan Gol. The overactive imaginations of farmers who weren't vigilant enough to protect their livestock from wolves."

"And the scale he showed us?"

Karaliene snorted. "It could be anything. He could have made it himself! No one has seen a dar'gaithin for *literally* thousands of years." She leaned forward. "Think, Tor. Just think. He's a murderer. He is asking for political asylum for another man wanted for the same crime—a man who may be a conspirator in what happened to your school, for all you know! Is this the kind of man a prince of the realm should be traveling with?"

Wirr scowled. "Davian verified Caeden's story about having lost his memory."

"The same Davian who set you on this journey to begin with." She held up her hand as he began to protest. "I believe you when you say he had no part in what happened. Don't worry, I'll keep my word—if you tell me he can be trusted, I won't tell anyone he's an Augur. But his ability has a very serious flaw if he is so easily fooled. I for one would not trust it implicitly." She paused. "And even if this Caeden truly has lost his memory, it does not make him innocent, either."

Wirr ran his fingers through his hair in frustration. He remembered this Karaliene. Good at arguing, not so good at listening. "So you'll not help us?"

There was silence as the two glared at each other, then Karaliene crossed her arms, coming to a decision. "I can arrange for you and your friend to return with us. It will be tricky—the Gil'shar know how many Gifted came with us, so it's going to take some explaining when we leave with two more. You'll have to act like just another Gifted; the Desrielites screen everyone at the border, and the entire country will know within days if Prince Torin sets off a Finder."

She pursed her lips. "This other man, Caeden, is a different matter. His description is everywhere; frankly I'm surprised you made it this far without being discovered. But he'll be recognized soon enough. Representative Lothlar was right, you know. If we give him asylum, it could very well mean war." She shrugged. "Handing him over might just offset the fallout of taking you with us, though."

Wirr's heart sank, and he gave a heavy sigh. "I understand," he admitted, "and you're being very generous with your offer. But I'm afraid I must refuse."

Karaliene blinked. "Pardon?" she said in disbelief.

Wirr grimaced. "Call me irresponsible if you want, Kara, but there is something about Caeden I trust. I believe him." As he was saying it, he was surprised to find it was true. "I know he's not making it up. I won't abandon him to be executed."

Karaliene took a second to compose herself. "You don't have a choice," she said abruptly. "You're too important. You'll come back with me if I have to bind you and drag you there myself."

Wirr laughed. "Do that, and I'll just come forward and tell everyone that I'm Torin Wirrander Andras, Prince of Andarra. Then I'll grant asylum for Davian, Taeris, and Caeden myself."

Karaliene scowled. "You wouldn't. Otherwise you would have done so long ago."

Wirr grinned. "I was trying to find a better way. Prevent a war and all that. But if you leave me no choice..."

For a moment it looked as if Karaliene was going to argue further; then her face fell and she gestured in disgust. "Very well," she said in exasperation. "Though I think you're a fool for doing this."

"Goes without saying," said Wirr.

Karaliene glared at him for a moment longer, but eventually couldn't stop the corners of her mouth creeping upward.

"You used to be so serious," she said with a wondering shake of her head. "What happened?"

Wirr shrugged. "I think...you get a different perspective when people treat you as an equal. It changes the way you look at things," he said, a pang of guilt and sorrow running through him as he thought about the school again.

Karaliene watched him, her gaze appraising. "I like you better this way," she admitted. "Just don't tell anyone I said that. There are going to be some very, very angry people once I get word of this back to Andarra."

"Which will be when?"

Karaliene considered. "I can't trust this sort of thing to a pigeon or a rider—I'll have to deliver it myself. So...a few weeks, maybe a little more?" She grimaced. "I know I gave you my word, Tor, but I *have* to tell our fathers something. And once they know you're alive, they're going to want a full explanation."

"Then tell them I'm here because I think the Boundary may be weakening—but that I'm heading home, and I promise to explain everything to them when I arrive. They don't need to know about

Davian, or Caeden, or Taeris for now." He held up his hand as Karaliene made to protest. "If you tell them, the only thing it will do is worry them more. Having that information won't help them in the slightest."

"What if you don't make it back?"

"If I'm not home in six weeks, you can tell them everything."

Karaliene scowled, but after a few seconds gave a reluctant nod. "On one condition."

"Which is?"

"That you let me send some protection with you." Karaliene brushed a loose strand of hair from her eyes. "Your father will skin me alive if I don't do that much. And at least this way I can give him *some* sort of reassurance."

Wirr hesitated, then nodded. "Done."

"Good." Karaliene released a deep breath. "I think I can manage that much without raising any suspicion. None of the Gifted, mind you—the Desrielites might be a little unhappy if we go back one or two short." She smirked at the thought. "I can organize someone to be at the northern gate of Thrindar at dawn tomorrow. I assume you won't be staying longer than necessary."

"I think that's a fair guess," admitted Wirr. "Thank you."

Karaliene inclined her head. "You know that if you're caught, you won't be able to claim any ties to the throne without starting a war?"

"I know."

They both stood, signaling the end of their conversation. "What should I tell the others?" Wirr wondered aloud.

"That's the least of your worries." Karaliene watched him for a moment, then abruptly stepped forward, giving Wirr a long, tight hug. "Be safe, Tor."

Wirr smiled affectionately. "Thanks, Kara," he said, returning the embrace.

At that moment the creaking of the door indicated someone had entered. Wirr and Karaliene leaped apart, turning to face the entrance.

The swordsman who had fought in the contest earlier stood in the doorway, hand frozen on the door frame as he stared at them. There was an awkward silence.

"I apologize, Your Highness," said the young man stiffly, giving a slight bow in Karaliene's direction. "I should have knocked."

He spun and vanished, shutting the door behind him.

"Aelric!" The princess's call came too late; he was gone. She turned to Wirr. "I am going to have to do some explaining later," she sighed, an exasperated look on her face.

Wirr hesitated. "Is that safe?"

"What?" Karaliene had been staring at the closed door; she waved him away distractedly. "Don't worry, Aelric is trustworthy. A bit full of himself at times, but eminently trustworthy." She saw Wirr's expression. "Oh, very well. I won't tell him who you are."

Wirr felt his eyebrows rise a little. "Are you two..."

"No." Karaliene frowned. "Friends, but not suited to each other like that. I just wish he felt the same."

They began to walk back through the corridors. "So do any of your friends know who you really are?" asked Karaliene, her tone curious.

Wirr grunted. "If there was one thing Father was exceptionally clear on before I left, it was that no one else was to know." He saw her surprised expression and scowled. "He said that anyone I told would have to be killed."

Karaliene grinned, though Wirr didn't see the humor. "I'm not judging," she said. They made the last turn, coming back in sight of the guards outside the room where Taeris and the others were waiting.

Karaliene put her hand on Wirr's shoulder, holding him back for a moment. She looked him in the eye.

"Do you even want to go back to Ilin Illan?" she asked quietly.

Wirr held her gaze for a moment, then glanced away.

"They must be wondering where we are," he said, gesturing to the door ahead.

Karaliene nodded thoughtfully. "Of course."

They walked the rest of the way in silence.

Davian stirred as the door opened and the princess walked in,
trailed by a drained, somber-looking Wirr.

The room had been uncomfortably quiet since they'd left, with only Dras and the other members of the princess's entourage occasionally chatting among themselves, and that at a whisper so that Davian and the others could not overhear. Taeris had made a few polite efforts at conversation, but had been bluntly ignored. He'd stopped trying after the first few minutes.

Everyone rose as Karaliene entered. She looked around to make sure she had everyone's attention, then spoke directly to Taeris.

"There will be no asylum," she said in a clear voice. From the corner of his eye, Davian could see Dras beginning to smirk. "Andarra will have nothing to do with helping a murderer, or one who has been accused of such"—she looked with disdain at Caeden, who flushed beneath her gaze—"but neither will we act to turn you over to the mercies of the Gil'shar. Tonight you will stay at the Juggler, an inn near the northern gate. I will send word you are coming; we have friends there and you should be safe. At first light tomorrow, you are to leave Thrindar and not return. You will receive no further aid, and any claim you make to have met with us here today will be denied."

With a final grim glance at Wirr, she spun and strode from the room, her entourage trailing after her. Dras lingered a moment in the doorway, shooting Wirr a long, curious look before following the others.

They were escorted from the stadium by a couple of soldiers; once they were outside, the men vanished, leaving Wirr, Davian, Taeris, and Caeden facing the milling crowds once again. There was a moment of silence as they all looked at Wirr.

Wirr returned their looks levelly.

"I suppose we should go and find this inn," he said.

Without anything further, he started off northward.

Davian exchanged glances with his other two companions, then sighed and set off after his friend.

Wirr had a lot of explaining to do.

The room was quiet.

Faintly from below, the boisterous sounds of laughter and men clapping to a musician's beat filtered through the floorboards, but from within the room there was only an awkward silence. They had eaten their meal in the common room in a similar silence; with the patronage the inn was seeing this evening, it had not seemed prudent to discuss their situation until they could do so in private.

Finally Davian took a deep breath and turned to Wirr, recognizing that his friend was not about to volunteer anything. "Well?"

Wirr looked at the floor, grimacing. "Well what?"

"Come on, Wirr!" Davian burst out in exasperation. "The princess knew you; she picked you out and you had a private conversation with her—at the end of which she told us that there would be no help from her! I've been patient with you for a long time about your past, and *especially* so since the El-cursed sha'teth, but…I think we're owed the truth now. We've come too long a way to have our plans fail like that without an explanation."

Wirr shook his head, still staring at the floorboards as if he could see through them and was watching something in the room below. "I want to," he said, desperation filling his voice, "but I don't know if it's a good idea." He looked up at Davian, his expression serious. "In fact, I'm fairly sure it's not. Otherwise I would have told you earlier. Years ago, Dav. I swear it."

Davian gaped at his friend. "I think the time for you deciding what's best has passed, Wirr," he said, his tone harder than he meant it to be. "Tell us, and we'll decide for ourselves."

Taeris, who had been watching Wirr closely, gently interjected. "Perhaps Caeden and I can go downstairs and get a drink," he suggested.

Wirr thought for a few moments, then nodded, his face clearing. "If you're thirsty anyway…"

"Parched." Taeris looked at Caeden, inclining his head toward the door. "Shall we?"

Caeden followed Taeris out the door. When it was shut, Wirr allowed his shoulders to slump, and he sat heavily on one of the beds. "I've made some mistakes, Dav," he admitted. "Perhaps one of them was not telling you the whole truth from the very start." He gestured, a resigned motion. "Ask your questions, use your ability. I will answer everything, complete and honest."

Davian felt some of his anger fade as he watched the forlorn figure of his friend. "Thank you, Wirr," he said quietly. He tapped his lips with a finger. "How do you know the princess?"

"She's my cousin," said Wirr, without a trace of humor.

Davian gave a disbelieving laugh, but his smile faded when Wirr's expression didn't change. "Seriously?"

"Seriously." Despite his obviously downcast mood, the corners of Wirr's mouth twitched upward as he watched Davian's reaction.

Davian felt his brow furrow as he tried to grasp this information. "So... you're..."

"Torin Wirrander Andras, son of Northwarden Elocien Andras. Third in line for the throne of Andarra, behind Karaliene and my father."

Davian shook his head, dazed. Wirr had to be making a joke... and yet there had been no black smoke from his mouth.

Davian just looked at his friend in stunned silence for a few seconds, feeling as though he were really seeing him for the first time. Wirr had always had natural bearing and presence; suddenly that made sense, was put into context. His polite avoidances of potential romances at the school were his being cautious rather than picky. And the way he'd never wanted to talk about what the future held for him at the Tol...

"You were never going to Tol Athian after you'd passed your Trials," realized Davian aloud, accusation in his voice.

Wirr shook his head. "I would have been taken to Ilin Illan separately, avoiding Athian altogether. I was meant to integrate into court life, keeping my abilities hidden. Ceasing all contact with the Tol and anyone associated with it." He hesitated. "The thing is, Dav—wherever the Vessel that created the Tenets came from, it's tied to the line of Tel'Andras. Tied to *my* bloodline. It was meant to be a way of ensuring that the Gifted would need to earn the trust of the royal family before the Tenets could be changed, but..."

Davian went cold as he processed the implications. He stared at Wirr in disbelief.

"You can change the Tenets? *By yourself?*" he asked, voice little more than a whisper.

Wirr held up a hand. "Not yet—hopefully not for some time, to be honest. My father and uncle were the ones tied to it. When Uncle dies, his connection will pass to Karaliene. And when my father dies, his will pass to me." He looked at Davian nervously. "So...you see why I didn't tell you?"

"Yes. Fates, yes, of course," said Davian, shaking his head. The burden of responsibility Wirr must have been living with, these past few years, was beyond anything Davian could imagine. He felt a chill run through him. "But if you remove the Tenets, wouldn't it mean another war?"

Wirr shook his head. "I have no intention of annulling the Tenets—I want to amend them, so there's a balance. Remember our discussion a couple of weeks ago? I'm not just Gifted, Dav. I'm my father's son. He and my uncle both know about me; they're the ones who put this plan into motion. The Treaty won't continue to be a tool of oppression, but I'm not going to allow the Gifted the absolute power they once had, either." Wirr's tone was quiet, but laced with a heavy seriousness and certainty that Davian had never heard from his friend before.

He digested what Wirr had said in silence for a while, still reeling over the revelations.

"So...your father knows about you—sent you to Caladel to learn how to use the Gift," he said eventually. "But he *created* the Tenets. Does he really want you to alter them?" The idea went against everything he knew about the Northwarden. Davian knew not to put too much stock in rumors, but over the years he'd heard so many about Elocien Andras that he'd assumed there had to be some truth to them.

Wirr hesitated. "Growing up, he hated the Gifted as much as anyone I've ever met," he conceded after a moment. "But when he found out I was one of them..." He shrugged, looking awkward. "I think it changed him. Changed the way he looks at us. He regrets making the Tenets the way they are, but he can't do anything about it now—he's already used his connection to the Vessel. That link can't be used again until it passes to me."

Davian frowned; it was still difficult to imagine the Northwarden's being sympathetic toward the Gifted, but Wirr wasn't lying. "What about your uncle, then? If he's in favor of this, why doesn't he just find one of the Gifted and amend the Tenets himself?"

"He and my father may agree that the Tenets should be changed, but neither of them trust the Tols, either," admitted Wirr. "It's the Gifted's role to actually say the oath once the Vessel is activated—all it would take is for them to change my uncle's wording on the spot, and there would be nothing anyone could do about it." He sighed. "I'm hoping he'll use me when I return, to be honest. I was too young, had no control over my abilities when all this was explained to me. But now..."

Davian nodded, dizzy at the thought. "So who else knows?"

"To the best of my knowledge, there was only a very small group who knew the whole truth—my father and uncle, the Council at Tol Athian. Talean and the Elders at Caladel." Pain flashed across his features at the last for some reason. "It feels good to finally tell you, though."

Davian inclined his head. "It can't have been easy, not being able to talk about it." He gave his friend a considering look. "So why didn't Karaliene give us asylum? Did you...pull her hair when you were children or something?"

Wirr grunted. "I did, but that wasn't the reason she said no. She figured she couldn't hide us, and the Desrielites would take it amiss if they found out she was trying to." He waved his hand vaguely. "Said it would start a war or something."

Davian grinned. "Just the man to be rewriting the Tenets."

Wirr smiled wryly, though the expression was still tinged with sadness. "Any other questions?"

Davian shrugged. "No doubt there will be more, but for now..." He brightened. "Oh, one very important one."

Wirr raised an eyebrow. "What's that?"

"Should I call you 'Your Grace' now?"

Wirr snorted. "No, no. Of course not. That's my father." He paused. "It's 'Your Highness.' Or 'My Prince,' if you prefer."

Davian laughed, but quickly sobered. "It goes without saying that I won't tell anyone, Wirr, but I think you should tell Taeris, too. He's risked his life to get us this far. He deserves to know."

Wirr grimaced. "I would have agreed a few hours ago, but..."

Karaliene was at his trial, Dav. She says the evidence against him was stronger than he told us. Witnesses that heard people screaming. And the men he killed, he supposedly tortured them. Disfigured them."

Davian listened in silence. "I cannot believe that," he said eventually. "Administration wouldn't have had any shortage of willing 'witnesses,' I'm sure. Still...what do you think?"

Wirr shook his head slowly. "We know why he killed those men. He certainly doesn't strike me as the type to take pleasure in killing, so if I had to guess whether the mutilation part was truth or an exaggeration...they could have been referring to knife wounds from the fight, for all we know." He shrugged. "He saved us. That's good enough for me."

Davian smiled, relieved. "Agreed."

Neither boy spoke for a few moments, and Wirr's face fell. "Dav, there's something else. Something big." Davian was unsure why, but from Wirr's expression he suddenly felt a wave of dread. As if, as awkward as the past few minutes had obviously been for Wirr, this was what his friend had actually been avoiding.

"What is it?"

Wirr tried to hold his gaze, but eventually looked away.

"I have some terrible news," he said quietly.

# Chapter 19

Asha stared out the window, still trying to come to grips with everything Elocien had just told her.

"And Wirr—Torin—could change the Tenets. By himself," she repeated, dazed.

"Only once I die, so hopefully not too soon," said Elocien wryly. "But yes. We suspect that's why these attacks have been happening—whoever was searching for him must have known he was at *a* school, but not which one. The first two attacks were probably to flush him out." He shook his head, expression rueful. "Which we knew at the time, and did everything we could to bring him home quietly... but it looks like we still obliged whoever was looking for him."

Asha nodded slowly, taking a moment to compose herself, to digest what the duke had revealed over the past few minutes. Wirr, the Northwarden's son. It was almost too ludicrous to contemplate... and yet she knew Elocien was telling her the truth. Now that she really looked, she could even see the physical resemblance between the two.

She closed her eyes, trying to sort through her churning emotions. Wirr was the reason Caladel had been attacked. Why Davian and her other friends had died. Her stomach burned with a flash of irrational, white-hot anger, which, thankfully, faded just as quickly. It was tempting to blame Elocien for bringing that danger to their doorstep, but it wasn't his fault—nor Wirr's, nor the Tol's. It was the fault of whoever had attacked. Whoever had targeted her friend in the first place.

"Who would even have known about his situation?" she asked eventually, trying to keep her voice steady. "It can't have been a big list."

Elocien shrugged. "Bigger than you would think—the entire Athian Council, for a start. Nashrel made it a condition of helping me. Said he wouldn't go behind their backs." He rubbed his forehead. "He knew Torin was at Caladel, but everyone else was kept in the dark about the specific location. That's one of the reasons I've been reluctant to exchange information with them."

"You think it's one of them?"

Elocien sighed. "Maybe. Truth be told, someone could just as easily have slipped up. A stray word near the wrong ear... it wouldn't have taken much."

Asha responded with an absent nod, still lost in thought. According to Elocien, Wirr's body hadn't been among the dead at Caladel, which meant that he might still be alive. It was wonderful news, of course... but even so she found herself frowning a little, the expression fortunately hidden from the duke's view as she gazed out the window.

It had been only an hour since she'd arrived at the palace, and yet as far as she could tell, Elocien had told her everything. *Everything.* She'd hoped he would be forthcoming, of course, but this much trust so soon after meeting her for the first time felt... strange. She couldn't say why, but the entire situation was making her uneasy.

She bit her lip. Perhaps, at least in part, she was uncomfortable because the revelations had changed things so much. She couldn't give the Shadraehin this information—couldn't have Wirr's plight used against his father, no matter how well-intentioned the Shadows were. She didn't know what the consequences of withholding the truth from Scyner might be, but that was something she would have to worry about later.

"I still can't believe Wirr's your son," she said after a while, even now bemused at the thought. "Sorry—Torin. It's going to take me a while to get used to that."

"I expect it will take him a while, too. Assuming..." Elocien's expression clouded, and he took a deep breath. "I just hope he's

safe. Not knowing if he escaped, or was captured, or..." He

shook his head. "It's been hard, searching for him without knowing who's behind all this, and especially doing it without Administration's knowledge. My resources have been more limited than I'm accustomed to."

"What *are* your resources?" asked Asha curiously.

"I have various people…some owe me favors, others are friends who have nothing to do with Administration and are smart enough not to ask questions." Elocien shrugged. "Here in the palace, there are only three people I trust. They're the ones I want you to work with." He stood. "Speaking of which—wait here. I'll find them and make the introductions. We can go from there."

Asha paced for a while once Elocien had left, still trying to process the implications of what she'd been told. Even the beauty on show outside the window—the immaculately kept gardens, and beyond, the elegant, clean lines of the city stretching away to the harbor far below—did little to distract her.

After a few minutes the sound of voices outside the door stopped her in midstep. She looked up as the duke entered, followed by three people close to Asha's age.

Elocien took a seat, gesturing for Asha to do the same. He stared at her intently for a few moments.

"So. These are the people you will be working with," he said eventually. "Ashalia—this is Kol, Fessi, and Erran. Perhaps the most important people in Ilin Illan right now."

Asha felt her brow furrow as she turned to the three, all of whom wore the simple clothing of serving folk. Erran she recognized as being the mousy-haired boy from earlier that day, the servant who had been with Elocien in Tol Athian. The one called Kol was enormous, all muscle; even sitting down he managed to loom over everyone else in the room. Still, when he looked at Asha his expression was more anxious than anything else.

The last of them, Fessi, was a girl about Asha's age, maybe a year older. She had dark, straight hair and a plump figure.

In all, they seemed entirely unremarkable.

"It's nice to meet you," said Asha politely, knowing her confusion was probably evident on her face.

There was a short, slightly uncomfortable silence, and then

Erran gave an awkward cough. "We're like your friend Davian," he explained. "We're Augurs."

The silence was longer this time as Asha stared between the three and Elocien in disbelief.

"I don't know what you're talking about," she said. It had to be some sort of trick. It *had* to be.

Elocien gave her an apologetic smile. "Yes, you do. Erran Read you, back at the Tol. I wouldn't have risked telling you about Torin or any of this otherwise."

"Sorry," said Erran, sounding sincere.

Asha shook her head, perhaps more dazed now than she had been after learning about Wirr. The duke was using *Augurs*? "But you're the Northwarden—an Administrator! I thought..." She trailed off.

Elocien's smile slipped, and he sighed. "You thought that I must want the Augurs dead. I understand. I helped write the Tenets and the Treaty, and I've done things in my past I'm not proud of. But I'm trying to make up for that now, Ashalia—particularly with what we are doing here." He grimaced. "As for the other Administrators, I rein them in where I can. Truly. If I hear about abuses of the Treaty, I punish those responsible as harshly as the law allows. But the types of people who are attracted to the job... well, I'm sure you've met enough of them. Let's just say it is an uphill battle."

Asha indicated her provisional acceptance of Elocien's explanation with a bemused nod, turning her attention to the three Augurs. The people she was going to be working with. They were so...young.

Erran glanced sideways at Elocien, who gave him a grim nod.

"You're not sure whether to believe us," observed Erran quietly. "Allow me to demonstrate."

Before Asha could react he took two quick steps forward and placed his hand against her forehead.


*The building was quiet.*

*Asha frowned. Even at this early hour, before dawn, Admin-*
*istration's main building should have been humming with activ-*

ity. There were lights flickering cheerfully in the windows, but no movement, no noise.

*Something was wrong.*

She walked inside, going cold as she saw the body. The young man who had been at the front desk twisted slightly as the breeze swept in the open front door. His face was purple and black, swollen, bloated folds of skin almost hiding the noose around his neck.

Asha touched the sword at her side, bile and unease swirling in her stomach. The motion was mostly for self-reassurance; whoever had done this had done it hours earlier. She headed toward the stairs, feet leaden, the utter silence feeding her dread.

Even after what she'd seen below, she was still unprepared for the sight that met her as she reached the second-floor passageway.

The hallway was lined with bug-eyed corpses, shifting and turning gently in an eerie, slow-motion dance as they hung from the rafters. Some of the distended faces stared blankly at her as she steadied herself against the wall, light-headed for a moment. Eventually she took a deep breath and started through the gauntlet of the dead, wincing whenever she had to push a limp, cold limb out of her path.

Most of the rooms she passed had more of the slowly twisting bodies. Men and women she knew, some little more than children—all of whom had been so eager to take the Oath, to come here and serve. She wondered what they'd thought in those last moments...or if they'd even known what was happening. There were no signs of struggle, no indication that any of them had put up a fight. Not anywhere.

Finally Asha reached her office. Her assistant, Genia, swung listlessly in front of the door. Bile threatened to rise in Asha's throat again as she remembered asking the young girl to work late the night before.

She looked away, collecting herself before entering.

At first glance her office seemed untouched...until she saw the slip of paper, out of place on the always-tidy desk. A note.

Hands shaking, she picked it up. There was only one word on it.

Stop.

*She crumpled the piece of paper and shoved it in her pocket, fear and horror melting away beneath sudden, white-hot rage. She should have known he was responsible for this.*

*The Shadraehin had gone too far this time.*

Asha gasped as the scene faded and the room snapped back into focus.

Erran lowered his hand, giving her an apologetic look before retreating to the other side of the room. She stared at him.

"What was that?" she whispered.

"A memory," said the duke. "My memory, from not more than a month ago. The Shadraehin's reaction to our trying to cut off his food supply."

He watched her expectantly.

Asha stared at him in disbelief for a long few seconds, heart pounding as she suddenly understood.

Erran had Read her at the Tol. They knew.

"How can I believe you?" she asked, trying not to let her hands shake. "How do I know you're not making this up, or that the Shadraehin was even behind it?" She shook her head. "How could a Shadow, or even a group of Shadows, do what you just showed me?"

"We don't know, but it happened. Memories aren't something Erran can create," the duke replied quietly. "It's not just that attack, though. Since we first heard of the Shadraehin a year ago, more and more Administrators have been turning up dead. Regular folk, too, sometimes. Each body is left with a note, explaining why the Shadraehin believed they had to die." He looked her in the eye. "I can show them to you. Or you can read the reports, if you need something further."

Asha stared at them for a few seconds, stomach churning. "Why are you telling me this?"

"You know the answer. When Erran Read you, he saw your deal with the Shadraehin. But he convinced me that you'd entered into the agreement without understanding the man you were dealing with—that you are, in fact, someone worth trusting." Elocien shrugged. "That, your history of keeping an Augur's secret, and the fact you were friends with my son convinced me to let you come this far."

"And now?"

"Now you know the truth, and you have a choice. Us, or him." Elocien's expression was grave. "I'm hoping that after what you just saw, you're not going to want to have anything more to do with him. I'm hoping that now you know about Torin, about what I'm trying to do for the Gifted, you wouldn't consider letting the Shadraehin use him as leverage. I'm hoping that my arranging such a prestigious position for you here will give you another avenue to help the Shadows, one that is less violent than the alternative he offers."

He sighed. "Under better circumstances I would ask you to help me capture him, too, but that isn't a game I have time to play at the moment. The deal is simple: you stay away from him and his people. You tell them nothing. You have *complete* loyalty to us."

Elocien hesitated. "And though your word on that is important, you should also know that Erran will be Reading you if you give it. Any hint of a doubt on your part, and he will erase your memory of everything you've been told here. It's tricky, but I've seen him do it before. You'd stay on as Representative, but would remember nothing of this. And you would be shut out of the investigation into the attacks entirely."

There was silence for a few seconds as Asha gathered her thoughts. Though she didn't want to believe it, somehow she knew that the duke's memory was real—that what she'd seen had actually happened. She shuddered as she remembered the eerie crowd of slowly swinging bodies. It wasn't as if she had experienced it in a detached way, either. She remembered *being there*. Remembered her disgust, her fury at the Shadraehin.

"You have my word," she said softly.

Elocien and the others all looked at Erran, who was staring intently at her. There were a few anxious seconds of silence, and then he nodded, giving her the slightest of smiles.

"She means it."

There was a collective sigh as the tension went out of the room, and Elocien smiled at her. "Then I am glad I took the risk."

"So is she," noted Erran.

"Don't, Erran." It was Fessi, her tone reproving. "She doesn't know how to shield herself yet. You've done your job. Leave her be."

"You'd do it if you were able to, Fess," Erran grumbled, but he kept silent.

On the couch Kol stirred for the first time.

"I cannot say I like this," he said bluntly, never taking his eyes from Asha. Something about his expression was cautious, almost fearful.

Elocien squinted at him. "It had to happen, Kol. I couldn't be your Scribe forever. You knew that."

"But it did not have to be *now*." Kol shook his head, clearly angry. "And not with *her*. How are we supposed to trust her, after she made a deal to spy on you—with the Shadraehin of all people? She may be loyal now, but what is to stop her from changing her mind again?" He held up his hand preemptively as both Elocien and Erran opened their mouths to protest. "I know what you are going to say, and it doesn't change my mind. In my opinion this puts us all in danger." With that he rose and walked out the door.

The girl called Fessi stared after him, her face set in a confused frown. "I apologize, Ashalia," she said, pushing a long wisp of hair from her face. "He's not usually like this...I don't know what came over him. We'll get better acquainted later, I'm sure." She hurried out the door after Kol.

"I think I know," murmured Elocien, so quietly that Asha wasn't sure she was supposed to hear it.

There were a few moments of silence, then Elocien sighed, turning to Asha. "That part didn't go as smoothly as I'd hoped," he admitted. "Don't worry about Kol—he's overreacting, but I'm sure he will calm down soon enough. Still...before we go any further, I do need you to swear to me that none of this will leave this room. I'm not just talking about the Shadraehin this time, obviously. Needless to say, if word of what we are doing here got out, it would be disastrous. Not even my brother knows about it."

Asha hesitated. "And what, exactly, *are* you doing here? There's clearly more to this than just trying to find out what happened at Caladel."

"That's true," conceded the duke. "We're protecting Andarra. The Augurs use their talents to help me inform my advice to the king. It's saved lives many times."

Asha's eyes narrowed. "That's all you use it for?"

Elocien shrugged. "I don't use it for personal gain, if that's what you mean."

"None of us would be doing this if he was," supplied Erran.

Asha hesitated, then nodded. There was no way to verify any of it, but for now she had no choice but to trust them.

"Very well," she said. "You have my word that I'll not speak of this to anyone."

The Northwarden glanced over at Erran, who studied Asha for a second, then nodded. "She's nothing if not truthful," he said cheerfully.

Asha avoided looking in Erran's direction, suddenly self-conscious. Knowing it was that easy for him to Read her sent a shiver up her spine, regardless of her having nothing to hide.

"So how do I fit into all this?" she asked, still a little dazed at the turn of events.

"Two ways." Elocien leaned forward. "The most pressing being that I cannot continue to meet with Erran or the other two in secret. As the king's brother, meeting with *anyone* privately is cause for speculation. If someone starts to notice I'm regularly going into a Lockroom with people who are, ostensibly, servants"—he paused, shooting Erran an apologetic look—"it will raise some questions."

"We've been getting by with me as Elocien's manservant," explained Erran, "but the problem is, I'm not very good at it. People around here tend to notice things like that, and then start wondering what the real reason is that the duke keeps me around. It's unlikely they'd guess the truth, but too much attention in itself could cause trouble."

"As Athian's Representative, you'll have an excuse to meet with me every few days," Elocien continued. "Normally that falls to the senior Representative, but I'll insist it's you. That shouldn't raise any questions; given who I am, I doubt anyone will think it amiss that I'm more comfortable with a Shadow than one of the Gifted. In fact, I've already started spreading it around that it was me who made Athian send a Shadow as one of their Representatives—a kind of penance for their return."

"But won't that draw more attention to me?"

"Yes, but it's the right kind of attention," said Elocien. "You'll be a curiosity for a few days, and then people will…dismiss you, to an extent. If you're only here because Tol Athian is being punished, they won't think of you as much of a threat." He gave her an apologetic look. "I want to be honest about what you should expect. People will ignore you, sneer at you behind your back, perhaps tell you to your face that you shouldn't be here. I doubt anyone outside of those you've already met will be friendly. But nobody will fear you, or watch your movements. And that's what we need."

Asha nodded, trying to keep the disappointment from her face.

"So I can meet with you without raising suspicion, and I can talk to the Augurs without anyone noticing," she said. "Is my sole purpose to be passing messages?"

Elocien smiled at that. "Not at all. As Kol so graciously brought up before, the main reason you're here is to become our Scribe."

"A Scribe?" Asha knew the word, of course, but Elocien had said it more like a title.

Erran spoke up. "You get to tell Elocien when to panic."

Elocien grunted at that. "Before the Unseen War, no one was allowed to act on an Augur's vision unless it had been confirmed," he explained. "The Augurs weren't allowed to discuss what they'd Seen with anyone, even amongst themselves—instead they had to write it all down and deliver it to the Scribe, who would then try and find other visions that contained similarities. If two Augurs had Seen the same thing, it was considered confirmation that it was going to happen."

Asha frowned. "But weren't the Augurs' visions supposed to be infallible?" She hesitated, glancing at Erran uncertainly. "Or was it because of what happened to the old Augurs, at the end…"

"No," Erran rushed to assure her. "Everything we've Seen so far has come to pass. Whatever the problem was twenty years ago, it doesn't seem to be affecting us."

"Then why wait for confirmation?" asked Asha, puzzled.

"Trust," said Elocien. "The trust placed in the Augurs was

absolute. Without checks and balances, it would have been too easy for someone to abuse their position, to take advantage by claiming to have Seen something that they hadn't." He shrugged. "I thought it was important to continue that tradition, even with only three Augurs. I've been filling the role, but aside from the difficulties we've already discussed, I'm often too busy to wade through every scrap of information I'm brought."

Erran spoke up. "We tend to have visions about ourselves, our friends or family—often about things that may be important to us, but not necessarily to someone like Elocien," he explained. "The further removed the events of a vision are from us—in time, distance or personal interest—the more important they seem to be. And those are the visions that other Augurs will also likely See."

Asha nodded slowly. It made sense, then; the Northwarden would hardly want to waste time wading through pages of information he couldn't use. "And once something has been confirmed?"

"The Scribe copies it into a single book—called the Journal— along with the names of the Augurs who had the vision. We all have access to it. The Journal is then used as a reliable source of information about future events," Elocien concluded.

Asha remained silent for a while as she processed what she'd been told. The system made sense, and she understood why they'd chosen her. It was a massive responsibility, though. One she knew without having to ask that she had no choice about accepting.

"You're placing a lot of trust in me," she observed.

Elocien nodded, expression serious. "Erran insisted."

Asha gave the young man a quizzical look. "Why?"

Erran returned her gaze steadily. "It wasn't a hard choice, once I'd Read you. You're smart. Honest. Loyal. You've been courageous, this past month, when a lot of others would have just given up after what you've been through. And most importantly, I saw how faithful you were to your Augur friend, back in Caladel. How determined you were to keep his secret." He shrugged. "Knowing that, you seemed like a good fit for the job."

Asha blushed a little and looked at the ground, not knowing what to say.

The Northwarden smiled slightly at her embarrassment, then stood, giving Asha's shoulder a light squeeze. "I'll leave you two to talk. I need to see whether Athian has sent someone over yet."

Asha nodded hesitantly, and Elocien slipped out the door, shutting it quietly behind him.

There was an awkward silence for a few seconds, then Erran said, "I'm sorry about Kol." He shifted in his seat. "He'll come around eventually, I'm sure."

"He looked quite upset."

"He was," conceded Erran. "You have to understand...I can be confident you won't betray us, but to the others you're a stranger who now has their lives in your hands. They'll accept you in time, but expect some suspicion for a while."

Asha frowned. "Can't they just Read me, too?"

Erran shook his head. "We each have our own strengths. Mine is Reading people, but I rarely have visions of the future. The others See more, and can do other things I can't, but they can Read perhaps one in every ten people. Only those with the weakest natural defenses." He gave her a small smile. "You're not in that group."

"But *you* can Read me." The thought made Asha more uncomfortable than she cared to admit. "Do you Read a lot of people?"

Erran nodded. "I've probably Read half of Ilin Illan, at one point or another," he confessed. "Just about everyone here in the palace, and then Elocien sends me down to the White Sword once a week, too. It's the most popular tavern in the city—you'd be amazed at the information you can pick up there." He grinned. "I can't say I dislike that part of the job, to be honest."

Asha smiled at that. "So is there anyone you can't Read?"

"Anyone who can shield themselves," admitted Erran. "And don't worry—we'll teach you how to do that soon enough. It's just a mental trick, no special powers required. With your training from Caladel, it shouldn't be too difficult to learn. But I promise I'll try to keep out of your head until you have."

Asha gave him an appreciative nod, and there were a few moments of silence.

"So how did all this come about?" she asked eventually, gesturing vaguely after the duke.

"Elocien found me a few years ago—or Administration did, to be exact. I was living on the streets of Ghas, and some of the criminal element there got wind of my...talents. They used me for a few months, but after a while, one of them decided that the reward for turning in an Augur was worth more than what I could do. Not really the most farsighted of men." He paused at that, rolling his eyes. "After the Administrators brought me here, when Elocien first came to meet me, I think he was going to have me executed."

Asha stared at him. "Really?"

"He was different back then," Erran rushed to assure her. "But I had the presence of mind to Read him before he could do anything. As soon as he realized I could get to people's secrets so easily, I became too valuable to waste. He helped me, got me a position as a servant in the palace. In return I'd Read visiting dignitaries, lords, the Gifted Representatives, anyone who might be trying to keep things from the king."

"You spied for him," said Asha flatly.

"Better than death." Erran's tone was mild. "We weren't friends and it wasn't something I was proud of, but it wasn't a bad life by most standards. And Elocien never abused the information I gave him."

"But he only had mercy because he wanted to use you?"

"At first. But...things changed." Erran hesitated. "I can't say why, exactly; one of the first things he made me do was teach him to shield himself. But he's not like that anymore. When Administration found Fessi and Kol, he rescued them, gave them homes here, hid them even from the king. If someone found out, he'd be executed for treason. He's risking his life, bringing us together."

"He's also getting access to your powers," Asha pressed, unconvinced.

"True," Erran conceded, "but he already had me. Adding the other two posed more risk than reward." He shook his head. "I know you've probably heard stories about him, and some of them are probably true. But whatever he was before, Ashalia, he's a good man now. One you can trust. I'll swear to it."

Asha nodded; she'd wait and see for herself, but Erran was obviously convinced. "I'll take your word for it."

Erran looked at her for a long moment, then sighed. "No you won't." He winced immediately. "Sorry...sometimes I Read people without thinking about what I'm doing. You'll watch Elocien and make up your own mind. That's fine. You'll see I'm right soon enough."

Asha nodded uncomfortably, suddenly feeling naked. She hadn't felt anything, but Erran had been inside her head as easily as that.

"How do you manage to keep all this a secret?" she asked, as much to take her mind off her discomfort as anything else. "Surely all it would take to get in trouble would be for someone to overhear you and the others talking."

Erran inclined his head. "I probably should have mentioned that already." He gestured to the walls around them. "This is what we call a Lockroom. It's shielded to all kinds of eavesdropping, both natural and Gifted—it's what your Elders would have called Silenced. Whatever you say in a room like this can only be heard by those within."

"Oh." Asha looked around, but could see nothing out of the ordinary about the room. "So you always meet in here?"

"No—there are several Lockrooms, actually, all around the palace. A relic from the Gifted era." He pointed to the doorknob. "They each have the same keyhole symbol, just above the handle. It's worth remembering because around here, you'll find that there is always someone listening. You should avoid even *mentioning* the word 'Augur' unless you're inside one of these rooms."

"Understood." Asha shifted in her seat. "Anything else I should know?"

Erran thought for a moment, then nodded. "There's the Journal, of course. You really should have a look at it. It's in Elocien's office—stay here, I'll get it for you."

He slipped out of the room, and only a few short minutes had passed when he returned with a leather-bound book.

"Have a look," he said, handing it to her.

Asha flipped through the pages. Most were blank, but the first twenty or so were filled with the same elegant, precise handwriting. She stopped at a page that had been marked with several asterisks.

*Vision—Kol*

*I was standing at the entrance to Fedris Idri, and people seemed to be fleeing Ilin Illan. It wasn't panicked, exactly, but the streets were full of travelers with carts, horses, anything to carry their possessions away from the city. Everyone looked worried and a few people were upset, crying. Fedris Idri itself was crowded, and from what I could tell at that distance, so were the docks. There didn't seem to be many ships left in the harbor, though.*

*I listened for a while to one man arguing with his wife— he was claiming that the invaders had no chance of reaching the city, and that everyone was overreacting. His wife replied that the battle was going to take place only days away, and that if General Jash'tar was not victorious against "the blind," there wouldn't be time to pack up and leave once they heard of it.*

*The weather seemed warm but not hot. The trees lining the Festive boulevard were losing their leaves—it was probably the end of summer or maybe autumn, rather than spring.*

Then a gap, followed by:

*Confirmation—Fessiricia*

*It was night, but from where I was in the Middle District, it looked like the entire Lower District was on fire. The smoke was so thick it was difficult to see through, but I definitely saw a group of soldiers running past, all in black armor. They were moving together at the same time, perfectly in step—but the strange thing was that there were no eyeholes in their helmets, no way they could have seen where they were going.*

*In the distance I could hear screams and the sound of a battle. I thought it was coming from the Upper District, toward Fedris Idri—but when I started to follow the soldiers to find out more, the vision ended.*

There were two more confirmations along a similar vein, one from Erran and another from Fessi. Asha's stomach turned as she read them. "How many of these have already come true?" she asked uneasily.

"Most of them," said Erran. "Unless something's really important, we only tend to See a day or two into the future." He paused, noting the page she was on. "Those ones are obviously further away than that... but they will happen eventually."

"You really think someone is going to attack Ilin Illan? And get inside the city?"

Erran nodded. "It seems that way."

Asha shook her head in dismay. "Do you think it has something to do with why someone is trying to hurt Wirr... Prince Torin? The timing seems..."

"Suspicious. I know," said Erran. "And certainly, anyone attacking Andarra wouldn't want the Gifted to be freed of the Tenets. But Elocien's still alive and as long as that's the case, Torin can't do anything to change them. I would have thought King Andras was more of a threat." He looked about to say something more, but remained silent as the door opened and Elocien walked in.

"The Athian Representative has arrived, Ashalia," he said without preamble. "He has asked to meet you."

Asha rose, suddenly nervous. "I'm ready."

"Good. You can use your real name, by the way—but if anyone asks, you're from the school in Nalean. I'll alter your records at Administration to indicate such." The Northwarden glanced at the book in Asha's hand, then at Erran. "You've shown her the Journal?"

"Yes."

Elocien gave him an approving nod. "Lock it back in my office for now; we'll keep it there until Ashalia's quarters have been arranged."

Erran ducked his head in acquiescence, accepting the Journal from Asha with a friendly smile. "I'll find you tomorrow sometime, show you around." He left.

"I should warn you," said Elocien conversationally as they exited the Lockroom, "I would not expect the warmest welcome from whomever the Tol has sent. I cannot imagine they will be pleased to be working with a Shadow."

Asha just nodded in acknowledgment. She suspected the same

thing.

Soon they were heading down a passageway into a part of the palace Asha hadn't seen before; a minute later they arrived at a large, sumptuously furnished waiting room. A man was within, his back to them as he looked out over the perfectly tended gardens. Elocien gave a polite cough.

The man turned, studying them. He was younger than Asha had expected—perhaps in his early forties, lean and athletic-looking, his movements reminding her more of a warrior's than an Elder's. His short black hair showed no signs of thinning or fading to gray. He smiled, and there was genuine warmth in the expression.

"Representative Michal Alac," said the Northwarden, "please meet Ashalia Chaedris, your new colleague."

Michal stuck out a hand, which Asha hesitantly shook. Thus far at least, she was seeing none of the displeasure she'd expected. Elocien, too, watched the exchange with eyebrows slightly raised.

"A pleasure to meet you, Ashalia," said Michal.

"You, too, Elder Alac."

"Please. Just Michal. No need for formalities between the only two Athians in the palace." Michal turned to Elocien. "Thank you, Your Grace. If you'll excuse us, I need to go over Ashalia's duties with her," he said politely.

Elocien nodded. "Of course." Once Michal's back was turned he gave a slight, nonplussed shrug of the shoulders to Asha, then left the room.

Michal sat, gesturing for Asha to do the same. "Elder Eilinar has told me that you are here because the Council thinks it could be advantageous. That in negotiations, some of the Houses might see the presence of a Shadow as Tol Athian reaching out, showing that we aren't above working with non-Gifted," he said quietly. "Let me say this straight out—I don't believe that is the reason. Not for a second. Fortunately, I also don't care. You're here, and you're my assistant. As long as you do this job to the best of your ability, whatever else you do in the palace is your own business."

Asha swallowed, but nodded. "I'll work hard," she promised.

Michal stared at her for a moment, then inclined his head. "Good." He leaned back, looking a little more relaxed. "Then let's begin."

# Chapter 20

Wirr woke and for a few blissful moments he just lay there, not quite sure where he was.

Then his memory returned. The slow, sickening realization that it hadn't been a nightmare twisted through him.

Everyone from the school in Caladel was dead.

He lay there for a while as the truth settled deep in his chest. How long had he slept? No more than a couple of hours, probably; grief had robbed him of his tiredness for much of the night.

He focused on his surroundings. It was still dark, only the faint glow of the street lamp outside providing the faintest of illumination. Soft breathing from the pallets on the floor indicated Davian and Caeden were asleep. On the opposite side of the room, though, a dark shape hunched on the edge of Taeris's bed. The older man was awake.

Wirr frowned after a couple of seconds, not moving, letting his eyes adjust to the gloom. He couldn't put his finger on it, but something was wrong.

A shadow shifted, and Wirr could just make out Taeris's scarred features. They were set in fierce concentration; his crisscrossed forehead glistened with sweat as he stared intently at something he was holding, mesmerized by whatever it was. Wirr moved his head ever so slightly to get a better view. Taeris appeared not to notice.

Wirr caught the dull glint of steel. A knife.

Taeris sat completely still, almost as if in a trance, but his expression told a different story. He was laboring, struggling against something unseen. Something that scared him. Wirr watched, keeping his breathing deep and even to ensure it sounded as if he were still asleep. Taeris just sat, motionless, staring at the knife with horror in his eyes, for a minute. Two minutes. Five.

Then, without warning, Taeris began to raise the blade toward his face—slowly, inch by inch. His breathing became shallower.

Just as Wirr was about to move, something seemed to break and Taeris's arm dropped again. His features relaxed; he pulled open his satchel and tucked the knife away. Once he was done he lay back down on his bed, and soon his breathing was deep and regular.

Wirr closed his eyes, trying to sleep again, but the image of Taeris's face stayed in his mind. Straining. Terrified.

He was still awake when the dawn came.

Davian stared numbly at the rising sun.

"So you think he might be dangerous now?" he asked, unable to summon enough energy to color his tone with emotion.

"I don't know." Wirr sounded as exhausted as Davian felt. "I just thought I should tell you. The way he was staring at that knife...like he was fighting it, afraid of it...it scared me, Dav. And this might be our last chance to part ways with him."

The knot of grief and anxiety tightened just a little more in Davian's stomach. He'd barely slept, and those few hours he had had been filled with nightmares. Asha, screaming for him to help as she died a bloody death. Mistress Alita, the Elders, Talean, all doing the same. No matter that he knew, rationally, that there was nothing he could have done. He still should have been there.

And now this.

"We won't survive on our own," he said.

"Karaliene was prepared to take just you and me. If we go back now, she still will be."

Davian hesitated. Thirdhand stories from the princess were one thing, but if Wirr had seen Taeris acting so strangely...

He glanced across at Caeden.

"No," he said tiredly. "That's the easy way out, but I'm not sure it's the right way."

Wirr just nodded, looking unsurprised and a little relieved. "I feel the same, I think—if there's even a chance that what Taeris says about the Boundary is true, then we need to get Caeden back to Tol Athian. But we should watch Taeris closely from now on."

"Agreed."

There was silence for a while, and Davian glanced again over the early-morning landscape. The sun had not been up long enough to banish the sharp chill from the air, nor completely burn away the light fog that lay across the nearby valleys. He stamped his feet to warm up, looking across once again at the archway of Thrindar's northern gate. A few people were already making their way to and from the city, but no one who looked as if they were there to accompany them.

"Are you sure Karaliene hasn't changed her mind?" he asked.

"They'll come," said Wirr, though he, too, glanced toward the gate again, searching for any sign of their promised allies.

They had been waiting for twenty minutes now. Taeris had been walking in aimless circles since dawn, occasionally muttering to himself as the sun rose higher and higher. The delay clearly wasn't pleasing him; Davian was beginning to feel exposed, too, standing as they were in plain sight of the city walls.

Suddenly there was a hail from the gate and he turned to see two figures approaching, leading several horses. He squinted. It was a young man and a young woman—both about his own age, slim and athletic-looking, and dressed in simple but well-made clothes that looked practical for traveling. Davian's heart sank a little. If this was the protection the princess had promised Wirr, it had barely been worth the wait.

Apparently Taeris was thinking along the same lines. "Is this all Princess Karaliene has to offer?" he asked Wirr, irritated, though quietly enough that the newcomers could not overhear.

Wirr raised an eyebrow. "Take another look," he replied.

Taeris frowned, turning back to those approaching. His eyes widened a little in recognition.

"Aelric Shainwiere," Taeris said as the two reached the group.

The boy inclined his head, and Davian realized that it was indeed the same young man they'd watched the previous day in the arena. Wearing unassuming clothes, and with his hair no longer bound, he looked markedly different.

Davian recognized the girl, too, now that he could look at her up close—she was one of the princess's attendants. Her dark hair was cropped to her shoulders, and she had lightly tanned skin that freckled beneath her eyes.

Aelric surveyed the group, his expression indicating that he was unimpressed with what he saw. "I have been ordered to accompany you on your journey," he said. "The princess has told me who you are. Most of you, at least," he amended, giving Wirr a baleful look. Davian's initial rush of excitement faded as he saw the disinterest in the young man's posture. Aelric clearly did not wish to be there.

The girl shot Aelric an irritated glare, then stepped forward. "My name is Dezia. I'm Aelric's sister," she said, looking vaguely embarrassed. "We've brought horses and some supplies. I hope there's enough for wherever we are going."

Davian glanced at the horses; their saddlebags looked full to bursting. They would have plenty of food for a while, at least.

Taeris quickly made some polite introductions, frowning all the while. "I mean no offense," he said once everyone had been introduced, "but why did Princess Karaliene send you? I'm sure she's told you that we need to stay...inconspicuous on the road. If someone recognizes you..."

Aelric snorted. "In these clothes? I barely recognize myself."

Dezia sighed, shooting her brother another irritated look. "The truth is, Master Sarr, Aelric has gone and done something rather foolish. He got drunk and admitted a little too loudly that he didn't...fight to his potential in the final bout yesterday."

"He threw the fight?" Davian's astonishment made him blurt out the question before he could stop himself.

Aelric scowled at him, but Dezia just nodded. "Yes," she said, glancing sideways at a sulky-looking Aelric, an odd note of pride in her voice.

"Why?" asked Davian in disbelief.

Wirr had been nodding throughout the conversation. "Politics," he said, in the tone of someone who had just put together several pieces of a puzzle. "An Andarran winning on Desriel's soil would have been a slap in the face to the Gil'shar. Small by itself, but given the delicate state of things right now..."

Dezia nodded, looking for the first time at Wirr, who straightened unconsciously under her examination. "That's right," she said. "He gave up a chance at fame, to be remembered as one of the youngest swordsmen ever to win the Song, in the interests of diplomacy. Even though the Song is supposed to be above all of that." Her expression darkened. "And then decided to risk his life hours later by having too much pride to pretend he'd lost fairly."

Taeris had been listening with a perturbed expression. "The backers know?"

Dezia turned to him, her concern showing through. "Yes."

Taeris grunted. "So you are in as dire need of escape from Desriel as us." Dezia nodded again, and Taeris sighed. "I suppose it could be worse."

Aelric gave him a fierce scowl. "You weren't my first choice, either, bleeder," he said in a low voice.

Davian stiffened, unexpected anger abruptly boiling at the forefront of his emotions. He walked over to Aelric until the two were face-to-face.

"I don't mind that you don't want to be here," he said softly, "but if you ever—*ever*—call one of us that again, we will set you and your sister adrift. Only one person needs to overhear that word being used, and we'll have the entire Desrielite army bearing down on us before we can blink."

Aelric didn't back down, but he gave a short nod. "As you wish," he said, the slightest note of contrition in his voice.

Taeris sighed as he watched the exchange. He turned back to Dezia. "And why are you here?"

"He's my brother. As embarrassing as that can be sometimes," she said with a scowl in Aelric's direction. Then she added, "But I can fight if I need to."

Taeris raised an eyebrow. "Sword?"

Dezia reached into a pack on the side of one of the horses. "Bow," she said, unwrapping an oiled cloth to reveal a well-made bow and a quiver full of arrows.

Taeris considered, then nodded. "Keep it close," he said. "There's no telling if, or when, we'll find trouble."

"Speaking of which. Where are we going?" asked Aelric. "Karaliene said that there was no way you'd risk trying to cross at Talmiel."

Taeris hesitated. "Deilannis," he said eventually.

There was a moment of silence as everyone stared at him. "Deilannis?" repeated Wirr, sounding slightly disbelieving. "Does it even exist?"

Taeris smiled, though there was little humor in the expression. "It's very much real," he assured Wirr. "I've been there once before."

Aelric frowned. "I've never heard of it."

"It was an ancient city. Built on an island in the middle of the river Lantarche, bordering Desriel, Andarra, and Narut," Davian supplied. He looked at Taeris worriedly. "I've read about it. I thought it was supposed to be...dangerous. Cursed, somehow." The stories varied as to what made the city so unsafe, but he remembered one thing clearly enough: they were unanimous in saying that those who went into the City of Mists did not return.

Aelric gave a scornful laugh. "Cursed?"

"*Occupied* would be a better word," said Taeris, unruffled by Aelric's reaction. "Something lives in there—and whatever it is, it *is* dangerous."

"Just stories, though, surely. Superstitious nonsense."

Wirr shot Aelric an irritated glare. "You'd never even heard of it a moment ago." The newcomer's attitude was obviously grating on Wirr as much as it was on Davian.

Aelric opened his mouth to retort, but Taeris cut in. "No one guards the bridges to and from the city, so it's our best chance of escape. It's also an indication of how perilous the city itself is," he added with a pointed look in Aelric's direction. "I wouldn't even suggest it if there were an alternative."

Aelric hesitated, then inclined his head reluctantly. "I suppose if the Gil'shar ignore it, it cannot be easy to pass through," he admitted.

"There is another benefit to crossing there." Taeris paused, glancing at Aelric and Dezia. "There are creatures pursuing us."

Dezia nodded. "The sha'teth. Yes, Karaliene explained."

"I see. Good. I'm...glad you know." Taeris shot a half-curious, half-irritated glance at Wirr. "I suspect that if we can avoid the sha'teth until we reach Deilannis, they won't follow us through. Years ago Tol Athian ordered them to investigate the ruins, and all five of the creatures refused to enter. Until last week it was the only time I'd ever seen them defy a direct order. We never found out why."

"Because entering the city would kill them."

There was a sudden silence as everyone turned to look at Caeden.

Taeris stared at the young man curiously. "Why do you say that?"

Caeden suddenly looked uncertain. "I...just know." He shook his head. "The same way I knew a Shackle would kill the one in Anabir."

Taeris rubbed his chin. "It's possible," he admitted. "The Law of Decay—the rate at which unprotected Essence normally dissipates—seems to work differently inside the city, which makes it all but impossible to use Essence there. So if a Shackle can kill a sha'teth, Deilannis could affect them in the same way, I suppose." He shrugged, though he continued to look at Caeden with slightly narrowed eyes. "Regardless, it's our only option now. And it's past time we were on our way." Leading by example, he took the reins of a horse from Dezia and mounted it in one smooth motion.

There were six horses, so each of the boys picked a mount he thought he could handle without too much trouble, and they started northward. Davian had a little difficulty adjusting; his horse was nothing like Jeni back at Caladel, his only prior mount. He winced as he bounced along, knowing without asking that he was going to be sore by the end of the day.

They rode without incident for a time, silent for the most part. Occasionally Dezia exchanged conversation with one or another of the boys, but she usually stopped under Aelric's disapproving glare. After she spoke briefly to Caeden, though, Aelric pulled the red-haired boy aside as they rode—away from the others, but close enough that Davian could still hear them.

Aelric's expression was affable enough, but his words were cold steel. "I know who you are," he said to Caeden softly. "I don't know whether you're innocent, as everyone else here seems so eager to believe—and I don't care. Under no circumstances on this journey are you to talk to my sister."

Caeden's eyebrows rose, but he remained otherwise impassive. "And if she talks to me?"

Aelric slapped Caeden on the back as if they were having a friendly chat, clearly unaware that Davian could hear him. "Politely remove yourself from the conversation."

For a moment Davian thought he saw a flash of anger on Caeden's face, but if it had been there, it was covered immediately with a pleasant smile and nod. "As you wish," said Caeden, not a trace of offense in his tone.

Aelric, apparently satisfied, rode on ahead. Caeden saw Davian looking at him and gave an uncomfortable shrug. The two rode side by side for a few minutes in silence.

"Do you dream at all, Davian?" Caeden asked suddenly.

Davian blinked at the question. "Sometimes," he answered. "Not often, though...and I don't really remember much after."

"I've been having dreams. Nightmares." Caeden shivered. "I can't remember much of them, either, mostly, but...they're bad. I wake up shaking and sweating most nights."

The admission came hard, Davian could tell. He gave Caeden a sympathetic look. "Given what you've been through—"

"No." Caeden cut him off. "It's not that. It's not about getting beaten. I dream about that sometimes, too, and it's awful. But this is something worse. Much worse." He was quiet for several seconds, and Davian wondered whether he should ask anything further about it. He was just about to speak again when Caeden shifted in his saddle, leaning closer.

"Do you think I did it?"

Davian stared at Caeden for a long moment. "Did what?"

"You know what I'm talking about," said Caeden, his tone reproachful. He jerked his head toward Aelric. "People like him tend to assume the worst about me—but I don't care what they think. You and Wirr, though...you're a different story. You've been nothing but friendly to me, but at the same time, I can see you holding back. Being cautious." He shrugged. "I don't blame you, I just want to know what you think of me. Honestly."

244    Davian chewed his lip; the subject made him a little nervous.

"Honestly? I think it's likely the Gil'shar lied about you. Taeris says you're probably a pawn in something larger that's going on, the same as me, and I think he's right. Besides—I've seen your face whenever you think about those accusations. I know the whole thing makes you sick to your stomach."

Caeden nodded slowly. "But?"

Davian took a deep breath. "*But*...everything's been so backward, this past month. I'm not sure I can trust my own judgment anymore." A stab of grief and fury cut through him as he thought about Ilseth Tenvar and Caladel, and he gritted his teeth. "I hope you're the person you seem to be, Caeden, truly. I like you. But I probably won't feel certain of anything until we reach Tol Athian and you get your memories back." He looked Caeden in the eye. "What do *you* think?"

Caeden grimaced. "I...don't know. Part of me wishes I could remember, so I don't have to wonder."

"And the other part is afraid of what you will find if you do?"

"Yes." Caeden didn't show much outward emotion, but Davian could see the pain in his eyes.

Davian hesitated, unsure of what to say. "I suppose...even if you find what you're afraid of, you'll still have a choice moving forward," he said eventually. "If you're a good man now...well, what you did in the past is in the past. There's no reason you can't continue to be a good man in the future."

Caeden thought for a while, then inclined his head. "That's good advice," he said softly. "And I appreciate the honesty."

Their horses drifted closer to the rest of the group, and the conversation died away after that, leaving Davian to his own thoughts again. To his grief. It was no longer sharp or threatened to come out in a burst of emotion, as on the previous night; instead it sat as a constant, grinding emptiness in the pit of his stomach, an ache that felt as though it would never recede.

For a while he brooded on his and Wirr's escape from Caladel. Ilseth had likely known what was going to happen; had he then been involved somehow? Perhaps even responsible? The more Davian thought about it, the more likely it seemed, and the angrier he became.

The day passed slowly, the group traveling in silence for the most part, constantly tense as they watched for any sign of pursuit from Thrindar. There was none, though, and they found a sheltered patch of ground suitable for making camp just as the rim of the sun was disappearing below the horizon.

Dusk was properly turning into night when they heard the sounds of a horse trotting up the road.

Other people had been scarce on the northern road, so Davian turned curiously from the newly made fire to watch as the figure rode at a steady pace toward them. The horse was reined in as the traveler came within range of the fire, and a familiar voice called out.

"El take you, Taeris, but you could have come by the temple before you left!"

Davian relaxed as the horse was urged a little farther forward, and Nihim's face became visible beneath his hood. Wirr grabbed the reins of Nihim's animal as he dismounted, leading it away to be tied with the others.

Taeris greeted the priest with a bemused look. "Nihim, what are you doing here?"

The tall man shrugged. "I heard the princess was less than gracious with your little party, and thought you might be headed this way. Despite omitting that minor detail when last we talked." He gave Taeris a meaningful stare.

Taeris just nodded, looking resigned.

Aelric, who had been listening, interjected indignantly. "Princess Karaliene was more than gracious!" he protested. "These men are criminals here; she gave them more than most others would have."

"That she did," Taeris assured Aelric soothingly.

Nihim glanced at Aelric, then raised an eyebrow at Taeris. "Don't tell me you've added a Loyalist to your group, old friend?"

Taeris smiled. "Nihim Sethi, meet Aelric Shainwiere, the finest swordsman to ever deliberately lose the Song of Swords."

Aelric scowled at the introduction, but Nihim chuckled. "Shainwiere, is it? Yes, I heard some mutterings about you before I left this morning," he said in amusement. "I suppose I can see why you might have joined Taeris's excursion out of the country. Nobody likes giving their life's savings to a man who deliberately and publicly dumps it into the nearest sewer. Makes them look somewhat foolish, one might say."

Aelric flushed, but didn't respond.

Nihim grabbed Taeris by the arm, murmuring something to him in a low tone. Taeris nodded, expression grave, and turned to the others. "I need to speak with Nihim privately for a time," he said. "Make sure someone's on watch while I'm gone." Without further explanation he and the priest walked out of the firelight and started down the road.

Davian frowned after them, wondering at Nihim's sudden appearance. The older men's secrecy hadn't bothered Davian back at the temple, but out here on the road it was different. If Nihim was coming with them, they should be told what was going on.

After a moment Wirr came to stand beside him, looking in the same direction.

"Do you want to go after them, or shall I?" the blond-haired boy asked in a conversational tone.

Davian smiled slightly. "I'll go. Tell the others I'm...relieving myself, or something."

Wirr just nodded, wandering back toward the rest of the group.

Following Taeris and Nihim wasn't difficult; the light was fading, and the two men strolled along the road, chatting amiably. Their conversation was inconsequential enough at first, but then there was a sudden silence, and when Taeris spoke again his tone was heavy.

"Is there any chance you'll turn back?"

Nihim smiled, shaking his head. "It's my time. We both knew it from the moment you walked into the temple with those boys. El help me, but I'll not hide from it any longer."

"So you're finally done with Marut Jha?"

Nihim spat to one side. "Every day I wore those robes I felt dirty. Yes, I believe I finally am. I can only pray that El forgives me for the things I've done while wearing them."

Davian crept a little closer, keeping to the thick brush on the side of the road. Nocturnal creatures were beginning to stir around him, masking any small noises he might be making.

"I wish I could have properly repaid you for saving her," Nihim said suddenly.

"There was never a need. You know that," said Taeris. "I'd make the same choice again if the opportunity came."

Nihim sighed. "But it lost you your chance to go home, sins forgiven. I know how much that meant. Now even more than I did back then."

"And now here I am, about to go home anyway, but this time with evidence. And if I can convince the Council of the danger, they'll trip over themselves in their haste to make amends. Who knows. Maybe they'll even decide not to hand me over for execution." Taeris shrugged. "Everything for a reason, old friend."

Nihim raised an eyebrow. "So you're going with them now?"

"I have to. When they were going to be traveling with the other Gifted, the risk was acceptable. But by themselves...even once we're through Deilannis, I can't just send them off with Caeden and hope for the best, not without knowing his purpose in all of this. There's still a very real chance he's dangerous."

Nihim inclined his head. "You won't hear any argument from me. Just...be careful."

Taeris grunted in acknowledgment, staring at the ground in contemplative silence for a few seconds. "Do you have any regrets?"

Nihim didn't respond for a moment, lost in thought. Then he exhaled heavily. "I do. Of course I do. But there's nothing that stands out—nothing that breaks my heart or plays on my mind. I served El as I thought best; beyond that, nothing is important."

Taeris smiled. "A good life, then?"

Nihim smiled back. "One that was worthwhile. That made a difference. I couldn't have asked for more than that."

Taeris looked at the ground again, swallowing. "You're taking this better than I am," he admitted, his voice catching.

Nihim laughed. "I've had twenty years to resolve myself to it. Twenty years of knowing I couldn't die. Twenty years of understanding that I was playing some small part in the Grand Design." He shook his head, putting a consoling hand on Taeris's shoulder. "It's more than I could have hoped for, probably more than I deserved. Don't mourn me, Taeris. There's no need."

Taeris nodded, releasing a shaky breath. "I wish I had your faith. It would be a comfort, given what's ahead."

Nihim just smiled. "One day," he said with certainty.

There was another long silence.

"We should get back," said Taeris eventually, glancing at the sky, which was now showing more than a few stars. "Those boys have been glaring daggers at each other all day. I think the princess may have saddled us with more trouble than help."

Nihim grunted. "I'm surprised she sent any help at all. And Shainwiere, whatever his faults, was a wily choice. Too many swords would have drawn attention, but that young man will be worth ten normal men to you in a battle. He may make the difference if a patrol catches you out."

Taeris frowned. "I know. I'm surprised as well, to be honest; Shainwiere needs to get out of the country, but there were easier ways for him to do so. It was generous of her to send him. She has some connection with young Wirr that I haven't been able to puzzle out as yet."

Nihim watched him, smiling. "That must rub the wrong way."

Taeris snorted. "You know me too well."

They paused, then turned back toward the camp. "The Boundary is going to fail soon. I'm sure of it. The time is finally coming and all I can see are the dark days ahead, old friend," said Taeris quietly.

Nihim clapped Taeris on the shoulder. "Then I suppose I'm leaving it to you to shine some light." His tone was nonchalant, but he wore a serious expression. Taeris considered him for a few moments, then nodded.

Now ahead of them, Davian darted away as quietly as he could.

He pondered what he'd overheard as he hurried back toward camp. Much of it made no sense to him—but even so, one thing was clear.

Taeris might be on their side, but he wasn't telling them everything.

# Chapter 21

Wirr yawned.

There was still no sign of Taeris and Nihim—or Davian, for that matter. No one had spoken much since their departure; he had exchanged a couple of friendly words with Caeden, but Aelric and Dezia appeared happy to keep to themselves.

Wirr was fine with that. Aelric and his attitude had been getting under his skin; every time the other boy spoke, Wirr had to stop himself from making a snide remark in return. Perhaps it was just the young man's obvious reluctance to be there, or perhaps it was his apparent belief that he was not among equals. Either way, Wirr was going to enjoy the moment Aelric discovered whom he'd been treating with such contempt.

Dezia, though...his eyes wandered over to her and remained fixed there. He inwardly cursed his lack of attentiveness to the girls at Caladel. Ignoring them had been the right thing to do, of course—but it had resulted in his being woefully inexperienced when it came to women.

Then he forced down the sudden, unexpected lump in his throat at the thought of the school. Those girls were all dead now. Because of him.

Dezia glanced up, catching his absentminded stare before he had a chance to look away. He felt the blood rushing to his cheeks, but she just smiled at him, murmuring something to Aelric—who looked displeased and tried unsuccessfully to keep her seated—before rising and making her way around the fire to join him.

"You look like you might be better company than my brother right now," she said cheerfully as she sat.

Wirr gave her a polite smile, trying not to show any of the grief still sharp in his chest. "That's a low bar, but I'll take it." He winced as soon as the words were out of his mouth. "Sorry. I didn't mean…"

Dezia grinned. "Yes you did. And you're right. Aelric is about as cheerful as an empty barn in winter when he gets like this."

Wirr smiled, relaxing a little. He looked toward Aelric, seeing the young man throwing a fierce scowl in their direction. "So there are times he doesn't look like that?"

Dezia sneaked a look at Aelric and then turned back to Wirr, giving a small laugh. "Occasionally. Around Karaliene, mainly." She sighed. "The princess told me what happened. She swore to Aelric that the two of you aren't…involved, but he's not the type to let something like that go easily."

Wirr frowned in confusion. "You mean he thought…" He shook his head, chuckling. "No."

"I know. But he doesn't know who you are, so he's not convinced." She rolled her eyes. "Though he should still be content to take Karaliene's word," she added, mostly to herself.

It took a few moments for what Dezia had said to sink in. "Karaliene told you who I am?" Wirr asked in a low voice, suddenly focused.

Dezia nodded. "Not the whole story, but enough. I hope you don't mind."

Wirr shook his head, smiling. "No. If Karaliene trusts you, so do I." He was surprised to find it was true. "You must be close."

Dezia gave a modest shrug. "We're friends." She cast an uncertain glance at Caeden, who was a small distance away but potentially still within earshot. "Perhaps we shouldn't be talking about this now, though."

Wirr hesitated, then stood, offering his hand to Dezia. "There's still a little light left. Perhaps you'd like to walk with me for a while?" Dezia raised an eyebrow. "To talk," Wirr clarified hurriedly. "I have plenty of questions about what's been happening back home, but I can't ask them around the others."

Dezia smiled. "Of course." She took Wirr's hand and allowed him to pull her to her feet.

They were about to stroll away when Aelric's voice cut through the quiet, thick with irritation. "Where are you going?"

Dezia sighed, turning back to her brother. "For a walk."

Aelric stood, anger now plain on his face. He crossed to them in a few quick strides and grabbed Dezia by the arm. "I don't think that's a good idea."

Wirr scowled. "Leave her alone, you fool," he said without thinking.

A heartbeat later he discovered he had the tip of a sword at his throat. The camp had gone deathly silent, the others watching in concern; the air had a tense feel to it, as if there were violence in it just waiting to happen. Wirr stayed perfectly still, not sure how far to trust Aelric's judgment.

"Perhaps you would like to duel with the fool," Aelric said in an icy tone. "First to draw blood?"

Wirr shook his head slowly. He was angry, but he knew he would be no match for Aelric.

Aelric stepped back, lowering his sword with a look of smug satisfaction. "Just as I thought."

"I'll duel with you."

Aelric's expression froze. Everyone turned as one to see Caeden reclining lazily on the ground, regarding the young swordsman with a half-amused, half-annoyed expression.

Aelric snorted. "Put a sword in the hands of a murderer? I think not."

Caeden merely raised an eyebrow at the insult. " 'Every man who holds a sword in his hand, holds murder in his heart.' "

"What?" Aelric looked bemused. Wirr didn't recognize the reference, either—Caeden was clearly quoting someone—but Aelric's hesitation lasted only a moment. "Very well," he snarled, striding over to one of the horses and locating a well-wrapped blade in one of the saddlebags.

He tossed the sword at Caeden so that it clattered to the ground at his feet.

"Aelric, stop," Dezia said in a worried tone. Wirr felt as

concerned as she sounded. The expression on Aelric's face was murderous.

"Caeden, don't do this," Wirr said seriously. "I appreciate it, but it's not worth getting hurt."

Caeden shook his head as he stooped to pick up the sword. He smiled as he hefted it in his hand, gauging its weight. "Thank you, Wirr, but I'll be fine," he said absently, giving the sword an experimental swing. To Wirr's surprise he appeared to know how to handle the weapon.

Caeden walked away from the fire, over to where Aelric was waiting. Wirr and Dezia backed away, giving the two boys plenty of room.

Aelric's expression reminded Wirr of a cat looking at a mouse it had finally cornered.

"Let's begin," he said, his smile confident. "Touch."

Caeden followed the form by tapping Aelric's outstretched blade with his own, and then they were on their guard, circling warily. Wirr watched with trepidation, wondering if he should intervene and stop the fight before it began. Aside from his personal concern for Caeden, an injury to either man could spell disaster for their journey, and Aelric's temperament was clearly not to be relied upon.

Suddenly Aelric attacked, faster than Wirr would have believed possible. Caeden's sword leaped up to meet the challenge; the sound of steel clashing against steel rang out as Aelric struck again and again in quick succession, raining down blows as Caeden desperately defended. Then the attack was broken off and Aelric was back on the balls of his feet, watching and circling, a little out of breath.

Wirr ran his hands through his hair in helpless frustration. "This is folly," he said as calmly as he could, addressing both combatants. "If one of you gets hurt, it puts us all in danger."

Aelric responded with another flurry of blows; for the first time, Wirr noticed how smoothly Caeden was responding. For every graceful move forward by Aelric, Caeden had a fluid counter.

And he was *fast*.

Wirr watched, mouth agape, as Caeden turned aside another of Aelric's attacks, his sword a blur, every small movement liquid. Beads of sweat had begun to form on Aelric's brow, and Wirr thought he saw a flash of concern on the young nobleman's face.

Then Caeden attacked.

Everything just...*flowed*; there was no telling where one move began and another ended. Caeden moved forward calmly, methodically, as if the motion cost him no effort, no energy at all. Yet his blade sang in front of him, impossible for the eye to follow, forcing Aelric back and back until they were almost at the road.

Aelric faltered.

Wirr watched in disbelief as Aelric's sword cartwheeled through the air, falling several feet away. Aelric stumbled backward and fell, raising his hands in surrender as the point of Caeden's sword rested above his heart.

A few long seconds passed in silence, everyone frozen.

Wirr turned his gaze to Caeden's face, suddenly nervous for a very different reason. The young man's expression had barely changed, but something in his eyes...

Wirr shivered, and it was not from the cold.

"Caeden," he called out.

The sound seemed to break something within Caeden, who slowly lowered his sword, eventually tossing it aside to join Aelric's.

"If you want to act the fool in future, be prepared for someone to call you on it," he said softly.

He turned and retreated to the campfire, sitting down without another word.

The others were still staring at him in shock when Davian emerged from the darkened road, a little out of breath. He nodded to Wirr, then frowned when he took in the scene before him.

"What's going on?"

"I'll tell you later." Wirr shook his head, still unwilling to believe what he'd just seen. He lowered his voice. "You hear anything interesting?"

"Nothing that made any sense." Davian glanced behind him. "They shouldn't be far—"

There was motion just beyond the light of the campfire, and then Taeris and Nihim were crashing through the surrounding brush, the urgency of their arrival drawing everyone's attention.

"Sha'teth. Get your weapons," Taeris said without preamble, quietly but with such force that everyone leaped to obey.

Soon they were all arranged in a tight circle with their backs to the campfire, silent, each one straining to see into the gathering gloom. Wirr's heart pounded, limbs heavy with dread, as he remembered their last encounter with one of the creatures.

"Which direction?" whispered Dezia to Taeris, her bow at the ready.

"Out there," said Taeris, gesturing a little to the left of where he and Nihim had emerged. "We cut through the forest on the way back, spotted it amongst the trees. It saw us, too, but..." Taeris shook his head, looking troubled. "It didn't attack. It seemed like it was just watching the camp."

"Isn't that a good thing?" asked Aelric.

"I suppose. Just...strange," replied Taeris, his expression uneasy as he stared into the darkness.

The silence began to stretch, the tension almost unbearable. Then the hush was suddenly broken by a low, hissing voice coming from all directions at once. It was difficult to tell, but Wirr thought it sounded female.

"*Darei ildos Tal'kamar sha'teth,*" it said.

"Where is it?" murmured Davian.

Wirr's eyes strained against the darkness, but he could see nothing out of the ordinary. "What did it say?"

Taeris didn't reply straight away. "I think it's telling us to hand Caeden over," he said eventually. To Wirr's left Caeden gave a small, nervous nod of confirmation.

"*Darei ildos Tal'kamar sha'teth,*" the voice hissed again. "*Sha'teth eldris karathgar si.*"

Taeris shook his head. "*Eldarei Tal'kamar,*" he called out. "*Sha'teth eldris gildin.*"

The low, rasping sound of the sha'teth's laughter filled the air. "Your Darecian is not what it once was, Taeris Sarr."

Everyone's head swiveled toward Taeris in surprise, but he ignored the looks. "What do you want?" he shouted into the darkness.

"You know what I want," came the whispery-hoarse voice. It was definitely female, Wirr decided. "Give him to me, and I will leave you unharmed."

"No." Taeris was emphatic.

"So quick to decide the fate of all," hissed the voice. "Perhaps your companions think differently?"

"No." It was Davian.

"No," Wirr added. He was echoed by Nihim and Dezia.

Aelric gave Caeden a long look. "No," he said into the darkness.

"Fools," whispered the voice.

There was silence.

After a few minutes had passed, Wirr could bear the strain no longer. "Do you think it's gone?" he asked no one in particular.

"Yes," said Taeris, relaxing his stance. "I think it has."

Wirr felt his muscles loosen a little as he took a deep breath. Beside him he could hear the others doing the same.

Caeden looked around at them. "Thank you," he said. He glanced across at Aelric, inclining his head slightly in acknowledgment. Aelric hesitated, then gave a brief nod back.

Taeris put a hand on Caeden's shoulder. "Nothing to thank us for, lad."

Dezia turned to the older man, frowning. "How did it know your name?"

Taeris shrugged. "When I was on the Council at Tol Athian, there were occasions I had to deal with the sha'teth. Apparently I made an impression," he said wryly. Then he frowned. "The bigger question is, why didn't it attack?"

Nihim coughed. "This may sound foolish, but...could it have been afraid? Or at least cautious? The way it was hanging back when we saw it, almost like it was hesitating..."

Taeris rubbed his chin. "Perhaps. We did kill one of its brothers, and nobody's done that before." He shook his head. "It's hard to say. Once I would have said no. But if they are truly out of Athian's control, there's no telling what else has changed."

Nihim accepted the statement with a thoughtful nod, and everyone began drifting back to their positions around the campfire. Wirr caught himself staring at Dezia again as she took her seat, until a gentle hand on his shoulder made him jump.

"Go easy," Caeden said to him, keeping his voice low. "I think you've antagonized Aelric enough for one evening."

Wirr glared for a moment, then gave a brief, rueful laugh. "I suppose you're right." He looked Caeden in the eye. "I didn't get a chance to thank you. What you did was...amazing. How did you...?"

"I don't know, exactly," admitted Caeden, sounding weary. "But I was glad to help."

They moved back to the fire. Conversation was stilted at first—everyone was on edge, listening to the sounds of the surrounding forest for any signs of attack. None came, however, and eventually the group lapsed into sporadic, distracted conversation until tiredness overtook their unease.

Wirr was normally quick to sleep, but tonight he found himself awake long after everyone else's breathing was deep and regular around him. He had his back to the fire, but he knew that only Nihim and Caeden were still up, having drawn first watch.

"You're troubled." It was Nihim breaking the silence, evidently addressing Caeden.

"That's nothing new," came the soft reply.

Wirr wondered whether he should move around, make it obvious he was still awake.

"More than usual, then," said Nihim.

There was a long silence, and Wirr was beginning to wonder whether Caeden was simply ignoring the priest when he responded, "I dueled. With Aelric."

"I see." There was a hesitation in Nihim's voice. "Aelric is an immensely talented swordsman. Losing to him—"

"I didn't lose." Caeden's voice was flat and low.

There was another long silence. "You must be an impressive swordsman."

"I suppose so." Caeden gave a bitter laugh. "Interesting skills for a simple farm boy."

"I think we both know that whatever else you are, you're no farm boy." A pause. "Neither of you was hurt?"

"No. But...I was angry. I...almost hurt him. I *wanted* to hurt him." Caeden choked the words out as if they were poison.

"And that scared you?"

"It terrified me."

"Good. That's good." Wirr could hear cloth rustling as Nihim shifted. "Everyone has a darker nature, Caeden. *Everyone*. Good men fear it, and evil men embrace it. Good men are still tempted to do the wrong thing, but they resist those urges. As you did. You have nothing to worry about."

There was a moment of silence. "That doesn't sound like the teachings of Marut Jha."

Nihim gave a soft chuckle. "Marut Jha doesn't trouble himself with definitions like *good* and *evil*. No—my priesthood here has never been anything more than a facade. My belief is in El, the One God."

"The god of the Augurs. The god of predestination."

"That's right." Nihim sounded surprised at Caeden's knowledge. "El sees everything, is in perfect and absolute control. The Grand Design, it's called. Everything that happens runs according to His purpose."

"Remind me to thank him for my last couple of months."

Nihim chuckled again. "I didn't say He was responsible, I said it runs according to His purpose. Shammaeloth has his influences over this world, too. He fights, but it's simply that he is in a war he cannot win, because every move he makes has already been accounted for by El."

There was silence for a few seconds. "Then why does El not simply finish him and be done with it? *Stop* every move he makes?" Caeden sounded irritated. "Terrible things happen all the time. It hardly feels like he's losing."

"The point is, he's not losing—he's already lost. What you see are his death throes. Shammaeloth was bound to this world in the Genesis War, and thus bound by time. He was trapped here, and now all he fights for is souls to serve him in his prison."

"He must not be doing a very good job. I haven't heard of many followers of Shammaeloth," observed Caeden, his tone dubious.

"It doesn't work like that. At the end of time, El will leave this world, taking those who gave Him their faith. When He does, what protection this world has will vanish, and it will fall to Shammaeloth to rule what remains—and only what remains—for eternity. Any who do not leave with El will be left here and serve him, like it or not."

There was a pause, Caeden obviously digesting this. "I can't     259 say I like the idea of not being in control of my own destiny," he said eventually. "If everything is already laid out, if there really is a Grand Design, wouldn't that mean we have no free will?"

Nihim grunted. "I can't tell you how many times I heard that same question debated, back in the Augurs' day," he admitted. "There are a lot of differing opinions, but I certainly think we have free will. Just because El knows each choice I'm going to make—even if He created me *knowing* it's the choice I would make—doesn't mean it's not mine." He sighed. "But perhaps it's still not free will as you would think of it. That's the natural arrogance of man, sadly. We want to believe that free will means complete independence from the plans of our creator."

There was a contemplative silence. "Tell me one thing, though," said Caeden after a while. "Since the Augurs fell...how can you still have faith?"

"Because my faith is in El. It was never in the Augurs or what they were once capable of," explained Nihim. "You can put your trust in something that's obvious, that's measurable or predictable—but that's not faith. Nor is believing in something that gives you no pause for doubt, no reason or desire to question. Faith is something more than that. By definition, it cannot have proof as its foundation."

There was another silence. "That makes sense, I suppose. It's something to think on," Caeden conceded eventually, sounding more polite than convinced.

"That's good. But you *should* think on it, Caeden. It's important, regardless of what conclusion you come to."

"Why?"

"Because it strikes me that a man needs to know what he believes before he can really know who he is."

Wirr didn't hear Caeden's response, but after a few more moments there was the sound of yawning, and Nihim chuckled. "I hope it's not the conversation, lad, but you look like you can barely keep your eyes open," he said. "Perhaps you should get some sleep. I can take the rest of the watch."

"It's not the conversation. Just a long day," Caeden assured him with another yawn. "You're right, though—I might take you up on that offer, if it's no trouble. Thank you." There were some scuffling sounds as Caeden made himself comfortable, and soon enough another note of regular breathing joined the others.

Wirr lay awake for a little longer, wondering at the conversation he'd overheard.

Eventually, though, his eyes shut of their own accord, and he knew nothing more until dawn.

# Chapter 22

Asha unlocked the door to her chambers wearily.

It was the end of only her fourth day at the palace, and so far the entire experience had been one long blur, with Michal proving to be a merciless teacher. She was woken each day before dawn so that he could tutor her; when he had to attend to his other duties, he made her work through entire tomes of genealogies, explaining that the blood ties among Houses motivated much of their politics. He would then return in the evening, drilling her on what she'd learned and refusing to let her leave until she displayed enough progress to satisfy him.

She sighed. There had been opportunity for little else; she'd barely had time to come to grips with what Elocien had told her about Wirr and the attacks, let alone do anything in her new position as Scribe.

Still, despite her exhaustion, she was far from ungrateful. The more she saw of the Shadows in the palace—treated much the same as those in the Tol, if not worse—the more she came to understand just how fortunate she was.

"Ashalia Chaedris."

Asha looked up at the sound of her name. The only other person in the hallway was a Shadow, a man in his midtwenties, heading straight for her.

"Do I know you?" she asked as he drew closer.

"The Shadraehin wants to know if there is news," said the man.

Asha repressed a scowl. "It's only been a few days since I got here," she pointed out.

"And yet you've been made Representative. It seems clear the Northwarden trusts you," the man noted. He drew a slip of paper from his pocket and offered it to her. "Instructions. A way to leave a message for us, should anything new come to light."

Asha hesitated, considering telling the man outright that the deal was off. But she knew that would only lead to recriminations, possibly violent ones given what Erran had shown her. And the Shadraehin couldn't know that she'd changed her mind, wouldn't have any reason to think that the Northwarden would have disclosed the attack on Administration to her.

"Thank you," she said, accepting the note. She turned away.

"As soon as you know something, make sure you tell him," said the Shadow softly. "He is eager to hear from you."

When Asha glanced over her shoulder, the man was already walking away. She stared after him for a few moments. Maybe it was the image of the swinging corpses in Administration still fresh in her mind, but something in the man's tone made her... uneasy.

Asha examined the piece of paper as she walked inside. It was the name of an inn in the Middle District, the Silver Talon, along with directions and a short list of names to ask for once she was there.

She paused for a moment. Then she wandered over to the fireplace—still burning, thanks to the ministrations of one of the servants—and tossed the note in.

The paper quickly caught, curling and disintegrating.

"What was that?"

Asha flinched, spinning to see an enormous, muscular frame reclining in one of her armchairs.

"Kol," she said in surprise, trying to sound pleased by the unexpected intrusion. "It's nice to see you." It wasn't, but this was the first time she'd encountered the big Augur since their brief introduction, and she was still hopeful of making a good impression.

Kol studied her intently for a few moments, as if trying to see inside her head. Perhaps he was, she realized with a stab of discomfort.

"Burning notes is a little suspicious," he rumbled.

Asha scowled. "It was instructions on how to meet with the Shadraehin's people, if you must know. I burned it because I'm never going to use it. Just as the duke asked."

Kol said nothing for a few seconds, then nodded. "Have you read through the papers Elocien gave you? The visions not in the Journal?" His tone was brusque.

Asha shook her head mutely, flushing, feeling as if she was being chastised even though there was no way she could have found the time. She'd managed to read all the entries in the Journal itself, but the duke had given her a ream of loose papers as well—all the visions that *hadn't* been confirmed. The ones she would need to read, in order to compare them against anything new.

"Then you should get started." Kol rose and crossed the space between them in two quick strides. His expression was so grim that Asha's first reaction was to shrink back defensively, but all the big man did was press a folded sheet of paper into her palm.

Then he was out the door, shutting it firmly behind him without another word.

Asha took a deep breath, partly relieved, but also a little annoyed at Kol's rudeness. She understood he had misgivings about her, but she'd done nothing to deserve such curt behavior.

She walked over and sat at her desk; once the lamp was lit and she was comfortable, she unfolded the paper Kol had given her and began to read.

*I found myself in a cavern, the likes of which I've never seen. Molten red rock glowed everywhere around me. There was no way to tell, but it felt as though I was deep underground.*

*I walked forward along a narrow path, through a tunnel, and then into a large room that had strange symbols carved into the floor. In front of me stood a creature. It seemed to be made of fire, in the shape of a man but with glowing skin and hair, undoubtedly not human.*

*Across from it, at the end of the room past all the symbols and standing beside a short stone pillar, was a plain-looking man with red hair. There was a sword on top of the pillar, and the man was in the midst of reading something on the blade.*

*" 'For those who need me most.' What does that mean?" he asked.*

*"Another question I cannot answer," said the creature.*

*"What does Licanius mean? It sounds Darecian. You could at least tell me that much," said the man.*

*" 'Fate.' The translation is more specific, but in your language it means 'fate,' " said the creature.*

*The man nodded, then picked up the sword. He shimmered for a moment, as if I were looking at his reflection in a pool of water, and then seemed to disappear entirely. I could still see everything else—the room, the creature—but he had vanished.*

*The next thing I knew I was back in the palace, and I recognized the scene straight away—it was just like the other times. Fessi, Erran, and Ashalia were kneeling next to me. We were in a Lockroom, and I was lying on the floor; when I looked down I could see that I was bleeding from many wounds. The pain was sharp, but fading fast.*

*I felt my head growing light, and then the dizziness became too much. The vision ended.*

Asha sat back, stunned.

It made sense now. No wonder Kol had been so brusque—and had looked so apprehensive when they'd first met.

Slowly she reached over and unlocked her desk drawer, then fumbled around until she felt the bundle of pages the duke had given her two days before. She drew it out, untied the string around it, and flipped through the pages one by one.

It wasn't long before she found another of Kol's entries, written a few weeks earlier:

*We were in a Lockroom. Fessi, Erran, and a girl I do not recognize were all kneeling next to me, looking upset. There was an excruciating pain in my chest, and when I looked down I could see blood pouring out of several wounds. Fessi was trying desperately to help, but I could see in the eyes of the others that it was too late.*

*Suddenly I felt dizzy; the room spun and the pain faded, replaced by a kind of dreamlike state. I tried to stay conscious as long as I could, but I also knew it would be of no use. I said something to Fessi, at the end—I can't remember what. I hope it was something meaningful.*

*I closed my eyes, and the vision ended.*

Asha just stared at the page for a long moment in horror. She knew this wasn't confirmation—a vision needed to be Seen by a different Augur for that—but if Kol had Seen this one twice, there was a good chance it wasn't just a dream.

Feeling sick, Asha began flipping through the rest of the papers. An entry in Fessi's delicate hand caught her eye:

*It was night, and I was in a strange city. Everything was made of stone, and it was all black—the roads, the walls, everything. As if fire had scorched every surface. The sky was darker than it should have been, too—perhaps it was just cloudy, but it felt as though it was always like that there.*

*The streets were empty, but I was running as fast as I could. I wasn't altering my passage through time, though. Maybe I couldn't for some reason? I was trying to be as quiet as possible, but I couldn't stop my footsteps from echoing off the cobblestones, and even that small sound was as good as shouting in a place like that.*

*Then there was a growl behind me and I turned to see a great wolfhound, so big that its face was at the same height as mine. There was something strange about its eyes—they were too intelligent for an animal, I think. The creature came toward me, and I turned to run but in front of me another one had appeared. They moved in slowly, taking their time, as if they knew I had nowhere to go. I screamed for help, but no one came.*

*The first creature finally attacked, and the last thing I felt was its teeth biting into my neck.*

Not long after that, there was an older entry by Erran:

*I was aware I was in a vision just in time to see Commander Hael driving a dagger into my stomach, screaming something at me.*

*Then I was waking up, lying on the floor of a Lockroom in the palace. There was blood everywhere—a disturbingly big pool of it on the ground where my face was. It was hard to orient myself, but when I checked my stomach, there was no wound. Most of the blood seemed to have come from my nose...and maybe my ears, which I thought was strange. Everything ached and I felt weak, nauseous; I tried to stand, but that turned out to be a bad idea. I collapsed back onto the floor, and everything went black.*

*When I woke up again, I was being led out into an unfamiliar courtyard. There were gallows there, which unfortunately meant that I got fixated on them and didn't take much notice of my other surroundings. The executioner watched us as we filed up beside him, and we all stood obediently in front of our assigned length of rope. I'm not sure why I wasn't struggling, but when I looked around at the people next to me, they seemed resigned to what was happening, too. I didn't recognize anyone. I wasn't sure if I was happy or sad about that.*

*We all just stood there silently as the executioner walked down the line, draping the nooses around our necks and tightening them. I watched him with a kind of detached fascination—I remember thinking I was glad he looked professional, because that wasn't the kind of thing I wanted to have botched.*

*I stared out over the courtyard, but it was empty. Shouldn't there have been a crowd watching something like that? Witnesses? I didn't think it strange at the time, though.*

*Then the trapdoor below my feet opened, and I got the sudden rush of falling for just a moment. Everything went black again, but this time I'm fairly certain it was permanent.*

Asha continued through the stack of papers in fascinated, horrified silence. Most of the visions were inconsequential: what was happening the following day, snatches of arguments or personal moments, but nothing of real significance. Hidden among them, though, she found repeated descriptions from each of the three Augurs—three identical visions written by Fessi and two from Kol. Erran's vision of the hanging was repeated, too, though not the first part about getting stabbed by Commander Hael—whoever that was.

She shivered as she stared at the pages. What must it be like, to See your own death? None of the three had been able to determine any timeline for their visions, though she couldn't decide whether they would consider that a blessing or a curse.

After a while she filed Kol's newest vision with the others and locked her desk drawer. She was tired, and it was only a few hours until she had to rise again.

Still, it took her a long time to get to sleep.

Asha groaned as a hand shook her by the shoulder.

"Go away, Michal," she mumbled.

"It's not Michal."

Asha forced her eyes open. "Erran?" She pulled the sheets a little higher.

The young man gave her a sheepish grin. "Sorry. I *did* try knocking."

"That's all right." Asha rubbed her face, slowly coming awake. "What time is it?"

"A couple of hours before dawn." Erran yawned. "A time no living creature should be awake, I know. But your Representative is a harder taskmaster than any of us anticipated."

"You don't have to tell me that." Asha shook her head. "Why are you here?"

Erran produced a slip of paper from his pocket that he handed to Asha.

"Nothing urgent," he reassured her. "This was just the only time I could get it to you. If Representative Alac keeps you this busy, you may be in for more of these late-night disturbances, I'm afraid. It's not the sort of thing we can just slip under your door."

Asha nodded. "Of course."

Erran coughed, then gestured to the door. "I should let you get back to sleep," he said apologetically. He turned.

"Erran."

The young man stopped. "Yes?"

"I read the other visions last night. The ones not in the Journal."

Erran turned, examining her face for a few moments in silence. "You have questions," he said eventually.

Asha shook her head, remembering what Erran had Seen. "How . . . how do you deal with it?"

Erran bit his lip. "How long until you need to meet the Representative?"

Asha shrugged. "An hour?"

"Enough time, then. Get dressed. I want to show you something."

"All right." When Erran didn't move, Asha pointedly looked at him, then the door.

"Ah. Sorry." Erran flushed, then exited.

Asha dressed hurriedly and soon joined Erran outside her room.

"So where are we going?"

Erran shook his head, indicating he didn't want to say outside a Lockroom. "You'll see."

They walked for a few minutes, turning down a series of increasingly bare hallways. This section of the palace was older and evidently less used; before long even the carpet underfoot had given way to hard gray stone, the occasional windows had vanished, and dust was evident everywhere. Only Erran's torch provided any light.

"The palace backs onto Ilin Tora," he explained as they walked. "These passages are cut directly into the mountain—like Tol Athian, but made by regular men, not the Builders."

Asha nodded; the passageways were well made, but the differences were obvious. Suddenly she was reminded of the similar journey she'd made with Jin, and she swallowed. "What's back here?"

"The old dungeons. Storage rooms." He shrugged. "Nobody uses this section of the palace anymore. Some of the deeper passages collapsed years ago, and given that the space wasn't needed, the cost of upkeep outweighed the benefits of having it available."

Asha looked around, a sudden chill making her shiver. The walls here were closer, rough, looming in the shadows cast by the flickering orange torch. "Then why are we here?"

Erran stopped in front of a large, thick-looking oak door with a keyhole symbol above the actual lock, then produced a key from his pocket. Despite the obvious age of the door, the key turned with a well-oiled click, and the door swung open without a sound.

"For this," said Erran.

Asha stared around in wonder as she entered the vast chamber, more a warehouse than a room. The torchlight didn't reach the roof, and there was no telling how far back the walls went. Row upon row of shelves stretched out into the darkness, each holding a variety of objects.

"What is this place?"

Erran shut the door. "Administration's stockpile of 'dangerous' Gifted artifacts. Every single thing they've confiscated from the schools and the Tols since the beginning of the war."

Asha stared at him blankly for a few seconds. "These are all *Vessels*?" she asked in disbelief, gesturing to the vast assortment of objects on the shelves.

"Mostly. There are some books thought too valuable to burn. Plenty of things confiscated for spite rather than because they posed a threat. But if you pick something up, chances are it's a Vessel."

Asha shook her head, dazed; given the price Administration put on Vessels, the contents of this room represented hundreds of thousands of gold pieces. Maybe more. "How do you..."

"One of the many benefits to having the head of the Administrators on our side. Aside from Elocien, there's only one other man who has access—Ionis, Administration's chief adviser in the palace. He rarely comes down here, though, so we should be safe."

Asha took a closer look at one of the shelves. The items on it looked innocuous enough. "What do they do?"

"All sorts of things. Administration took anything they thought could be used as weapons, but nearly half were confiscated because the Tols couldn't give a satisfactory answer as to what they were for. Some fire bursts of energy, plain and simple.

Some can blow a hole through ten feet of stone, or put people to sleep, or create illusions." Erran smiled. "Some allow you to turn invisible."

Asha paused. "*That's* why I didn't see you come into my room, back at the Tol." She'd wondered about that a few times since she'd arrived, but other questions had always taken precedence.

"We didn't want anyone to know we were there until we could talk to you." Erran moved over to a nearby shelf and picked up a torc. Its shape was similar to the twisting, sinuous one of a Shackle, but this one gleamed silver, not black. "This is what we used. We call it a Veil."

Asha frowned. "How did Elocien use it, though? He doesn't have a Reserve."

"Neither do I." Erran gave her a crooked smile. "As long as these are filled with Essence beforehand, they'll work. Without a Reserve to tap into, they last about an hour before the Essence decays."

Asha frowned. "What do you mean, you don't have a Reserve?"

"None of us Augurs do." Erran shrugged. "We can use Essence, but we get it from external sources. We're not like the Gifted in that respect."

"Oh." Suddenly Davian's struggles with Essence made a lot more sense. The thought, like all those involving Davian, came with a sharp pang of loss. "So...do you have the Mark, then?"

"I don't—we only get one if we use quite a large amount of Essence at once. Fessi doesn't have one, either, but Kol got his before we realized what would happen. He has to keep his arm covered all the time now."

"I see." Asha stared at the torc in Erran's hand. She hadn't missed being Gifted more than at that moment.

Erran bared his forearm, then touched the open end of the torc to it. Immediately the metal twisted, became fluid, melding itself to his skin until his arm was rippling silver in the torchlight.

Then he vanished.

Asha blinked. "Erran?"

"Still here," came Erran's voice. Suddenly he was visible again, the silver torc back in his hand. He held it out to her with a grin. "Want to try it?"

Asha hesitated. A part of her did want to—badly—but she

knew, deep down, it would just be a disappointment. A hollow echo of what it was like to use Essence. She shook her head.

"Why did you bring me down here?" she asked, looking away.

Erran's smile faded as he saw the expression on her face. Nodding to himself, he moved over a few shelves and located a bound book. He handed it to her silently.

"What's this?"

"The Journal from before the war."

Asha stared down at the tome in her hands. "The...*Augurs'* Journal?"

"Yes." Erran gently opened the book for her, then flipped through some pages. "Here. Read some of these."

Asha did so, her frown deepening as she scanned through the pages of visions. One entry spoke of an earthquake in the south, destroying the city of Prythe. Another described a massive fire in Ilin Illan, with the palace burning to the ground, along with many of the other buildings in the Upper District. A different vision foretold an assassin's taking of Emperor Uphrai's life, plunging the Eastern Empire into civil war. Each one was long, detailed, and confirmed by other Augurs.

"None of these happened," she said eventually.

Erran nodded. "You want to know how I deal with what I See?" He gestured to the Journal. "I hope I'm like them. I hope I'm wrong."

Asha stared at him, then back at the book in her hands. "So the invasion you foresaw..."

"No. Don't get the wrong idea," said Erran hurriedly. "Nothing Fessi, Kol, or I have Seen has *ever* failed to come to pass." He sighed. "Honestly, I don't think it's *likely* that I'm wrong, Ashalia. We have to assume that everything we See will happen. But... it still gives me hope. And that's something."

Asha flipped farther through the book, a little stunned. Her brow furrowed as she came to the end. "There are pages missing," she said, pointing to some ragged edges near the spine.

"Quite a few," agreed Erran. "We think whoever recovered the Journal after the Night of Ravens must have taken them before handing it over to Administration. With the Augurs and their Scribe dead, there was no way to know what was in them."

Asha nodded. She kept looking through the book for a while, then handed it back. "Thank you," she said sincerely. Erran had been right. Knowing just how wrong the Augurs had been once before...it helped, somehow. Made their visions just a sliver less terrible.

Erran inclined his head. "It's only right that you have all the facts. You're as much a part of this as us now. You need to know it's possible." He put the Journal back in its position on the shelf, then gestured to the door. "We should head back before Representative Alac comes looking for you."

Asha gave an absent nod, but her mind was on something else. She stared around at the rows upon rows of Vessels stretching away from them. "The invasion...wouldn't some of these be able to help against whatever is coming?"

Erran shook his head. "The First Tenet would still prevent the Gifted from using them. Even from charging them, in most cases—it's still intent to use Essence against non-Gifted." He sighed. "We thought about it long and hard, believe me. But many need a Reserve to even work, and most of those that don't still need the mental training to control them. The Veils are an exception—and there are only three of them. Nearly everything else was designed to be used by the Gifted."

Asha nodded, disappointed. "Of course." She hesitated. "One last question before we leave. Who's Commander Hael?"

Erran's expression twisted, and he took a few seconds to reply. "I don't think you would have seen him—he's only around the palace now and then. He's in the army, as you've probably already deduced. Big man, gray hair, long scar above his left eye?" He gave an uncomfortable shrug once he saw the description wasn't familiar. "I've Read him, a couple of times, just to be sure. He doesn't even know who I am, and he's not an especially violent man. So...I have no idea why he would stab me." He stared at the ground, and Asha could tell he didn't want to talk about it any further.

"Sorry," said Asha. "I shouldn't pry."

Erran shook his head. "No, it's fine. I've just never talked about it with anyone before."

"Not even Kol and Fessi?"

"Especially not them." Erran raised an eyebrow. "We can't discuss our visions, remember? Otherwise this whole system is pointless."

"Oh, of course. That...must be hard." Asha was silent for a moment. "What about Elocien?"

"Elocien?" Erran seemed not to understand what she was asking for a second. Then he gave a short laugh. "To talk to about this sort of thing? No, we never did. It's just...not the same." He shuffled his feet, looking impatient. "We really should hurry. The last thing we need is the Representative asking questions about where you were at this time of the morning."

Asha nodded her agreement. They exited the room, Erran locking the door behind them, and began walking back into the main structure of the palace.

Asha was relieved to see that Michal wasn't already waiting when they reached her rooms. She said a quick good-bye to Erran, then slipped inside, wondering if there was time for a quick nap before Michal arrived.

She'd barely climbed back into bed when there was a knock on the door.

Muttering to herself, Asha opened the door to find Michal waiting. He looked at her with a pleased expression.

"You're already up," he said with an approving smile. "Good to see you're getting into a routine."

Asha opened her mouth to correct him, then just gave a resigned nod, falling into step alongside the Elder. "So what are we studying this morning?"

"Something a little more practical, actually." Michal glanced behind them to make sure no one was listening, then lowered his voice. "There was an interesting piece of news last night—it's worrying, but it's also something that could significantly change our position here. Once it becomes public knowledge, we may get more visitors than I can handle. I need to prepare you to meet with some of the minor Houses by yourself."

Asha frowned, taken aback. "What was the news?"

"An unknown army has been sighted within Andarra's borders,

to the north." Michal grimaced. "Invasion, from the sounds of it."

Asha went cold. Michal was still talking, but she didn't hear whatever he was saying.

The Augurs had been right. The attack on Ilin Illan was coming.

# Chapter 23

Wirr couldn't help but smile as Dezia laughed, admiring the way her deep blue eyes shone when she was enjoying herself.

They were sitting a little way away from the others, within sight of the camp but not so close that anyone could overhear their conversation. Evening was falling, and Taeris had just told them that by his estimate, they were less than a day from reaching Deilannis.

As a result the group was in good spirits. Since the sha'teth had spoken to them ten days earlier, the only trouble they'd encountered had been occasional Desrielite patrols along the road, all of which they had avoided easily enough. Taeris and Nihim were wary because of how straightforward their passage had been—both insisted that the sha'teth would not have given up its pursuit—but their fears had done little to dampen the mood.

Wirr's own mood was as close to positive as it had been since they had left Thrindar. He still grieved for his friends; he knew he probably would for a long time. But the pain was fading, settling. Becoming bearable. For the first time, he felt as though he was moving forward again.

He glanced across at Davian, smile fading as he wondered whether his friend felt the same way. He hoped so. They'd spoken little of the school in recent times; the days on the road had been long, and there had been few opportunities for truly private conversation.

"You're worried about him." Dezia had followed his gaze.

Wirr gave an absent nod. The others knew about what had

happened at the school—after a few days of traveling, it had seemed better to just get it all out in the open. Still, despite everyone's heartfelt sympathies, Dezia was the only one who had managed to make Wirr feel comfortable discussing it. "I've tried talking to him a couple of times, but...I don't know what to say. He's lost so much."

"As much as you," Dezia pointed out quietly.

"No." Wirr shook his head. "It's been hard for me, too, but... he's been at that school all his life. He was a servant there before he ever got the Mark. Those people were my friends, but they were his family."

And there had been Asha, too. The pain Wirr felt for her loss, he knew Davian felt tenfold. But that wasn't his grief to share.

Dezia looked at him for a long moment. "You think he blames you."

"How could he not?" Wirr asked softly. "He says he doesn't, but it's my fault."

"It's the fault of whoever did it," Dezia said in gentle rebuke. "Davian's still grieving, Wirr—you both are. Even I can see that. If he's not talking much, that's probably his way of dealing with what he's going through. Some people just need space. I wouldn't assume it's because he's angry with you."

Wirr sighed. "I hope you're right."

There was silence for a while, though it was a companionable one. Eventually Dezia lay back, gazing up at the stars.

"Was it difficult, when you first went to the school?"

Wirr frowned. "Difficult?"

"Leaving Ilin Illan. Pretending to be someone you're not." She raised her head to look at him. "I mean—I've spent a lot of time around Karaliene, so I can imagine how people would have treated you in the palace. To go from that to nothing..." She shrugged. "It seems like it would have been a difficult transition."

Wirr shook his head, feeling a pang of sorrow as he did every time he thought of the school. "Maybe a little, at first—but there were things at Caladel that I never could have had as a prince. Things I hadn't even imagined growing up in Ilin Illan."

"Like what?"

"Anonymity. Free time. Real friendship."

Dezia nodded slowly. "I suppose I can see how you would make that trade," she conceded. She cocked her head to the side. "Is that why you left with Davian?"

Wirr grunted. "Karaliene asked me the same question."

"Your cousin can be very insightful."

"Sometimes." Wirr shook his head. "Honestly, I don't know. I came because I thought it was important to find out what was going on with the Boundary, with the sig'nari. And especially because I didn't want Dav to be out here alone. For all his intelligence, he's naive in many ways; he'd never been out in the real world before. He needed me along." He shrugged. "But I won't lie. The thought of going back to Ilin Illan, leaving my friends in the school behind and pretending I'd never been there, didn't sit well, either. Maybe that influenced my decision, maybe it didn't. It's hard to say."

There was silence for a few moments, then Wirr turned to Dezia. "What about you?"

Dezia frowned. "What about me?"

Wirr gestured around him. "You said you came because of your brother, but I remember most of the girls from the Houses—even if they were somehow forced to come on a journey like this, they would be kicking and screaming most of the way. I haven't heard a word of complaint from you."

Dezia raised an eyebrow. "Are you saying I'm not ladylike?"

Wirr grinned. "I'm saying that you had the opportunity to stay with Karaliene and enjoy an easy trip back to Ilin Illan, but you chose to come with us. I know a lot of that is from loyalty to your brother, but you don't strike me as someone who's pining to be home, either."

Dezia smiled. "I suppose that's true," she admitted. She thought for a moment. "Life in the palace can be...difficult, sometimes. I don't hate it, but I'm in no rush to return to it, either."

"Any particular reason?"

Dezia gave an awkward shrug. "Being the king's ward, and friends with Karaliene, isn't always the easiest position to be in."

Wirr nodded slowly. "People see you as an easily accessible way to influence her...and maybe my uncle, too?" he deduced.

"Exactly." Dezia sighed. "Most days someone manages to corner me, trying to convince me of one thing or another.

A tax should be raised. A law should be changed. The king should know about this nobleman's bad behavior. And there are always…'incentives' for me, should I decide to help." She shrugged. "Recently it's changed from that to suggestions about whom I should be marrying. Houses sending their sons to court me, after Karaliene turns them away." She scowled. "That I hate most of all. And a lot of them don't understand that persistence won't change my mind."

Wirr frowned. "They won't leave you alone?"

Dezia shook her head. "Several of them were apparently told by their fathers to woo me at all costs. I've had more expressions of undying love in the last few months than I would want to see in a lifetime." She gave a small, humorless laugh. "Though that may stop now."

"Why's that?"

Dezia hesitated, looking embarrassed. "I shot one of them. Just before I left." She paused. "In fact, it may have been why Karaliene insisted I come with her and Aelric. I…wasn't too popular with House Tel'Shan."

Wirr gave her an incredulous stare. "Shot? As in, with an arrow?"

"Accidentally, and only in the shoulder. It wasn't much more than a graze," said Dezia defensively. "Denn Tel'Shan. He said he'd do anything for me, so I said I needed someone to hold up targets while I practiced." She winced at the memory, but the edges of her mouth still curled upward slightly. "The idiot didn't realize it was a joke. Then when I tried to back out by explaining to him that it was *really dangerous*, he got quite upset—said I was insulting him by suggesting that he wasn't courageous enough to do it. So I let him." She sighed. "I didn't mean to hit him, of course, but he flinched on the first arrow. Not my proudest moment, even if he did bring it on himself somewhat."

Wirr stared at her in astonishment for a moment, then gave a disbelieving laugh. "No wonder you agreed to come with us."

Dezia punched him on the arm in a reproving manner, but she smiled back.

Wirr shifted. "So how does Aelric take all of this?"

Dezia smirked. "Not well. And being the swordsman that he

is, he *is* rather handy to have as an older brother." Her smile widened a little. "Most of the time."

Wirr grinned back.

They spoke for a while longer until the smells of cooking wafted over to them, and they reluctantly made their way back over to the others. The rest of the evening proved to be uneventful, and soon Wirr was lying down to sleep, a warm feeling in the pit of his stomach whenever he thought of Dezia.

In the back of his mind, though—and as hard as it was to remember sometimes—was the unavoidable truth of his position. He was a prince of the realm. There was a good chance that when the time came, his father would tell him with which girls he could socialize. Or, more to the point, with which House he should be allying himself.

Still, out here, in the open air and away from the eyes of the nobility and his responsibilities, he could dream.

◈

*Davian frowned at the dusty plain stretching out before him.*

*Where was he? A moment ago he had been bedding down to sleep on the road through the Menaath Mountains; his mind was clear, sharp, with none of the fuzziness he would have expected from a dream.*

*He looked around, trying to get his bearings. Behind him was a thick tangle of forest, but the trees were unlike anything he'd seen in Desriel. In front was a vast plain, in the middle of which a mountain range rose abruptly, majestically, silhouetted against the setting sun. The tallest mountain was cut in two, as if a great knife had carved a thin slice from its very core; the orange sunset shone directly through the gap, making each half of the mountain stand out in sharp relief.*

*Though he'd never been here before, Davian recognized it; many artists had rendered this very image on canvas. He was looking at Ilin Tora.*

*He shifted his attention back to the plain. Dotted across it, small groups of men in black armor moved with mechanical efficiency as they built fires and cooked food. Davian frowned as he studied them. Many were wearing helmets in addition to their* armor—but where there should have been a slit or holes for eyes, there was only smooth, dark metal. How could they possibly see what they were doing? Yet each man moved with an assured air, none looking even slightly troubled by their apparent lack of vision. Over each face was inscribed a single large symbol: three wavy vertical lines encapsulated by a circle. An insignia, perhaps?

Davian just stood for another minute or so, eyes narrowed as he observed the proceedings. Each fire was manned by a single soldier without a helmet, who simply watched as the other men went about their tasks. Commanders of some kind, presumably, though there were certainly a lot of them. He shivered as he watched. The entire picture was...unsettling.

Was he dreaming? He could feel the last of the day's heat still radiating from the ground, the dryness of the air in his lungs. He pinched himself sharply on the wrist, wincing as the pain registered.

No, not dreaming. He was here.

Suddenly he noticed a tall, helmetless warrior with an authoritative air striding among the fires. Motion ceased where he passed; even those who appeared to have no way of seeing him paused in their tasks, turning to watch. He left the hush of expectation in his wake.

The man stopped in the center of the camp and raised his hand; immediately soldiers everywhere leaped to their feet, leaving what they were doing and pressing toward him eagerly. There was unmistakable excitement, a sense of anticipation that was palpable.

The general, as Davian thought of him, waited until every eye was on him. His features were rugged, with scars crisscrossing his face liberally. His black hair was shoulder length, tied back.

He gazed over his men calmly. His eyes were hard and proud.

"Two thousand years," he said, barely loudly enough to be heard by the men in front. He shook his head. "Too long."

There were murmurs of agreement among the soldiers, but the general raised his hand, silencing them immediately. He stood straighter, taller, pride in his stance. This time he shouted so that all could hear him.

"Two thousand years our people have waited for justice. Two thousand years of survival, of struggle, of sacrifice. But our time has finally come! We have broken free of our prison. We are at last ready to face our ancient foe, and you who have passed through the ilshara unscathed are truly worthy of this fight.

"You all know me, or know of me. My name is Andan Mash'aan, Slayer of Lih'khaag, Second Sword of Danaris. My trust is in the steel on my hip and the men at my side. My faith is in the plans of the Protector and our resolve to carry them out."

He looked out upon them with a fierceness that made Davian take an involuntary step back. "By all these things, by my name and honor, by my life itself, I swear this one thing to you. When our task here is complete, this country will burn. Her rivers will run red. Her armies will be like dust beneath our feet. Her women will scream and her children will weep."

He raised his sword, screaming the last with fire in his eyes. "Andarra will fall. We will have our revenge."

The roar of approval rolled over Davian like a wave, thunderous in his ears.

⚜

Davian shivered despite the afternoon heat.

The road had disappeared and the forest had become thick, almost impassable, as the day progressed, slowing them to a crawl as they hacked their way forward and upward through hundreds of years of undisturbed growth. Something about the forest was unsettling here; the shadows writhed and shifted in ways that did not marry with the movement of the trees, and it felt as though eyes were on them at every moment. The trees themselves were thick, bent and twisted, looming over them as if angered by their intrusion. No birds sang, and Davian had not heard the sounds of any other wildlife since early in the morning.

He hadn't mentioned his odd dream of the previous night to anyone, not even Wirr. He'd spent the entire morning telling himself that it meant nothing—that Taeris's talk of dangers beyond the Boundary had somehow brought it on—but deep down he knew that wasn't true. He remembered every detail as if he had actually lived through it. He *never* remembered his dreams.

Though he did his best to ignore the knowledge, what he'd seen had to have been Foresight.

In some ways the development was actually a welcome distraction, something else to focus on. Too often since Thrindar he'd found his thoughts drifting to Asha. Picturing her face, her smile, and then gritting his teeth at the fierce, aching pain those memories produced.

He missed her. He'd never be able to speak with her again, never have a chance to tell her how he really felt. There was still a deep sadness at the death of Mistress Alita, Talean, all the others, too—but the thoughts of Asha were always worse, always more intense.

He looked up as Taeris, who was leading the group, sliced through some more vines and emerged onto what appeared to be a cliff top. The scarred man stopped, turning to the others with a half-relieved, half-worried expression.

"We're here," he announced.

Davian reached the top of the rise, his eyes widening as he took in the sight, troubles momentarily forgotten.

They were at the edge of a downward slope that was almost steep enough to describe as sheer; several sets of broken stairs wound their way sharply downward to what appeared to be the remnants of a small village below. No movement was visible in the streets; the buildings were crumbling shells, each one missing its roof and at least one wall. The stillness was eerie in the fading light.

Beyond the group of houses, the ground vanished into a vast chasm; the sound of distantly thundering water echoed even to where they were standing. Davian realized that if he were to go to the edge of that chasm he would be able to peer down and see the white, churning waters of the Lantarche River far below.

A massive bridge stretched out at least a hundred feet over the abyss, maybe more, before vanishing into thick mist. It was made of a white stone that gleamed in the last rays of the day; no cracks or joins were evident, as if the entire thing had been carved from one enormous piece of rock. From this distance it looked wide enough to comfortably take five men walking abreast—perhaps even wider. Despite its length, Davian could not see any supports;

it simply extended out in a smooth, straight line until it was eventually swallowed from view.

It was the mist, however, that made him pause. Unnaturally thick and dark, it hung like a shroud in the middle of the chasm; it devoured the waning sunlight, making the entire scene feel colder and darker than it should have. Staring out at it, Davian suddenly realized he could make out vague shapes within it—the very tops of houses and other structures within the city. If he had not seen those, he might not have believed there was anything at all between the two sides of the gorge.

"Deilannis," Wirr murmured beside him in an awestruck voice.

Taeris dismounted. "We will have to leave the horses," he observed regretfully.

"Will they survive?" protested Dezia.

"There's a good chance they'll make their way back to the road." Taeris gestured to his own mount, which was whickering softly, rolling its eyes so it didn't have to look upon the city below. "Animals have a sense about this place—they want to get away from it as quickly as possible. By the time they lose that feeling, they should be back where someone will find them."

Dezia looked as if she was going to object, but then took another look at the narrow, crumbling steps and remained silent. They began unpacking their mounts, taking as much food and water as they could comfortably carry. Taeris quickly fed each horse in turn, then gave it a slap to send it on its way. As he'd predicted, the animals didn't need much motivation, moving back along the path the humans had carved through the forest at a steady trot.

The group made its way carefully down one of the many stairways, which were etched straight from the rocky sides of the cliff. The steps were narrow and quite steep; Davian forced himself to focus on each one, taking care not to slip. Grass and weeds had long ago begun creeping through cracks in the stone; though the stairs had doubtless once been well maintained, shale and other loose rubble now made the descent a dangerous undertaking.

Finally they had picked their way safely to the bottom. The thundering of the Lantarche was louder now, though the air remained unnaturally absent other sounds. The sun had slipped below the horizon, and the dark, empty husks of buildings glowered at the party as they trudged through the narrow streets. An occasional gust of wind blew a loose window shutter that was somehow still on its hinges, making everyone flinch and look around nervously.

"Perhaps we should make camp for the night here, and cross Deilannis in the morning," Aelric suggested.

Taeris hesitated, then gave a reluctant nod. "It wouldn't hurt to be rested when we try the city," he agreed.

They made a rudimentary camp and settled in, trying to ignore the sinister feeling of the abandoned town around them.

A couple of hours had passed when a prickling on the back of Davian's neck made him twist in his seated position. He looked up; at the top of the cliff-side stairs, silhouetted against the fading light, stood two figures. The wind was blowing, yet their cloaks did not seem to move.

"Taeris," he said, not taking his eyes from the scene.

Taeris followed Davian's line of sight and inhaled sharply. "Get to the bridge. Run."

Davian sat rooted to the spot for a few more seconds.

The figures moved.

Suddenly they were starting down the stairs; they seemed to move casually, almost lazily, but their progress was terrifyingly quick. There was a flash of light, and the earth in front of Davian erupted, showering him with shale.

Spurred into motion, he and the others scrambled to their feet and ran.

They were already close to the bridge. Davian knew that it could not have taken him more than twenty seconds to reach its edge, but it felt like an eternity; around him bursts of power flew past, any one of which would have torn his body apart if it had struck him. Some of the houses, already decaying, collapsed entirely as bolts of light smashed through their foundations, sending clouds of dust and grit into the air.

He was the last to reach the bridge; without hesitation he ran onto its smooth surface, the roaring of the Lantarche far below crashing in his ears. A few paces in he slipped, tumbling. The stone was so smooth that it didn't even badly graze his skin; he rolled over, scrambling to his feet.

He turned to see how far behind the sha'teth were, and let out a cry of terror.

The two figures stood at the very edge of the bridge, less than five feet from Davian. The shadows hid their faces, but he could feel the malice, the frustration, in their gaze. Vaguely, behind him, he could hear someone calling his name—Aelric, he thought— but all his senses were consumed by the black-cloaked creatures in front of him.

For a long moment, Davian was sure he was going to die.

Then he was backing away as fast as he could. The sha'teth just stood there, watching him. The bolts of Essence had stopped.

A hand clasped his shoulder from behind; he leaped, heart racing, before he realized it was Taeris's.

"What are they doing?" Davian whispered, eyes still fixed on the sha'teth.

"Either they cannot cross, or they refuse to," Taeris puffed, out of breath from the sprint. He glanced over his shoulder, toward the mist-wreathed city. "The Law of Decay is warped from the edges of the bridges inward. They know that if they try to attack us with Essence now, it would simply...dissolve before it reached us."

"But why did they wait until now to show themselves?" asked Dezia, looking puzzled. "They've had our trail for nearly two weeks."

"Perhaps they were trying to force us into the city all along." It was Caeden, watching the creatures at the edge of the bridge worriedly. Nobody said anything to that, but the mere possibility sent a shiver down Davian's spine.

Taeris shook his head. "No. The first must have been waiting for the second. He just got here too late." He bit his lip as he stared at the sha'teth. "First she speaks Andarran. Then she waits for reinforcements at the risk of losing us. A survival instinct. Something *is* different," he murmured, almost to himself.

Suddenly one of the creatures—Davian could not tell which one—spoke. "He belongs to us, Taeris Sarr," it hissed. "Give him over and you may yet live." The voice was not angry, or even insistent. It was completely devoid of emotion.

Taeris just motioned in the other direction. "Ignore them," he said quietly. "Let's move."

No one voiced a complaint, and they started silently along the long, open bridge. After a minute Davian looked back. The sha'teth were still just standing there, watching.

Then the mists closed around him, hiding the creatures and the desolate town from view.

He turned his head forward again, facing into the thick white murk.

They had reached Deilannis.

# Chapter 24

Wirr took a deep breath, heart still hammering.

He threw a nervous glance over his shoulder, relieved to see that the mists had finally hidden the sha'teth and their unsettling stares from view. He slowed his pace a little, breathing evening out as the end of the bridge became visible up ahead. A flight of stairs led sharply downward; below, stretching away into the fog, the rooftops of hundreds of abandoned buildings were barely discernible through the haze.

Taeris came to a gradual halt at the top of the stairs, and everyone followed suit. Wirr gave an involuntary cough as he stared into the city. The atmosphere here was thicker, damp and hard to breathe. The mood of Deilannis was even heavier and more oppressive than it had looked from the outside.

"Are we safe?" Wirr asked Taeris.

Taeris looked around at the forbidding mists, then nodded, though his expression was still grim. "From the sha'teth at least."

Dezia shivered, walking up to stand beside Wirr. "What if we get through, and they're waiting for us on the other side?"

"They won't be. There's not a crossing for at least two hundred miles in any direction. Even with their speed, it would take them several days to get there." Taeris paused, then rummaged around in his bag, producing four Shackles. "Before we go any further…"

Wirr sighed. "They're really necessary?"

"We've already talked about this," said Taeris, his tone firm. "You all need to wear one. The Contract will let me sense you—if we get separated, it's the only way I'll be able to find you."

Aelric looked at the Shackle with obvious distaste. "I'm still worried about what happens if you *don't* find us. I don't want to wear that thing for the rest of my life."

Taeris gave a long-suffering sigh. "If I don't find you then either I will be dead, in which case the Shackle will come off of its own accord, or you will be dead, in which case you won't terribly mind."

Dezia pushed past her brother, rolling up her sleeve. "We know. We're happy to do it," she said, glaring at Aelric.

Taeris nodded as if there had been no issue, touching the Shackle to Dezia's wrist. The young woman stared as the torc sealed itself, touching it lightly. "I don't feel any different," she reassured Aelric.

Aelric hesitated, then reluctantly submitted himself to the same process. He gave an irritable tug at the twisted metal band once it was on, but did not appear to suffer any ill effects. Davian followed, and then Taeris held up the last Shackle to Wirr, gesturing for him to come forward.

"What about Nihim?" asked Wirr, realizing the priest didn't have one.

Taeris shook his head. "There aren't enough Shackles." He turned to Nihim. "If you're separated..."

"It's fine," said Nihim. "I've studied maps of Deilannis. If it happens, I can figure out the way through."

Taeris and Nihim exchanged a look, so brief that Wirr immediately wondered if he'd imagined it. Then Taeris was turning back to him. "Your turn."

Wirr sighed. He hated Shackles. He wasn't as badly affected as some Gifted, but whenever he wore one he still felt significantly slower, weaker. He held out his arm, and Taeris touched the torc to it.

Pain lanced through Wirr's head.

He gave an involuntary cry as his knees buckled; he scrabbled desperately at the metal as it slithered around his arm, trying his utmost to rip it off. It was hard to breathe...

And then he was lying on the cool, smooth stone of the bridge. He took a few long, shaky breaths, vision clearing to reveal everyone crowded around him, their faces taut with concern. Taeris was kneeling at his side, the Shackle back in his hand, his face pale.

"Wirr. Can you hear me?" Taeris asked urgently. "Are you all right?"

Wirr groaned, elevating himself on one elbow. "A little dizzy, but...I think I'll be fine."

Taeris exhaled in relief. "Good." His brow furrowed. "What happened? Have you ever had a reaction like that to a Shackle before?"

"Never." Wirr climbed to his feet with Davian's assistance. "I sometimes get a little shaky or nauseous, but that was..." He shook his head, at a loss for words.

There was silence for a few moments.

"Should we be wearing these?" Aelric asked nervously.

"Whatever happened to Wirr happened as soon as he put the Shackle on. You'll be fine," said Taeris, waving away the question. His eyes never left Wirr.

"I think I'm going to have to risk Deilannis without a Shackle," noted Wirr, still a little groggy.

"I think you are," agreed Taeris. "Just...don't try to use Essence while we're in the city. Under any circumstances."

Wirr frowned. "I thought you said it has no effect here."

"It doesn't. And we have no idea why." Taeris rubbed his forehead. "For all we know, it's by design. Essence could be dangerous here, somehow."

"Or it could attract whatever guards this place," pointed out Caeden.

"Exactly." Taeris acknowledged Caeden with a nod. "Regardless of the reasons—if you're not going to be wearing a Shackle..."

"I'll be careful," promised Wirr.

"Good." Taeris gave him an appraising look. "Can you walk?"

Wirr nodded; his head still ached, but everything else appeared to be functioning normally. "I'll be fine."

Taeris turned to Nihim, holding out the Shackle in his hand and raising an eyebrow.

"Not a chance," said Nihim firmly.

Taeris gave the ghost of a smile. "Then we should move." He turned to the others. "Keep the talking to a minimum. Whatever's in here, we want to do as little as possible to attract its attention."

Without anything further they headed down the stairs from the bridge and into the city itself.

After a few minutes of walking in uneasy silence, Wirr found himself next to Taeris. "So you've been through the city from Narut," he said conversationally, trying to provide himself with a distraction.

Taeris gave an absent nod, never pausing in his scanning of the road ahead. "The Narut and Desriel bridges are actually quite close together," he said quietly. "Unfortunately, the Andarran bridge is on the other side of the city. According to the maps, anyway."

"You've never been there?" Wirr kept his voice low, but he couldn't stop it from taking on a slightly panicked note. "How can you be sure you know the way?"

Taeris shrugged. "Now you mention it, I'm not sure I even recognize the layout of these streets. Don't tell the others, but I think we may be lost."

Wirr's eyes widened, then narrowed as the corners of Taeris's mouth twitched upward for a brief moment, betraying the scarred man's amusement at Wirr's expense.

"That was not funny," Wirr grumbled.

Taeris did not take his eyes off the road ahead. "It was a little funny. Now be quiet."

Wirr lapsed into silence.

Despite his admission, Taeris walked the route they were taking with confidence, and whenever he made a turn it seemed to be because he recognized certain landmarks along the way. They progressed in almost complete silence, none of them straying farther than the reach of the torches, fixing their eyes on the road ahead. Everyone walked with their heads slightly bowed, as if trying to ignore the buildings in their peripheral vision.

Wirr found himself doing the same; looking too closely at his surroundings only fed his unease. Every road was clean and every building looked as if it were newly made, with not a hint of rot or decay. As if it was being maintained.

"I'm beginning to think the sha'teth had the right idea," he whispered to Davian. "This place makes my skin crawl."

A sharp look from Nihim silenced Davian before he could reply, and they pressed on mutely.

They made their way mainly along the one road, which was

wide enough that their torchlight barely penetrated the mists as far as its edges. Soon they came to a giant archway that, like the rest of the city, was still wholly intact. Sitting atop the arch itself was a pike; impaled on it sat a leering skull, the bleached white seeming to glow in the surrounding gloom. It was the only skeletal remains they had seen since entering the city.

Wirr felt a chill as he looked at it. There was something... *wrong* about it, aside from the obvious. Something disturbing, though he couldn't put his finger on what.

Davian had noticed it, too. "Creepy," he muttered to Wirr, shivering.

Caeden stepped toward them, having overheard. "This is the entrance to the inner city," he said, staring at the skull. "The Door of Iladriel. When we pass through, we will be in Deilannis proper."

Wirr raised an eyebrow at him. "How do you know that?"

Caeden shrugged. "I just do," he said distantly, gaze shifting to the stone structure itself. Then he frowned, turning to Taeris. "I... would not have thought this was the fastest way to the Andarran bridge."

Taeris had stopped in front of the archway. He looked at Caeden for a long moment, his gaze inscrutable. "You're right," he said. "This is the southern entrance to the inner city. I only know the way from maps—the originals of which are almost two thousand years old. I didn't want to get lost."

"What lies in there?" asked Aelric, eyes searching the darkness beyond the archway for any sign of movement.

Taeris shook his head. "No one knows. I don't believe anyone has passed through this part of the city since Devaed's time."

The group was silent as it digested this information. "We could go back," suggested Dezia.

Taeris shook his head. "The sha'teth are not fools. They will have split up, one of them staying on the Desriel side to ensure we don't double back."

For a moment everyone hesitated, then Dezia stepped forward.

"Then I suppose we shouldn't delay," she said. Before anyone could stop her, she was striding through the archway.

Davian exchanged a look with Wirr. Taking deep breaths to

steel themselves, they moved beneath the archway's grinning skull and into the inner city.

❧

Davian beckoned to Caeden, who was staring at the enormous archway as if mesmerized.

"Caeden!" he hissed in a harried whisper. The sound jerked Caeden into action; the young man took a last look at the archway and hurried after them into the inner city.

Davian took a long glance at the archway himself, wondering what Caeden had been looking at. The Door of Iladriel, he'd called it. A memory. Had there been something else, though? Something he wasn't telling them?

He shivered again as he looked up at the skull piked atop the stones. If Caeden was concealing something, he was probably doing them a favor.

Everyone was deathly silent now as they walked; Davian often found himself holding his breath, so intent was he on hearing any sound that was out of the ordinary. As they crept closer to the center of the city, he began to notice subtle changes in their surroundings. The mists thinned, and a gray light gradually became apparent, illuminating everything in drab monochrome. The buildings here were mostly the same as in the outer city, untouched by the ravages of time—however, some had smashed windows or doors crumpled inward, and others bore the scars of fire.

Occasionally Davian thought he caught a glimpse of movement from the corner of his eye, but every time he spun, there was no one there. He could see his tenseness reflected in the faces of the others, including Taeris. Something about this place felt very wrong.

Soon he began to notice that the structures in this section of the city were less cramped, grander and far more distinctive than the close-packed houses they had already passed.

Dezia suddenly stopped.

"What is it?" she whispered, staring at Caeden. The others stopped, too, all turning to Caeden curiously.

The young man bit his lip. "I...know this place," he said, keeping his voice soft. Despite some uncertainty, there was also excitement in his tone.

He took a couple of steps forward, pointing to an enormous building with giant columns of white marble. "We are in the main street of the city. That is the Great Library of Deilannis." He pointed to a structure a little farther down the road. "That is the Ashac Temple, where worshippers would go each Seventhday to hear the word of the One God preached." He pointed again, confident now, this time to a wide roadway that curved off to the left. "That road is known as the Scythe. Follow it for another five minutes, and you would come to a massive marketplace." He smiled, a flush of excitement on his cheeks. "I think from here, I could even guide us to the Northern Bridge."

Taeris placed his hand on Caeden's shoulder. "That's good, lad." Davian could see a mixture of fascination and concern in his eyes. "I don't wish to dampen your enthusiasm, but—do you actually recall being here? I've not been into the inner city before, but I do recognize many of these buildings from the texts I've collected over the years. Are you sure you're not simply remembering things you've read?"

Caeden shook his head, still staring around, absently rubbing at the wolf tattoo on his wrist as he did so. "I don't think so."

Taeris gave Caeden a considering look for a few moments, then just nodded. "Let me know if anything else comes back."

They moved on, drawing ever closer to the center of the city. Soon they came to a fork in the road, and Taeris led them without hesitation to the left.

Caeden stopped in his tracks.

"Taeris," he called quietly, uncertainty in his voice. "I think that's the wrong way."

Everyone paused, and Taeris turned to Caeden. "I know where I'm going," he whispered firmly, so that everyone could hear. "I know you think you remember this place, but I am quite certain."

Caeden didn't look convinced, but eventually inclined his head. "If you're certain," he said, reluctance still clear in his tone.

They walked for a few more minutes until Taeris abruptly signaled a stop, looking up at an unusual structure on the side of the road. It was less a building than a spire, twisting at impossible angles as it stretched skyward and only twenty feet wide at its base, just large enough to accommodate the broad double doors set into its facade. Davian couldn't quite see, but he suspected it stretched well back from the street.

Suddenly a piercing shriek cut across the silence. Davian spun, trying to determine the direction from which it had come, but all was still.

"What was that?" asked Aelric, his voice thick with apprehension.

Taeris shook his head. "Stay alert," was all he said, casting a longing glance toward the building. He took a deep, steadying breath. "And stay here. I'll return soon."

"What?" whispered Wirr in disbelief. "You're going in there? Why?"

Taeris didn't have time to respond before another cry came. This time it was deeper, clearly a man's voice; the sound was so full of pain that Aelric's sword was out of its sheath before anyone else could even move. He held it for a moment, wary, scanning the road ahead before slowly sheathing it again. No one chuckled at the reaction. Davian felt blood pounding in his ears, his muscles tensed.

Then he strangled a yell. He'd been looking at one of the buildings, and for the briefest of moments there had been someone standing in the doorway and staring straight at them. The expression on the man's face had been... quizzical, with neither alarm nor malice in his gaze.

Then the stranger was gone again. Vanished.

"What?" hissed Taeris, his tone a mixture of fear and anger at the comparative loudness of Davian's cry.

Davian didn't take his eyes from the building. "There was a man in that doorway," he said, gesturing toward where he had seen the figure.

Taeris's eyebrows rose. "Are you sure?"

Davian nodded mutely.

Taeris grimaced and looked about to say something else when Caeden gasped, pointing in a different direction. They all spun to see a young woman standing in the middle of the road, looking at them with an expression of curiosity. Taeris made to step toward her, but even as he moved, she was gone again.

"Illusions," muttered Aelric. His comment was punctuated by another scream, though this one sounded farther away.

Taeris shook his head slowly. "I don't think so."

Suddenly Wirr let out a roar of warning, and Davian spun to see a figure standing only a few feet away from them. The hair stood up on the back of his neck. At first glance he thought it was a man, though it stood head and shoulders above even Nihim, who was the tallest of the group. Then he saw the reptilian visage, the cold black eyes regarding them with undisguised rage.

Davian's eyes traveled down its body and he saw that rather than legs, it stood erect on a thick tail that trailed out behind it. Its skin was an oily dark green, almost black in the dull light of Deilannis. Thick, well-muscled arms stretched toward Dezia, who was closest to it.

Everything happened at once. There was an odd ripple of white light in the gray; Taeris screamed "No!" as the creature turned, distracted, a look of what could only be called surprise on its ugly face. Then it vanished.

Taeris rounded on Wirr, whose hands were still outstretched, his expression frozen in shock. The ripple faded, but Davian could see clearly that it had emanated from his friend's body.

"You tried to use Essence, didn't you!" Taeris hissed, looking as though he was about to strike the boy.

Wirr nodded, his face pale.

Balling his hands into fists, Taeris groaned as a cry went up from somewhere in the city. Unlike the other sounds they had heard, this was completely inhuman, a high-pitched keening that made Davian's blood freeze.

Taeris turned to Caeden, and Davian knew the older man was now genuinely frightened.

"You know the way to the Northern Bridge?" he asked.

"I think so."

Taeris pushed Caeden into motion, back the way they had come. "Then run."

Caeden stumbled into a quickly accelerating jog, and Taeris turned to the others. "All of you, follow him and do not let him out of your sight! He knows the way out."

Caeden was already disappearing down the street, and Davian

didn't need a second invitation. Wirr, Aelric, and Dezia set off at a dead run; Davian was close behind as another shriek sounded, this time much, much closer. Whatever was coming, it was moving faster than should have been possible.

Suddenly he realized that he could not hear Nihim or Taeris behind him. Risking a glance over his shoulder, he saw Nihim gripping Taeris by the arm, the two men talking in low tones. Davian hesitated, then turned, sprinting back toward them.

"Let me go, Nihim," said Taeris furiously.

Nihim shook his head. "No." He tugged on Taeris's arm. "There will be other chances, but if you leave those children to their fate, you'll never forgive yourself."

Taeris hesitated, his face a mask of frustration. "El damn you." Then he spun, spotting Davian. "What are you doing?" he bellowed. "I said RUN!" He followed his own advice, and then the three of them were sprinting after the others.

The mist, which had barely been in evidence a moment earlier, abruptly thickened until Davian could see only a few feet ahead. Taeris and Nihim were lost to view. Suddenly Davian heard a muffled cry in front of him, and he had to leap to one side to avoid stumbling over a body writhing on the ground.

He stopped, kneeling. It was Nihim; the priest was holding his ankle, face twisted in pain.

There was another cry. The creature couldn't be more than a few streets away now.

"Can you stand?" Davian asked in an urgent whisper.

Nihim sat up and pushed him hard in the chest. "Run, lad!" he said, wide-eyed. "There's no point us both dying!"

"Neither of us is going to die." Davian said the words more as a prayer than as encouragement.

The mist was so thick now that even breathing felt difficult; he felt more than saw Nihim's form, at one point stepping clumsily on the man's arm. Muttering an apology, he grabbed the priest under his armpits and hauled him into the shelter of the nearest building, wincing as he dragged him over the shattered remains of the door.

This was one of the buildings blackened by fire, though the roof and all the walls were still intact. He propped Nihim up against
the nearest wall, facing away from the street and hidden from the

view of anything outside. Davian collapsed beside him, trying to slow his breathing, straining for any sound of approaching danger. There was nothing, though. The silence was eerie.

They stayed that way for several seconds. Then the dark mists swirling around them thickened even more and the shriek sounded again, this time so close it seemed to be right on top of them. Davian and Nihim sat motionless, barely daring to breathe.

After a few moments, Davian risked glancing out the door. The mist was getting...*darker*, eddying and churning until it was more of a cloud of black smoke than fog. He shuddered. The swirling darkness spoke of nothing but death and decay.

The air grew colder as Davian watched the darkness coalesce in the middle of the street, distending and contracting until it finally formed itself into the silhouette of a man. It was unlike any man Davian had seen before, though; its skin was completely black and glistened in the dull gray light. Its hands were curved and elongated, more clawlike than anything else, and its limbs and torso were unnaturally thin.

A horrible snuffling sound erupted from it; it turned toward him and Davian sank back, covering his mouth in horror. Though its face was distorted by the fog, he could see that the creature had no eyes, a mouth filled with rows of razor-sharp teeth, and a gaping, circular hole where its nose should have been.

It raised its smooth, hairless head. The snuffling sound came again, and Davian realized with mounting terror that it was sniffing out a scent.

Then it opened its mouth wide and keened in triumph, a sound so loud and shrill that Davian and Nihim both had to put their hands over their ears.

It came into the building slowly, deliberately, as if it knew its prey was nearby and didn't need to rush. It moved for Davian with unhurried, almost lazy steps, a blade coalescing in its hand. In the corner of his mind not consumed by fear, Davian realized that the blade that was about to kill him was the same blade he'd seen the sha'teth use.

Nihim moved before Davian could stop him. He stumbled awkwardly to his feet, throwing himself between Davian and the creature.

"You cannot have him. He is not supposed to die," he said, lifting his chin in defiance. "You cannot—"

The blade moved forward in slow motion. Nihim screamed.

The following moments passed in a blur for Davian. Nihim crumpling to the floor, blood spilling from the gaping wound in his stomach. The creature moving forward through the mist as if nothing had happened.

Then it stood in front of him, its hideous, eyeless face studying his. Davian braced himself for the death blow, but the creature stopped, cocking its head and sniffing the air.

"*Ilian di,*" it said in a low, gravelly voice. It sounded angry, perhaps even disappointed. "*Sha di Davian.*" Davian's eyes widened when he heard his name, but he did not move.

Suddenly the creature exploded apart, disintegrating back into its wraithlike form, merging once again with the surrounding mists.

The unnatural, awful chill vanished from the air. They were alone once again.

# Chapter 25

Stunned, Davian didn't move until a moan from Nihim spurred him into motion.

He knelt beside the priest, whose eyes were tight with pain. Davian looked at Nihim's wound in despair. He tried to cover it with his hands, but the hot, sticky blood just pumped out between his fingers.

"What can I do?" he asked, knowing he was powerless to help.

Nihim exhaled, his breath bubbling, taking a moment to compose himself. "It knew your name," he said eventually. His tone would have been conversational had it not been forced out through gritted teeth. "That's odd."

"Yes." Davian rubbed his eyes, still trying to process what had happened.

"You made it leave," said Nihim, his voice weak. "How? What did it say to you?"

"No! No, I didn't do anything. It sounded ... it sounded like Darecian, but I don't know what it said." Davian ran his hands through his hair, mindless of the fact that they were still covered in blood. "We need to get you back to the others. Taeris will be able to help you."

Nihim laughed, though it came out as more of a hacking cough. "*You* need to get back to the others," he corrected him. "I fear I'm not going anywhere."

"I'm not leaving you behind."

Nihim coughed again. Already he looked paler, weaker. Then he drew a deep breath, putting a hand on Davian's shoulder.

"You're a brave lad," he said. "A good boy, and I appreciate the effort. But there's no point. I'm fated to die here."

Davian processed the statement in silence. "You mean...this was Seen?"

Nihim nodded, even that small movement causing his face to twist in pain. "By an old Augur friend, more than twenty years ago. I've been wondering for a long time when this day would come." He gave a short laugh, a desperate, almost delirious sound. "It seems it's finally here."

Davian shook his head in disbelief, cradling Nihim's head so that the priest would not hurt it against the cold stone floor. "Then why come?"

"To prove a point to Taeris," wheezed Nihim, a rueful smile on his lips. He held up his hand preemptively as Davian opened his mouth. "No time," he said in a whisper. "Go."

Davian half stood, then gave an angry shake of his head, crouching down again. "Fates take it. I'm not going to leave you here." He grabbed Nihim and lifted him as gently as possible.

Nihim gave a soft laugh, which turned to a moan as Davian began walking. "Stubborn," he gasped.

Davian crept out into the street again, barely able to carry the weight of the priest. He began moving in the direction in which he had last seen Caeden running, trying to ignore the blood still flowing freely from the gash in Nihim's stomach. He didn't know much about such wounds, but he was certain that Nihim would not survive long without assistance.

"I need to rest," groaned Nihim after a couple of minutes. "Just for a moment. I swear."

Davian considered protesting, but in truth his arms were ready to give out anyway. He came to a shaky stop, seating the priest on a nearby piece of rubble and turning to face him, careful not to let his emotions show. Nihim was dying, and there was nothing, *nothing* he could do about it.

Nihim looked up at him. "Listen, lad, there are some things you should know. Taeris hasn't told you everything."

"You should save your strength."

Nihim shook his head. "He's been waiting for you, Davian. He knew you would come," he said weakly. "There's a text from the

Old Religion, written by a man called Alchesh, an Augur from two thousand years ago. It talks of the man who will one day stop Aarkein Devaed from destroying the world. Taeris believes that man is you. He thinks that..." He trailed off into a coughing fit, blood seeping from his mouth.

Davian frowned; delirium was clearly setting in. "We can talk about this when we see Taeris," he said gently.

Nihim shifted, groaning at the motion. "Don't condescend to me, boy. Listen. The Augur who told me about today...he told me I'd be with someone very important. At the end." He coughed again, more weakly this time. "Someone whom the Augurs had seen on so many occasions in their visions, over the years, that they considered him to be the center point of this time—the fulcrum on which things in this era turn."

Davian stared at Nihim with determination. "This clearly isn't the end, then."

Nihim gave a weak chuckle, though it quickly died out. "An optimist. I like that." He paused for a second. "There's something else, Davian. Taeris has a link to you. It's dangerous for him. You need to break it, else he will die." His breath was coming shorter and shorter now. "When you..."

Nihim trailed off. His eyes had gone wide, and he was staring over Davian's shoulder with an expression of disbelief. He opened his mouth to speak, but no sound came out, and for a moment Davian thought he had passed away.

Too late, he realized that something was coming.

He turned, but the blast caught him in the side. Suddenly he was spinning wildly, tumbling through space. There was agony, as if a hand had reached into his skull and begun squeezing. A scream ripped from his throat, though whether it was from the pain, the terror, or simply the shock he wasn't sure.

It was like nothing he had ever felt before, ever *imagined* before. It was as if he had been cast into a raging river of gray smoke, a river of emptiness, of nothing—and the currents were trying to crush his mind, tear it apart, do whatever they could to utterly destroy him. He felt pulled in a thousand different directions at once, but unable to go anywhere. The buildings, the road, Nihim—they had all vanished, dissolved into the endless torrent of twisted void.

He struggled to breathe. It was impossible to say how long he had been in this state—seconds, minutes, or hours—but Davian was filled with a sudden certainty that if he did not escape, he would cease to exist.

Acting on pure instinct he found himself trying to calm his mind, employing every technique he'd ever learned while trying to use Essence. For a terrible moment, he understood that Essence did not—*could* not—exist here.

Suddenly there was something else. Cold and dark. Flowing though him.

He immediately felt an easing of the pressure on his mind. The sensation was still terribly unpleasant, but what had been a raging torrent around him now moved more slowly, flowing almost calmly past in comparison. He floated in the void, composing himself, the chill substance coursing through him like blood. Looking too closely at the gray smoke streaming past hurt his head, but he tried anyway.

Soon enough he noticed something. A gap, an area lighter than the space around it. He gazed at it, trying to focus in on it, ignoring everything else. It was a beacon in this surreal place—but how to reach it? He knew without looking that he had no physical body here, no legs to carry him.

Instinctively he fixed the light in his mind, then *willed* himself toward it...

...and the light was directly in front of him. Whether he had gone to it, or it had come to him, he did not know.

He studied the gentle glow. It was...familiar. Inviting. He stared into it for what seemed like only a moment...

...and groaned.

Davian's head felt as though someone had taken to it with a hammer. He lay still for several seconds, eyes closed, as he tried to assess the situation.

What had happened? He had been in Deilannis, and then... the void. That torrent of gray emptiness. He shifted, feeling cold, chiseled stone beneath him. So he was no longer in that place, at least. He had his body back. That was something.

Slowly he forced his eyes open. A high stone roof greeted his gaze, sturdily made but otherwise unremarkable. It was dim in here, though the light was still bright enough to hurt his eyes until they adjusted. How long had he lain there? Had he been returned to Deilannis, or was he somewhere else? A jolt of adrenaline ran through him as the memories started to come back. Nihim. With an effort he raised his head and looked around.

He was lying atop the altar of what appeared to be a vast temple. Columns stretched away into the darkness in all directions; Davian could not see any walls, any edges at all to whatever this room was. The illumination was coming from a skylight in the roof, but it must have been the only one in the room, for outside the small pool of light—in the center of which Davian now lay—nothing was visible. Everything in the room had a cold grayness to it; though there were no mists, Davian had the immediate sense that he was still somewhere in Deilannis.

"Welcome, Davian. Be at ease. No harm will come to you."

Davian scrambled to his feet, looking around apprehensively for the source of the words. "Who's there? How do you know my name?"

The disembodied voice chuckled, though it was a joyless sound. "*That* is a story."

Davian slowly stepped back, until he was pressed against the stone altar. "Show yourself."

There was movement from the shadows, and a man stepped forward into the light. His appearance was unremarkable— mousy-brown hair cropped short, a plain, slightly lumpy face, neither tall nor short, fat nor thin. Yet he carried himself with an air of authority.

There was something else, too, something almost unnoticeable but definitely there. Though there were no physical signs of it, the man's eyes were old. Weary beyond reckoning.

The stranger slipped something into his pocket, frowning at Davian. Davian tried to shift, to place the altar between himself and the other man, but suddenly found he could not move his feet.

"Do not try using your powers. They will have no effect on me," said the man absently as he walked closer, squinting as he stared into Davian's face. He wore a puzzled expression. As he drew near he stopped, a sharp intake of breath making a hissing sound as it passed through his teeth.

"You have only one scar," said the man in disbelief. He looked shaken.

"Yes. One scar. Now tell me who you are and what I'm doing here!" Davian tried not to let panic seep into his tone.

The plain-looking man appeared not to hear him. "Impossible," he muttered, now standing only a few feet from Davian, who was still powerless to move. The stranger began circling him, staring at him with morose fascination. "I was so sure. *So* sure. Perhaps the old fool was right after all." The energy went out of him.

"Are...are you going to kill me?" Davian asked, unable to keep the nervousness from his voice. The man seemed completely mad.

The stranger stopped at the question. He gazed long and hard into Davian's eyes, then let out a loud laugh, a raucous sound that echoed off into the shadows. "I'm hoping we can avoid that," he said with a wry shake of his head.

Davian swallowed, not entirely comforted. "Then what do you want of me?"

The man did not reply, continuing to study Davian with an intent expression. Finally he sighed. "I will release you, but only if you swear not to run."

Davian nodded. "I can do that."

The man moved to stand directly in front of him, placing a hand against Davian's forehead. He closed his eyes. "Now repeat after me: 'I swear I will listen to what you have to say, and judge it fairly. I swear I will not harm you or try to escape from you.'"

Davian felt his brow furrow in confusion, but seeing little alternative, repeated the words. A jolt of energy flashed through him, and there was a brief burning sensation on his left forearm. He jerked, glancing down.

For the first time he realized that his Shackle had somehow fallen off and was lying on the altar next to him; where the Gifted Mark had once been on his arm, there was now a simple circle of light. As he watched, the circle faded, dissolving into his skin and vanishing.

"What was that?" he demanded. "And where is my Mark?"

The man frowned. "That was a binding," he said. "It enforces your vow to me. As to the other...I don't know to what you are referring."

Davian paused for a moment, taken aback. "My *Mark*. From

being Gifted." When the man still stared at him blankly, Davian shook his head in disbelief. "You haven't heard of the Tenets? They bind the Gifted and the Administrators to one another, stop us from using our powers in certain ways."

The stranger cocked his head to the side. "Interesting," he said. "A binding applied to *every* Gifted. Impressive. I wonder which one of them did that." He looked at Davian thoughtfully. "What symbol did it leave?"

"It was the outline of three people within a circle. A man, woman, and child." Davian stared at his arm. He'd lived with that brand for so long now, had known with such certainty that it was permanent. It was unsettling to see clean skin there again.

"Of course it was," muttered the man, mostly to himself.

Davian frowned at him. "So where did it go?" he asked again.

"These Tenets, as you call them, don't exist yet. Thus you're not bound by them."

Davian screwed up his face. "I don't understand."

The man gestured, and Davian found his feet were no longer anchored to the ground. "All in good time, Davian. Now follow me."

Davian hesitantly trailed after the stranger into the shadows.

Once the darkness had closed around him and his eyes had adjusted to it, Davian could see that they were in a very, very large room—a hall of some kind, he assumed. Its size was the only thing spectacular about it, though; there were rows of stark gray columns, a smooth stone floor, an arched roof high above—and nothing else.

They walked for around thirty seconds before they came to a doorway, which opened into a narrow corridor. After the cavernous hall, the passage made Davian feel almost claustrophobic.

"Who are you?" asked Davian as they walked.

The man did not turn around. "My name is Malshash."

"Well, Malshash," said Davian, encouraged by the response, "can you tell me where I am?"

They were at the end of the passageway; Malshash grabbed one of the double doors in front of them and swung it wide.

Davian sighed. The mists were not as thick as they had been when the creature had attacked, but they were there.

"I'm still in Deilannis," observed Davian, his tone flat.

"Yes."

Davian walked outside, turning to examine the building he had just exited. To his surprise he recognized it. It was the same building Taeris had been so interested in—the one he had nearly stayed behind to enter, despite the danger. The memory reminded Davian of the threat, and he looked around with apprehension.

"The creature," he said to Malshash in a low, urgent tone.

"We're safe," Malshash assured Davian. He started off down the road, in the direction opposite to that in which Taeris and the others had gone. Davian tried to stand his ground, but discovered that his feet were moving to follow Malshash.

"Wait!" Davian called softly. "My friends may still be here! One of them is badly hurt—the creature wounded him. If I can just find him..."

Malshash did not stop, or even turn. "If your friend was wounded by Orkoth, he is dead." His tone held no emotion. "Even if he is not, there is no way for you to return to him."

"But he's only a few hundred feet the other way!" Davian protested, voice louder now as frustration and anger crept in.

Malshash shook his head. "There is no one here but us, Davian. I would know if it were otherwise." He held up his hand peremptorily, still not looking back as he spoke. "No more questions. There will be time later."

They walked for a few minutes, Davian throwing nervous glances over his shoulder, until they came to a large two-story house. Malshash entered, gesturing for Davian to follow. They passed through the entryway and into a large kitchen, where a small fire crackled merrily in the corner, casting a warm glow across the room that was in stark contrast to the cold whites and grays so prevalent in the rest of the city.

Malshash motioned Davian into one of the seats at the table, then began opening cupboards filled with food. Davian watched in surprise as the man began preparing a meal, though his absorbed expression suggested his thoughts were elsewhere.

"You *live* here?" Davian asked.

Malshash gave an absent nod. "For now."

Davian watched in silence until Malshash set down two meals
on the table.

"You must be hungry," said Malshash, gesturing for Davian to eat.

Davian's stomach growled, and he realized just how hungry he truly was. There was cooked meat of some kind—beef, he thought—and vegetables. It was simple fare, but to Davian it looked a feast.

Ravenous, he had eaten several mouthfuls before he realized that Malshash had not touched his food. He stopped, eyes narrowing, a flash of panic racing through him.

Malshash saw his reaction and gave him a slight smile. "I'm not poisoning you," he reassured Davian, taking a quick bite of his own meal to prove the point. He leaned back, sighing. "So. You have questions."

Davian swallowed his mouthful, nodding. "What happened to me? How did I end up in that building?"

Malshash paused. "What do you mean?"

"One moment I was on the road out of this El-cursed city. Then I was...somewhere else. Everything was gray, and I was being thrown around. I thought I was going to be torn apart, but I saw a light and headed toward it. The next thing I knew, I was waking up. You know the rest."

"You...you don't know what that was?"

"Should I?"

Malshash rubbed his forehead, for some reason looking shaken. "I suppose not. But for you to have survived the rift with no training, no idea what you were doing...it's remarkable."

"The rift?" Davian leaned forward, but even as he did so he realized that his eyelids were getting heavy. He yawned, long and loudly. The heat of the fire, combined with his full stomach, was making him drowsy—but far more so than it should have been. "What is this?" he said through another yawn. "You drugged me?"

"No. It's just a side effect. The shock must have kept you awake until now."

Davian felt his head getting heavy. He leaned forward until his head touched the table. "Side effect of what?" he mumbled.

If Malshash answered, Davian didn't hear it. He slept.

# Chapter 26

Wirr burst through the edge of the mists.

He collapsed upon the smooth white stone of the bridge, savoring the sight of the night sky and luxuriating in the feel of fresh air on his face. Even the roaring of the river below was musical compared to the sullen silence of the cursed city behind him. The stars were out, though no moon was in evidence; still, Wirr thought the cloudless heavens were as beautiful a thing as he had ever seen.

He twisted in his seated position to watch as Aelric and Dezia came stumbling from the thick blanket of fog, followed quickly by Caeden and then Taeris. From within Deilannis he could still hear occasional shrieks as the creature hunted, but the sounds were distant now.

Suddenly he went cold. He stared at the group on the bridge for a long moment.

"Where are Davian and Nihim?"

Taeris looked around at that, paling. "Nihim tripped," he said after a moment, "but I didn't see what happened to Davian." As one they looked at the mists, as if expecting the remaining two men to emerge at any moment.

Nothing happened.

In the distance the creature shrieked again, but this time the sound was different, more urgent. It sent a shiver through Wirr like none of its previous cries.

Still short of breath, he struggled to his feet. "We have to go back." He started forward shakily toward the white curtain of fog.

Taeris grabbed his arm in a viselike grip, stopping him in mid-step. He looked Wirr in the eye. "Don't be a fool," he said quietly.

Wirr struggled forward for a moment longer, but he knew Taeris was right. The last vestiges of energy drained from him and he slumped to the ground, staring back at the city.

"They must be lost," he said, hearing the desperation seeping into his voice. "They'll be hiding. But you can find them..."

Taeris closed his eyes for a long moment, and Wirr knew what he was about to say next.

"Wirr," the older man said, his tone gentle. "I can't feel Davian anymore. My Contract with his Shackle was broken."

Wirr just gazed blankly at Taeris for a moment, a sick feeling in the pit of his stomach, then shook his head in denial. "What does that mean?"

Taeris bowed his head, and everyone else looked away as the meaning of the Gifted's words struck home. "They are dead, Wirr," Taeris said, his voice thick with emotion. "It's the only explanation."

With that he slowly started walking along the bridge, toward Andarra.

Wirr, Caeden, and the others didn't follow, just stared back into the mists, listening numbly to the shrill, staccato screeches of the creature.

This time, it sounded triumphant.

Wirr perched on a boulder dangerously near the edge of the chasm, letting the roar of the Lantarche wash over him, his expression blank as he stared out toward the roiling mists.

Most of the others had long since fallen asleep; the travails of the night had taken a toll, as he knew they should have on him, too. Still, he didn't turn as the sound of crunching gravel indicated someone approaching.

"I would prefer to be alone," he said quietly.

Aelric seated himself beside Wirr on the stone, not responding. They sat like that in silence for several minutes, just watching the mists; the moon had risen, and the fog glowed with an ethereal silvery light in the middle of the gorge. Wirr thought about asking

Aelric to leave, but his heart wasn't in it. As much as he wanted to lash out at something—anything, in fact—he was grateful for the company.

"It wasn't your fault," said Aelric suddenly.

Wirr didn't react for a moment, but for some reason he didn't understand, the words ignited a cold rage inside him.

"What makes you think I blame myself?" It came out as more of a snarl than anything else.

Aelric ignored his tone. "Because I can see it. Right now you're sitting here, playing back every moment from today and thinking of all the things you could have done differently that would have saved your friend. You're feeling guilty for a single moment, a single mistake. An accident." He looked at Wirr with a serious expression. "Tell me I'm wrong, and I won't say anything more about it."

Wirr opened his mouth to do just that, but shut it again without making a sound. Aelric was right. He *had* been playing back every moment of the day in his head, wondering what he could have done differently. Cursing himself for not having enough self-control to be silent, not being smart enough to resist reaching for Essence in a panic.

He gave a heavy sigh, then pondered the tone of Aelric's voice for a moment.

"You sound like you might know what that feels like," he said grudgingly.

Aelric chuckled, though there was no joy to the sound. "There's some truth to that."

Wirr looked at him, frowning. "What happened?" The pain in Aelric's voice had caught him by surprise. Since they'd met, Wirr had seen only bluster, swagger, and no small amount of belligerence from the young man.

Aelric stared into the chasm. "Do you know how Dezia and I came to be at court?"

Wirr shook his head. "Not the details. Dezia only said that after your father died, King Andras took you in."

Aelric nodded. "We lived with my father," he said, voice soft as he remembered. "He was vassal to Gerren Tel'An, a nobleman, but with no holdings of his own. The Tel'Ans all looked down on him, but he didn't mind so long as we had a roof over our heads and food on the table.

"One day I was playing with Lein Tel'An. We used to practice against each other with training swords, but that day we broke into the armory and found some real short swords. We were fourteen, thought the swordmaster was an old fool who couldn't see we were ready for the real thing."

Wirr leaned forward. He remembered Lein: a skinny boy with golden hair and a shy smile. He'd been one of the better Tel'Ans. One of the few boys his age Wirr hadn't completely disliked, in fact, though they'd not spoken often.

Aelric continued, "We were careful at first, but once we got used to the weight of the blades, we were swinging hard and fast. Just like real warriors." He grimaced at the memory.

Wirr stared at Aelric, aghast. "You killed him?"

Aelric blinked in surprise, then gave a slight smile. "Fates, no," he said with a chuckle. The smile faded. "I cut off his right hand. I was overconfident and slipped, and the sword went clean through his wrist." Aelric shook his head, and Wirr could see him reliving the moment in his mind. "The second son of House Tel'An was crippled, and I was at fault."

"And Lord Tel'An wanted you punished?"

"He wanted me flogged."

Wirr stiffened. "But…at that age…"

"It could have killed me," finished Aelric. "A fact my father knew all too well. He demanded that the king be consulted before the punishment was carried out, but Tel'An was having none of it. The day after the accident, I was brought into the town square and tied to the flogging post. My father tried to stop them, first with words, then with his blade." He stared at the ground. "He was never much of a swordsman, and there were just too many of Tel'An's men. They killed him."

Wirr gazed at Aelric for a moment. "I'm sorry."

Aelric inclined his head. "It was a long time ago."

"Did they still flog you?"

"No." Aelric sighed. "My father's death put a stop to the proceedings. That night the king received word of what Tel'An had done, and sent for Dezia and myself. Tel'An was furious, but even he was not fool enough to defy the king."

He paused for a few moments in remembrance, then turned to face Wirr. "What happened with Lein…it was an accident. Carelessness. A moment of madness that changed the course of my life, and Dezia's, forever. I still regret it, every day, but…it gets better. The pain is still there, even now…but it does fade."

Wirr nodded slowly. Taeris and the others had told him that he shouldn't feel guilty for what had happened in Deilannis, but their words had been hollow, meaningless, however well intentioned. Aelric, though, understood that the pain of his mistake wouldn't be so easy to simply put aside. Strangely, Wirr found that more comforting.

They were silent for a time. "So is that why you became so good with a sword?" Wirr asked eventually.

Aelric hesitated. "In part, I think that's probably true. It took me a while to pick up a blade again, though. Almost a year after I got to court." He gave a rueful smile. "To be honest, I was…not highly regarded at the palace, to begin with. I shirked my responsibilities and hid from my tutors. I suspect it was only Dezia's friendship with Karaliene that saved me from being sent back to Tel'An within the first few months."

"What changed?"

Aelric chuckled. "Unguin heard that I'd been showing some promise, before the accident. Once he found out all the details, he insisted on training me—wouldn't take no for an answer. Made my life such a misery that it ended up being easier to just turn up for drills every morning."

Wirr looked up in interest. Unguin was the palace swordmaster; Wirr had been given many—mostly unsuccessful, but still beneficial—lessons under his tutelage. "He must have seen something in you, for him to be so persistent." That was the truth. Unguin was a no-nonsense man, straight as an arrow and with little patience for the pretensions of the nobility. If he'd gone out of his way to tutor Aelric, there was more to the young man than Wirr had initially credited.

Aelric shrugged. "He said that my skills weren't anything

special, but my motivations were. That I wouldn't just understand why control was more important than strength or speed—I'd live by the concept." He gave a short laugh. "And I suppose he was right. Once I picked up a blade again, I didn't stop working at it until I was certain that what happened with Lein would never happen again. I worked as hard as I could, as long as I could, every day...though Unguin would tell you otherwise, of course."

Wirr smiled. "He sounds like a hard man to please."

"You would know, I suppose."

There was silence for a few seconds as Wirr hesitated, processing the comment, trying to see if there was a meaning he had somehow missed. Finally he looked sideways at Aelric, who was still staring into the chasm.

"Karaliene and Dezia are like sisters," said Aelric, not looking at Wirr. "After I walked in on you hugging Karaliene, Dezia swore to me there was nothing between you. She wouldn't betray Karaliene's confidence, but I know she wouldn't lie to me, either." He shrugged. "If it wasn't that, the only other person who could be that familiar with the princess would have to be a relative. It was easy from there. You look a lot like your father."

Wirr shook his head in chagrin. "You've known all this time?"

Aelric allowed a half smile to creep onto his face. "Since the second day." He paused, the faint trace of amusement quickly disappearing. "As, I assume, has my sister."

Wirr nodded mutely.

Aelric gave a slight shake of his head, looking frustrated at the confirmation. "You'd think she'd have learned from my example," he muttered in a wry tone. He rubbed his forehead. "Look—I can't tell either of you what to do, and maybe this isn't the best time to bring it up. But if it hasn't been clear, I don't think you and Dezia getting attached to each other is a good idea."

Wirr flushed. "It's not like that."

"I'm not an idiot, Wirr. Torin. Whatever you want me to call you." Aelric said the words gently, only a hint of reproach in his voice. "The two of you are becoming close—anyone with eyes can see it. Once we're back in Ilin Illan, though, how long will it take for your father to start pairing you off with one of the girls from the Great Houses? A month? Two? The more time you spend with Dezia now, the harder that will be for her. For both of you."

Wirr was silent for a few moments; he wanted to protest, but Aelric wasn't wrong. "Nothing's happened between us," he said eventually.

Aelric gave him a tight smile. "And I believe you, if for no other reason than Dezia's too smart to cross that line." He sighed. "I'm not suggesting you should stay away from her, or that you shouldn't be friends. Just...don't spend so much time together, especially off by yourselves. There's no point letting those feelings develop. Do it for my sister's sake, if not your own."

Wirr's heart twisted. Aelric was only repeating what Wirr already knew—that his friendship with Dezia needed to remain just that—but it didn't make confronting the fact any easier, especially tonight.

Still, he nodded a reluctant acknowledgment. He understood why Aelric was concerned, and also why he hadn't waited to talk about this. The older boy hadn't mentioned it explicitly, but they both knew that grief could cause people to make poor decisions. Wirr hated to admit it, but in Aelric's position, he would probably be doing the same thing.

Wirr's response had apparently satisfied Aelric, and the conversation drifted to lighter topics. It did not take Wirr long to grudgingly decide that he was beginning to respect the older boy, maybe even like him a little, despite his first impressions. Aelric knew without having to ask that Wirr was keeping a vigil, waiting to see if Davian would miraculously emerge from the mists of Deilannis during the night. Rather than pointing out the foolishness of the task, he seemed content to simply keep Wirr company.

Finally the conversation ceased and they lapsed into a companionable silence, each lost in his own thoughts. A silent understanding had passed between the two young men, and both were content to sit there quietly as the night slipped by.

Dawn came too soon, yellow and bright. Wirr and Aelric rose and headed back to camp. The others were already awake; no one needed to ask where they had been.

They gathered up their meager possessions, the silence somber. Soon they were on the move again, upward for a time along stairs similar to those on the Desriel side of the city. They crested the steep hillside, then began to walk the gentler slope downward. Wirr glanced back over his shoulder, watching as the mist-bound city was lost from view.

He turned forward again and swallowed a lump in his throat, forcing himself to finally admit the hard truth.

Davian was gone.

# Chapter 27

Asha gave an inward groan as she saw the line of nobility waiting outside Elocien's study.

She gritted her teeth, ignoring the stares as she passed. It had been weeks since she'd been officially introduced as Tol Athian's Representative, but more often than not, she was still looked at like something akin to a dog that had suddenly learned how to talk. The worst of the offenders were people like those waiting for Elocien. They wouldn't be happy about what she was about to do...but the duke had sent for her, and it had sounded urgent.

The hallway had gone silent at her appearance, but now a low, annoyed muttering started up behind her as she knocked on Elocien's door. It was well known that she was only at court through the Northwarden's insistence, and few people tried to hide their disapproval away from Elocien's sight. This would only serve to reaffirm their opinion that she didn't know her place.

There was silence for a few moments, and then the door opened. A man Asha didn't recognize peered out at her with a frown.

"The Northwarden is busy," he told her, his tone stern. He tried to shut the door again, but Asha jammed her foot in the crack.

"Tell him that it is Representative Chaedris. He sent for me."

The wiry man hesitated, then gave a sharp nod. A few seconds later the door opened again and the duke appeared, ushering out a disgruntled-looking older man.

"This will not take long, Lord si'Bandin," Elocien said. He turned to Asha; his expression was smooth but she could see a strange combination of concern and excitement in his eyes. "Representative Chaedris. Please, come in," he said politely.

As soon as the door was shut, the Northwarden's manner changed. He collapsed wearily into a chair, but despite his obvious exhaustion, he appeared upbeat.

"Ashalia. Thank you for coming," he said with a tired smile, gesturing for her to take a seat. "I have news of Torin. He's alive."

Asha stared at the duke for a long moment, barely daring to believe her ears. She sat, a sudden burst of emotion dizzying her. She'd hoped, of course, but to have it confirmed…

She laughed delightedly. "That's wonderful!" She was about to say more when she realized that the man who had initially opened the door was still standing by another chair in the corner. She hesitated.

The duke caught her glance and nodded to himself.

"Ah—of course. How rude of me. Ashalia, meet Laiman Kardai, my brother's closest friend and most trusted adviser."

Laiman grimaced at the introduction. He was an unassuming-looking man, thin in both body and face, with wire-rimmed glasses that lent him a scholarly air. "Until recently, anyway," he said with forced cheerfulness, running a hand through his mousy-brown hair. He nodded to Asha. "A pleasure to meet you. I've heard much about you from Duke Andras." He gave a slight smile. "And from others, too, these last few weeks. You've managed to make quite a stir."

"Not deliberately," Asha assured him drily. She bit her lip, glancing again at Laiman. She was ecstatic about Torin, but she could hardly have this discussion with Elocien while there was a stranger in the room.

Elocien followed her gaze. "Laiman knows everything, Asha. About Torin, and about the Augurs. You may speak freely in front of him."

Asha tried not to look surprised; after all Elocien's talk about keeping the Augurs a secret, he had told the king's closest friend? Still, it was hardly her place to question the duke's judgment.

She relaxed a little, allowing her smile to return. "So…where is he? What happened to him—is he safe?"

"Details are scarce at this point," Elocien admitted. "We do know for certain that a couple of weeks ago, he was in Thrindar."

Asha stared at the duke. "In *Desriel*?"

Elocien nodded grimly. "He made contact with Princess Karaliene at the Song of Swords—she let me know as soon as she arrived home this morning. He's on his way home, too, apparently." He rubbed his forehead, looking as though he didn't quite know whether to be pleased or irritated at the next part. "She says he didn't even know about what happened at Caladel—that he'd left before the attack, to investigate the weakening of the Boundary…it was all very vague, to be honest. I don't think he told her much at all."

"The Boundary? The one up north?" Asha frowned, trying to remember what she knew of the far north. "Does that mean…"

"I don't know." Elocien sighed. "These invaders—the Blind, as they're being called now—*are* coming from the north. If Torin thought there was a problem with the Boundary—enough of a problem to risk sneaking into Desriel—then I suppose it's possible they're from Talan Gol. Some sort of…distant Andarran relative, maybe, descended from those who were trapped in the north when the Boundary was first created." He shrugged, glancing across at Laiman. "We'll find out soon enough, anyway."

Asha frowned. "What do you mean?"

Elocien hesitated. "We've heard nothing conclusive, but the early reports have been worrying. Refugees describing soldiers with inhuman strength and speed, slaughtering everyone in their path—adults and children, resisting or not." He shook his head. "Those fleeing are terrified, of course, so it's impossible to say how much of that is actually true, but King Andras has still decided to send the army out to meet the Blind. Nine thousand men, all told."

Asha stared at him in horror. "But you know what happens," she said, a note of protest edging into her tone. "The invasion reaches Ilin Illan. Surely that means…"

"A lot of those men may be going to their deaths. I know," said Elocien. "This is why I had to tell Laiman exactly what was going on. The king wanted to send *everyone*, Asha. All fifteen thousand troops, leaving the city defended by only a handful of soldiers. My pleas were doing nothing, but Laiman got him down to nine thousand."

"It's still many more than we wanted," added Laiman quietly, "but it was the best I could do. Given the circumstances."

"The circumstances?" repeated Asha.

Elocien glanced at Laiman, who gave him a brief nod.

"My brother is acting...irrationally," said Elocien. "We've been noticing small things for weeks, but since war was officially declared it seems to have become much worse. *Much* worse. He rants against the Gifted, but is perfectly content to have Dras Lothlar as one of his closest advisers. He has started refusing to see all but his most trusted lords, advisers, and servants. Karaliene came home this morning after being away for months, but he's not even changing his schedule to see her. I've *never* seen him do that before." From the duke's tone, he was genuinely worried. "We know something is wrong, but no one is in a position to find out what."

"What about the Assembly?" asked Asha. "Can't they step in?"

"Andarra is at war, so the Assembly has been dissolved until further notice." Laiman's tone was calm but Asha could see the concern in his eyes, too. "It was announced yesterday. His Majesty has absolute control over the country until the Blind are defeated. And he *insisted* on sending the troops. At the urgings of Dras Lothlar, I might add," he said, unable to repress a scowl.

The Northwarden leaned forward. "Nine thousand is more than we should be sending, but...there are other things to consider. We have people, thousands of people, outside the city in the path of the Blind. Those troops will give them a chance to escape. And even if our soldiers don't stop the invasion, we don't know what impact they will have. Sending them may weaken the enemy enough that we will be able to defeat them once they breach the city. We could gain valuable intelligence on who they are, what they want, and how they fight."

Asha processed what Elocien had told her for a few seconds, then gave a reluctant nod. "I hadn't thought of that."

Elocien's tone became milder. "Just remember, Asha, that even if what the Augurs See is inevitable, it doesn't mean we can just wait for it to happen. Fessi saw the Blind inside the city, yet we're still going to man the Shields at Fedris Idri when they come. Why? Because even though good men will die, and those walls will eventually be overrun—who knows how many of the enemy will be killed in the process? The damage we do them there may end up making the difference between victory and defeat." He sighed. "Regardless, all we can do is make preparations based on what we know. And I promise you, I am doing that."

Asha inclined her head nervously; when Elocien put it in such a matter-of-fact way, the prospect of invaders inside the walls suddenly felt more real. She'd been imagining that Fessi's vision had meant that the Andarran soldiers would simply wait for the Blind inside Ilin Illan, make their stand from deep within the city. That what had been Seen would come before any blood had been shed.

But she saw now that the duke was right—knowing they were going to lose the battle for the Shields didn't mean they could, or even should, avoid it.

She took a deep breath, a little dazed. Elocien watched her sympathetically.

"How is everything else going?" he asked after a moment, his tone gentle. "Is the Shadraehin still pressing you for information?"

Asha grimaced, nodding. "They're contacting me once every couple of days now," she admitted. The messages were always essentially the same, and yet...in the last few, she had begun to sense more than a hint of impatience.

Elocien frowned as he watched her reaction. "If it becomes anything more than them just making contact, you let me know straight away," he said quietly. "I can't see any reason for the Shadraehin to think you are anything but loyal—he must have known your getting information from me could take a while, months even. Still, there are measures we can take to protect you if you feel the need."

Asha gave him a grateful nod, silent for a moment. Then she stood, suddenly remembering the long line of impatient nobility outside. "I should let you get back to your meetings, but thank you for letting me know about Torin," she said, managing a small smile. "It really is wonderful news. Do you know when he will be back?"

Elocien returned the smile, standing too. "If there are no complications...soon, I would hope. I'll keep you informed if I find out anything more specific." He sighed, glancing at Laiman. "But for now it's back to hearing every single House tell us why their interests should be protected against this invasion, I suppose."

"Yes. Let the tedium resume," agreed Laiman reluctantly. He nodded politely to Asha. "It was a pleasure meeting you, Ashalia. I'm sure our paths will cross again."

The duke opened the door, and the murmuring from the gathered nobility outside stopped once more as Asha made her way past. She tried to stare straight ahead as she walked, but she still caught a couple of the half-disgusted, half-irritated looks she had already grown accustomed to.

Rubbing her forehead, she made her way back to her rooms. She had only a little time before her next lesson with Michal, but it was enough to catch up on some rest, and a chance to try to process everything she'd just been told.

Her bedroom was still dark; getting up before sunrise meant she rarely thought to draw back the thick curtains. She left them closed and wearily lay down on her bed.

"Asha."

The male voice made her sit up straight in alarm.

"Who's there?" she said, trying to make the fear in her voice a warning. She scrambled to light the lamp beside her bed, raising it with a shaking hand.

A figure shifted in the shadows at the corner of her room. There was a clinking sound, metal against metal. Then the intruder moved forward, into the light.

"It's good to see you, Asha," said Davian softly.

Asha stared in disbelief. She had to be dreaming, hallucinating. The man standing in the corner of the room was Davian, but... he looked older.

*Much* older.

Gone was the skinny boy from Caladel. Muscles rippled beneath Davian's light shirt, which was tattered and bloodstained. There was a strange scar, almost a tattoo, scored onto his neck—three wavy vertical lines, all within a circle. And his face not only had the old scar from Caladel but another one, worse, running across the other cheek just beneath his eye. It looked deep, painful, not fully healed. Week-old stubble made him look

324    even more disheveled.

Davian's entire body was bound by a black, glistening chain with thick links, the metal writhing in the lamplight as if alive. He shifted, and the metallic clinking echoed through the room again.

Worst of all, though, were his eyes. They were old. Full of pain as he looked at her.

"Is this a dream?" asked Asha, dazed. "You...you're not real. They said you died. At Caladel."

"They lied." Davian made an awkward step back as Asha swung out of bed. "Please, don't come any closer. It's dangerous."

Asha stopped. She wanted to go to him, touch him, just to make sure he was really there. "Why?"

Davian grimaced, staring at the ground. "I don't have time to explain. I'm...restricted in what I can say. Who is the Shadraehin?"

Asha shook her head in confusion at the sudden switch. Was this some kind of elaborate trick? "A man called Scyner," she said slowly. "Why?"

Davian grimaced again, still staring at her. "She's telling the truth. She doesn't know." He gave a moan of pain as the black chains tightened around him. "You have my word, Rethgar," he added through gritted teeth.

"Dav?" Asha took a hesitant half step forward in concern before remembering Davian's warning. "What's going on?"

"We know you have met with the Shadraehin. You helped her." Davian spoke in a monotone, and he stared at her intently, trying to communicate...something. A warning.

"Her?" Asha shook her head. "Scyner is a man."

"Scyner is just the Shadraehin's lieutenant. A prewar, though. Don't trust him." The black chains flexed; though Davian didn't cry out this time, she could see from his expression how much it hurt.

"Dav—" Asha made to move forward.

"*Stay back.*" Davian's words were like a whip, stopping her in place. "Ashalia Chaedris, for your part in assisting the Shadows, you have been found guilty." He hesitated, clearly reluctant to say the next part. "The sentence is death."

A chill ran through Asha at the words. "*I'm* a Shadow, Dav," she said softly, holding the lamp higher in case he hadn't been able to see her face.

Davian gave her a tight smile. "You won't always be, though."

The black chains shivered and Davian let out an involuntary groan, sinking to his knees. "She doesn't know anything. And this is the furthest we can go before Tal'kamar—"

The chains tightened again, and this time Davian's expression turned to one of grim anger. He closed his eyes.

The chains froze, turned gray as steel.

Davian kept his eyes closed. "They can't hear us now, but I can't do this for long, either," he said calmly, his voice finally gaining a hint of the warmth she remembered. "I know this must be confusing, but there's no time to explain so you are going to have to trust me. You'll be making a deal with the Shadraehin soon—the real one. When you do, I need you to tell her that Tal'kamar is taking Licanius to the Wells, and that the information is a gift from me. Can you do that?"

Asha swallowed the myriad questions she wanted to ask, instead giving a bemused nod and repeating the message.

"Good. Thank you, Ash." Davian took a deep breath. "Now, this is equally important. When you find out that I'm at Ilshan Gathdel Teth, don't come after me. I'm fine. The Venerate can't kill me, but they will kill you—you are the one they want. I'm just the bait. Remember that."

He opened his eyes, and the chains began slowly moving again, starting to bleed back to their original oily black. A shiver ran through Davian's body, and he looked as though he'd been drained of blood, of life. "Don't tell anyone else that you saw me. Especially not me. They've Read...they've Read so many of us now. There's no telling whose mind is safe, these days." He shook his head as he saw her baffled expression. "I'm so sorry. You'll understand when the time comes."

The chains tightened, jerked backward. Davian silently locked eyes with her as he was pulled into the shadows.

Then he was gone.

# Chapter 28

*Davian frowned.*

*He was atop a low hill, which afforded a good view over the entire moonlit valley below. All around him were tents, some with lights still burning inside, but most dark. The moon was at its zenith and almost full; the night was clear, allowing the silvery light to illuminate his surroundings almost as if it were daytime. The air was cold and crisp, and he shivered, rubbing his hands together for warmth—even though he suspected he was not truly there. Just as before.*

*At the edges of the camp, quite some distance away, he could see sentries patrolling. In other areas campfires burned, and a few men still gathered around them, laughing bawdily at jokes or stories being told by their comrades. There was a banner flying at the camp's center, three clashing golden swords set against a field of red. This was King Andras's army, then—perhaps sent out to meet the invading force he had foreseen last time? Why was he here, Seeing this? All seemed well.*

*Then he saw it. A shadow, silent, flitting from one tent to another. He stared, squinting, wondering for a second if he was imagining the whole thing. Then it came again, the slightest of movements, black against black. It moved into the next tent, noiseless, unnoticed by any of the men still awake.*

*Davian walked over to the tent, hesitant despite knowing that nothing here could see or harm him. He slipped inside, restraining a gasp as his eyes adjusted to the gloom.*

The tent housed ten men, all lying motionless on their camp beds. Even in the dim light he could see the dark gashes running along their throats, and the slow, muted sound of dripping echoed dully around the tent. Blood onto the dirt, Davian realized sickly. He stumbled outside again, straining for another glimpse of the shadow. He had a suspicion, but he needed to find out exactly what it was before the vision ended.

Another flicker of movement caught his eye, and he dashed over to where he'd seen it. This time, as he entered the tent, he knew it was still there. The sounds of men breathing as they slept indicated it had not yet finished its grisly work.

He took an involuntary step back as he finally saw what was responsible for the killings. A figure stood above one of the beds, swathed in black, a dagger in its hand. Yet the dagger was not made of metal but rather shifted and swirled, forged from shadow itself. The blade caressed another man's neck, and blood fountained forth. The creature silently moved on to the next camp bed, its unsettling, flowing gait all too familiar.

A sha'teth.

Then it froze. It turned slowly until it was facing Davian.

Davian stood stock-still. It could not see him; it must have been startled by something else. These were events yet to come. He was not actually here.

A wet, snuffling sound came from beneath the creature's hood; it bowed its head and began moving toward him, not directly, but testing the air like a dog closing in on a scent. Much as the Orkoth had.

"I can smell you, Shalician," it whispered. The voice was harsh and low, rasping.

Davian clenched his fists, terrified. It couldn't know he was there. The creature crept closer and closer, Davian still too afraid to move, until it stopped in front of him.

It looked up, into his eyes, and Davian saw the hideous face beneath its hood. Pale skin was crisscrossed with unmentionable scars; its eyes were disturbingly human, its gaze unseeing and yet focused. Its ruined lips curled in contempt.

"You should not be here," it hissed into his face.

Davian awoke with a shout.

He thrashed on his bed for a few seconds, pain arcing through his head. Malshash was above him, wide-eyed, holding him down by the shoulders. Davian forced a hand up to his face; when he took it away again it was covered with blood.

He tried to speak, but no words came out. The pain roaring in his ears suddenly began to subside, and his vision blurred.

He slipped into unconsciousness.

Davian awoke.

He sat up sharply as he remembered where he was, what had happened. To his surprise he was lying in a large, comfortable bed. He leaped up and crossed to the window to discover he was on the second floor of a house—presumably the same one that Malshash had taken him to earlier. The dull gray mists made the passing of time difficult to calculate in Deilannis, but his instincts said he had been asleep for several hours at least.

He was still dressed, but his clothes showed no trace of blood. He examined where he'd been sleeping, but there were no bloodstains there, either. Had he been dreaming? The army, the sha'teth, and then waking...it had all felt so real.

He wandered downstairs, listening for any sign of movement and finding his way to the kitchen once he was satisfied he was alone. It was, indeed, Malshash's house; the fire still burned in the hearth, and a meal of porridge and bacon had been laid out on the table. The smell made his stomach growl, despite his having eaten just before he slept.

He stared at the food suspiciously for a few seconds, but eventually hunger overcame his caution and he sat, wolfing down the meal.

"I see I should have prepared for two," an unfamiliar voice observed drily from behind him.

Davian leaped to his feet, knocking over his chair in his haste. He spun to see an elderly man, perhaps in his late sixties, though apparently still hale and spry enough to move around without making a sound. His hair was shoulder length, gray but with streaks of the black it must once have been. His hazel eyes twinkled in amusement as he watched Davian.

"Who are you?" asked Davian, caught between fear and irritation.

The man blinked, then laughed. "Ah, of course. How foolish of me." He stepped forward. "I am Malshash."

Davian shook his head. "I met Malshash yesterday. You are not him."

"And yet I am." The man claiming to be Malshash took another step forward. "As I told you yesterday, we are the only two people in Deilannis. I would know immediately if it were otherwise."

Davian allowed his tensed muscles to relax a little, though he remained cautious. "I don't understand," he admitted.

"I am what you would call a shape-shifter," said Malshash, busying himself serving another plate of porridge. He paused. "Actually, that isn't entirely true. I have...borrowed...a shape-shifter's ability. Temporarily." He shrugged. "As a result, I must use it at least once each day. If I do not, the ability reverts to its previous owner. Which—and you will need to trust me on this—would *not* end well for either of us." He smiled to himself, as if he had just said something amusing. "Needless to say, if you see someone in this city, it will be me."

Davian shook his head. "I've never heard of someone who can change their appearance."

Malshash snorted. "Of course you have. You must have heard of Nethgalla? The Ath?"

Davian screwed up his face. "Well, of course I've heard of her, but that's just..." He blinked, stopping short. "You stole the *Ath's* ability?"

Malshash grinned. "Don't worry. She's not coming for it anytime soon." He gestured to the half-eaten meal in front of Davian. "Eat. It will help restore your strength."

Davian scowled. "And why am I weak to begin with?" he asked irritably, though he didn't need a second invitation to continue the meal.

"Two reasons," said Malshash. "The first being that you lost plenty of blood last night. I assume it wasn't a deliberate act on your part, using your Foresight in the middle of Deilannis? For a while there, I wasn't entirely sure you were going to live, even with all logic to the contrary."

Davian paused. "So I didn't imagine that?"

Malshash gave him a wry smile. "I'm afraid not. I took the liberty of suppressing your ability before you had another episode, though. You're no longer in danger."

Davian shook his head in confusion, then decided to let the matter slide until he had his bearings a little better. "You mentioned there were two reasons?"

Malshash nodded. "You stepped through time to get here," he explained in a calm, matter-of-fact tone. "Or, more to the point, you stepped outside of time. For a moment—a millionth of a millionth of a moment, and an eternity—you existed elsewhere."

Davian gave a humorless laugh. "I don't understand a word of what you just said."

Malshash sighed. "You will. Or at least you'll need to, if you ever hope to return to your own time."

Davian paused midbite. "What do you mean?"

Malshash looked at him, expression serious. "This moment here, now? It is about seventy or so years before you were born."

Davian stared at the plain wall of what was now, apparently, his room.

He had not reacted well to Malshash's revelation. He had laughed at first, thinking it a joke; when Malshash had insisted it was true he had flatly refused to believe it, calling the man a liar and a fool.

And yet deep down, he'd known. Perhaps had known before Malshash had even told him. The sick feeling in his stomach was fear, and he was afraid because there was so much he didn't understand.

In the end he'd stormed off back to this room; Malshash had let him go, evidently deciding it was best to leave him to his own devices for the time being. Davian knew he would have to go and apologize soon. He needed Malshash; the mysterious man seemed to know everything important about what was happening, including how to get him home.

Davian had been working up the courage, and the energy, to go back downstairs for the last hour now. There had just been so much happening—not only today, but over the past few weeks. He'd always thought of himself as mentally strong, able to adapt no matter what was thrown at him. But this, on top of everything else ... whenever he tried to think about it, it felt as though his head were burning up.

He eventually rose and, steeling himself, headed back downstairs. Malshash was still sitting at the table, sipping a warm drink. The shape-shifter glanced up at Davian as he entered, but said nothing.

Davian sat himself opposite Malshash. "I am sorry," he said quietly. "I said things—"

"Not your fault," interrupted Malshash. "I wish there had been a better way to tell you, but it's not something that's easy to digest, no matter how you're informed."

Davian snorted. "There's truth to that." He ran his hands through his hair. "Let us say, for the time being, that I believe you. That I have somehow traveled eighty, ninety years into the past."

Malshash inclined his head. "I'll explain as best I can." He paused, thinking. "You remember the room where we met?"

Davian nodded. "The one with the columns, and the altar in the middle."

Malshash chuckled. " 'Altar.' Yes, I suppose that's about right," he mused. "That's actually called a Jha'vett. It is set in the very center of the city. The exact midpoint." He looked up expectantly, but Davian just gave him a blank stare back, not understanding the significance of what Malshash was saying.

Malshash sighed. "Three thousand years ago, a race called the Darecians came to Andarra as refugees, fleeing the destruction of their homeland. They conquered this continent and immediately began building Deilannis—a city that no native Andarran was allowed to enter, in which only High Darecians could live. They did all this because the city was, in fact, a weapon."

"The entire city?"

Malshash nodded. "Possibly the greatest weapon ever made, though in some ways even the Darecians didn't understand that at the time. Every building here, every street, every stone, is made to capture Essence—and it all leads to the Jha'vett. That 'altar,' as you called it, is the focus of immense energies. The High Darecians, at the height of their knowledge and power, spent a hundred and fifty years making it."

Davian felt his eyebrows rise. Every story of the Darecians spoke at length of their powers, their abilities with Essence. "What does it do?"

"It tears a rift," replied Malshash seriously. "It allows someone to leave time itself, to step outside the stream of time and shift themselves elsewhere along it. Forwards. Backwards. Whenever they wish." He shook his head. "They built it so that they could go back, to before the Shining Lands were destroyed. They wanted to warn their people of what was coming. To perhaps kill the man who destroyed them, before he could do it."

Davian gaped. "Is that possible?"

"No one really knows, but...I am beginning to think not." Malshash sighed, deeply and with regret.

"So they failed?"

"Not exactly," said Malshash. "The Jha'vett works, as you can tell. But if any of the Darecians went back, they weren't able to change anything." He jumped up, grabbed a handful of flour from a bag on the shelf, then came back and dumped it on the table. He drew a line through it. "Imagine this is time. The Darecians believed that going back to a point in time will create *this*." He drew a branching line from the original. "An alternate timeline, where things are different depending on what has been changed. Where you could go back in time, kill your parents before they ever meet, and still live out the rest of your days in a reality where you are never born." He drew more lines. "They believed that there are infinite realities, where each choice of each person creates a new world. So possibly they went back in time, succeeded, and are now living out a different reality from this one."

He erased the extra lines. "*However*, there may be only one timeline. One set of possible events. The Augurs have been reinforcing that theory for years, but it's not something anyone wants to believe. We like the idea of infinite possibility. That nothing is inevitable." He sounded frustrated. "Yet the more I see, the more inevitability seems to be the way of it. One timeline. No second chances."

Davian frowned. "I was nowhere near the Jha'vett when all this happened. So how did I get here?"

Malshash shifted, looking uncomfortable. "There was a man. Aarkein Devaed. He was amongst those responsible for the destruction of the Shining Lands; when he invaded Andarra, he went ahead of his army and tried to use the Jha'vett for himself." He paused. "Instead of getting it to work, though, he just...damaged it. Now sometimes the energies in the city become misdirected. Escape, flow outward. Ripples like that are rare, but if you weren't at the Jha'vett, it's the only explanation."

"There were apparitions, just before the Orkoth attacked," said Davian, remembering. "People appearing and disappearing right in front of us. Would that have been caused by one of these... ripples?"

Malshash gave a thoughtful nod. "I would think so. Different times bleeding into each other, most likely. I've seen it happen once before." He hesitated as if reminded of something, then fished around in his pocket, producing a ring with a slightly guilty expression. It was silver, made of three plain bands that twisted together to form a distinctive pattern, irregular but flowing.

Malshash held it up. "Before we go any further, you should know: I used the Jha'vett to draw you here with this," he admitted awkwardly. "I needed something of yours, something personal. Something that meant a great deal to you."

Davian looked at him in puzzlement. "What is it?"

Malshash raised an eyebrow. "It's your ring."

Davian shook his head. "I've never seen it before. It's not mine." The ring was distinctive; he'd certainly know if he'd ever owned something so fine.

"Ah. Then it will be," said Malshash with a slight shrug.

Davian scowled. "How is that possible? How can something be important to me if I've never even seen it before?"

Malshash shrugged again. "Remember, you were outside of time when it drew you. There was no future, no past. *When* it is important to you is not relevant. At some point it will be."

Davian stared at him for a few seconds. "I think I'm going to have to take your word on that."

Malshash gave him an amused half smile in response and then

tossed the ring to Davian, who caught it, examining it closely. It was unadorned with jewels, but the pattern created by the bands' twisting together was intricately done.

"What am I to do with this?" asked Davian.

"Keep it on you," said Malshash. "Wear it. Don't stray too far from it, ever. It's the anchor that is holding you here in this time. If you get too far away, the pull of your own time may become too strong, draw you back into the rift."

Davian stared at the ring. "Surely that would be what I want? I could go back?"

"No." Malshash shook his head, expression serious. "It's remarkable you survived the journey here, Davian. A miracle. Most people caught in a rift are ripped apart by the sheer force of the transition; if they aren't, they go mad, their minds unable to process the absence of time."

Davian frowned. "Most people?"

Malshash shifted. "Everyone who has ever entered a rift, to the best of my knowledge," he admitted. He sighed. "You will go back, I promise. But you need to hone your Augur abilities, train using kan before you can continue your journey."

Davian looked at Malshash in open surprise. "You can teach me?"

Malshash grinned. "Ah, did I forget to mention? I'm an Augur, too." He continued to smile as he watched Davian's shocked expression, then stood. "Finish up your meal, then rest a little more. I will return in the afternoon and we can begin your training."

Before Davian could recover enough to speak, Malshash had left the room. Davian stared after him, mouth still open, for several more seconds.

"Yes, you forgot to mention that," he eventually muttered to himself.

He returned to his meal, not knowing whether to feel excited or afraid.

A few hours passed before there was a knock on Davian's door.

He had been lying on the bed, tired but unable to sleep, still struggling with the concepts Malshash had tried to explain that morning. He leaped up and opened the door, relieved to find that Malshash's appearance had not changed since breakfast.

"Come with me," said Malshash.

Davian trailed after the shape-shifter. They walked out of the house and down a street, neither toward the center of the city nor toward one of the bridges.

"Where are we going?" Davian asked.

"The Great Library. I can teach you some things, a few tricks here and there, but much would be better coming straight from the Darecians."

Davian nodded, falling silent. They walked at a casual stroll; Davian constantly had to slow to match Malshash's pace, his skin crawling as the mists caressed it. "Aren't you afraid the Orkoth will attack?" he asked nervously.

Malshash shook his head. "We need not fear Orkoth."

Davian was not going to be put off. "Why?"

Malshash stopped in exasperation. He closed his eyes, gesturing in the air.

The mists thickened and a cry came, earsplitting and chilling to the bone. Davian made to flee but suddenly found his shoulder gripped by Malshash, whose eyes were open again.

The Orkoth formed in front of them, as nightmarish as Davian remembered it. Its eyeless gaze sent a shiver down his spine... however, the creature did not seem aggressive. Instead it just stood there, motionless.

Awaiting orders, Davian realized with horror.

"*Adruus il. Devidri si Davian,*" said Malshash, gesturing toward Davian.

"*Devidri si Davian,*" repeated the Orkoth.

"*Sha jannin di,*" said Malshash. The creature bowed— bowed!—and disintegrated into black smoke. Within seconds the mists had faded again.

"You see," said Malshash. "Nothing to fear. Orkoth knows you now. He will not attack you."

Davian gaped for a few moments at Malshash's back as the older man kept walking, then had to jog to catch up.

"Why can you control it?" he asked quietly.

Malshash waved the question away. "A use of kan. Simple enough when you know how." He turned, raising an eyebrow at Davian. "I'm sure you have more important questions, though?"

Davian was tempted to pursue the matter, but some of the questions he had thought of in the past few hours came bubbling to the surface. "When I go back," he said, "will I go back to the same time as I left? Can I save Nihim?"

Malshash shook his head. "If what I suspect is true, then…no. A part of you—the shadow of a shadow of you—remains in your present. That is what will draw you back, when you're ready. As much time as you spend here, the same amount of time will have passed when you return." He shrugged. "The Jha'vett bends the rules, but it seems it cannot break them entirely."

Davian nodded; he'd hoped it would be otherwise but somehow the answer didn't surprise him. "Why did you bring me here?" he asked. "How did you get this ring?"

Malshash didn't stop walking. "I did it to see if I could change things," he said softly. "And I had the ring because you…left it. Left it for me, I suspect."

"So we've met before?"

Malshash shook his head. "Not exactly. But our paths have crossed—in my past, your future. Briefly. I was trying to prevent you from going to that time," he admitted, looking uncomfortable. "But you must have dropped the ring knowing what I would do with it, I suppose. Knowing this younger version of yourself would end up here." He laughed, a little bitterly. "Clever."

Davian hesitated, trying to grasp what Malshash was telling him. "So…you know my future, then?"

"Not really." Malshash gave him an apologetic smile. "Before yesterday all I knew was your name, and that you were able to travel through the rift. I *did* see you at a distance, that one time… you had another scar, on the other side of your face. That was a long time ago for me, though." He shrugged. "That's all I can offer, I'm afraid."

Davian sighed, massaging his temples. "Then why choose me?"

"You were the only person I knew of who had survived the rift. This was…a first step. A relatively simple way to see if the past could be altered."

"So you wanted to use the Jha'vett to change something?"

Malshash stared straight ahead. "Yes. And the reasons behind that are my own." His tone indicated he would say no more about it.

They walked for a few more minutes in silence, until finally they came to a large building with white marble columns at the front and an enormous dome. They climbed the stairs and stopped in front of the massive double doors, which were closed. Malshash gestured at them, and they swung open without a sound.

"The Great Library of Deilannis," he said, indicating Davian should enter.

Davian gaped openly once they were inside. A gentle yellow glow bathed everything, similar to the lighting used in the library back at the school at Caladel. They were in a large room—massive, really—and every wall, every *inch* of wall, was filled with books. They stretched away into each corner; farther along Davian saw an open doorway, through which it seemed there was another room also full to the brim with tomes.

"How are we supposed to find anything in here?" he asked, both awed and a little dismayed.

Malshash grinned. "Fortunately, the Darecians were a rather clever people." He guided Davian over to a short, squat pillar in the center of the room, atop which was a translucent blue stone. "Place your hand over this, and think of what you need to know."

Davian touched the stone lightly. "But I don't know what book I need."

"You don't need to know the name of the book. Just think of what you're trying to find out."

A little skeptical, Davian took a deep breath and concentrated. He was there to learn to use his Augur abilities, so he could go home. That was what he needed.

The stone beneath his palm began to glow; Davian snatched his hand away as if burned, though there had been no physical sensation. A thread of blue light crept from the stone, slowly but surely stretching out, moving toward the wall until it came to rest touching the spine of a small red book. Another tendril appeared, this time drifting in nearly the opposite direction, eventually attaching itself to a book on the other side of the room.

Three more tendrils appeared, Davian watching in stunned silence. When it became clear there were to be no more, he walked over to the first book, which itself now glowed with the gentle blue light.

He took it carefully off the shelf. It didn't have a title, so he flipped it open to a random page.

His eyes widened as he read. It was a discourse, thorough and frank, on the best ways to practice reading another person's thoughts. He flipped to a different section; this one talked about natural offshoots of being an Augur. Even his own ability—the ability to sense deception—was briefly discussed.

He read on in fascination. There were methods to subtly engage a person's thoughts, in order to manipulate them. Implied rules, discussions of moral implications. Techniques of focus, ways to achieve clarity when two minds were linked.

It was all there, written plainly and simply, as if it were nothing at all remarkable.

He was lost for a while, flicking pages back and forth in complete fascination. After a time there came a polite cough, and he looked up to see Malshash watching him in amusement. Davian flushed, realizing he had been caught up for several minutes now.

"Sorry," he said, a little abashed. "It's amazing."

Malshash smiled. "You'd be wise to at least skim all of them," he said, gesturing around. Davian glanced up to see that the other books touched by the tendrils of blue light were still glowing. "The Adviser is rarely wrong. It will have picked out only the very best books to satisfy your query."

Davian looked at the blue stone. "It's called an Adviser?" He gave a slight smirk.

Malshash rolled his eyes. "*I* call it that...you can call it what you want. Just use it. Learn the theory, and I'll help you put it into practice." He gestured around grandly. "All the knowledge of the Darecians is here, Davian. They weren't perfect, but they were more advanced than any other civilization that has walked this earth. Believe me." He turned, heading toward the doorway. "You know the way back? I will be gone for a few days."

Davian froze. "You're leaving?"

"Only for a short while."

"But…" Davian floundered. "I thought you were going to train me?"

"I will," Malshash reassured him.

"What if someone else comes?" pressed Davian. The thought of being left alone in the city frightened him. "Am I safe from the Orkoth?"

Malshash grunted. "I told you, Orkoth won't harm you now. And there is no one and nothing else here to fear."

Davian gave an uncertain shrug. "So I'll just…see what I can find?"

Malshash smiled. "Good. Study hard. The faster you understand the basics, the faster you will be able to return home."

Without anything further he turned and left.

Davian stared after him for a few moments, feeling cast adrift. He hadn't known what to think of Malshash—still didn't; the man clearly didn't want to reveal much about himself—but the presence of another human being had been comforting. Left so completely alone now, Davian was struck by just how silent the building was, how empty the city felt.

Shaking off the sensation as best he could, he turned back to the book in his hand. Whatever else the events of the last few days had done, they had delivered him an amazing opportunity to learn about his powers—his hopes for which had been dashed since the moment he'd realized Ilseth Tenvar had lied to him.

His face hardened into a mask of determination as, for the first time in a while, he allowed himself to think about the man who had fooled him into this journey. Who had probably known in advance that Asha was going to die.

He would learn these abilities, and find a way back to his own time. Do his best to stop whatever was going on with the Boundary.

And after that he would seek out Ilseth Tenvar.

# Chapter 29

Caeden woke.

He climbed slowly to his feet, wincing as he stretched stiff muscles. It was just past dawn; the sun had not yet risen above the mountains behind them.

They were only a day past Deilannis, yet already he felt...less. The overpowering familiarity he'd felt in the city—his recognition of buildings, streets—had faded almost as soon as they had left the mists. He'd felt *stronger* there, more confident.

Now it was all a distant memory, and the old feelings of helplessness had returned. He didn't know who he was. Didn't know why Davian had been sent to find him, or why he was connected to the Vessel Taeris was carrying, or what he was involved in.

Worst of all, he didn't know if he'd done what he'd been accused of.

He rubbed the Shackle on his left arm, trying to ignore the constant glow of the wolf tattoo there. Its light never faded; Taeris still had the Vessel on his person somewhere, though Caeden hadn't sighted it since Thrindar. There were moments he'd considered trying to find it—there had been opportunities, while Taeris was asleep—but caution had won out each time. Taeris said it could be dangerous, and the scarred man had helped him, *saved* him. Caeden had to put aside his uncertainties and trust in his companions.

Still, the lure of the box was almost more than he could bear, sometimes. None of them spoke about it, but everyone knew that there was a possibility it was meant to restore his memories. And as much as Caeden dreaded that happening, not knowing the truth was worse by far.

Sighing, he glanced over toward the rest of the group as they began to stir.

Everyone's mood, Caeden's included, had been understandably morose since the loss of Davian and Nihim. Caeden had liked Davian, and his conversation with Nihim after his duel had been a comfort, too. He'd felt their absence keenly since Deilannis, and still sometimes found himself glancing over his shoulder, scanning the horizon for them.

He often caught Wirr doing the same thing. Despite Taeris's grim assurances, none of them really felt as though the other two were truly gone.

He stretched, nodding to Taeris, who was already up and had evidently been on watch. Though Caeden tried not to let on, Taeris's scars sometimes made him uncomfortable. They were a constant reminder of what the Gil'shar had accused him of doing to the villagers' bodies.

Taeris nodded back, looking thoughtful, then walked over to him.

"Can I trust you?"

Caeden blinked, taken aback by the question. "Yes. Of course," he replied after a moment.

Taeris locked eyes with him for a long few seconds. Then he reached down and, before Caeden realized what was happening, touched the Shackle on his arm.

There was a cold, slithering feeling, and the metallic torc dropped to the ground. Caeden shook his head in surprise. He suddenly felt lighter, more energetic. Free. Even the tattoo on his wrist seemed to pulse brighter. It had been so long since he'd felt this way, he'd barely remembered what it was like.

Aelric, who was standing a little way off, rushed over when he saw what was happening. "What do you think you're doing?" he exclaimed.

Taeris raised an eyebrow at him. "I've been thinking about this all night, Aelric, and Caeden has earned our trust. We have monsters hunting us—going through Deilannis has gained us some respite, but they won't have given up. And you saw how powerful those creatures are. We need every advantage we can get."

Aelric scowled. "You still can't let him free," he said grimly. He turned to Caeden. "I'm sorry. I'm not saying I think you're a threat to us, but after what you were accused of in Desriel..."

Taeris scowled back. "He's been with me for many weeks now, Aelric. He *saved* us in Deilannis, and I'm risking my life to bring him before the Council. I feel warranted in making this decision."

Caeden frowned. Taeris's voice was suddenly...small. Far off. He tried to focus on what else was being said, but the sounds all blurred together.


*He stood on a hilltop, a breathtaking vista below him—green fields and rolling hills for a short distance, and beyond that the ocean, glittering like diamonds in the afternoon sunlight. A pleasant warm breeze ruffled his hair gently. He was suddenly aware he was holding hands with someone; he looked to his side, heart leaping to his throat.*

*The most beautiful woman he had ever seen was standing next to him. Her alabaster skin was flawless. Her long black hair was loose, cascading down her back almost to her waist, shining in the sunlight. She had a perfectly oval face, with full, red lips and cheeks rosy from the climb up the hill. Her eyes were blue, not like the ocean or the sky, but something deeper, stronger, more indefinable. She turned to him, smiling, and those eyes shone as they gazed upon him. So focused. As if he were the only thing in the world, or at least the only thing of importance.*

*The image faded, the color draining away from the scene. He was standing outside a massive city. Even from a distance away the walls loomed ominously; at a glance he thought they were at least a hundred feet high, probably more. They were made from black stone, jagged edges everywhere.*

*Above the walls rose the city itself. It was built atop a peak; Caeden couldn't see any buildings near the wall, but could easily make out roads and structures farther toward the city center. Nothing moved within, though. There were no guards, nor any* gates he could see. Massive fires burned at various points around the top of the wall, the red-orange of the flames the only color in an otherwise drab landscape.

It was night, the moonlight casting a strange silver pallor over everything. He was in a field, though most of the grass was dead, or at least struggling to survive. He looked over his shoulder. There were no trees in sight, with the flat, barren fields stretching on as far as the eye could see in all directions. All was silent here. No wind, no animals.

Then he was somewhere else. It was day again, he thought, but the sky was blacked out by billowing smoke from burning homes. Around him he could hear the screams of people as they died, not quite drowning out the quieter cries of panic and confusion. The smoke shifted and twisted around him; suddenly two dark silhouettes were visible through it. They were humanoid in nature, but too tall, too thin.

Then he could see them properly. Covered in black scales, the creatures stood at least nine feet tall; their bodies were slim and sinuous, with no necks to speak of. Their heads were shaped like snakes', and when they looked at him, he saw the rows of tiny, sharp teeth that filled their mouths. The two creatures watched him for a moment, lashing their tails as they stared hungrily. There was something eerily intelligent about their expressions.

Then they were gone into the smoke, moving faster than he would have believed.

He was kneeling. He looked up to see the smoke had gone; he was in an underground cavern of some kind, the roof stretching upward so far that he could barely see the top. He was sweating; a little way to his left a pool of molten rock bubbled threateningly.

In front of him was a being that appeared made of pure fire, its skin smoldering and writhing, even the strands of its hair glowing with energy. Its eyes, though, contemplating him, were undeniably human.

The creature was holding a sword, and Caeden knew that the sword was important somehow. It bent the light around it, drank it in, but Caeden could still see the symbols inscribed onto the blade, words in a different language. They were familiar to him, but he didn't have time to concentrate on them.

"You are unworthy," said the creature holding the sword. Its voice was rough, deep, and knowledgeable. "You have come for Licanius, and so may not have her."

The scene shifted yet again, but this time the sensation was different, though he couldn't say how. He stood in the center of a large, open field; it was night, and a gentle breeze made the long grass seem as though there were silvery-black waves sliding over the ground. Everything was in stark contrast, with the moonlight almost blinding, and the shadows as dark and impenetrable as pitch. He looked down. He was wearing a black tunic of fine silk, the threads snug against his skin. It was a familiar feeling. A good feeling.

In the distance, emerging from a copse of swaying birches, he saw a man approach. As he came closer, Caeden could see that he was tall, muscular, with chiseled features and a wide, welcoming smile. The man raised his hand in greeting; hesitantly Caeden raised his in return. A sense of familiarity flashed through him. Somehow, from somewhere, he knew this man.

"Tal'kamar!" the man called when he was closer, a jovial, welcoming note in his voice. He strode over, and before Caeden could react he was being wrapped in a fierce embrace. "I knew you'd find your way here eventually! It is good to see you, old friend."

Caeden blinked. "Is this actually happening?" He knew as soon as he said the words that it was. The previous images had been vague, hazy—memories, perhaps, though seen in a detached sort of way. This was something different.

The man chuckled. "Of course! We're in a dok'en. Your dok'en, actually." His smile slipped a little. "You're serious?"

Caeden's heart leaped. This man knew him—appeared even to be friends with him. "I'm sorry," he said earnestly. "I know it sounds strange, but I have no memory of anything beyond a month or so ago. If you know me..."

The man's smile faded entirely. "Then it is true," he said, sadness in his voice. He sighed. "My name is Alaris." He put his hand on Caeden's shoulder. "We are friends, you and I. Brothers."

Caeden leaned forward. "You can tell me who I am? How I came to be here?"

Alaris nodded. "Yes, of course," he said in an amiable tone. He glanced around. "There may not be time right now, though."

"Why?"

Alaris gestured. "Look for yourself."

Caeden looked back over his shoulder. A black shadow had fallen over some of the field; where there had once been a wide expanse of open grass, there was now nothing to be seen. As he watched, the shadow inched forward some more. He turned back to Alaris, panic welling up inside him.

"What happens when the shadow reaches us?"

Alaris smiled. "Nothing, to you. It's your dok'en."

"'Dok'en'?" The word was familiar, but Caeden couldn't recall its meaning.

Alaris rolled his eyes in amusement. "A place you created some time ago, Tal'kamar. Once you had many of these lying around, and I knew where you'd hidden most of them...but this is the only one that I know of now. You must not have lost all of your memories, to find your way back here." He looked around with a frown. "Dok'en are always based on real places, though, and I'm not sure where this was in real life. The Shattered Lands, perhaps? You were always fond of traveling there." He checked the oncoming shadow again. "Regardless. You're not doing a terribly good job of keeping this place stable, and I really do need to leave before everything disappears, so let's make this quick. Where are you?"

Caeden hesitated. The man knew him, but was he trustworthy? Eventually he shook his head. "People are hunting us, and I do not know you," he said. "I'm sorry."

Alaris looked exasperated, but gave a reluctant nod. "I understand." Then he frowned. "Wait. 'Us'?"

"The people I am traveling with," elaborated Caeden, still unsure how much to reveal. "Gifted."

Alaris looked displeased at that. "And who is hunting you?"

"Creatures. They're called sha'teth."

Alaris's expression froze, and Caeden thought he saw a flicker of fear in his eyes. "I see," he said quietly, all humor vanished.

"You know of them?"

Alaris glanced over Caeden's shoulder, clearly distracted by the oncoming shadow. "You could say that. A tale for another time, my friend." He grabbed Caeden by the arm. "You are in serious danger, Tal'kamar. If the people you are with find out who you really are, they will kill you without a second's hesitation. We are at war, and though they may not seem like it now, they are the enemy." His expression was deadly serious.

Caeden shook his head, refusing to accept the statement. "They have already risked their lives for me."

"Because they don't know who you are," countered Alaris. He eyed the field behind Caeden nervously. "Read them. If you don't find they're capable of what I say, then forget I ever spoke ill of them."

Caeden shook his head. "I . . . don't know how," he said, a little embarrassed.

Alaris looked at Caeden, his expression pitying. "I see," he said softly. "It's like that." He hesitated. "I'm sorry, Tal'kamar. There simply isn't time to explain."

He started backing away; Caeden turned to see that the shadow was almost upon them. "The dok'en is about to fail, Tal'kamar," said Alaris. "Once that happens, we cannot use it again. I may not see you for some time." He paused, looking conflicted, then came to a decision. "In Ilin Illan there lives a man called Havran Das. Find a way to get to him, without your companions knowing. He's a merchant dealing in fine wines, and someone who is . . . reliable. I will contact him myself; he will be able to help you."

Caeden shook his head. "Why should I trust you?"

Alaris gripped Caeden's arm. "Because we are brothers, and we have a bond that not even time can break." He closed his eyes. "Until we meet again, my friend. It was good to see you."

"Wait! One more question." Caeden clenched his fists; he was afraid to ask, but he had to know. "I was accused of a crime, from before I can remember. Killing people . . . slaughtering them for no reason." He watched Alaris closely, dreading the answer. "Is that the kind of man I am? Would I have done that?"

Alaris hesitated.

"No, Tal'kamar," he said softly. "Never without a reason."

He faded just as the shadow touched Caeden.

"Caeden," came Taeris's voice.

He shook his head, trying to focus. The world around him bled back into view, slowly regaining color and clarity. He was on the ground. Taeris was looking at him anxiously and the others were watching from a little distance away, concern on their faces, too.

"Take it easy," Taeris advised as Caeden struggled to rise. "You collapsed."

Caeden took a moment, then levered himself upward. The momentary disorientation had passed.

"I'm fine," he said, getting to his feet. Still, his stomach lurched. *Never without a reason.*

"What happened?" asked Wirr.

Caeden stared at the worried faces around him for a long moment. Then he glanced at Aelric, who was clearly still concerned that his Shackle had been removed.

"Just a dizzy spell," he assured everyone.

Taeris hesitated, then gave him a gentle clap on the back. "Probably a side effect of having the Shackle on for so long," he said. "Are you able to travel?"

Caeden gave a silent nod of confirmation, his thoughts already elsewhere.

*Havran Das.*

He fixed the name in his mind as he began helping the others break camp. He didn't know if he could trust Alaris, but one thing was certain.

He was going to find out more once they reached Ilin Illan.

# Chapter 30

Wirr poked at the fire with a stick, keeping a thoughtful silence.

He glanced across at the three sleeping forms lying at the edge of the flickering light. Caeden had made his excuses and retired early tonight; though apparently recovered from his sudden collapse that morning, he'd seemed a little off throughout the day. Aelric and Dezia had soon followed, leaving Wirr and Taeris on first watch.

The lack of conversation had suited Wirr. He needed time to gather himself after the madness of the past couple of days.

His thoughts, as they often did now, drifted to the friend he'd lost. Wirr forced himself to picture Davian's face—to once again accept the accompanying pain and regret that settled heavily in his chest. He knew he should have been smarter than to shout out, to try to draw on Essence.

He recalled that moment. The dar'gaithin, the shouting. The desperate sprint after Caeden, back the way they had come.

Then he frowned. Since leaving Deilannis, something had been tugging at the corners of his mind, small but insistent. This time he realized what it was.

"What was in the building?" he asked abruptly, tone low so as not to wake the others.

Taeris blinked, shaken from a reverie of his own. "Pardon?"

Wirr leaned forward. "The building," he repeated. "In Deilannis. You were going to go inside." His frown deepened as he remembered. "You led us there, didn't you? You knew it wasn't the way out. Caeden even told you, but you ignored him."

Taeris stared at Wirr for a moment. "Yes."

Rage began to boil up inside Wirr; it was all he could do to keep his voice low. "Why? Davian and Nihim died, Taeris! My friend and your friend died because you wanted something so badly, you were willing to risk all our lives for it. So you will tell me what was in that building." His voice was cold and hard, anger sitting just beneath the surface.

"A weapon," said Taeris, looking more resigned than surprised at Wirr's tone. "A weapon that was built to defeat Aarkein Devaed himself. Lost for thousands of years." He sighed. "The time approaches, Wirr, when we may need a weapon against whatever is waiting for us in the north. So...yes. I risked lives."

Wirr felt some of the anger drain away, but far from all of it. "And what would this weapon be?"

"I don't know," admitted Taeris. "That's part of the problem. We need to know what it is, how it works, *before* the time comes to put it to use."

Wirr shook his head. "You should have told us. We had a right to know," he said furiously. "Why now? You've lived in Desriel for years. Why wait?"

Taeris bowed his head. "Because it was only supposed to be Nihim," he said, voice aching.

Wirr frowned in confusion. "What do you mean?"

Taeris took a deep breath. "Before the Unseen War, Nihim was approached by an Augur, who told him he would die in Deilannis—but in the process, supposedly, of helping one of the most important men of our time. The Augur also told him— promised him!—that no one else would die. That all others traveling with him would be safe." He shook his head. "I thought... I thought it gave me a free pass, Wirr. Nihim insisted on coming, said it was his time. I thought that knowing he was the only one who died would give us impunity to investigate. That it was perhaps my only chance to do so safely." He looked up. "I'm sorry."

Wirr saw it then—the guilt that was crushing Taeris, as real and raw as his own.

It didn't matter, though. In some ways it was worse; Wirr had been shouldering the burden of Davian's death, when in reality

that responsibility was shared.

"So you risked our lives, based on a vision an Augur told you twenty years ago. Despite knowing that their visions stopped coming to pass," he said in quiet disbelief. He stood, hands shaking, almost too angry to think. "I'm going for a walk."

Taeris grimaced. "That's probably not the best idea—"

"Enough, Taeris," Wirr snarled as softly as he could. "I'll stay nearby in case there's trouble."

He walked off into the darkness, the jumble of emotions that had died down since Deilannis back now, worse than ever. He'd just pushed them down before, but he knew he needed to deal with them this time.

He found a log still dry despite the damp of the evening, well away from the fire, out of earshot of the rest of the camp. He sat, staring at nothing for several long minutes.

Finally the tears began to fall. The frustration, the anger, the pain all bubbled to the surface, and he let them out, weeping harder than when he'd heard about Caladel—as he hadn't done since he was a child, the day he'd discovered he was Gifted.

There was nothing left. Everything from the past three years, everything he'd valued, was gone forever.

He didn't move for a long time.

It was an hour later when Wirr returned.

Taeris watched him silently, nodding as he sat down on the opposite side of the fire. Wirr stared at the other man for a long moment, then cleared his throat.

"I'm not sure I can forgive you," he said, keeping his voice low. He held up his hand as Taeris opened his mouth. "Perhaps in time. However, I understand what you were trying to do. I understand that you thought we were safe." He set his face in a grim mask as he leaned forward. "But the secrets have to stop *here*. Here and now. If you'd just explained what we were doing beforehand, we might have agreed to help. Us knowing might have changed things...we might be young, Taeris, but we're not children. We're on your side. You don't need to lie to us."

Taeris considered, then slowly inclined his head. "True. But that needs to go both ways."

Wirr grimaced; he'd thought long and hard about this, and he knew he was just as guilty as Taeris when it came to keeping secrets. He nodded. "Very well. Allow me to start." He rose, crossed to the other side of the fire, and extended his hand to Taeris. "I am Prince Torin Wirrander Andras."

Taeris gave the hand a blank stare. "The son of Elocien Andras." The shock on his face made it very hard for Wirr not to laugh.

"I am," said Wirr, allowing himself a smile.

Taeris let out a long breath, puffing his cheeks out. "That makes no sense."

Wirr's smile faded, and he lowered his hand. This was not the reaction he had been expecting. "Why not?"

"Because I've met Elocien Andras. The man that I remember would have killed his son if he'd turned out to be Gifted." Taeris looked Wirr in the eye. "He's the one who sentenced me, you know."

Wirr shrugged. "He changed. When I was growing up, he did hate the Gifted. But when he found out I was one, he wasn't angry." He smiled at the recollection. "I was so scared. I'd been brought up calling them bleeders, and then to discover I was one of them...I thought he would disown me, but he didn't. He arranged everything. The falsified trip to Calandra. Secret meetings with Athian to get me placed discreetly in a school. He risked everything for me. He was amazing."

Taeris scratched his head. "He was a Loyalist, though. He *created the Tenets*," he said in disbelief. His eyes widened as the implications struck home. "And—fates, lad. The Tenets. You'll inherit your father's connection to the Vessel?"

Wirr gave a small nod of affirmation.

Taeris shook his head, dazed, silent for a long moment. "Administration are not going to be very happy when they find out," he said eventually.

"I've already thought of that," observed Wirr, his tone dry.

"Of course. Of course." Taeris looked at Wirr, still stunned, evidently reassessing him. "I assume this means you won't be coming with us to the Tol."

Wirr nodded. "That would be best. I'll head for the palace with

Aelric and Dezia once we reach the city. My father's hoping to keep my abilities a secret until I'm well established at court—maybe longer—so I'll need to stay away from the Tol where possible, in case I'm recognized."

"A wise choice." Taeris looked at Wirr consideringly. "You've given some thought as to how you'll change the Tenets, then?"

"I have, but I'll think about it more when the time comes. It's hopefully a long way off." Wirr raised an eyebrow. "You don't advocate removing them entirely?"

Taeris grunted. "No." He said nothing more on the subject.

There was silence for a while, then Wirr said, "So you knew my father?"

Taeris shook his head. "Apparently not," he said quietly. "But I've met him. Spoken with him." He didn't look pleased at the memory.

Wirr shifted. "I remember him talking about you, you know. He didn't tell me all the details—I got those from Karaliene, in the end—but he did say you were the perfect example of why the Treaty was necessary. Of why no Gifted could ever be trusted." He sighed. "That was only a few months before I discovered I had the Gift."

"I thought you were reluctant to trust me, to begin with," Taeris admitted. "Now I understand why."

Wirr looked at the scarred man intently. "There's something I've been wondering about. The man my father was talking about, the man Karaliene described to me, was a monster. They were *afraid* of you, Taeris. Karaliene I can understand—but my father? If there had been some conspiracy to convict you, surely he would have known about it."

Taeris shrugged. "Perhaps he truly believed I'd used Essence to kill those men. Any Administrator in his right mind would be afraid of someone who could break the Tenets."

The words rang true, but there was something in Taeris's eyes when he spoke. A hesitation, a flicker of worry.

Wirr scowled. "No more secrets, Taeris. You understand the enormity of the trust I've placed in you by revealing mine. I won't tell anyone, but for my own sake I need to know. I need to be able to reconcile what I was told with the man I see before me."

He leaned forward. "I saw you that night, in Thrindar. With the knife. So tell me the truth, Taeris. How *did* you get all those scars?"

Taeris grimaced, then after a few seconds gave a slow nod. He glanced over his shoulder to make sure everyone else was still asleep before he spoke.

"Very well," he said quietly. "The truth is, I was in Caladel when I saw Davian being tailed by a group of men. There weren't any Administrators around, so I followed at a distance to make sure nothing happened to the lad. When he passed the tavern, the men grabbed him and dragged him inside.

"There was an Administrator coming out just as I went to go in. I asked him to help, but he said the boy wasn't Gifted and so there was nothing he could do." Taeris's mouth curled in distaste at the memory. "So I went in. They'd already started roughing him up."

Wirr nodded. Davian never spoke of that day—Wirr knew his friend had blocked out the memories—but from what he'd heard, Davian's injuries had been many and severe.

"I pleaded with them to stop, but they held me down, too. Told me there was nothing I could do to stop them, that by the Tenets I couldn't take action against them." Taeris winced. "Your friend was a brave lad. He took the punches and the kicks in silence.

"Then one of them noticed the Mark on Davian's arm. I don't think it was there until the beating; I assume his body had never needed to draw enough Essence to activate the Tenets before. But once they saw it, the mood changed. They were only roughing him up a bit when they thought he was just a servant. When they saw he was Gifted..." He trailed off for a moment.

"One of the men who'd had too much to drink brought out a knife. A big man, not the kind of man any of the others would have tried to stop, even if they'd wanted to. He was screaming something about his father dying at the hands of the Augurs, and that anyone even associated with them was...diseased." He looked sick at the memory. "He started cutting into Davian's face. Davian was screaming, but everyone else was just watching. Silent."

Wirr shivered. He'd always known that what Davian had been

through must have been awful, but he'd never envisaged it this graphically before. "Then what happened?"

Taeris hesitated. "Then the man stopped. They all just... stopped. The ones who were holding me down let me go. The one holding the knife turned it so that the edge was against his own face and... started cutting." He drew a deep breath. "Then we all started doing it. All at once. Those of us who didn't have a knife went and found one from one of the tables. None of us made a sound, but that didn't mean it wasn't agony." He touched his cheek absently.

"Davian just stood there, watching us, the blood pouring down his face and neck onto his shirt. I could see it, though. He was doing it. He was controlling us, somehow."

"*What?*" Wirr exploded. He felt his face grow red with anger. "You're going to blame *Davian* for what happened?"

"You asked for the truth," said Taeris softly, checking to see none of the others had woken. "My Reserve saved me, but everyone else died. All at the same time, just dropped to the floor; as soon as they did, I could control my body again. I checked them but there was no heartbeat, no breath. Nothing. And when I went back to Davian, he'd fallen unconscious from the loss of blood.

"I had to make a choice, so I used Essence to save him. That drew the Administrators, and once they saw the bodies they wanted an explanation." Taeris shrugged. "I knew what the penalty was going to be, regardless of how it had happened or who had done it. I was an old man already, Davian just a child. It was an easy decision to tell them the lie."

Wirr felt a chill run down his spine. "And Davian never remembered?"

"Thank El," murmured Taeris. "Knowing him as I came to over the past few weeks, I don't think he would ever have forgiven himself if he'd found out." He leaned forward. "This is important, though, Wirr. I don't believe he knew what he was doing. The look in his eyes... it was vacant. Like he wasn't even really there. I think what he did was from a pure survival instinct, nothing more."

Wirr gave a slow, reluctant nod. "And your scars? What I saw in Thrindar?"

Taeris sighed. "Since that day...I've been linked to Davian, somehow, and it's as if there's some remnant of that moment in my mind. I wake up sometimes and I've cut myself. Or I have the knife in my hand. I never remember any of it, but I've always been able to sense where Davian is, so it seems likely that there was some sort of connection still there. After Deilannis..." His gaze dropped to the fire. "It was like a pressure inside my head disappeared. Now Davian's gone, I don't think it's going to happen anymore."

Wirr processed what Taeris had told him. It made sense. Davian's Augur powers had saved him, somehow. Taeris, believing the boy was meant for something more, had taken the blame.

"You finding us that night in the forest wasn't a coincidence," he realized.

Taeris shook his head. "I *was* in the area because of Caeden, originally...but when I realized Davian was so close, I started tracking you. Trying to figure out why you'd come to Desriel," he admitted. He gestured to his face. "Honestly, I'd hoped he was there for me. I thought perhaps he was tracking me down so he could sever the connection. But when I realized he didn't know what had happened, didn't have control of his Augur abilities... well, he'd been through enough already. There didn't seem any benefit to adding to the poor lad's burden."

Wirr was silent for a long time.

"You did the right thing, Taeris," he said eventually.

Wirr had more questions, and he knew that Taeris probably had more for him, but after the revelations of the evening they were both content to just sit, mulling over what they had learned. Wirr had been staring into the fire for so long that he started at a sudden tapping on his shoulder.

It was Aelric. "My turn," he said with a tired smile. "Get some rest."

Wirr tried to sleep, but for a long time all he could think of was Davian and what Taeris had said. For some reason Wirr believed him, though there would be no way of ever proving the story.

His last thought before he finally slept was that he wished Davian could have known just how much Taeris had sacrificed for him.

# Chapter 31

Asha reclined in the armchair across from her bed, smiling as she listened to Fessi's idle chatter.

It was late, but for once Asha didn't mind. She'd arrived back at her rooms to find the youngest of the Augurs waiting to deliver another vision to her, but it hadn't taken long for the slightly awkward formalities to turn into a more relaxed, friendly conversation. They had been talking for a while now; the other girl had an open, laid-back personality that had put Asha immediately at ease.

Asha hadn't yet read the slip of paper she'd been given, but judging from Fessi's demeanor it wasn't urgent. Despite the hour, Asha hadn't pushed for Fessi to leave so she could look at it, either. She had no desire to interrupt the first pleasant conversation she'd had in what felt like months.

And more than that, it was helping to keep her mind from what had transpired the previous afternoon.

Between Davian's appearance yesterday and the ever-looming threat of the Blind—which no one in the city yet seemed to be taking seriously—she'd been distracted all day, much to the vexation of an obviously frustrated Michal. All she had been able to think about was Davian. Whether his presence had been a dream, a vision . . . or real. Whether he was alive, or whether her subconscious was somehow feeding her false hope. Every time she had almost convinced herself of one, she began to vacillate.

"So you said it was through one of your visions that Elocien found Kol?" she asked, before she got caught up in her own thoughts again.

Fessi nodded. "Several of them, actually. It wasn't until I saw him drawing Essence from a forge that I realized why I was Seeing him so often." She hesitated, a smirk and a slight blush spreading across her face. "Before that, though, a few of the visions were... interesting."

Asha gave her a quizzical look. "How so?"

Fessi coughed. "The visions didn't always show him when he was... appropriately dressed, I suppose you would say."

Asha stared at her for a moment in surprise, then laughed.

"Don't tell him I told you that. I was never able to bring myself to admit it to him."

Asha shook her head in amusement, then sobered a little as her thoughts turned to the big man. What he'd Seen. "How *is* Kol?" she asked tentatively. "I know he wasn't happy when I showed up..."

Fessi made a dismissive gesture. "He's fine. He knows we needed a Scribe, and he knows Erran wouldn't have chosen you unless you were absolutely trustworthy, no matter what happened with the Shadraehin." She shrugged. "He can be a bit of a storm cloud when you don't know him, to be honest. He doesn't tend to open up to people until he's known them for a while, and until then, he just comes across as big and grumbly. But once you get past that... he's a good friend."

Asha raised a questioning eyebrow at the warmth in Fessi's tone, and the other girl's cheeks reddened a little. Asha didn't say anything, though.

They sat in silence for a few seconds, then Asha gestured to the piece of paper on her desk. "So. Is this anything urgent?"

Fessi sighed. "Not unless you're worried about me getting a scolding from Trae tomorrow."

Asha winced in sympathy; Trae was the head cook and from what Fessi had previously indicated, not exactly an affable sort of fellow. In a small way, Fessi's description of him reminded her of Mistress Alita back at Caladel.

She pushed down a sudden wave of sadness at the thought, but the association with the school had already dragged Davian to the front of her mind again. For a few seconds, all she could think about was how he'd looked the day before. Old. Tired. Scarred

and chained.

"Are...you all right?" Fessi frowned in consternation. "Did I say something wrong?"

"No. It's..." Asha rubbed her forehead tiredly. "It's nothing."

Fessi's eyes narrowed. "You may know how to shield yourself now, and I may not have Erran's skill, but I can tell it's not nothing." The black-haired girl hesitated, then leaned forward, her expression serious. "Look—I know what it's like, not having anyone to talk to. Elocien was always too busy for anything more than debriefing, and I obviously couldn't discuss my visions with Kol or Erran, either. Honestly, tonight is the first really open conversation I've had in a long time—and I appreciate that. So if there's any way I can return the favor, I'm happy to listen."

Asha hesitated. She almost refused out of instinct, accustomed as she was by now to keeping things to herself...but she didn't. She liked Fessi, knew the other girl could be trusted. And Asha hadn't had the opportunity to talk to someone—*really* talk to someone—in a very long time.

She couldn't let Fessi know about Davian, of course; whether he had been real or not, admitting to anyone that she'd seen him seemed like a bad idea. But everything leading up to that was another matter.

So Asha slowly, hesitantly told Fessi about Caladel. About her time in the Tol, about what had happened in the Sanctuary with Jin and Aelrith and the Shadraehin. It was hard, at times, but it also felt good to get it off her chest—to be able to share the burdens of the last couple of months with someone who actually seemed to care.

Fessi listened the entire time in attentive silence; when Asha had finished, the other girl quietly began relating her own story. How someone in her own close-knit village had betrayed her to Administration when they'd realized she was an Augur. How Fessi's family had refused to even say good-bye to their teenage daughter, who was presumably being taken away to be executed.

And how terrified she had been, every time she thought of her own death. How she couldn't sleep some nights, knowing what was coming.

They talked a while longer after that, but eventually there was a natural break in the conversation and both girls stood, knowing it was getting into the early hours of the morning. They exchanged a warm embrace at the door.

"No matter what you went through before this, Asha, I'm glad you're here now," said Fessi as they parted.

"As am I," said Asha with a smile. She meant it.

Once back in her room, Asha busied herself getting ready for bed. She would have only a few hours until Michal woke her, but for once the thought didn't make her scowl.

An abrupt knock on the door made her jump; she shook her head, giving a rueful smile at her own startled reaction. Fessi must have forgotten something.

She opened the door absently, barely having time to register the black-veined face behind the fist blurring toward her.

Everything went black.

Asha groaned.

She was lying on her side on a hard wooden floor; she groaned again as she shifted, her head throbbing. She slowly forced her eyes open, the eyelid on the left struggling to break free of the sticky, semidried blood that she suspected ran all the way down her face and neck.

There was light, too bright to look at initially. A lamp. With an awkward motion, she twisted and rolled into a seated position against the timber wall. Her hands were tied behind her back, but she didn't need to check to know she must have a serious gash on her forehead; aside from the pain, there was a brown circle of blood on the floor where she'd been lying. She took a deep breath, trying to focus.

The small room was lit only by the lamp on the table; there was a seat next to that, but otherwise her surroundings were bare. A door at the far end of the room was shut, and looked solidly made. It was doubtless locked, but Asha slid herself over to it anyway, levering herself to her feet and barely managing to get her hands on the doorknob.

She scowled as it refused to turn. Just as she'd expected.

She assessed the rest of the room, forcing herself to stay calm. There was no point in calling out; if she couldn't hear anyone outside then there was likely no one around to help. And she didn't want to draw the attention of whoever had brought her here. This might be her best, or only, opportunity to find a way out.

She made her way back over to where she'd started, feeling at her bindings as she went. The knots were tight, but she thought she might be able to undo them, in time. Whoever had tied them must have been in a hurry. Or, she hoped, simply careless.

She frowned as she recalled the man who had attacked her. He had definitely been a Shadow...which more than suggested that the Shadraehin had become tired of her lack of answers. But Scyner hadn't struck her as an impatient man, nor did he have any reason to think she wasn't doing her best to fulfill her side of the bargain. It might be taking longer than he had anticipated—but kidnapping her? It didn't feel right, didn't feel like something he would gain any advantage from.

She heard the scraping of boots outside the door and quickly lay back down, resting her head back in the tacky pool of reddish-brown blood. The lock clicked and the door creaked as it swung open.

"Still out," growled a deep voice as heavy footsteps clomped into the room. "You shouldn't have hit her so hard, Teran. Shadraehin won't be happy if he finds out we hurt her."

"The Shadraehin won't be happy if he finds out we *touched* her," came the dry response. "And as for hitting her so hard, I apologize. Next time I'll try and hit the person I'm trying to knock out with just the right amount of force." This man sounded sharper, more eloquent. There was a pause, and then he continued, "Besides, she's awake. Get up, girl. I can see the bloodstain from where you moved."

Asha hesitated, then rolled into a sitting position, staring at the two men as calmly as she could.

The man closest to her was Teran, the one who had hit her. A portly Shadow with a round, cheerful face, he was the least likely looking kidnapper Asha could have imagined.

The other she recognized from around the palace, though she had never interacted with him. He was muscular, thickly built, probably someone who served in a heavy labor capacity.

"Why am I here?" she asked quietly. Her head still swam a little from the pain, but she did her best not to show it.

The big man scowled, but Teran just gave her a slight smile. "Direct. I like that." He grabbed the chair from beside the table and swung it around so that it faced Asha, then sat on it. "I think you know why you're here, Ashalia. We very much would like the information you promised the Shadraehin. The information you *owe* him."

Asha scowled. "As I already explained to the many messengers you sent—I don't have it yet. The duke doesn't trust me enough to tell me everything." She shook her head, doing her best to look irritated rather than scared. "Why would I lie about this?"

"I don't know," admitted Teran. "But we've been keeping an eye on you, and fates take me if you're not in the Northwarden's inner circle. Fates, he made you a Representative! You're holding out on us, Ashalia." He leaned forward. "I'm sure of it."

Asha stared at him steadily. "Perhaps it would be better if you got the Shadraehin to come down here himself, clear all of this up." If Davian had been right and the Shadraehin was actually a woman, these two appeared to be unaware.

The big man shifted, looking uncomfortable, but Teran simply smiled at her. He rose, stepped forward, and casually backhanded her across the face; the force of the blow sent her reeling, her vision blurring as new pain joined the already pounding ache of her skull.

"So you overheard us talking. Congratulations," Teran continued, as if nothing had happened. "The thing is, Ashalia, the Shadraehin wants us to keep an eye on you until you hold up your end of the bargain. Which wasn't a problem until the other day, when he informed us that we were to stay up here and keep watching you even if this army, these 'Blind,' reach the city—that no matter how dangerous it gets, we are not to go back to the Sanctuary until he has his information."

His expression twisted. "And when I can see that you're keeping me here in harm's way, that upsets me. So you're going to keep your end of the Shadraehin's bargain, or I'll start making things...unpleasant for you." He leaned forward, touching Asha's cheek gently.

Asha jerked away, giving Teran a furious glare.

"We'll give you some time to think it over," said Teran.

He nodded to the other man and the two left, locking the door behind them.

Asha swallowed, staring around the room in desperation, but this inspection revealed no more opportunities for escape than before. She took a deep breath, trying to order her thoughts. She was bound, and even if she hadn't been, her chances of overpowering both men were next to none. She would be missed soon enough at the palace, of course—but no one would know where to look for her.

By the time the door opened again, maybe a half hour later, she knew what she needed to do.

"I'll tell you what you need to know," she announced to the two men as they entered.

The big man's eyes lit up, but Teran stared at her with suspicion. "You don't strike me as the type to give up so easily."

Asha glared at him. "I was always going to hold up my end of the bargain. I just don't have the proof yet," she explained in a grim tone. "The information I have is useless to the Shadraehin without that."

"So what is it?"

"The Northwarden discovered that a faction within Administration is behind the attacks." It was one of the more credible theories she'd formed after the Sanctuary, when she'd been waiting for Elocien to find her at the Tol. Asha stared Teran in the eye, willing him to believe her. "He's trying to cover it up, but there are documents that prove it. Signed orders."

Teran snorted. "And I suppose you want us to just let you go, so you can retrieve them?"

Asha did her best to look disdainful. "Even if you did, I can't just go and get them. The duke has been using me as a go-between for an Administrator who was involved, but who doesn't want anything more to do with it. That's who has agreed to get the documents for us—and once he'd given them to me, I was going to head straight for the Silver Talon and hand them to the Shadraehin's people there." She scowled at the two men. "So as you can see, a few more days, and none of this would have been necessary."

Teran eyed her narrowly. "We're not letting you out to meet him."

"Then go yourself." Asha shook her head in disgust. "The White Sword. I was supposed to be there each night this week, and he'd meet me when he could. His name's Erran. Big man in a blue cloak. He's hard to miss."

Teran looked at her, wavering. "And what do we say to him?"

"Tell him Elocien sent you to collect the documents instead of me. Don't worry, he's not too bright. He'll hand them over."

Teran stared at her for a long moment, then gave a sharp nod. "Good enough. But if a week passes and there are no documents, things will go very, very badly for you."

"He'll be there," said Asha, with more confidence than she felt. Erran had told her that Elocien regularly sent him to the White Sword for information...would he try Reading people there, once he and the others realized she was missing? She could only hope so.

The door closed, and Asha settled back down against the wall, closing her eyes and breathing deeply to slow her pounding heart. She'd look for another way out soon; she couldn't pin all her hopes on this plan working.

At least now, though, she felt that she had a chance.

Asha's heart sank as she awoke in the cold, and the dark, and the damp.

Her muscles, stiff from disuse, screamed at her as she shifted. The rope around her wrist—retied and viciously tightened by Teran after she'd managed to slip the knot three days earlier—burned where it chafed against her skin. She winced as she felt the slickness of her hands, blood trickling down from where the cords had bitten too deeply as she'd struggled against them.

She stared around blearily, though there was never anything to see in the utter darkness she was left in each night. Something had woken her, and it wasn't the pain, or the stench, or even the gnawing hunger. She'd had one meal since she was captured, and Asha was fairly certain that had just been to keep her alive until her story was confirmed—until Teran had the evidence he so des-

perately wanted.

She winced as she rolled her shoulder, wondering if anything was broken. Teran had kicked her, hard, when he'd returned this evening from another unsuccessful trip to the White Sword. Asha could see his mistrust mounting each time he came back empty-handed, but she pressed her case, putting everything she had into sounding convincing.

She had to. She knew now that her captors were too thorough, too alert for her to escape on her own. She still kept looking for a way out, but all her hopes were realistically pinned on Erran.

She wasn't sure how long had passed, but she'd almost fallen into a restless sleep again when she heard the soft voice.

*Asha.*

She flinched and looked around, peering into the murk. "Who's there?"

*Quiet. It's Erran. I'm outside.* A pause. *I've linked our minds. Just think your responses, don't say them out loud.* Another pause. *Are you all right?*

Asha took a couple of deep, shuddering breaths of pure relief. *I've been better. Glad you're here, though.* She hesitated. *You're alone?*

*Kol and Fessi are here, too. Elocien wanted to send men, but I Read the Shadow you sent to the White Sword. Teran. He'll kill you if he gets even a hint of a problem. He's got a plan to kill Pyl, too, if it comes to that. Then blame your death on him and say he was trying to save you.*

*Of course he does,* thought Asha grimly. She'd never heard his name, but Pyl must be Teran's partner. *So you'll sneak me out?*

*Fessi just went through the house; she's figured out which door is your room. Pyl's on guard, and Teran's asleep. She's going to come in, take the keys from Pyl, unlock your door, and get you out before anyone knows what's happening.*

Asha hesitated. *I'm hurt, haven't had much to eat or drink. Tied up, too. Not sure how fast I can be.*

*Doesn't matter. You'll see. Just get ready.*

Asha shook out her muscles as best she could, then as quietly as possible raised herself to a standing position against the wall. Her shoulder felt as if it were on fire; when she looked down she could see the black, red, and purple of an ugly bruise through the torn and bloodied cloth of her shirt. She staggered a little once she was upright, and her vision swam.

*Here she comes.*

"Fates."

Asha blinked. The door was open, the light from a lamp outside spilling in, hurting Asha's eyes. Fessi was standing a couple of feet in front of her; the word had been whispered, but the horror on the other girl's face told Asha just how much of a mess she must look.

"I need cleaning up," whispered Asha with a weak smile.

Fessi shook her head, then reached out and grabbed Asha's arm—not, thankfully, the one attached to her bad shoulder. The Augur closed her eyes for a moment, then quickly released the cords that bound Asha's wrists.

"All right. Let's move," Fessi said. "Don't let go of me for any reason."

Asha leaned heavily on her friend as they made their way toward the doorway, Asha certain with every step that Pyl or Teran would appear in their path. As they reached the door and gazed out into the room beyond, though, Asha frowned.

Pyl's back was to them as he shuffled cards at the table, but that wasn't what Asha noticed. He was moving…sluggishly. *More* than sluggishly. She watched, eyes wide, as individual cards inched through the air from one hand to another, slowly enough that as one flew out of Pyl's right hand, she could have walked the ten feet between them and plucked it out of the air before it hit his left.

It wasn't just Pyl, though. The air itself felt thicker; the candle on the table flickered, but so gradually that in each moment it looked completely frozen. Asha clutched at the black-haired girl a little tighter as she understood what was happening. Fessi had said just the other night that her best ability, her Augur talent, was to slow time. It seemed she hadn't been exaggerating.

Asha made to move toward the back door, but Fessi gave a silent shake of her head. She shut the door behind them. Locked it. Then she guided Asha over to where Pyl sat, the cards still moving between his hands, and calmly placed the keys back on his belt.

Then they were away, out the back door and into the fresh, cool night air. It was late enough that the streets were empty, but Fessi didn't stop slowing time until they were in the shadows of the alley opposite and standing alongside Kol and Erran, who were watching the house pensively.

Both boys blinked as the girls appeared in front of them; Fessi collapsed against Kol, the strain of what she'd done clearly taking a toll. The street was dim, but there was enough light to see by, and both Kol's and Erran's eyes widened as they took in Asha's appearance.

"Fates," breathed Erran, with almost the same horrified intonation Fessi had used. "Are you all right?"

"It looks worse than it is," said Asha weakly, her voice hoarse. It was probably true; her clothing was torn and bloodied, her hair matted with the dried blood that was also caked across her face. "I could use something to drink, though."

Erran scrambled around in a bag he'd obviously brought for the occasion and passed her a flask. Asha drank, sighing as the cool liquid slid down her throat.

She handed the flask back, then noticed Kol's expression for the first time. He was still silent but his eyes were hard, cold with fury.

"It's all right, Kol," she said gently. "I'm fine."

"It's not all right. If the men who took you treated you like that, they're not going to back off just because you escaped. We need to send a message." Kol spoke through gritted teeth, then turned to the other two. "I'll be back in a few minutes."

Fessi shook her head in alarm. "You don't want them to see your face, Kol."

"Then I'll just have to make sure they don't want to remember it," he said.

He stalked toward the door they'd exited, little more than a massive shadow in the darkened street, his stride determined.

"Pyl's big," said Asha, concerned. "I know Kol is, too, but two against one—"

Kol reached the door and drew back his fist.

There was a ripple in the air around his arm; it wasn't quite Essence, but the energy was palpable. When his fist connected, the door didn't just break or swing open. It *splintered*, sending shards of wood flying into the room beyond. There was a cry of

367

surprised pain as Pyl was evidently struck by at least one of the pieces.

"We'd better make sure he doesn't kill anyone," muttered Fessi.

The three of them made their way to the doorway, Asha peering in nervously.

Kol already had Pyl pinned to the ground, facedown; the big man was struggling, but it made no difference against Kol. The Augur grabbed Pyl's arm and gave it one strong jerk backward; Asha winced as there was a cracking, popping sound, ligaments and bones snapping. Pyl began to scream, but Kol silenced him by grabbing a handful of hair at the base of his skull and smashing his face into the ground.

The door to the bedroom opened and a disheveled Teran emerged, a knife in his hand. He took in the scene with a surprisingly calm expression.

"I'll kill you if you come any closer," he told Kol.

As if he hadn't heard, Kol walked toward him with ground-eating strides; Teran's eyes widened as he realized his threat had had no effect. He swiped at Kol with the knife, but Kol came in under the swing, grabbing Teran's wrist and twisting. There was a sharp snap, and Teran shrieked in pain as the blade fell to the ground.

Kol spun the portly Shadow around as if he were a rag doll, shoving him against the wall so that the entire building shook. Asha gave a nervous glance around the street, but the racket didn't seem to have raised any alarms. They were in the Lower District, not a wealthy neighborhood from the looks of it. There wouldn't be many of the watch down here to call upon anyway.

Kol leaned forward against the struggling Teran. "If you touch her again. If I see you again. If anything untoward *happens* to her again, regardless of who's responsible. I. Will. Kill. You," said Kol, the fury in his voice unmistakable. "I would kill you right now if I didn't have to worry about the body."

Teran's face twisted into a sneer. "The Shadraehin—"

"I'm not afraid of the Shadraehin." Kol grabbed the man's arm and pulled backward; again there was a popping sound as ligaments snapped. Teran's face went white. "Do you understand?"

There was silence; Kol snarled, giving Teran's arm another tug.

*"Do you understand?"*

"Yes," gasped Teran.

Kol drew back Teran's head and smashed it against the wall; Asha flinched, wondering how many teeth Teran had lost to the impact.

Her would-be captor slumped to the ground, unconscious.

Kol stared at the man in disgust, motionless for several seconds. Finally Fessi stepped over to him, putting a hand on his arm.

"We need to go, Kol," she said softly.

Kol nodded, and the four of them left the dingy building. Fessi gave Kol and Erran a meaningful glance as they began to walk, and the two boys hurriedly moved so that Asha would be able to lean on them if she needed to.

"Thank you," she said quietly, her gaze including all three of her rescuers. Kol and Erran gave solemn nods in response, and Fessi just smiled, giving Asha's good arm a light squeeze of reassurance.

They navigated the sleeping city, all the way back to the palace, in silence.

⚜

It was late morning, three days after the Augurs had rescued her, when Kol knocked on her open door.

"Kol!" She smiled at him, rising from her desk. "Come in."

Kol entered hesitantly. "How are you feeling?"

"Michal healed me the morning after we got back, so...much better." Asha rotated her shoulder to prove the point.

Kol smiled. "That's good." Asha gestured to a chair and the big man sat, looking awkward. "I wanted to come and check on you earlier, but Elocien said it was best to let you rest."

Asha nodded. "I needed it," she admitted. Though her body had been healed, today was the first day she'd felt ready to face other people again. Even after all she had already been through over the past few months, this last week had been hard.

"Representative Alac didn't mind?"

Asha shook her head. "He says I should take as much time as I need." She gave a slight smile, gesturing to a thick tome sitting on her bedside table. "That isn't to say he didn't leave me anything to do if I felt so inclined, though."

Kol snorted. "Sounds about right." He glanced around the room, noting several arrangements of flowers. "Seems you're suddenly rather popular."

Asha rolled her eyes. "You could call it that, I suppose." The Houses hated to be outdone by each other, even when it came to false sympathy. Bouquets and gifts had been arriving in a steady stream almost since she had returned.

She sighed. It had been impossible to get her back into the palace without her battered state being noticed, and though Elocien had tried to be discreet about ordering the arrest of two other Shadows straight after her arrival, someone had still made the connection. The rumors had been everywhere within a day—the Shadraehin had attacked one of his own, kidnapped the only Shadow in the city who held a position of relative power. Proof positive that he had no intention of ever trying diplomatic means to help the Shadows.

To make matters worse, Elocien's men had arrived at the house in the Lower District to find it empty. Teran and Pyl were still out there, somewhere.

"Even si'Bandin sent me something," she eventually continued in a wry tone, shaking off the unpleasant train of thought. "And that man looks at me like I'm a diseased dog that's in need of putting down."

Kol grinned. "Don't be such a cynic, Ashalia. I'm sure every one of the Houses' gifts came from a place of love and concern." Then his smile faded and he took a deep breath, suddenly awkward again as he stared at the ground. "Look, before we go any further...I wanted to apologize. Apologize for my behavior toward you since you got here. You've been through so much these past few months, and I've been acting like..." He trailed off.

Asha studied him. "I understand why, though. I don't blame you," she said quietly. She gave him a friendly smile. "And anyway, I suspect I can find it in my heart to forgive you. You helped rescue me, probably saved my life—and you certainly made sure Teran and Pyl won't come after me again. You didn't have to do any of that."

"Still." Kol clenched his fists. "What I've Seen...that's not your fault. It doesn't justify the way I've been treating you." He took another deep breath, finally looking her in the eye. "I'm just...I'm scared, Ashalia. I'm scared that it's going to happen soon, and there isn't anybody I can talk to about it. I find it hard enough to deal with the everyday things I See, but knowing *that* is coming..." He sighed. "I've wanted so many times to tell Fessi and Erran, but even if I could, it would just be a burden on them as well."

Asha nodded slowly; Fessi had said much the same thing last week. "I may not be your first choice, but if you need someone to talk to..."

Kol gave her a small smile. "Thank you." He rubbed his face, looking relieved. "That's not the only reason I'm here, though. I've come to collect you, on Elocien's instructions. Apparently there's something you need to see."

Asha hesitated. "We may as well go now, then," she said reluctantly, forcing down a sudden pang of nervousness. She hadn't been outside her rooms since the night she got back.

They left, and Asha's churning stomach eased a little as they made their way along the palace hallways. She still tensed up whenever she saw another Shadow, and she knew that might be her reaction for a while to come. Even so, it became easier the longer they walked, and Kol's hulking presence alongside her lent a certain physical reassurance, too.

Soon they were at the duke's office, and Kol bade her farewell. Once she was inside and the door was shut, Elocien gestured to a closed wooden box that sat on the floor in the middle of the room.

"This arrived about an hour ago. The guards at the gate were asked to deliver it to me, but I have no doubt that it was meant for you as well." He walked over to the box, then hesitated. "You should probably sit."

Frowning, Asha took Elocien's advice.

Elocien carefully levered up the lid, and Asha shuddered as she realized what was inside.

Teran and Pyl's severed heads stared up at her, their bloodied expressions taut with fear. Sitting atop the heads, flecked with dark red, was a note. Asha stared in horror for a moment, then leaned forward, a chill running through her as she read it. It was inked in the same neat, precise handwriting she'd seen in Elocien's memory, from the night Administration had been attacked.

There were only two words on the slip of paper.

*I apologize.*

"It seems you were right about the Shadraehin not ordering the kidnapping," Elocien observed softly. "He's making sure I know, so that Administration doesn't retaliate—and making sure you know he didn't betray you at the same time."

Asha shuddered. She'd despised these men for what they'd done, had even taken satisfaction in watching Kol's treatment of them. But this...she hadn't wanted this. She turned away, feeling sick.

"At least he doesn't think I'm holding out on him, then," was all she said.

She spoke with Elocien a little longer, but soon enough she headed back to her rooms, suddenly too tired to be afraid. She'd seen so much violence over the past few months, more than she'd thought was possible. What had happened to Teran and Pyl...it almost didn't surprise her.

Even so, as she lay back on her bed and closed her eyes, she knew she wouldn't be able to get their final expressions from her mind for a long, long time.

# Chapter 32

Davian glanced up from his reading at the sound of footsteps echoing around the stone corridors.

His muscles tensed as he stood, facing the doorway into the library. Despite Malshash's assurances, he remained cautious at all times in Deilannis. There was something too...*wrong* about the city for him to be able to relax.

It had been four days since the shape-shifter's abrupt departure. Davian had broken from reading during that time to eat and sleep, but nothing else. Partly it was due to the enormity of the task; every time he thought he'd exhausted a topic, the Adviser directed him to books with fresh information on the same subject. Partly it was an escape.

Mostly, though, he'd discovered a fierce determination within himself, a hunger to be able to do what these books described. He'd never realized it before, but he'd watched his peers use Essence for so long—effortlessly, it had seemed—and been deeply envious.

Now, perhaps, it was finally his turn.

A man not much older than him entered the room, smiling boyishly when his eyes alighted on Davian. He had bright-red hair, a strong jawline, and a crooked nose. He waved in a familiar fashion.

"Malshash?" Davian asked, his tone hesitant.

The man gave a cheerful nod. "In the flesh." He looked in a particularly good mood; he sauntered up to Davian, glancing at the array of tomes spread out across the table. "How have you progressed?"

Davian shrugged. "I've done plenty of reading. Kan doesn't strike me as the sort of power to rush into, though, so I've been waiting for you to return before going further." Though he tried to sound casual about the last, in truth he was itching to see whether the theory he'd been devouring would actually work.

"Good lad." Malshash gave him an approving nod. "You think you've grasped the basic concepts?"

Davian nodded. "The mental techniques sound simple enough. I've actually come across a few of them before, when I was trying to use Essence. They shouldn't be too much trouble." He was being modest. Every mental technique he'd ever tried—quite a few, in his years at the school—he had perfected. They had just never resulted in his being able to use Essence.

Malshash smiled. "But you understand that the two—Essence and kan—are very different?" He watched Davian closely, and Davian's breath shortened a little. He got the distinct feeling he was being tested.

"Kan is an external force," he said. "Whereas Essence is usually drawn from within the body, kan is drawn from a single source—one that seems to have its physical location here, somewhere in Deilannis. Although kan can be used from anywhere in the world, it is easiest to access and control here in the city."

Malshash nodded encouragingly. "That's accurate. What else?"

"Essence is energy. In the case of the Gifted it's a piece of our own life force, extracted and converted into something that can physically affect things." He bit his lip, straining to explain what he'd understood from the books. "Kan is not energy. You couldn't make a fireball with kan, or lift a feather. You can't heal with it. But it can *affect* energy. It seems to…sit above Essence, somehow. As we manipulate the world with Essence, so we manipulate Essence with kan."

Malshash gave him an approving look. "You've been reading Delatroen, I see. Very good." He smiled. "And what does he have to say about the consequences of this hierarchy?"

Davian stared at the ground for a long moment, trying to remember. "Two things. Firstly, that kan allows us to access things that Essence alone cannot touch—things that are not physical—specifically, he mentions thoughts and time as instances of that. And secondly, kan allows us to use Essence with a level of finesse and efficiency that is not possible otherwise. He gives the example of drinking from a pool. Manipulating Essence by itself is like scooping the water with your hands, whereas using kan to do it is more like using a cup."

Malshash smiled. "I always liked that analogy." He paused. "There's more to it, though. He was only talking about one aspect of their interaction."

Davian nodded, feeling his brow furrow. "Kan can also be used in other states to siphon, absorb, or store Essence. I read a little about Imbuing—making Vessels. The kan stores Essence in the Vessel indefinitely, preventing decay, until its function is triggered. In some cases it can draw Essence from whoever is using it, too." He thought of the Vessel that had brought him and Wirr to Desriel. "It seemed quite advanced."

"It is," said Malshash drily. He nodded in approval, though. "There's only one other thing you failed to mention, though it's rarely spoken of in texts so I can hardly blame you for omitting it. Kan, in its natural state, absorbs Essence because the two were never designed to coexist. They *can* be used together—with training—but they are by no means complementary."

"They were never designed to coexist?" repeated Davian.

Malshash waved away the query. "A story for another time. For now, all you need to know is that when learning to use the two combined, you must understand the quirks of each. Knowledge of one in no way imparts knowledge of the other."

"That probably won't be an issue, anyway," muttered Davian, meaning the comment to be to himself.

Malshash gave him a puzzled look. "What do you mean?"

Davian stared at the floor, embarrassed. "I...struggle, when it comes to using Essence. I've never been able to even access my Reserve."

Malshash frowned. "Of course you can use Essence," he said slowly. "I've seen you do it."

Davian frowned back. "When?"

"After coming through the rift." Malshash scratched his head. "Your body was nearly wasted away when you appeared on the Jha'vett. You regenerated in seconds, though. You actually *glowed*, you were using so much Essence."

Davian shrugged. "I've been trying for years with no success," he admitted.

Malshash's frown deepened. "Stand still," he instructed. He came and stood in front of Davian, putting his hand against his forehead. A wash of energy flooded through Davian's body, startling him. He flinched backward to see Malshash looking at him in shock.

"What is it?" asked Davian.

Malshash just stared at him through narrowed eyes. "Of course," he muttered, almost to himself. "It makes sense. I should have seen it earlier." He laughed. "I should have *felt* it earlier. But it's very subtle. Unnoticeable unless you're looking for it."

Davian scowled. "What are you talking about?"

Malshash thought for a moment. "Do you know why no one else has ever used the rift to pass through time, as you did?"

Davian shook his head mutely.

"It is because no living thing can pass through it and survive," said Malshash. "The energies of the other realm are pure kan; they are drawn to Essence, and when they find it, they tear its source apart. Obliterate it." He paused. "You don't have a Reserve, Davian—in itself, not so unusual for an Augur. Beyond that, though, your body generates no Essence. Not just no excess. None *at all*."

Davian shook his head. "That makes no sense. Everything living needs Essence."

Malshash gave a delighted laugh. "That's the trick, Davian! You're using kan to get it. You draw it in from around you—any source you can find. The body does not need much, truth be told." He shook his head. "I thought it was a miracle you'd picked up how to use kan so quickly, making it through the rift as you did. This is why. You've been using it unconsciously since the day you... well, since you died."

Davian paled. "I don't understand."

"It's very simple." Malshash sat in a chair, gesturing for Davian to do the same. "At some point in your life, you died. I don't know when—probably very young, though, earlier than you'd be able to even remember. So your ability to produce Essence failed. But somehow your instincts kicked in, and you began drawing

Essence from around you using kan instead." He shrugged. "You must have been doing it ever since. Stealing a little from here, a little from there. Sometimes from people, sometimes from your environment. If you were raised around the Gifted, it would have been too easy."

Davian felt a chill run through him. "You mean...I'm *dead*?"

"No, no." Malshash gestured impatiently. Then he hesitated. "Well...yes. In a way. You *are* just as alive as anyone else. Your heart still beats, your blood pumps, you need food and sleep. But...differently, I suppose. I meant that at some point, your body expired. Perhaps it was only for a few seconds, perhaps it was minutes—I don't know how long it takes for a source to flicker out completely. But now for your body to function as it should, you need to draw your Essence from external sources."

Davian shook his head, dazed. "What does that mean?" He ran his hands through his hair. "I think I understand what you're saying, but...what are the implications?"

Malshash shrugged. "Nothing to be worried about, I would think. You do it instinctively, like breathing, so you shouldn't be in any danger—and as far as I can tell you don't draw enough to put anyone around you in harm's way. So long as you don't lose your ability to use kan, you're no different from anyone else."

Davian was silent. He had *died*? He thought back to the day he'd been branded with his Mark, the day he'd woken up in the school unable to move from his injuries. Had that been when it had happened? Thinking about it—that somehow in the past he had actually *died*—made him twist inside.

"I can't say I'm entirely comfortable with the concept, nonetheless," he admitted in a shaky voice.

Malshash nodded. "I understand. But it saved your life. You couldn't have survived the rift otherwise." He grinned at the irony. "It was meant to be, Davian. You have this power for a reason. And the good news is, your body is well adapted to kan. Which means we can take a few...shortcuts. You'll be home in no time."

Davian brightened at the prospect. "When do we start?"

Malshash clapped him on the back. "We'll begin this afternoon. For now, though, we should get some food. I haven't eaten today."

Davian nodded, caught between dismay at the news he'd been told, and the hope that he would soon be returning to his own time.

He followed Malshash silently, lost in thought.

Davian cleared his mind, trying to sense kan.

It was only a few moments before he could feel it. It was less something physical, and more an absence. Like a shadow rather than light.

"Good," murmured Malshash. Davian ignored the comment. This was the easy part.

They had been practicing for a couple of hours now. It was a frustrating process, though Malshash appeared unfazed by Davian's lack of progress. If anything, the mysterious man seemed encouraged by how quickly Davian was able to sense kan, and even to an extent control it.

"Now," said Malshash, "I've walled off most of my mind, but left a specific memory open for you to see. My memory will become yours, though you will be able to see it as distinct from your own. All you need to do is use kan to will yourself inside my mind, to connect to me."

"Is that all," said Davian through gritted teeth, a bead of sweat trickling down his forehead. Kan was stubborn and slippery; using it for even a few seconds was like grasping at shadows. What was worse, the process of entering another's mind was delicate; it required a deft touch and more mental concentration than Davian would have previously believed possible. Malshash said kan was more difficult to wield than Essence, and Davian believed him. If Essence were this difficult to control, the number of Gifted able to use it effectively would be far smaller.

Still, this time he managed to keep it in his mind, keep his focus sharp as he reached out tentatively toward Malshash. He felt himself push *through* the kan, using it to make his will a reality.

He mentally reached Malshash and felt a barrier, something stopping him. He pushed again.

The world blurred for a moment; he lost concentration and everything dropped away, including his sense of kan. He gasped, holding his head, feeling as if a bucket of cold water had been dumped over it.

He looked up. Malshash was watching him intently. "Well?"

Davian felt a chill run through him. "You were on the road yesterday. You passed a merchant who sold you food." He snorted. "You ate all the good stuff before you got back here."

Malshash considered him for a few more seconds, then broke into a wide smile. "Exactly right."

Davian smiled back, still examining the memory in his head. It was an odd feeling. He knew the recollection wasn't his, but he could picture the open fields, the fair weather, the greedy smile of the merchant knowing he could charge double for food so far from a town. It was remarkable.

"Can we try again?" he asked, elated.

Malshash shrugged. "I'll have to choose a different memory and isolate it, but yes, I think so."

Davian gave an eager nod. "So is that all there is to it?"

Malshash laughed. "It's a start. But learning to really understand memories...that's tricky." He paused. "For example. You just said I ate all the 'good stuff.' Was that your assessment, or mine?"

Davian opened his mouth...and hesitated.

"I suppose...yours," he conceded eventually, brow furrowed. "I don't really care for figs."

"And the weather was..."

"Fair?" Davian replied, a little uncertainly.

Malshash grinned. "Was it? Were there no clouds, or was it just brighter than I'm accustomed to here in the city? Or was I simply in a good mood?"

Davian shook his head. "I don't think there were clouds. I can't picture any. But now that you mention it...I don't know," he admitted.

Malshash clapped him on the shoulder. "And that's the hard part. Even though you relived that memory far more clearly than I ever could have, it's not just a sensory record of what happened. You're experiencing the memory as *my mind* remembers it. Everything is always seen subjectively, colored by emotion. Memories can even change over time, be affected by new information. Reading a memory one day can be a different experience from Reading that same memory the next."

"So you can't take what you see for granted?"

"Exactly. That's not to say it's completely unreliable; it just needs some experience to interpret what you see. And...you have to be careful. Once you Read someone's memory, it becomes yours, too. If you're not careful, that can change you."

He paused, watching Davian to make sure the seriousness of that statement had sunk in before continuing. "Once you've mastered memories, there's still learning how to Read what someone's thinking at that exact moment. *That* is difficult. Even people who haven't been trained have natural barriers protecting their thoughts. You need to learn to get around those, without harming them."

Davian frowned. "They could get hurt?"

"Yes." Malshash's expression was solemn. "All these powers are dangerous in some way, Davian. You can't just go forcing your way into someone's mind, not without the mind pushing back. If you do, it can have serious consequences. Their mind could be permanently damaged; in some cases they may even die from the experience."

Davian paled, thinking back to what Taeris had told him about the smuggler Anaar. "Why didn't you tell me this before we started training?"

Malshash waved away his concern. "I have everything else walled off. Don't worry, Davian. You can't hurt me."

Davian nodded in relief. "Good."

Malshash held up a finger in warning, though he had a half smile on his lips. "By the way—you should know that I always shield my mind from being Read. It's natural for me now; I do it without thinking. So don't imagine you can try it sometime when I'm not ready."

Davian grinned; he hadn't really considered the possibility. Then his smile faded. "Have you Read me?"

"Oh yes." Malshash chuckled as he saw the horrified expression on Davian's face. "Only a little, now and then. To get myself...acquainted with what kind of man you are." He waved his hands in a dismissive gesture. "Don't worry. You're a good one, in case you were wondering."

Davian found himself caught between a scowl and a smile;

eventually he gave up and chose the latter. "You will have to show me how to shield myself, then," he said in a begrudging tone.

Malshash nodded. "It's easy enough. Visualize a box in your mind; anything you want to protect—memories, thoughts, emotions—you lock away inside that box. Anything you don't need to protect, you leave outside." He shrugged. "It's a mental trick, not anything to do with kan. The mind has its own natural defenses; as I said, it already goes to some lengths to protect our thoughts. For some reason, though, this tricks it into raising even stronger defenses. Most of the time, that makes it impenetrable."

Davian looked at Malshash warily. "It sounds a little easy. How do I know you're not just telling me this so you can continue to Read me whenever you want?"

Malshash sighed. "You told me that your one ability up until now has been to see when people are trying to deceive you," he said. "Use it on me. I won't take offense."

"It doesn't work on anyone who can shield themselves," Davian pointed out.

"Of course it does. Shielding can mask it, but when you see that someone is lying, your mind is in some small way connected to the other person's. And believe me, people *know* when they're lying—it's not something you can fully hide away, no matter how skilled you are. The signs might be different—may be too subtle for most other Augurs to pick up—but someone with your specific talent should still be able to tell."

Davian shook his head. "Not that I've noticed." Then he paused. "Tell me something false, then true, then false again."

Malshash crossed his arms. "I have never met you before. It is seventy years before you were born. Traversing the time rift back is not a risk."

"And again?"

Malshash repeated what he had said, and Davian sighed.

There it was. A slight pain, a pressure on the temples that he automatically tried to massage away, on the first and third sentences. It had been there all along, and he just hadn't known what to look for. He wasn't sure whether to be happy—his confidence in his ability had been badly hurt after Tenvar's betrayal—or furious that he hadn't figured it out sooner.

He decided to choose the former. "It works," he said with a tight smile. Then he raised an eyebrow. "Though for all I know, you could be messing around in my head about this, too."

Malshash chuckled. "Sorry, Davian, but I'm not *that* interested in what you're thinking at any given moment." He grinned to soften any perceived insult.

Davian smiled. "Of course. Sorry."

Malshash shrugged. "I can't blame you, I suppose. Once you know what people with these abilities can actually do, it becomes a lot harder to trust them." He gave a small yawn, glancing around. "That's probably enough for today, anyway. Nightfall is coming." He began walking back toward their house.

Davian squinted at the mists surrounding them, but could detect no change in the light. That was the way it always was in Deilannis: a constant dull gray, enough light to see by, but never bright, never cheerful. Still, Malshash had seemingly been living here long enough to know when day became night.

"So we continue working on Reading tomorrow?" Davian asked, trotting to come up alongside Malshash. This version of the shape-shifter was tall, and his long legs meant his stride was hard to match.

Malshash shook his head. "No. You've grasped the concept quickly enough; we don't have time to waste mastering each ability. Tomorrow we move on."

"So that's it? That's all you're going to teach me on Reading?"

"I didn't say that," said Malshash, a little irritably. "If there is a chance, we will revisit it."

Davian frowned. "You talk as if there may not be time to do that."

"There may not be," Malshash admitted after a pause. He glanced down at Davian's right hand, on which he wore the ring. "I never meant you to be here for more than a few hours, a day at the very most. I used that ring to draw you here, but the natural laws of time will eventually try to reassert themselves. You need to be as rounded as possible when that happens."

Davian shook his head in confusion. "I don't understand."

"That ring is what binds you to this time," explained Malshash. "But it's a tenuous link. Remember what I said, about a shadow of a shadow of yourself being left in your own time? Your body has a specific place in the time stream, and every moment you're here, you're fighting against it. Every moment you're here, the time stream works harder to correct what it perceives as a mistake. Eventually it will find you, try to draw you back."

Davian scratched his head. "And we *don't* want that."

Malshash snorted. "Not if you want to stay alive." He sighed, softening. "I know I've said it before, but this journey through the rift will be just as dangerous as your last, Davian. Perhaps more so, because you won't have anyone in your own time lighting a beacon to find your way home, as I did for you here." He stopped, his expression deadly serious. "These skills, in and of themselves, will not help. But being able to see kan, to manipulate it at will, use it competently—*that* will be invaluable. It's the only thing that can protect you on the trip back." He gestured at nothing in particular. "Which is why we train, why I had you read as much theory as you could, and why we are not waiting to master everything. Because any day, at any moment, you could find yourself back in the rift."

Davian paled as Malshash spoke. He was silent for several seconds. "Why didn't you say something before?" he asked.

Malshash sighed. "Do you think you would have been able to concentrate on studying those books if you'd known?"

Davian thought about it. "No," he admitted reluctantly. "I suppose not."

Malshash nodded in a satisfied manner. "But now we're training?"

"It will make me work harder, push myself further."

Malshash grinned. "So there is your answer. It was for your own benefit."

"It doesn't mean I have to like it," muttered Davian.

"No, it doesn't," agreed Malshash cheerfully.

They walked the rest of the way in silence.

# Chapter 33

*Caeden stood in the courtyard. Sweating. Nervous.*

*The nine towers of Ilshan Tereth Kal rose high above him, surrounded him on all sides—improbably tall and impossibly beautiful, evoking calmness and strength in their design, just as the Builders had intended. The crystal walls glimmered and shone in the dawn, streaks of blue energy flowing through them, swirling and dancing, traversing the castle at random. They were the guardians of Tereth Kal, not quite sentient but not without intelligence. They, too, were beautiful to behold, though he had seen what they were capable of when the Velderan had attacked. A sight no man before him had seen. A sight no man was meant to witness and live to tell of it.*

*Ordan glided into the courtyard. Caeden had been around the Shalis enough now to recognize their moods, subtle though the signs usually were. Today Ordan was determined.*

*The Shalis mage stopped in front of him, his sinuous red skin glistening in the light. He was at least nine feet tall at full extension, though out of politeness he tended to contort his body slightly, which allowed him to speak to Caeden face-to-face. Despite the red serpentine body, and the complete lack of legs, there was a human aspect to Ordan that some of his brethren lacked. But then, Ordan was the one who had spoken for him. Who had convinced the Cluster to let him train here, who had vouched for him despite his many struggles to learn what was needed. He was the most human of his kind.*

*"Is today the day, Tal'kamar?" Ordan asked, the hissing lisp of his voice barely noticeable now.*

"May Dreth send it be so," replied Caeden. The words were formal, but the sentiment was heartfelt.

"Then let us begin," said the Shalis.

The energy crackled toward him, abruptly and so fast he barely had time to react. He connected to his Reserve and envisaged a shield, a pulsing barrier through which Ordan's bolt could not pass. He threw up his hands to cast it just in time; it appeared and the bolt dissolved in a sputter of blue electrical fire.

"Good," said Ordan. "But remember—no gestures, no words. These are the signs of a mind poor in discipline. A mind that needs trickery as a crutch to perform its tasks."

Caeden grimaced, but bobbed his head in acknowledgment. He'd been here two years now, honing his focus, training himself mentally to do things other Gifted would consider impossible. And he could do them now—do wondrous feats that would make most men gasp in awe. Not the Shalis, though. They still looked at him as a child, or more accurately as an animal they were teaching to talk.

Ordan struck again, and this time Caeden forced his hands to his sides. His barrier still appeared, but it was too weak; a small portion of the bolt sizzled through, striking him on the shoulder. He grunted in pain, gritting his teeth as he glanced down at the seared skin, which was already blistering. He knew the Shalis would not heal it for him, nor would they approve if he did it himself. It was only through trials, through pain, that mastery of Essence could be achieved.

He growled, mainly to himself. He was better than this. He circled Ordan warily, watching for the telltale glow—so small it was almost invisible—that indicated he was about to strike. When Caeden saw it, instead of raising a shield he dove to his left, going on the attack. He imagined Ordan's chest bursting into flame, then let the power flow from his Reserve, as much as he could without risking Ordan's life.

Ordan blocked the attack easily, then sighed. "You still hold back," he said. To most people the words would have sounded angry—most of the Shalis's speech sounded that way—but Caeden understood that this was a gentle reprimand, an almost-fond rebuke. "When you fight for your life, will you do so then?"

Caeden shook his head. "Of course not. But I have no wish to injure you."

Ordan just watched him, the sinuous lines of his body swaying gracefully. "You know my people will bring me back. You know you can defeat me. You could leave this place today, Tal'kamar. You could return to Silvithrin and fight the Shadowbreakers. Why do you hesitate?"

Caeden paused, searching his heart for the truth. "I fear that in returning to fight them, like this, I may become like them," he said quietly. It was a hard thing to admit, but the Shalis did not believe in subtlety, false modesty, or lies. They were wise. Perhaps, with this admission, Ordan could help him.

But the serpentine man only sighed. "We each have our temptations, Tal'kamar. We each have our own battles that must be fought." He paused. "But you must fight them, my friend. You cannot hide from them. Otherwise you will never be more than you are."

Caeden nodded, though he had hoped for more reassurance. Still, what his friend had said made a lot of sense. He couldn't hide from what was coming, just as his people could not.

"Again, then," he said, tone grim, taking the stance.

They circled, and this time he felt oddly at peace, no longer nervous. When Ordan's attack came he didn't even break stride; the barrier dissolved the bolt long before it reached him. He dug inside himself, then pictured Ordan bursting into flame. Not just his skin, but his insides, his entire body from head to tail. The Shalis were vulnerable to fire, but he drew more from his Reserve, letting the power build up. More. More.

He released.

Ordan was expecting the blast, but his shield was nothing compared to the power of Caeden's blow. The shield shattered and Ordan screamed in pain as tongues of fire engulfed him; his scaly skin began to shimmer and then melt as the intense heat devoured all. Caeden made himself watch, though it tore him up inside to do so. His friend would be reborn, as the Shalis always were. He knew it would be painful for Ordan, hated himself for doing this. Yet it was necessary. Ordan was right. He needed to return home.

387

Another Shalis—Indral, he thought, though they all looked very similar—came and busied himself next to Ordan's smoking body. Gently he picked it up, powerful arms having no trouble lifting the corpse. He turned to Caeden.

"He will be proud of you, Tal'kamar," he said in his unusual high-pitched voice. The words were blunt, but Caeden thought he detected a hint of respect in them. That was something, coming from Indral, who had always been against his being allowed to train here.

Caeden stared at the corpse sadly. "Will I be able to speak to him before I leave?"

"No." Indral was emphatic. "You have completed your training, and Ordan will not return for months yet. Rebirth in the Forges is a slow process. You will need to be gone before then." Indral was not being rude, Caeden decided, only practical. The Shalis were like that: blunt, often difficult to read.

He felt a wave of regret as he glanced around. He would never see this place again, of that he was certain.

"Tell him it was an honor," he said to Indral quietly.

"I will, Tal'kamar. Farewell." Indral slithered off with Ordan's body.

Caeden flexed his burned shoulder, grimacing in pain, then moved off toward his quarters. He needed to pack.

He was going home.


Caeden woke, a light sheen of sweat on his brow.

He rolled onto his side, gazing up at the predawn sky. Another dream. As the others had, this one was already fading; even now he could grasp only the odd detail here and there. The snakelike creature he'd been friends with—so similar to the dar'gaithin. The strange fortress where he'd lived, if only for a time.

He hadn't told the others about the dreams. Alaris's warning still echoed in his head, and, as he had tonight, sometimes he saw things...if he told them the truth they'd think he was crazy, or worse, a threat. Taeris's removing his Shackle had meant a lot. Caeden didn't want to force him to put it back on.

Soon enough the others were awake, and they were traveling

once again. The roads had been heavy with traffic over the past few days—and many of the travelers had borne ominous news. There was trouble in the north, an invasion of some kind. Details were scarce, but Caeden could see how Taeris was beginning to look more worried with each mention of it.

He rubbed the tattoo on his arm absently. The fact that this invasion was from the north—where the Boundary lay—had not been lost on him. That glowing wolf's head, always in the corner of his vision, was a constant, unsettling reminder that he was likely connected somehow.

They proceeded for a while in companionable silence; at about midday the road forked, and the steady stream of people coming the other way suddenly stopped. For several hours after that, they walked without seeing anyone, and the silence of the group gradually became an anxious one.

Late in the afternoon, Taeris held up his hand, signaling that they should halt.

"Do you smell that?" he asked. He turned to the others, seeing the answer to his question in their wrinkled noses, and Dezia holding a kerchief to her face.

There was a stench on the breeze that had just sprung up, the sickening smell of rotting meat. Not just a whiff, though, as would happen if an animal had died nearby. This was strong and constant.

"What is it?" asked Wirr, almost gagging.

Taeris shook his head. "I'm not sure," he said in a worried tone, "but I think we're going to find out soon enough."

They kept moving along the road, which was still deserted. As Caeden crested the next rise, he let out an involuntary gasp, freezing in his tracks as he took in the scene before him. Behind him he could hear equally horrified sounds from his companions as they saw what he was seeing.

The bodies were everywhere.

They lined the road for hundreds of feet ahead, draped over piles of gray stone rubble. Many of the corpses were sliced open and already rotting under the hot sun; black carrion birds flocked wherever he looked, pecking at eyes and entrails with ecstatic fervor, barely bothered by the arrival of living humans.

To Caeden's horror, he realized some of the bodies had been carefully arranged in lewd embraces. In some places men's heads had been removed and sewn onto the bodies of women. He forced himself to look even closer. Some of the men's heads were on children's bodies, too.

He turned and retched, vaguely relieved to hear he was not the only one doing so.

His stomach emptied, he forced himself to turn back to the scene. With a chill Caeden realized that the piles of stones he could see were all that remained of a large township.

"Gahille," said Taeris, dismay in his voice. "I've been here before. This was a big town. It had its own wall, and a garrison to protect it."

The wall was gone now, only a few stones jutting up from the grass a reminder of it. There were no buildings left standing. Just a flat expanse that stretched out ahead, broken by the small hills of stone that indicated something had once stood there.

"Who could have done this?" whispered Caeden. He felt another wave of nausea.

"The sha'teth?" asked Aelric. He was doing better than the others. Still, he looked a little unsteady as he surveyed the carnage.

Taeris took a deep breath, trying not to breathe through his nose. "No," he said after a moment. "The sha'teth would not bother to do this. They haven't changed that much. Whoever, or whatever, was here reveled in what they were doing."

"We should see if there are any survivors," said Wirr.

Taeris shook his head. "I'm not sure if that's a good idea. It could still be dangerous."

"I'll not feel right if we leave without at least looking," pressed Wirr.

Aelric stepped forward, nodding. "I agree. We need to look."

Taeris sighed. "As you wish," he said, though his tone was heavy with reluctance.

They walked forward slowly, checking for any sign of life, each of them now breathing through a kerchief to lessen the chance of sickness. Some of the corpses were entirely rotten, while others looked almost fresh; the stench of death was overpowering at times, making Caeden's eyes water.

Ahead of him Taeris sent out a thin stream of Essence—nothing strong enough to be detected by any nearby Finders, presumably, but sufficient to clear most of the smell. It wasn't enough to make the air entirely breathable, but it was an improvement.

From the line of trees up ahead, there was suddenly movement. Taeris held up a warning hand to the others.

Two people hurried toward them; they stopped in the middle of what would have been the town square, clearly unwilling to run the gauntlet of the dead. Taeris urged his companions toward them.

Thanks to a stiff breeze, the air was much clearer in the middle of the town, enough so that Caeden felt comfortable lowering his kerchief. As he drew closer to the newcomers—a woman and a young boy, perhaps fifteen—he could see their red eyes, their ragged clothing, and the cuts and bruises on their hands. They had been running, then. Possibly for days.

"Who are you?" called the boy as they approached. "What are you doing here?"

Caeden and the others stopped just short of the two. "We are travelers," said Taeris, tone gentle, seeing the fear and suspicion on the strangers' faces. "On our way to Ilin Illan. What has happened here?"

Something seemed to break in the woman, and she rushed forward, embracing Taeris and beginning to sob. He stood there awkwardly for a few moments, unsure what to do.

"I'm sorry," the woman said eventually, stepping back in embarrassment and wiping her eyes with a dirty sleeve. "We've not seen another living soul for three days. Not since it…" She broke down again, and the young boy hurried forward to comfort her.

"We were attacked," said the boy. His tone was devoid of hope, and his eyes looked dead to Caeden. "Soldiers in armor black as night, men with no eyes. Our watch tried to fight them, but they were so fast." He shivered at the memory. "It wasn't really a battle. None of the invaders died at all."

Caeden took a step back, a chill running through his veins. He'd been worried about his potential involvement in whatever was going on, but this…this was worse than anything he'd feared.

Taeris, too, looked at the boy in dismay. "This was the invaders' doing?"

The boy nodded, still comforting the weeping woman, whom Caeden assumed was his mother. "Word came only a few hours before they got here."

"Who are they?" Taeris asked, clearly unsettled. "Where did they come from?"

"The riders who came to warn us said they were from the north. From beyond the Boundary." The boy rubbed his hands together nervously, glancing around as if he expected the enemy soldiers to reappear at any moment. "Don't know about that, but they weren't natural, I promise you that. Stronger and faster than normal men, and like I said, their helmets had no holes for them to see out of. It was something twisted, no doubt about that." He spat to the side. "The bleeders are rising up again, maybe."

Taeris winced, and Caeden saw Wirr scowling from the corner of his eye. "The Gifted are still bound by the Tenets, lad," said Taeris. "But I believe what you say." He gestured to some of the larger stones left from the destroyed houses. "Please, sit. Tell me what happened. As much detail as you can."

The boy shook his head. "I wish I could, but me and my mother ran once we saw what they were doing. Ran into the forest and just kept going for the entire night, until we were too tired to go any further." He rubbed at the cuts on his arms. "They weren't like our soldiers would have been. People were screaming for mercy, but they wouldn't listen. They killed the men, and then what they did to the women..." He trailed off.

Taeris patted him on the shoulder. "It's all right, lad. You've been a great help already." He guided both the boy and his mother over to a stone on which they could sit. "What are your names?"

"I'm Jashel. My mother's name is Llys," the boy said, still scratching at his arms.

"I'm Taeris," said the scarred man. He glanced toward the trees from which the two had emerged. "How long have you been hiding in the forest, Jashel?"

"Three days," said Jashel. "We came back yesterday, and the soldiers were still here, camping in the town. They were pulling down the buildings one by one, and dragging the corpses out to the road. Placing them like they are now." He bit his lip. "They left last night. We were still trying to decide what to do when you showed up—we would have gone for Naser, but my mother has something wrong with her leg. It would be too hard for her to walk all that way."

Taeris nodded. He reached into his knapsack and drew out a loaf of bread, offering it to Jashel. The boy took it hungrily, breaking it in two, thrusting one half at his mother and then wolfing down the other.

Caeden watched him eat in silence. What this young boy had been through these past few days was beyond what any person should ever have to endure.

"We need to bury them," announced Jashel, his mouth still full of his last chunk of bread.

Taeris blinked, glancing back along the road. Caeden followed his gaze. There were hundreds of bodies. "They'll get a proper burial, Jashel, I promise," Taeris said as gently as he could, "but there are not enough of us to do it."

Jashel's face started to go red. "They're my friends," he said angrily. "My father is out there. He fought knowing he was going to die, so we could get away! He deserves a burial!"

Taeris tried to hold Jashel's gaze, but couldn't. He looked away. "I'm sorry, lad."

"It's not your fault, sir." It was Llys, talking again for the first time since breaking down in Taeris's arms. She moved across to give Jashel a fierce hug. "We can't do it, Jashel," she said to her son. "I understand. I want to as well. But there are too many." She smiled sadly at him. "We are alive. We need to worry about surviving. Your father would have wanted that."

Jashel looked like he was about to argue, then sagged, burying his face in his mother's shoulder. He let out a couple of long, heaving sobs. Caeden looked away awkwardly.

"Is there any way we can help?" Taeris asked Llys after a while. "We can give you supplies enough to see you to Naser."

Llys shook her head. She drew up her skirt, revealing a blackened and swollen ankle. "I'm not going anywhere for a while."

Taeris hesitated. Then he stepped forward, kneeling beside Llys and placing his hands around her evidently broken ankle. He closed his eyes.

Llys's ankle began to glow as Essence flowed through Taeris. By the time he took his hands away—only a few seconds after he had begun—the ankle's swelling and bruising had disappeared.

"That should make it easier," he said with a small smile, looking drained.

Llys wiggled her ankle in astonishment. "You're Gifted," she said quietly.

The knife was in Taeris's belly before any of them realized what was happening, and everything seemed to move in slow motion after that.

Taeris emitted a single low moan before collapsing, and Caeden knew straight away that the blade had gone in deep and long, a killing blow. Mother and son both had daggers in their hands, their dead eyes suddenly registering with Caeden. Absently, through the sudden fear, he wondered how he hadn't seen it earlier. They weren't just tired, terrified. It was as if there was no life in them at all.

And though he couldn't say why, he knew exactly what it meant.

Caeden dove at Llys, wresting the blade from her hand before she could stab Taeris again, but she kept fighting, clawing at his face, his arms, anything she could touch. She hissed, her eyes wild and red-rimmed, moving with inhuman speed and strength.

To Caeden's left Aelric's sword struck like lightning, spearing young Jashel through the neck just before the boy's blade descended on Dezia's exposed back. Then there was a blinding blast of Essence, and Caeden felt the attack stop, the woman in front of him slumping to the ground as if her bones had turned to jelly. He looked over his shoulder to see Wirr standing there, panting, his arms outstretched.

Caeden dropped to his knees beside Taeris as the others crowded around. A ghastly gash ran the length of Taeris's stomach, exposing intestines and other innards; blood pooled around him on the stone of the road, dark and smooth. The Gifted's eyes were still open, but his breaths were shallow and had a horrible bubbling sound.

Taeris was dying.

Caeden turned to Wirr. "He needs healing," he said urgently.

Wirr ran his hands through his hair. "I don't have enough Essence left in my Reserve to heal him. Even if it were full, I'm not sure I could repair a wound that bad." He hesitated. "You need to do it."

Caeden looked at Wirr, horrified. "I don't know how."

"You have to try and remember." Wirr grabbed Caeden's hand and forced it against Taeris's stomach. "I know you can do this, Caeden. Close your eyes, try and sense your Reserve. Then you need to tap into it and infuse the wound with raw Essence. If Taeris gets enough, his own body will do the rest."

Caeden swallowed, heart pounding. "I'll do my best." He began to close his eyes.

"Wait." Wirr grimaced. "Maybe I spoke too soon. It's not like firing a bolt of energy. It's gentler than that, trickier. You don't hurl it, you let it flow. Like a stream." He bit his lip. "That's very important, Caeden. If you can't get the difference, the energy will be too forceful. That would kill him."

Caeden paled. "Is there some way I can practice?"

"There's no time." It was Aelric. He placed a hand on Caeden's shoulder. "He's almost gone, Caeden."

Caeden gave a resolute nod, turning his attention to Taeris. He positioned his hands over the gash in Taeris's stomach, ignoring the blood welling up between his fingers. Then he took a deep breath and closed his eyes, searching out his Reserve. Trying desperately to remember how he'd done it in his dream.

The warmth of Essence was flowing through him, out of him, before he knew what was happening.

As quickly as it had come the feeling faded and Caeden sat back, drained. The wound had closed, only the raw pink of a newly healed scar now visible, but Caeden could not see any indication that Taeris's chest was rising and falling. Wirr dropped to his knees beside the Gifted, ear over Taeris's mouth, listening for any sign of life.

There was nothing for several seconds…and then Taeris gave a violent, hacking cough, his entire body contorting with the effort. He sat up and turned, vomiting the remaining blood from his stomach. When he'd finished he slowly turned back to Caeden and the others, hand on the freshly healed wound.

"Seems taking that Shackle off was a good idea," he said weakly.

Caeden gave him a relieved smile and allowed his tense muscles to relax a little, from the corner of his eye seeing the others doing the same. He helped Taeris stand. The older man tested out his muscles gingerly for a few seconds; once satisfied he could move without pain, he wandered over to where his attacker had fallen. Llys's eyes were closed, but her chest rose and fell rhythmically.

"We need to take her with us," said Wirr.

Taeris sighed. "No, lad. I saw her eyes, just before she stabbed me. Her body may still be sound, but her mind is gone. Following orders, but making use of her memories to achieve them." He rubbed his beard, expression thoughtful. "I've seen this once before, a long time ago—we called them Echoes. These ones were left behind deliberately, a trap for anyone who came after. Especially Gifted, apparently."

"I think he's right," added Caeden. He flushed a little at everyone's surprised looks. "I don't know how I know, but I thought the same thing when they attacked."

Dezia stared at the woman in disbelief. "But she told us her name. They were upset about what had happened."

Taeris shrugged. "And that was likely the case, before they were changed. But the people that they were no longer exist."

Wirr scowled. "So you're saying we should just kill her?"

"That's exactly what I'm saying," said Taeris softly. "It gives me no pleasure, but it is what needs to be done. If we leave her, she'll kill others."

"We don't know that!" protested Dezia.

Taeris gave her a sorrowful look. "Didn't you notice how the last group of bodies we saw coming into town didn't match the others? They were fresher, and were wearing traveling cloaks, not work clothing. There were children amongst them. I thought it was odd at the time..."

Caeden's stomach churned as he glanced back down the road. He hadn't spotted that.

Beside him Dezia's face twisted as she realized what Taeris was saying. She looked at Llys in horror. "We can't kill her," she said, though her voice was more uncertain now.

"What would you have us do?" asked Taeris. "There are three options. One, she comes with us. We don't even have rope to tie her up with, let alone know anything about her capabilities given what's been done to her. Two, we could leave her. She could come after us, or she could lay in wait for more people here. Or three, we can kill her." He folded his arms. "She's *dead*, understand. Something else is using her body and memories to trick people. She's no longer human." He raised an eyebrow at Wirr. "Unless you think you've somehow found a way around the First Tenet?"

Caeden grimaced, and Wirr turned away, looking sick. Taeris was right. Wirr had blasted Llys with Essence, something he shouldn't have been able to do.

"We should at least wait until she wakes up," Wirr said stubbornly. "We need to make sure."

Taeris groaned. "She will just try to fool you again, but..." He threw his hands up in the air. "Very well. You think you can restrain her?"

Wirr nodded. "I should be able to." He hesitated. "Do you think it's still wise to be heading for Ilin Illan now? Coming in behind this army?"

"Yes. If anything, this means it's more important than ever we reach Tol Athian quickly, before they get to the city. Otherwise we may not be able to get inside to restore Caeden's memories," said Taeris. "We'll take the eastern road, go around them. We should be able to get to Ilin Illan days before they arrive."

Wirr shook his head. "The southern road is the quicker route. I doubt we can beat them there by much."

"Look around you, Wirr." Taeris gestured at the rubble that surrounded them. "This army isn't in any hurry. Regardless of whether what Jashel told us was true, they certainly took the time to take down these buildings brick by brick. There are no signs of them using fire—probably because they didn't want the smoke letting people know they were coming. But they have managed to destroy every structure here nonetheless, and done horrible, unspeakable things to the occupants. It all takes time, time a normal army wouldn't bother wasting."

Caeden stared at the remains of the town. "Why do you think they did it?"

Taeris scratched his beard. "Could be that they're trying to draw the king's forces out of Ilin Illan, to engage them in the field rather than meet them on the city's walls. These things seem designed to taunt."

Suddenly there was a moan from the prostrate woman on the ground, and all five of them took a wary step back. Llys shook her head groggily, getting slowly to her feet. "What happened?" she asked in bemusement. Then her eyes fell on Jashel's corpse and a scream ripped from her throat, a heartrending sound full of pain. Heedless of the onlookers she rushed over to her son, cradling his head in her arms.

"No, no, no," she sobbed, repeating the words over and over again as she rocked back and forth, the boy's blood smearing across her already-dirty dress. "No, no, no."

Taeris glanced sideways at Wirr, seeing the dismay and sorrow on his face. He groaned, grabbing the golden-haired boy by the shoulder.

"You are only making this more difficult for yourself," he warned Wirr. "She'll act exactly like Llys until the moment she can strike. The creature inside of her is making use of her memories, just as it is borrowing her body. Trust me on this."

"Listen to him, Wirr," said Caeden worriedly. He, too, had no doubt the woman was still dangerous.

Wirr scowled at both of them. "You don't know that! Either of you," he protested. He turned to Taeris. "You say you've only seen this once before, and it was years ago. You don't even know if there might be a way to cure her, to save her! We *can't* just kill her."

He shook off Taeris's grasp, moving over to the woman and kneeling beside her.

"I'm sorry," he said, tone gentle. "What can we do to help?"

Llys just kept on weeping, her body racked with deep sobs. Wirr turned to look at the others helplessly.

Behind him Llys moved like a cat. She snatched the dagger from her dead son's hands and spun, blade arcing toward Wirr's heart.

Before anyone else could react, Dezia drew her bow and fired.

The arrow sped past Wirr's ear and took Llys in the eye; the woman gave a single scream and then collapsed, motionless. Everyone else stood there, frozen to the spot; even Taeris looked shocked by the speed at which events had turned.

Wirr twisted in his crouching position to look at the corpse behind him, then rose.

"Thank you, Dezia," he said sadly.

Taeris grimaced, then stepped forward. "We need to move. There could be more of them out there, for all we know. This area isn't safe."

The others gave him silent acknowledgments and they moved onward, away from the horrors of Gahille. Though no one suggested it, they traveled late into the night. None of them wanted to be closer to the desecrated town than they had to be.

They walked in heavy, stunned silence, but every time someone glanced in his direction, Caeden couldn't help but flinch a little. They didn't show it, but his companions had to be wondering anew about his role in all this—what his connection was to these invaders. They had to be asking themselves just how far he could be trusted.

And after what he'd just seen, he couldn't blame them.

He gritted his teeth and marched on.

# Chapter 34

Asha stared at the ring in the palm of her hand.

"You seem preoccupied."

She started as Erran's voice came from just behind her ear. She spun, flushing.

"Sorry," she said, shaking her head. "What were you saying?"

"I was saying that ring goes with the weapons." Erran gingerly removed the thin silver circle from her grasp. "It creates a focused burst of air."

Asha frowned. "Doesn't sound terribly dangerous."

"It's strong enough to punch through a wall," Erran assured her.

"How do you know?"

"Best we don't talk about that." Erran placed the ring next to a pair of copper gauntlets on the shelf. "But it certainly doesn't need testing. As denoted by the fact it was on the 'weapons' shelf."

Asha shook her head again, flushing. "Sorry." When Elocien had suggested that she help Erran sift through Administration's stockpile of Vessels—to look for something that could potentially be used against the Blind—she had thought it sounded like an interesting diversion. The reality had been that though Erran needed someone on hand in case he injured himself testing a new device, there wasn't a lot she could do to assist him otherwise. Even watching the process was relatively dull; Erran was always cautious and only ever fed a trickle of Essence into each device, often with no result. With little else to keep her occupied, her thoughts kept drifting.

It had been a week since the Shadraehin's grisly gift had been delivered, and as her residual fears after the kidnapping had gradually eased, her focus had more and more turned back to Davian. His appearance in her room seemed an age earlier now, and sometimes she doubted her memory of the event. Even so, when she thought about it—*really* thought about it—she knew she hadn't been dreaming.

"It's all right." Erran gave her a quizzical look. "Is…something wrong? You've been awfully quiet this morning."

"No. I'm fine."

"Well…best you pay attention, if you can. We're not filing books here. Some of these things really could be useful, and I'd hate to miss something."

"Sorry," Asha repeated, more contritely this time. Erran was right. She needed to concentrate.

She wandered over to an unsorted shelf, picking up an abstract symbol carved from some sort of blue-green rock. "How much chance do you think we have of finding something we can use?"

"Almost none," replied Erran cheerfully. "I've done this a few times now. The Veils are the most useful thing we've found by a long way, and that was more than a year ago now." He shrugged. "It's just a slow process. I'm not supposed to put too much Essence into any one Vessel—safety reasons, aside from not wanting to get a Mark or set off any Finders—so most of the time, testing does nothing. As you've no doubt concluded," he added with a wry grin.

Asha gave him an absent nod in response, suddenly noticing a pile of small black discs heaped on another shelf of sorted Vessels. She knew what they were—had witnessed enough people being made into Shadows, even if she couldn't remember the experience herself.

She stared at the pile, her thoughts already beginning to drift again as Erran turned back to his task. She mentally replayed what Davian had said to her, as she'd often found herself doing over the past few days. Felt herself flush with anger as she considered what it meant if he'd really been there.

It would mean that she'd been lied to by Ilseth. It would mean that the story of how she'd become a Shadow was just that—a

story.

This time the frustration and anger settled in her stomach, burned steadily rather than faded. It was too much. She was *tired* of being used, *tired* of not knowing what to believe. She needed to find out what was real.

She took a deep breath.

"If I let you Read me, do you think it's possible you could access the memories from when I was made a Shadow? The ones from the morning of the attack at Caladel?"

Erran stopped what he was doing, gaping at her.

"What?"

Asha turned to face him. The anger was still there, hot and low, with nowhere to escape. "Can you access the memories I've lost?" she asked succinctly.

"Why...why would you want to do that?" Erran looked flustered.

"Because I think the man who made me a Shadow might have lied about the reason why," said Asha. "Can you do it?"

Erran slowly put down the Vessel he'd been holding, shaking his head. "I...don't know," he admitted after a moment. "There are a lot of variables. If the memory has just been walled off, rather than erased...maybe. But it could be dangerous. There has to be a reason Shadows lose that memory, Asha. It's probably a defense. Messing with the mind when it's trying to protect you... I have no idea of the consequences." He frowned. "And even if I could access the memory, I'd have to break down whatever barriers are in place to get at it. Which means that it won't be shut off from *your* mind anymore, either. I just don't think—"

Asha spun, stiffening, as a metallic scratching sound echoed through the room.

Erran paled. He heard it, too.

Someone was unlocking the door.

"No time," he murmured, snatching up something from the shelf nearby and tossing it to Asha. She caught it before realizing what it was. A Veil.

Without hesitating Asha pressed the open end of the silver torc onto her arm.

Everything...shimmered.

A moment later the door swung open. A tall, thin, blue-cloaked

Administrator strode through, freezing when he realized a lamp was already lit. His eyes moved straight to Erran, who was now standing with his back to the door, examining a shelf.

"What are you doing in here?" said the Administrator angrily, his voice booming around the warehouse.

Erran turned, and Asha shook her head in silent admiration at his nonchalant expression. "Administrator Ionis," he said politely, giving a slight bow. "Duke Andras asked me to store something for him in here."

The man called Ionis crossed his arms. "I recognize you. That servant that kept spilling drinks when I met with Elocien a few weeks ago." He shook his head. "I don't believe you. This area of the palace is strictly off-limits, and the duke knows it."

Erran looked hurt. "Duke Andras will confirm he asked me," he said in an injured tone. He reached into his pocket, producing the ring Asha had been handling a few moments earlier. "See? I was just trying to decide where it goes."

Ionis studied the ring with narrowed eyes. "It goes wherever there is a space. There's no order to any of this junk." He shook his head, taking an object of his own from his pocket and tossing it on a nearby shelf. "Give me that, and come with me. I'm not letting you out of my sight until I speak to Elocien, so I hope for your sake you're telling the truth."

"Of course, Administrator. I'm happy to help."

Ionis gave a brusque nod. "You're alone in here?"

"Yes."

Ionis looked around suspiciously but eventually nodded again, apparently satisfied. "Then let's go."

"Just let me get the duke's key. I left it lying around on one of these shelves," said Erran, his tone embarrassed. "I wouldn't want it to be locked in here. It might be a while before someone can come down here again to fetch it."

He started walking toward a shelf near where Asha stood. It took her a couple of moments to realize his words had been directed at her.

Moving as quietly as possible she slipped around the Administrator and through the still-open door, breathing a sigh of relief as she emerged into the passageway beyond. Erran had been right;

the door required a key to unlock it, no matter which side of it you were on.

Once outside she set off at a light jog for the main section of the palace.

As soon as she was certain she was alone, she removed the Veil from her arm. Her first thought was to head for her rooms—after such a near miss, she wanted nothing more than to collapse onto her bed and rest—but after a moment she made for Elocien's study instead.

Fortunately there was no one waiting outside today; either Elocien had dealt with all the concerned nobles, or he had grown sick of them and had ordered them to leave him alone. Asha suspected the latter.

She knocked, relieved to see Elocien when the door opened.

The duke frowned around at the empty hallway. "Ashalia. This isn't the best time…"

"It's urgent, and it won't take long."

Once she was inside, she drew the Veil from her pocket, showing it to Elocien. "I was helping Erran look for something we could use amongst the Vessels," she said quickly. "An Administrator came in while we were there. Ionis, I think his name was. I hid with this, but Erran didn't have time. He told Ionis you sent him down there to store a ring."

Elocien nodded calmly, as if this was entirely expected. "Thank you, Asha. Ionis won't be happy, but he rarely is. Don't worry. It will be fine." He paused. "You should probably use the Veil again, though."

Asha frowned. "Why?"

A knock came at the door.

Asha pressed the silver torc back onto her arm as Elocien rose. He made sure that she was no longer visible, then opened the door.

"Ionis! What a pleasant surprise," said the duke in an amiable tone, stepping back to let the Administrator in. "And Erran, too, I see. How can I help you?"

Ionis made no move to enter. "This young man says you gave him this key"—he handed the storeroom key to the duke—"and sent him to put something in the Old Section?"

"That's correct. A silver ring," confirmed Elocien. "Erran has been with me for years. I trust him."

Ionis's face tightened, and he reached into his pocket and handed the ring across to Elocien before turning to Erran. "You may go," he said curtly.

Erran nodded, looking relieved, then vanished down the hallway.

"Would you like to come in?" asked Elocien, gesturing inside his study.

Ionis's eyes bored into the duke's. "He shouldn't have been down there, Your Grace." He made no move to enter.

Elocien sighed. "Do you really think I would have sent him if I didn't think he was trustworthy?"

"That's not your decision to make. Administration won't be happy. Your Grace."

Elocien leaned forward slightly, and his tone changed. It was still friendly, but the words had steel beneath them this time. "Administration answers to me. As do you. You would do well to remember that."

Ionis matched Elocien's gaze, unperturbed. "As you say." He moved to walk away, then hesitated, turning back. "What happened to you, Your Grace?"

The duke frowned. "I don't know what you're—"

"Yes you do." Ionis studied Elocien's face closely. "You used to believe in our purpose here. The importance of the work. You know the worst part of today? I believed that boy, even before I came up here. A few years ago I wouldn't have even had to check with you. I would have *known* he was lying." He shook his head, eyes narrowed. "Something changed, but I was never able to figure out what."

"I don't know what you're talking about, Ionis," said Elocien, sounding weary.

Ionis gazed at the Northwarden for a few more seconds, then snorted in disgust. "Of course you don't."

He spun on his heel and vanished down the hallway.

Elocien watched him go, then closed the door. "You can take it off again."

Asha didn't respond for a moment. She'd been half listening to the conversation, but there had been something else that was distracting her. Something she'd noticed when she'd put the Veil on the first time, but had been too flustered to pay any attention to.

The Veil was drawing Essence from her. From her Reserve. It was only a thin stream of energy, but... it was definitely there.

She closed her eyes, reaching out for Essence herself. There was nothing there... but the momentary disappointment faded as she considered the possibilities.

The art of making Vessels had been lost hundreds of years earlier, so very little was known about their operation. But if they could tap a Shadow's Reserve...

It meant that becoming a Shadow hadn't destroyed her Reserve, only blocked it off.

It meant that, just maybe, Davian had been right. There *could* be a cure, a way to reverse it.

Trembling, she released the Veil from her arm, allowing herself to fade back into view. Elocien looked at her in concern as he saw the expression on her face.

"What's wrong?"

Asha hesitated, a dozen thoughts flashing through her mind at once.

If this was true for all Vessels, and all Shadows, then the implications of what she'd discovered were enormous. Shadows lost their Marks, were not bound by the Tenets. They could use Vessels however they chose. Use the weapons. Perhaps not as effectively as the Gifted—most Shadows were Gifted who had failed their Trials, after all—but each one could still count for a hundred normal soldiers, if they could be convinced to defend the city.

On the other hand, she trusted Elocien, but... he was the Northwarden. Was this something he would feel obliged to warn Administration about? Because given how much Administrators already feared the Shadraehin, and by extension all Shadows, she shuddered to think what the reaction might be to news such as this.

Then she thought of the visions in the Journal, and she knew there wasn't really a choice. The Augurs had Seen the Blind inside the city. This wasn't information she could withhold.

"I think... I'm fairly certain the Veil was drawing from my Reserve," she said, voice shaking a little.

Elocien stared at her blankly for a few moments. "Your Reserve," he repeated.

"I know how it sounds." Asha rubbed her forehead, staring at the torc in her hand. "But it's not my imagination."

Elocien shook his head. "You must be mistaken. If Shadows could use Vessels, we would know about it."

"Would we?" Asha looked him in the eye. "Shadows have only been around since the war, and given how we're treated...I cannot imagine many of us have even had the chance to *see* a Vessel, let alone touch one. We're mostly Gifted who failed our Trials, remember. I know the Shadows at the Tol wouldn't be allowed anywhere near Athian's Vessels. And Administration wouldn't let a Shadow anywhere near...anything." She shrugged. "And let's be honest. I don't know many Shadows who would make the knowledge public, even if they did find out."

Elocien stared at her for a few seconds, then tossed her something small that glinted as it spun through the air.

"Prove it."

Asha caught the object neatly and opened her hand, staring down at what she held. The silver ring from the storeroom. "Erran says this can punch a hole through a wall."

"That was the first Vessel Erran ever tested, and he poured enough Essence into that thing to punch a hole through Ilin Tora," said Elocien drily. "Just a trickle should be fine."

Asha nodded, holding the ring out in front of her. She was about to close her eyes when Elocien coughed.

"Even so, if you could please point it away from my head..."

Asha gave him a crooked smile, adjusting so that she was facing Elocien's bookcase. She took a deep breath. Concentrated.

At first there was nothing. Then...a connection. A sense of energy building up in the ring.

She released it.

Then she was flying backward, crashing against the far wall hard enough to rattle her teeth as Elocien's carefully stacked shelves of books and documents exploded into a fluttering, chaotic mess of papers. Dazed, Asha accepted Elocien's help as she struggled to her feet, eyes wide.

They both stood for a few moments, surveying the carnage.

The point of impact on the bookcase had splintered the shelf, and there was a circular series of cracks in the stone where the blow had dinted the wall behind.

"Fates," said Elocien. He looked at the wall, then Asha, then the wall again.

"Fates," he repeated dazedly.

They spent the next few minutes tidying the mess as best they could, silent until the worst of it was cleared, each lost in their own thoughts. Eventually Elocien sat, gesturing for Asha to do the same, and stared at her like a puzzle to be solved.

"Assuming this applies to all Shadows, and not just you," he said quietly. "You're not bound by the Tenets?"

Asha shook her head. "Not from what I can tell."

Elocien rubbed his forehead. "I need time to think about this." He grimaced. "In the meantime I need your word. You don't breathe a word of this—not to anyone. Not even to the Augurs. If this ever got out…" His frown deepened. "Panic. Overreaction, from Administration and probably from a lot of common folk, too. Which ends badly for the Shadows. And then, any Shadows who manage to get hold of a Vessel…" He looked sick. "I know a lot of Shadows are good people, Asha, but a lot of them hate Administration for making them the way they are. Not sure I can blame them, either, but giving them weapons like that…"

Asha nodded; she'd had time to process the implications now, and she knew that what the duke was saying was true. "You have my word," she assured him. "What about for defending against the Blind, though?"

Elocien shook his head. "No. Not even for that." He held up a hand as Asha made to protest. "And regardless, the Shadows are disparate, disorganized, and have little allegiance to the city. Even if we sent word out, there's no way we could arrange them into any meaningful group."

"There's one person who could." Asha raised an eyebrow. "Who already has."

Elocien stared at her in pure disbelief.

"After what they've done? After what they did to you?" He shook his head. "No. We're not there yet."

"That wasn't him. And we know the Blind get inside the city—"    409

"We *believe* they do," corrected Elocien. "But right now, we have an army of nine thousand good men standing in their way, not to mention the Shields at Fedris Idri. I'm worried, Asha, but not worried enough to give over some of the most powerful weapons ever created into the hands of murderers. Particularly ones who wouldn't hesitate to turn those weapons on us once the battle's over." He held up a hand as he saw Asha's face. "I'm not saying I won't consider it. But we're not there yet."

Asha gave a reluctant nod, then offered the ring back to Elocien.

The duke hesitated for a moment, then shook his head.

"Keep it," he said. "Just don't let Ionis see it." He paused. "And it probably goes without saying, but be very careful of Ionis if you come across him in your duties as Representative. He's a zealot—the worst kind. Give him the opportunity, and he'd wipe out every Gifted and Shadow in existence."

Asha inclined her head. "I will be."

They talked a little more after that, but before long Asha made her excuses and headed back toward her rooms. She wanted to be alone for a while, to gather her racing thoughts. To try to calmly determine what this all meant.

She shook her head, still dazed, as she made her way along the palace hallways, rolling the silver ring idly in her hand. Her Reserve was intact, just…blocked off, somehow. Could Davian have been right? Was it possible to somehow *undo* having become a Shadow?

Then she frowned, coming to a gradual halt as she realized something else. For the first time, Asha felt certain that Davian had actually spoken to her that day—had been there in the room with her. She *knew* that it hadn't been some kind of odd dream.

Asha slipped the ring onto her finger, and walked on. She had a lot to think about.

Erran looked up as Asha entered the Lockroom.

"Quick thinking earlier," he said once she'd shut the door. "I gather Ionis wasn't too happy with Elocien?"

Asha shook her head. "Decidedly unhappy." She sat opposite the Augur, silent for a moment. "Before he interrupted us—"

"It's dangerous, Asha," interjected Erran, his expression serious. Their conversation from the storeroom had obviously been on his mind, too. "I couldn't guarantee your safety."

Asha took a deep breath. If Davian was really alive, then Ilseth had lied to her—lied to everyone—about why she'd been made a Shadow. And there had to be a reason for that.

"I don't care," she said quietly. "I want you to try and restore my memories." She set her features into a grim mask of determination and looked Erran in the eye, daring him to refuse her.

"I want to remember what happened at Caladel."

# Chapter 35

Davian grinned as he walked around Malshash, watching the almost motionless man.

The stone he had dropped only a split second ago continued its gradual fall away from his outstretched hand, inching toward the ground. Davian had now been observing its descent for at least a count of ten.

They had spent the last few days working on this ability, one of the hardest to master according to Malshash, and one of the most relevant to Davian's return through the rift. The mysterious Augur had been hesitant about using it here in Deilannis—he was worried about what the effects might be, this close to the Jha'vett—but his determination that Davian learn the ability had won out.

It had been frustrating at first; aside from trying to use Essence, Davian had never had so much trouble learning anything in his life. Even now he sweated with the strain of concentration, letting time move all around him but letting it touch him as little as possible. It had been a difficult concept to explain for both Malshash and the authors of the books he'd read, and now Davian understood why. It was like trying to stand in a stream of water without getting wet.

He leaned down, grabbing the stone in midair, allowing the time bubble—as he thought of it—to encapsulate it as well. That was important, otherwise the stone would in reality be moving at speeds its structure could not handle, and would likely disintegrate or melt. He moved a few paces away from Malshash and then relaxed, allowing time to crash back into him. It was momentarily disorienting, but he quickly recovered.

Malshash blinked, then realized the stone had vanished from in front of him. He looked up at Davian, who opened his palm to display the smooth rock, grinning.

Malshash smiled back. "Excellent, Davian." The praise was genuine, but he seemed less enthusiastic today for some reason.

Davian still had not been able to figure out the enigmatic stranger, who this morning wore the face of a handsome young man with jet-black hair, dark skin, and deep, piercing eyes. At times Malshash acted distant, like today; at others he was jovial, friendly. Mostly, though, Davian thought he seemed sad. Occasionally he would catch Malshash watching him train, and there would be such a look of pain on his face that it almost made him stop.

He didn't intrude as to why, though. Whenever he asked personal questions of Malshash, the Augur simply went quiet. Those matters were something Malshash clearly had no interest in talking about.

Davian accepted the compliment with an inclined head, the feeling of accomplishment a warmth in his belly. "Necessity is a wonderful motivator," he said in a dry tone. Then he grinned. "I have to say, though, that kan is...amazing. These abilities, this power, is more than I could ever have dreamed. I've never experienced anything like it."

Malshash studied him for a moment. "I understand," he said quietly, "but be very wary of enjoying yourself too much. Most Augurs learn these powers as they grow up—are taught their proper applications over the course of years, not weeks."

Davian's smile faded. "What do you mean?"

Malshash shrugged. "Augurs are supposed to train in each power for a year and a day before they are allowed to use it in the real world. You're going to have a grand total of a few weeks for all of them, *if* we're lucky. On top of that, you've been striving for your powers for so long, and now you're receiving them all at once. On the one hand, that will make you more appreciative of them. On the other, it could make you overeager to use them."

Davian raised an eyebrow. "So...you don't trust me?"

"It's not that," Malshash rushed to assure him. "It's only that I've seen firsthand what power like this can do to the best of people. I'm not suggesting it will happen to you. But believe me, you will be tested. You'll have opportunities—many opportunities—to use kan in ways that will benefit you, but are not strictly... moral. It's a constant temptation, Davian. There is a reason why the training is supposed to take so long. You need to be prepared for the new choices these powers give you."

Davian nodded, though he still felt vaguely irritated at the suggestion that he would abuse his abilities. "Of course."

Malshash watched him for a moment longer, then nodded in a satisfied manner. "Good." He stroked his chin. Davian often wondered whether his real form had a beard, for it was a habit of his, regardless of the face he wore. "Which power should we try next?"

Davian didn't have to think; he knew which one he wanted to try the most. "Foresight."

Malshash hesitated, then shook his head. "I'm sorry. I suppressed that ability for a reason, Davian. It's just too dangerous here."

"But surely it's the closest ability to traveling through the rift itself," pointed out Davian. "Isn't it worth the risk?"

Malshash looked uncomfortable. "It doesn't matter. I gave up the power to See some time ago," he confessed. "I don't have the knowledge of how to do it."

"*What?*" Davian frowned in confusion. "You...gave it up? Why?"

"It doesn't matter." Malshash rubbed the back of his neck tiredly, his tone indicating he wished to discuss the topic no further. "I can't See, and so I am of little help to you in that regard."

Davian scowled. "Why not just tell me?"

Malshash met his gaze, a chill in his stare. "Because it's *none of your business*, Davian." He held up his hand. "I know that's not a satisfactory answer, but it's all you're going to get. So please. Let it go."

Davian grimaced, but nodded his acquiescence. If Malshash wanted to be mysterious, that was his prerogative, so long as he taught Davian what was needed to get home. "Fine. If you don't

415

know how to See, do you at least know something about it? The books all said that the visions inevitably come to pass...but as I told you, in my time the Augurs were overthrown after their visions stopped coming true. What does that mean?"

Malshash hesitated. "If what I've come to believe here, these past couple of weeks, is true...it means they were tricked, Davian. It's as simple as that."

"So you don't believe the future can be changed?"

"I did, once. I...hoped it could be," admitted Malshash. "But from what I've seen...the future can no more be changed than the past."

Davian frowned. "So our fate is set, no matter what we do? We can't change anything?"

Malshash inclined his head. "I think so—though perhaps that's not the best way to think about it," he said quietly. "The future may be immutable, but it's not because our choices do not change anything. It's that they already *have* changed things. The decisions you make tomorrow are the same as those you made yesterday—still your choices and still with consequences, but unalterable. The only difference is your knowledge of the decisions you made yesterday."

Davian screwed up his face. "I don't understand."

Malshash sighed. "When you came to this time, you momentarily stepped *outside* of time. A place where time doesn't exist. Nothing to separate events from one another, or to give them length. They happen simultaneously and for eternity." He shrugged. "In short, all that will happen, has already happened. It's just that we are experiencing it through the lens of time."

Davian shook his head. "I don't accept that. There has to be another explanation."

Malshash grunted. "You're not a believer in El, then?"

Davian frowned at the question. "Not especially. That religion has been all but destroyed in my time—in Andarra at least."

Malshash raised an eyebrow. "Has it now," he murmured. He nodded to himself. "I see. Because of what you told me about the Augurs."

Davian nodded. "As soon as they began to get things wrong, people started losing faith. After the Unseen War, the Loyalists decided it meant either El had never existed, his plan had gone awry somehow, or that he was dead—and that in any case, no one should be worshipping him."

Malshash sighed. "Such is the way of weak men," he murmured. "Daring to believe only in what can be seen, touched, and measured."

Davian frowned. "I thought the logic made a kind of sense."

Malshash shook his head ruefully. "It does—that's the problem. It was always a danger, priests pointing to the abilities of men as proof of the existence of God. Already, even in this time, they are becoming reliant on the acts of the Augurs to proclaim El's existence. It sounds like it will destroy them."

"So you believe?" asked Davian.

Malshash hesitated. "In His existence? Yes," he said slowly. "Do you know why the Augurs were thought to prove it?"

Davian nodded, thinking back to what Mistress Alita had taught him. "El was supposed to have the perfect plan, to be in complete control of the world. The Grand Design. You can't have a perfect plan if men can determine their own futures—and the Augurs were proof that the future was set." He raised an eyebrow. "Until they started getting things wrong."

"Exactly." Malshash sighed. "Everyone thinks of us as great men. Wise. Untouchable. But you're an Augur, Davian. You don't think you could be tricked?"

Davian made to protest, then hesitated. He thought back to how Tenvar had fooled him at the school. "I suppose I could."

"And if a great power—an ancient, malevolent power—bent its entire will to fooling you?"

Davian paled. "Is that what happened to the Augurs?"

"Maybe." Malshash shrugged. "I can only speculate."

Davian frowned. "You said an ancient power. A malevolent power." His eyes narrowed. "Were you talking about Aarkein Devaed?"

Malshash grimaced. "No."

"He really exists, though?" Davian shuffled his feet nervously. "He's still alive, after all this time?"

Malshash chuckled, though the sound was humorless. "Oh yes. He is very much alive." He rose, indicating the end of the conversation. "Enough about that. We should take a break for a meal, and then continue your training."

Davian gave an absent nod in response. For a moment he wanted to pursue what Malshash had said...but even as he opened his mouth the desire left him, replaced by excitement at the prospect of learning new skills. "Can we try shape-shifting next?" he asked, unable to keep the eagerness from his tone.

Malshash shook his head. "Another skill that is too dangerous," he admitted. "There's a good reason you didn't know about it before you came here. No Augur who has discovered the ability has ever passed on its knowledge. That alone should tell you how unsafe it is."

Davian sighed. Along with Seeing, shape-shifting had been the ability he'd been most looking forward to learning. "I'll take the risk," he said stubbornly. He grinned. "If you've seen me in the future, it means it can't kill me, right?"

"True, but it isn't relevant to what you need to know to get home." Malshash gave him an apologetic shrug. "We don't have time for anything extra, Davian. Your bond here will begin weakening soon. It's already been two weeks; I'm surprised there have been no problems as it is. And I still don't believe you're ready to face the rift again."

Davian thought about protesting, but decided against it. "Very well," he said reluctantly. "I think I'll stay here and do some reading, if you want to eat."

Malshash hesitated, but nodded. "I'll bring back some food. See you in an hour or so." He turned and walked through the door, leaving Davian alone in the Great Library once again.

Davian sat for a while, lost in thought.

Then he came to a decision. He moved over to place his hand on the Adviser and closed his eyes, concentrating.

The blue line shot straight for one of the books on a nearby shelf. Davian grabbed it, then flipped through until he found what he was looking for: the section entitled *Shape-shifting, best practices.*

He scanned the text, frowning. The entry was only a page long—but he knew that in the other books he'd read, shape-shifting was mentioned only briefly, too, if at all. It appeared Malshash had been right about its knowledge not being passed on.

The description in this book of how to undertake the process was vague, but it sounded simple enough. Davian read the section a few times to make sure he understood everything, then closed his eyes.

He held a picture of Wirr in his mind. The book specified that the shape-shifter needed only a passing familiarity with the appearance of whomever they were trying to change into, an "imprint" of the person, but Davian thought it would be safest to pick someone he knew well. He drew on kan, let the dark substance settle into his flesh, cooling and warming at the same time. He pictured Wirr in his mind as clearly as he could, then willed his own flesh, his own face, to look the same.

Immense pain tore through him.

A scream ripped from his throat as he fell to the ground. Every nerve ending in his body felt as if it were being burned by ice, and his eyes felt as if someone were scraping hot knives across them. He could feel his ribs expanding, his bones growing, his muscles contorting themselves into position around his changing ligaments. His skin stretched until it felt as though it would break apart. He tasted blood.

Then it was over. He lay on the cold stone floor for several minutes, drifting in and out of consciousness, his mind trying to recover from what had just happened. Eventually he forced himself to kneel, then stand. He shuffled unsteadily on shaky legs that were longer than he was used to. He was taller; everything looked just a little farther down than normal.

Despite the aches, despite the memory of the fierce, unimaginable pain, he smiled to himself. It had worked.

He hurried down a corridor into a room which he knew contained a mirror. As he came within sight of his reflection, he froze, staring in horror.

His features, his body, were normal enough. But they were not Wirr's.

The reflection in the mirror was of an older man, at least in his thirties. He had dirty blond hair and was of a size with Wirr, but there the similarities ended. He had a hooked nose and small, beady black eyes. When Davian tried to smile, his lips curled upward into a sneer instead. His skin was weather-beaten rather

419

than tanned—the skin of a sailor, perhaps? Whoever the man was, Davian was quite certain he had never seen him before.

Davian scowled as he continued to examine his new visage. This man had facial scars, too; if anything, they stood out more than Davian's. That had been one of the fantasies he'd had about shape-shifting—that he could finally wear a face that wasn't marred.

"Davian? Where are you?" It was Malshash calling out, apparently having returned sooner than expected. Either that or Davian had been unconscious longer than he'd realized.

For a second he considered trying to turn back, to hide what he'd done. But he knew immediately that it would not work, and was too dangerous besides. He was probably fortunate to have survived the first transition alone. He needed Malshash's help to return to his normal body.

He slowly walked back down the corridor to the main chamber. Malshash was laying out some food on a nearby table, his back turned.

"I'm here," said Davian, flinching as the voice emanating from his throat was deeper, huskier than his own.

Malshash whirled in alarm. Before Davian knew what was happening he was frozen to the spot, unable to move, though he could feel no bindings holding him in place. He stared at Malshash pleadingly.

"It's me," he said, hanging his head. "I shape-shifted. I...I'm sorry."

There was silence. Davian raised his head again to find Malshash just looking at him, seeming more horrified than angry.

"Whose form is this?" asked Malshash eventually, sounding shaken.

Davian grimaced. "I'm not sure. I pictured my friend Wirr, but ended up like this. They look vaguely similar, but I don't believe I've ever seen this man before."

Malshash swallowed, looking disturbed. He waved his hand in the air, and Davian found he could move again. "You must have seen him before," Malshash said softly. "There is no other explanation." He seemed...off. Not just concerned, or shocked. He appeared suddenly wary of Davian. As if he'd arrived expecting a mouse and instead found a lion.

Davian shrugged. Even without the odd sensation of being in someone else's skin, he didn't like this body at all. It ached everywhere, particularly the fingers, which he could barely move without a dull pain shooting through his hand. "I'm sorry," he repeated, his tone heavy with contrition. "It was a foolish thing to do. And it *hurt*." He scratched his head. "Can you help me change back? Preferably without the pain this time," he added with a shallow smile.

Malshash shook his head. "If you did this safely one way, all you need to do is picture your own face and do the same." He sighed. "As for the pain...I'm afraid that's unavoidable. It happens every time you change."

Davian paled. He desperately didn't want to go through that again.

Then he realized what Malshash was saying.

"But that means..." His eyes widened. "You do that *every day*?"

Malshash grunted. "It certainly wakes me up in the morning."

"But why?" exclaimed Davian. The thought of facing that pain each and every day chilled him to his core. "Why not just return to your own form?"

Malshash sighed. "I've already told you, Davian. The talent I have for it now was taken from the Ath herself. If I don't use it once during each day, it will return to her and the consequences would be...unpleasant. Much worse than the pain. Not to mention that I'd be stuck in whatever form I happen to be in at the time." He shrugged dismissively. "Believe me, if there were a better choice I would take it in a heartbeat."

Davian gave a reluctant nod. "I suppose I should just get this over and done with, then."

"Do you want me to leave?"

"No. It's probably safer if someone is watching over me."

Malshash inclined his head, moving over to a nearby chair and taking a seat.

As Malshash had said, the process of shape-shifting was just as painful in reverse. By the time the echoes of Davian's screams had faded from the Great Library, though, he found himself fully aware of his surroundings. That was one thing, at least. The disorientation was not so bad changing back.

421

Malshash walked over to where he lay, offering his hand and dragging Davian to his feet. "You're back," he confirmed after a moment. He shook his head in amazement. "You pick things up so quickly it's frightening, Davian." His expression hardened. "But never try something like that again. Understand? These early lessons are by far the most dangerous. You may not kill yourself, but there are plenty of ways you could be badly injured playing around with kan."

Davian bowed his head. "Of course," he said in a penitent tone, his face burning. Inwardly he kicked himself for his impatient overconfidence. Malshash had said these powers took a year and a day *each* to learn under normal circumstances. His teacher knew how important it was for Davian to grasp them; Malshash was pushing as hard as he thought possible. Davian had to trust him.

Malshash clapped Davian on the back. "I think this afternoon we should revisit what we've done so far. Make sure you haven't forgotten anything."

Davian smiled. "You mean I should slow down for a few hours." He shrugged. "Agreed."

They sat down to eat the meal Malshash had brought. Davian wolfed down his generous portion of bread and fruit, a little surprised at the end that his stomach was still growling. He'd been eating more and more the last few days, but it rarely satisfied his hunger. Still, he'd been working harder than he ever had before. No doubt it was simply a side effect of that.

They eventually resumed their work, Malshash acting as if nothing untoward had happened that morning. Still, to begin with, the image of the stranger's face in the mirror bothered Davian from time to time. He was *sure* he'd never seen the man before. There had to be a good explanation for it.

Eventually he became engrossed in the drills Malshash had set him, forgetting about it and all his other troubles for a time.

He didn't even pay any attention to Malshash's occasional glances toward him. Uncertain. Contemplating.

Worried.

# Chapter 36

Wirr stretched, his muscles taut more from nervousness than from traveling.

Though he'd already begun to suspect, Taeris had just informed them that they were now less than a half day's travel away from Ilin Illan. The place where he'd grown up; the place where he was not simply Wirr, but Torin Wirrander Andras, prince of the realm. People would be bowing and scraping whenever he was around. They would always smile at him, even if it was through gritted teeth. He was leaving a world and a life he loved to return to one where most people he met wore a mask.

He'd begun seeing familiar landmarks over the past couple of days. They'd passed the Eloin Marshes this morning; yesterday they'd traveled through the midsize town of Goeth, where he had distant relatives with estates. Now, in the distance, the tip of Ilin Tora was just barely visible against the horizon. Every step he took felt heavier with reluctant inevitability. He'd known this day would come, though he'd wished against it constantly.

"Which problem are you worrying about?" came a soft voice at his side.

He started, whipping his head around. Dezia was walking beside him, looking torn between amusement and concern.

He smiled at her, though he knew the effort was a weak one at best. "I'm trying to give them all a fair shot at ruining my day," he said lightly. He couldn't help but widen his smile as the corners of Dezia's mouth turned upward. A moment later he looked away, feeling as if he'd been punched in the stomach. Being home meant seeing Dezia far less, too. If at all.

"Which one is winning at the moment?" she asked.

Wirr grunted, glancing around. They were slightly separate from the others, able to have a conversation without being in danger of anyone's overhearing. "Going back to court," he admitted. "Pretending to be someone I'm not."

Dezia's eyebrow rose a little. "As opposed to the last few years?"

Wirr sighed. "You know what I mean. I won't even be able to look sideways at one of the Gifted for the next few years. And there will be...other restrictions on what I can do, too. Who I can spend time with."

Dezia nodded slowly. "I know." She gave a small smile. "Though that doesn't mean you won't run into people. Coincidentally."

Wirr grinned. "Certainly. Sometimes you can't avoid running into people," he agreed readily. His smile faded. "But still...it won't be the same as out here." He shook his head in frustration. "I won't even be able to help to find out what happened at the school. It will be nothing but lessons in politics, and maybe military tactics, for the foreseeable future."

"As long as there *is* a foreseeable future," observed Dezia, "the rest will work itself out." She reached over and squeezed his arm, a reassuring touch.

Wirr gave a grim nod in response. The past couple of days they had been moving very much against the flow of travelers; the closer they got to the city, the more people there appeared to be leaving it. Many were hauling carts and wagons filled to the brim with personal items. Some said they were leaving the city only as a precaution against the oncoming army, and expected to return once word came that the king's forces had defeated the enemy. But others were not so certain.

"Do you believe what people are saying about the invaders?" he asked. "That they're stronger and faster than normal men should be?"

Dezia shrugged. "I'm not sure. On one hand it's only a rumor, and it could be blown entirely out of proportion—I doubt we can trust what Jashel and Llys told us. On the other...we saw our-selves what they're capable of. They obviously have *some* pow-ers." She sighed. "It is going to be a difficult time for your uncle."

Wirr nodded. They had already heard murmurs against the king—rumors suggesting he had started to take a hard line against the Gifted, just when he should be courting them and considering the possibility of modifying the Tenets. It was hard to know how much was true, and how much was just people's nervousness—it was only grumbling, the odd word here and there—but the message was clear enough. People were fright-ened by what they'd heard of the Blind. They wanted the invaders defeated by any means necessary.

"Whatever the Blind are, it sounds like what we saw was hardly the worst of what they've done," Wirr noted. Word had begun to trickle in a couple of days earlier from those refugees who were brave, or foolish, enough to come to Ilin Illan to help fight. Villages burned to the ground, entire towns razed. Men, women, and children—regardless of whether they resisted, fled, or surrendered—being slaughtered and left for the animals. "I hope we're making the right choice, going back to the city."

"Given the circumstances, it's the only thing we can do." It was Taeris interjecting; he'd drifted closer to them and had evidently overheard. He lowered his voice, looking at Wirr. "Before we reach Fedris Idri, Caeden and I will need to part ways with the rest of you."

Wirr nodded; he'd known it would probably be necessary. "If there's any way I can help..."

Taeris shook his head, looking up ahead at the steadily growing silhouette of Ilin Tora. "No. Needless to say, Wirr, even though it's been a few years and my face has...changed, once inside the city I'll need to tread lightly. I was known to a lot of the Adminis-trators. If I'm caught...well, the last thing you need is to be asso-ciated with me."

Wirr acknowledged the advice with a nod, though it left a bitter taste in his mouth. Taeris was right; he couldn't afford to be found traveling with any of the Gifted, let alone with two accused of murder.

"Still. There must be something I can do, even if it's not

directly," he said. "My name won't carry much weight in political circles just yet, but Karaliene will be back from Desriel by now. I can probably convince her to use her connections, put pressure on the Council to help you, should things not go well at the Tol."

Taeris raised an eyebrow. "To do that you would need to tell her that Caeden and I were in the city. And she didn't exactly take a shine to us when we last met."

Wirr nodded. "True—but a lot has changed since Thrindar. You warned us about the Boundary weakening before the invasion began, and that will count for something. I know my father and uncle won't believe a word of your theory, but Karaliene's always made up her own mind about things. I think I can convince her."

Taeris looked dubious, but nodded. "I leave it to your judgment, Wirr," he said quietly.

"Then I'll try. If you fail at the Tol, come to the palace and ask for Aelric or Dezia. I'll make sure they know what to do. At worst, they have to turn you away."

Taeris clapped Wirr on the shoulder. "That's very generous. I hope it won't come to that, but should the Council be unwilling to listen, I'll take you up on that offer. There won't be many other places for us to turn, to be honest."

Wirr inclined his head. "I'll also be listening for any notable arrests in the city. If the worst should happen and you get caught, I'll see what I can do with Administration. It will be risky, but aside from anything else, getting Caeden's memories restored is too important at the moment."

Taeris smiled slightly. "You're a handy man to have around, Wirr." He glanced over at Caeden. "I should let him know what to expect, I suppose," he murmured to himself, detaching himself from the group.

Wirr took a deep breath, glancing across at Dezia. "So I suppose this is it. Everything changes," he said, tone grim despite his best efforts. Ilin Tora was now clearly visible up ahead; Wirr could even make out the gap in the mountains where Fedris Idri lay.

Dezia nodded, almost to herself. "Everything changes," she repeated quietly.

Caeden looked up as Taeris tapped him on the shoulder.

"We're nearly at the city," the scarred man informed him. "We should talk about what's going to happen next."

Caeden nodded. "I'd been wondering." He'd already gathered that Taeris was not on the best of terms with the Tol, and actively wanted by Administration. The end of their trip was going to be no easier than the rest of it, it seemed.

"First, we're going to split up from the others soon. Before we reach the city."

Caeden frowned. "Why?"

Taeris shrugged. "Justified or not, we've been accused of crimes, and the others have not. Aelric and Dezia have reputations to protect, and it's in Wirr's best interests if he's not associated with us, either. Starting out in the Tol can be hard enough without that sort of introduction."

"Oh." It made sense...still, he felt the slightest sting of betrayal. It was irrational, he knew, but the others were his closest—only—friends.

Taeris saw his expression and gave him a sympathetic smile. "It was my decision. I insisted," he added. "The others understand the logic behind it, but it's not something they would have asked for."

Caeden opened his mouth to reply.

Without warning, screams split the air.

Everyone froze as chaos erupted on the road just ahead of them. Travelers in front of them scattered, fleeing across fields, away from a figure swathed in black. A figure hard to focus on, as if somehow deep in shadow despite the noonday sun shining on it.

It was surrounded by bodies—four, Caeden thought. None of them moved.

Taeris gripped his shoulder. "Get ready," he muttered. "There's nowhere to run this time. We can't beat it without you."

The sha'teth was coming now, walking steadily toward them, though it was covering the distance at an unnatural speed for its gait. Dezia had already unslung her bow and was notching an arrow; Caeden watched in stunned fascination as she loosed and the creature moved smoothly to one side, impossibly fast, the arrow clattering harmlessly to the road behind it. Aelric was trying to push his way forward, sword drawn, but to Caeden's relief Wirr dragged the other boy back again. Steel would have no place in this battle.

In moments the creature was standing only twenty feet away.

"You were warned, Taeris Sarr," it hissed. Its face was covered by its hood, but Caeden could feel the malice of its gaze on him. "I told you that all you needed to do was relinquish him, and no one else would die. Now your companions will all pay for your foolishness."

Caeden closed his eyes, concentrating. He knew what to do.

He moved several paces in front of the others, stretching out his hands toward the sha'teth and tapping his Reserve.

A torrent of energy exploded from him, a blinding wave of yellow-white light. *This* was power. He gloried in the strength he felt, how vivid the colors of the world were, how *right* the feeling was.

He released Essence, panting a little from the exertion, almost laughing at how easily it had come to him.

Then he stumbled as the memory crashed into him.

*The cold wind of Talan Gol swept silently through the deserted stone streets, sending a shiver down his spine. He increased his pace. Seclusion was an area of Ilshan Gathdel Teth where no living thing survived for long, and powerful though he was, he had no desire to find out why.*

*He glanced to his right; Gellen was walking alongside him, lost in thought, apparently unperturbed by where they were. That was his way, though. Unflappable, silent unless spoken to but always observing, always thinking. A strong successor to Chane.*

*"What do you think?" he asked Gellen.*

*Gellen continued as if he hadn't heard for a few moments, then sighed. "I think even from here, there must be a way to use them. To turn their existence to our advantage. The Gifted have no idea of the powers they are meddling with, creating these sha'teth—I doubt they would be able to stop us taking their new toys away from them."*

Caeden nodded; he had been thinking much the same thing. "To do that, He would need to send one of us across."

Gellen didn't look at him, but Caeden saw the slightest tensing of muscles in the other man's face. "Dangerous ground, Tal'kamar," he said softly.

Caeden grimaced, but nodded. It *was* dangerous ground. Still. "Vote for me."

"I've voted for you the last three times. People are beginning to talk. He is already suspicious."

Caeden shrugged. "That doesn't matter. We can't create sha'teth ourselves, and won't be able to until the power of the ilshara has been broken. When that happens, the attack will already be under way. The Andarrans have five of them. Five! If they still control them when the time comes, what do you think will happen to our forces?" He paused. "I am the only one who can do this, Gellen. You know that."

Gellen grunted noncommittally, but Caeden knew his point had been made. They walked on in silence for a while, then Gellen said, "He thinks you are planning to overthrow him, you know."

Caeden blanched. "What?" The exclamation rang out over the empty streets, and he clapped his hand over his mouth. Whatever lurked in Seclusion, the last thing he wanted was to attract its attention.

Gellen glanced around, more from caution than from any nervousness. "All your trips Outside. You're neglecting your duties at the Cyrarium. And the incident with Nethgalla didn't go over well, either."

Caeden snorted. Inwardly he didn't know whether to be amused or fearful. "Where did you hear that?"

They had reached a black iron gate; with a gentle push Caeden opened it enough for them to pass through into the building beyond.

"Around," replied Gellen.

Caeden frowned. "Needless to say, it is untrue." In some ways it couldn't be further from the truth.

"Of course," said Gellen smoothly.

They walked inside without another word.

As Caeden's vision cleared, his triumphant smile faded.

The sha'teth stood exactly where it had. Its hand was outstretched, and a black, translucent rippling bubble surrounded the creature's body.

The sha'teth lowered its hand, and the bubble disappeared. It gave a rasping laugh. "You truly have forgotten, haven't you, Tal'kamar," it said to Caeden softly. Pityingly. "Aelrith was caught by surprise when you attacked him, and Khaerish and Methaniel were craven. But I am neither unprepared nor afraid." It stood motionless, waiting.

Caeden hesitated, still shaken by the memory. As with the earlier one, aspects of it were crystal clear—but there was no further knowledge, no sudden rush of information to tell him who he'd been. He could picture Gellen and knew his name, but knew nothing more of him outside that memory. And what he'd said about the sha'teth...

"Who do you serve?" he asked the sha'teth suddenly, muscles tensed in case the creature attacked.

The creature chuckled. "Are you not the one who set us free? Who do *you* serve, Tal'kamar?" it replied, quietly enough that the others could not overhear. "I can never keep track."

Caeden felt the blood drain from his face. He dared not look back at the others. "I serve my friends, and Andarra. Whatever ties I had in my past life are gone." He said the words with as much confidence as he could muster.

The sha'teth laughed again in its raspy voice. "You cannot escape yourself forever."

Suddenly a glow surrounded it, and time seemed to slow. Bursts of light erupted from the sha'teth's chest, streaks of power that headed toward the other four members of Caeden's party. He knew instantly that should those bolts touch them, they would be dead.

There was only a moment to stop them; even with his newfound control of Essence, he couldn't shield them all.

He couldn't choose, though. He wanted to save them all. He *needed* to save them all.

Desperately, he willed the bolts to stop.

Dark bubbles, exactly like the one that had surrounded the sha'teth, sprang up around Caeden's companions. The bolts sizzled into the surface of each one and simply vanished, gone as if they had never existed. The sha'teth gave an angry hiss as it realized its attack had been thwarted.

"So. You have forgotten some, but not all," it said.

Caeden nodded, trying to hide the fact that he was as surprised as the sha'teth that the bubbles had appeared. "Not all," he repeated grimly. He stretched out his hand once again toward the creature.

This time, though, he didn't use Essence. There was something else there, the same thing he'd used to create his companions' shields. The bubble appeared again around the sha'teth, but Caeden simply *pushed* at it. He felt it move, flex beneath his pressure. He closed his eyes, then imagined himself ripping the bubble away, tearing it like a piece of parchment.

There was a shriek, and he opened his eyes to see the sha'teth on the ground, writhing in pain.

"No!" it screeched, angry and despairing. "It is not possible!"

Caeden walked over to it, ignoring the cautioning cries of the others, who hadn't moved since the sha'teth had first appeared. He stood over the creature, then leaned down and pulled back its hood.

Beneath there was a man's head, but it was disfigured, pale, and scarred. That was not what made Caeden take an involuntary step back, though. The creature's eyes stared back at him with pain, with anger. Human eyes.

Aside from its glare, the sha'teth showed no further outward signs of distress. It had stopped writhing, and was instead staring up at Caeden. It wore an almost curious expression.

"You should know. I was the one who killed him," it whispered. It wasn't a confession; there was no trace of sadness in the statement. It was gleeful.

Caeden frowned. "Who?"

The sha'teth scowled. It tried to rise, but Caeden knelt on its chest, forcing it back down. For some reason it was evidently unable to use its powers at the moment. "And I had so looked forward to telling you," it hissed, disappointed.

"You must finish it, Caeden!" called Taeris. "Don't let it distract you!"

Caeden hesitated, then leaned forward. "Who are you talking about?" He clenched his hand into a fist. "Why did you come for me?" he whispered, low enough that the others could not overhear. "Who wants me, and why?"

The sha'teth gave a rasping laugh. "I will tell you—but it will be so all your friends can hear. So they can know what kind of man you truly are." It raised its voice, calling out the words. "Can you all hear me?"

Caeden moved without thinking. He drew back his hand, letting Essence flow through him and into his fist. Then he drove it down into the sha'teth's disfigured face.

There was a blinding light, and a final scream from the creature.

When Caeden's vision cleared, all that remained was a pile of ash.

He knelt there, silent and trembling, for what felt like an age. Finally a hand clasped his shoulder. He looked up to see Taeris watching him, concerned.

"Are you hurt?" the older man asked.

Caeden forced himself to stand, still trying to comprehend what had happened. He had killed the creature. Had it been the right thing to do? Would it have told the truth about who he was—and if it had, would he have liked what it said?

He stared at the pile of ashes morosely. There could be no knowing now.

"I'll survive," he said softly.

Wirr came to stand next to him, looking at the ashes on the road in fascination. A gentle wind sprang up, scattering some of them to the grass on the roadside. "How did you do that, Caeden?" he asked. "The shields you gave us. I've never seen anything like it. It wasn't Essence."

Caeden shook his head. Already the memory of how to use that power was hazy again, though he knew it would not fade entirely. There was something about Essence—something about wielding it—that seemed to stimulate his memories, bringing them to the fore. He still wasn't sure if that was a good thing or not, but it was valuable knowledge nonetheless.

"I don't know," he admitted to Wirr. "I just reacted instinctively, and they appeared."

"Just in time," noted Taeris. He clapped Caeden on the back. "You saved our lives, lad."

Caeden forced a smile. "Perhaps it can go some way to paying you back for bringing the sha'teth down on you in the first place," he said wryly.

"That's hardly your fault."

Caeden started. It was Aelric who had spoken, still standing a little distance away but looking at him with an expression of vague approval. "We owe you a debt, Caeden."

Not knowing what to say, Caeden gave Aelric an appreciative nod. The five of them stared at the remains of the sha'teth for a moment longer, then Taeris said, "We should get moving before those other travelers come back and start asking questions."

Caeden glanced up. The road ahead was empty aside from scattered belongings and the four bodies a little farther along; everyone else had fled, running as hard as they could until they had lost sight of the road altogether. Still, many of them had left what were probably their only possessions behind. It would not be long before some of them began to venture back.

"What about the bodies?" asked Wirr. "We can't just leave them."

Taeris grimaced. "We have no choice. Those who come back will see they get a proper burial, I'm sure."

They began walking again, carefully navigating around the blood-soaked section of road where the corpses lay. After a few minutes, Taeris matched his stride to Caeden's.

"So. It seems you're an Augur, too," he said, keeping his voice low. "Wirr was right. That wasn't Essence you used to save us."

Caeden didn't respond for a few seconds. He'd guessed as much, but at the moment it felt like just one more thing to worry about. "It was instinct," he eventually reiterated, not taking his eyes from the road ahead. "I don't know how I did it."

Taeris grunted, looking dissatisfied but seeing he was not going to get any further comment on the matter. "What did the sha'teth say to you, just before the end?"

Caeden shrugged. "It was spouting nonsense. Nothing that made sense."

Taeris raised an eyebrow. "Such as?" He scratched his beard. "It might be important."

Caeden hesitated. He had no intention of telling Taeris what the sha'teth had been going to reveal. "It said it had killed him. When I asked who it meant, it just acted disappointed that I didn't know." It was at least some of the truth, hopefully enough to satisfy Taeris's curiosity.

Taeris thought for a moment. "Another mystery," he sighed eventually, rubbing his forehead. "The sooner we get your memories back, lad, the better."

"No argument here," Caeden replied heavily.

They kept walking. In the distance Fedris Idri was now clearly visible, and farther along the road he could see more people heading toward them. A steady stream, in fact.

They were almost to Ilin Illan.

# Chapter 37

Asha watched as Erran shifted uncomfortably in front of her, clearly reluctant to proceed.

The young man took a deep breath, exchanging worried glances with Elocien, Kol, and Fessi, who had gathered for the occasion and were looking on from the corner of the room. Then he turned back to Asha.

"Are you sure you want to do this?"

"I'm sure," Asha affirmed, though her stomach twisted as she said the words. In truth, the certainty she'd felt the previous day had faded.

"Ashalia," interjected the duke, his tone gentle. "Do you really think Elder Tenvar lied to you?" He hesitated. "It's not that I don't believe you, but I wouldn't want to see you go through this for no reason."

Asha turned to him. "I need to know," she said simply.

Elocien inclined his head, and Kol and Fessi both gave her encouraging smiles, though the concern in their eyes was obvious. Erran hadn't minced words when he'd explained the dangers of trying to restore her memory.

In front of her, Erran sighed. "All right." He paced back and forth for a couple of seconds, rubbing his hands together in a nervous motion. "All right. Ready?"

Asha nodded.

Erran stopped in front of her, leaned forward, and pressed his fingertips against her temple. There was nothing for a few moments and then the slightest pressure at the back of her skull, like the beginnings of a headache.

The feeling began to build, gradually at first, but soon enough Asha's head was throbbing with it.

"Erran," she said uncertainly. "I'm not sure if—"

The pressure burst.

A gentle warmth flooded through her head. It wasn't an unpleasant sensation, but it made her gasp nonetheless. Her thoughts were suddenly scattered, jumbled.

Erran stepped back, lowering his hand. His eyes were full of horror.

"Fates. I'm so sorry."

And then the memory came crashing back into her.

There was pain behind Asha's eyes, but she forced them open anyway.

She stared around, trying to get her bearings. What had happened? Jagged-edged images flashed through her mind and she sat up sharply, heart pounding, panic threatening to take over.

Someone had attacked the school. Everyone was dead.

"Ashalia."

She turned to see a blond-haired Administrator watching her with a worried expression. He looked...familiar. She stared at his face for a few seconds in confusion.

"Do you recognize me?" asked the man, his tone gentle.

"Yes," said Asha slowly. Her memories began to order themselves, and the fear subsided. Faded into grief. "Duke Andras. Elocien."

"Good." Elocien looked relieved. He leaned forward, taking her hand and squeezing it. "We were worried."

"We?" Asha looked around with some effort, but only she and the duke were in the room. It was her sleeping quarters, she realized after a few seconds.

"All of us. It's almost dawn; the others went to bed a few hours ago. You've been asleep for nearly a day."

Asha struggled up into a sitting position. "That long?"

Elocien nodded. Then his expression sobered. "Erran told

us what happened. What you saw, before Tenvar made you a Shadow." He shook his head. "That note from Torin...I never knew about it. I suspect the Council didn't, either."

Asha smiled as she remembered. *Davian and I have had to leave.* "He's alive," she murmured, still barely daring to believe it. Then her smile faded, and a wave of fury washed through her as her thoughts cleared and she was able to analyze the new memories, come to grips with them. "What have you done about Elder Tenvar?"

Elocien grimaced. "We're watching him."

"We need to lock him up." She thought of everyone who had died at the school, of the bloodied corpses of her friends, and her expression hardened. "At the least."

"I understand, but...it's not that simple," Elocien cautioned her. "Tenvar is Gifted. There are rules that prevent us from simply marching into the Tol and arresting him. Laws that I cannot break without undeniable, airtight proof." He gave Asha an apologetic look. "As long as he is inside the Tol, he's under the Council's jurisdiction, and the Gifted are the only ones who can bring him to trial and punish him. It's part of the Treaty."

Asha stared at him in disbelief. "But he made me a Shadow against my will. He lied about Davian. I *remember.* And Erran saw, too—"

"Which no one can know," Elocien pointed out gently. "As for you remembering—how are you going to explain that to the Council? You can point the finger all you like, but unless they really believe you've got your memory back, all it will do is warn Tenvar that we know what he did." He sighed. "Watching him... it's the best we can do, for now. I promise you, as soon as we get the opportunity to do more, we will."

Asha shook her head, still trying to clear it. She should have realized that. "You seem very calm about all of this."

"I've had the entire day to be angry," said Elocien. "And believe me, I was." He stood, putting his hand on her shoulder in a reassuring gesture. "If you're feeling well enough, I should get the others. They will want to know you're awake."

Asha nodded, lying back down and staring at the ceiling as Elocien left, trying to sort through her churning emotions. Grief and horror at what had happened. Fury at Tenvar. Fear at knowing what he was capable of.

She took a few deep, steadying breaths as she mulled over what Elocien had said about the Gifted, about Tenvar's immunity so long as he was inside the Tol. A plan began to form, just an idea at first, but fully fledged by the time Elocien returned with the Augurs.

After receiving delighted hugs from the others—particularly from Erran, whose relief was so evident it made her laugh—she turned to Elocien.

"I think I have a way to solve our problem with Tenvar. To have him locked up," she announced.

Elocien frowned. "We can't risk an incident between the palace and Tol Athian, not at the moment. Tensions are already high and rising as it is, with my brother's recent outbursts against the Gifted," he warned her.

"It wouldn't involve you or anyone else here," Asha quickly assured him. "If it fails, the worst that happens is that Tenvar knows I've remembered." She outlined her idea, her four companions listening in attentive silence. There was a pause once she'd finished as everyone considered what she'd proposed.

"It's still a risk for you, though," noted Erran eventually, his tone uneasy. "There's no telling what Tenvar's reaction will be."

"I can handle it," Asha told Erran, locking eyes with him. After a moment Erran nodded his acceptance, and the other Augurs soon followed suit. They were concerned for her, but none of them was going to try to convince her out of it. For that, she was grateful.

Elocien hesitated for a second longer, then inclined his head, too.

"So you'll need a meeting with Councillor Eilinar. And access to the storeroom in the Old Section," he observed.

"That should do it."

Elocien nodded, more to himself than to Asha.

"I'll see what I can do," he said quietly.

Asha threw open the door to Ilseth's study as hard as she could, the resultant crash echoing down the hallway.

Ilseth jumped up, eyes wide for a moment. Then, seeing who it was, he sank back into his chair again, trying his best to look unconcerned.

"How can I help you, Ashalia?" he asked with cool politeness. "You really should be more gentle with the door."

Asha paused for a long moment. Then she turned and closed the door carefully, taking a key from her pocket and, with a quick twist, locking it.

Ilseth frowned. "Where did you get that?"

"It doesn't matter." Asha slipped the key back into her pocket.

"I suppose it doesn't," said Ilseth, looking more amused than concerned. "What would you like to say to me?"

Asha stared at him. "I want you to know that I remember."

"Remember what?"

"Everything." Asha swallowed a lump in her throat. "I know Davian was missing, not dead. I know you made me a Shadow against my will. I know you had something to do with what happened in Caladel." She clenched her fists, trying to contain her anger. "And now you're going to tell me exactly what."

Ilseth just smiled a pleasant, nonchalant smile, though his eyes betrayed a sliver of shock. "I have no idea what you're talking about." He sighed. "Perhaps you're confused. I know Shadows have very vivid dreams about their past, sometimes—"

"Don't patronize me. I'm going to get your confession."

Ilseth smirked. "How? Force?" He chuckled. "Ashalia, you may be safe from Essence thanks to the Tenets, but don't for a second think that you can overpower me."

Asha reached into her pocket and drew out a small black disc, holding it between her forefinger and thumb for Ilseth to see. "Familiar?"

Ilseth's smile slipped, though he still didn't look concerned. "You're a Shadow, Ashalia, in case you've forgotten," he said, his tone verging on mocking. "You can't use that."

"But I don't need to use it." Ilseth was wrong about her ability to activate the Vessel, but she didn't need him to know that right now. "I just need it to make contact with your neck. Or have you forgotten how it paralyzes? I certainly haven't." She stared confidently at him. "One touch, and you won't be able to move. And

I'll be able to do whatever I like to you. You can feel everything, you know. See everything, hear everything. But you can't make a sound." She gave him a cold smile. "We could be here for hours, and no one would know."

There was a long silence. "You don't have it in you," said Ilseth eventually.

"There was a time I didn't," admitted Asha. She gestured to her face. "Before you did this to me."

She took a step forward.

Ilseth scrambled up from his desk, scowling at her. "Why even bother? This section of the Tol has no Remembering, child. Even if I said what you wanted to hear, no one else would believe you. You'll be thrown in prison. If you leave now, though... I won't chase you. I swear it."

Asha laughed in his face. "You swear it? That's reassuring." She took another step forward. Ilseth took a corresponding step back, looking concerned now, even though the desk was still between them.

For a few seconds Ilseth contemplated the locked door; realizing that there was no way to safely slip past Asha and the black disc, he dropped all pretense of calm. "You're a stupid little girl," he spat furiously. "You were supposed to die with all the others. And you *will* die now, I promise you. But it won't be quick like them. I'm going to give you over to the Venerate. Do you know what they will do to you? You'll *beg* for death."

Asha took another step forward, reaching the desk. "Where are Davian and Wirr?" she asked, steel in her voice.

"I wouldn't tell you even if I knew," snarled Ilseth, tensing himself to spring at her.

Then suddenly he was flying backward, as if an unseen hand had gripped him and slammed him against the wall. He shouted in alarm, struggling against invisible restraints and staring at Asha in wild-eyed disbelief.

"It's not possible," he gasped. "You can't be—"

"Enough."

Ilseth's head snapped around at the voice from the other side of the room, though Asha didn't take her eyes from his panicked features. From the corner of her vision, she could see Elder Eilinar appear as he removed the Veil.

"He knows more than he's saying," said Asha, tone cold, still not looking around.

"No doubt," said Nashrel wearily, "but he's said enough to damn himself, and this need not get dangerous. We'll get the rest from him, don't worry about that." He stared at Ilseth with a mixture of sadness and disgust. "I defended you when Ashalia made her accusations."

Ilseth looked as though he was about to protest his innocence; then, seeing the expression on Nashrel's face, he spat in his direction instead. "You are a fool, Nashrel," he said, making another furious attempt to free his hands. "And you have no chance of getting information from me. You should have let the girl torture me." He gave Asha a leering smile.

Asha stepped forward and pressed the black disc against Ilseth's neck.

The Elder's face and body immediately went still.

"What are you doing, Ashalia?" Nashrel asked. His tone was curious rather than worried.

Only Ilseth's eyes were alive now, rolling between her and Nashrel as they spoke. Nashrel didn't know. All she had to do was to place a finger against that disc, let it tap her Reserve, and Ilseth would suffer the same fate he had given her.

She raised her hand . . . and then let it fall again.

"It was the only way to improve his company," she said, taking her eyes from Ilseth's face for the first time since she'd entered. She glanced across at Nashrel. "You'll send word to the palace of any information you get, as we agreed?"

"Of course." Nashrel watched Ilseth with a thoughtful expression. "This will stay between you, me, and a few select Elders I know I can trust. But if we have word of your friends, we will tell you immediately."

"Thank you, Elder Eilinar."

She looked at Ilseth again, pinned helplessly to the wall. Suddenly feeling sick, she turned and left the room.

She did not look back.

# Chapter 38

Davian cracked his knuckles, giving Malshash a confident grin.

"I'm ready."

Malshash smiled, shaking his head. "You've spent half your life trying to use Essence. What makes you so sure you can do it now?"

Davian shrugged. "That wasn't really my fault. I was being taught to look for it in the wrong place," he pointed out. "At the school I was always told that the only way to access Essence was to tap into my Reserve—the internal pool of Essence that every Gifted's body produces. But I'm not Gifted; I don't even have a Reserve. As an Augur I needed to be extracting it from the world around me instead."

Malshash inclined his head. "True enough, but knowing that isn't even half the battle. You still need to learn to control Essence, to harness it properly. Remember it's an energy, active, a force in and of itself. Nothing like kan."

Davian smiled. "I've probably studied more about the nature of Essence and how to use it than any Gifted my age," he said wryly. "I've always felt that if I could just access it, I could use it as well as anyone."

Malshash grinned. "Very well. This is the final skill I can teach you, so let's see whether your abilities are a match for your confidence."

Davian took a deep breath and reached out, feeling the kan all around him, permeating everything. It had been almost indistinguishable at first, but now—only a couple of weeks into his training—he could touch it, grasp it almost without needing to think. Malshash never said so, but Davian could see the look in Malshash's eyes after he'd picked up the basics of a new skill in an afternoon, an hour. He was good at this. *Very* good. It came to him as naturally as breathing.

He concentrated, extending his senses using kan, looking for the telltale glow of Essence. Malshash pulsed with it, but he knew better than to try to extract any from him—Davian would likely just end up hurting his teacher by accident.

He focused harder. A little way down the road, he caught the faintest glimpse of a glow through the mists, which were especially heavy today. He moved forward, concentrating on the luminescence.

Slowly the haze around the light thinned, revealing a tall oak tree. Its glow was far from bright, but it definitely had Essence running through it. Davian reached out.

Something blocked him.

He pushed against it, gently at first, but with increasing frustration. There was a space of a few meters around the tree that he could not seem to enter with his kan-enhanced senses. He scowled, opening his eyes.

"I can see the Essence flowing through the tree," he said in irritation, "but I can't get to it."

Malshash crossed his arms, a smile threatening to creep onto his face. "But you were so confident a moment ago."

Davian looked at him wryly. "Fine. I don't know everything yet," he said in as humble a voice as he could muster. "What am I doing wrong?"

Malshash raised an eyebrow. "You didn't wonder how there are trees growing here, healthy and well maintained?"

Davian looked again. Sure enough, the oak trees lining the street were neatly trimmed; they had clearly been set there as part of the city planning. He frowned. "You're right. They should all be dead, surely?"

Malshash shrugged. "They're like the books in the library. Preserved in their original state." He gestured around. "This place was built to absorb small amounts of Essence from almost everything except the human body, then channel it to the Jha'vett.

Because of that, there were a few things the Darecians had to shield against kan. If they hadn't, I doubt the trees would have grown here in the first place, let alone survived unchanged for a couple of thousand years." He slapped Davian on the back. "Anyway, all you need to do is go up to one and touch it. That will put you inside the shield, and you won't be blocked."

Davian rolled his eyes. "So I wasn't doing anything wrong after all."

Malshash grinned. "Not as such, I suppose."

Davian began walking toward the nearest tree but then hesitated, turning back.

"How am I still alive?" he asked quietly. "I thought you said I had to get Essence from outside my body to live."

Malshash was silent for a moment. "You're getting it sporadically from what I can tell," he admitted. "I've tried to see on a few different occasions, but the lines of Essence are so fine, so thin, that even I have a hard time making them out. And I actually know what to look for, so that is quite an accomplishment." He sighed. "I'd rather hoped you wouldn't wonder too much about this. You draw some from the fire each night and each morning. The library is shielded from the rest of the city; when you're in there you draw it from the Adviser, I think." He paused. "Occasionally, when you run low, you draw some from me."

Davian stopped in midstep. "From you?" It obviously hadn't hurt Malshash, but the thought of stealing someone else's Essence—their life force—made his skin crawl.

Malshash made a reassuring gesture. "Tiny amounts," he said. "And you've needed it to help you concentrate."

Davian blinked. Now that he thought about it, he'd barely slept these past couple of weeks. An hour or two each day, perhaps? How was that possible? His brow furrowed. Why had that not occurred to him before as being odd?

He sighed, focusing again on their topic of conversation. "But if I were alone, without a fire, on these streets for long enough..."

Malshash shrugged. "I don't know for sure. My recommendation is to not put yourself in a situation where you find out."

Davian grunted. "Good advice," he said, his enthusiasm dampened as the reality of the dangers he faced struck home once again. Malshash had been pushing him harder and harder these past few days; though he'd said nothing, Davian knew the time must be approaching when he had to return, go back through the gray void. He twisted the ring on his finger nervously. Despite Malshash's apparent confidence in Davian's abilities, he'd pulled no punches when it came to the perils of the rift.

Davian shook his head, clearing it again before striding up to the tree he had been looking at before and placing his hand against the rough, dry bark. He closed his eyes.

He could feel the Essence now, pulsing and vibrant within the tree. He carefully drew kan around it. It was different from the kan he normally used—that would have engulfed the Essence in a moment, extinguishing it completely. Instead he positioned the kan and then...*hardened* it, for want of a better word. Partly it was how Malshash had described it, but partly it was what felt natural. It was this new form of kan that he used to draw the Essence toward his body.

Nothing happened at first. Then the glowing stream slowly poured toward him, into his hand and up his arm, into his chest. He felt warmth and life flow through him, intense and beautiful. He opened his eyes to see his hand glowing with raw energy.

He spun and flung the Essence at a nearby wall.

It didn't have the effect he'd hoped. Rather than causing the wall to explode into pieces, the bolt of energy simply rippled and vanished, absorbed into the air. Of course; Malshash had just been telling him how the entire city was an enormous conduit for Essence. He should have tried something else.

His body still buzzing, he stepped away from the tree, examining it in fascination. The leaves, which had been a bright green against the dull grays of Deilannis only moments earlier, were now shriveled and black. The trunk and branches, too, looked as though they had been wasting away for years. He gave the withered trunk a gentle tap, then leaped away as the entire tree collapsed in a puff of black dust. He coughed furiously, trying to get the taste of dead wood from his mouth and lungs.

"What happened?" he asked.

"You took the life force from the tree," Malshash replied, his gaze fixed on where the oak had once stood. Now there was only a pile of ash-like grit littering the stone. He shook his head, looking disturbed. "You took *all* of it, Davian."

Davian finally managed to clear his throat. "Is that good?"

"It depends on how you look at it, I suppose," said Malshash, sounding undecided on the answer himself. "It's certainly... unusual. I've seen it done before, but only in times of great need, great stress. And it was certainly not good then." His expression twisted. "Regardless, it seems like that lesson went rather smoothly. Away from Deilannis, I have no doubt you will be able to draw large amounts of Essence, should the need arise."

Davian grinned. "Definitely good, then."

Malshash held up a cautioning hand. "You must be very, very careful with this ability, Davian," he said softly. "What you did to that tree? You could just as easily do that to a person. Accidentally, if you are not careful."

Davian looked back on the pile of black dust and paled. "It could kill them?"

Malshash nodded. "Your body is used to drawing on anything it can to survive; I can only assume that's why you're able to take so much. But if you drained a human being like that... well, Essence is their life force. Remove it completely, and I think you can guess the consequences."

Davian nodded. "I'll be careful," he promised. He gave Malshash a cautious look. "Aside from that..."

Malshash laughed. "It was very impressive, Davian. The bolt you threw looked like it would have blown the wall apart if we were anywhere else."

"It was less spectacular than I'd hoped," admitted Davian. "If only it were—"

He cut off with a grunt as pain flooded through his stomach, and every limb went suddenly weak. He collapsed to the ground with a moan, clutching at his belly. It felt... empty. Painfully so. He was *so* hungry.

Malshash rushed forward, dropping to his knees beside him. Without a word he drew an apple from his pocket. Davian took it and devoured it; as he ate the pain lessened, and soon he was able to sit up straight again.

"What was that?" he asked, dazed.

Malshash rubbed his hands together nervously. "Your bond here is weakening, Davian. It has lasted much longer than I would have thought possible, but it's finally happening. Our time together is drawing to a close."

Davian took a couple of deep, steadying breaths. "Now?"

"No." Malshash shook his head. "We still have a few hours—I think waiting until this evening would be best, maybe even tomorrow morning unless these attacks start increasing. That at least gives us the opportunity to run through a couple more exercises, get you as prepared as we can."

Davian stared at the apple core in his hand. "How did you know I would need this?"

Malshash sighed. "Remember what I said, about a shadow of a shadow of your body remaining in your own time? It's still a physical presence, Davian. And it's had neither food nor water in the last couple of weeks."

"So...I'm dying? In my time?"

Malshash ran his fingers through his hair. "It's all just theory, but I suspect so. Your body there won't need sustaining like a normal person's would, but eventually it is going to need nourishment."

"So that's why I've been so hungry," muttered Davian. He scowled. "You leave this until now to tell me?"

"I didn't think you needed the added pressure."

Davian just grunted, in no mood to argue. "So what now?"

"What you just felt was a stronger connection with your body in your own time. The rift is trying to correct the anomaly of your being here. It's trying to send you back," said Malshash. He sighed. "All we can do is break your binding to my time. Choose when to begin the process."

"By destroying this," said Davian, holding up his hand to display the ring.

"Exactly," said Malshash. He gave Davian a considering look. "I think we should practice your Reading, one more time. It's probably the best exercise for mental focus, and you'll need all you can get once you're in the rift."

Davian hesitated. "What about Control?" He'd been wondering whether Malshash would teach him that, ever since he'd read about the ability. He'd been stunned to learn it was truly possible—there had always been rumors of the Augurs being able to manipulate other people's thoughts, but nobody had ever really believed them. Even back when the Augurs still ruled, he knew that people had been skeptical of such a power's existence.

Malshash shook his head. "No. Control is like shape-shifting—ill-advised, and very dangerous." He looked Davian in the eye. "This time you need to trust me. Don't try it."

Davian gave a noncommittal shrug. "Very well. Reading it is," he said, trying to keep the disappointment out of his tone. He took some deep breaths, calming his mind. "I'm ready. What am I looking for?"

Malshash shrugged. "I've left a few things open, this time. See what you can find."

Davian nodded. He closed his eyes, pushing through the kan until he was inside Malshash's mind. He still hadn't quite grown used to the feeling: he knew who he was, knew all his own thoughts, but if he tried to think of something—anything, really—it would be Malshash's mind to respond, not his own. And Davian could then examine that response with his own mind.

He composed himself for a second, then began searching through Malshash's thoughts and memories.

Most were still hidden within the locked box, he soon discovered. The ones that were not were fairly dull, and all recent. What Malshash had had for his meals the last few days. How amazed he was at how quickly Davian had picked up kan. His sense of urgency about getting Davian back to his own time, keeping him alive. There were other feelings associated with that—sorrow, pain—that Davian did not understand, could not access the exact memories to explain. Emotions were much harder to hide than specific recollections of events.

He thought to find out where Malshash had lived, before he came to Deilannis. He was confronted with the locked box again. He wondered where Malshash had received his Augur training. The locked box. He wondered why Malshash had been so upset to discover Davian could shape-shift. The locked box. Davian felt his frustration turn to anger. What was the point of this ability if people could just hide things so easily?

He wondered why Malshash had given up his ability to See. The locked box.

Rather than move on, Davian imagined himself directly in front of the box. He concentrated, gripping the lid with his hands and *pulling*.

The lid came open, and he heard a gasp of horror from Malshash.

*He was in a large, long room, filled with table upon table of people talking and laughing, all dressed in fine suits and elegant gowns. He felt his heart swelling as he gazed out across the crowd from his position, his own table slightly raised above everyone else's. So many people. His friends and family, come to celebrate with him. A feeling of pleasant warmth flooded through him, not just from the fine wine they had been drinking.*

*This was happiness.*

Detached, Davian forced himself to stay alert. He knew this feeling. He was reliving the memory, unable to alter it in any way, but experiencing it exactly as Malshash had. He knew he'd somehow broken into Malshash's locked box, knew this memory was supposed to be personal, but had no idea how to stop it now.

*He glanced to his left, and his breath caught in his throat. The most beautiful woman he had ever seen sat beside him. Her long black hair was straight and gleamed in the light of the lanterns. She was slim, with an oval face, large blue eyes, and a delicate mouth. Her full lips curled upward slightly as she saw him watching her, and she leaned toward him.*

*"See anything you like?"*

*Davian felt himself grin in return. "I think you know the answer to that." He looked around. "Is it wrong to wish your own wedding were over?" he whispered conspiratorially.*

*The woman—Elliavia was her name, Davian suddenly*
*knew—leaned forward and gave him a long, passionate kiss. In*

the background he could hear a few people starting to hoot and whistle. "Not at all...Husband," she whispered back.

Davian sat back, trying to drink it all in. This was the moment. It was perfect, better than he could have imagined, than he could have hoped for. He looked again at Elliavia. She was amazing. He knew, perhaps more deeply than he'd known anything before, that he didn't deserve her. No one deserved her. Perhaps that was where he'd been so lucky. He'd been the closest thing she'd found to a good match.

A servant came and touched Ell lightly on the shoulder, whispering something in her ear. She nodded, then leaned toward him again, her lips tickling his ear she was so close. "I will be back in a moment, my love," she said, her eyes shining as she looked at him.

He squeezed her hand. "I'll be waiting."

He watched her slip away after the servant, so beautiful in her white wedding dress. Once she was through the door he returned his attention to the festivities, nodding politely as people came past his table, offering their congratulations. His face hurt—it actually hurt!—from the effort of smiling so much, but he didn't mind in the slightest. He was not by nature a man who found happiness easily, but tonight most certainly qualified.

A half hour passed. He found himself glancing toward the door his wife had disappeared through, expecting to see her reappear at any moment. It remained closed, though. He scanned the crowd, but the servant who had come to fetch her was nowhere to be seen, either.

Finally he called over another weary-looking young man who was serving drinks. "Excuse me," he said, "but have you seen my wife?"

The boy stared at him for a moment to see whether he was joking, then glanced around the room as if expecting to see Elliavia standing somewhere obvious. Finally he shook his head. "I'm sorry, Lord Deshrel. I haven't."

Davian felt himself frowning, and sighed in vague exasperation. It seemed he would need to find her himself. He rose, navigating through the jumble of chairs that had been abandoned in midaisle, then slipped through the door Ell had gone through.

There was a short passage, lit by a single torch, and then another door that opened into the castle courtyard. He felt his frown deepen. He didn't know Caer Lyordas well, hadn't realized this door led outside. Why would Ell have needed to come out here?

The courtyard was lit, but it was a gusty night and some of the torches had guttered out—this area was unattended, as most of the guardsmen tonight were focused around the feast. Davian found himself meandering aimlessly, a little light-headed from the wine, around the side of the castle.

Then he spotted it. It was just a flash, a glimpse of white against the dirty black of a ditch. Uncomprehending, he wandered over, peering into the gloom.

The cry was out of his throat before he realized what was happening. He was in the dirt, the cold mud, screaming for help, cradling Ell's bloodied head in his lap. Her eyes stared sightlessly up at him, the jagged gash along her throat still leaking dark-red fluid. Her dress was muddied everywhere, and torn in such a way that he did not want to think about what else might have happened to her. Even as he wept, he carefully, tenderly made her private again.

There were shouts behind him as people ran to answer his screams. He heard gasps of horror as the first to arrive took in the scene, but he didn't turn, couldn't take his eyes from Ell. He rocked her back and forth gently, sobs ripping from his throat, tears spilling onto her beautiful, cold face.

No. It couldn't be this way. He would not let it be this way.

He delved into his Reserve, drawing deeply, more deeply than he ever had before. All of it, in fact. He closed his eyes, putting his hands against Ell's clammy skin and letting his Essence flow into her. He could feel the wound on her neck close, the bruises she had sustained all over her body fade away. He pushed more, willing her heart to begin beating again, willing her life to return. He drained himself, past the levels he knew to be dangerous. He could take it.

But when he opened his eyes, Ell still lay there, staring up at the murky sky. Her chest was still, her skin cold.

He didn't know how much time had passed when he felt the hand on his shoulder. It was Ilrin, his teacher from the Academy.

"Who did this?" Ilrin asked, his voice shaking. His eyes held horror, anger, pain, sorrow. Ell had been his student, too.

Davian found himself looking around. His gaze fell on a young man; it took him a moment to place him, but when he did his grief flashed into white-hot fury. It was the servant who had led her out here. Led her to her death.

He was on his feet in an instant; moving faster than he would have believed possible he slipped through the steadily growing crowd until he had both hands around the young man's throat. "Tell me what happened," he growled. He barely recognized his own voice.

The blood had drained from the boy's face. "It was the priest," he managed to choke out. "The one who married you. He asked me to fetch your wife out here."

Davian looked at the young man and felt only rage. He had drawn Ell out to her death. He was a part of it.

His Reserve was already refilling. He let Essence infuse his arm, giving it the strength of ten men, and then twisted.

The servant's neck snapped like a twig. A low moan went up from the stunned onlookers.

Davian felt himself whirl, scanning the crowd. The priest. A holy man, supposedly. He had done this. People leaped from his path; a few of his friends called out to him, pleaded with him to stop, but none moved to get in his way. They knew better. They could all try to stop him, and it would be meaningless, nothing to him. He would brush them aside like flies. He would find the priest and kill him, slowly and painfully.

It didn't take him long. He sent his vision high above the castle, scanning the surrounding lands; almost immediately he spotted the lone figure scrambling along the north road, slipping on loose shale as it hurried down the steep hillside. The plain brown robe was obvious, even from this distance, even in the gloom.

He moved, faster than he had ever moved before, and yet somehow with a cold deliberateness, a calm that belied the raging fire inside him. He walked, but those around him stood like statues. The wind seemed to slow so that he could barely feel it, and even the fire of the torches moved sluggishly. He took one off its bracket as he passed, leaving the castle and streaking northward. 453

Somehow he knew that anyone watching would see only a blur of orange light, nothing more.

He walked in front of the priest, setting his feet firmly in the portly man's path. Davian wanted to see his face. He wanted to see his expression when he realized he was going to die.

The priest skidded to a stop when he saw Davian in front of him. His cheeks were flushed with exertion, but the rest of his skin was pale as a ghost. His expression was one of pure terror.

"Mercy," he muttered, falling over as he moved backward as quickly as he could. Even sitting down he tried to scramble away, his eyes wild. "Mercy. It was not me. I swear it by El. It was not me."

Davian took in the priest's muddied clothes. His arms were bare, and Davian could see long scratches on them. Any semblance of calm evaporated.

He reached out with Essence, holding the terrified man down. Then he concentrated on the man's hands. The priest screamed as the little finger on his left hand snapped backward with a sharp crack. Davian released it and moved on to the next finger. Crack. The middle, the forefinger, the thumb. Then the other hand. Crack. Crack. Crack. Davian barely knew what he was doing. All he wanted was for this man to feel the pain he was feeling now. To feel worse.

He moved on. He broke every toe, the priest's screams intensifying until finally they died to almost a whimper.

Davian frowned. That wouldn't do. The man had felt nothing yet.

He concentrated. He fed Essence into the priest, allowing the broken bones to mend themselves. He hadn't bothered to straighten them; most healed at ghastly angles, deformed and likely still agonizing. Even so, the worst of the pain would be gone.

He changed the flow of Essence, pointed it at the man's blood. Heated it. A little at first, then more, until he could feel it boiling. The priest screamed properly this time. Prolonged cries of pain, gut-wrenching screams of agony. Davian watched impassively, feeling nothing. Not satisfaction. Not sorrow. This was not revenge. This was justice, plain and simple.

454

Ensuring he still fed enough Essence into the man to keep him conscious, he turned another sliver of energy into a razor, thin and sharp. With one flick of the wrist, he castrated him.

The priest made no noise now—just lay there, back arched, spasming. His mind was trying desperately to shut down, but Davian concentrated, made sure it was aware of every moment of what was happening. Bubbling blood spilled out into the dirt, hissing as it hit the cold ground. This was how he would die. Bleeding out in slow agony.

Davian made sure the man had absorbed enough Essence to keep him conscious to the end, then leaned forward until the priest was focused on his face.

"For Ell," he said softly.

He turned and walked back up toward the castle.

He'd come farther than he'd realized; it was a good mile back to Caer Lyordas from where he was. How had he come here so quickly? He tried to remember. Everything was a blur...

Suddenly it came crashing in on him. What had happened. What he'd done. He dropped to his knees and vomited, retching until his stomach was empty. Once he was finished, he stood shakily and kept walking to the castle. In a distant kind of way, he knew he was in shock.

A crowd of people were waiting for him outside the gates, but he pushed by them, barely even hearing their questions and meaningless offerings of sympathy. He moved straight past them, back to where his wife's body lay. Someone had moved her from the gutter, laying her in the middle of the courtyard, her hands carefully folded over her breasts. Despite the position, she looked anything but peaceful. Her dress, torn and bloodied, told the true story.

He stood over her, looking down vacantly. Inside he felt... nothing. An emptiness so profound that it made it difficult to breathe. It was all so meaningless. She was gone, gone in a moment, and suddenly nothing that was to come mattered anymore.

"No." The word came from his throat unbidden. He knelt, cupping her cheek with his hand. "No."

He reached deep inside, drawing once again on Essence. 455

*Despite all his efforts tonight, his Reserve was nearly full again. But he knew somehow, instinctively, that even with all his powers he could never generate enough Essence to bring her back. He needed more. So much more.*

*He reached out. He could feel the Essence all around him, everywhere in the castle and its surrounds. The trees and grass. The torches on the walls.*

*The people.*

*There was no time to think; every second he delayed made it harder to bring her back. He drew in Essence, then let it flow into Ell. Her entire body glowed with the soft yellow light, but it wasn't nearly enough. As his Reserve came close to dry, he started pulling Essence from around him. Vaguely he could sense the grass withering; in the distance over the wind he could hear trees collapsing to the ground. The torches winked out around the castle one by one.*

*It was still not enough.*

*There was a scream from somewhere in the castle as the first person fell, dead, drained of Essence. Screams started up elsewhere, but they were cut off as Davian snatched away their life force, taking it into himself and then letting it flow into Ell. In his mind the area became darker and darker, until there was no Essence left. No life. Nothing but him.*

*He'd drained his Reserve long before, but he knew there was more. He was so close; he could almost see her breathing again, could almost see a tinge of red returning to her smooth cheeks. He tapped into his own Essence, the force that was sustaining his body. All he had left.*

*He felt his limbs growing numb; his hand slipped from Ell's cheek, the link finally broken. Had it worked? He strained to see her face, her chest, anything that might indicate if she was alive. But he was so tired.*

*He closed his eyes.*

When he opened them again, he was back in Deilannis opposite Malshash. He stood there for a long moment, aghast, unsure what to say. Malshash wore a similar expression, though his was mixed with something that sent a shiver of fear through Davian. White-hot anger.

Davian blinked, suddenly making a connection. Malshash's form today was familiar. The man from the wedding, the one who had tried to comfort him. Ilrin.

It took him only a moment longer to make other connections. None he could put names to, but many of which he remembered clearly. All of them men whose form, at one time or another over the last couple of weeks, Malshash had chosen to take.

Malshash just stood for a few more moments, staring at Davian, panting as if he had been running a race.

"Prepare yourself, Davian," he snarled eventually. "You leave this place today."

He spun without another word, stalking off down the road and into the mists.

# Chapter 39

Davian bit at his fingernails.

He sat on the steps at the entrance to the Jha'vett; he assumed this was where Malshash would find him, though the shape-shifter hadn't said so explicitly. Several times in the last couple of hours he'd considered going to search him out, but each time he thought of it, he remembered the expression on his teacher's face.

Davian shivered again at the memory of what he'd seen. Not just seen—*experienced*. Davian had lived Malshash's grief, lived his rage. The emotions had been more powerful, more raw, than anything he'd ever felt. He knew that what Malshash had done was horribly, horribly wrong. Yet he had *been* Malshash, felt the irresistible need to mete out justice, to try everything—*anything*—to bring back his wife.

It made him sick to his stomach every time he thought of it, and yet somehow he also understood.

He suspected he now knew Malshash's reason for being in Deilannis, too. The shape-shifter had been trying to do exactly what Davian had done and travel to the past—except Malshash had thought to *change* his past, and Davian's arrival had apparently proven that he could not. Though it was hardly his fault, Davian felt a sliver of guilt for denying Malshash that hope.

After a few more minutes a figure emerged from the mists, trudging down the road toward him. Davian stood as Malshash approached. The shape-shifter still wore the same face, but somehow looked as if he had aged terribly. His gait was unsteady, weary, his expression sad rather than angry.

Malshash stopped a little distance away from Davian, unable to meet his gaze, preferring instead to stare at the ground.

"So. Now you know," he said. "I am sorry you had to see that."

Davian blinked. He had expected a tongue-lashing at best. "I'm sorry I pried where I had no right," he said, genuine remorse in his tone.

Malshash barked a short laugh. Then he shook his head, sighing, any trace of amusement vanished. "I should probably say the same thing." He walked up to Davian, and before Davian could react, Malshash's hand was on his forehead.

He gasped as a cold sensation washed through him, sharp but brief. When Malshash removed his hand, the world suddenly felt both clearer and duller.

"What did you do?" Davian demanded.

"I removed my influence from your mind," said Malshash, sounding tired.

Davian gaped at him. "You've been Controlling me?" He took a step forward angrily. "All this time?"

"No." Malshash looked guilty, but his tone was firm. "Not Controlling. Influencing. Feeding. *Focusing.*" He gave a small smile. "Your mind is exceptional, Davian, have no doubt about that. But no one can learn what you have learned in a couple of weeks. Not without help."

Davian opened his mouth to protest, but was suddenly struck by just how hard he'd been studying and practicing. He had been sleeping one, maybe two hours a day, and hadn't questioned it. The oddity of it hit him. He knew that it had before, too— remembered thinking it curious before now—but somehow he'd never been motivated to follow up on the thought.

"You've been keeping me awake. Alert," he said, some of his initial anger dissipating.

Malshash shrugged. "That, and keeping you focused on the task at hand. A little too focused, apparently." He shook his head, chagrined. "You have a hundred different questions about the things I know. Some of them I wouldn't answer, the rest I couldn't, and none of that was going to be conducive to your studies. With the time we had, Davian, you couldn't just get no answers. You had to forget there were questions." He screwed up his face. "I truly am sorry, but you needed to be ready. If I hadn't done this, you wouldn't have had a chance of surviving the trip back through the rift."

Davian clenched his fists. Some of those questions were already coming back to him, and he didn't know which ones to ask first. "At least tell me one thing."

Malshash gave him a wary look. "It depends on the question," he warned.

"You said that you stole your shape-shifting ability from the Ath. That you gave up your ability to See." He gestured in confusion. "I've read nothing like that, anywhere in the library. I've never heard of it even being *possible*. These abilities are all just applications of kan, aren't they? If you can do one, why not another?"

Malshash rubbed his chin. "That is too complicated a question to answer properly right now," he said. "The short version is, it's just a very complex use of Control. I'm linked to the part of the Ath's mind that understands shape-shifting—not the theoretical knowledge, but what you would call the talent, her unique mixture of instinct and experience. When I shape-shift, I use both her talent and my own. When she tries to shape-shift, she hits a kind of mental barrier. As long as I hold the link, it's like at a very deep level, she just can't grasp how to do it."

Davian gave a thoughtful nod, accepting the explanation. "And when you gave up Foresight?"

"It was the same," admitted Malshash. "I could try to See right now, but it simply wouldn't work—any natural sense I have for it is completely blocked."

"But why? Why give away your ability?" He frowned. "And to whom?"

Malshash sighed. "I gave it away because of what you saw before," he said quietly. "Seeing can work in both directions, forwards and backwards. Not many people know that. Most people with the talent are naturally focused on what is to come. But I..." He shook his head. "When I See, I go back there. I was reliving it, again and again, every time I closed my eyes. I couldn't make it stop any other way." He paused. "Whom I gave it to is not your concern, though."

461

Davian opened his mouth, but grunted as another attack punched into him. It felt as if his stomach were eating itself from the inside. He doubled over, gasping for breath. He knew it would pass—there had been three since he'd begun waiting for Malshash—but they seemed to be increasing in intensity.

Malshash watched him, looking troubled. "There's no more time, Davian. We need to do this now."

Davian nodded and followed Malshash into the building and along the long corridor. As they walked, more and more questions filled Davian's head. He scowled to himself.

"Tell me one last thing before I leave," he said.

Malshash hesitated, then nodded. "Very well."

"Why do you wear the faces of the people at the wedding? The ones who..."

"The ones I killed," finished Malshash. He looked at Davian with an expression of immense sadness. "You haven't figured it out yet, have you?"

"Figured out what?"

Malshash hesitated. "A shape-shifter can only take the form of someone who is dead," he said eventually.

"Oh." Davian lapsed into silence. Malshash was watching him expectantly, but Davian didn't know how he was supposed to react to that news. Idly he wondered again about the identity of the blond-haired man he had changed into. Whoever it had been was dead? It didn't bring him any closer to determining who it was. He wondered why Malshash had thought it so important to hide that detail from him.

They were in the enormous room now, and Davian could see the Jha'vett itself, lit up between the columns. As they approached, Malshash reached beneath his cloak and drew something out—an object that fit into the palm of his hand, shining slightly even in the dull light. They stopped just short of the altar, and Malshash held out the object for Davian to see.

"We need to do one last thing before you go."

Davian stared in disbelief. The small bronze box gleamed, the strange symbols on it as alien as ever to his eyes. He stepped forward, snatching it from Malshash's grasp and examining it

closely.

There could be no doubt. This was the same Vessel that had guided him to Caeden.

He shook it at Malshash. "Explain."

Malshash shook his head. "There's no time." He put one hand over the box and the other on Davian's forehead; there was a flash of energy, a warmth flowing through him for a moment. Without asking, Davian knew that Malshash had just linked him to the box.

Davian just stared at him, incredulous. "You lied to me, didn't you? You said you didn't know anything about my future...but that was before you showed me how to see lies through a shield."

Malshash didn't deny it, tucking the box back into his pocket. He faced Davian, looking him in the eye.

"I tell you this, I tell you everything—and that's not safe for either of us. The only secrets a mind cannot give up are those it doesn't know," he said softly. "You taught me that, Davian."

Davian looked at him, head spinning. "*I* taught you—"

Another attack hit him without warning and he cut off, falling to his knees. Pain ripped through his stomach, his chest. He felt as if he might burst open at any moment.

Malshash ran to him, then looped a supporting arm under him and steadied him. They made their way over to the altar. Malshash helped Davian to sit on it, then held his hand out, palm up. Davian reluctantly slipped the silver ring off his finger.

So this was it. The moment had finally come. His stomach hurt too much for him to feel the butterflies, but he knew they were there.

"Just tell me," groaned Davian, not taking his eyes from the ring. "Should I be trying to get that box to Caeden—the man it leads me to in my time?"

"Yes," snapped Malshash, his tone impatient. "Now clear your mind, Davian. It's time to concentrate."

Davian gritted his teeth—he had so many more questions he wanted to ask—but he gave a reluctant nod. He knew that aside from the training he'd been doing, there was no real way to prepare for what was coming. Even Malshash had admitted that everything he knew of the rift was theoretical. Davian was probably the only person ever to have survived it, and now he had to do it again.

Malshash placed the ring on the ground, then knelt and put his hand over it. He hesitated, though, twisting so he could look up at Davian.

"I have something I need you to remember. A message from me," he said. "That it was worth it. It changed me. And...I am so very sorry."

Davian frowned, repeating the message as he noticed a glow beginning to shine out from beneath Malshash's hand. "Who is it for?"

Malshash didn't reply for a few moments, then lifted his hand. All that remained of the ring was a small pool of molten metal on the ground. He stood, turning toward Davian. Even as he moved, Davian realized he was beginning to fade.

"It's for you, Davian," said Malshash softly. "You'll understand one day."

The gray torrent washed him from view. Davian was once again within the rift.

⚮

The river of gray nothingness was just as terrifying as before, but this time Davian's mind reacted with instinctive discipline. After the first few moments of chaos, he found himself concentrating, focusing on the flow rather than struggling to break free of it. As he did so it gradually slowed, until it was a gentle stream rather than a raging river. He hovered within it, not comfortably, but no longer fearful of being torn apart by the raw power of this place.

He floated for a moment, or an hour, or a day—there was no way to tell here. The longer he looked, the more he could see differences in the gray. A lighter patch here, a darker section there. Places he could go to, if he so wished. *Times* he could go to.

But that was not where the flow was taking him. Time was trying to correct itself; though Malshash had not said so, it seemed only logical to Davian that the forces within the rift would therefore try to take him back to where he was supposed to be. So he passed by the distinct sections he made out—portals, as he thought of them—and waited patiently for a sign.

When that sign came, it was unmistakable. To one side the
grays were banished by a shining light, so bright that it reminded

him of pure Essence. He pushed himself forward, not struggling, but guiding himself toward the light. He reached out to touch it.

He groaned.

How long had he been lying there? The stone was cold and rough against his cheek. His body felt drained, and hunger and thirst stabbed at him everywhere. He rolled, trying to get his bearings.

Nihim's sightless eyes stared at him glassily.

The pool of blood surrounding him had long since dried, black and flaky where Davian was lying in it. Davian stared sadly at the priest's body, the memories of what had happened rushing back. Somehow he'd hoped Nihim had survived, had miraculously been saved. It shouldn't have come as a surprise that the priest had bled out on the ground next to him, but it did.

From the corner of his eye, Davian spotted something a little way away from Nihim's corpse. Forcing himself to his knees, he reached over to the satchel, slowly unbuckling it and emptying its contents on the ground. Some fruit, well and truly rotten. Some tough strips of salted meat, which he wolfed down without a second thought.

Best of all was the canteen of water. Though he was tempted to try to down it all in a single gulp, Davian forced himself to take small sips, wetting his throat and moistening his lips only. There was a fountain a few streets away, but Davian had no idea if it would still be running in this time.

He was still awfully weak. He briefly thought about trying to bury Nihim's body, but dismissed the idea as impractical—not only was he not strong enough, but almost the entire city to the outskirts was paved. He nodded a silent, sad good-bye to the priest, then set off down the street.

Despite knowing it was ninety years later, Davian felt completely at home; nothing in the city seemed to have changed at all. Still, it was with some relief that he arrived at the Central Fountain to see it in proper working order. Without wasting another second he opened his canteen and drank, savoring the cold, refreshing liquid as it flowed down his throat.

It barely helped, though. His muscles were stiff and aching; every step sent a jolt through his entire body. He stumbled over to    465 one of the few remaining trees, then leaned against it and drained it of its Essence. He felt better as it blackened and crumbled, but not strong. He made his way gradually to the next, and the next, until they were all gone.

He felt healthier—but far from whole. Still not well enough to make it out of the city. The rift had sucked his body dry of Essence, had weakened him too much.

He slowly made his way to the house where he and Malshash had stayed, but when he arrived it was empty, the cupboards bare. There wasn't even any fuel for a fire.

He closed his eyes, trying to think. He needed Essence. The Jha'vett was probably too far, even if he was willing to risk going near it again. Deilannis sucked Essence dry almost everywhere else...everywhere but a few places, like the Great Library. He was in no state to get out of the city, but he could make it there.

It took him almost thirty minutes, by his estimate, to shuffle to the library. Like everything else, the enormous domed building was exactly as he remembered it, every detail identical to how he'd left it nearly a century earlier. Too weak to do anything except marvel at the fact, he stumbled inside, relieved to see the cool blue light of the Adviser glowing in the main chamber.

He collapsed against the short column, placing his hands over the blue light. He could feel it this time, now he knew what to look for. He wasn't controlling it, but his body was reaching out toward the Essence, sucking it in.

He drew a deep breath as his muscles relaxed, the ache of his head and stomach fading. He straightened, flexing his arms and legs experimentally.

"Not bad," he muttered to himself.

He turned to go, then hesitated. He was in the Great Library, knew how to use the Adviser. Before, when he'd been there, his mind had been influenced by Malshash. He could see that clearly now. All the knowledge of the world at his fingertips, and he hadn't even been curious?

He knew he should leave, but he also knew that the opportunity he had right now might never come again.

He placed his hands over the blue light of the Adviser and closed his eyes. What topics did he need to know about? He'd already read plenty of books on Augur abilities; he probably wouldn't benefit much from more of those. What he *did* need was information on the threat that was coming to Andarra. He needed to know more about Aarkein Devaed. He needed to know more about the invaders he'd seen.

He pictured their armor in his mind. That strange symbol, the three wavy lines.

He opened his eyes. A single tendril of blue light was snaking out, beyond the room. Davian hurried after it, eventually discovering where it had come to rest. A thick tome, bound in black leather, sitting beneath a pile of other books on a table in the corner.

Davian picked it up and dusted it off. It had no title on the cover, so he flipped it open.

"*A Collection of Darecian Fables*," he said, reading the title aloud. An odd book to have information on Devaed, but this had been the first the Adviser had chosen. It had never steered him wrong in the past.

He hurried back, ready to collect the next tome. When he came to the main chamber, though, he stopped dead.

No more tendrils of light emanated from the Adviser. The blue glow of the column itself was dimmer—much dimmer, in fact.

Davian rushed forward, crouching so that he was at eye level with the light.

"No," he muttered in frustration. "Not yet. Not now." He stood, placing his hands on the Adviser and concentrating on Augur abilities. He knew there were books on that topic here— plenty of them.

When he opened his eyes, the light in the Adviser had gone dead.

"Two thousand years," muttered Davian in disgust, "and you couldn't hang on for another ten minutes." He gave the column a light kick, doing more damage to his toes than to the Adviser.

He knew what had happened. Like any Vessel, the Adviser stored a certain amount of Essence—and when it ran low, it drew on the Essence of the Gifted using it. Except Davian had drawn from it instead, draining the remaining Essence from the device, sucking it dry to restore his body to full health. It was a trade he'd had to make, but that knowledge made him no less irritated at the situation. The Adviser could be recharged, of course...but only with another source of Essence. Something not readily available to him at the moment.

Reluctantly slipping the sole book he had managed to find under his arm, he left, making his way out of the Great Library and down past the silent buildings of Deilannis. Orkoth would be around somewhere, but Davian knew he had nothing to fear from the creature, so he walked without concern for being seen.

Despite his lack of success at the Great Library, his heart was lighter than it had been in a while. He was back in his own time. More than that, he was able to wield the power of the Augurs— and Essence as an added bonus.

He paused, the thought reminding him of what had happened after his first trip through the rift. He pulled up his shirtsleeve. The skin was still smooth beneath; despite his being back in his own time, his Mark had not returned. Interesting. Perhaps if he avoided using too much Essence, he could keep free of the Tenets altogether.

Davian imagined Wirr's face when he revealed his bare forearm, told him what he'd just been through. He smiled to himself. Wirr no doubt assumed he was dead. Though the thought should hardly have been amusing, his friend's expression simply at seeing him walk into the palace would no doubt be something to remember.

Then, for the first time in weeks, his thoughts drifted to the school.

During his time under Malshash's influence, his grief—so sharp just before Deilannis—had been...muted. Almost forgotten, so focused had he been on study. Now he was fully himself again, the pain of what had happened at Caladel returned—but it was fainter, an ache rather than an open wound. Sadness rather than anguish.

For the first time, he felt as if he'd moved on. That things were going to get better.

He made his way to the Northern Bridge, walking quickly but not hurrying. In some ways he had grown fond of the city over the past couple of weeks, and there was beauty in its design when one could observe it without fear. He drank in the familiar sight of the gracefully sloped buildings and perfectly smooth roads, silent and shrouded in the pervasive eerie white though they were. This was the last time he'd see them. He had no intention of ever coming back, of risking any sort of proximity to the rift again.

Then he was crossing the bridge; after a few minutes he broke through the edge of the fog and into warm, bright sunlight. He squinted as pain shot through his eyes, unaccustomed as they were to the direct light of day. Once they had adjusted he stood there for a few moments, face toward the sun, drinking in its warmth. Its *life*. He could feel it now, he realized, even without concentrating. His body was drawing energy from the light and heat, sustaining itself.

He consciously reached out and drew in a little more, grinning at the sudden flush of energy. He felt *good*. Perhaps better than he ever had in his entire life.

He kept walking until the bridge, the mists, Deilannis itself had disappeared from view. Headed east.

It was time to go to Ilin Illan.

# Chapter 40

Caeden allowed himself to be ushered through the tunnels of Tol Athian, trying not to look intimidated.

Taeris had headed straight for the Tol once they'd parted ways with the others; though the scarred man had ducked his head a few times when he'd spotted blue cloaks up ahead, the journey through Ilin Illan's streets had been uneventful. There had been an empty quality to the city, though—a sense that things were too quiet. Everyone looked on edge, and it all only served to bring home the reality of what was coming.

When they'd arrived at the Tol it had quickly become apparent that they were expected; as soon as Taeris had asked to see Councillor Eilinar, they had been immediately Shackled and escorted inside. From the way Caeden had three men flanking him, it didn't feel as if they were being welcomed, either.

Finally they were shown into a small room, an office of some kind.

"Wait here," said one of their escorts, his tone brusque. The door closed, the clicking of the lock punctuating the command.

Caeden looked at Taeris worriedly. "What's happening?"

Taeris rubbed his forehead. "The Tol must have had advance word that I was coming," he said, looking grim. "Karaliene, maybe, or..." He cursed.

"What?"

"Dras. The snake." Taeris groaned. "He was angry, at Thrindar, and he knew where we were heading." He shook his head. "I hope I'm wrong, but—"

The lock clicked again, and the door swung open.

Three Gifted strode into the room, two men and a woman, the last one inside closing the door behind them. The first, clearly in charge, stopped and studied Taeris with cool hazel eyes.

"Taeris. It has been a while," he said eventually, stepping forward and offering his hand. There was no smile, but if the action wasn't friendly, it at least held a measure of respect.

"Nashrel. It's good to see you," said Taeris, gripping the man's hand and shaking it firmly. "You don't seem surprised to see me."

"We had word. An anonymous note, about a week ago." His gaze shifted to Caeden. "Said you were alive, scarred, and that you were likely to turn up with an accused mass murderer."

Taeris sighed. "Dras, then."

Nashrel raised an eyebrow at that. "Lothlar?"

"Ran into him in Desriel. It's a long story."

"I'm sure." Nashrel paused, still watching Caeden. "Is it true?"

"Another part of that long story."

"We might have to hear it soon, then." Nashrel turned. "You remember Elder Haemish and Elder Ciahn? I didn't want to risk gathering the entire Council in case an Administrator got wind of it, but these two... volunteered to be here."

"Insisted on it, actually." Haemish was an older man, wrinkled, with graying hair that would have made many people look distinguished, but that on him just aged him further. He spoke with a sneer. "Thought it would be a good idea to make sure you weren't coming back from the dead to cause more divisions, Sarr. The damage you did five years ago was enough."

"That's enough, Haemish." Ciahn was perhaps in her early forties, an attractive lady with a strong bearing. She smiled at Taeris. "I'm glad you're alive, Taeris. None of us thought you deserved that sentence." She glared to her right. "None of us."

Haemish muttered something under his breath, but gave a reluctant nod.

Nashrel turned to study Caeden again. "So your young friend here..."

"Caeden." Taeris gestured to the Elders. "Caeden—as you've probably gathered, these are Elders Nashrel, Haemish, and Ciahn. We can trust them."

Caeden nodded. "Pleased to meet you," he said politely.

Nashrel and Ciahn nodded back, but Haemish glared at him with ill-concealed disgust. "So you're the murderer." He turned to Taeris. "You have a lot of explaining to do."

"Haemish. Please." Nashrel gave Taeris an apologetic look, but then sighed. "He's right, though. It's probably time we heard that long story of yours."

⚶

Caeden flushed under the stares of the three Elders as Taeris finished explaining the events of the past few months.

After a few seconds of silent study, Nashrel shifted.

"Show us your arm," he said quietly.

Caeden rolled back his sleeve, revealing the wolf tattoo, but otherwise bare skin beneath.

"That doesn't prove anything," pointed out Haemish. "We would know if the sha'teth were no longer under our control."

"Would we?" asked Ciahn.

Haemish scowled. "I suppose...maybe not." He rubbed his forehead, then looked at Taeris. "But tell me this. Do you still think it's Aarkein Devaed behind all this?"

Taeris hesitated. "Yes," he conceded. "You know I do."

"And there it is," Haemish said with satisfaction. "Sha'teth thinking for themselves. An enemy that can create Echoes, supposedly one of Devaed's favorite tricks. Ancient monsters in the mists of Deilannis. And Taeris Sarr at the center of it all, bringing us the solution to our problems, saving the day. Fulfilling the old prophecies and proving Alchesh Mel'tac wasn't truly mad, just like he always said." He raised an eyebrow at Ciahn. "Sound familiar?"

"That was a long time ago, Haemish," said Ciahn reprovingly.

Taeris reddened as he listened to the conversation. "I'm not asking you to believe, Haemish. Just help Caeden regain his memories, find out what this Vessel does. And if you don't believe he's Gifted, just test him—you can see for yourself just how strong he is. At worst you'll be gaining a powerful ally."

Haemish shook his head. "At worst, Sarr, we'll be reminding a murderer who is not bound by the Tenets how to fully utilize his powers." He sighed. "This invasion from the north—these 'Blind'—are just men. They don't have dar'gaithin, or eletai, or any of the old monsters alongside them. We can agree that they're dangerous…but that is why the Council has already made a decision about them."

Taeris stiffened. "Which is?"

"Unless the king changes the Tenets, the city can fend for itself. If they don't want our help, we'll do what is safest for us—which is to stay behind these walls. If the invasion succeeds in taking the city, then we will negotiate." Haemish stared Taeris in the eye.

Taeris looked at him for a long moment in disbelief, then turned to Nashrel, horrified. "Is this true?"

Nashrel, who had remained silent up to this point, gave a tired nod. "I'm afraid so," he said quietly. "I was against it, but some of the rhetoric we've heard coming from the palace lately…it's dangerous talk, Taeris. The king has always felt like a neutral party when it comes to the Gifted, but these past few weeks, he's sounded more like a Loyalist." He looked at the ground. "We have to start thinking about ourselves."

"But you won't be able to hide behind your walls. Not like in the war," said Taeris, his tone urgent now. "These people won't negotiate. I told you what we saw in Gahille!"

"What you claim you saw." Haemish sighed. "Taeris, we went through this five years ago, and it nearly tore the Tol apart. Devaed is *dead*, if he was ever even alive. We need to face the reality of the invasion, not pretend it's some ancient evil come to destroy us."

Taeris groaned. "You're being obtuse, Haemish."

Haemish stiffened, but Nashrel held up his hand. "You lied to us once, Taeris. He has a right to question."

Taeris said nothing for a moment. "What about Ilseth Tenvar? You said yourself he was a traitor, a conspirator in the deaths of hundreds of Gifted students—and I told you that he sent the Vessel to Caeden before I knew any of that. Surely that verifies at least part of what I've said. And surely you want to understand more about what Tenvar was involved in, too." Taeris gave Nashrel a steady look. "You know me, Nashrel. We may have differing views about many things, but I'm not a fool. I haven't risked my life, come back here just to tell you a lie."

Nashrel held Taeris's gaze for a few seconds, then sighed. "I know," he said reluctantly. He looked around at the other two Elders. "He makes some valid points, and this isn't a choice that should be left to us alone. We need to discuss it with the others." He turned back to Taeris. "Whatever we decide, though, no one here will turn you in to Administration. You have my word."

Taeris looked relieved. "Thank you," he said. "Please, take what time you need. Caeden and I can wait—"

"*You* can wait here. We owe you that much." Nashrel shook his head slowly. "But we do not know Caeden, except for what you've told us, and what we know of his crimes. It would be irresponsible of me to have him wait anywhere except for in a cell."

Caeden felt his heart sink, and his muscles tensed. They were going to lock him up? Every nerve in his body screamed for him to do something; his thoughts immediately flashed back to the last time he had been imprisoned. He clenched his fists, and light beads of sweat began forming on his brow.

Taeris glanced at Caeden with a worried expression. "Alleged crimes," he corrected. "First I need your word that he will be released back into my custody as soon as you have made a decision, either way. And that he will come to no harm in the meantime."

Nashrel looked at him with vague surprise. "Of course," he said sincerely.

Taeris glanced at Caeden, giving him the slightest of nods. "He means it. You will be fine," he murmured.

Caeden gritted his teeth but nodded back, forcing himself to relax.

Taeris turned back to Nashrel. "Very well."

Nashrel hesitated. "One other thing. We will need to take custody of the Vessel."

"What?" Taeris frowned. "I would prefer—"

"This isn't negotiable, Taeris."

Taeris glowered but inclined his head, reaching into a pocket and drawing out the bronze box. As always, it shone like the sun to Caeden's eyes.

Taeris reluctantly gave it to Nashrel. "Can I at least hang on to the other one?" he asked.

Nashrel paused in his examination of the box. "The other one?"

"The other Vessel I found in Desriel." Taeris held up a smooth black stone, about the size of his palm. "I haven't been able to determine what it does yet, but it seems harmless enough. Nothing to do with Caeden, though."

Nashrel stared at the stone for a long moment, and Caeden thought he saw a glimmer of recognition in the Elder's eyes.

"What is it?" asked Ciahn.

Nashrel didn't respond for a few seconds.

"I...don't know," he said slowly. "But we should hang on to it."

Taeris scowled, giving up the second Vessel to Nashrel, too. But as he did so, Caeden thought he saw a flicker of acknowledgment pass between the two men. An understanding.

Then it was done, and Taeris was gripping Caeden's shoulder. "Don't worry. You won't be locked up for long," he said in a reassuring tone.

After Nashrel had talked to someone outside, Caeden found himself being led away. He and his escort descended a flight of stairs until they came to some basic cells, carved out of the bedrock of Ilin Tora itself. They were little more than small caves with doors made of steel bars; once Caeden was inside he realized there would only just be room to lie flat on the ground, and when he stood straight, his head was only inches from the roof. He felt a flash of gratitude that fate had not made him any taller, and that despite his experiences he had no particular fear of confined spaces.

The jailer locked the door and moved a little way down the hall to a more open part of the passageway, where his desk and chair sat. "No funny business, and we'll get along just fine," he called as he wandered away.

Glowing Essence orbs lined the hallway outside, but the cells themselves were quite dark. Caeden shifted, trying to see if there was anyone in the cell opposite. He moved forward to the bars, squinting as the light hit his eyes.

Suddenly a face appeared in the opposite cell, and Caeden could see a Shackle glinting on the other man's arm. The stranger smiled, a wide grin of triumph.

Even through the bars, Caeden could tell that the man was staring at the bared tattoo on his wrist. The glow of the wolf's head was weaker—Taeris and the Vessel must be a good deal farther away now. The other prisoner wouldn't be able to discern the light, of course, but the tattoo itself was still plain enough to see.

"*Dreh Kaaren si,*" the stranger said quickly. "*Sha tehl me'athris dar?*" It was clearly a question, but Caeden had no idea what the man was saying.

Caeden shook his head. "I'm sorry," he said. "I have no idea what language you're speaking."

The man looked at him in shock for a few moments, then vanished from his doorway, retreating into the gloom of his cell.

The jailer called out from his desk. "Nonsense words, lad," he confided. "Ignore him. That one's scheduled for the lower dungeons—he's just here temporarily. We think his mind's gone. Only stands to reason the first thing he says since being locked up is gibberish."

Caeden frowned. He hadn't understood what the prisoner had said, but the sound was too regular, too structured to be nonsense. And the language was…familiar. As if, if he concentrated hard enough, he might be able to ascertain the meaning of the prisoner's words.

"Who is he?" he called out.

Caeden could hear the jailer spitting on the ground. "Name's Ilseth Tenvar," he said. "He had something to do with that bad business in the schools recently. Not sure what, exactly; they don't tell me much. But he's supposed to be in here, don't you worry about that. Not a man you want to be making friends with."

Caeden nodded, though mostly to himself, as he knew the jailer couldn't see him. He stared at the cell across the hallway, trying to see into the murk. He remembered Davian and Wirr talking about this man. The one who had tried to send him the Vessel.

And Tenvar had known him, recognized him, despite what the jailer said.

He settled down in the corner to wait, knees drawn up to his chest, all the while keeping a close eye on the cell opposite.

Despite the two layers of thick steel bars between them, he did not feel particularly safe.

It was hours later when someone finally unlocked his cell door and escorted him back to the main tunnel.

He smiled in relief when he saw Taeris waiting for him.

"What did they say?"

Taeris scowled. "Exactly what Haemish said. There's no proof. There's no indication that the Blind are anything more than men. Helping you is too much of a risk." He shook his head in disgust. "Their theory is that the Blind are a race of people descended from us—from the Andarrans that were trapped behind the Boundary during the Eternity War. The Council agrees that they're dangerous, but not that they are anything...worse."

"So they won't restore my memories?"

"They were almost willing to, and then..." Taeris sighed. "I have a long history with the Council, Caeden, and that has gone against us. I'm sorry for that. A few of them argued that the risk was worth it. Some even believed me, but most of them are just... angry, at the moment. They feel betrayed by the king. The argument was, why take a chance restoring your memories for the good of the city, when the city doesn't even seem to want their help?"

"But they're in danger, too," Caeden protested.

"They don't see it that way. Tol Athian withstood everything Vardin Shal and the Loyalists could throw at it during the Unseen War. They don't believe the Blind will be any different."

Caeden was silent for a moment. "So what now?"

"We go to the palace. I was speaking to Aelric and Dezia earlier today, and they think there's a chance they can convince the princess to help. With her influence behind us, we might still be able to change some minds at the Tol."

Caeden gave Taeris a dubious frown, remembering the disdainful way Karaliene had looked at him in Thrindar. "Are you sure that's a good idea?"

"I never said it was a good idea," observed Taeris drily. "But it's the only option we have right now."

They walked out of the Tol. It was midafternoon, and the streets were busier now. Taeris appeared lost in his own thoughts, but eventually Caeden tapped him on the arm.

Taeris turned. "What is it, lad?"

"I have something to ask you," Caeden said hesitantly. "I heard someone say something in the dungeons. I couldn't translate it this time, but...it sounded like the same language the sha'teth use. Is that possible?"

Taeris frowned. "I don't know. Maybe," he said slowly. "Do you remember what they said?"

Caeden screwed up his face, trying his best to remember the words. "*Dreh Kaaren si, sha tehl me'athris dar.*"

Taeris's eyebrows rose. "'Honored lord, has the time finally come?'" he translated. His expression became focused. "Who said this, Caeden? And who did they say it *to*? This language is... old. Rare." He stopped, forcing Caeden to look him square in the eye.

Caeden shook his head, suddenly sick to his stomach. He knew what it would look like if he told the truth. What it would do to Taeris's trust in him.

"I don't know. I couldn't see them from my cell, just heard the words."

Taeris bit his lip. "I know Ilseth Tenvar was in those cells," he said, almost to himself. "But it sounds like perhaps Athian has more than one traitor in its midst." He started walking again, lost in thought.

Caeden stared after him for a moment, then trotted to catch up, grimly returning his attention to the road ahead.

Perhaps the Council had been right not to trust him after all.

# Chapter 41

Wirr stared up at the palace gates with trepidation.

In times of peace they stood open, an invitation for anyone, no matter their rank, to come before the king or one of his Judges and have a complaint heard. They were shut today, of course. Several guardsmen stood at attention in front of them, and assembled in a vaguely threatening manner when Wirr and the others approached.

"Move on," said one, a grizzled-looking veteran whom Wirr didn't recognize. His tone was firm. "Only members of the court or those with appointments may enter today."

Aelric raised an eyebrow. "Don't recognize me, Ethin?"

The man stared at Aelric for a moment, then started. "Young Shainwiere!" He rescanned the group, his eyes coming to rest on Dezia. "And your sister. Of course, of course." His gruff manner had vanished. "My apologies. Princess Karaliene asked that you and your party be brought to her as soon as you arrived, no matter the time, day or night."

Aelric hesitated. "I'd... hoped to get cleaned up first." He indicated his clothes, which were showing the wear and tear of travel, not to mention the odd bloodstain.

Ethin smiled. "No offense, Aelric, but if it's a choice of displeasing you or the princess, you're out of luck." He slapped Aelric on the back in a familiar fashion. "I heard you did well at the Song?"

Aelric grunted. "Not well enough, I'm afraid."

Ethin gestured for another guard to open the gate, then led them through. "Second's still an impressive achievement, lad.

And there's plenty of years left in you, too," he said cheerfully. He glanced across at Dezia. "I trust you're well also, Dezia?"

Dezia smiled. "Just glad to be home, Ethin."

The guardsman closed the gate behind them. "I hope we can keep it that way," he said as they headed into the grounds. "You've heard about the Blind, of course?"

Aelric inclined his head. "We crossed paths with some of what they left behind. It was not pleasant."

Ethin nodded, expression solemn. "It'll be a relief once General Jash'tar has dealt with them. Never seen him in action myself, but if he's as good as people say he was under Vardin Shal, I'm sure he and the rest of our men won't have too much trouble." He glanced around, then lowered his voice. "Just a warning, though—the Houses haven't been especially happy with things here lately. General Parathe's in charge of the defenses now, and I think his reputation for being better at tactics than motivation is starting to show. He's been having some issues keeping the troops that are still here in line." He hesitated. "And the king...well, let's just say that Karaliene will be glad to see you. She could use some friends about now."

Wirr listened with interest. That the Houses were causing problems was hardly surprising, and certainly nothing new...but Ethin's tone had indicated something more was going on. Something serious.

They made their way through the palace corridors. Little had changed; every time they rounded a corner Wirr found himself reliving another childhood memory. He'd played with Karaliene in these halls. He smiled briefly as they passed a large floral vase on a pedestal. That was at least one thing that was different; when he was a child, such decorative displays had been removed, lest they meet an accidental demise at his and Karaliene's hands.

But those days, unfortunately, were long gone. His smile faded as his thoughts returned to what lay ahead.

Ethin guided them to the princess's quarters, pausing outside to let Karaliene's attendant know who was there to see her. After a moment inside, the woman returned.

"The princess will see them immediately," she said to Ethin.

Ethin nodded. "Time for me to go back to my post, then,"

said the grizzled guard. He nodded to Aelric. "Good to see you again, lad."

Aelric smiled. "You, too, Ethin."

Wirr, Aelric, and Dezia entered Karaliene's chambers. Wirr was surprised to see that they were relatively unadorned; the princess had been fond of decorations and finery in her earlier years. Karaliene herself reclined, apparently at ease, in a chair over to one side—but the dark circles beneath her eyes, covered though they were with makeup, betrayed her. Wirr had never seen her looking so tired.

She gave a brief smile when she saw them, a glimmer of relief flickering across her face before her usual calm, composed look was restored.

"You may leave us, Nelisi," she said to the older woman, her tone polite but firm. The attendant curtsied and shuffled from the room.

As soon as the door had closed Karaliene leaped from her chair, her smile returning. "You're safe!" she exclaimed, hugging first Dezia, then Aelric, then Wirr. "It's been so long, and with the Blind coming..." She let out a deep breath.

"It was a near thing, Your Highness," said Aelric. He waited for the princess to sit, then sat in one of the chairs opposite. He peered at her, eyes narrowing. "You look exhausted." He paused, reddening, as he suddenly remembered whom he was talking to. "I apologize, Your Highness. That's not to say..."

Karaliene, much to everyone's surprise, threw back her head and laughed. She quickly contained her mirth, but traces of amusement still played around her lips. "That might be the first honest thing I've heard in weeks," she said, shaking her head. She gave Aelric a rueful smile. "You can dispense with the formalities, Aelric. Nobody can hear us in here. And, honestly, you're no picture of health yourself." She gestured pointedly to Aelric's torn and bloodstained clothes.

Aelric smiled back in relief, happy she hadn't taken offense. "I'm just glad Ethin recognized me."

"That was a stroke of luck," agreed Karaliene. She paused, looking at Wirr. "What of the others you were traveling with?"

"Taeris and Caeden went to Tol Athian, to see if they are

willing to restore Caeden's memories," said Wirr. He looked at the ground. "Davian...didn't make it."

Karaliene's smile slipped. "I'm so sorry, Tor."

There was silence for a few moments, and then Karaliene glanced up at Aelric. "You know who this is now?"

Aelric just nodded, looking slightly abashed.

"Good. Then I don't need to tell you again how important it is to keep the details of your journey a secret?"

"No. We won't say anything," Aelric assured her.

Karaliene nodded her acknowledgment, then looked at Dezia, smiling. "I'll hear all about the trip later, I'm sure...but first I should catch up with Torin."

Dezia inclined her head, then grabbed her brother and pulled him out of the room.

"So," Karaliene sighed once they had left. "It seems I owe you an apology."

Wirr raised an eyebrow. "How so?"

"You warned me about the Boundary. Weeks before the invasion." Karaliene grimaced. "I should have listened."

"You believe me now?"

"I believe at least some of it—and I'd be foolish not to at least consider the rest. There have been no signs of any dar'gaithin, but the things we've been hearing about the Blind..." Karaliene shook her head.

"And my father?"

"Isn't sure what to think at the moment. I told him you'd ended up in Desriel because you were investigating the Boundary, and that you'd promised to explain everything to him when you got back. That at least got him thinking about where the Blind might be from." She looked him in the eye. "He's going to want to know everything, Tor."

"I know. But I've already figured out how to tell him most of the story, without letting on about Taeris and Caeden." Wirr hesitated. "I assume you didn't tell him...?"

Karaliene snorted. "That you were traveling with a man he'd sentenced to death? Of course not."

"Good." Wirr exhaled. "Because I told Taeris to come here, if he wasn't successful at the Tol. I told him that we might be able to help…convince the Council of Caeden's importance, if necessary." He held up his hand as Karaliene made to protest. "Only if they fail, in which case they'll have no other option. I didn't offer without giving it some serious consideration, Kara. We both know that there are ways you can pressure the Tol without ever having your name brought into it." He stared at her pleadingly, willing her to understand. "Caeden's key to all this; we need to help them any way we can. As long as they both stay out of Administration's sight, it shouldn't be a problem."

"Except that I will knowingly be giving one accused mass murderer, and one convicted one, free access to the city!" Karaliene looked at him in disbelief. "I said that I believed there was something to Sarr's claims, not that I thought he was in any way trustworthy. I don't feel comfortable with this, Tor."

Wirr grimaced. He'd hoped he wouldn't have to do this—hated the thought of tainting Davian's name even just with Karaliene, who hadn't known him. But Davian was dead, and Taeris and Caeden needed help.

He took a deep breath. "Taeris made a false confession, three years ago. He didn't kill those men." He quickly, bleakly explained the true events of that day to Karaliene, who listened to the story in silence.

"You believe him?" she asked once he was finished.

"Yes. It all fits—everything from why Administration thought he'd broken the First Tenet, to how he got his scars."

Karaliene sighed. "It would explain much," she admitted, still sounding reluctant. "It's hard for me to make a judgment for myself—but if you honestly believe that's the truth, then I will, too. Should Taeris and Caeden require it I will reach out to some of my contacts, see how much we can lean on the Council without them knowing who's behind it." She frowned at him. "But before I do that, I expect to speak to your new friends. My help *will* be conditional. And I hope neither of our fathers find out, else fates save us both."

Wirr exhaled in relief. "Thank you, Kara. I owe you," he said sincerely. Then he leaned forward in his seat. "How *is* your father?"

Karaliene looked sick. "What have you heard?"

"That he's been ranting against the Gifted. That it doesn't seem like he will be willing to change the Tenets, no matter the cost." Wirr frowned. "It doesn't sound like him."

Karaliene sighed. "It's not," she said, pain evident in her voice. "He's...sick, I think. I can't explain it. One moment he'll be fine—almost normal—and then the next he'll fly into a rage. He's always tired, and paranoid about everything and everyone. *Especially* Tol Athian. When word of the invasion came, he thought it was a trick. A trick by the Gifted to get him to change the Tenets." She shivered. "That was his *first* thought."

"Why would he think that?"

"I don't know." Karaliene rubbed her forehead. "He refuses to believe the Blind are a real threat to the city, despite what they've done so far. He virtually ignores your father, and I'm finding it harder and harder to get past his guards to see him, too. He won't even listen to Laiman Kardai half the time, and those two have been friends for near twenty years." She hesitated. "He sweats, his skin is gray, he often doesn't eat his meals. People are saying it's just stress, but...I'm worried."

Wirr felt a chill. "You think the Blind have something to do with it?"

Karaliene gestured. "I don't know; that's the problem. I tried talking to him about it, and he just laughed it off." Her face twisted. "And I daren't bring it up with any of the Houses."

"Not if you don't want a coup on top of everything else," agreed Wirr.

Karaliene nodded tiredly. "So there you have it—it's been a long couple of weeks. But fates, it's good to have you back. I've missed you."

Wirr grinned. "Missed you, too, Kara." He raised an eyebrow. "So what now?"

Karaliene gave the ghost of a smile. "Now, we get to have a feast to celebrate the return of Torin Andras, back from his glorious triumphs in Calandra. I'm sure the generals here will be dying to hear of your exploits."

Wirr groaned. "Is that really necessary? There *is* an army coming this way, after all."

Karaliene shrugged. "The Houses will think that more of a reason, not less. Partly because everyone wants a chance to become your new closest friend, of course. And partly because most of them are fools, and they'll welcome any chance to ignore what is happening rather than confront it."

Wirr laughed. "It *has* been a rough couple of weeks, for you to talk like that."

Karaliene rolled her eyes. "You have no idea. They're vultures, Tor. You would not believe the number of none too subtle offers I've already had to make me queen if I tell the Assembly my father's unfit to rule. At a price once it's done, of course." She shook her head in disgust. "Regardless. They will all want a feast. And it will look suspicious if you return to too little fanfare."

"Wonderful," said Wirr drily.

Karaliene raised an eyebrow. "You're going to have to get used to this again, you know."

"I know." Wirr bit his lip. "Speaking of which…I should probably go and see my family. No one else knows I'm back except for you."

Karaliene smiled, her expression softening. "Of course. You must be eager to see them. And I *know* they will be delighted to see you. Your father's been so worried, Torin."

Wirr grimaced. He wondered exactly how much trouble he was going to be in for going to Desriel. At least it would be a private scolding, he consoled himself, and only after the—hopefully happy—reunion. "Lead the way," he said.

Karaliene hesitated. "First let me arrange for some quarters so that you can rest. And bathe," she added, taking in his weary expression and ragged clothing. "Your mother would likely faint if she saw you in this condition. Another hour or so of waiting won't kill them."

Wirr grunted. "Good point."

He trailed after Karaliene, mentally steeling himself for what was to come, the whirlwind of attention and false smiles that he had dreaded for so long.

There was no turning back now.

Wirr waited nervously.

He had just spent the last two hours being clucked over by the palace tailor, an older man who had nearly had a heart attack when he'd seen what the prince was wearing. First Wirr had been bathed by some servants—a most uncomfortable experience in and of itself—and his hair had been cut to the latest style of the city. His beard, which had grown out to be quite scraggly since Thrindar, had been trimmed down to a neat goatee.

Then he'd been given a torrent of information regarding the latest news from Calandra, most of which he doubted he'd remember if anyone quizzed him. Still, it was enough to get by. He could always plead tiredness if the questions became too in-depth.

Now he was waiting for his family—his father, mother, and younger sister—to come and greet him. He didn't know whether to feel excited or anxious. Would they have changed in the last three years? Would they still see him as they once had, or had the time away colored their opinions of him?

He fiddled with his sleeves again, frowning at the lace on the cuffs. The entire suit felt odd, uncomfortable, against his skin after so many years. It made him feel like a child again, no longer able to choose what he wore.

The sound of the door opening made him flinch. He spun to see his father's familiar blue-cloaked frame in the doorway, with his mother and Deldri peering in behind. They all stared for a moment, silent, each as if surprised to see the other was really there.

Then there was a blur of motion and he was being swept up in a fierce hug by his father, squeezing out a laugh as the pressure on his ribs made it hard to breathe. Elocien had always been so reserved; this was an unexpected display of emotion, though not unwelcome. They were soon joined by two more bodies as Geladra and Deldri joined in the hug, his mother emitting a couple of sobs as she held him in her arms.

Suddenly he couldn't keep from smiling. As much as he had dreaded returning here, he *had* missed his family—even his father, with whom he had never truly gotten along.

"It's good to see you," he said, grinning, as they all finally separated.

Geladra gave him an affectionate smile, dabbing at her eyes. "We've missed you." She stepped back, examining him. "Calandra has been good to you, Torin. You look strong and healthy."

Wirr nodded, still smiling, though the comment sent a pang of guilt through him. His mother and Deldri hadn't been told where he'd been—didn't know, even now.

"The last few years were more than worthwhile," he said honestly. "You got my letters?"

"We did," said Deldri, her tone reproachful. "You could have described some of your battles in them, though." Though neither his father nor his mother looked much different—a little more tired around the eyes, perhaps, and his mother with slightly more gray in her hair—the changes in Deldri were dramatic. Gone was the chubby nine-year-old, and in her place was a slim, confident-looking girl who was tall enough now to look him in the eye without craning her neck.

Wirr smiled. "There wasn't much to tell, really. Sometimes the barbarians attacked our fortress, but they were never organized enough to pose a real threat."

Deldri nodded. "I heard you came back with Aelric Shainwiere," she said suddenly.

Wirr blinked in surprise. "I...yes, we met on the road back."

"What's he like?" Deldri leaned forward, her expression eager.

Geladra sighed. "You can harass your brother for gossip another time," she said in a stern tone, rolling her eyes. "We have much to catch up on." She sat down, and everyone followed suit.

They talked for an hour or so, soon lapsing into the comfortable style of conversation that Wirr knew came only with being related. He kept talk of Calandra to a minimum, instead focusing on what had been happening in the others' lives. His mother and sister did most of the talking; Deldri especially chattered on for quite some time, much to Wirr's astonishment. When he had left, she had been so quiet that he would often forget she was even there.

Finally Geladra glanced at Elocien, who gave her a slight nod in return. "We should go," she said, tugging on Deldri's arm. "Your father and Torin have other things to speak of."

Deldri pouted but acquiesced, rising and giving Wirr an abrupt, affectionate hug before leaving. Wirr grinned as he watched them go.

"Deldri is growing up," he said.

The duke nodded absently. "Too fast," he sighed. "I've already had Houses asking whether their sons might be a suitable match."

"Already?" Wirr shook his head. "They really are vultures."

Elocien stared at him for a moment, then chuckled. "I see your time away has done nothing to dampen your dislike of them," he said with amusement. His smile faded, expression turning serious. "I'm so relieved you are safe, Torin. When the news came about the school..."

Wirr grimaced. "I suppose I have some explaining to do."

He spent the next hour relating his last couple of months to his father. He told Elocien most of the story, including Davian's true role; as much as it hurt, there was little point in keeping his friend's ability a secret anymore. In the end he omitted only Taeris's real name, and the fact that Taeris and Caeden had accompanied them back.

Elocien was surprisingly understanding throughout the tale, so much so that for a moment Wirr considered telling him the truth about Taeris and Caeden as well...but he dismissed the idea as soon as he'd had it. Those two needed every opportunity to convince the Tol to restore Caeden's memories, without Administration's interference. And he remembered his father's opinion of Taeris, all too clearly. "A monster" was what he'd called him three years earlier. "The very worst of the Gifted."

No. He couldn't say anything. The risk was too great.

When Wirr had finished, Elocien let out a long breath.

"You've been through so much," he said, shaking his head in wonder. "I want to be angry at you for going to Desriel, but... it seems that running away ended up saving your life. For that I am truly grateful." He leaned back. "I should tell you, too—we found out about the Elder who tricked your friend into leaving. Tol Athian has him safely locked away in their dungeon, but he refuses to say anything."

Wirr felt his eyebrows rise; with all that had happened, he'd almost forgotten how this had all started. "That is good news," he said, nodding. He determined to pay Ilseth Tenvar a visit at some point.

Elocien leaned forward. "So. Your letters seemed to indicate you were happy enough, but tell me. How did you find the last few years?"

Wirr thought for a moment. "They were the happiest of my life," he said sincerely. The sentiment was laced with sadness and regret, though. Any thoughts of his life at the school always would be now.

Elocien smiled. "I'm glad. I always wondered whether it was the right choice, sending you there." He bit his lip. "Given what has been happening here, I suspect it was the best choice I've made in a long time."

"You're talking about Uncle?"

Elocien nodded. "He's...ill, Torin. I think he—"

A knock at the door cut him off; after a few seconds the door opened and a young woman appeared. A Shadow, Wirr realized absently, not really paying attention.

The girl's eyes were on his father. "Duke Andras," she began in a formal tone, "I have some news I think..."

She trailed off.

Wirr started as he realized the girl was staring at him, mouth agape. He flushed, shuffling uncomfortably...and then frowned. There was something familiar about her. He looked up, studying her black-scarred features properly for the first time.

"Asha?" he whispered in disbelief.

Suddenly he was being wrapped in a fierce embrace.

"Wirr!" Asha was hugging him so tightly it was difficult to breathe. "It's really you?"

Wirr laughed, though it was a mostly stunned sound. "It's really me, Ash." Remembering where he was, he dazedly disentangled himself and glanced over at his father, who was looking on in amusement.

"Asha is from Caladel," he explained to Elocien. "She can be trusted, though—I'll swear to it. It's not a problem that she knows where I've been, these past few years." He turned back to Asha. "Asha, this is going to come as a shock, but I need to tell you something."

There was silence for a moment as Elocien and Asha exchanged amused glances.

"I know, Wirr. Or is it Torin now?" said Asha, green eyes sparkling.

Wirr gaped at her in silence for a few seconds.

491

"How?" he asked.

"Your father told me."

Wirr glanced at Elocien, who nodded his confirmation; Wirr rubbed his forehead, trying to come to grips with the information. "But...why?"

"Because I trust her," said the duke simply.

Wirr shook his head in disbelief. "I...but you..." He trailed off, dumbstruck.

Asha laughed. "As eloquent as I remember."

Wirr smiled back, heart lighter than it had been since he'd first heard about the attack at Caladel. "How is this possible? How did you get away, and how are you here?" His grin slipped a little. "And fates, Asha...why are you a Shadow?"

"Slow down, Wirr. Too many questions at once. It's a long story." She paused. "Though something you should also know... I'm one of the Representatives for Tol Athian now."

Wirr stared at her, certain she was joking. When she stared back, entirely serious, he just shook his head.

"I must be dreaming," he muttered, though the smile didn't leave his face.

Asha suddenly bit her lip. "Wirr. Is Davian with you?"

Wirr's smile faded, and he looked away. "Ah. I'm so sorry, Ash." His voice cracked. "He's...we lost him."

Asha watched Wirr for a few seconds, then shook her head. "Did you see him die?" Her tone was calm.

Wirr paused, thrown a little by her response. "No, but...he's gone, Ash. I want to believe he might have survived, too, but—"

"He's not dead, Wirr." There was certainty in Asha's voice. She stared at him for a long moment, then looked away. "I know he's not dead."

Elocien coughed. "You two have a lot to catch up on," he observed. He gripped Wirr by the shoulder. "I have other matters that need seeing to right now, but you can stay for a while, talk. Once people know you're back, your movements are going to be watched fairly closely. You may not get an opportunity like this for some time."

Wirr nodded, rising and embracing his father. "It's good to

see you."

Elocien smiled at his son. "You, too."

"Elocien," Asha called out before he departed. "Can I tell him..."

Elocien gave her a slight nod. "That's fine." He left.

Once his father was gone, Wirr turned back to Asha, a wide smile on his face. For the first time in a long time, his heart was light.

"Now," he said, still grinning. "Tell me everything."

# Chapter 42

Caeden shuffled his feet, unable to hide his discomfort.

He glanced again around the spacious, well-lit room, its luxurious furnishings just as intimidating as the other finery he'd seen on his way into the palace. Aelric reclined in a well-cushioned chair in the corner, looking relaxed. Taeris was also seated, but in stark contrast to Aelric was visibly tense, leaning forward and staring absently at the thick carpet, his shoulders hunched.

Caeden understood his apprehension. Their entrance to the palace had gone surprisingly smoothly once Aelric had vouched for them at the gate, but that had been the easy part. Now they needed Karaliene herself—Karaliene, who had so obviously mistrusted them in Thrindar—to believe them. To *help* them, rather than turn them over to Administration. Even given Aelric and Dezia's relationship with the princess, Caeden still expected armed guards to burst through the door and arrest them at any moment. From the way Taeris looked, Caeden suspected the older man was thinking the same thing.

The rattle of the doorknob turning made him flinch, and he straightened as Taeris and Aelric both rose. The other two men bowed as Karaliene slipped into the room, alone; after a moment of relief Caeden quickly, awkwardly copied them.

There was silence for a few seconds as the princess studied him and Taeris, and Caeden flushed beneath her disapproving gaze. Even so, just as he had at Thrindar, he couldn't help but stare a little, too. It wasn't just that Karaliene was attractive—though she undoubtedly was, and he was far from blind to the fact. But she had a... presence. A way of commanding the attention of everyone in the room, just by being in it, that Caeden found more than a little mesmerizing.

He dropped his eyes again before his staring became too obvious, and Karaliene fortunately didn't seem to have noticed. She sat, gesturing for the others to do the same.

"I cannot stay long, but I wish to make one thing clear before we begin," said the princess to them as they took their seats. "I am here because people I trust believe you can help fight the Blind. That does not equate to me trusting you." She tapped her teeth with a manicured fingernail, watching them intently. "Now. My understanding is that Tol Athian's Council is refusing to help you, and that you would like me to use my influence to see if their minds can be changed. Is this correct?"

Taeris blinked, looking a little taken aback at Karaliene's straightforwardness. "It is, Your Highness."

Karaliene hesitated, glancing across at Aelric for a moment before continuing. "I *am* willing to do this," she said, her tone heavy with reluctance. "My name would not be directly involved, but some of the Houses have been trying to gain my favor for a while now. I can think of at least one that has a loose alliance with Athian, and would be willing to pressure the Council to help you, without asking too many questions about who you are."

"Of course, Your Highness," said Taeris quickly. "I can't tell you how—"

Karaliene held up a hand, forestalling him. "I haven't finished. There are conditions." She looked Taeris in the eye. "Fortunately, I have had your... past explained to me. That, and the fact that you warned us about the Boundary before anyone had even heard of the Blind, is in your favor. I am satisfied that you are truly here to help."

Taeris's eyes betrayed a glimmer of surprise, but he nodded in mute acknowledgment.

Karaliene's gaze hardened as it switched to Caeden, who shrank a little beneath it. "Your companion, on the other hand, remains a mystery. He has been accused of a terrible crime, regardless of where it was committed—and there has been no evidence to suggest that he was not the perpetrator, not even from his own lips. I am taking an enormous risk letting a man like that into my city, regardless of who has vouched for him. As such, I will require something more from him." Her tone was cold, and she still addressed her words to Taeris, as if even speaking to Caeden was distasteful to her.

Caeden stared at the ground, swallowing. It was harsh treatment, but for all he knew it could be justified. "I am willing to do whatever you need of me, Your Highness," he said, keeping his tone meek. If they could not convince the princess to help them, their chances of making any progress with the Tol were slim.

Karaliene nodded, then walked over to her desk and picked something up out of one of the drawers. Caeden paled as he recognized the black torc in her hand.

"You want me to wear a Shackle," he said quietly.

"Yes. And I will be the one to bind you," replied Karaliene, looking him in the eye. "Other people have vouched for you, believe you could be the key to defeating the Blind—and they may well be right. But ultimately, I am the one giving you refuge here. You're my responsibility while you are in Ilin Illan." She arched an eyebrow at him. "So these are my terms. You will wear the Shackle, and under no circumstances will you leave the palace grounds without my express permission. Agreed?"

Caeden hesitated. He knew there was little choice in the matter, knew that they were beyond fortunate to have the princess's help at all. But the thought of putting a Shackle on again made him cringe.

And... it would mean he had no way to slip out, no way to speak to Havran Das without the princess's knowing he had left.

Eventually, though, he took a deep breath and bared his left forearm, holding it out toward Karaliene.

"Agreed."

The princess examined him for a moment longer, and his breath caught as he locked gazes with her. Her expression became a hint more disapproving after a second, and Caeden reddened as he realized he was staring again; he looked away awkwardly, only to blush further as he saw Aelric glaring at him from the side. He finally fixed his eyes firmly on the ground, flinching as Karaliene touched the cold metal to his forearm.

The black metal turned to liquid, slithering and molding itself to his skin. The world immediately became duller, more gray, as if some of the color had been leeched out of it. Caeden sighed, then smoothed down his sleeve again.

Karaliene paused, then gave a satisfied nod. "I can feel the link."

Then she turned back to Taeris, evidently done with Caeden. "You may stay here, too, if you wish—there are few enough Administrators around, so it's as safe a place for you as any. You should both be able to pass as servants; I'll have someone organize quarters and some appropriate clothes. Use the servants' entrance if you want to come and go without attracting too much attention. Just don't wander too far into the main parts of the palace, and try to keep your excursions to the evenings, when there are fewer people about. If an Administrator does happen to recognize you, there will be nothing more I can do to help you."

"Understood. Thank you, Your Highness," said Taeris.

Karaliene inclined her head and then glanced across at Aelric, who was still scowling at Caeden. "Aelric. Can you please show these two to the east wing, and have Bacira make up some quarters there—maybe use the rooms near the gardens that 'Zia and I sometimes use for study? They're near enough to the other servants to not arouse suspicion, but isolated enough that no one should really notice that they are being occupied."

Aelric finally tore his gaze from Caeden, bowing to the princess. "Of course, Your Highness."

The princess considered them for a moment; her eyes again met Caeden's, and again his stomach fluttered. He looked to the side straight away this time, inwardly cursing himself. Reactions like that could only land him in trouble here.

Oblivious to Caeden's thoughts, Karaliene gave them all a tight nod, indicating she was leaving. The three men stood in deference.

"I'll set things in motion," she said to Taeris. She slipped out the door.

There was silence for a moment, and then Aelric gestured to the hallway. "We should get moving. The quicker we get to the servants' wing, the less likely you are to be spotted," he said, eyes hardening a little when he looked at Caeden.

Caeden flushed again, but nodded, silently grateful that things had gone so smoothly. He and Taeris exchanged relieved glances, and then they trailed after Aelric.

Caeden lay on his new bed, staring at the ceiling.

He'd been trying to sleep for hours now, battling both the warm evening and his own frustrations in search of rest. A breeze sighed through the open window, providing momentary relief from the heat and accompanied by the distant murmuring of the city below. It was well past midnight by his reckoning, but from the sounds of it, Ilin Illan was far from asleep, too.

Despite its being only his first night at the palace, this new situation was already beginning to chafe at him. It would take time for Karaliene's political machinations to achieve anything at the Tol, and Caeden accepted that. But that didn't mean he should be sitting idle. He felt sure he could be doing something—*anything* other than just lying around, hoping that either Taeris or the princess could eventually convince the Council to help him.

He stared out the window and pondered again how best to contact Havran Das, the merchant Alaris had talked about. He'd ventured outside his room earlier for some fresh air and taken careful note of the guards' routine patrols, even spotting a small supply gate he thought would be unattended at night. The only other brief excursion from his quarters had been to the library, where, much to his delight, he'd found more detailed maps of Ilin Illan than he'd had time to look over.

Havran Das's store had been easy to locate—it was clearly marked, large and in the upper city, quite close to the palace itself. An influential and successful man, then. Caeden didn't know whether that made him feel better or more nervous... but for the moment it barely mattered. All the information he'd gathered was useless if he couldn't find a way to slip his Shackle.

He sighed, staring resentfully at the black metal sitting snug around his arm, a constant reminder that Karaliene could pinpoint his location at any time. For all the finery around him, he was effectively just a prisoner once more.

He gave the Shackle a gentle tap, wondering if there was any way to remove it. Nothing happened except for a slight metallic ring. He closed his eyes, concentrating, trying to will it to fall off. He wanted it gone, *needed* it gone, so he could find out who he really was.

Still nothing. He scowled, opening his eyes again and gazing morosely at the ceiling. Traveling here, he'd felt as if he had a greater purpose; the blazing light of his tattoo and the sense of urgency Taeris had lent their journey had done little to dampen that. But he was isolated here in his room, the time already beginning to drag—and with the Vessel now secured in Tol Athian, his tattoo gave off only a dull, flickering glow. It all combined to make him feel cast adrift, as if his opportunity to get answers was starting to slip away.

The need to take action settled in his stomach, almost painful. He was tired; he should just try to sleep. Everything would seem less upsetting come morning.

But the knowledge remained that even if he felt better then, he would still be no closer to understanding who he was. What his purpose was in all of this. He gritted his teeth as the frustration built in his chest, intense and hard.

The Shackle retracted, dropping noiselessly from his arm and onto the quilt.

Caeden stared at it, stunned, for a few moments. It had come off. He'd done it, though he had no idea how.

Then he felt a flash of panic. Karaliene would know. Wouldn't she? The princess was most probably asleep at this hour; perhaps it would go unnoticed, at least for a time.

He waited in the darkness, frozen to the spot for several minutes, listening for the sound of soldiers rushing to his door. No one came. Gradually he relaxed, sitting up on the bed and staring at the Shackle. He could try putting it back on, but he had no idea when—if ever—he'd be able to take it off again.

And even if he was able to reactivate it, he doubted it would still be linked to Karaliene. This might be his only opportunity to act before his newest custodian realized something was amiss.

Heart pounding, he fumbled around in the darkness for his clothes. Once dressed he slipped out into the corridor, nerves taut as he strained for any sign of discovery.

The hallways were all but empty at this hour and he made quick time, soon locating an exit to the palace grounds that he thought would be unguarded. Holding his breath, he cracked the door open, waiting for a shout to indicate he'd been mistaken.

There was only silence, with the occasional snatch of city noise in the background. He slipped through and gently shut the door behind him.

The thick shrubbery and moonless night made staying out of sight relatively easy, much to his relief. He secreted himself behind some bushes, keeping his breathing calm and steady, straining for the sound of the next patrol. Once he thought he heard a noise behind him—the crunch of leaves underfoot, perhaps—but when he spun, there was no one there, and he put it down to his imagination.

Minutes passed, and finally the orange flame of a torch began bobbing toward him. He held his breath as two guards walked past his hiding spot, both looking alert but neither showing signs of having spotted anything unusual.

Then they were past. Forcing his legs to move, he dashed forward, staying low and ready to dive into cover at the first sign of another patrol. He arrived at the supply gate to find that it was much as he'd hoped, secured from the inside with a solid latch but not needing a key.

He opened it cautiously, then used a sliver of Essence—so small it would surely be undetectable—to hold the latch up, leaving the gate accessible from outside. By his estimate, the Essence wouldn't decay for at least a few hours. To a casual glance from any passing patrols, though, nothing would seem amiss.

He slipped out into a side alley, unlit and without shops or buildings of any kind. He kept his pace steady as he walked toward the main street, trying not to run despite his instincts. If anyone saw him, he wanted to look as innocuous as possible.

At the end of the alleyway he stopped, mentally revisiting the route he needed to take as he peered cautiously around the corner. In the distance he could see the four men standing guard in front of the palace's main gate, from their body language more bored than anything else. That was good. The last thing he needed was to be challenged by an overzealous sentry.

He waited for a few moments until he thought none were looking in his direction, then exited the alley and began walking away, keeping to the shadows where possible. He didn't look back, and there were no shouts from behind him.

Caeden's racing heartbeat slowed a little once the palace was lost to view, though he remained tense as he hurried along. Even at night the splendor of the Upper District was remarkable; the wide, sweeping streets were lined with enormous mansions set well back from the thoroughfare, each artfully lit up to display the impossibly detailed, seamless white stonework facades that stood as the enduring trademark of the Builders.

The wonder of the journey was marred, though, by the heavy sense of apprehension that lay draped over everything. Despite the late hour, several buildings still had windows illuminated, and he overheard more than one heated conversation emanating from the grounds of Ilin Illan's wealthiest residents. He couldn't make out the specifics of any of them, but the entire city just felt…uneasy.

He soon arrived at Havran Das's shop. He considered the building for a few minutes; the street was well lit, so there was little chance of his breaking in unnoticed. However, there did appear to be an upper floor to the shop—it was possible Das lived here as well as traded.

Taking a deep breath, Caeden walked up to the door and rapped on it as loudly as he dared.

He stood in silence for what seemed like minutes; he was almost about to leave when the sound of a bolt being slid back echoed around the street, and the door opened a crack. A bespectacled, middle-aged man peered out at him.

"What do you want, lad?" he asked sharply. "Do you know what hour it is?"

Caeden gave a nervous cough. "I'm looking for Havran Das."

The man stared at him for a moment, sizing him up. Evidently deciding Caeden did not pose much of a threat, he opened the door a little wider. "I am Havran Das," he said, suspicion thick in his tone. "Who in fates are you?"

"My name is Caeden." When the man still stared at him blankly, he added, "Alaris said you would be expecting me."

Havran took an unconscious step back at the last part, his

entire demeanor changing. He smiled, but for a moment Caeden saw a combination of fascination and fear in the merchant's eyes.

"Of course. Of course," Havran said, opening the door wide and gesturing for Caeden to enter. "Please. Come in."

Caeden did as he was asked, and the other man shut the door behind him, sliding the bolt back into place. He held his candle high, providing enough light for Caeden to navigate between the shelves of bottles. Finally they came to the back of the shop, where Havran indicated he should take a seat at a long table. Caeden did so uncertainly, still not sure what to expect from this meeting.

"So," said Havran as he sat opposite. "Alaris told me a little about your situation, but even he didn't know much. He certainly didn't tell me you would be in this body. Perhaps if—"

It was the slightest flicker of the eye, from Caeden's face to over his shoulder. If Caeden's senses had not already been so heightened from nervousness, he might not have noticed it at all.

As it was he reacted on instinct, spinning to the side and to his feet.

A blade cleaved the air where he had just been sitting, splintering the chair in two.

Caeden moved without thinking, elbowing his would-be attacker in the face. He heard the crunching sound of a nose breaking but didn't pause, allowing his momentum to take him behind the armored man's back. In one smooth motion he grabbed both sides of the assassin's helmetless head and twisted it as hard as he could, downward and to the side.

The snap of the man's neck was deafening in the silence of the shop.

Then Havran was scrambling backward away from Caeden, who felt a sudden rage burning in his stomach. He'd been set up, betrayed. Had anything Alaris told him been real? He started toward the cowering merchant, then picked him up by the shoulders with Essence-enhanced arms and slammed him against the wall.

"Why?" he hissed.

Havran cringed away, refusing to meet Caeden's gaze. "Tal'kamar, wait! It's not what you think!" he shrieked, plainly terrified.

A woman's scream from outside cut through the quiet of the night.

Caeden hesitated for only a moment; then he released the merchant and was moving, heading for the door. He heard Havran dashing out of the room behind him, but another shriek came, this time clearly only just outside. He slammed back the bolt and burst out of the shop, freezing as he took in the scene before him.

Fifty or so feet down the road a young woman was surrounded by five armored men, four of them watching as the other held her from behind, hand over her mouth. She was kicking and clearly trying to bite her attacker's hand, but Caeden could see her struggles were already weakening.

For a moment the man's hand slipped, and Caeden got a good look at the woman's face. He paled as he recognized the fair skin, the delicate features.

It was Karaliene.

She'd felt him take off the Shackle and decided to follow him, almost certainly, but there was no time to worry about that now. He gritted his teeth, then took off at a dead run toward the group.

He was still thirty feet away when he was first noticed; the man who had seen him murmured a word of warning, and all five men were facing Caeden in an instant. His heart skipped a beat as each one of them drew a sword, their black armor barely visible in the gloom.

Though none of the men were wearing the distinctive helmets, Caeden had no doubt who they were. He kept running. He was not going to leave Karaliene to the Blind.

The man closest gave a wide, greedy smile when he realized Caeden was unarmed; he stood calmly in an attack stance, perfectly still, as Caeden rushed toward him. Just as Caeden came within range the man moved, catlike, far quicker than should have been possible. His sword snaked out, streaking toward Caeden's neck.

Time slowed and Caeden let his instincts take over, just as he had against Aelric.

He slid beneath the arc of the sword, coming in under the man's defenses. Then he twisted and kicked upward into the left knee of his opponent, intuitively knowing that his altered passage through time meant that the blow in reality would be delivered much faster, and therefore much harder. He winced as he felt the man's ligaments snap, the knee bending sideways; a shout of surprised pain ripped from the soldier's throat as he crumpled to the ground.

Caeden regained his footing smoothly, snatching the man's sword from the air as it fell and then spinning forward, slashing his attacker's throat in one fluid motion. *Four.*

The smiles of the dead man's companions had vanished now. The one holding Karaliene hit her hard on the head, sending her slumping to the ground. Caeden watched her fall helplessly, hoping that the blow had not caused her any serious injury.

The four remaining soldiers moved as one toward him, fanning out, surrounding him so that he was no longer able to see them all at once. He knew he was still slowing time—Karaliene's fall appeared to take several seconds—but these men were clearly less affected. A little sluggish compared to him, perhaps, but not as much as he would like. He couldn't allow them to settle, to get any advantage.

He lunged forward, slipping gracefully between two whirring blades, one so close that he felt it brush a few strands of his hair. Caeden brought his own blade around in a vicious arc, the edge slicing into the exposed neck of the man to his left. His opponent began to fall without a sound; before the body could hit the ground Caeden snatched a dagger from its belt and spun, throwing it at one of the men who had moved behind him. It caught the unsuspecting soldier in the eye, blood fountaining through his fingers as he died clutching his face.

*Three. Two.* Their armor was well made—almost impenetrable to a normal weapon, he suspected—but these men had neglected to wear their helmets. Their laziness, or overconfidence, was going to kill them.

The two remaining soldiers faced him grimly, spacing themselves so that he would have to concentrate on one or the other. He'd vaguely hoped that they would run, having seen what had become of their comrades. But the expressions on their faces were intent, focused. As if his success so far had only intrigued them.

The one to his right feinted; when Caeden flinched toward

him the one to his left came in hard and fast, stabbing with lethal accuracy. Caeden was faster, though. He moved *forward*, toward the thrust and slightly to the side, spinning so that the steel passed just by his ribs. He went down on one knee in the same motion, grabbing the man's leg with his free hand and lifting.

Before his opponent hit the ground Caeden rolled toward the other soldier, anticipating the attack. Steel sparked as it hit the stone of the street where he had been a moment earlier. Caeden focused, then thrust upward at the second man, into the thin slit that allowed movement for the knee. He was rewarded with a scream of pain as his blade bit home.

He slid the blade back out before it could get caught, then rose, severing the man's head from his shoulders as he tumbled forward.

*One.*

The soldier he had tripped was back on his feet, panting but still with an oddly intent look in his eye. There was no fear that Caeden could see. At first he thought that was strange, but then he considered what he must look like to his opponent. Calm. Composed. Focused.

Exactly the same.

Before he could think on it any further, the final soldier was upon him, raining down a fierce array of blows. Caeden blocked them all—not easily, but not feeling that he was likely to lose now, either. He allowed the soldier to exhaust his attack, then put several feet between them.

"Who are you?" he asked, breathing heavily. "Why are you here?"

The man stopped, blinking as if surprised by the question.

"We are here to stop you, Tal'kamar," he eventually replied, his voice emotionless.

The soldier threw himself forward, but it was a tired thrust and Caeden sidestepped it with ease. He acted on instinct, bringing his sword up so that his opponent's momentum carried him into it. The blade sliced across his face, biting deep but not delivering a killing blow.

The man growled, blood spurting down his cheek, then turned to face him again.

Caeden stretched out his hand without thinking.

A blinding torrent of power and light washed through him, exploding from his palm and slamming into the man's chest. It should have vaporized the soldier where he stood, but much to Caeden's astonishment he simply stood there, neither advancing nor retreating as his armor drank in the Essence, extinguishing it.

Caeden stopped, cursing as he realized that every Finder in the city would now be pointed at him. He had to end this, and quickly.

He swiveled, flicking his sword underhand at the other man. The blade caught the soldier square through the mouth, blood fountaining as the man stared at Caeden in horrified disbelief. He was dead before he hit the ground.

Caeden stood there for a few more moments in silence, breathing hard, surveying the scene. Bloodied bodies lay everywhere. In the distance he could hear the whistle of the city watch; the fight had taken only a minute, perhaps less, but someone must have heard the clash of steel. There was doubtless a legion of Administrators heading in his direction now, too. He had to move.

He knelt by Karaliene, emitting a sigh of relief when he saw she was breathing. He hoisted her onto his shoulder—mentally apologizing for the indignity—then hurried away as fast as he could, disappearing down a darkened side street just as the urgent whistles of the watch sounded as if they had made it onto the scene.

Havran Das—who hadn't shown his face during the entire fight—would have to wait for another day.

Caeden suddenly discovered he was tired. Exhausted, in fact. The adrenaline was wearing off, and whatever he'd been doing to slow down time was no longer working. He had to think of what to do with Karaliene.

She knew, of course. She knew he'd slipped his Shackle, left the grounds—breaking the only two conditions she'd set for her hospitality. If he took her back to the palace, she would have him thrown in a dungeon as soon as she awoke. At the least.

Then he thought of what he'd done, how easily he'd killed those men. He shivered a little as the reality of it set in; it had been surreal at the time, almost as if he were watching himself do those things. He hadn't taken pleasure in it, certainly—but it hadn't upset him as he knew it should have, either.

He swallowed. Perhaps he belonged in a dungeon.

He thought furiously as he half walked, half jogged along the deserted streets. Was there even an alternative? He couldn't prevent Karaliene from returning to the palace; one thing of which he was certain was that he wasn't capable of kidnapping or killing her. He was relieved to discover that, though in his current situation it presented its own series of problems.

In the end he decided that there was nothing for it but to return to the palace and accept the consequences. Even though she had been unconscious for most of the fight, Karaliene would hopefully feel some sliver of gratitude toward him for saving her. The prospect seemed a slim one at this point, but he clung to it.

He made it back to the supply gate without any issues, relieved to find that it was still unlatched, despite the princess's presumably having used it after him. He shut it properly behind him, then hid in the bushes until the patrol passed by again, covering Karaliene's mouth for fear she would wake up and give him away. Heart pounding so loud he was worried he wouldn't hear the guards coming, he made it back inside without incident.

The trip to Karaliene's quarters was trickier. He already knew where to go thanks to Aelric's thorough rundown of off-limits areas earlier that day—the problem was that there would be plenty of guards stationed along the hallways leading up to the royal chambers. Caeden found a safe corner and let Karaliene's limp body rest against the wall, flexing his tired shoulder. She was heavier than she looked.

He stared at her for a moment. She looked strangely peaceful, her hair tousled but still shining in the dim light.

Then he shook himself. If anyone found him with her like this, it was unlikely he'd even last until the princess awoke to explain matters. He needed to get her back to her chambers.

He closed his eyes, taking a deep, steadying breath. She must have slipped away from her bedroom without being noticed; none of the guards would have let her wander off alone in the middle of the night. And, therefore, she must have had a plan to get back in.

He carefully picked her up again, then found the nearest exit, moving around the outside of the palace until he was reasonably sure he was below Karaliene's rooms. They were on the top floor, but Caeden remembered having seen a slender set of spiral stairs leading up to the balcony.

Holding his breath, he started up them as quickly as he could, praying that the dim starlight was not enough for anyone to see the silhouette clambering upward. It was slow, exhausting progress with the princess over his shoulder, and he felt more exposed the higher he climbed. His skin crawled, and every moment he expected to hear cries of alarm.

Finally, though, he gained the upper balcony, relieved beyond measure to see that one of the windows had been left ajar. He opened it a little wider and climbed awkwardly through, careful not to make any noise. There would doubtless be guards posted outside Karaliene's quarters; any suspicious sound and they would come rushing in.

He carried Karaliene over to her bed, laying her gently across it. He held his breath as she started to stir, but the princess simply rolled over into a more comfortable position, eyes still shut. Caeden exhaled, then exited through the window again, closing it until the latch clicked neatly behind him.

He paused for a moment on the balcony, awestruck by the view. This was the highest accessible point in all of Ilin Illan; before him the city was laid out like a living map, the outline of every building discernible in the starlight. The gracefully sculpted white stone structures seemed even more cohesive from here, each unique and yet unified with the others, each a piece that fit to its neighbor with liquid elegance. Beyond the streets he could see a ship slipping down the silvery-black river, visible only thanks to its bobbing lights.

Even with the details obscured by darkness, it was breathtaking.

But he didn't dare tarry to enjoy the sight, especially here where an errant glance from a guard would undo him. He turned for one last glance at the princess, to ensure she was still sleeping.

He froze.

Karaliene was sitting up in her bed, eyes open, staring through the window at him. There was a look of curiosity on her face, but no alarm.

Caeden didn't wait for her to cry out. He fled for the stairs at a dead run, getting to the bottom just ahead of a patrol. He made it back to his own quarters unseen, out of breath as he finally shut the door and collapsed onto his bed, heedless of the bloodstains that marred his clothing. He felt the cold metal of the Shackle press against his back.

Without hesitation he reached around and grabbed it, then placed it against his arm.

Nothing happened.

"It won't work. You can't put it on yourself," came a deep voice.

Caeden leaped to his feet again, relaxing only a fraction when he saw its owner.

Taeris was standing in the doorway to the adjoining room. He had evidently been waiting for Caeden's return; the older man was watching him closely—not fearfully, exactly, but with an abundance of caution.

Caeden found himself coloring, and he let the Shackle fall to the ground with a clatter. The full toll of the night finally crashed down on him, and he sank back onto the bed, holding his head in his hands.

"I'm sorry," he said.

He truly was. He'd betrayed Taeris's trust, hedged his bets so that he didn't have to choose a side. He realized now that it was time to make that choice.

Taeris gave him the slightest of smiles, though his expression was still stern. "You came back. That's a start." He walked over to the bed, seating himself next to Caeden and putting a hand on his shoulder.

"But it certainly seems we have much to talk about," he added quietly.

# Chapter 43

Caeden watched as Taeris leaned back, evidently trying to absorb everything he'd just been told.

Caeden had spent the past half hour explaining the events of the evening and, to a lesser extent, what had precipitated them. About how Alaris had contacted him through the dok'en, had warned him against revealing information to the Gifted. Had warned him to distrust them completely.

"Why didn't you tell me sooner?" Taeris's expression was more thoughtful than angry.

Caeden looked at the ground. "Alaris said that if you found out who I truly was, you would kill me."

The scarred man nodded slowly. "You were scared."

Caeden's cheeks burned. "I should have trusted you," he said, his voice catching. "I don't know why I didn't. You've shown me nothing but kindness and good faith since we met."

"Trusting someone is one thing, lad. Trusting them with your life is another entirely. I can't say that this has made things any easier for us here, but...I understand." Taeris's tone was gentle, with only a hint of the frustration he surely must have been feeling.

"Thank you," said Caeden softly. He paused, then gave Taeris a cautious glance. "How long were you waiting?"

"I came as soon as I felt that Essence blast. Not many of the Gifted around here could have produced that," Taeris observed drily. He rubbed his forehead. "The men you fought. You're certain they were Blind?"

"I think so. They didn't have the helmets, but they were wearing black armor. They were a good deal faster than normal men, too."

"And yet you killed all five of them." Taeris raised an eyebrow.

Caeden hesitated. "I can do what they do, only...better. And without the armor."

"You think it's the armor giving them these powers?"

"I'm sure of it." Caeden had already had some time to think about this. "Slowing your passage through time like that is an Augur ability; those five men couldn't all have been Augurs. Combine that with the way their armor absorbed Essence..."

Taeris gave a thoughtful nod. "And as I said, I felt the blast from here. This is bad, Caeden. Very bad. It means that even if the Gifted get a chance to fight, we're going to be less effective than we'd hoped."

"I know."

There was silence for a few seconds, then Taeris began pacing. "The question is—how did they get in? The city is supposed to be locked down; everyone is being searched as they enter. Men transporting black armor would certainly have been stopped." He paused, frowning. "Unless, of course, they have been here for some time. Waiting." He glanced at Caeden. "When did you make contact with Alaris?"

Caeden calculated. "Just after Deilannis. A month ago, perhaps?"

Taeris nodded to himself. "A week before the invasion began. Those men could have been sent ahead to help Das kill you—they could have slipped into the city as recently as a couple of weeks ago." He stared worriedly into space as another possibility occurred to him. "Or they may have been sent ahead for a different purpose entirely, and Alaris simply took advantage of their presence here."

Caeden swallowed. "A different purpose...like what?"

"Scouting. Sabotage. Fates only know." Taeris was silent for a few seconds as he considered it some more, then shook his head. "Regardless—the Blind are clearly afraid of you, Caeden. Whatever is locked away in that memory of yours, it's evidently something they don't want uncovered." He rubbed his chin. "When you spoke to Alaris, did you tell him where you were going?"

"No." Caeden hesitated, grimacing as he recalled the conversation. "He knew I was traveling with Gifted, though. He probably could have guessed where I was headed...but he couldn't be certain, so maybe Das was the bait. He knew that if I really wanted answers, I'd have to come here. Sooner rather than later, too, once I heard about the invasion."

"That sounds like it would be about right." Taeris bit his lip. "Unless..."

"Unless what?"

Taeris sighed. "I've been thinking a lot about the Blind, Caeden, and there's always been something that hasn't quite made sense. They've never acted like a conquering army, trying to maintain control of the territory they've gained. And if they were sent by Aarkein Devaed, why just a thousand men? We know there are at least dar'gaithin out there as well, so why not send them, too—everything he has?"

He leaned forward. "But think about the timing of all this. If you're such a threat to them...maybe when Alaris made contact with you and realized that you might get your memories back, it forced them to act early. The Boundary is weak, but we know it hasn't collapsed yet, not completely—why not wait until that happens, and send everything they have at once?" He nodded to himself. "I think...there's a possibility this entire attack is about you, Caeden. I think they may have lured you here, and are coming for you before you can remember anything. While you're vulnerable."

Caeden felt a chill as he considered the possibility. "So I'm responsible for even more deaths," he observed, his tone heavy.

"No. You can't think like that. This has to be a precursor to Devaed's real attack; the only reason he would send an advance party like this—giving us warning, time to prepare for whatever comes after—is if you are somehow a threat to him. Perhaps his *only* threat." Taeris shook his head. "It's only a theory. But if I had to guess, I would say that he can't risk you remembering... whatever it is you know."

Caeden shifted uncomfortably. "Even if you're right, I'm not going to be able to remember anything from a cell," he pointed out. "The princess knows I took off the Shackle, saw me sneak out. It's only a matter of time before I'm locked up." He rubbed his forehead, glancing at the door, still half expecting guards to come crashing through it at any moment.

"We will have to see how Karaliene reacts before we make any plans," Taeris admitted. "If she wants to clap you in irons, then we will have to adapt. But I suspect she will at least hear you out—and from everything you've told me, there's a good chance she will be grateful."

Caeden gave Taeris a puzzled look. "Grateful?"

Taeris smiled, looking amused. "You *did* break her trust, Caeden, but...you also saved her life. You saved her and brought her back here, when you could have escaped and left her to her death. You may think what you did was the logical choice, but some people aren't as naturally good-hearted as you." He shrugged. "Growing up here, Karaliene's probably seen more of the selfish side of human nature than you and I put together. I'm sure that on some level, she'll appreciate the sacrifice you made."

Caeden frowned. He wanted to believe Taeris, but it had been his fault that Karaliene was in danger in the first place. Besides, her disapproving glares from earlier that day were too fresh in his mind for Taeris's words to give him any comfort. "And if she doesn't throw me in prison?" he asked.

"Then nothing changes. I keep pressing Tol Athian to use the memory device, and hope that Karaliene's contacts are helping our cause in the background."

Caeden sighed. "So for now, I just...wait?"

"Yes. If you run then Karaliene will assume the worst, and this opportunity we've been given here will be for nothing." Taeris shook his head. "And anyway—if things go badly with her, we do have a last resort."

Caeden raised an eyebrow. "Which is?"

Taeris hesitated, then drew a small, smooth white stone from his pocket.

"I gave Nashrel the other Travel Stone, back at the Tol. I'm hoping he stored it with the other Vessels in Tol Athian." He stared at the stone grimly. "It's not charged yet; I've only been able to use the smallest trickle of Essence here in the palace. But it should be ready in a couple of days. It was my intention only to use it if the

Blind got too close to Ilin Illan, when there was no longer any chance of convincing the Council to help. But if you get locked up, we can use it earlier. Break you out, if need be."

Caeden looked at the white stone with trepidation. "Won't Tol Athian know we're there if we use it, though?"

"Oh yes," said Taeris with an emphatic nod. "The Elders will detect the portal as soon as we open it inside the Tol—we'll have only minutes to both locate and use the Vessel that can restore your memories. If that."

"And if the other Travel Stone is somewhere else in the Tol?"

"Then it will be a short trip." Taeris slipped the stone back into his pocket with a sigh. "But there's no benefit to worrying about any of that right now—it may be an option we'll never have to use. The best thing you can do at the moment is try to sleep, if you can. Whatever action Karaliene is going to take, it seems likely at this point that she isn't going to take it until morning."

Caeden inclined his head. "Thank you, for being so understanding about all of this. And...I truly am sorry for not telling you about Alaris sooner. I know I've caused a lot of trouble this evening."

"I'm just glad you know which side you're on now," said Taeris with a tight smile. He gave Caeden a slight nod, and slipped out the door.

Caeden stared into space for a few minutes after he'd gone, lost in thought. Eventually he gave a tired shake of his head and decided to follow Taeris's advice, lying down on the soft bed and closing his eyes, trying to ignore the knot of worry in his stomach.

Still, it was a long time before he could sleep.

Caeden yawned.

For a moment he lay in his comfortable bed, blissfully sleepy, aware that something had happened the previous night but not quite remembering what.

Then the memories returned and he sat up straight, any semblance of tiredness gone.

The world outside the open window was still dark, but Caeden could detect a hint of gray in the black night sky. It was morning, albeit still before dawn. That was a good sign; he'd half expected to be woken sooner by guards with instructions to haul him off to the dungeons. The princess had evidently decided against that course of action—or at least decided to hold off on it.

He rose and dressed, enough time passing that he was almost beginning to relax when a sharp knock at the door made him freeze.

"Open up," came a stern voice from the other side.

Caeden glanced at the open window and for a brief, wild moment considered running. He wouldn't get within a hundred feet of the wall before being stopped, though.

He walked over to the door and opened it, trying to look calm.

Outside he was surprised to see Karaliene herself, flanked by two burly and very displeased-looking guards. Her arms were crossed and a frown was plastered across her face; even so, the sight of her made Caeden's heart skip a beat.

Then he took a deep breath, focusing. This was the *princess*—and she currently held his fate in her hands. He couldn't afford to let himself be put off balance, no matter how lovely she looked.

"Your Highness," he said formally, remembering to bow just in time. "How can I help you?"

"You can help me by having a conversation with me." Karaliene strode forward, grabbing his arm and steering him back inside. "In private," she added with a glare, stopping her two body-guards in their tracks. She shut the door in their faces.

Caeden waited for the princess to take a seat, then sat opposite her, his heart pounding and a heavy feeling in his stomach. This was it. He tried to tell from Karaliene's face what his punishment would be, but her expression was inscrutable.

"You sneaked out of the palace last night," Karaliene observed, her tone flat. "You found a way to remove your Shackle."

"I did, Your Highness," acknowledged Caeden.

Karaliene leaned forward. "You broke the two conditions I had for allowing you to stay here. The *only* two conditions."

Caeden swallowed. "Yes. I…" He sighed, not knowing where to begin, what to say. His shoulders slumped a little. "I apologize, Your Highness. I made a mistake." He put every ounce of sincerity he had into the statement.

Karaliene watched him for a long moment, eyes narrowed. She looked...puzzled. As if she had been expecting an entirely different reaction.

"Were you trying to run?" she asked. "How did you get out of the Shackle?"

Caeden was silent for a few seconds, trying to think of how best to explain everything. "I wasn't running. I planned to come back," he said. "I was told that there was a man in the city who knew something about my past. I went to visit him, but it was a trap." He couldn't keep the bitterness from his tone.

Karaliene studied him, looking skeptical. "And you couldn't have just asked for my permission to see him?"

"It was...complicated," said Caeden, the words stumbling off his tongue. He winced, knowing how evasive and vague the answer sounded.

Karaliene frowned a little, but still looked more perplexed than angry. "Then you should probably do your best to explain it," she said quietly.

Caeden hesitated but eventually sighed, nodding. He could see from the princess's expression that anything short of the whole truth would probably land him in the dungeons.

He took a deep breath, and told her everything he could about his meeting with Alaris.

His throat was hoarse by the time he was done. Karaliene watched him for a long few seconds, her expression unreadable. Then she rose, crossed to the basin, and poured a glass of water. She sat back down opposite Caeden, offering him the drink silently.

He gave her an appreciative nod and took a long swig, using the moment to brace himself for whatever was about to come.

"They were Blind, weren't they?" said Karaliene, her voice soft.

Caeden blinked in surprise at her gentle tone, but nodded his confirmation. "I think so."

"And you killed them all?" Karaliene watched him closely. "The Administrators found the bodies last night—it's supposed to be a secret, but the entire palace has been talking of nothing else this morning."

Caeden nodded again, a little awkwardly this time. "I had to," he admitted. He didn't mention that he had left Havran Das alive. If the man had information about who Caeden really was, then Caeden needed to find him before anyone else.

Karaliene bit her lip. "My uncle has ordered Dras Lothlar to examine their armor. Is that what made them so quick? When they caught me, it was like...I was stuck in glue. Every time I tried to hit them, one of them would catch my wrist before I could swing." She shivered. "And they were *strong*. Stronger than they should have been, I'm sure. That wasn't my imagination, was it?"

Caeden shook his head. "No," he said quietly.

Karaliene looked at him in silence for a while. Gone were the hard, disapproving glares from their earlier meetings. Now she just seemed...curious. "I saw you," she said eventually. "I saw you move toward them. You were so fast. And graceful, like..." She shook her head at the memory. "You were almost a blur, even compared to them." She raised a questioning eyebrow at him.

Caeden shrugged. "It's the same as what happened with the Shackle. I have these...other abilities, when I need them. I can't control them, though. That's one of the reasons Taeris wants me to get my memory back—so I can understand those abilities, use them against the Blind." He hesitated. "He thinks I may be an Augur."

Karaliene nodded. "That sounds about right," she murmured, almost to herself. She bit her lip. "So what do you want?"

Caeden stared at her blankly. "Want?"

Karaliene made an impatient gesture. "For saving me. We both know you didn't have to do it."

Caeden frowned. "Of course I had to do it. Those men would have killed you." Taeris had said much the same thing, but he couldn't understand it—leaving Karaliene to the Blind had never been an option, and the idea that anyone thought it had been was vaguely offensive. "It wasn't for some sort of reward."

There was a long silence as Karaliene continued to stare at him like a puzzle in need of solving, until Caeden began to grow uncomfortable.

Finally the princess leaned forward. "So you knew that being caught outside the palace could end in your being thrown in prison. You knew I'd followed you. Despite that, you fought off five men, then carried me back here—not just to the palace, but to my own rooms." Her eyes narrowed. "And you want nothing for this?" Her face was impassive, not giving away even a hint of what she thought of the concept.

Caeden hesitated. "Not being thrown in prison would be nice," he said cautiously.

There was another long silence, then Karaliene gave an abrupt, disbelieving laugh.

"You're serious." She gave a rueful shake of her head, eyes shining for a moment as she looked at Caeden.

He smiled back, a little dazed. "So...you're not angry?"

Karaliene stared at him, a half smile on her lips. "No." She brushed a stray strand of blond hair back behind her ear. "It seems I have misjudged you," she added, sounding as if she rarely made such admissions. She glanced toward the door. "Have you seen much of the palace?"

Caeden shook his head.

The princess stood. "Then perhaps I should show you around."

Caeden stood, too, noting the still-dark sky outside the window. "At this hour, Your Highness?"

Karaliene gave him an amused look. "I would like to continue this conversation," she said, still smiling, "but I'm not sure that the two men outside your door would believe that was what was happening in here if we stayed much longer. They don't need to accompany us, but they will certainly be more comfortable if we're not locked away together."

Caeden gave a nervous laugh, trying not to look flustered. "Then lead the way, Your Highness. I'd be honored."

Karaliene snorted. "And no need for the formalities, Caeden. You saved my life. In private you can call me Kara."

Caeden ducked his head, still a little bemused at the turn of events. "I will."

They walked to the door. Karaliene opened it and immediately she was cold and formal once again; to Caeden's eyes she grew six inches, somehow seeming to tower over the muscular bodyguards waiting outside.

"You may leave us," she said in a peremptory tone. "I am going to show Caeden around the grounds. Your presence is no longer required."

The shorter of the men gave her a nervous look. "Highness, if I may suggest—"

"No." Karaliene cut him off with a slicing gesture. "No discussion. I know my father and uncle worry about me, but I'm old enough to make my own decisions."

The guard opened his mouth to protest, but one look from Karaliene silenced him as effectively as a slap to the face. Caeden tried to hide his amusement, but he still got a dirty stare from both men as they wandered off, their expressions sullen.

Once the men were out of sight, Karaliene relaxed again, and they began walking—not aimlessly, exactly, but at a companionable stroll, chatting about small things as they went.

Caeden's nervousness soon faded away. The princess was easy to talk to, even charming now that she had dropped her formal facade, and Caeden found himself enjoying the conversation. At certain points, though, he had to remind himself of their respective positions. There was a warmth to Karaliene's expression now when she looked at him, and she certainly showed no signs of wanting to be elsewhere...but she was still the princess. He knew that this newfound friendliness was nothing more than her expressing her gratitude.

Even so, time passed faster than Caeden would have credited, and it felt like only a few minutes later that they came to a balcony overlooking a wide-open courtyard, the now-midmorning sun bright in the sky. A squad of soldiers trained below, their swords flashing sporadically in the light. Caeden and Karaliene just watched for a while, the pleasant mood of the conversation lost as the reality of what was coming set in. The men below wore grim expressions; no one laughed or joked as they worked.

"I wish I could understand why these men have been acting so carelessly," said Karaliene softly.

Caeden glanced at her. "What do you mean?"

Karaliene sighed. "General Parathe has been reporting to my father that they have started to just...take days off. Drinking and carousing, presumably. One day they fail to report for duty; the next day they just turn up and act like nothing is wrong. Parathe disciplined them at the start, but the problem is so widespread now that he cannot afford to. If General Jash'tar cannot stop the Blind, we will need every man we can get."

"Let's hope it doesn't come to that," said Caeden.

Karaliene turned to him; he felt his heart skip at how close she was standing. "That's what everyone else is saying, though—and that's why I'm worried," she said in a low tone. "My father, the Houses—they're so confident that our advantage in numbers is all that matters. And until last night, I might have agreed with them, but now..." She shivered, shaking her head. "I know Laiman Kardai and my uncle have been preparing the city for a siege since the first day they heard about the Blind, so I suppose we at least have that. But aside from those two, everyone else just seems to think that this invasion is a chance to play politics."

Caeden glanced across at her; Karaliene's tone was bitter. "How so?"

Karaliene hesitated, then grimaced. "Thanks to my father's... instability, I've heard rumor of at least two of the Great Houses planning for the possibility of ruling. Not planning to rule, of course; that would be treason. But making sure that if there is an empty throne in the near future, they would be nearby to sit in it." She shrugged. "And I'm a complication to those sort of plans, as you can imagine."

Caeden looked at her in disbelief. "Surely they wouldn't risk making things even more unstable. Not now."

"You really haven't spent much time around men of power, have you?" Karaliene said with wry amusement. "Take last night. In your place, half of the nobility would have demanded a heavy reward for saving me, and the other half would have just let me die." She smiled, though with a hint of sadness.

Caeden looked at her with horror. "I'm sorry," he said sincerely. "That must be hard."

"Don't misunderstand, Caeden. I'm a princess; there are plenty of benefits, too. I don't have to face many of the everyday trials that most people go through." Karaliene's smile faded. "But at times like this? Yes, it can be hard."

They watched the soldiers for a while longer, then Karaliene said, "Who do you think they are?" She made a vague gesture to the north.

Caeden paused to think. "I believe what Taeris believes," he said after a moment. "That these men have been sent by Aarkein Devaed." 521

The princess nodded. "There was something...*wrong* about that armor last night. It made me feel sick just being in contact with it."

"Then you believe, too?"

The princess shook her head slowly. "I don't know. It all still seems so surreal. A bedtime story brought to life." She looked at him, expression curious. "Why do you believe?"

Caeden shrugged. "I just know," he said quietly. "Somehow, I know that he's not just a myth. When I think of him, I think of someone to be feared." He sighed. "I seem to know a lot of things that no one else does, though."

Karaliene considered. "Perhaps that's why your memories were removed," she suggested. "Perhaps you found out too much about Aarkein Devaed?"

Caeden rubbed his forehead. "Maybe." It was similar to Taeris's suggestion—it could certainly explain why the invaders seemed to be after him—yet he didn't think it was correct. But then, he couldn't even give a reason as to why he thought that. It was all very confusing.

Karaliene saw his disconsolate expression and hesitantly reached out to lay a hand on his forearm. "Whatever it is, I'm sure you will get to the bottom of it."

Caeden's breath caught and he froze, as if Karaliene were a bird he could accidentally scare off with a sudden movement. The princess didn't remove her hand straight away and for a long moment they just stood there, watching the soldiers.

Then there were footsteps behind them and Karaliene turned smoothly, letting her hand slip to her side again.

Caeden turned as well, cringing to see Aelric striding toward them. With the possible exception of the king or the Northwarden, Aelric was the last person he'd wanted to see him with the princess. He'd heard the young swordsman talk of her often enough over the past month or so to know that he was hopelessly in love with her. The black expression on his face as he looked at Caeden did nothing to dispel that notion.

"Your Highness," said Aelric stiffly, bowing to Karaliene. "I've been looking everywhere for you. Your uncle was most upset when he discovered you had dismissed your guards—especially to wander off in the early hours of the morning with a servant." He shot an accusatory glare at Caeden. "I thought it best to find you before he did, lest he start taking too close an interest in who it is you're with."

Karaliene hesitated, for a moment looking as if she was going to protest. Then she gave an exasperated sigh. "Very well." She turned to Caeden. "I'm sorry, but I really should go."

Caeden smiled. "I have no doubt you have more important things to do, Your Highness. I'm honored to have received as much time as I have."

Karaliene smiled at him warmly. "I hope we can talk again," she said. "Soon." With a final, irritable glare at Aelric, she walked back toward the palace.

Aelric made as if to follow, then stopped, frowning. He turned back to Caeden. "What was that all about, then?" he asked. There was nothing untoward in the question or his demeanor, but Caeden could sense the underlying tension.

Caeden gave an awkward shrug. "The princess offered to show me around the palace."

Aelric scowled openly now. "That's not what I meant." His eyes narrowed. "Yesterday she could barely stand the sight of you. Now she's talking to you like you're her best friend?" Caeden breathed a sigh of relief. It at least sounded as if Aelric had not seen Karaliene's hand on his arm, however brief the contact had been.

Caeden gestured, indicating ignorance. "I don't know why she changed her mind."

Aelric stared at him for a few seconds in silence. "Very well," he said eventually, "but let me make this clear." He leaned forward, lowering his voice. "If I find out you're using some sort of Augur power to influence her, I will end this." He looked conflicted. "I have no wish to see you harmed, Caeden. I believe that there is something...special about you. But if it means protecting Karaliene, I won't hesitate to tell Elocien and the king about you."

Without anything further, he spun on his heel and stalked off, leaving Caeden to stare after him worriedly.

# Chapter 44

Davian's stomach rumbled as he walked into the tavern.

The smell of stewing meat dragged him forward, despite his knowing he didn't have enough coin in his pocket to pay for it. He'd covered a lot of ground over the past week and now he estimated that at the same pace, he was only a few days away from Ilin Illan itself. Fortifying his body with Essence had given him stamina he'd once only dreamed of; whenever he began to tire, he simply drew more from the world around him. He'd slept twice since leaving Deilannis, both times only briefly, and more because he was worried about the effects of staying awake for so long than because he needed to.

The one thing Essence hadn't been able to do, however, was stop him from being hungry. His stomach growled again, sucking at his insides. He glanced around. The village was small and so was the tavern; there were only a few patrons tonight, mostly farmers from the looks of them.

"Evening, friend." A pretty girl planted herself in front of him. "Can I help you?"

Davian winced. He knew how he looked—disheveled, clothes ragged, a pack on his back that was clearly empty. More like a potential thief than a customer.

"I'm out of coin," he admitted. "But I'm willing to work for a meal. Anything you need doing. You don't have to feed me until after I'm done, but—"

"That's fine." The girl's expression softened. "We'll work something out later. You look exhausted. Take a seat and I'll see what Cook has to spare."

Davian gave her a grateful smile in return. The girl was striking, with long legs and green eyes that shone in the firelight. For a second she seemed almost familiar...though he couldn't say of whom she reminded him.

He collapsed into the nearest chair, relieved to rest despite knowing he didn't need it. It wasn't too long before the serving girl was back, placing a large plate of steaming meat and vegetables in front of him.

Davian looked at it in astonishment; at the few places that had been willing to trade food for work, the meals had been stingy at best. "I can't tell you how much I appreciate this," he said sincerely.

"Times being what they are, we can all use a little help."

Davian nodded, his expression serious. He'd heard about the invaders at the first big town he'd come across after Deilannis, and had pushed himself hard ever since. He had abilities now—a way to help Wirr and the others, help fight whatever was coming from the Boundary. He had to get to Ilin Illan before it was too late.

"Any word on the invasion?" he asked between mouthfuls.

"Folk are saying King Andras has sent out troops, but...a lot of people are getting out of the city." The girl flashed him a pretty smile, sliding into the chair opposite him.

Davian paused midmouthful, suddenly aware of just how attractive the girl was. Her tight-fitting outfit showed off her full figure to good effect, and he forced himself to focus on his plate as she leaned forward.

"That's good the king is sending troops," he said, a little distracted. Then he remembered his vision, the one from Deilannis, and grimaced. "Hopefully."

"Hopefully," agreed the girl with an easy smile, amusement dancing in her eyes. "I'm Ishelle. You can call me Shel."

"Nice to meet you, Shel. I'm Davin. Davian." Davian shook his head, flushing as he corrected himself. His mind was sluggish.

Ishelle's smile changed, and she looked...sad. "You don't remember me, do you?"

Davian frowned. He opened his mouth to ask what she was talking about, but suddenly his tongue felt thicker than usual, and the only sound that came out was an odd gurgling. He tried to focus on Ishelle's face, but everything was blurry.

With a rising panic, he realized the expression on her face had not been one of sadness. It had been one of guilt.

He tried to stand, but the hard wooden floor of the tavern rushed up to meet him.

Everything faded.

❦

Davian shook his head, then groaned at the motion.

His skull felt as though it were about to split in two, and movement only made matters worse. His mouth was dry and his eyelids gummed, but when he tried to move his hands to rub his face, he found that they were tied to his sides. He turned his head, looking around blearily from his position on the bed.

The room he was in was nondescript. The bed and a couple of chairs were the only pieces of furniture that he could see; the timber floors and walls were bare. A small window provided what little light there was, the illumination clearly originating from a street lamp, indicating that it was still night.

Vaguely he began recalling the events of earlier in the evening. Ishelle had clearly drugged him with something—why, he had no idea—but if she believed she could keep him tied up, then she was going to be surprised.

He closed his eyes, reaching out with kan. There were sources of Essence everywhere—including people—but he chose to draw it from the fire that burned in the kitchen. He needed only a little, not even enough to extinguish the flames.

He solidified the Essence, made it razor sharp, and then sliced through his bonds, grimacing as he remembered where he'd learned that trick. Once free he stood and stretched muscles stiff from disuse, feeling almost casual as he surveyed his surroundings.

Absently he realized he had a Shackle around his arm. It made little difference to him—it stopped him only from drawing Essence from within, something he couldn't do anyway—but it was an irritation. He concentrated for a moment, intrigued. The Shackle was just a layer of kan, containing Essence within the body. Of course. He pushed at the metal on his arm with kan for a few moments, experimenting. The Shackle suddenly retracted, falling to the floor with a clatter.

He grinned to himself.

He strode to the door, drawing a little more Essence from the fireplace to ease the ache in his muscles. Immediately they felt looser, stronger. He reached for the door handle.

"Very impressive," came a voice from behind him.

He spun, ready to defend himself. A man stood in the corner of the room; Davian was certain he had not been there a moment before.

"Who are you?" Davian drew in the remaining Essence from the fire, as well as a little from the heat of the kettle that had been boiling atop it. Not much, but enough to do some damage if required. "Why did you take me prisoner?"

The man smiled. "Prisoner?" He sighed. "I must apologize for Ishelle's . . . less than subtle method of delaying you. She had strict instructions to keep you here until I arrived. I'm afraid she was a little overzealous."

Davian scowled. "You haven't answered my question."

The man sighed again. "My name is Driscin Throll. I am an Elder from Tol Shen," he said, offering his hand. When Davian didn't shake it, he dropped it with an impatient roll of his eyes. "You're not a prisoner. You are here for me to make you an offer, nothing more. All I ask is that you hear what I have to say, and then you may continue on your journey."

Davian gave him a suspicious glare. "Very well." He concentrated, pushing through kan and searching out Driscin's mind. He would find out exactly what this man intended before he agreed to anything.

As he stretched out, though, he found himself blocked by an invisible barrier. He frowned, probing the shield, trying to push past it, but it was no use. Driscin's mind was being protected by another source of kan.

Driscin saw the surprise on his face and smiled. "As I said before. Impressive," he said thoughtfully. He glanced toward the door. "You can show yourself now, Shel."

Davian turned, expecting to see the door swing open. Instead there was a shimmering in the air, like a mirage in the desert; in an instant Ishelle stood before them, having seemingly appeared from nowhere. Davian took a half step back.

"Haven't seen that one?" the young woman asked with a cheeky grin.

Davian's eyes widened. "You're an Augur?" It was the only thing that made sense. Essence alone couldn't make someone invisible, he was certain. Ishelle must have been using kan somehow. She'd been the reason he couldn't Read Driscin, too, no doubt.

"Surprise," said Ishelle.

Davian stared at her for a moment. "You drugged me," he said, his tone accusatory. His head was beginning to clear of the effects of whatever she had given him, but he was still a little foggy.

Ishelle's expression changed to something approaching apologetic. "I had to make sure you didn't go anywhere. Driscin was only a few hours away, but you have a nasty habit of disappearing for long periods of time."

Driscin waved his hand dismissively. "We'll get to that later," he said. "Suffice it to say, we know who you are, Davian."

Davian leaned forward. "And who is 'we'?" He focused on the strange man. He'd know if they lied to him, at least, even if they tried to mask it.

"The sig'nari. You might know of us as the Prefects," replied Driscin. "We serve the Augurs, are their eyes and ears, carry out their wishes. And search out new Augurs, when they appear."

Davian's eyebrows rose. "The sig'nari?" he said dubiously. "I've heard this story before."

"It's the truth," supplied Ishelle. "I'd heard rumors about them for years before they found me."

"At the beginning of the Unseen War, we went into hiding," continued Driscin. "But we kept watch. We waited. When one Augur dies, another is born within a few years; that is the cycle. So we knew that on that night, when the war began, new Augurs would soon be brought into the world. We have been vigilant ever since."

Davian frowned. "Let's say I believe you, at least for the moment. How did you find me?"

"Talmiel." Driscin watched him closely. "A man there of...somewhat unsavory repute helped two young boys across the border into Desriel. He robbed them, but immediately afterward he collapsed. Almost died. Three days later he awoke with no memory of the incident at all, and two years of his life missing into the bargain." Driscin shrugged. "Talmiel is a superstitious town at the best of times. Word spread, and one of my men heard the tale. From there we managed to piece together your journey as far as Thrindar."

Davian grunted. "And after that?"

"I found you," spoke up Ishelle.

"Shel has an unusual gift, even for an Augur. One touch, and she can know where someone is for the rest of their life," explained Driscin.

Davian stared at the young woman. "I remember you," he said suddenly, eyes widening. "The girl from the market. I bumped into you, knocked you over." Ishelle smiled, and Davian sighed. "Or so it seemed."

Ishelle leaned forward. "I tracked you all the way to Deilannis, but once you entered the city it was like you just...vanished. We knew you were on your way to Andarra so I waited here, assuming you'd come along this road eventually." She scowled. "Waited here, in this backwater village, for a month. A *month*. I was only days away from leaving when I felt you again." Her eyes narrowed as she stared at him. "How did you do it? I've never had *anyone* disappear from my tracking before."

"Maybe I'm just special," said Davian.

Ishelle narrowed her eyes at him and he restrained a smile, relaxing a little. Whatever their methods, he was beginning to believe that these people had no intention of harming him.

Davian leaned back. "So how many Augurs have you found thus far?"

Driscin shifted. "Including you and Ishelle? Two." He held up his hand. "Understand, this is no easy task. It was difficult enough back when the Augurs were ruling; it's a thousand times harder now that the Treaty exists."

"I suppose I can see that," Davian conceded. He crossed his arms. "So. You were going to make me an offer."

"Come with us." It was Ishelle, her voice pleading. "Help me find others like us, Davian. We can teach them; we can teach each other."

Davian shook his head. "To what end?"

"This invasion came from Talan Gol," said Driscin seriously. "We don't know much about it yet, but it seems clear the Boundary is weakening. Without the Augurs there will be no way to strengthen it against whatever threats are beyond."

Davian hesitated. "And I do want to help with that," he admitted, "but the invasion hadn't started when I was in Thrindar." Driscin wasn't lying, but he clearly wasn't telling Davian everything, either.

"True," said Driscin. "I suppose that has been a more recent shift in our focus. Originally our aim was simply to gather the Augurs—to keep them hidden from Administration, let them learn from one another. Then to eventually pave the way in the Assembly for the Treaty to be changed. Maybe have the Augurs return to a semblance of power one day." He shrugged. "Ultimately that's still our goal."

Davian stared at Driscin in bemusement, thinking back to some of his conversations with Wirr. "I don't know much about politics, but that doesn't sound like something that could happen anytime soon. Maybe not in my lifetime," he said quietly.

"It was always a long-term plan," admitted Driscin, unfazed by Davian's pessimism. "But as it happens, this invasion may have changed that. Thousands have died, and as awful as that is, it has also reminded people of how important the Gifted are."

He leaned forward. "The way the king has been acting towards us over these past few weeks is starting to make people nervous—it's shining a light on the fact that Andarra's most powerful weapon, its best defense, could be made impotent by one man's prejudice. When all this is over, I guarantee that there will be an argument for changing that—renewed support for the Tols both in the Assembly and amongst the people. Andarra may not like us, but they are beginning to recognize our value. And the more that happens, the more sway we will have."

Davian gave a slow nod. "That's good for Tol Shen...it doesn't mean anyone will feel differently towards the Augurs, though," he noted.

"When we tell everyone that the Augurs are the only ones who can seal the Boundary, I suspect that may change, too," said Driscin. "It should be enough to have the Treaty amended, to remove the ban. That's more progress than we could have dreamed of a few months ago."

Davian leaned back, heart rate increasing a little as he assessed what Driscin was saying. Much still had to go right, but he couldn't see any flaws in the logic. It *was* possible. "And if that happens, you want the Augurs to be overseen by Tol Shen. You want *me* to join Tol Shen," he concluded after a moment, enthusiasm suddenly waning again.

Driscin nodded. "The Athian and Shen Councils are too at odds to work together on something like this, and any association with Athian is political poison at the moment. The Augurs need to be unified, allied with somebody...reliable, if the Assembly is to ever take them seriously. Tol Shen is the only realistic option."

Davian shook his head, unable to hide his reluctance. It all seemed perfectly reasonable—and yet he knew Tol Shen's reputation. They were power hungry, manipulative. The idea of their exerting any measure of control over a group of Augurs, over him, made him uncomfortable.

"No," he said after a moment. He glanced at Ishelle. "Once these invaders have been defeated, I will work with you to fix the Boundary—but that's all. I don't want to join Shen."

Ishelle rolled her eyes. "Because we're all evil, I assume?" she said, sounding more amused than annoyed. "That's what they teach you in Athian, isn't it—that Tol Shen is more interested in power than what's right, while every single Gifted from Tol Athian is a shining beacon of the standards of El himself?"

Driscin spoke up before Davian could respond, making a calming gesture in Ishelle's direction. "You've grown up in an Athian school, and you're reluctant. I understand." He rubbed his forehead. "If you are concerned about the types of people you associate with, though, perhaps you should take another look at your friend Taeris Sarr before coming to a decision."

Davian flushed. "You're talking about what he did three years ago? That's a poor example to choose, Elder Throll. I was the boy he rescued—he saved my life by killing those men. Hardly a black mark against him in my book."

Driscin shook his head. "But you don't know the whole story," he said quietly. "Haven't you ever wondered where you came from? Before the school, I mean."

Davian stared at the Elder, puzzled. "Of course I have."

"We think that Taeris knows," said Driscin. "What we *do* know is that he is the one who brought you to Caladel as a child, who dropped you at the school's doorstep. He's followed you, followed your progress your entire life. It was no coincidence that he found you in Desriel, nor that he was there that day three years ago."

Davian shook his head again. "He would have told me something like that," he said, with more confidence than he felt.

"There's more," said Driscin. "He *set up* that encounter in Caladel, Davian. He told those men you were from the school. He *wanted* them to attack you, so that you would be forced to defend yourself, to discover you had powers."

Davian scowled, his head spinning. "I don't believe that." It couldn't be true—though there was no black smoke, nor any pain in his temples to indicate Driscin was lying. Davian snorted, ignoring the sudden sick feeling in the pit of his stomach. "How could you possibly have information like that?"

Ishelle shifted. "You surely didn't think I'd miss the opportunity to Read you and your companions, back at Thrindar? There wasn't time to get everything from him, but Taeris was far too preoccupied with finding a way out of Desriel to worry about shielding himself." Her lips curled upward. "I know what you were thinking when you bumped into me, too, by the way." She winked at him, and he felt himself blush furiously.

Davian took a few seconds to recover, then shook his head. "No. Either you're mistaken, or this is some sort of trick. Taeris isn't like that."

Driscin sighed as he saw Davian's defiant expression. "Perhaps this is something you need to resolve for yourself."

"And how can I do that, exactly?"

"Ask him." Ishelle stepped forward, placing her hand on his

shoulder. "You know how to see whether people are deceiving you—I've watched you do it for the last few minutes. You *know* we're not lying to you, Davian. You owe it to yourself to at least find out if we're right."

Davian gritted his teeth; he still wanted to argue the point, but he knew it would just look as if he were being unreasonable. "No matter what I find, it won't change my mind about Tol Shen," he said, a little defensively now.

"I don't understand. Where else would you go?" Ishelle crossed her arms. "You don't know anyone at Tol Athian, even if they were willing to take you in. The only other survivor from your school was Torin Andras, and you can be certain he won't be spending his time around the Gifted."

"How did you..." Davian trailed off, grimacing. "Oh. Well, if you know that, then you know we're friends. I can do more by working with Wirr—Torin—than I could by joining Tol Shen, anyway."

Driscin shook his head. "Don't delude yourself on that front, lad," he said, his tone gentle. "He's a prince of the realm, the Northwarden's son. You might be friends, but whatever passed between you at the school, don't imagine you're equals. Even if he wants to welcome you at the palace gates with open arms, he won't be able to."

Davian frowned. "Meaning?"

"Meaning if you stay in the city to aid Prince Torin, you'll be forever hiding, living your life in the shadows. It will be years before he can afford to be publicly associated with an Augur, regardless of how soon the Treaty is changed. Years before he can acknowledge your existence." He looked at Davian with a serious expression. "Your influence would be limited at best. It would be a waste of your talents."

Davian gave Driscin an angry stare. The Elder's argument was sound, but it wasn't what Davian wanted to hear. He'd assumed that once he made it to Ilin Illan, made contact with Wirr, things would work out somehow. That he'd find a way to stay, to help the only friend he had left.

Driscin sighed as he watched Davian's expression. "You are not convinced—that's fine; perhaps we can change your mind in time. You at least agree that the Boundary needs to be sealed?"

Davian nodded slowly. "Yes."

"Good." Driscin stood. "Then do what you must, for now—go to Ilin Illan, help where you can. But think about what I've told you—and once these invaders are defeated, come and find me at Tol Shen. If you still want only to seal the Boundary and return to Ilin Illan, then there will be no pressure to join us permanently. You have my word."

He nodded to Davian, then gave Ishelle a tight smile. Without further pleasantries he left the room.

There was a long silence as Davian and Ishelle looked at each other awkwardly.

"Am I free to leave?" asked Davian eventually, his irritation at the way he'd been treated bubbling to the surface again, making him sound ruder than he meant to be.

Ishelle held up her hands in mock defense. "You are. But I thought perhaps a full stomach might make you a little less prickly," she said, with a smile to show she was only teasing. She gestured to some buttered bread on a tray next to the bed. "You must be hungry. You should eat."

Davian gave the tray a mistrustful glance.

Ishelle laughed as she saw his expression. "Nothing unusual in the bread. I swear it."

Davian thought about refusing the offer, but at that moment his stomach growled. He hadn't eaten since the small amount of drugged food he'd managed to ingest. And it would look petty. And he might not get another opportunity to eat properly until he reached Ilin Illan.

Scowling, he took a cautious bite of the bread. When he was still able to move his arms and legs satisfactorily, he wolfed down the rest, all the while watching Ishelle with a wary expression. Despite her apparently having intended him no harm, he couldn't bring himself to trust her again so soon.

He finished, wiping his mouth with his sleeve. "I'll be on my way," he said, standing. "I've wasted too much time as it is."

Ishelle frowned. "To Ilin Illan? Tonight? Surely you need some rest." She gestured to the bed. "You can have this room free of charge, if you like." She grinned, a dimple appearing in each cheek. "As compensation for being drugged."

"Thanks," said Davian in a wry tone, "but I don't need it."

Ishelle kept smiling, unfazed. "How about we make a deal. To show there are no hard feelings, at least take a free meal. A *proper* meal. No drugs. And my company for the evening."

Davian snorted. "You almost had me until the last part." Ishelle continued to smile at him cheerfully, and he wilted, sighing. A proper meal was too good to pass up. "Very well," he said reluctantly, making a weary gesture in the direction of the door. "Lead the way."

They made their way downstairs into the common room. The innkeeper, a short, rotund woman of middle age, was soon bringing them their meals. When Ishelle offered to pay, the innkeeper refused, insisting that Ishelle's coin was no good to her.

Ishelle shrugged at Davian's questioning glance. "I've been here a month. She likes me."

"Your knowing exactly what she's thinking has helped, I'm sure," observed Davian. He'd seen the thin lines of kan stretching from Ishelle to the innkeeper. Minute, almost unnoticeable, but definitely there. His new companion had been Reading her.

"Nothing wrong with that."

Davian snorted, shaking his head. Malshash had been clear about this, but it was barely more than common sense. Common decency.

Ishelle looked at him with genuine surprise. "You disagree?"

Davian gave an emphatic nod. "Yes. These people...*regular* people, they have no way of defending themselves against us. What right do we have to go prying inside their most personal thoughts?"

Ishelle shook her head. "You haven't Read many people, have you? Most of them deserve everything that's coming to them." She sighed, waving away his scowl. "Don't pout. I'm not asking you to do it."

Their meals arrived, and the two began eating. They were silent for a while, then Davian paused as he saw Ishelle looking at him with a curious expression. She smiled, leaning back and dabbing at her mouth with her napkin. "So tell me about Caladel," she said. She waved her hand impatiently as Davian gave her a wary look. "Not the attack; I know all about that. What was it like, growing up in an Athian school?" She shook her head. "I always thought it would be so...boring."

Davian sucked in his breath; it stung to hear the destruction of the school mentioned so flippantly. "I'd prefer not to talk about it," he said, trying unsuccessfully to keep the stiffness from his voice.

Ishelle grimaced when she saw his expression. Her shoulders slumped a little.

"I'm sorry," she said after a few awkward moments. "I know I can be...blunt. Driscin says I rely on my abilities so much, I don't really know how to talk to people anymore. Maybe he's right."

Davian hesitated. She sounded...uncomfortable. Genuinely embarrassed.

He paused for a few more seconds, then sighed, leaning forward.

"It wasn't boring." He took a mouthful of food, chewing as he thought. He swallowed. "There was always a lot to do. Studying, practicing." He scratched his head. "Sometimes we got sent outside of the school to run errands."

Ishelle raised an eyebrow. "I think you and I have different definitions of 'boring,'" she said with a gently mocking smile. Despite that, Davian thought he could detect a hint of gratitude in her tone.

He shook his head in chagrin. "I'm not explaining it very well. My friends were there," he clarified. "It was...simple. The school was my home. It may sound monotonous—it *was* monotonous, I suppose—but for the most part, I loved my life there." With another twinge of sadness, he realized just how true that statement was.

Ishelle shook her head. "I cannot imagine being forced to stay in the one place all those years," she admitted. "It sounds like just another prison, barely any different from what the Tols must have been like during the sieges. Essence and kan are both dull unless you can go out into the real world and actually *use* them."

Davian leaned forward, glad of the shift in conversation. "I take it you aren't a student at one of Shen's schools, then—you never got the Mark? Because if you had, there wouldn't have been much choice in the matter," he added drily.

"No, thank the fates." Ishelle gave him a half-apologetic shrug. "I work in the kitchens at Tol Shen, when I'm not out with Driscin trying to find other Augurs. But Driscin always made sure I didn't draw enough Essence to be bound by the Tenets." Ishelle frowned. "You did, though, I take it?"

Davian hesitated, then nodded. "I don't remember it, but... yes." He fell silent as he thought about that day, thought about what Driscin had told him earlier. He had a sudden urge to ask Ishelle exactly what she'd seen when she had Read Taeris... but he knew that whatever the answer, he wouldn't believe a word of it until he spoke to Taeris himself.

The moment passed, and Ishelle evidently sensed that Davian didn't want to speak further on the subject. The conversation turned to lighter things as they ate, and for a while Davian actually found himself relaxing.

Soon enough, though, their plates were cleared and he remembered the long journey he had ahead. He sighed. He still mistrusted Ishelle, but the meal *had* been a pleasant respite from the road. "I should go soon," he observed. "Before I do, though—is there anything else you can tell me about this invasion?"

Ishelle shrugged; it might have been Davian's imagination, but he thought he saw a flash of disappointment on her face. "The Andarran army was about to meet the invaders, last I heard. Hopefully that will be the end of it."

Davian shook his head. "No. A while back, I... saw something. The invaders, camped outside Ilin Illan. That's why I'm trying to get back there. If there is going to be a siege, they will need all the help they can get." He raised an eyebrow at her. "You could come. Two of us could make a real difference."

Ishelle hesitated. "No," she said slowly. "I don't think that's for me."

Davian grunted but nodded, having not really expected a different response. "Have you heard if the king is going to change the First Tenet, to let the Gifted fight?"

Ishelle shook her head. "Nothing beyond what Driscin said earlier. King Andras has made some strong statements against the Gifted in the past few weeks... if those are anything to go by, it's not likely." Her eyes narrowed. "You *have* been isolated, haven't you? Tell me, Davian, in truth. Where did you disappear to? How did you do it?" Her eyes burned bright with curiosity.

Davian grimaced; he had no desire to talk about Deilannis. He could see the determination in Ishelle's eyes, though—her desire to know how he'd escaped her for so long.

He quickly came to a decision. "Let's trade. If you tell me how to make myself invisible, I'll tell you how I avoided your tracking."

Ishelle considered for a moment. "You first."

Davian smiled, knowing he had her hooked. "Not a chance."

"Nothing else you want to know more?"

"Invisibility," Davian replied in a firm tone.

Ishelle sighed. "Very well." She played with her hair idly. "It's not terribly difficult, once you get the hang of it. Encase yourself in a kan shield, but rather than have the kan absorb Essence, make it redirect it—a little like when you draw it out of the environment, I suppose. Bend it around yourself, so it's as if the Essence is passing through empty space." She grinned. "It was an accident, to be honest. Driscin and I were testing ways of deflecting attacks one day, and surprise!" She made a dramatic gesture. "Driscin nearly had a heart attack."

Davian smiled. "I can only imagine."

Ishelle grinned. "Driscin thinks it works by bending the light," she continued. "The Essence drags it around the shield, rather than letting it through."

Davian glanced around at the other occupants of the room. "I probably shouldn't test it right now," he said regretfully.

"Try it on an object. Something small so no one notices," suggested Ishelle.

Davian gave her an approving look, then concentrated. He covered his bowl in a tight mesh of kan, then altered its properties so that it redirected Essence as Ishelle had suggested. Nothing happened; Davian adjusted the hardness of the kan a little, making it act almost like a mirror.

The bowl wavered in front of him, then vanished.

Davian's eyes widened, and he felt himself grinning. "This could be useful," he mused.

Ishelle beamed. "You have no idea," she said with a wink. She leaned forward. "Your turn."

Davian looked her in the eye. "I've changed my mind, actually."

Ishelle gaped at him for several seconds.

"You lied to me?" she eventually choked out in quiet, outraged disbelief.

"Fair is fair," replied Davian cheerfully. "You should have been checking. And anyway, you drugged me. I think we might be even now."

Ishelle stared at him, caught in a mixture of shock, annoyance, and amused chagrin. "You're serious. You're not going to tell me."

Davian shrugged. "Perhaps we can make a new deal. I'll tell you if you come to Ilin Illan."

Ishelle looked at him through narrowed eyes. "Tempting, if I thought you would hold up your end of the bargain." She shook her head, smile rueful. "I suppose I'll just have to wait until Tol Shen to get it out of you, then." She hesitated, looking him in the eye, suddenly serious. "Speaking of which. You *are* going to come, aren't you?"

Davian inclined his head. "As soon as this invasion has been defeated—but as I said, it will just be until we figure out how to seal the Boundary." They both stood. "Thank you for the meal," Davian added sincerely.

Ishelle nodded. "Thank you for the company," she said with a small smile, apparently willing to forgive his deception. "And keep safe. I don't want you dying until I get that answer from you." She nodded toward the stairs. "If you change your mind about staying the night, you can have the room upstairs. First on the left. It's paid for until tomorrow, and I thought you might like somewhere familiar to sleep."

She flashed a pretty smile at him and, before he could respond, spun on her heel and disappeared out the door.

Davian stared after her for a moment, not sure whether to be irritated or amused.

He shook his head, but despite his best efforts he felt a small smile force its way onto his face.

Still smiling, he walked up the stairs to the room, then shut and locked the door behind him. He had no intention of staying the night, but before he left, he was going to take advantage of the lamplight and the comfortable bed.

He was going to keep searching through his book for information about Aarkein Devaed.

# Chapter 45

Davian lay on the bed, opening the book he had taken from the Great Library and flipping through to where he'd left off, rescanning the pages as he went for any clue as to why the Adviser had picked it out.

He was almost to the end of the thick tome, and thus far the book had been exactly what it had seemed—a collection of old fables, interesting enough but meaningless as far as he could tell. A few pages further on, though, a small picture at the beginning of one of the stories caught his eye. Frowning, he studied it carefully.

The image was of a soldier. Whereas most of the other drawings he'd seen in the book were rudimentary, even abstract, this one was detailed, as if the soldier had actually posed for the picture. The man's armor was shaded so that it had a dark aspect to it, but the headpiece was what caught Davian's eye. There were no gaps for eyes, and over the face a sole symbol was inscribed. Three *S* lines, drawn vertically, and circled.

The same symbol he'd seen in his vision.

Hands shaking slightly, he moved on to what was written beneath.

*Hail, king of traitors!*
*We who knew you mourn what was lost.*
*Only a shadow remains:*
*A whisper where once a shout,*
*A pond where once an ocean,*

*A flickering candle where once the sun itself.*
*Hail, king of corruption!*
*We who serve you despair for what is to come.*
*You will break the Oath,*
*You will shatter the Path,*
*You will sing the Song of Days as a dirge.*
*Your people will weep tears of ice and blood*
*And only the fallen will know peace.*

He flipped slowly to the beginning of the story and began to read.

## The Impossible Tasks of Alarais Shar

*(Translated from the original High Darecian)*

*In the Shining Lands, the immortal king Alarais Shar once reigned.*

*He was known as one of the great kings; perhaps the great king. He forged a treaty with the vicious northern Qui'tir. He led the final battle against the Darklands and was victorious, sealing their domain away from the mortal world forever. He was wise in his rulings, swift and decisive in dispensing justice, and beloved by his people.*

*Much was his immortality discussed. Steel could not pierce his skin; fire did not burn him, and his bones did not break. No one knew the source of his longevity, but of all the mages in the Shining Lands, he was the most powerful.*

*One day Alarais heard of a new power rising to the east, a king who had united the lands of Kal and Derethmar. He determined to seek out this new king. He hoped to discover an ally, but the reports he had heard of the new king's victories disturbed him greatly, and so he held out little hope.*

*He rode for many miles and eventually came to the great city of Kyste. Once beautiful and proud, the buildings now lay mostly in ruins, and the people stared blankly at Alarais as he rode by, their clothes little more than rags, their stomachs distended from lack of food. The dead lay in the street next to piles of refuse. Though they had been the Shining Lands' sworn enemies, Alarais wept when he saw what had befallen Kal's people.*

*By the time he reached the palace itself, Alarais was filled with a burning anger. His eyes blazed with righteous fury as he was led before the man who had conquered Kal, and who now did so little for its people.*

*The man on the throne of Kal was not what Alarais had expected. As a man he was impressive. Tall, strong, and handsome, the new king looked every inch a warrior, a hero. But as Alarais looked at him, he seemed to shimmer, to pulse and fade with a strange, otherworldly energy. He appeared more an ethereal being, an apparition rather than a mortal.*

*Still Alarais was unafraid, and what he had seen in the city was still fresh in his mind. He stood before the throne proudly, waiting for the king to address him, as was proper. But the shimmering man simply watched him, until Alarais could take the silence no longer.*

*"I am Alarais Shar, king of the Shining Lands." He paused, but the man on the throne said nothing. "I had come to see if a bond of friendship could be forged between our lands. But I have seen the state of Kyste. I have seen her people's suffering, and cannot fathom the reason for it. Why do you not help them?"*

*Still there was silence. Just when Alarais had determined to leave and return home, the shimmering man spoke. "I am Ghash, Seer of the White Temple, Herald of Shammaeloth. The ones of which you speak are beyond saving. This I have Seen."*

*"How can you say this?" cried Alarais in frustration.*

*"I have Seen the destruction of those who still live here," replied Ghash. "I have Seen what is to come. To help them now would be wasteful."*

*Alarais did not understand. "If you see their destruction, then why not save them?"*

*"Because what has been Seen cannot be undone. No efforts of yours or mine can change their fate."*

*"I cannot accept that," said Alarais stubbornly.*

*"And yet you must," said Ghash, "for I have long known your fate, too, Alarais Shar. The Shining Lands will fall, and you will come to serve me willingly. Together we are to conquer the world."*

Alarais laughed, and Ghash saw that he would not easily be convinced. "Allow me to prove what I say," he said. "I will set you three tasks. If you can complete any of the three, I will withdraw from these lands. If you cannot fulfill even one, though, you will serve me, and the Shining Lands shall be mine."

Alarais replied, "I cannot accept this challenge without first knowing what tasks you will set."

Ghash nodded. "So be it," he said. "Hear the tasks I would give you: first, to find a subject worthy of your kingship; second, to find a man worthy of your friendship; and third, to find a woman worthy of your love."

Alarais laughed. "These are weighty tasks indeed, mighty Ghash. How long might you wait for me to complete them?"

Ghash smiled. "I am like you, Alarais—untouched by time. Search for however long you need. I know you to be a man of honor. Once you know a task to be impossible, you will tell me. Until then I will not move against your realm." He paused. "I ask only that you speak of your quest to no one, including those whom you bring here. Should you do this, I will know, and will consider all three tasks to have been failed."

Alarais thought for a long time, but could not see any reason to refuse. "I accept," he said.

They bound the bargain in blood, and it was witnessed by Ghash's court under the Old Law.

Wasting no time, and confident of his success, Alarais returned to the Shining Lands full of hope. Many years passed, and Alarais finally found a man he thought more worthy a subject than any he had seen before: a warrior named Jadlis, fiercely loyal and brave. Alarais traveled with Jadlis back to Kyste, coming before Ghash, his spirits high.

"Mighty Ghash," he said, "I have successfully completed your first task. This man is named Jadlis. His skill is immense. His bravery is unquestionable. His loyalty is fierce and endless. He is a subject most worthy of my kingship."

Ghash examined Jadlis silently for some time, and Alarais's confidence grew within him. Then Ghash spoke.

"As king," he said to Alarais, "Would you be willing to die for your people?"

"Of course," replied Alarais. "As any good king would."

"Then your subjects should be willing to die for you, also."

Alarais hesitated. "Yes," he replied grimly.

Ghash turned to Jadlis. "You would die for your king?"

"I would," replied Jadlis proudly.

"And if he commanded you to die here and now?"

"Still." Jadlis was unmoved.

"Why?"

"For the love of my king. My country."

Ghash shook his head. "No. You would because the readiness to do so brings you glory—respect in the eyes of your friends, your fellow soldiers, even your king. To be unwilling to die would be traitorous, cowardly. You are willing to die, but you do not want to die. It is simply preferable to the shame. You would die because there is not a better choice."

"That is not true," said Jadlis stoically.

"But it is!" cried Ghash. "Yet what if I told you there was a better way? A choice, where you earned respect rather than shame for living?"

Jadlis frowned. "If it is better for my king that I die, then there is always shame in living."

Ghash smiled slyly. "Very well; here is my offer, Jadlis. Your king has been given a task. It matters not if you do not complete this task for him, for he may try again. To fulfill this task, though, he will ask you to sacrifice your own life."

"Then I will!" cried Jadlis.

Ghash held up his hand. "But what care has the king if he commands you to do this? Should he not love you as a subject, seek to keep you from harm if there is a better way? True—if you obey, then your king will have succeeded, and you will have died with honor." He paused. "But if you refuse his command, I will give to you these lands. I will make you king in your own right. Your wife will be your queen, your children your heirs. You can make peace with the Shining Lands, which I wish only to destroy. Men will honor you for your life, not your death." Ghash placed a hand on Jadlis's shoulder. "You fight to uphold the ideals of your king, and that is a fine lot. But you could be so much more. Do so much more. Your king chose you because of your worthiness, your honor. That is how I know there would be no better man as king of this realm."

Then Ghash turned to Alarais. "Now he knows what is at stake. Command him to kill himself."

Alarais shook his head. "I will not."

Ghash frowned. "There is no other way to fulfill this task. You are willing to make the ultimate sacrifice for your subjects. One worthy of your kingship must be willing to do the same."

Alarais's heart was heavy now, but he knew Ghash spoke truly. "Jadlis," he said quietly. "You are a true and loyal subject. I would ask that you take your life for this cause, for the sake of your king and the Shining Lands."

Jadlis thought for a long time, then shook his head. "I am sorry, my king, but he is right. I can do more for the Shining Lands by living," he said to Alarais. Then he turned to Ghash. "I accept your offer."

At those words he fell dead to the floor.

"The first task is failed," intoned Ghash. "The most loyal of your subjects refused your command, and so was unworthy of your kingship."

Alarais left without a word, disappointment and sorrow mixing a bitter taste in his mouth.

A hundred years passed, and eventually the pain of Alarais's first defeat faded. He met a young man named Diadan, a noble of the Shining Lands who came into his inheritance early through tragic circumstances. With no family, Diadan had come to Alarais for advice on how to manage his affairs.

Alarais was first a mentor to Diadan, then, after a few years, a true friend. Despite Alarais's many years his body had never aged, so he rarely found someone young enough to stay with him on the hunt and in dueling, but intelligent and wise enough to hold his interest in conversation. Yet Diadan excelled in all these areas, and proved himself many times over to be a loyal and trustworthy friend, never seeking to betray Alarais's trust for his own ends. Alarais presided at Diadan's wedding, and Diadan became the king's right hand.

Time passed. After thirty years of unwavering friendship, Alarais decided that Diadan was the man to fulfill the second task. The two men journeyed to Kyste and came before Ghash.

"Mighty Ghash," said Alarais, "I bring before you a man with whom I have a bond stronger than stone. A man to whom I would entrust my life, and who I know would do the same to me. A man my equal in honor, in courage. My friend. This is Diadan."

Ghash considered Diadan silently. "This is the one you would put forward to fulfill your second task?"

"Yes," replied Alarais.

Ghash turned to Diadan. "Your friendship with Alarais is strong."

Diadan nodded. "He is my brother in all but blood."

"And yet," pointed out Ghash, "not by blood. He ages not. You do."

"That is true," acceded Diadan. "I cannot keep pace with him as once I did. But that is our lot. I no more resent him his eternal youth than he resents me my looks." He gave Alarais a grin.

"I speak not of resentment," said Ghash softly. "I speak of something a man, any man, may wish for. The chance to be young again, to be forever in the prime of his life. To attain knowledge and wisdom but never have his body fail. To have the vitality and strength that an aging body can never summon. If I offered you this gift, freely and without condition, would you take it?"

Diadan did not pause. "I would," he said.

Ghash nodded, then turned to Alarais. "I know your heart, Alarais. Advise him as a friend, and see if he trusts you as a friend."

Alarais groaned inwardly. Long had Diadan yearned for just this thing, and many times they had talked of what it *meant. It was, perhaps, the one thing they had never truly agreed on. "Diadan, my friend," Alarais said earnestly, "we have often talked of my long youth. You know the pain it has wrought me. I see those I love wither and die; you would see the same for your wife Siana, your children, your grandchildren. There are some pains and failures I still remember from a thousand years ago, clear as if they were yesterday. I beg of you, though I know your heart and how tempting it must be. Do not accept this gift."*

*Diadan heard the words of his friend, yet, as before, they made little sense to him. "But Alarais, think of it! We could ride as when I was young. We could adventure together once again. The deaths of those I love would hurt, yet we would still have the chance to spend the entire span of their lives together. That alone is worth the price!"*

*Alarais saw which way his friend was deciding, and thought to warn him. He made to cry out, but Ghash raised his hand, and all words fled from Alarais's lips.*

*Diadan turned to Ghash, his face glowing with excitement. "I accept your offer," he said.*

*At those words he fell dead to the floor.*

*"The second task is failed," intoned Ghash. "The greatest of your friends refused your advice, and so was unworthy of your friendship."*

*Alarais dropped to his knees and wept for his dead friend. Then he left Kyste without saying another word, the burden on his heart almost too heavy to bear.*

*For generations Alarais mourned the death of his friend. The final task weighed on him, and yet he knew that Ghash would know if he simply stopped trying to fulfill it. So he searched, but was never satisfied. A thousand beautiful, intelligent, interesting, honorable women passed through his court each year, but he found none of them more special than the others. The price of immortality on love was too high, the pain too great. Only for a great love would he take such a risk. Alarais had never wed for exactly this reason.*

*Five hundred years passed, and Alarais met Teravia, the Shard Princess. Few women Alarais had ever seen could* match her beauty, and yet it was her wit that drew him to her, and her warmth and kindness that slowly turned his heart. She was wise with the purity of innocence, witty but never mean-spirited, charming but never ingratiating. And beyond all that, above all, she loved Alarais. Not just as a powerful king, an honorable warrior, an intelligent strategist. She loved him as a man, with all his faults and failings. And he loved her in return.

Their wedding was celebrated throughout all the Shining Lands.

Their marriage was the stuff of legend. Teravia was beloved by the people of the Shining Lands; as queen she was as wise as her husband, and a time of unprecedented peace lay across the realm. Alarais had never been happier than when he was with Teravia.

It was a great love, a true love, and yet Alarais did not tell Teravia about the third task. He did not ask her to accompany him to Kyste to see Ghash. Diadan's death—and Jadlis's before him—still weighed on his mind, and the thought of losing Teravia was more than he could bear. And so he waited, telling himself each year that he would try the next.

Sixty years passed, and Teravia became gravely ill. The country ground to a halt as word spread of the queen's sickness, with every man, woman, and child hoping against hope that she would be miraculously healed.

Her time drawing to a close, Teravia met with her friends, then her children, to bid them farewell. Finally the only one left was Alarais, who knelt by her bed holding her hand. Even aged, even on her deathbed, she was beautiful.

Teravia smiled when she saw him. "Husband," she whispered, "why do you look so sad?"

And so he told her. About Ghash and the three tasks. About Diadan and his failure. As Alarais spoke, Teravia's smile turned to a look of pain and sorrow.

"Why did you not take me to see Ghash, all these years?" she asked. "Do you not think our love is true?"

"Our love is more than true. It is a great love," said Alarais, tears in his eyes. "But I was afraid. Afraid of losing *you before your time, as I lost my friend Diadan."* He closed his eyes. *"This burden I could not have borne."*

Teravia looked on her husband sadly, squeezing his hand. *"You should have trusted me,"* she whispered. *"I would not have failed you, my love."*

Her grip loosened and her gaze faded. With those words Teravia, Last Queen of the Shining Lands, passed on.

Alarais looked on her and wept bitter tears, for he knew in his selfishness he had not only lost his chance to prove Ghash wrong, but left Teravia believing she had not had his trust.

When his eyes cleared, he was before Ghash in Kyste once again. How he had come to be there, he did not know.

*"You have broken our agreement, Alarais. You spoke of our accord to another."*

Alarais nodded. *"I did."*

Ghash leaned back. *"Yet she is dead. I will overlook your mistake, should you wish it."*

Alarais shook his head. *"I finally found a woman worthy of my love,"* he said softly, *"only to discover I was not worthy of hers."* He straightened. *"I concede to you, mighty Ghash. You spoke the truth; the tasks you set me were impossible. I will serve you as you see fit. The Shining Lands are yours."* He spoke truly, for his spirit, and his heart, were broken.

Ghash rose from his throne, eyes burning. *"It is done!"* he proclaimed joyfully. He fitted Alarais in the black armor of Telesthaesia and charged him to lead his army against the Shining Lands.

Alarais did as he was commanded, slaughtering those he had once sworn to protect. The Shining Lands, without a king and facing a force unlike any they had ever seen, fell swiftly into chaos and destruction.

So ends the story of the Impossible Tasks of Alarais Shar.

Davian stared at the book thoughtfully for several minutes.

It had made no mention of Aarkein Devaed; if it had not been for the picture at the beginning, he would not have thought this story had anything to do with Devaed at all. Was Alarais Shar actually Aarkein Devaed? Or was Ghash? Or had he made a mistake by picturing the symbol when using the Adviser, leading himself to a book that held no useful information at all? He gritted his teeth in frustration.

He read the story again, but gleaned no more from it than the first time. Finally, reluctantly, he snapped the book shut, drew some Essence from the lamp, and got to his feet.

He'd probably have time to examine it again, and read the remainder of the stories in the book, once he reached Ilin Illan.

For now, though, he needed to keep moving.

# Chapter 46

Asha gaped a little as she entered the ballroom.

She'd never been in this part of the palace before. A vaulted ceiling held thousands of tiny crystal lanterns that reflected softly off the polished black marble floor, highlighting the dazzling designs of inlaid white marble and gold. Tables lined the enormous room, each filled with gleaming silver platters and goblets. Arched stained-glass windows let in the last of dusk's light; these depicted various scenes—battles, moments from legend—in stunning color and detail.

"Impressive, isn't it?" murmured Michal from next to her.

Asha nodded. "It is, but...they still shouldn't be going ahead with this. Not now," she said quietly as they were ushered to their seats. She rubbed her forehead, trying not to sound bitter. "I just don't understand why everyone is trying to hide from what's happening."

Michal was silent for a few seconds, then glanced at her sideways. "You're not just talking about tonight, are you?"

"No." They'd had a meeting at Tol Athian earlier that day, in which Elder Eilinar had informed them that if the Tenets were not changed, they would not be joining in the defense of the city. "The Gifted could make a real difference healing the wounded in a battle. I understand that they're angry, that they feel like they're being asked to go out and fight without any way to defend themselves. But to hide in Tol Athian while the city gets attacked is just..." She shook her head in frustration.

Michal gave her a reassuring smile. "I actually agree, but it's not going to come to that. General Jash'tar and his forces will have dealt with the Blind soon enough. And if for some reason they do not, I'm sure the king will reconsider." He shrugged. "As for tonight, the Northwarden is perfectly within his rights to celebrate the return of his only son."

Michal glanced around, then lowered his voice. "Besides, I suspect the king will use it as an excuse to show himself in public. Quiet all these rumors that have been swirling about him."

Asha sighed, but didn't argue further. She gazed around at the people already filling the room, every one clad in finery that made her new red dress look almost shabby by comparison. She recognized many of them; some she'd met in her role as Representative, and others Michal had previously pointed out. There were plenty of minor Houses, as always—si'Bandin, si'Dres, and si'Kal were all near her table, laughing and drinking. The Great Houses—Tel'Rath, Tel'Shan, Tel'An, and Tel'Esh—were all well represented, too, but their lords seemed less jovial.

She took a deep breath, letting some of her frustration fade into the background as she focused on her surroundings. "The Great Houses," she said softly to Michal. "They don't usually speak together so publicly, do they?"

Michal followed her gaze. "No," he said, frowning. "They don't usually speak together at all."

Asha watched for a moment longer, then glanced over with interest at the king's table. Princess Karaliene was already there, as were a couple of others she did not recognize. As she watched, Dras Lothlar, the Gifted adviser from Shen, came and sat only two seats away from Karaliene. The princess shot him an angry look, but Lothlar ignored it.

"We've done better than I expected, being seated here," murmured Michal. They had people seated either side of them, but the chatter of the crowd was loud enough that no one would be able to overhear. He shot a dark look at the king's table. "Though I could say the same for Shen. Something odd is going on there, mark my words."

"The princess wasn't too happy to see Representative Lothlar sitting there," said Asha.

"I saw that. Ionis didn't look pleased, either. Though that's not really a surprise." Michal made a discreet gesture to where the tall, severe-looking Administrator was sitting.

At that moment a horn sounded and the room quickly fell silent, all eyes turning to the king's table. Introductions were made by a herald and everyone rose as King Andras himself entered; though Asha didn't think the king looked as sick as some people had claimed, he did seem pallid, almost fragile as he walked. As if he were much older than his fifty years.

Behind him came the duke, regal in his formal attire, even his fine blue cloak for once looking far more for show than practical. He was followed by Wirr—or Torin, as she now had to think of him. Even after their afternoon together a few days earlier, she almost didn't recognize her friend; he was as finely attired as his father and looked self-assured as he came to a stop at the seat of honor, to the right of the king.

"You and everyone else," whispered a voice in her ear.

She started, turning to see the young woman sitting next to her giving her a conspiratorial grin.

"Sorry?" said Asha.

The girl gestured toward the king's table. "Our young prince. All grown up," she said. "Every unmarried girl in the room is having the same thought right now." She glanced around. "Some of the married ones, too, I'll wager."

Asha flushed. "I wasn't..." She trailed off; the young woman had already twisted away again, staring hungrily at Wirr. Asha restrained the urge to snicker.

The first course was served and Asha ate absentmindedly, barely responding to attempts at conversation by Michal and the others around her. She knew she was being somewhat impolite— Michal even shot her a few irritated glares—but every time she caught a glimpse of Wirr, her mind wandered.

She wished again that she could tell her friend about Davian. When she and Wirr had spent the afternoon swapping stories, that had been the hardest part—watching his face as he'd hesitantly, despondently described their flight from Deilannis. The moment that Taeris had told him the connection had been broken. There had been such pain there that Asha had almost spoken up, despite Davian's warning not to.

But she'd kept silent, and the moment had passed. The rest of that afternoon had been the happiest she could remember in months. Wirr, for his part, had been thrilled to discover Asha was living in the palace—and suitably astonished by the reasons why. If Elocien hadn't returned after a while to confirm he was working with the Augurs, Asha didn't think Wirr would have believed it.

She couldn't help but smile now as she watched her friend. As dinner progressed, small groups of people—usually in twos or threes—were brought up to be formally introduced to the prince. Everyone bowed, many brought gifts. All looked vaguely intimidated by him.

Time passed, and soon there was an usher touching Michal on the shoulder. The Athian Representative rose, gesturing for her to do the same.

"Try to be a little more attentive than you have been so far," Michal whispered to her as they made their way between the tables toward Wirr, a hint of irritation in his tone. "We have this one chance to make an impression—and the prince is going to notice that you're a Shadow. Regardless of whether he already knows, it's going to be a point of conversation. So be prepared to do some talking."

Asha didn't know whether to be embarrassed or to laugh. In the end she did neither, instead inclining her head in acquiescence.

Asha kept her eyes firmly on Wirr, who was deep in conversation with the young woman sitting between him and Princess Karaliene—the king's ward, from what Michal had said—and didn't notice who was approaching. When he looked up, his eyes flashed with amusement as introductions were made.

"Michal. Ashalia." Wirr nodded politely. "A pleasure to meet you both. You are the Representatives for Athian?"

Michal bowed, and Asha remembered to curtsy just in time, trying not to smile as she did so.

"We are, Your Highness," said Michal. "It is a pleasure to meet you, too."

Wirr inclined his head, then leaned back, studying them openly. "So. A Shadow as a Representative," he said, looking at Asha with a raised eyebrow. "An unusual choice."

"One that we have not regretted, Sire," Michal assured him. "Asha is a quick study; she'll one day make an excellent addition to the Assembly. I could not have asked for more."

Wirr nodded, looking thoughtful. He stared at Asha intently. "High praise," he said, the faintest hint of amusement back in his eyes. "And I've heard good things from other sources, too. I'm impressed."

Asha kept her face smooth. "Thank you, Your Highness. That means so much to me," she said with as much sincerity as she could muster.

The corners of Wirr's mouth crept upward, and he was about to say something more when an older man—one of the generals, Asha thought from his uniform—hurried past, going straight to King Andras and whispering something in his ear. The king glowered at whatever the man had said, then shooed him away, gesturing to Elocien.

The duke paled as the news the king had been given was relayed, then stood, heading straight for Wirr. He frowned for a moment when he saw Asha sitting opposite Wirr, but relaxed again once he realized that Michal was there, too. He bent over Wirr's shoulder.

"You're needed, Son," he said, his voice calm. "Our army has been broken." The Northwarden glanced across at Michal and Asha. "You two should come as well. I think Tol Athian may need to have some say in what happens next."

"Of course," said Michal, looking sick.

Asha's stomach churned too as she processed the news. Despite having known what was coming, she'd still been clinging to the hope that it would turn out differently.

They trailed after Elocien and Wirr, leaving the hubbub of the feast behind them as they moved into an adjoining room. The king had already seated himself, and he gestured for everyone else to follow suit. Princess Karaliene was there, as were Laiman Kardai and Dras Lothlar, the latter looking especially displeased to see Michal and Asha.

The group was soon completed by Ionis, who looked even more disgruntled when he realized that both Tol Athian and Tol Shen were represented.

"What are they doing here?" he asked irritably, gesturing at Michal and Asha.

"I invited them," said Elocien. "This discussion will doubtless revolve around the Gifted. They have just as much right to be a part of that conversation as us, Ionis."

Ionis muttered something inaudible, but subsided as the duke looked at him steadily. Once the Administrator was seated, a middle-aged man—a general named Parathe, if Asha remembered correctly—stood.

"Jash'tar's forces haven't just been broken. They have been decimated," announced Parathe. There was a heaviness to his tone, a despondency that made Asha's heart sink.

Everyone just stared at the general for a moment, with more than one face going pale at the news.

"How?" asked Elocien. "They were told to dig in, to hold them up. Possibly to negotiate, if that was an option. But to retreat if necessary."

Parathe shook his head. "It wasn't in open battle. The Blind stopped marching when they saw our men coming; they'd been dormant for a couple of days. Jash'tar thought they were intimidated, might even want to talk." He sighed. "To be honest, Your Grace, we're not sure exactly what happened. It seems that our men were overconfident and didn't set an adequate watch. The enemy sneaked in under cover of darkness somehow, while many of our people were sleeping. Killed most of the men in their tents before the alarm was even raised, then swept in and finished the rest off. There were only a few survivors."

There was a stunned silence. "How many is a few, General?" Wirr finally asked.

"Four hundred or so," replied Parathe. "Maybe five, depending on how many managed to scatter to the forests nearby."

Asha swallowed, and she could hear Michal's sharp intake of breath beside her.

The duke just grimaced. "You're certain the others are all dead?"

"Yes." Parathe stared at his clasped hands, unwilling to look anyone in the eye. "And that report is days old now. Depending on how hard the Blind have been pushing, they could be here in a couple of days. Maybe less."

Elocien leaned forward; he wore a calm expression but his knuckles were white as he gripped the table. "Do we at least have any new intelligence?"

Parathe nodded. "We know that they move in squads of ten men: nine with those strange helmets, and one who sits back from the fighting like a commander. They all seem to be well trained—hard to fight individually, but especially cohesive as units." The general sighed. "Other than that, Your Grace? No. Only what we already knew."

"Which is that there's something unnatural about them," growled Ionis, shooting Dras and Michal an accusatory look as if it were somehow their fault.

The Northwarden took a deep breath, then laid a hand on his brother's shoulder. "This is an enormous loss, Your Majesty," he said. "I know you're against it, but there is no other way. We need to change the Tenets, allow the Gifted to fight." Parathe inclined his head in agreement.

"I concur, Your Majesty." It was Dras. "I can have a contingent from Tol Shen ready to defend the city walls by dusk tomorrow." Michal, reluctant though he looked to be agreeing with Dras, nodded, too.

"You know my thoughts, Your Majesty," interjected Ionis. "Administration has an obligation to protect the people, and the Tenets are what allow us to perform that function. Changing them is taking a short-term view." He shot a hard look at the duke, as if daring the other man to reprimand him. Elocien scowled, but said nothing.

The king stared vacantly at the table for a few moments, then shook his head. "No."

There was silence as everyone exchanged questioning looks, then Elocien cleared his throat. "Brother, surely you don't mean—"

The king slammed his fist down onto the table, suddenly and violently, making everyone jump. "I mean NO!" he roared. His face had turned bright red, and spittle came out of his mouth when he spoke. Sweat clung to his brow in great beads now, and there was no doubt in Asha's mind that he was a very sick man. "Don't you see, Elocien? Ionis is right. This is what they want. It's what they've always wanted." He sneered at Dras, then twisted to glare at Michal and Asha. "You bleeders are probably behind all of this. I should have you all hanged for traitors. Every last one." He stood as if to carry out his threat immediately.

Dras had gone deathly pale. "Your Majesty, I . . ." He trailed off helplessly, clearly not sure what to say.

"Kevran, please sit down." Elocien looked more troubled than Asha had ever seen him. "We can lay blame later, but right now we need a plan to defend Ilin Illan. The Gifted are our only—"

"We have our six thousand. We have the city guard," interrupted the king. He had calmed again, though he was still a little wild-eyed. "We have the four hundred returning to us. We have citizens who will fight. The Blind have no ships; they cannot come by river, so the only way into the city is through Fedris Idri. This is the most defensible city ever built. We will prevail without the Gifted." He gestured. "I tell you this as a courtesy, not to seek your advice. It is my decision, and mine alone, to make."

Parathe opened his mouth to protest, but a quick glance from the duke silenced him. The general gave the slightest of nods to the Northwarden, unseen by the king. Elocien could obviously see that arguing the point now would only cause more trouble.

"And what of the Gifted, Your Majesty?" asked Wirr quietly.

"The Gifted can fight like real men if they wish, with sword and shield. Or heal the wounded if they are too afraid. But they will not use their powers for violence whilst I rule." The king looked around, his glare defying anyone to gainsay him. "You are dismissed."

They rose silently, stunned, and began filing out of the room. Asha glanced toward Wirr, hoping to catch his eye, but he appeared to have been waylaid by the king and was not looking in her direction.

Once outside she found herself walking alongside Michal as the others went their separate ways.

"What did you make of all that?" asked Michal, keeping his voice low.

"I think those rumors about the king being ill were fairly accurate," Asha said worriedly. "He's not in control."

Michal sighed and gave a grim nod. "I agree. And suddenly

it seems I share your concern about Tol Athian's recent decision, too. I'm just not sure what anyone can do about it." He glanced across at her. "Are you going to leave?"

"Leave?" Asha looked at him in surprise. "No. Of course not."

Michal watched her for a long moment, then let out a breath, evidently satisfied. "Good. A lot of the nobility will, once they find out—first thing tomorrow morning, I suspect. Maybe even tonight." He smiled, shaking his head. "I would understand if you decided to go, but...just let me know if you do. Seems I'm becoming fond of you, Ashalia. I'd be worried if you suddenly disappeared again."

Asha smiled back. "You're staying?" She hadn't thought for a moment about leaving, but she suddenly realized how tempting it must be for a lot of people.

"Yes. I'm going to go back to the feast now, try to convince as many people as possible to stay and fight. Try and get as many people as we can behind the idea that now is the time for the Tenets to be changed, too. I know how King Andras looked, but maybe, if there's enough pressure..." He sighed. "It would help if you were to join me. Would look less like I was arguing for my own interests."

Asha nodded and was about to agree when she caught sight of Elocien down the hallway. She hesitated.

"I'll come if I can," she promised, "but there's something I must discuss with the duke first."

Michal looked about to protest, then nodded reluctantly. "If you can, then," he agreed.

Asha gave him an apologetic glance, then hurried after Elocien, falling into stride alongside him just before he turned the corner.

"Representative Chaedris," the duke said politely, nodding to her. He glanced around, seeing that there was no one within hearing distance. "I know we shouldn't be surprised, but I hadn't imagined it would be this bad. Or happen so quickly."

Asha watched the duke as he walked. "I know," she said. "And I think it's time we reached out for some aid."

The duke scowled and shook his head, though not with his usual air of certainty. "No. These are dangerous people, Ashalia, and they still think you owe them something. I'm not going to send you to beg for their help, not after everything you've been through."

"But it's my choice to go, and it's something we need to do," observed Asha. "The Shadraehin can organize the Shadows, and we can provide them with weapons that may make the difference when the Blind get here. I know you can't do this officially, that Administration will never go for it. But let me try. If we don't try everything in our power to save the city, it's no different from your brother refusing to change the Tenets."

Elocien said nothing for a few seconds, but eventually he slowed, then stopped altogether. He looked Asha in the eye, silent for a long moment.

Then he gave a reluctant nod.

"Let's discuss the details in my study," he said quietly.

⁂

Wirr rose to leave, head still spinning from what Parathe had just told them.

Almost nine thousand men, dead in some sort of ambush. It didn't take a military mind to understand that those losses were extraordinary. Unthinkable.

"Torin." It was the king. "Stay. I would like to speak with you."

Wirr gave a slight bow and sat again, waiting patiently for the others to file past.

Once everyone was gone, Wirr cast a cautious glance across at his uncle. Karaliene hadn't been wrong about his condition. He was drawn, sweating, and gray, a shadow of the man Wirr remembered.

"What can I do for you, Uncle?" he asked eventually as the silence began to stretch.

Kevran didn't reply for a moment, then leaned forward so that his face was close to Wirr's.

"I have only one question for you, Torin. Whose side are you on?"

Wirr resisted the urge to flinch back. "What do you mean?"

The king glowered. "Don't play the fool. I know where you've been, these past few years," he said, irritation thick in his tone. "I helped send you there, remember. You're one of them. Or you were. So my question is, are you Gifted or are you a prince? *Whose side are you on?*"

Wirr shook his head. "I would like to think it is not a case of sides."

"The Treaty would suggest otherwise," observed Kevran. "Or perhaps you have forgotten the meaning of that word. Treaties cannot be made without there first having been a war."

Wirr bit his lip. His uncle spoke in a slightly breathless, manic way; anyone else, and Wirr would have said he was insane. "I will always do what is best for Andarra, Uncle," he said after a moment. "But I don't see myself as being on one side or another."

"Then you have grown up to be a fool." Kevran leaned back, looking disappointed. "The Gifted are traitors. Their power is a disease, a stain on the world. They are untrustworthy. Each and every one of them."

Wirr bit back an angry retort. The way the king was acting, he knew that to protest would only be putting himself on dangerous ground.

"Is that all, Your Majesty?" he asked stiffly.

The king inclined his head, making a dismissive gesture.

Wirr stood slowly and left, shaken. What had happened to his uncle? The man he remembered had had no love for the Gifted, but nor had he hated them. If anything, it had always been Kevran who'd had the calm head, and Elocien who had spouted the rhetoric.

He was so caught up in his worries that he almost walked straight into Dras Lothlar, who had been waiting in the hallway outside. Wirr excused himself, but when he tried to move around the other man, Dras stepped into his path again.

Wirr scowled as his already frayed temper threatened to snap, but held his tongue and looked at the Shen Representative steadily.

"Can I help you?"

Dras smiled at him, a look so predatory that it made Wirr shiver. "I just thought I should introduce myself, Your Highness," he said in an obsequious tone. "I am Dras Lothlar, Representative for Tol Shen."

"I know who you are, Representative Lothlar," said Wirr, trying to sound irritated rather than anxious. Had Dras recognized him from Thrindar? Wirr looked different now: hair trimmed, a light beard, fine clothes rather than rags. And in Desriel they had spent only a few minutes in each other's presence. "As you can imagine, I have some very important things to discuss with my father. So if you wouldn't mind..."

Dras didn't move. "How was Calandra, these past few years, Your Highness?" he asked, his gaze intent. "Whereabouts were you stationed?"

"Ildora," said Wirr automatically. He'd had these details drilled into him over the past few days.

"Ah, I remember Ildora. Lovely place." Dras sounded relaxed, but Wirr could still see the focus behind his eyes.

"I don't know about that. I saw plenty of good men die defending it against the barbarians. It doesn't bring back fond memories."

Dras's expression didn't change. "I suppose you've been to the inn there? The Juggler?"

Wirr hesitated. He'd been told plenty about Ildora, but he had no information on the names of the inns there.

And...the Juggler was the inn that Karaliene had sent them to in Thrindar. His heart sank.

"No," he replied.

"No?" Dras looked surprised. "Not once? I remember it being very popular when I was there." He frowned. "Perhaps I'm misremembering. Perhaps that inn was somewhere else."

Wirr forced himself to keep his breathing steady. The man knew. "If you don't want anything, Representative, get out of my way," he growled.

Dras smiled. "Of course, Your Highness. My apologies." He stepped to the side.

Wirr stalked away, not looking back but unable to stop picturing the smarmy expression on the Representative's face. The Shen Gifted should be thinking of ways to defend the city, not playing these games as if nothing were amiss.

Doing his best to banish Lothlar from his mind, he headed for his father's study, arriving just as the door opened and Asha emerged into the hallway. They stared at each other in mild surprise for a second, and then Wirr gave her a rueful smile.

"Interesting night," he observed.

Asha nodded her agreement. "Remind me to stay away from your parties in the future," she said drily. She slipped something into her pocket—a key, Wirr thought—then gave him an apologetic squeeze on the shoulder. "I'd stay to talk, but Michal needs my help, and then after that—"

"It's all right. Go." Wirr hesitated. "And Ash, if I don't see you again before the Blind get here..."

Asha smiled at him. "Then I'll see you after," she said firmly.

Wirr watched her go, even now still barely believing it was really her. Asha's having survived the attack at Caladel was astonishing, miraculous. And her new place here at the palace—what his father had been building with the Augurs, these past few years—was even more so.

He sighed, then walked inside to find Elocien flicking through some papers. The duke glanced up as Wirr entered.

"I'm glad you're here, Torin. We need to go back to the feast," he said, pushing himself to his feet.

Wirr gave him a blank look. "The feast? Surely everyone will have gone."

"They won't know what's happening for another couple of hours." Elocien ushered him out the door. "Which means we have exactly that amount of time to convince anyone capable of fighting that there's still a chance. That there's no need to panic."

Wirr grimaced. "We need to lie, you mean."

Elocien sighed.

"Yes. We need to lie," he agreed.

Wirr just nodded, and they walked back toward the ballroom in heavy silence.

# Chapter 47

It was the very early hours of the morning, the moon still high, when Davian caught his first glimpse of the palace.

He exhaled as he took in the grand structure, clearly his destination despite being partially obscured by a combination of high walls and the expansive, immaculately kept gardens beyond. The enormous white columns and elegant arching entrances he could see through the gate were impressive, even after his time in Deilannis. The knot of worry that had been sitting at the base of his skull loosened a little. After all that had happened it was a relief, almost surreal, to finally be here.

He rubbed his neck tiredly as he approached the gate, which was an ethereal silver in the moonlight. Aside from the guards there was no one on the street; as with the rest of the city he'd seen, everything was impressive, and yet it felt...empty. Deserted. His footsteps crunched in the postmidnight hush, and all four men at the gate were watching him with narrowed eyes before he got within fifty feet.

"No entry to the palace," said one of them, stepping forward. His tone brooked no argument.

Davian held up his hands to show he meant no harm. "I need to see Aelric or Dezia Shainwiere," he said, his tone polite. "It's urgent."

The guard shook his head. "Sorry, lad, but no visitors. And if the Shainwieres are even awake, they'll be helping prepare the city defenses—I can't disturb them."

"I have information about the invasion."

The guard raised an eyebrow, looking skeptical. "Do you now. That's convenient. Perhaps you can tell me, and I'll relay it to those who need to know."

"I need to give it to them directly." Davian rubbed his forehead. "Could you please just tell them that Davian is here to see them?"

The guard scowled. "Fates, lad, what part of 'no entry' don't you understand? Even if they knew you, I couldn't let you through at this time of night."

Davian sighed. He hadn't wanted to do this, but the man was clearly not going to be swayed.

He concentrated, reaching out with kan.

He almost lost his grip on the connection, so surprised was he by how easy it was to slip inside the guard's mind. Once he was through, though, it wasn't like Malshash's thoughts—cold, ordered, and distinct. Everything here was...a mess. Emotions tangled with sensations tangled with memories, each coloring the others until none were entirely recognizable.

Davian focused on the present, trying to block out everything else as Malshash had taught him. There was nervousness about what was coming, a sense of dread. And suspiciousness of Davian, certainly no inclination to let him through the gate.

He looked deeper, trying to find what would change the man's mind. The guard knew who Aelric and Dezia were, though only from afar; they registered as two faces, little more.

He turned his thoughts to Wirr—to Prince Torin. *That* was a different story. A powerful figure, an intimidating one in this man's life. One word from the prince and his life could be changed, for better or for worse.

Davian barely stopped himself from shaking his head in disbelief at the thought.

He withdrew the sliver of kan, sighing. "If you're comfortable with the consequences once Torin discovers his friend has been turned away..." He trailed off, turning as if to leave.

"Wait. What?" The guard's voice had taken on a nervous note. "The prince? You never mentioned—"

"I shouldn't have had to." Davian shook his head, doing his best to look irritated. "I asked for the Shainwieres because I knew Tor would be busy. But I'm an old friend of his. From Calandra," he added, remembering where Wirr was supposed to have been for the past few years. He stepped forward, looking the man in the eye. "Davian. And it's urgent."

The guard hesitated, and Davian pressed home his point. "Just tell him I'm here. If he doesn't know who I am, or doesn't want to let me in, you can lock me up." He gave his most confident smile. "But he'll want to see me."

The man hesitated a moment longer, then nodded briefly and disappeared through the gate.

A few minutes later someone else appeared from within the grounds, a harried look on his face. He was older, finely dressed.

"Davian?"

Davian nodded.

"My name is Laiman Kardai. Come with me. Quickly, please." He turned to one of the guards. "Trevin. You trust me?"

"Of course, Master Kardai," said the man.

"Tell anyone who asks that he left," Laiman said, jerking his head toward Davian. "Walked off, didn't say where he was going."

Trevin bit his lip, then nodded. "We can do that." The other two men with him nodded their silent agreement.

Davian frowned but hurried after the older man, through the gates and magnificent grounds and into the main building. Once inside, Laiman took a couple of sharp turns, then ushered Davian into an unoccupied room.

He shut the door and leaned against it, exhaling in what appeared to be relief.

"What's going on?" asked Davian in confusion.

"You've...caused a bit of a commotion, I'm afraid," said Laiman, gesturing for Davian to have a seat. "Not through any fault of your own. Prince Torin will be along to see you shortly, I'm sure."

"What happened?"

Laiman sighed. "There was a feast earlier tonight, and several lords stayed around afterward to discuss the defense of the city. The prince was part of that meeting, along with his father, uncle, and a couple of Administrators. We were just finishing up when word came that one of Torin's friends from Calandra was at the gate." He shook his head, a weary motion. "We both know where Torin's actually been these last few years, but until now few others did."

Davian hesitated, for a moment unsure how much he could admit to this stranger. Then he frowned, picking up on the last part of Laiman's statement. "Until now?"

"King Andras...lost control when he heard." Laiman looked dazed at the memory. "I don't know how else to describe it. He stood up and, in front of everybody, revealed where Torin has been. The fact he's Gifted. Claimed that this was Torin's way of letting his 'bleeder' friends into the palace so that they could kill him, overthrow him." He shrugged. "The duke did his best to calm him, while I slipped away. I don't think anyone else saw us coming inside, so if Trevin keeps his word—which he will—you should be safe in here for a while."

Davian gave him a stunned nod. "Thank you."

"Don't mention it. I've heard Torin's entire story, and I know who you are. *What* you are. We can use all the help we can get against what's coming." Laiman looked grim. "I should get back before I'm missed, though...or shut out altogether," he added, sounding bitter. "Stay here. I'll make sure Torin knows where you are."

He slipped outside and shut the door behind him, leaving Davian alone and shaken.

Perhaps thirty minutes passed before the door opened again. Davian rose in anticipation, his smile broad as he took in the first of the two figures in the doorway. Wirr was almost unrecognizable with his fine clothing and neatly trimmed hair.

Davian's attention shifted to the girl next to him; they locked eyes, and for several moments neither of them moved. She was a Shadow, but Davian recognized her immediately...and yet it couldn't be.

Then she was rushing into the room, and they were embracing.

"Asha?" Davian could barely choke out the name, overcome with a flood of emotion. He held her away from him for a moment, peering into her black-scarred face, scarcely daring to believe it. He swallowed hard as unexpected tears threatened to form in his eyes. Even as a Shadow, she was the most beautiful thing he'd ever seen. "How...?"

Asha grinned in delight at the look on his face. "It's a long story, Dav."

Wirr gave a cough as he entered the room. "Good to see you, too, Dav. Glad you're not dead and everything."

Davian laughed dazedly, elatedly, grabbing Wirr and pulling him into the embrace. "Fates, Wirr, you have no idea how good it is to see you again. After Deilannis..." He shook his head, smile finally slipping a little. "Laiman said I've caused trouble for you. I'm sorry."

"Not your fault." Wirr stared at the floor, his brow furrowed as he said the words. "My uncle is very sick; I'm sure it would have come out eventually." He rubbed his face. "Word's already spreading, though, and I have no idea what the consequences are going to be. I can't stay around here for long."

"Neither can I, Dav." Asha looked torn as she said the words. "You have no idea how much I want to sit down with you, tell you everything that's been happening... but Wirr caught me just as I was leaving. There are things I need to do before the Blind get here. Important things. I've only got a few minutes." She gave him a rueful smile.

"She never believed you were gone." A guilty expression spread across Wirr's face. "I shouldn't have, either...I never would have left you in Deilannis, but Taeris lost his connection with your Shackle, and..."

"It's all right, Wirr," Davian reassured him. "There was nothing you could have done. Believe me." His gaze returned to Asha, head spinning. "So if you're alive... is everyone else...?"

Asha's face twisted. "No," she said gently. "Just me."

Davian nodded; there was the momentary pain of having that flicker of hope crushed so quickly, but the joy of seeing Asha again was stronger by far. "It's still a miracle," he said, unable to wipe the smile from his face.

Wirr gripped him by the shoulder, as if testing to see if he was truly there. "So what happened? Where have you been?" He hesitated. "Is Nihim with you?"

"No." It was Davian's turn to grimace. "He died in Deilannis. As to the rest, it's difficult to explain quickly. If you really have to go..."

Wirr nodded, looking frustrated. "I really do."

Davian sighed; he understood the need, but this reunion with his friends was going to be all too brief. "Any ideas as to what I should be doing next, then? This was as far ahead as I'd thought," he admitted. "I have control of some of my Augur powers now. There must be some way I can help."

Wirr and Asha exchanged glances. "You can Read people?" asked Asha.

"Yes. Why?" Davian smiled slightly at the odd expression on his friends' faces. "Don't worry. I'm not going to Read either of you."

Wirr shook his head, remaining serious. "It's not that, Dav." He hesitated. "It's Ilseth Tenvar."

Davian felt his expression twist in sudden anger at the name. "Where is he?"

"Locked up in Tol Athian," supplied Asha. "But he's not talking."

"Asha and I were discussing this a few days ago," continued Wirr. "That box for Caeden, the attacks to find me...we know it's all connected to this invasion."

"And if I Read Tenvar, there's a chance we might find out something useful about the Blind," finished Davian, unable to keep the reluctance from his tone. He rubbed his forehead, a sick feeling in the pit of his stomach. He badly wanted Ilseth to answer for what he'd done, but suddenly the thought of facing him made Davian queasy. "Caeden didn't get his memory back, then, I take it?"

"The Council refused to help him," said Wirr. "I don't know the details, but I think Taeris is still trying to convince them."

Davian was silent for a moment as he processed the information. "And Tenvar's said nothing?"

"So far as we've been told," said Asha, a little bitterly.

Wirr grimaced, nodding. "Things have been...strained between the palace and the Tol, as you can probably imagine if you've heard anything about how my uncle's been acting. The Council has all but cut off communications now; we asked to see Tenvar the other day and they refused us entry. As is their right under the Treaty, unfortunately."

Davian gave a thoughtful nod. "So you can't get me in," he said. "If I want to see Tenvar, I'll probably have to tell them that

I'm an Augur." He rolled back his sleeve, revealing the smooth skin where his Mark had once been. "They're going to take some convincing if I don't."

Wirr and Asha both stared in silence for a few seconds.

"Fates," murmured Wirr. "How..." Then he shook his head, looking frustrated. "No time; you'll just have to tell us everything when all this is over. But you're right—you *are* going to have to tell them you're an Augur. That's one of the reasons we haven't sent any of ours yet."

Davian gave him a puzzled look. "Our what?"

"Augurs." Asha grinned at Davian's expression, which he felt turn from bemusement to outright disbelief as he stared at her. "A long story. Only one of them can really Read people, though, and he's too valuable at the palace at the moment. If we expose him to Athian, it would be too risky for him to come back and assume no one from here will find out."

Davian was silent for a long few moments as he digested what Asha had said. "Tenvar managed to lie to me. He knows how to shield himself. I'm not sure there's any use sending anyone to Read him, to be honest," he said eventually, a little dazed.

"We know, Dav. The chances of getting anything useful are slim—we just thought it might be worth trying." Asha laid a reassuring hand on his arm. "If you don't think it is, though, I'm sure there are other ways you can help." At her side Wirr nodded his agreement.

Davian thought for several more seconds, then shook his head. "No," he said quietly. "I'll do it. If there's even a slight possibility we can get answers from him, then we should try."

Wirr quickly related how to get to the Tol and then glanced at the door, clearly anxious to leave. "I hate to go so soon, Dav, but I need to get away from here before an Administrator finds me. The El-cursed Fourth Tenet is an awfully dangerous thing right now," he said, looking nervous. "I'm going to head to Fedris Idri until my father sends word that everything is under control; it's unlikely Administration will try anything while I'm surrounded by my uncle's soldiers. Find me there if you discover anything important." He embraced Davian. "Fates, it's good to have you back. When this is all over, we'll celebrate your return from the dead. Properly."

"I'd expect nothing less." Davian turned to Asha, and they both hesitated for a second. Then she wrapped him in a long, tight hug, her cheek against his.

"Be careful," she said softly. "We have some things to talk about when this is all over."

Davian gave her a gentle squeeze. "I know. You, too, Asha."

Wirr was standing impatiently by the door. "You can find your own way out?"

Davian nodded. "As long as the guards at the gate won't stop me."

"They won't," Wirr promised. "Give me five minutes to speak to them, then head out."

With that he left. Asha paused in the doorway, giving him one last, brilliant smile over her shoulder before she followed suit.

Davian sat, still trying to comprehend everything that had just taken place. Asha was alive. It didn't seem possible, was too good to be true. After all he'd endured over the past few months, this was a ray of hope, of happiness, he'd not dared to think was possible.

Suddenly the door was opening again, and Davian leaped up warily.

"Davian?" A scarred face peered into the room.

"Taeris!" Davian relaxed again, smiling. He gave a soft laugh of relief. "Is everyone I know at the palace today? How did you know I was here?"

"A friend mentioned it." Taeris's expression was wry. "Word tends to get around when the man we're depending on to defend us goes completely mad."

"Ah. Yes." Davian crossed the room and embraced the older man. "It's good to see you again."

"You, too, lad. Fates, you, too." Taeris smiled, and Davian suddenly noticed a long, pink scar across his cheek, overlaid on some of the others. It looked fresher, newly healed.

"Where's Caeden?" Davian's heart suddenly dropped. "Is he all right?"

"He's fine," Taeris rushed to assure him.

"And his memories?"

Taeris took a deep breath. "Nothing so far—but given how

close the Blind are getting, I'm going to see if we can do something about that in a few hours." He outlined his plan to break into Tol Athian using the Travel Stones.

Davian gave a thoughtful nod once he was finished. "I'm about to go there myself," he said. "If there's any way I can help keep them off your backs, I will."

"I appreciate that, lad." Taeris smiled. "So. Where have you been?"

Davian opened his mouth to reply, then hesitated. He didn't believe what Driscin had told him, and yet...the man from Tol Shen hadn't lied.

"I'll explain in a moment, but first I need to know something. When was the first time you saw me?"

Taeris blinked, surprised by the question. "The day you were attacked, of course," he said, looking puzzled. "Why do you ask?"

Davian stiffened. It was faint, but it was there—pain in his temples.

Taeris was lying, and trying to mask it.

"I see." He was silent for a moment, trying to contain his suddenly roiling emotions. "Tell me...did you plan it? When I got this." He raised his head, pointing to his scar. "Did you get those men to rough me up so that I would get scared, be forced to find my powers? Was it all a plan that went horribly wrong? Is *that* why you saved me?"

Taeris paled. "Of course not," he said hurriedly. "Who has been telling you this? I'd never..." He trailed off as he saw Davian's expression.

Once again, that faint but insistent throbbing. Another lie.

Davian couldn't take it anymore, couldn't stand to be in the same room as this man.

"I have to go, Taeris," he said softly, hurt and disbelief making his voice tight. "Just...don't follow me."

He walked out without another word, blocking out whatever Taeris called after him, emotions churning. He hadn't found the allies he'd expected at the palace, but at least he had somewhere to go now. Something to do.

It was time to get some answers from Ilseth Tenvar.

# Chapter 48

Asha walked through the silent city streets as dawn broke, a smile plastered across her face despite the task that lay before her.

Davian was alive. She'd known it, but it still hadn't truly felt real until she'd seen him, felt his arms around her. It had been hard to leave him again so soon, but she knew she couldn't afford to delay in trying to contact the Shadraehin. The Blind were on the march, and could be at the city within a couple of days—maybe earlier. There would be time for a proper reunion once all this was over.

Her smile faded. There would be time, *if* they survived.

The empty streets and hurriedly boarded-up stores around her were a stark reminder of what was coming. Last night's news had traveled fast; nearly everything was closed, silent, and the few civilians walking the streets looked nervous and spoke to each other only in hushed tones. Even to Asha, who had been out in the city only a few times, the scene was surreal. There was a heaviness, a deep sense of impending doom hanging over everything like a thundercloud.

She headed toward the Silver Talon, one of the smaller taverns in the Middle District, and the only name she remembered from the note she'd burned a month or so before. It was hardly a foolproof plan, but she didn't know her way to the Sanctuary. This was the only place she could think of to contact the Shadraehin.

She soon arrived outside the tavern, a two-story brick building that, like everything else in the street, was closed and empty. After a minute of peering vainly through windows into the murky interior, Asha gave up and settled down on the doorstep.

It was a half hour later when crunching footsteps indicated someone's approach.

She looked up to see a thin, distinguished-looking man striding toward her, the black lines on his face stark against his pale skin.

"Ashalia Chaedris?"

She nodded.

"Come with me."

Asha scrambled to her feet, giving a silent sigh of relief. She followed the man through a series of desolate back streets, the echo of their footsteps often the only sound. Her guide ignored her for the most part, swiveling his head occasionally to make sure she was keeping up, but otherwise keeping his eyes fixed on the way ahead.

They made their way into the residential section of the Middle District, and before long the Shadow came to a halt outside one of the smaller houses, opening the front door.

"The Shadraehin is waiting," he said, gesturing for Asha to enter.

Inside was dim, the curtains drawn, but Asha could see Scyner reclining in a chair near the window. He was flanked by two huge Shadows, who both gave her suspicious stares. Scyner gestured cheerfully for her to sit.

"Ashalia!" he exclaimed. "Very clever, asking half the Shadows in the palace directions to the Silver Talon. I had three separate reports saying you were on your way there."

"I assumed you probably had someone following me anyway, but I wanted to be sure," said Asha, trying to keep the bitterness from her tone.

"Indeed," said Scyner. He leaned forward. "I want to begin by saying that I had no knowledge of Teran's and Pyl's actions until after the event. It was...unfortunate."

"I think they would agree," said Asha quietly, forcing down the twist of fear in her stomach.

Scyner stared at her for a moment, then chuckled. "I suppose they would." He straightened. "So. It seems like an odd time to be delivering information, but I take it you have news?"

"No. Not about the Northwarden, anyway."

Scyner watched her for a few seconds, silent. "Teran insisted that you never meant to tell us anything," he said eventually. "He was telling the truth, wasn't he?"

"Yes," said Asha. "Once I found out the truth about you."

Scyner's eyebrows rose a fraction. "Honesty. Surprising, but I can respect that." He scratched his head. "However, it leaves me in something of a quandary. We made a deal, Ashalia. You have broken it, and you know what happens to those who break deals with me. Why not just lie?"

"Because I don't have time for lies," said Asha grimly. "And I have something you're going to want more."

Scyner sighed, shaking his head. "Maybe so, but I think I'd prefer to keep you restrained for now. At least until I hear what it is you have to say." He nodded to the two men standing on either side of him, who started forward.

Asha stretched out her hand.

There was the briefest moment of Scyner staring at her in puzzlement. Then his two bodyguards, already halfway across the room, flew backward and slammed into the wall, one shattering the window as his flailing arm hit it.

Both men collapsed to the floor, unconscious, as Scyner scrambled up from where his chair had been overturned by the powerful gust, his eyes wide.

"Now," said Asha, trying to keep her voice from shaking, "I would like to talk to the real Shadraehin, please. There's something I need to discuss with her."

⋙⋘

Only a few minutes had passed when the door opened again.

The woman who entered was a Shadow, and yet somehow she was also startlingly beautiful, even the black lines on her face seeming to accentuate rather than mar her soft features. She was young—older than Asha, but only by a few years. Even so, she moved with confidence and grace as she swept inside, taking in the crumpled forms of Scyner's bodyguards with an amused glance before turning to face Asha.

"Ashalia Chaedris," she said, a slight, lilting accent evident even in Asha's name. "It seems you are full of surprises today."

Asha stared at her. "You're the Shadraehin?"

579

"I am. Do not bother asking for proof. You will not get it."

Asha inclined her head; though the woman was certainly young, something about her bearing had convinced Asha the moment she had entered the room. She took a deep breath. "I've come to ask the Shadows to join the fight against the Blind."

The Shadraehin raised an eyebrow in amusement. "It would be safer by far to flee," she observed, her odd inflection making the cadence of the words sound almost musical. Whatever the accent was, Asha didn't recognize it. "I take it from what Scyner just told me that you do not wish for us to simply take up swords?" Her eyes flicked to the ring on Asha's finger, then back again.

Asha bit her lip. "Shadows can use Vessels," she explained, feeling a sense of dread as she said the words. It was out now, and no turning back. "I have access to Administration's stockpile. For each Shadow you can gather, I can have a powerful weapon in their hands by nightfall."

The Shadraehin studied her for a long moment, and Asha flushed under her cool gaze.

"I am interested," said the other woman eventually. "Once you give us these weapons, though, what is to keep us from simply leaving?"

"Nothing, I suppose," said Asha. "Except that the Sanctuary is here, and as little as you may like the way things are run aboveground, this is your home." She took a deep breath. "And you don't strike me as the type to run. Or to break deals, for that matter."

The Shadraehin gave a slow nod. "True enough." She tapped at her teeth, looking thoughtful. "And after the battle is over? Assuming we hold the city?"

Asha grimaced. "To an extent, that is going to be up to you. Administration is going to want you to return the Vessels, of course. If you don't...I have no idea what their reaction will be."

"But regardless, they are going to see Shadows as a real danger—all Shadows, not just my people. And we will be defenseless if we return the Vessels," noted the other woman.

Asha nodded. "I know," she said softly. "And I will not blame you if the Vessels are not returned. I want your word on one thing, though. You'll only ever use the Vessels for self-defense. No going after Administrators, no killing. There's no point having you defend the city if you're just going to tear it apart afterward."

The Shadraehin was silent for a long moment. "You would take my word?"

"Do I have reason not to?"

The other woman gave her the slightest of smiles. "No. And you have it. I cannot make promises for every Shadow who has a Vessel, of course, but for my part, I will insist that their use is for self-defense only." She touched two fingers to her heart, then the same two fingers to Asha's forehead. "Let it be so known. We have a covenant," she said formally.

Asha inclined her head, letting out a breath she hadn't realized she was holding. She wasn't sure how far the Shadraehin's word could really be trusted, but it was the best she could have hoped for.

"Where should I deliver the Vessels?" she asked.

"I'll have people gather at the Silver Talon at dusk. From what I've been hearing, there will be no Administrators left in this part of the city to notice. Or anyone else, for that matter," said the Shadraehin.

Asha nodded. "How many?" There were hundreds of catalogued weapons in the storeroom, so she wasn't worried about there not being enough.

"A hundred should suffice."

Asha's eyes narrowed. "I'll provide one Vessel per Shadow you can get to that inn. No more."

The Shadraehin nodded. "And I expect there to be about a hundred present."

Asha frowned, taken aback. It was good news, of course; the more Shadows there were, the better defended the city would be. But she'd expected twenty, maybe thirty at best. People had been abandoning the city even before the previous night's news, and the Shadows—even the Shadraehin's people—hadn't had any good reason to stay. In fact, they'd had less reason to remain than most.

Unless the Shadraehin had asked them to stay, of course.

Asha was silent for several seconds as she studied the other woman.

"You knew," she said.

The Shadraehin kept her face smooth, but Asha saw the tiniest flicker of surprise in her eyes. "What do you mean?"

"You knew Shadows could use Vessels. You knew I'd bring you this deal." Asha thought back to what Teran had said, about his having to spy on her even if the Blind were at the gates. His instructions not to touch her, even if she didn't deliver on her agreement. She looked the Shadraehin in the eye. "It doesn't change anything, you have my word—but tell me the truth. Did you know this would happen when you sent the Northwarden to me?"

The Shadraehin just stared at her for a few moments. Then she gave a small laugh.

"Too many," she sighed, shaking her head. "I did not think you would notice."

"Then you *did* know?"

"Not as such. I knew we would be fighting the Blind with Vessels, and I knew that Administration were the only ones with a significant number of them. Putting you close to the Northwarden was one of several ways I thought it might happen."

Asha paused. It galled her to think that the Shadraehin had planned to get a hold of the Vessels, but ultimately it mattered little. "So are you…"

"An Augur? No." The Shadraehin sounded amused. "I'll tell you how I knew, if you're willing to tell me how you knew Scyner was not in charge. Or how you found out that I am a woman."

"I'm afraid I can't do that."

"I suspected as much." The Shadraehin gave a regretful sigh. "A mystery for another time, then." She stood, indicating the meeting was over. "Oh, and Ashalia. Neither Scyner nor I will be at the Silver Talon, so I will be letting my people know that they are to follow your lead. They will do whatever you need them to, and go wherever you ask."

Asha felt her eyebrows rise, but she quickly nodded. It was a lot of responsibility, but it still made her feel more comfortable than if the Shadraehin were to be giving the orders.

"One last thing," said Asha as she stood, too. "I have a message for you, though I don't really understand it. A gift from someone

called Davian."

The Shadraehin smiled. "A gift from someone I do not know?"

Asha ignored the other woman's amusement. "The message is that Tal'kamar is going to take Licanius to the Wells."

The Shadraehin froze. For a fraction of a second she looked both excited and terrified, though the expression was quickly smoothed over, replaced by one of intense curiosity. She stared into Asha's eyes for a long moment, eyes focused.

"You are certain that was the message?"

Asha nodded, shivering a little under her gaze.

"And that was all?"

"Yes."

The Shadraehin didn't move for a few seconds, rubbing her thumb and forefinger together absently. "Davian," she murmured. "Excellent. Please tell him that I am in his debt." She gave Asha a considering look, then the slightest nod of respect. "Now, however, you and I are both needed elsewhere, so you will need to see yourself out. It was a pleasure to meet you, Ashalia. I feel certain our paths will cross again."

She gave Asha a final smile, then crossed to the door and left.

As quickly as that, it was done.

Asha did as the Shadraehin had suggested and found her own way out, not for the first time wondering exactly what Davian's message had meant. It didn't play on her mind for long this time, though; once back on the street she took a deep, steadying breath, then started back toward the palace. She already had the key to the storeroom, and a Veil would allow her to go to and from it several times without being detected.

She watched a patrol sweep through the street ahead of her, the soldiers' every motion taut with nervousness. She understood exactly how they felt.

Things were coming to a head, and she had no idea how they were going to turn out.

It was almost time.

# Chapter 49

Davian stared ahead grimly as he walked alongside Elder Eilinar down yet another flight of dimly lit, rough stone stairs, deeper into the heart of Tol Athian.

"You're angry," noted Nashrel, giving him a sideways glance.

"Yes," Davian replied bluntly, too frustrated to be polite. He gritted his teeth for a few seconds in silence, then scowled, unable to contain his exasperation. "You and the Council are making the wrong decision. Having Gifted available to heal the wounded would save many lives."

Nashrel made a calming gesture. "I'm on your side, Davian. If I had my way, we would be at the Shields as we speak," he said calmly. "But the others did make some valid points. The palace can hardly expect us to help, not if they're not willing to change the Tenets so that we can at least defend ourselves."

"But you won't even talk to them," said Davian in frustration.

"And as we told you, if changing the Tenets is not a part of the discussion, there is little point."

"But if you just—"

"It's not just the king's stubbornness regarding the Tenets, Davian." Nashrel stopped and turned to him, a serious look on his face. "This vitriol we've been hearing from him—these open threats against the Gifted—isn't something we can just ignore. You have to understand...all of us remember the Unseen War like it was yesterday, and what we've heard coming from the palace has been stirring up old memories. Old fears."

"So the solution is to hide in here and hope it all goes away?"

585

Nashrel frowned at that. "Show a little respect," he said quietly, anger just beneath the surface. Davian colored, knowing he'd overstepped, but Nashrel started walking again before Davian could respond. "I know you're frustrated, but the Elders on the Council went through things during the war that you can only imagine. Since then, being behind these walls is the only way many of them can feel safe. Fates, I can name four Elders who haven't left the Tol in near twenty years! These are deep-seated fears, Davian—not the kind that can be easily overcome. Especially not when they are fed by the king like this."

Davian shook his head. "Maybe you're right," he conceded. "But it doesn't excuse the way they're abandoning everyone. It doesn't give them the right to bury their heads in the sand while the Blind threaten their city. Even the Gifted from Tol Shen have realized that."

Nashrel didn't respond for a while. The stairwells and passageways narrowed more the farther down they traveled; here Davian would be able to touch both walls simultaneously with his elbows if he tried. The rock of Ilin Tora itself had slowly transformed from the carefully carved light brown of the upper levels to a jagged, menacing black, roughly hewn and almost volcanic in its appearance. The air was musty, and there was such a fierce chill to it that Davian shivered despite his thick cloak.

Eventually the Elder sighed. "There's some merit to what you're saying, Davian. And the news about Shen surprised me. But the Council has made its decision; what's done is done." He shook his head. "Just be glad they agreed to let you see Tenvar. I wasn't sure they were going to do that much, to be honest, after you... expressed your displeasure about our decision not to fight. And Tol Athian is not in the habit of giving strangers free access to prisoners, either."

Davian grunted. "I can't say I appreciated having to Read them like it was some kind of parlor trick, though," he said in disgust.

"They needed proof that you were really an Augur—some guarantee you weren't lying—before they could let you down here. It was not unreasonable." Nashrel gave a slight smile. "Anyway, Fethrin and Ielsa certainly regret making you do it."

Davian snorted. "They brought that on themselves."

"That they did," said Nashrel in amusement.

They turned down another passageway; here Essence orbs had been replaced with traditional torches, so sparsely placed along the hallways that it was almost pitch-black in between them. The only sound was the constant echoing of the two men's boots on the hard stone, and even that faint noise was quickly swallowed by the darkness.

They emerged into a long hallway, wider and better lit than those preceding. Rather than unbroken black rock, the passage here was lined with iron doorways that had small barred windows. From the occasional cough, Davian could tell that the dungeon had at least a few occupants.

Finally they came to a stop in front of a cell, one of the last in the hallway. Dark though it was, Davian could make out the crouched human form within. He waited until Nashrel unlocked the steel-barred door, then turned to the Elder.

"I'd prefer not to go in there unarmed."

Nashrel hesitated, then drew a short dagger from his belt. "Use this for anything but self-defense, and Augur or not, I'll have you thrown out of the Tol. Immediately."

Davian nodded. "Of course."

"Davian!" came a familiar voice from inside the cell. "I see the Gifted know what you are now. And haven't turned you in yet. Good for you." Tenvar walked forward so that his face was pressed up against the bars of the tiny window. He looked as if he hadn't washed in days, and his beard was growing out to give him an entirely unkempt look.

Davian glared at him, fury burning in his stomach. "Stand back," he growled.

Tenvar did as he was told.

Davian opened the door with one hand, gripping the knife in the other. He doubted Tenvar could overpower him in his evidently weakened state, but there was no point taking the chance.

Davian entered the cell warily, but Tenvar had taken a seat on the opposite side of the small room. Despite his condition he looked relaxed, even a little smug, his legs crossed and reclining as if the stone bench were the most comfortable chair in the world.

Davian felt another flash of anger. "I've come to find out who you're working for. And how to stop the Blind," he said, keeping his tone as calm as he could manage.

Tenvar smiled. "Ah, so that's what they decided to call them. How unoriginal. And they're here already, are they? Faster than I expected," he said cheerfully. "Thank you for that information. Nobody had told me I would be rescued quite so soon."

"Rescued?" Davian gave a bitter laugh. "You're not going anywhere, Tenvar. I'll see you dead before I see you free."

"Threatening my life?" Ilseth sighed. "Davian, you forget that I know you a little. Not well, perhaps, I'll grant you that. But enough to know that you're no murderer. You don't have a violent bone in your body."

Davian said nothing for a moment, then took a deep breath. He wasn't here to argue with Tenvar or rise to his taunts. He was here to Read him, plain and simple.

He concentrated, reaching out until he could feel Tenvar's mind. He was immediately, unsurprisingly, presented with a locked box.

Davian examined the box in silence. There were other memories outside it but Davian didn't bother to look at them; if Tenvar didn't feel the need to hide them, they were unimportant. He tried to remember how he'd broken into Malshash's box, but the longer he stared at Tenvar's, the more impregnable it seemed to become.

"I'm shielded, Davian," said Ilseth, his tone relaxed, even slightly amused. "I've kept my thoughts private for forty years. From before the *real* Augurs fell. You're not breaking in."

Davian didn't reply, but allowed his focus to wane for a few moments. Ilseth was putting all his concentration into maintaining that shield; even if Davian tried forcing the box open he would probably fail. He needed Ilseth's attention elsewhere.

His stomach churned a little, but it needed to be done.

He leaned over and, as coldly as possible, plunged his knife into Tenvar's thigh.

Tenvar screamed in surprised pain; even as Davian pulled the knife out again, he slammed into Tenvar's mental box with everything he had. It disintegrated, and Davian moaned as Tenvar's agony flooded through to his own mind. He ignored the pain, clenching his fists.

Behind him he could hear Nashrel yelling something, rushing into the cell. If Davian was going to get information, he had to be quick.

He searched for a way to stop the Blind, but to his frustration he discovered that Tenvar knew very little of the invasion. It made sense, he supposed; if he'd had something so vital in his memories then Devaed would surely have found a way to have him killed, tucked away in a Tol Athian dungeon or not.

Davian moved on to the question that had been burning inside him for so long now. Why had Tenvar given him the Vessel, sent him away before the slaughter of everyone else in the school?

He located the memory he was after, then took a deep breath.

*Davian waited.*

*The small room was dark and dank, and had a musty smell that made him sporadically wrinkle his nose in disgust. A jumble of discarded boxes were heaped in the corner, where the damp had already contrived to rot through some of them. Otherwise the room was empty. There were no windows this far beneath the surface, of course, but his lamp, set down in the middle of the room, lit the black stone walls well enough.*

*He hoped this meeting would not take long. Being discovered in this section of Tol Athian, so deep beneath the ancient foundations, would result in questions he might not easily be able to answer.*

*He began to pace, tracking an imaginary path along the cold stone floor. He had received this summons so abruptly, so directly, that he did not know what to expect. For the thousandth time he pondered the possibility that it was a trap. The message had been written in an ancient Darecian dialect; there were only four or five people in Andarra who still knew that language, so a ruse was unlikely. Why he was being called upon at this vital moment, though—now, when he was so close to succeeding—he simply could not imagine.*

*He ran his fingers through his hair as he marched back and forth, mentally categorizing the possibilities. None of them were good.*

Behind him the lamp went out, plunging the room into darkness.

He froze in midstep, a shiver running up his spine as he heard the door to the stairwell creak shut. The hair at the base of his neck began to prickle.

"You have come," a deep voice rumbled in approval.

Davian turned. The room appeared lit again, but this time with a cold, unnaturally pale luminescence. In front of the closed door stood the faint outline of a lone man, cloaked and hooded, face shrouded in shadow. The stranger made no move to enter the room farther.

"I would not refuse a summons from the master we serve," said Davian. The man had to be using kan to manipulate Essence, illuminating the room but keeping himself in darkness. Not a trap, then—something more terrifying by far, in fact, though Davian could not fathom how one of them could be on this side of the Boundary.

They weren't a myth, then. This was one of the Venerate.

The hooded man nodded, oblivious to Davian's train of thought. "That is good," he growled. "Then you would not refuse a task from him, either." Davian thought he must be altering his voice somehow; certainly no one could naturally sound so gravelly. Distracted by the concept, he took a few moments to comprehend the stranger's words.

"It would be an honor to serve Lord Devaed in any task," he said, almost tripping over the words in his haste to respond. The Venerate were not to be trifled with, but the question burned within him—he hesitated a second longer, swallowing hard, working up the courage to continue. "Before we proceed...if I may ask...why now? I mean no disrespect, but what could be worth risking my place here, so close to the end?" He had worked too hard, sacrificed too much, not to know.

There was a long silence; though Davian could not see beneath the other man's hood, he could feel his gaze burrowing into his skull.

"Do you know why I chose this place to meet?" The words were spoken so softly that Davian barely heard them.

He shifted, his sense of unease growing. "No."

"I chose it because the walls here have no Remembering." The man raised his hand, brushing the stone with his fingertips. "In this room, Tenvar, I can do whatever I please."

There was no warning.

Davian gasped as the index finger of his right hand began to burn; a second later a shriek ripped from his throat as agony coursed through him, nerves screaming as they were sliced open. He grasped the finger tightly but to no avail; he collapsed on the floor as it began to tear open from the tip downward, fingernail and then flesh slowly splitting in a shower of blood and pain, the bare bone itself splintering as impossibly fine strands of Essence pulled it carefully, inexorably, in opposite directions.

"Stop!" he sobbed, writhing helplessly. Already the finger was split down to the second joint. He moaned, heart pounding wildly, trying to focus on anything but the pain. "Stop," he choked again.

After what felt like an eternity, the force exerted upon his rent flesh vanished. Essence flowed around him; his hand began to cool, and something dropped wetly to the floor. The pain eased. He sat up from his prostrate position, then turned away and retched, the bile acidic in his throat. The small, pulpy mass of twisted and torn flesh next to him was all that remained of his forefinger. On his hand the dark red blood had vanished, and a smooth, scarred stump sat where the finger had been taken off. Only a throbbing remembrance of pain remained.

"That is a reminder," the man said quietly. "I chose only a finger, to punish your insolence. I could as easily have chosen something more...important." Davian shuddered, scrambling backward away from both the mangled digit and his attacker, until his back was pressed against the cold stone wall. The man paid his actions no heed. "You are not here to question," he continued, "but to serve as your master sees fit. Do you understand?"

Davian nodded, eyes wide with fear.

"Now. We received your message. You think the escherii's attacks have finally borne fruit—that the heir is hiding in Caladel?"

Davian swallowed, his nod vigorous this time. "Nashrel    591 insisted on holding the Trials there early this year. It's for reasons of efficiency, supposedly, but that's a weak excuse at best—it seems clear they are trying to get the boy out of harm's way." He paused. "I have already made sure I am part of the group going there. If my suspicions are correct, Eilinar will reveal the true purpose of the journey just before we leave."

"Good." Suddenly the stranger was moving, striding across the room; Davian pressed farther back against the wall, as if trying to sink into the stone itself. The man stopped directly in front of him, towering over him.

Then, in one smooth motion, he retrieved something from beneath his robes. He held it out to Davian.

"Take it," he instructed.

Davian leaned forward hesitantly, then removed the item from the man's gloved hand, almost snatching it in his haste to retreat again. He managed to drag his gaze downward for a moment, giving the object a quick glance. It was small, small enough to fit snugly in his palm, and appeared to be a metallic cube of some kind.

As Davian took the object, the man's sleeve pulled back slightly. Davian saw it for only a moment, but there was a symbol tattooed on his wrist—the ilsharat, the symbol of the Boundary, he thought—that flickered with light as Davian touched the box. He looked back up straight away, knowing he was not supposed to have seen what he had. The other man, fortunately, appeared not to have noticed.

"There is a boy in the school at Caladel called Davian. He is an Augur—barely aware of his abilities; however, he knows how to discern deception. You know how to counter that?"

"Of course," said Davian, still dazed.

"Good. You are to give him that box, and tell him that he needs to deliver it for you. It doesn't matter what reason you give, just ensure it is something that he can believe, and that it motivates him sufficiently to go through with it. Allow him to leave the school safely and undetected."

Davian nodded. He had a hundred questions, but he knew better than to ask most of them. "Where is he to take it?"

"North," replied the man. "Tell him to head north. He will know where to go thereafter."

*Davian coughed. "My lord, if there were something more spe-*
*cific, perhaps it would be easier to..." He trailed off, realizing*
*what he was saying. "As our master wishes. What of the heir?"*

*"He dies, as planned. Along with the rest," said the man. "No*
*survivors, no one to confirm that Davian is missing. Understand:*
*this is even more important than killing Torin Andras. Davian*
*must deliver the box at all costs."*

*Davian repressed a frown. That was explicitly different from*
*what he'd been told before. Still, there could be no doubt that this*
*man had been sent by Aarkein Devaed. Whatever had caused the*
*change in plan, it seemed he was not to be privy to it.*

*He gave a weak nod. "It must be important," he said cautiously.*

*The man paused. "It will ensure our master's return from his*
*exile in Talan Gol. It will ensure our victory, Tenvar." He leaned*
*forward. "Is that motivation enough for you?"*

*"I will not fail you," Davian managed to stutter out, but the*
*other man had already spun and was heading toward the door.*
*A shadowy swirl of kan covered the messenger as he reached*
*the heavy oak and he melted through the wood, vanishing from*
*sight. As soon as he had gone, the room was once more plunged*
*into darkness.*

*Davian huddled farther into the corner, eyes squeezed shut,*
*nursing his hand and choking back the sobs that threatened to*
*explode out of him now that he was alone.*

*He did not move for a very, very long time.*

Davian gasped as he dragged himself out of Tenvar's mind, stumbling backward and then crashing to the ground as Nashrel tack-
led him.

He allowed himself to be dragged to his feet and shoved bodily
against the wall, mind still reeling from the impact of forcing his
way into Tenvar's thoughts, as well as what he'd just seen.

"Give me the knife," said Nashrel, his voice high with tension.
"And don't move."

Davian released his grip on the bloodstained blade, letting it fall
to the ground, his mind spinning. The stranger had been linked to
the box, just as Caeden was. What did that mean? That Caeden

was associated with him, somehow? That the box had been linked to someone else initially? It hadn't been Caeden himself; the man in the hood had been too tall, too thin—and the hand Davian had seen had been wrinkled, the hand of an older man.

Another thought struck him. Given what the stranger had said at the end, why would Malshash have told him to follow through on getting the box to Caeden... unless Malshash wanted Devaed to be freed? Davian went cold at the thought. He'd never once considered it before, but after what he'd just seen...

He clenched his fists. The memory had told him a little... but not enough. And in many ways it had only raised more questions.

"What did you do to him?" Nashrel's voice broke through Davian's train of thought.

"I'm sorry. I wasn't trying to kill him," Davian reassured the Elder. "I just needed to disrupt his concentration so I could get to his memories. I knew you'd be able to heal the wound. He'll be fine."

"I'm not so sure about that."

Davian frowned, twisting from his position pressed up against the stone wall to see what the Elder was talking about.

Ilseth lay, mouth and eyes wide open, on the floor. Nashrel had already used Essence to heal his leg wound, but the man's expression was... vacant. Lifeless. His chest rose and fell, but it was as if a light had gone out behind his eyes.

Davian grimaced. Malshash had warned him about the possibility of doing permanent damage.

For a moment he felt glad, as if perhaps some form of justice had been done.

Then he recoiled at the thought, felt bile swirling in his stomach. He'd wanted vengeance for those who had died at Caladel, certainly. For what had happened to Asha. But he wasn't the kind of man to take it with violence.

Was he?

Davian swallowed. His emotions had been... murky, ever since he'd accessed Malshash's memory back in Deilannis. He still felt as if he'd done those things at the wedding, killed all those people. Just as he now rubbed at his forefinger, vaguely surprised to find it intact.

He shook his head to clear it. He would deal with whatever this was later. For the moment he had more important things to worry about.

He shivered as he remembered the hooded man's words to Ilseth. *It will ensure our victory.*

Then he froze.

"We need to leave," he said to Nashrel suddenly.

The Elder grunted. "*You* certainly do. Because I warned you what would happen if you used that knife."

"No." Davian looked at him, urgent. "There's something you need to know. We need to get to wherever you store your Vessels."

Davian's heart pounded as he explained. Whatever else happened, whether he was an enemy or just a pawn in all that was happening, Caeden needed to be kept far, far away from that box.

※

Caeden sat on the low stone wall next to Kara, silent as he digested what the princess had just told him.

He stared out over the empty courtyard, the only other people in view a pair of distant guards going about their predawn patrol. The space would be full of soldiers soon enough, and given the news, today more than ever the mood during their training would be somber. The Blind had defeated General Jash'tar's army. Were coming straight for the city.

Caeden shivered a little, and he wasn't entirely sure it was just from the crisp night air.

He glanced across at the princess, chest constricting a little as he realized that this meant his time with her was rapidly drawing to a close. These early-morning conversations between them had become a routine over the past week; Kara would slip out of her rooms without her father's guards' realizing, knock at his door, and the two of them would come out here and spend hours just... talking.

He knew the princess was being nothing more than friendly, but Caeden had begun to live for those times. Though he'd often enjoyed his talks with Wirr, Davian, Taeris, and the others, the specter of his past had always hovered over those exchanges. Around Kara that never seemed to be the case. Their conversations were more relaxed, lighter somehow, even if the topics were    595 serious; with her, for just a few hours each day, he was able to forget all the problems that he faced—that they all faced—and just take pleasure in someone else's company.

Today, however, was different. Kara had looked exhausted when he'd opened his door this morning, and now he knew why.

"How soon until they arrive?" asked Caeden, his stomach churning.

"A couple of days—maybe less, if they push. Nobody is really sure." Kara watched Caeden's expression. "What are you and Taeris going to do?"

Caeden hesitated. He hadn't confided Taeris's contingency plan to the princess—not due to a lack of trust, but rather because Caeden didn't want to put the princess in yet another awkward position. Knowing her as he now did, Caeden had no doubt that if he told Kara that he and Taeris were intending to break into the Tol, she would feel guilty for not acting on the information. Would feel party to whatever happened as a result.

But he realized now that he couldn't leave her completely in the dark, either. She hadn't made him put the Shackle back on—if he left without warning, she would think he'd just run away, abandoned the city. Abandoned her.

Before he could speak, though, he spotted a harried-looking Taeris hurrying toward them. Caeden grimaced, but nodded to the older man and stood.

"Caeden," said Taeris in half-irritated relief when he got a little closer. His eyes widened as he recognized Caeden's companion, and his demeanor transformed. He gave a low bow. "Your Highness. I...I'm afraid I will need to borrow Caeden for a while."

Kara nodded slowly. "That is fine, Taeris," she said, suddenly the cool and formal version of herself that Caeden now saw only on occasion. She turned to Caeden with the hint of a wry smile. "Perhaps there will be an opportunity to continue this sometime later today."

She began to walk away. Caeden watched her go in frustration, knowing why Taeris had come to find him.

"Your Highness," he abruptly called after her. "Please wait a moment."

He hurried over to the princess, ignoring Taeris's surprised look.

"I'm not sure we will get the chance to speak again before the Blind arrive, Your Highness," Caeden said in a meaningful tone, locking gazes with Kara. "I think other matters may...keep me away."

Kara looked between Caeden and Taeris for a few seconds, then nodded in understanding. Her eyes were suddenly sad.

"Then we will just have to wait until after everything is over," she said softly. She stepped forward, her lips brushing against his cheek. "Fates guide you, Caeden."

Caeden swallowed, blushing. "You, too, Kara," he said, quietly enough that Taeris couldn't overhear.

Kara just nodded, then turned and disappeared back into the main palace building without another word.

Caeden watched her go, then turned to Taeris and opened his mouth to explain.

"I...don't want to know," said Taeris gruffly, shaking his head. There was something approaching an amused smile on his lips, though it faded almost immediately. "You've heard about the Blind?"

"Just then," said Caeden. He hesitated. "The Travel Stone is really our only option?"

Taeris nodded. "It is now, and we should think about using it straight away. It's early enough that we might catch some of the Gifted still asleep in the Tol, maybe buy ourselves a couple of extra minutes to get the memory device working." He glanced around. "We can't just open the portal out in the open, though; the last thing we need is someone seeing and trying to interfere. Doing it from my quarters would be best."

Caeden nodded, and they started toward Taeris's rooms.

After a few minutes they rounded a corner and Taeris issued a soft, panicked curse. Caeden looked up at him in alarm as the scarred man faltered, breaking his stride for a moment as he stared down the hallway ahead.

Caeden followed his gaze. A blond-haired man in a fine blue cloak was walking toward them, though he was absorbed in reading some papers in his hand and hadn't yet noticed their presence. Caeden glanced at Taeris, who had now bowed his head, evidently doing his best to hide his face from the stranger.

The Administrator looked up just before they were past and came to an abrupt halt, holding up a hand to indicate that they should do the same.

"Taeris Sarr," he said once Taeris had stopped, a quiet certainty in his voice.

Taeris's shoulders slumped, and he nodded. "Duke Andras," he responded dully.

Caeden's stomach twisted. The duke was one of the people whom they had been desperate to avoid, whom Taeris was certain would turn them over to Administration.

The duke studied Taeris and Caeden for a long moment.

"Try not to be seen," he said.

He turned his attention back to his papers and walked off without another word.

Taeris and Caeden both gaped after the Administrator for a few seconds.

"Why didn't he raise the alarm?" asked Caeden.

Taeris shook his head in confusion. "I...I don't know," he admitted. "But let's get moving before he changes his mind."

They made it to Taeris's rooms without further incident; the few other people they passed in the hallways all appeared distracted, hurrying about their business and paying little heed to the two men.

Once they were inside, Taeris turned to Caeden, still looking a little shaken.

"Before we do this—I need to make one thing clear, Caeden. This was a last resort for good reason. I can get us in, but not out again. If we let the Gifted catch us, they will lock us up and we'll be of no help to anyone...so whatever happens, you're going to need to get free. Fight your way out if you have to, but make sure you get to the Shields by the time the Blind get here. Even if that means leaving me behind."

Caeden didn't reply for a moment, wanting to protest, knowing that this was his last chance to change his mind. He'd suspected that this would be the way of things, ever since Taeris had told him the plan...was he really capable of fighting his way out of Tol Athian, though? He knew he probably had the raw strength; if his memories were fully restored, he would, hopefully, have the skill as well.

But whether he would be able to do it without hurting any-one was another matter entirely. Despite their stubbornness, the Gifted were to a large extent innocent in all of this, and Caeden had no desire to injure anyone at the Tol. Deep down, though, he understood that an escape without casualties might turn out to be impossible.

And he *did* need to escape—needed to do everything he could to fight the Blind.

"I understand," he said reluctantly.

Taeris gave him a relieved nod. "Are you ready? Once we start this process, Administrators will be on their way. We won't get a second chance at it."

Caeden took a couple of steadying breaths. "Ready."

Taeris put his hand above the Travel Stone and closed his eyes. A stream of white energy started pouring from him into the stone; he stayed like that for several seconds before stopping the flow with a slight shudder.

He picked up the stone from the table and held it out, away from his body. The Vessel began to glow; a shimmering line of light appeared in front of Taeris, spinning and expanding until it formed a circle twice Caeden's height and just as wide.

Then it vanished, replaced by a hole that simply hung in the air. Caeden peered through it into what appeared to be a vast storage room.

He glanced at Taeris, who made an impatient gesture.

"Go. Quickly," the Elder said through gritted teeth. "I can't hold it open for more than a few seconds."

Caeden braced himself, then tentatively stepped through the hole. He'd expected some sort of sensation or resistance, but it was no different from stepping through a doorway.

Taeris followed and the portal blinked shut behind him. He moved quickly over to a nearby table, then scooped up a polished black stone and pocketed it before turning to Caeden.

"Now," he said, "Let's find this device."

Caeden barely heard the words.

On a shelf, not far from where the stone had been, was the bronze box.

To Caeden's eyes it burned like the sun, though he knew only he and Davian saw it that way. Taeris probably hadn't even noticed it yet.

The tattoo on Caeden's wrist was shining brighter than ever, too, even through the fabric of his shirt.

"Where should we look?" asked Caeden, not taking his eyes from the Vessel.

Taeris shuffled his feet, casting a nervous glance toward the door. "It's large. A pillar of stone, about three feet tall if I remember correctly. If we just—"

Taeris's voice faded into the background.

Caeden stepped forward, reached out his hand, and picked up the bronze Vessel from the shelf.

The explosion nearly tore him from his feet.

He stumbled backward, throwing a hand to his eyes to shield them from the intense red light that had erupted in front of him. Taeris was yelling something at him, screaming it, but there was a roar of power that drowned out everything else.

When Caeden's eyes finally adjusted to the brightness, he felt a stab of fear. Before him was an enormous vortex of pure red fire, swirling and coalescing, stretching from roof to ceiling. He stared at it for a few moments in shock, then glanced down at the box in his hand. It was warm, but its glow—so bright a moment before—had vanished.

As had the glow from his wrist.

"What is it?" he screamed to Taeris.

"I don't know!" Taeris yelled back, only just audible. "We should leave it be, though! There's no telling what it does!"

To his left the door to the storeroom burst open.

Caeden turned to see a wild-eyed Davian rushing inside, followed closely by a red-cloaked man he recognized as Elder Eilinar. Both men stared at the vortex in shock, then headed straight for Caeden.

"Caeden!" screamed Davian, seeing the box in his hands. "Put it down!"

Caeden barely heard, even his shocked delight at seeing Davian alive registering as only a minor distraction. Somehow he knew that the vortex was meant for him. He was supposed to step into it. It would take him...he wasn't sure where, but it was somewhere he wanted to go. Somewhere he *needed* to go.

He shook his head.

"I'm sorry," he yelled, including both Davian and Taeris in the apology. "I have to do this."

"Caeden! Don't!" It was Taeris. "We need you here!"

Caeden closed his eyes. Breathed steadily.

Then he spun and sprinted as hard as he could toward the tunnel of fire. He could sense Taeris and Davian both moving to stop him, but he was too fast. He was always going to be too fast.

He leaped into the vortex at full speed, bracing himself.

There was heat, the briefest instant of feeling as if the flames were dancing on his skin. The shouts behind him faded.

And then he was somewhere else.

# Chapter 50

Wirr stood alongside Aelric and Dezia atop the First Shield, staring apprehensively out over the steadily darkening green of the rolling plains beyond Fedris Idri as they waited for the first sign of the enemy.

The Blind were coming, and fast. The report had arrived an hour earlier from one of General Parathe's scouts, who had ridden his horse near to death in his urgency to return. The invaders were no longer taking their time; they had seemingly marched throughout the previous night, pausing for neither sleep nor food. They were likely to reach the city walls by nightfall.

Now afternoon was waning to dusk, and the gates below were finally shutting. Wirr flinched as the massive doors sealed the city, the ominous boom echoing around the narrow pass.

Then the sound faded, leaving almost utter silence. At least a few minutes earlier there had been the low murmur of voices from the several hundred men manning the First Shield, even the occasional nervous laugh. Now that had died away too as the sun began to slip below the horizon.

Wirr felt a hand on his shoulder, and he turned to see Aelric looking at him with a serious expression.

"Are you sure you want to be up here?" the young swordsman asked quietly. He glanced across at his sister, including her in the query. "It's not like the Second Shield isn't going to need defenders."

Wirr winced, glancing around to check that no one had overheard. His father had warned him that the fighting would reach Ilin Illan itself, and Wirr in turn had felt the need to tell Dezia and

Aelric. That didn't mean he wanted the soldiers to know, though. For most of the men, the hope of victory—the belief that it was attainable—was what gave them the courage to fight.

Dezia evidently knew that too and gave her brother a withering look, shaking her bow at him. "We've already discussed this. My skills are going to be all but useless once it comes to hand-to-hand combat," she said in a whisper. "I may as well make a difference while I can."

"And I can be most effective healing the wounded from up here, getting them back in the fight quickly," added Wirr. "No different from the Shen Gifted." He glanced across at the nervous cluster of red-cloaked men and women, who stood together at the city end of the wall, back a little from the front lines. There weren't many of them, but it was more than Wirr had expected from Tol Shen. And their presence would make a real difference.

Aelric grunted as he followed Wirr's gaze. "Fair enough. Just… stay as far back as you can once everything starts, both of you. You're no good to anyone if you get hurt," he said gruffly, turning his gaze back out onto the plains.

Wirr exchanged a small grin with Dezia; her brother had already said something similar a few times in the past hour. He clapped Aelric on the back. "We will," he assured the young man.

On a whim Wirr wandered closer to the edge of the wall, tentatively leaning forward to see the hard stone below, marveling again at just how high up they were. A mild wave of vertigo washed over him before he drew back. The First Shield—the outermost of Fedris Idri's defenses, atop which he now stood—was at least fifty feet tall, allowing anyone manning it to see for miles across the plains in any direction.

Height wasn't its only advantage. Despite the narrow pass, the Shield's depth allowed hundreds of people to be atop it at once. At the front its thin parapet tapered upward everywhere into sharp points, jagged but elegantly symmetrical, as if rows of enormous swords had been carved from the stone itself.

He'd tested one of the edges of those impossibly thin stone spikes himself, drawing blood from the lightest of touches. His father had once explained that the Builders had created every edge of the parapet to be razor sharp; any attackers clambering over it would inevitably be cut. And the tapering shape of the parapet itself meant that ladders could never sit flat against it, could never jut out above it in order to bypass its dangers altogether.

Even so, none of it made Wirr feel any safer.

"So what news from General Parathe?" he asked after a moment. "I saw you speaking to him a few minutes ago."

Aelric shrugged. "He says there's likely to be about a thousand of the Blind. They're not going to fit more than a couple of hundred into the pass at once, though, so that's something." He hesitated, glancing along the line and lowering his voice. "He's worried about how these men are going to hold up in a battle. Many of them were left out of Jash'tar's force for a reason—Parathe said a lot of them have had discipline issues lately. Difficulty completing their drills sometimes. Gone for a day or so doing fates know what, then back and pretending like nothing's wrong. Not men he particularly wanted to have to rely on."

Wirr grimaced. "Just what we need."

Aelric grunted his agreement. The three of them stood side by side for a while, the heavy silence pressing on Wirr's shoulders like a physical weight. He was so lost in thought that he jumped when a hand clapped him on the shoulder.

Wirr turned.

"Davian!" he exclaimed.

Davian smiled tiredly, then gave a short laugh of surprise as he was enveloped by embraces from Aelric and Dezia.

"Wirr said you were alive, but I wasn't sure I believed him until now. It's good to see you, Davian," said Aelric.

"You, too," said Davian. "I just wish it were under better circumstances."

Wirr's heart sank as he saw the expression on his friend's face. "Tol Athian...?"

"Did not go well." Davian paused, then gave Aelric and Dezia a hesitant glance.

"They know about you, Dav," said Wirr, a little apologetically. "There didn't seem to be much point hiding the truth after Deilannis."

Davian inclined his head, looking more relieved than anything else, and related what had happened at the Tol.

"Fates," murmured Wirr when he was done, a sick feeling in his stomach. "So only the Shen Gifted to heal the wounded, and now we have to keep an eye out for Caeden, too. And the Council locked Taeris up?"

Davian nodded. He looked about to say more when there was a shout from down the wall, followed by a low murmuring as soldiers began to point out toward the plains. Wirr looked up, squinting in the fading light.

Fires had begun to dot the horizon.

Aelric turned to Davian, his voice tight. "Things are going to get messy up here soon. Are you going to be able to fight?"

Davian didn't respond for a moment, staring out over the plains as if he could see something the others couldn't. Then he shook his head slightly as if to clear it. "There's no point me try-ing to use Essence—there aren't enough sources nearby, and even if there were, I'd be bound by the Tenets as soon as I drew enough to be useful. I might be able to use kan, though." He bit his lip. "I could use a sword, too, if there are any to spare."

Wirr gave him a skeptical look. "A sword? Dav, we can find one for you, but . . . is there really any point?"

Davian hesitated, then glanced across at Aelric.

"Aelric. I will understand if you don't want me to, but . . . may I Read you? If you let me, I can access your memories, relive some of your training. I don't think it will give me anywhere near your level of ability, unfortunately—I've read that physical skills don't translate very well due to the bodies being different—but even just knowing some of the basics would help."

Aelric stared at Davian, wide-eyed, for a long few moments. He licked his lips, looking nervous, and Wirr felt sure he was going to refuse.

Then he sighed. "That's all you'll see?"

"Yes," Davian assured him.

Aelric gave a slow nod. "Anything I can do to help."

Davian inclined his head gratefully, then stepped forward. He touched Aelric lightly on the forehead and closed his eyes, stand-ing like that for several seconds. Wirr and Dezia looked on with silent curiosity. As far as Wirr could see, there was nothing to indicate anything unusual was happening.

After a few more moments Davian opened his eyes again, stepping back. "Thank you."

"That's all?" Aelric rubbed his forehead where Davian's hand had been, looking uneasy. "I didn't feel anything."

"That's all," said Davian with a smile.

Wirr stared at his friend, fascinated. "Did it work?"

Davian shrugged. "I should get myself a sword...after that, I suppose we'll know soon enough."

Wirr went to help Davian secure a weapon; by the time they returned to Aelric and Dezia, sunset was vanishing into dusk, leaving only a slowly fading glow and plunging the flat plains that approached Ilin Tora into a deep murk.

They had been standing there for less than a minute when Wirr spotted a flicker of movement in the distance. A few moments later, a horn blasted from somewhere down the wall.

"Here they come," muttered Aelric.

A mass of glinting black resolved itself from the gloom that covered the plains, moving faster than Wirr would have believed possible as it surged forward into the narrow pass. It was hard to tell in the fading light, but Wirr thought there were a couple of hundred men rushing into the enclosed space below—three hundred at most.

"Where are the rest of them?" he wondered aloud, nerves making his voice tight.

Aelric shook his head. "This is just the first wave. They know that having more than two hundred men in here at once is a waste of energy."

Wirr didn't respond, chewing at his lip as Dezia walked forward to join the other Andarran archers at the front of the wall. The order to draw rang out, and Dezia notched an arrow, her actions deliberate and her hands steady. Wirr couldn't help but admire her composure.

Then the Blind were in range and arrows were raining down upon them. Wirr's heart sank as he watched the men below rush onward, unfazed. The archers fired again, and again, but it didn't seem to matter. Wirr didn't see a single enemy soldier falter, let alone fall.

The oncoming black mass hit the wall like a wave as the last of the light faded from the sky.

The next few minutes passed in chaos.

All along the First Shield, screams rang out as attackers started appearing like wraiths along the battlements, reaching over with preternatural speed and strength to pull soldiers over the wall and to their deaths. They were little more than black shadows, silent, appearing from nowhere and vanishing behind the parapet again within moments.

Wirr had already begun retreating when a darker shape against the night sky shifted in the corner of his eye. Davian leaped forward, blade whipping out; there was no sound except that of metal on metal, but his sword met solid resistance and the owner of the armor was sent flying backward into the darkness.

"They're not using ladders," Davian warned Wirr. "You should get further back. They could be coming up anywhere."

"How is that possible?" asked Wirr.

"It has to be the armor," interjected Dezia, who had also retreated a little, but was still smoothly firing off arrows whenever she caught sight of movement. She allowed herself a quick glance along the battlements. "It must allow them to climb the wall somehow."

Wirr followed her gaze. There were plenty of men crowding along the parapet, but already it looked as though the Andarran front line was thinning. Replacements were being ushered up the stairs at the back, but Wirr could already see the futility of it. The Blind might be heavily outnumbered, but each attacker was going to be worth too many defenders.

"It's blocking kan, too," added Davian grimly, his sword lashing out at another Shadow. His movements didn't look anywhere near as assured as Aelric's, but Wirr could tell Davian knew how to handle a blade now. "I can't push it past those El-cursed helmets."

"Wonderful," said Aelric, already a little out of breath. He flinched back as another blade slashed out from the blackness. "We're not going to last an hour if we can't see them. I take it neither of you can do anything about that?"

608    Wirr hesitated, then closed his eyes, tapping his Reserve.

Focused inward. Cautiously he drew from the pool of molten light, then...*twisted* it. Condensed it, made it brighter, as he'd done countless times before.

Nothing happened.

"El-cursed Tenets," he muttered. He issued a frustrated shake of the head to Aelric as the other man backed away from the edge of the wall for a moment, giving Wirr a questioning glance. "It's still trying to use Essence with the intent to cause harm to non-Gifted."

Things passed in a blur after that. Wirr was reluctant to leave his friends, but he knew he was needed elsewhere; soon enough he had joined the Gifted from Tol Shen, healing those soldiers who were still able to stagger away from the front lines. Wirr was the strongest of the group, and he threw himself into the work. It was all he could do to concentrate, to block out the screams of the injured, the scent of men soiling themselves, and the hot, sticky feel of blood.

Finally, though, his Reserve began to empty, and he looked up to see the Andarran line was dangerously thin, threatening to break. Even as he did so, a horn rang out with two quick blasts. The signal to fall back, abandon the First Shield.

He headed for the stairs, numb as he glanced back to see black-clad soldiers pouring over the parapet, dispatching anyone too slow to retreat.

They were losing.

⟡

Asha stared up at the Second Shield in horror, stomach churning as the screams of the dying echoed around the pass.

She glanced behind her at the long line of Shadows that followed in her wake, suddenly uncertain. Were they too late? Word of the Blind's sooner-than-expected attack had reached them only an hour earlier; though she'd done her best to organize the Shadows quickly, she could see that the First Shield had already fallen.

She stared for a moment longer, then drew a deep, steadying breath and grabbed the arm of the nearest soldier. "Where's General Parathe?"

The man blinked at her in surprise, his gaze shifting over her shoulder to take in the small army of Shadows behind her. "I'm not sure if—"

"Just tell me," said Asha, putting as much cool anger into her tone as she could manage.

The soldier blanched, then gestured toward the top of the wall.

Asha gave a sharp nod. She turned to Gaell, an older Shadow who had helped her distribute the Vessels to everyone else.

"Keep everyone here. I'll see where they want us," she told him.

Gaell nodded, turning to let the others know as Asha hurried off. Several soldiers paused to give her curious looks as she shouldered her way toward the Second Shield, but none moved to stop her.

Asha climbed the stairs two at a time, quickly spotting General Parathe once she was at the top. She was about to head toward him when there was motion to her left, and a blue cloak suddenly stood in her way.

"What do you think you're doing up here?" the young Administrator asked, his tone grim.

"I'm here to help," Asha replied, staring the man in the eye. "I just need to speak to the general. Please let me past."

The Administrator stared at her in disbelief for a few moments.

"Nonsense. Get off the wall," he sneered eventually. "You're only going to get in the—"

Asha gestured, a small movement. She'd managed to practice a little with the ring today, knew enough to control its strength now. And there wasn't time for this.

The Administrator stumbled backward as if shoved hard in the chest, tripping and sliding several feet before coming to a sprawling halt.

Asha walked past, ignoring the startled stares from those around her who had seen what had happened.

"General Parathe," she called when she was within hearing range.

The general looked up, frowning a little when he saw who it was, but waving her through the cordon of men surrounding him.

"Ashalia, isn't it?" said Parathe, examining her with undisguised curiosity. "The Athian Representative."

Asha nodded. "I'm not here in that capacity right now, I'm

afraid," she said. "But I do have a hundred Shadows with me, and we all have Vessels that can be used as weapons. Just tell me how we can help."

The general stared at her for a few moments in silence.

"Do you now," he said softly, a flicker of hope in his weary eyes. "Anything that can get rid of this El-cursed darkness?"

Asha nodded; there were a few Vessels that would create plenty of light, even if that wasn't their primary purpose. "Some that can heal people, too," she said, noting a wounded man being carried down the stairs.

Parathe nodded slowly, staring out into the darkness toward the First Shield.

"Send a few of them up," he said. "Let's see what you can do."

Asha nodded, exhaling in relief and hastening back to find the others. The presence of the Shadows had already caused a small stir on the ground, but thankfully the soldiers there had too many other concerns already to have become confrontational. Soon she was hurrying back up to Parathe with a small group of Shadows in tow, and the general quickly allocated them to various points along the wall.

"Where do you want me?" she asked Parathe as he sent the last man on his way.

The general shook his head. "I need to keep you safe," he said. "I don't know any of these people, and they don't know me. If they listen to you, I have to make sure you don't come to any harm."

Asha grimaced, but accepted the general's logic with a reluctant nod.

Parathe turned to the muscular man at his right, a tall soldier with gray hair and an old, thin scar above his eye. "Hael. Give the Shadows the order."

Asha stiffened at the familiar name. This was Hael—the man from Erran's vision? In the back of her mind, she suddenly wondered where the Augurs were in all this. She watched the middle-aged man as he signaled to two Shadows standing at the back of the Shield. He looked no different from, and no more threatening than, any of the other soldiers along the wall.

She turned her attention to the Shadows he had motioned to.

Each held a long, thin white rod; at Hael's gesture they pointed the Vessels at opposite sides of the pass and closed their eyes.

Two lines of light burst into existence, molten streams of twisted energy pulsing along the smoothly cut walls of Fedris Idri, throwing everything into sharp relief. For a moment everything paused; even Asha, who had been expecting it, was shocked at the sudden brightness.

She looked over toward the edge of the Shield, now able to see the black-armored men as they scrambled over the parapet. She shivered as she took in the unsettling, eyeless helmets—and then her stomach churned as she recognized the design etched onto the front of them.

It was the symbol she'd seen on the side of Davian's neck, that night he had appeared in her room. The one that had been cut into his skin.

She gave the attackers her full attention now. In the distance, atop the First Shield, she could see more of the Blind standing among the Andarran corpses that were littered across it. These had no helmets, though.

They just... stood there, motionless. Watching.

"Asha?"

The familiar voice interrupted her thoughts, and she tore her gaze away with a shiver to see Wirr kneeling beside a wounded man only a few feet away, staring at her in surprise. Her friend let the last traces of Essence vanish into the man's newly healed side, then stood, hurrying over to her. "What are you doing here?" he asked, concern in his tone.

A long horn blast echoed along the wall, the signal Parathe had arranged for the Shadows to attack.

The area in front of the Second Shield exploded into a cauldron of light, wind, and fire.

The soldiers along the top of the Shield stopped as one, watching in awe as the pass below vanished under wreaths of thick, swirling smoke, which flickered an ominous red with the light of the fierce flames beneath. Several men covered their ears as shrieks of power ripped through the night, bolts of Essence sizzling down from the Second Shield into the maelstrom.

A thunderous gust of wind suddenly swept down, catching up

the black-clad men clambering over the wall and casting them back out into space like rag dolls. Asha watched as they vanished, screaming, into the cloud of crimson smoke. She spotted one or two holding on and flicked her wrist at them; they sailed off into the air like the others as Wirr looked on, frozen to the spot, openmouthed.

"Prince Torin!" It was Parathe, shouting over the cacophony that still thundered around the pass. "The Shadows look to have things under control for the time being. Get some rest!"

Wirr glanced around, spotting the group of Shadows who had joined the Gifted and had started healing some of the wounded. He sagged with visible relief, and for the first time Asha realized just how pale and drawn he looked. She didn't know how many people he'd healed, but it was evident he'd pushed himself to the brink.

Even so, Wirr looked about to protest before eventually giving a reluctant nod. "You fetch me if I'm needed!" he yelled to Parathe. He threw a questioning glance at Asha, but she shook her head, indicating that she was going to stay. She was needed up here.

Wirr gave her a tired smile, squeezing her arm in farewell before joining a trail of weary soldiers limping down the stairs.

Soon the initial thunder of the Shadows' attack quieted, and an eerie hush descended on the smoke-filled pass. The silence was still broken by an occasional ear-piercing shriek as one or another of the Shadows fired bolts of energy into the chaos below, but the ringing in Asha's ears slowly faded.

Finally confident that the Blind had broken off their attack, she crept forward to the edge of the Shield and peered down. Smoke still obscured some of the gap between the First and Second Shields, but enough was visible to know that the Blind had withdrawn, regrouping atop the First Shield and out of range of the Shadows' weapons.

There were plenty of bodies below, and her stomach lurched as she realized that few of the ones she could see were clad in black. Either the Blind had dragged away their dead, or—more ominously—not many of those who had been blasted off the Second Shield had been killed by the fall.

"We've pushed them back for now," said Parathe as he joined her at the parapet. He stared down into the smoke-filled pass below, his expression pensive. "Those flames are too hot even for them to get through, I suspect...but there's only stone down there. Nothing that will burn of its own accord."

Asha gave a thoughtful nod. "If we rotate fresh people onto those Vessels every so often, we should be able to keep the fires going indefinitely," she said in response to the implied query.

Parathe exhaled, a relieved sound. "Thank the fates," he said. "If you hadn't arrived when you did..."

He was silent for a few moments, then clapped her gently on the shoulder. "I'm heading down to check how everyone is faring below, but stay alert. If you see anything, have someone fetch me. You've given us an advantage, but these El-cursed Blind don't strike me as the type to give up. It's not over yet. Not even close," he concluded, gazing through the shimmering red haze toward the First Shield.

Asha watched as Parathe walked away, wondering if the general knew exactly how true those words really were.

"Not even close," she repeated quietly.

Wirr flinched as another shriek of power cut the air, echoing off the walls of Fedris Idri.

He glanced back up toward the top of the Second Shield, swaying a little as exhaustion threatened to get the better of him. He knew he needed to sit down, to rest, but already the screams of the dying were beginning to weigh on him. Even with the Shen Gifted and the Shadows still on the wall, he was one of only a handful of people who could truly help the wounded.

"I wonder how long they can keep that up," came a voice from behind him.

Wirr turned to see Davian following his gaze upward. His friend looked haggard, but uninjured.

"Davian!" He embraced the black-haired boy in relief. "I lost track of you. I didn't know..."

Davian gave him a tired grin. "Can't say it wasn't a near thing, but I'm all right. And Aelric and Dezia are, too; they're around here somewhere. We all fell back after the Shadows...did what they did." He shook his head dazedly at the memory, as if still unwilling to believe what had just transpired.

Wirr knew exactly how he felt; he was still trying to comprehend the implications of the Shadows' ability to use Vessels. "Did you see Asha?" he asked.

Davian frowned. "She's here?"

Wirr was about to reply when he spotted his father approaching, walking alongside a fatigued-looking General Parathe. Wirr gave Elocien a weary smile, and the two embraced.

"My father," he explained to Davian after stepping back again. "And General Parathe."

Davian shook hands awkwardly. "Pleased to meet you, General. Your Grace."

The duke gave an absent nod, though his eyes were still fixed on the top of the Second Shield. "And you, Davian. Torin has told me all about you," he said. "We have much to discuss once this is all over."

Wirr smiled when he saw Davian's expression. "He really does just mean a discussion, Dav—nothing sinister. I promise."

"Of course," said Davian quickly, though Wirr could still see a hint of nervousness in his nod. Wirr turned to Parathe. "How are they doing up there, General?"

"Well enough, for now," said Parathe. "The Shadows say they can do what they're doing indefinitely. It at least buys us some time." He hesitated, casting a cautious glance at the duke. "And perhaps if the king changes his mind..."

"No. No chance." Elocien shook his head. "If anything, my brother is worse. I spoke to him not an hour ago, told him we were being beaten back. He still won't take action. I suspect he'll let the city burn before he lets the Gifted fight, in his current state." He rubbed his forehead. "I shudder to think what he'll do when he hears about the Shadows."

Parathe looked sick at the news, but nodded. "We'll just have to manage with what we—"

Two bodies landed with a crashing of armor against stone, not twenty feet from where they stood.

All four men stared in shock for a moment, then as one turned their gaze upward as panicked shouts began echoing along the Second Shield.

Wirr squinted against the bright light shining down from the walls of the pass. The sporadic flashes from the Shadows' weapons had stopped; there was plenty of motion atop the Shield, but he couldn't tell what was going on at this distance. No one had sounded the retreat, and there were too many men atop that wall to have been overwhelmed so suddenly.

Yet without warning another two pairs of screaming men plummeted from the sky, crashing to their deaths against the floor of the pass.

"Fates," muttered Parathe. He turned to a nearby soldier, who was looking in horror at the motionless bodies. "Nihk. Find out what in fates is going on up there."

The soldier nodded, taking two steps toward the Shield.

Then he spun, sword out and flashing. The man who had been standing guard next to him cried out in alarm, but he was too slow. Nihk's blade embedded itself in his skull with a sickening, wet crunch.

The next few moments passed as if they were minutes.

Everyone stared in frozen, stunned horror as Nihk wrenched his blade free. Then Parathe and two of the other guards went for their swords. Nihk turned to the general, lips curled back in a rictus of rage as he leaped, sword outstretched, its connection with Parathe's chest inevitable.

And then the blade had vanished from Nihk's hands, and reappeared through his neck with Davian holding the hilt.

Nihk slumped to the ground, eyes glassy as blood spurted onto the stone.

Parathe stood frozen, his hand on his hilt. "Thank you," he said to Davian, dazed. "But how—"

"No time." Davian gestured.

Wirr turned to where he was pointing, suddenly aware of how close the surprised shouts of the men had become. He stared around in dismay.

Andarran defenders everywhere were turning on each other; soldiers were drawing their swords and lunging at their comrades, apparently heedless of any harm they might come to themselves.

Duels were breaking out all along the pass, men defending themselves desperately against those who moments earlier had been their allies. In less than thirty seconds, the relative calm between the Second and Third Shields had descended into chaos.

"We've been betrayed," said Parathe, his voice hollow.

Wirr found himself shaking his head as he briefly replayed Nihk's attack, remembering the man's dead eyes.

"No. I've seen this before." He turned to Parathe. "They're called Echoes, General. I don't know a lot about it, but the Blind are controlling them, somehow."

"They're not doing this of their own volition?" Parathe gave Wirr a hopeful look. "Is there any way to snap them out of it?"

Wirr grimaced. "No. It's not them anymore," he said reluctantly. "Anyone who's an Echo is already dead. Tell your men not to hesitate."

"He's right." It was Davian, who was staring at the nearest Echoes with a perturbed expression. "I can't Read them. They're just...empty," he finished, shivering.

Parathe gave Davian an uneasy glance, then turned back to Wirr. "Are you certain about this, Your Highness?"

"Quite." Wirr extended a hand as one of the Echoes nearby made straight for their group. There wasn't much left in his Reserve after all the healing he'd performed, but it was enough.

A bolt of white light sped from his fingertips, blasting the man he'd spotted backward.

"They're dead," he repeated grimly in response to the surprised look of the others. "Or at least no longer human. I wouldn't have been able to do that otherwise."

Parathe looked sick. "We have to fall back to the Third Shield," he concluded in a heavy tone. Before he could give the order, though, Parathe's second-in-command, Hael, rushed through the fighting toward them.

"Sir," he gasped to Parathe. "The enemy have taken the harbor and the Lower District. They're pressing us hard, trying to get to the Third Shield. If they reach it, we'll be trapped."

Parathe paled. "How is that possible?" he demanded.

"No one knows, sir. Only that they're inside the walls. We need to fall back if we hope to defend the Upper District."

Parathe didn't hesitate. "You're right. There's no way we can fight the Blind if they're coming at us from both sides." He cursed. "Sound the retreat, Hael. We'll regroup at the palace."

Parathe turned to Elocien. "We need the El-cursed Gifted, Northwarden. No two ways about it," he said, his expression grim. "The palace is the strongest defensible position in the city, but even with the Shadows I don't know how long we'll be able to hold it."

A horn blast sounded the retreat, and the Essence lighting the pass abruptly blinked out. Suddenly Wirr froze, glancing up at the top of the Second Shield, where the chaos sounded worst.

"What is it?" Davian asked, seeing his expression.

"Asha is up there."

Davian was moving before Wirr realized what was happening.

He sprinted after his friend; they made it almost halfway to the stairs before two armor-clad Echoes stepped into their path.

"I don't have any Essence left, Dav," Wirr warned. He saw Davian hesitating. "They're not human anymore. Trust me."

Davian nodded silently. He stretched out his hand as the Echoes closed in on them.

For a moment nothing happened. Then one of the attackers roared, knees buckling as a line of pulsing Essence appeared between him and Davian. The man's face...withered, as if he were aging at an incredible rate; his skin became sallow before finally disintegrating, leaving only a fine white dust that drifted, smokelike, in the wind.

The second Echo hadn't paused in his wild rush toward them; Davian turned to face him, releasing the Essence he'd drawn. It wasn't a bolt, though, as Wirr would have expected, but something...thinner. Harder.

The energy sped toward their attacker, taking him in the neck and slicing clean through. The soldier's head bounced grotesquely on the ground toward them, carried by his momentum.

Neither boy moved for a moment.

"So...I see you can use Essence now, too," said Wirr, a little out of breath as they stepped over the decapitated body and pressed forward.

Davian nodded, eyes fixed on the way ahead. "As long as I don't draw too much at once," he muttered, more to himself than to Wirr. Wirr didn't understand the comment, but Davian didn't elaborate and there was no time to ask about it.

They managed to avoid further confrontation until they reached the top of the Second Shield, where they were once again brought to an abrupt halt. This time four Echoes stood in their way, not moving yet, but their dead eyes focused on the two boys.

"I don't think I can take them all. I'm tired, and it's getting harder and harder to use kan," said Davian as he drew his sword, his tone grim. "But I'm not leaving her. I—"

The Echoes sailed clear over the parapet, spinning away to crash to their deaths on the hard stone below.

Davian and Wirr both flinched back; when they looked up again, Asha was hurrying through the space where the Echoes had just been.

"You need to get out of here," she said bluntly as soon as she saw them. "Follow me. I don't have a lot left in my Reserve, but it should be enough to get us back to the Third Shield."

She slipped past them without waiting for a response.

Davian exchanged a vaguely rueful glance with Wirr, and then the two of them turned and hurried after her.

Asha cleared their path twice more before they reached the temporary refuge of the Third Shield. Wirr's father was waiting for them there, a clearly anxious Parathe and Hael standing by the duke's side.

Elocien nodded his relief to Wirr, and without a word the group headed toward the city. As they emerged from Fedris Idri, though, Parathe held up a hand, bringing them to an abrupt halt.

He frowned, cocking his head to one side.

"I don't hear any fighting," he realized. "We should have been able to—"

He cut off in midsentence with a choking sound, eyes wide with pain.

Behind him Hael stepped away, the dagger in his hand dripping blood. He bared his teeth, eyes glazed, as Parathe dropped to the ground, dead before he hit the cobblestones.

Before anyone could react he leaped forward toward a paralyzed Wirr, dagger lashing out in slow motion.

It all happened in a moment. Elocien roared as he leaped in

front of his son, taking the blade squarely in the stomach. Davian, who had been several strides ahead with Asha, was suddenly there and ramming his sword through Hael's chest. Both Elocien and Hael crumpled to the ground, the former moaning in pain, the latter twitching once and lying still.

Wirr finally found the ability to move; he dropped to his knees beside his gasping father, pressing his hands in vain against the fountain of blood pumping from Elocien's rent flesh. He closed his eyes. Healing a wound this severe would take a lot of Essence; he would need to use everything he had left. He just hoped it would be enough.

"No, Torin." Flecks of foamy blood appeared at the corner of the duke's mouth, but his tone was firm, even at a whisper. "No healing."

Wirr stared at his father in shock. "But you'll die!" he protested. He furiously wiped away tears that he hadn't even realized he'd begun to shed. "I can save you!"

Elocien gave him a sad, affectionate smile, clasping Wirr's hand in his own. "But you must not," he murmured. "We've been tricked, Torin. They'll be coming through Fedris Idri. We need the Gifted to fight, else we all die, not just me."

"But—"

"*Promise me*, Torin." Elocien's grip began to weaken, but his tone was edged with urgency. "I'm starting to lose focus; if I get confused, I need you to know that this is what I want. Changing the Tenets is all that matters now. I need you to swear to me that you will let me go."

Wirr stared at him for a long moment, then sat back, letting his shoulders slump. The tears ran freely down his face now. "I promise."

The duke sighed in satisfaction. His eyes glazed for just a second and he coughed, then moaned in pain. When he looked up at Wirr again, his gaze was...different. Panicked.

"Torin?" he whispered. "What is happening?"

Wirr paused uncertainly, then swallowed a lump in his throat. The loss of blood was starting to disorient his father. "You were stabbed," said Wirr, keeping his tone as gentle as he could. "You saved me."

Elocien groaned. "You're older. I don't understand."

Wirr held his father's hand tight. Elocien was fading fast. "Everything's all right. I'll be here until the end."

Elocien shook his head in desperation. "No. I don't want to die. Help me." He grabbed Wirr by the shirt, pulling him close so that all Wirr could see was the fear in his eyes. "Help me, Son! I beg of you. I know you can heal me. Do not let me die."

Wirr looked away. "I'm so sorry," he said, barely choking out the words. "You told me not to." He swallowed. "I love you, Father."

"No," whispered Elocien. "No."

His hand went limp, and his eyes stared sightlessly into the night sky.

Wirr just knelt there, racked by sobs as he bent over his father's body. He stayed like that for several seconds; then he took a deep, shuddering breath, forcing down his emotions and wiping his face, doing his best to regain a semblance of composure. There would be a time for grieving, but for now he needed to make sure his father's sacrifice had not been in vain.

"Oh, no."

Wirr's head snapped up at the horror in Asha's voice. She was staring at Elocien's motionless form as if she had just understood something terrible.

"I'm so sorry, Wirr," she said softly, dazedly. She shook her head, looking at both him and Davian. "There's something I have to do. I . . . I have to go."

She hurried off before either of them could respond.

Wirr watched her go, too numb to wonder at her reaction. "Raise the alarm," he said dully to the soldiers nearby, who were looking on in mute dismay. "The Blind have tricked us. We need everyone back to the Shields."

He watched the men leave, then turned to Davian. "And we need to go to Tol Athian."

Davian was still staring at the three bodies on the road, bloodied sword hanging limp in his hand. "Why?"

"Because it's time to end this," said Wirr heavily. He got to his feet. "It's time to change the Tenets."

# Chapter 51

Asha darted through the eerily deserted palace hallways.

Most able-bodied people willing to fight had left for Fedris Idri hours earlier; only the city's governing structure remained here now, along with a scant few who had chosen not to flee despite being unfit to assist in the defense. Asha's footsteps echoed as she hurried along, doing her best not to panic whenever she thought of what was happening at the Shields, trying instead to focus on locating the next Lockroom.

And trying to decide whether she was hoping to find Erran there, or was worried that she would.

Erran had been in a Lockroom in his vision—Asha had even stopped back at her room to read his description again, to make sure there weren't any further clues in it as to his location. There hadn't been, unfortunately—nor had there been any indication of exactly what was going on.

No hint as to why he had Seen Elocien's death as if it had been his own.

She was fairly certain that was what had happened; the description fit, and Hael's death meant that the man wouldn't be stabbing Erran anytime soon. As to what that implied...a theory had begun to form as she'd made her way back to the palace, and it was one that made an increasing amount of sense the more she thought about it.

She just desperately hoped it was wrong.

"Asha!"

Asha looked over her shoulder to see Kol and Fessi hurrying toward her, and stopped just long enough for them to catch up.

"Have you seen Erran?" she asked them.

Fessi shook her head. "Elocien told us all to stay here until he sent for us," she said in a worried tone. "But Erran disappeared a couple of hours ago. We were just looking for him."

"I think he's in a Lockroom," said Asha.

Kol frowned. "Why do you say that?"

"He foresaw it." Asha hesitated. "He needs our help."

Fessi and Kol glanced at each other. "There's a Lockroom a few corridors over. It's Erran's favorite. He goes there to be alone, sometimes," said Fessi.

Asha nodded. "Lead the way."

When they arrived the door was locked, but it took only one solid blow from Kol to open it. Asha's heart sank as she took in Erran's prone form in the middle of the room, a pool of blood around his head.

The three of them rushed in and knelt beside the young Augur's prostrate body. Blood seeped from his eyes, his ears, his mouth—but, Asha realized with a relieved sigh, he was still breathing. She checked his pulse. It was faster than it should have been, but regular.

Fessi gently cleaned away the worst of the blood with a handkerchief, then grabbed a pillow from one of the couches and laid it under Erran's head. As she did so, his eyes fluttered and he gave a racking cough, sending flecks of blood onto his shirt.

"Just breathe, Erran," said Asha. "You're alive. You're going to be all right."

Erran groaned. "I'm going to have to take your word on that."

"What happened?" asked Kol.

Erran hesitated, then glanced up at Asha. As soon as she saw the guilt in his expression, she knew her suspicions had been right. Her heart sank.

"Tell us," she said softly. "Everything."

Erran gave a slow nod, then winced at the motion. He levered himself up onto one elbow, his gaze encompassing all three of them.

"I've been...keeping something from you. From all of you,"

he said, his voice small. "Do you remember what I told you about how Elocien and I met?"

"Of course," said Fessi.

"It's only partly true." Erran swallowed. "The Administrators did find me, and they did bring me to Elocien. He came into the cell where I'd been tied up, and..." He grimaced, squeezing his eyes shut against the memory.

"It's all right, Erran," said Asha, her tone gentle.

Erran took a deep breath, giving her an appreciative nod. "He started beating me. He didn't ask me any questions, but whenever he was taking a rest, he'd tell me a story. Each time it was about one of the previous Augurs he'd captured. The ones...the ones he'd already killed."

Fessi took a step back, paling. "That's not true. Elocien wouldn't have done that."

"Not the Elocien you know," agreed Erran quietly. "He was about to kill me, and something just...snapped. I was inside his mind, somehow. I made him stop, made him take me down. I was just going to get him to let me go, maybe try and make him forget all about me, and then I thought..." He gave a slight shrug. "There were going to be others."

Kol sat heavily as what Erran was saying sunk in. "You've been *Controlling* Elocien?"

"Not always directly, but...yes. For the past three years." Erran stared at the floor, unwilling to meet anyone's gaze. "To start with I just sat in this room most of the day and made sure that he didn't try to kill anyone. I don't know why, but after a while the link became...more permanent. Easier to sustain, to control. And then my feelings, my ideas, began replacing his. Bleeding into him, I suppose. He started to think like me. Started doing what I would have done in a situation, but of his own volition." He grimaced, looking awkward. "After that I just made sure that when I felt the old Elocien starting to take over again, I suppressed him."

There was silence for a long few moments as they all tried to process what Erran had told them.

"He really murdered the other Augurs he found?" asked Fessi, distress evident in her tone.

Erran gave her a sad nod. "Four of them. One was eight years old."

The blood drained from Fessi's face, and she looked away. "Then...you did the right thing, Erran. I wish you'd told us, but...you did the right thing," she said softly.

Kol hesitated, then put a muscular arm around Fessi, nodding his silent agreement.

"So why tell us now?" the big man asked.

Erran bit his lip, glancing at Asha.

"Elocien was killed, Kol. About an hour or so ago," said Asha gently.

Kol looked at her, shocked, and he took a moment to respond. "What happened?"

"The Blind fooled us into leaving the Shields, and..." Asha trailed off as she thought about that moment, remembered how Elocien had jumped in front of Wirr. How the duke had pleaded with his son not to save him, so that the Tenets could be changed.

Erran saw her expression, and gazed at the ground. "He was wounded," he finished. "The details don't matter."

Asha stared at Erran, uncertain how to feel. She'd put her trust in Elocien. She'd *liked* the man.

"You sent Torin to Caladel," she said suddenly, feeling sick.

Erran nodded. "It was right near the start, before I got full control. Elocien would have killed him, eventually. There was so much rage and fear when he looked at his son...sometimes I could barely manage it. So I had to send him away."

Asha swallowed. Wirr had been so happy, so proud to discover how much his father had changed. "Torin must never know."

Erran opened his mouth to reply, but somebody else spoke first.

"Augurs," murmured a voice from the doorway. "So it's true, then."

Asha spun.

Scyner stood at the entrance to the Lockroom, his stance casual as he leaned against the door frame. It was impossible to know how long he'd been there; the door had been broken by Kol's blow and none of them had thought to try to close off the room anyway, so concerned had they been for Erran's well-being.

"Scyner," said Asha, confused. "What are you doing here?"

"Following you. Seeing if Teran's babbling held any truth," said the Shadow. He rubbed his forehead. "Honestly, the Shadraehin and I thought he was making it up, trying to find a reason for us to spare his life. I suppose we owe him an apology."

There was a shocked silence.

"What does the Shadraehin want now?" asked Asha, her voice flat and hard.

Scyner sighed, seating himself on the nearby couch. "So businesslike," he said sadly. "The Shadraehin was actually very happy with the Vessels, Ashalia. That was always her goal. But I knew there was something more to you. The fact you were left alive in Caladel, and then the way Aelrith reacted to you…" He shrugged. "I thought you might have something more to offer. And, it seems, you do." He indicated the Augurs with a lazy smile.

In the corner Kol snorted. "You cannot think we are going to help you."

Scyner raised an eyebrow. "You don't mind if I let the king know what's been going on with his brother these past few years, then?"

"You're very confident we'll give you that opportunity," said Kol. "Or even let you leave this room."

Scyner leaned forward. "Try to stop me, and I will kill you."

Kol laughed humorlessly. "You think you can kill three Augurs?"

Scyner smiled at him.

"I killed twelve in one night, once," he said. "And they were far more accomplished than you."

There was dead silence as Asha and the others processed Scyner's words.

Suddenly Kol stiffened. He stared around the room, his eyes widening, face draining of blood as recognition spread across his features.

"Fates," he murmured to himself, a strangled sound. He turned to the others, gaze lingering on Fessi for a long moment.

"Run," he said, voice catching.

Asha realized what was happening a split second too late.

"Kol, no! Wait!" she screamed, moving to grab at him.

With a roar Kol leaped at Scyner.

The next few seconds passed in slow motion. Scyner was on his feet before Kol had crossed half the distance between them, a blade in his hand. He stepped forward to meet Kol's charge, his arms blurring as he stabbed him once, twice, three times in the chest, the blows cold and clinical despite the incredible speed at which they were delivered.

Fessi vanished from beside Asha, only to reappear behind Scyner, evidently intent on subduing him. But Scyner twisted faster than Asha could follow; his hand lashed out and caught the black-haired girl squarely in the face. Her body spun around from the force of the blow, and she crumpled to the ground, unconscious.

Erran struggled forward furiously, but Asha grabbed him, able to restrain him in his weakened state. Then she shifted a little, stretching out her hand and letting what little Essence she had left in her Reserve flow into her ring.

Scyner made a casual gesture in her direction.

Asha slowly lowered her hand again, trying not to let it shake. The energy building up in the ring had just... vanished.

"Disappointing," growled Scyner as he surveyed the carnage in the room. "It did not have to be this way." He walked toward the door, then paused.

"Aelrith is dead, Ashalia. He knew that was going to happen as soon as he saw you," he said quietly. "But I spoke to him that day, before he left. He wanted to kill you, but couldn't. Do you know why?"

Asha shook her head mutely.

"He said it was because Aarkein Devaed wanted you alive," said Scyner. "You've been marked by him, and none of his creatures can touch you." He stared at her for a long moment. "I wonder why that is."

Asha felt the blood drain from her face. It couldn't be true, and yet... there was something about Scyner's tone. An arrogance that said he wouldn't bother telling her a lie.

Scyner glanced down to where Fessi lay as the girl began to stir, then turned to leave. "One more thing. The Shadraehin thinks your King Andras is being Controlled, much like the duke was." He nodded toward Erran. "I don't particularly like the idea of the

Blind running the city, so please get him to figure out by whom. The last thing we want is for the king to suddenly announce we're surrendering." He tapped at his teeth with a fingernail, gazing at Erran thoughtfully. "You'll hear from me again soon. Hopefully under more civil circumstances, next time."

He disappeared out the doorway, his footsteps echoing down the hallway as Asha and Erran rushed to Kol's side. The big man was still breathing, but his breath bubbled whenever he exhaled, and the look of pain on his face told Asha he didn't have much time.

In the corner Fessi was stirring. She raised her head groggily.

"What..." She saw Kol and gave a cry of dismay. She was kneeling beside him in an instant.

Kol looked up at his friends, eyes tight with pain. "He was an Augur," he coughed, body spasming. "An El-cursed prewar Augur."

"Be quiet, Kol. You need to rest," whispered Fessi. She looked around and Asha knew she was searching for a large-enough source of Essence, but there was none. Fessi pressed her hands desperately against Kol's chest, but he just shook his head, giving a rasping, hacking laugh. Blood seeped from wounds everywhere, and it began to dribble from the corners of his mouth, too.

"I don't think you have enough hands, Fess," he said in amusement.

His eyes glazed over, and his enormous chest became still.

Fessi just knelt there, head bowed over him, her long hair hanging onto his chest. Silent sobs racked her body; dazed, Asha knelt by her side, putting an arm around her shoulder.

Then Asha, too, had tears trickling down her cheeks. It couldn't be true. Kol was too big, too strong to die. He would wake up, and later they would all laugh at what a scare he had given them.

Erran carefully knelt opposite the girls, expression stunned, eyes glistening. Gently he lifted Fessi's hands from Kol's bloodied chest, then drew the large man's eyelids closed.

All three of them knelt there for several minutes in silence, in shock, grieving the loss of their friend.

Eventually Fessi looked up, and when her eyes met Asha's, they were cold.

"You knew. You tried to stop him," she said. "You knew, and you let him come here."

"Fessi!" It was Erran. "This wasn't Asha's fault, and you know it." He took a deep breath. "I'd read his vision, too, you know. There was no way of knowing this was…"

He trailed off, overcome with emotion. Fessi didn't respond, just bent her head over Kol's body again, not moving.

Asha finally sat back, her mind reeling. It had all happened so fast. And as little as she wanted to face the fact, there was still a battle going on—there was no time to grieve, no time to take stock. Especially not if what Scyner had told them was true.

"Erran," she said quietly. "What Scyner said…"

Erran took a deep breath, then straightened. "It's possible, I suppose," he admitted. "I've considered it before—a few times— but the physical symptoms just don't make sense. I tried to check a couple of times anyway, but…" He grimaced, giving a reluctant nod. "Being connected to Elocien all the time did make sensing kan harder. I might have missed something."

Asha bit her lip. "Then we need to speak to someone about this. Even if we do discover the king is being Controlled, we can't exactly march in there and tell people to stop listening to him. We need someone who will know how best to handle a situation like that." She looked at Erran. "Can Master Kardai be trusted?"

Erran inclined his head. "Yes."

"Then let's find him." Asha gave Erran a doubtful glance as she registered just how unsteady he was on his feet. "Are you going to be able to do this?"

"Not much of a choice," observed Erran, his tone grim.

Asha nodded. She brushed a loose strand of hair from her face and looked across at Fessi, who was still on her knees beside Kol. The other girl hadn't reacted to anything that had just been said.

Erran followed her gaze. He hesitated, then reached over to Fessi, placing a comforting hand on her shoulder.

"Fess," he said gently, voice catching. "I know this is hard, but we might need you. We will come back for Kol. I promise."

Fessi didn't respond at first. Then she shook her head, her eyes lingering on Kol's motionless features.

"If you need me, I'll be here," she said.

After a few moments, Erran nodded. He got gingerly to his feet, accepting Asha's arm for support. They paused in the doorway as they left, watching as Fessi stroked the hair back from Kol's face.

"We need to go, Asha," said Erran quietly.

Asha nodded, swallowing a sudden lump in her throat.

She made sure Erran had a firm grip on her arm, and they began slowly limping toward the Great Hall.

The doors to the Great Hall were open, much to Asha's surprise.

One of the guards outside recognized her and, after a moment's hesitation, waved her and Erran straight through. Asha frowned uneasily as she entered. The enormous room was nearly empty, its only occupants a small group of people talking in hushed tones off to one side. The throne up on the dais was, disconcertingly, vacant.

She exchanged worried glances with Erran, then headed toward the circle of people. The group looked to be mostly made up of men from the Great Houses, but she breathed a sigh of relief as she recognized Laiman in among them. The king's adviser spotted her a moment later, smiling and murmuring a quick apology to his companions before walking over.

"Ashalia!" Laiman had dark circles beneath his eyes, but his demeanor was almost cheerful. "What can I do for you?"

Asha indicated the empty throne. "What's happened? Where's the king?" she asked, unable to keep the anxiety from her tone.

"Sleeping." Laiman lowered his voice. "Whatever was afflicting him seems to have just…stopped. It was only a few minutes ago. One moment he was ranting about the Gifted again, and the next…" He shook his head. "It was like something just snapped. He almost collapsed, didn't know what was going on. But when I told him about the Blind, he immediately put Karaliene in charge until he was well enough to resume his duties."

Asha glanced at Erran, who gave a small, nonplussed shrug. She turned back to Laiman. "Do you know what changed?"

Laiman hesitated, then nodded. "The Tenets," he said softly. "We don't know what the new ones are yet, but Dras felt it happen. It couldn't have been more than a minute later that the king came to himself." He shook his head at her bemused expression. "I don't know the significance of it, either, but for now I'm just grateful. Karaliene knows what she's doing, and if the Tenets are different, I'm hoping it means the Gifted can fight."

Asha shook her head, a little dazed, relieved to hear that Wirr had been successful but unsure how it could possibly have affected events here. "So what happens now?"

"Now? There's little else left but to get everyone we can to the Shields," said Laiman grimly. He glanced back over toward the gathered lords. "Speaking of which..."

Asha nodded her understanding. "Thank you, Master Kardai," she said. "Fates be with you out there."

"And with you, Ashalia. Erran." Laiman nodded to them both, then hurried back toward the gathered noblemen.

Asha and Erran left the Great Hall again and began heading back toward Fessi and the Lockroom, silent for a time as they walked.

"What do you think it means?" asked Asha eventually.

Erran shook his head. "I don't know," he admitted. "The Tenets shouldn't affect kan. I'm glad the king is free of whatever was wrong with him, but... it makes no sense."

Asha just gave a frustrated nod, having reached much the same conclusion.

They arrived at the Lockroom to find Fessi sitting on the couch, still staring listlessly at Kol's prone form. She didn't look up as they entered.

Asha gave Erran a hesitant glance, then crouched down in front of Fessi. "Fessi. The king has recovered," she said. "The Blind are still attacking, though. It's time we went to the Shields to see how we can help."

Fessi looked up, but at Erran rather than Asha. There was a second of silence as the two gazed at each other, and then Fessi gave a small nod.

Erran coughed, suddenly awkward.

"We've... decided to leave, Asha," he said in an apologetic tone, looking uncomfortable as he said the words. "You're certainly welcome to come with us, though."

"What?" Asha looked between the two of them, stunned. They

must have been communicating using Erran's ability; Asha felt a stab of anger at having been so bluntly excluded. "You can't leave now! And besides, there's no way out."

"There are still some smaller ships in the harbor—the Houses left them there as a way to retreat, should the Shields fall," explained Erran. "They won't be guarded now, and there are more than enough for us to take one without putting anyone in danger."

Asha gave him an incredulous stare. "Do either of you even know how to sail?"

"Elocien did." Erran looked her in the eye. "We can't stay, Asha. Surely you must see that. With Scyner out there, knowing what he knows…he's either going to try and use us, or turn us in. Until we can figure out a way to deal with him, it's not safe for us here. Or you, for that matter." His tone was earnest. "Please. Come with us."

Asha hesitated for the briefest of moments, then shook her head.

"I can't. I suppose I understand, but…I just can't." She paused, then laid a hand on Fessi's shoulder. "I will take care of Kol's burial, though. I promise."

Fessi looked up at her for the first time since Asha had entered the room.

"Thank you," she said softly.

Erran watched for a moment, his expression sad, then took two quick steps and embraced her. "Fates be with you, Asha."

"You, too, Erran." Asha looked down at Fessi. "And you, Fess. I'll be thinking of you. Be safe."

Fessi gave her a tight, tearful smile. "We'll see you again, Asha." Her voice shook a little, but there was hardness behind her eyes, too. "We'll be back to deal with Scyner soon enough."

She stood, reaching over and taking Erran's hand in her own.

They vanished.

Asha didn't move for a long moment, twisting the ring on her finger nervously. The Augurs' abrupt departure had suddenly given her pause, made her wonder whether it was really worth her going back to Fedris Idri. Her Reserve was close to drained; she wasn't sure how much more she could do in battle anyway. And it felt wrong to leave Kol like this, alone on the floor…

But she knew straight away that those were just excuses. She took a deep breath, squaring her shoulders. Even if she was able to summon only one final blast with her Vessel, returning to help at the Shields was the right thing to do.

She took a long last look at Kol's lifeless form, grief still heavy in her chest.

Then she turned and left, heading for Fedris Idri.

# Chapter 52

Wirr rolled his shoulders, sensing more than seeing Elder Eilinar's glare.

There was a stony silence as the group walked deeper into the Tol, broken only by the occasional nervous cough from one member of the Council or another. Wirr scowled to himself. His arrival at the Tol, and his announcement that he was going to change the Tenets, had been met with open arms. His insistence that Davian accompany him to do so had not.

He glanced across at his friend, who was walking alongside, evidently lost in thought. The Council had been furious at Wirr's obstinacy, going so far as to call Davian a threat after what he'd done to Ilseth Tenvar. Eventually, though, Elder Eilinar had relented—if not graciously.

Wirr could still feel the man's anger emanating from him whenever they locked gazes, but he didn't care. He was here for one purpose only: to fulfill his father's dying wish. To make sure his sacrifice had not been in vain.

"I would have understood, you know," murmured Davian suddenly, as if reading his thoughts. "You didn't have to rile them on my account."

Wirr shrugged. "I needed someone with me for this. Someone I can trust."

Davian inclined his head. "Still. I'm not sure that I blame Elder Eilinar. I probably wouldn't want me involved in this, either, after what happened this morning."

Wirr gave him a stern sideways glance. "What you did to Tenvar was an accident, Dav," he said. "You were doing what needed to be done—and honestly, it's not like the man didn't deserve it."

Davian grimaced, but nodded. He watched his friend for a moment. "How are you holding up?"

Wirr gritted his teeth, swallowing a sudden lump in his throat. He'd managed to push what had happened to the back of his mind for now, and he wanted it to stay there, to keep the emotions at bay until this was done. "There will be time for grief later. This is what my father wanted," he said grimly.

Davian gave him another nod, accepting the statement in silence.

After a while they came to a halt in front of a large, solid-looking steel door; Elder Eilinar pressed his hand against its surface, releasing the wards that protected it. Once he was done, he produced a set of keys and opened it, holding it ajar so that everyone could pass through.

Wirr stared around the chamber within as he entered. It was entirely empty of furnishings except for a thick, squat table in the center, which itself looked carved from the same black rock as the rest of the room. In all, it seemed unremarkable.

Nashrel waited until all the Elders were inside and then walked over to the table, placing a hand on it with something approaching reverence as he closed his eyes. He murmured a few words under his breath, and Essence began flowing from him into the stone.

Wirr watched, wide-eyed. The table turned a deeper shade of black; suddenly the torches on the walls were reflected by its now-glistening dark surface. Then there was a rippling, a shimmering in its center; it began to stretch and morph as something new rose out of the stone.

Wirr stared. It appeared to be an ornate shield—but too large, taller and wider than even the largest of men, impossible to wield.

"This is the Vessel through which you will need to rebind the Tenets, Your Grace," Nashrel explained to Wirr, eyes not leaving the shield. "You must place your hand on it, keeping a steady stream of Essence flowing into it, and speak the vows that you want all the Gifted to be bound by."

Wirr frowned at the shield. "That's it?"

Nashrel nodded. "Your new vows should take the place of the old ones. Beyond that..." He shrugged. "The Tenets have never been successfully changed, and this Vessel was not made by us, so I cannot speak as to any other consequences."

Davian and Wirr both stared at the shield. Its steel was almost as black as the table beneath, and as Wirr took a closer look, he saw that it was covered by hundreds of finely inscribed symbols.

"Who *did* make it?" Wirr asked abruptly. "Where did it come from?"

"Only the Loyalists know the answer to that question," said Nashrel. His glance flicked to Wirr, then away again.

"Why doesn't someone just destroy it?" asked Davian.

Nashrel shook his head. "That is why it is left in Athian's care, hidden, and not at the palace. If it were destroyed, we suspect that the Tenets could not be undone. Its terms would last forever."

"Then perhaps that is what we must do," came a deep voice from the entrance.

Wirr spun, heart sinking as soon as he saw the blue cloak. All the Administrators were supposed to have left, called to fight at Fedris Idri.

Then he grimaced as the man stepped forward into the light.

"Ionis. I'm sorry, but this is how it has to be," Wirr said quietly. "We need the Gifted to be able to fight, else the city will fall, and we'll all die."

"Then we will all die, Your Grace," replied Ionis, his tone calm. "An unpleasant fate, and yet preferable to having the bleeders running things again. I lived through those times, Prince Torin. I'll not return to them."

Wirr turned back to the shield, away from the Administrator. "You don't have a choice."

"Actually, I do. Prince Torin, I command you by the Fourth Tenet. Do not use Essence unless I tell you to."

Wirr gasped as his hand froze, only inches above the shield. He scowled, concentrating, willing his hand downward. Instead he found himself pulling back, away from the metallic surface.

He took a couple of steps away from the table, until it was well out of reach. Then, able to move freely again, he rounded on Ionis.

"Administrator, you must do as I tell you. Fates, man, I'm the prince; I'm the *Northwarden* now! Release me to do as I wish, or I'll have you strung up for treason!"

"I'm sorry, Your Grace, but I won't be doing that." Ionis looked…composed. Almost unconcerned. With good reason, too, Wirr realized dully. So long as the original Tenets remained in place, Ionis was safe. "And I suspect that of the two of us, once King Andras finds out what has happened here today, it might rather be you looking at the hangman's noose," the Administrator added.

Wirr flinched, remembering his last conversation with his uncle. "What do you want?"

Ionis leaned forward, and Wirr shuddered as he caught the look in his eye. There was a hint of mania there, an unmistakably zealous fire. "I want you to create a new, single Tenet. That any man, woman, or child who is Gifted must take their own life."

Wirr felt himself pale, and there were gasps of horror from around the room, which had been utterly silent up until now. "You can't," he said suddenly. "You're an Administrator; you took the Oath. The Third Tenet binds you just as much as us— you cannot cause harm, physical or otherwise, to any of the Gifted."

Ionis inclined his head, looking unperturbed. "And perhaps if our positions were reversed, that would stop you. You may not realize it, but for some Administrators, their interpretation of 'harm' means that they cannot act to even *upset* one of the Gifted deliberately." He took a step forward, eyes glittering in the torchlight. "But not me. This power, the 'Gift' as you call it—it is a disease. I believe that, more deeply than I have ever believed anything. So you see, Prince Torin, doing this to the Gifted…it is not causing them harm. Far from it. It is putting them out of their misery. It is *helping* them."

Wirr shivered under Ionis's gaze. He didn't want to believe the man, and yet there was something in his eyes, a fearsome certainty that what he was doing was right. In that moment, Wirr knew that the Administrator truly thought that he was doing the Gifted a kind of twisted favor.

"You're insane," he said softly. "We could help, Ionis. We could fight the Blind."

"The long term is the only thing that matters, Your Highness," said Ionis.

Wirr just stared at the blue-cloaked man, aghast. He tried to make his body move toward Ionis but it wouldn't budge; subjective or not, the Third Tenet prevented him from taking any action with the intent to hurt an Administrator.

His jaw clenched in helpless frustration. He'd known this was a weakness; it had been one of the most pressing reasons to keep his abilities a secret in the first place. His father had always been concerned that an Administrator would find the temptation of having a prince under their control too hard to resist.

And apparently, Ionis had seen the same flaw—seen the opportunity. All that remained now was for him to give the order.

The Administrator leaned forward. "Prince Torin, by the Fourth Tenet I order you to—"

Suddenly Ionis's smug expression faltered, and he stopped in midsentence. His eyes widened, and his breath came in short, ragged gasps. He spun, looking directly at Davian as his body began to spasm.

"What are you doing?" he groaned, collapsing to the floor.

Wirr turned to Davian. His friend was making no outward appearance of effort, simply staring at the Administrator with a grim expression. There could be no doubt, though. Thin tendrils of light streamed from Ionis's violently shaking form into Davian, vanishing as soon as they touched the boy's skin.

Suddenly the stream halted.

"Release him," said Davian quietly. "Please. I have no wish to do this. Release him to change the Tenets, and I will let you live."

Ionis gave a racking cough, looking twice the age he had a few moments before. He stared at Davian in utter fear, and for an instant Wirr thought he was going to comply.

Then he twisted away with an effort of will, shouting the words.

"Prince Torin, by the Fourth Tenet I—"

He cut off in a desperate, rage-filled shriek.

Ionis's body began to age, wrinkles appearing on his face, his skin sagging and creasing, his features becoming gaunt. Then his skin and muscles began to wither and decay, slowly at first but with increasing speed, until the white of the bone underneath began to show through.

As the last wisps of light were sucked from the corpse, even the skeleton itself collapsed in a slight puff of powdery white dust.

Wirr stared at the small pile of grime on the floor, a chill running down his spine.

"I had to," said Davian softly. He shook his head, his hands and arms glowing with the light of the Essence he had drained from Ionis. "I had to be sure he didn't say it."

Wirr looked up at his friend, for the first time really seeing how much Davian had changed since Deilannis. He was...harder now. As if whatever he'd gone through over the last couple of months had sucked the innocence out of him. The changes were subtle, but they were there. It was still his old friend, but a bleaker version. A more world-weary version.

A moment later the full consequences of what had just happened hit home, and the pain of how close he'd come became sharp in his chest.

"I can't change the Tenets now," he realized, shaking his head in steadily growing dismay. "Ionis is dead; he can't rescind the order. I can't use Essence."

There was silence for several seconds, then he felt a hand on his shoulder. "What if we remove the Fourth Tenet?" Davian asked.

"What do you mean?"

Davian gestured toward the shield on the table. "Ionis only stopped you from using Essence, not from altering the Tenets," he observed. "You said you needed someone here that you trusted. Trust me now, Wirr. If you'll let me, I'll change the Tenets exactly as you ask—word for word. From what you told me, all you need to do is stand there. I do the rest."

Wirr found himself suddenly, unexpectedly smiling. He hadn't been called Wirr in weeks now. It felt good to hear the name aloud again.

He inclined his head. Whatever he'd been through...Davian was his friend. He *could* trust him.

"Then let's get started before there are any other complications," he said, glancing again at the pile of dust on the floor
640 where Ionis had been standing.

Davian nodded. "Good idea. What I took from Ionis should be enough, but we do need to be fast. I have to hold Essence outside my body if I want to use it, and I can't stop it decaying anymore than you could."

Wirr strode over to the shield and hesitantly placed his hand against it. As Davian had suspected, now his intent was not to use Essence, he was able to touch the Vessel. Davian gave him a tight smile, then placed a hand on the shield, too.

"Your Grace, if I may interject." It was Nashrel, looking on with a worried expression. "I mean no offense to young Davian here"—he nodded politely at Davian—"but if you need someone else to assist you after all, I would...feel more comfortable if you used one of the Elders instead. After what happened to Ilseth Tenvar, one of the Gifted and a man ostensibly under our protection..." He shook his head. "At the very least, perhaps you should be writing down the exact wording of the Tenets you are going to create. The current ones took months of discussion and negotiation before they were settled upon. Let us take a few minutes to go over them with you, advise you on how best to—"

Wirr shook his head. "I've known these words for years, Elder Eilinar," he interrupted gently. "And I mean no offense to the Council, but I don't trust anyone else to help me. It's that simple." He turned back to Davian. "Now. All you need to do is repeat after me, and keep a steady flow of Essence going into the shield. The Vessel should do the rest."

Davian nodded, taking a deep breath and glancing around at the Elders, who were all watching with keen interest. "I'm ready."

Wirr closed his eyes, remembering the words.

"'I swear I shall not use Essence to harm or hinder non-Gifted, except in cases of self-defense or for the purposes of protecting Andarra.'"

Davian hesitated.

"'I swear I shall not use Essence to harm or hinder non-Gifted, except in cases of self-defense or for the purposes of protecting Andarra,'" he repeated, a thin line of Essence flowing from him into the shield.

Wirr released a breath he'd been unconsciously holding. He *did*     641 trust his friend, but if Davian had chosen to alter the wording, there would have been nothing Wirr could have done about it.

The symbols on the shield had begun to glow with an intense blue light. It was working.

Wirr continued, " 'I swear I will not use Essence with the intent to deceive, intimidate, or otherwise work to the detriment of non-Gifted, except in cases of self-defense or for the purposes of protecting Andarra.' "

Davian said the words back to him, enunciating carefully and clearly.

Wirr smiled as the symbols glowed blue again. " 'I swear that as no Administrator may kill or bring harm of any kind to me, I shall not kill or bring harm of any kind to an Administrator.' " After Ionis, Wirr had decided to tweak that Tenet a little.

Davian repeated the phrase word for word. When he was done, Wirr took a deep breath, then gave Davian a shaky grin.

"That's it," he said softly.

Davian let out a long breath as the symbols on the shield began to fade.

He should have felt ecstatic at changing the Tenets—felt *something*—but instead his gaze was drawn to the pile of dust that had once been Ionis.

Leaving the Administrator alive had been too great a risk. If Ionis had had even a few more seconds, managed to finish his sentence, then Davian's only option would have been to stop Wirr in the same manner. Even with so many lives at stake, he wasn't sure he could have done that.

He frowned as he thought about what he'd done. A detached part of him understood, perhaps for the first time, how deeply experiencing Malshash's memory had affected him. Killing a man in cold blood—even a man such as Ionis, even in defense of something far greater than himself—should have shaken him to his core.

It hadn't.

He rubbed his forehead, glancing down at the smooth skin on

his forearm. After all of that, had it been worth it? He exchanged glances with Wirr. Nothing seemed to be happening.

"I did everything I was supposed to do," Davian said worriedly. "Did it—"

Wirr's eyes rolled into the back of his head, and he collapsed.

Davian dashed forward to help him, but a sudden flash of pain—mild, but noticeable—on his exposed forearm made him hesitate. He glanced down to see the familiar tattoo forming, glowing slightly, just as the symbols on the shield had a moment earlier. He'd bound himself to the Tenets again, even if they were different this time. Bound all of the Gifted, in fact.

He felt a stab of concern, of doubt. Had he done the right thing? He turned his attention to the Council members, watching as they examined their own forearms in fascination.

As quickly as it had come, the pain and the light faded.

"Is it done?" asked one of the Council members.

Nashrel stared at his arm, then at Wirr's prostrate form. "I believe it is," he said slowly. "There is only one way to find out, though. Marshal everyone." The other Council members began filing out, whispering among themselves.

Davian knelt by Wirr. He was still unconscious, but his breathing was regular and deep.

"He's alive," said Davian with relief. He took off his well-worn cloak and created a makeshift pillow. Wirr's head had hit the stone floor hard when he'd fallen, but there was no blood.

Nashrel nodded his acknowledgment. He crouched down on the other side of Wirr and placed his hand on the prince's forehead, a small stream of Essence trickling out of him.

"He's fine," said Nashrel after a moment. "We're a long way from any beds here, though. It's probably safer if we wait until he wakes up before moving him."

Davian nodded. "I'll stay," he said. "I'm sure you have other things to attend to."

Nashrel inclined his head, turning to go. Then he hesitated.

"Nobody would have blamed you, you know," the Elder said quietly. "I saw your expression. You were tempted to change what he said, at least a little."

Davian shook his head. "No. He trusted me, and he's thought about this a lot longer than I have. It wouldn't have been right."

Nashrel gave a thoughtful nod. "I'm not sure any of us would have felt the same," he admitted. "But maybe it's for the best. And those new Tenets may still be restricting, but fates take me if they aren't an improvement."

Suddenly there was a flurry of activity at the door, and a younger man in a red cloak hurried inside.

"Elder Eilinar," he said, out of breath. "We're getting reports that some of the Blind are inside the Tol."

Nashrel stared for a moment, then snorted. "In the Tol? How? They cannot have breached the Resolute Door," he said dismissively. "Someone is seeing things, Ralyse. The Blind haven't even made it past Fedris Idri yet, else we would have heard. And there is no other way..."

He trailed off, paling.

"Most of our people are already on their way to the Shields?" he asked. Ralyse nodded, and Nashrel bit his lip. "Warn everyone else to be wary, then. And have someone watch the El-cursed stairwells to the lower levels." He turned to Davian. "Can you carry him?"

"I think so."

"Then we need to seal this room, and get moving."

Davian grabbed Wirr by the waist and slung him awkwardly over his shoulder. His friend was heavy, but not so much so that Davian couldn't manage the weight.

"Taeris warned us," Nashrel muttered to himself as they hurried along the tunnels, back toward the main part of the Tol. "He said the sha'teth had returned, and we didn't listen."

"Probably the one thing he didn't lie about," murmured Davian under his breath.

Soon enough they reached a part of the Tol Davian recognized. The passageways, normally full of red cloaks, were completely empty. Nashrel frowned at the deserted corridors but said nothing, pressing on.

Just as Wirr was becoming too heavy a burden for Davian to bear, Nashrel gestured to a nearby room.

"There's a bed. Set him down in there and rest for a few moments; I'll return when I find out what in fates is going on."

Davian did as Nashrel suggested, closing the door behind him. The silence of the Tol was making him nervous, and it had obviously unsettled the Elder, too. The Gifted had sent on several of their people to the Shields already; Wirr had insisted that happen before he changed the Tenets. Even so...there still should have been *someone* left in this section.

Davian waited for a while, occasionally checking on Wirr, trying to stay calm. Ten minutes passed. Thirty. An hour.

Then the shouting began.

Davian's first reaction was to open the door to see what was going on, but suddenly a scream of pain broke through the commotion, cut short as abruptly as it had begun.

Then a brief silence, followed by the sounds of heavy footsteps in the hallway outside.

Davian hurried over to where Wirr lay on the bed, looking around and trying not to panic. There was nothing in here he could use as a weapon, and he knew that neither kan nor Essence would be effective against the Blind, even if he was willing to risk a close-quarters fight in the same room as his unconscious friend.

Clenching his fists to stop them from shaking, he carefully drew a mesh of kan around both himself and Wirr.

There was a scratching at the door, and the handle turned. Davian hardened the layer of kan, praying fervently he was remembering how to do it correctly.

He turned, holding his breath as the door swung open to reveal the Blind soldier.

The man had removed his helmet, but the black-plated armor was the same as Davian had seen in his vision. The soldier's eyes swept the room, and for an instant they paused on the bed, as if he'd noticed something amiss. Davian held completely motionless, willing Wirr not to choose this moment to stir in his sleep.

Then the man was shutting the door again, apparently satisfied the room was empty.

Davian waited a few seconds, then took several shaky lungfuls of air. He slumped onto the bed next to Wirr, putting his head between his knees as he tried to slow the pounding of his heart.

A few long minutes later, Wirr gave a small moan, then stirred.

"What's going on?" he asked Davian, rubbing his eyes as he

propped himself up. "Where are we?" He winced. "Fates, my head hurts."

"Still in the Tol," said Davian. He recounted the events of the past hour to Wirr.

Wirr shivered once Davian had finished, looking nauseous. He took a deep breath, staring at the tattoo on his forearm. "So we need to get out of here," he said. "The Tenets are definitely changed?"

Davian nodded. "I think so. The Council certainly did, too."

Wirr levered himself out of bed. "Then we should get moving."

He was halfway to the door when it swung open.

"Taeris!" Wirr exclaimed.

Taeris winced, limping inside and putting a finger to his lips.

"Not so loud, Wirr," he muttered as he shut the door.

Davian stared at Taeris for a long moment. He still felt a deep, burning anger toward the man, but now wasn't the time to bring it up. The issues between them would have to wait.

"What's going on, Taeris?" he asked, tone grim. "I thought you were locked up."

"I was." Taeris gave the door a nervous glance. "Nashrel came to let me out when he realized what was happening. He told me where you were before he..." He grimaced, looking at the ground. "He didn't make it."

"He's dead?" Wirr paled. "Fates. What's happening out there?"

"Most of the Gifted that didn't head for the Shields are dead. The Blind have mostly moved on into the city, but there are a few groups sweeping the Tol, looking for survivors." Taeris spoke quietly, but Davian could hear the anxiety in his voice. "The new Tenets do let us use Essence in combat, but the Blind's armor is still making it hard to fight them, especially in enclosed spaces."

"How did they even get in here?" asked Davian.

"Nashrel thought they were coming through the catacombs." Taeris looked sick. "There's a network of old tunnels, deep beneath the Tol, that supposedly have an exit out past Ilin Tora. No one knows where that exit is, though." He rubbed his forehead. "Those roads are a labyrinth, but Nashrel said the sha'teth have been using them. It's how they get in and out of the city unseen when they go about their...business."

Davian felt a chill. "So the sha'teth are here? Helping the Blind?"

Taeris nodded. "It would seem so."

Wirr grimaced. "And the Tol didn't guard this entrance, I take it?"

"They didn't think they needed to, and I don't blame them," said Taeris. "The catacombs come out next to the Conduit, something the Builders created to help power the Tol. Any living thing coming that close to it should have died within seconds." He shook his head. "The Blind's armor must have protected them against it, somehow."

There was silence for a few moments, then Davian shifted nervously. "So what do we do now?"

Taeris chewed at his lip, expression thoughtful. "There's nothing more we can do here. If we want to help, we need to get back to the fight."

Davian and Wirr both nodded; Davian helped his friend to his feet, glad to see that Wirr's strength seemed to be returning.

Taeris opened the door a crack, peering through cautiously before beckoning for the boys to follow.

They started out through the Tol at a silent half jog, Taeris going ahead and checking around each new corner. After a minute they entered a new hallway and Davian faltered.

Crumpled, lifeless bodies littered the way ahead. They were all Gifted, from their red cloaks. He knelt by the closest one— a young man, no older than Davian—but the Gifted's chest was still, and his eyes were glassy as they stared at the roof. Davian stood unsteadily.

"It's like this everywhere," Taeris warned him.

They moved on; every new corridor greeted them with eerie, unsettling silence—and, in a few cases, more bodies. A couple of the corpses were holding daggers, which Wirr collected as he went. Davian wasn't sure how much use they would be against swords; even so, he didn't refuse the one that Wirr offered him.

A few tense minutes passed. Davian's eyes and ears strained for any hint of danger, but it was still without warning that the two black-armored men wandered into the passageway up ahead.

Though they were not wearing the distinctive helmets, there was no doubting who they were.

Before anyone could move, Davian felt Wirr gathering Essence; his friend threw it at the soldiers, aiming for their exposed heads. To Davian's dismay, the bolts evaporated just before they made contact.

He took a deep breath and focused, following the failed attack with one of his own. It was just as he'd found while fighting at the Shields, though, despite the missing helmets. The two men seemed to have an invisible barrier around them that Davian's thread of kan simply could not penetrate.

"Looks like we missed a couple," snarled the man on the left.

Wirr and Davian both took a faltering step back and drew their daggers as the men began walking toward them; though they started more than thirty feet away and appeared to be moving at an almost casual pace, they were covering the space between unnaturally fast.

"Your knives, boys. Throw them now," said Taeris urgently.

Davian and Wirr both hesitated for a split second, then did as Taeris instructed, throwing the blades wildly at the oncoming soldiers.

Taeris stretched out his hand.

The daggers stopped for a second in midair as if frozen in time, then spun, their blades pointing straight at the approaching men.

The soldiers were fast, but Taeris was faster. The daggers blurred forward; the Blind might not have needed their helmets to stop Essence, but steel was another matter. They yelled something incomprehensible as they saw the danger too late.

Taeris sunk a dagger into each man's left eye.

The soldiers crumpled to the ground, pools of scarlet forming on the stone around their heads. Davian leaned weakly against the wall, staring at Taeris, who was busy reclaiming their blades from the bodies.

"So the new Tenets really are working," he said eventually.

Taeris gave a tired nod. "We were just lucky they weren't wearing their helmets. Fully armored, we would have had to run." He handed the boys a dagger each, the blades now smeared with red. "We should get moving. We're not far from the gate."

Davian nodded, accepting the dagger and trying not to look at the corpse it had come from. His stomach churned. Fighting the Blind with their helmets on, without the advantage of the Shields... Tenets changed or not, he shuddered to think of how the Andarrans were going to fare. For the first time, he couldn't see how this was a fight they could win.

Still, they had to try. He took a deep breath to steady himself, nodding to Taeris.

"Lead the way," he said quietly.

They headed down the corridor at a jog.

# Chapter 53

Caeden looked around the massive cavern in despair.

This one was nearly identical to the many others he'd already crossed, and he was beginning to wonder if he was moving in circles. His head spun a little from the oppressive heat as he examined the expansive maze of narrow paths ahead. Slim walkways of hewn black stone crisscrossed the vast, open space, their treacherously sheer sides plummeting into the seething river of molten rock far below.

Some paths ended abruptly, their crumbling edges highlighted by the fierce glow that emanated upward, tingeing everything an angry red. Others appeared solid enough... but that made the prospect of walking on them no less daunting. He'd already had several secure-looking footholds threaten to crumble beneath his weight.

Caeden wiped sweat from his brow, taking a deep breath to ensure he wasn't getting light-headed again. The heat hadn't been a problem at first, but he'd been wandering this network of caves for hours now, following the inexorable flow of lava in search of an exit. Dehydration was beginning to rob him of his balance. Along these narrow walkways, that could easily result in a quick but painful death.

Still, he knew there was nothing to be gained by waiting. Keeping his eyes fixed on the path ahead, he started forward once again.

He rubbed at his wrist absently as he inched his way through the cavern. The wolf tattoo had vanished as soon as he'd touched the bronze box at the Tol, and even now he couldn't help but notice the absence of its familiar glow, which had tugged at the corners of his vision for as long as he could remember. Taeris had once suggested that the link would remain only until it had physically been completed. It appeared he'd been right.

After a few minutes of carefully picking his way across the cavern, he paused, allowing himself some rest. Ahead the path disappeared into the gaping black maw of yet another tunnel. He squinted toward the exit, heart suddenly leaping. There was something about the tunnel entrance—something new. A series of markings, etched in a semicircle into the rocky wall around it.

His need to rest faded as he edged closer, a surge of excitement running through him. He couldn't read the strange symbols, yet they were also somehow familiar.

Then he knew why he recognized them.

Digging into his pocket, he drew out the bronze Vessel that had brought him here, holding it up so that the light from the red river below illuminated it.

He smiled in triumph.

The writing wasn't identical, but…there could be no doubt. The inscriptions on the box were in the same language as the markings around the tunnel entrance.

Replacing the Vessel in his pocket, he ventured cautiously into the darkness.

He took several deep breaths as he entered; the air here was much cooler, and he straight away felt more clearheaded. He hurried forward, eager now. This passage was longer than the others he'd been through, and he was soon forced to create a small ball of Essence to light the way ahead.

It was a full ten minutes before the tunnel began to lighten again, and Caeden paused uncertainly as he reached the exit.

Instead of yet another cavern, he was at the entrance to a large room, black stone walls smooth and straight. It was the floor that had made him hesitate, though. Fine cracks ran everywhere, along which crimson lava flowed in tiny rivulets, lighting the room a virulent red.

For a moment Caeden thought the ground might be unstable,

but then he took a half step back, squinting. The cracks were too regular, too straight to be natural.

The lava was creating a series of symbols.

They were similar to those he'd seen outside the tunnel, he soon realized—clearly the same language. The design pulsed and glowed, the floor shimmering through the haze of rising heat.

A warning. He wasn't sure how he knew, but he was certain of it.

He tore his gaze from the symbols, studying the rest of the room. It was empty except for a short stone pillar set at the far end, with a single naked sword balanced across its peak.

Caeden stared at the blade curiously. Something about it looked...alive. It gleamed not with the eerie red of the lava, but rather with a white light, like that of Essence.

There was nothing else in the room, nor any other exits he could see. As if this room had been built specifically to house the sword, nothing more. Almost like a shrine.

He hesitated. He felt as though he'd intruded, stumbled across a place where he had no right to be. Yet the box had brought him here, was clearly connected to this place somehow.

And he knew he couldn't go back the way he'd come. He had a couple of hours at best before dehydration got the better of him. He wouldn't survive on those narrow walkways for long.

Cautiously, Caeden placed one foot into the room, testing the stone underfoot. It seemed firm. Taking a deep breath, he put his whole weight onto it, stepping completely inside.

There was a grinding sound behind him and a hidden door slammed shut, neatly bisecting the chamber and the tunnel.

Caeden stared at the blocked exit in horror. He looked around, trying not to panic, but his gaze met only solid stone. There was no other way in or out that he could see.

"You have intruded once again, I see," came a soft voice from behind him.

Caeden froze, then slowly turned.

A man now stood between him and the sword, though Caeden had no idea where he had come from. He resisted the urge to shrink back against the wall. The stranger's skin glowed a smoldering, writing red—darker than the light from the molten rock in the floor, but not by much. His hair and clothes appeared made of strands of lava itself, but...his eyes were human. Blue and calm, intelligent.

Watching Caeden closely.

"I...I'm sorry," stuttered Caeden, taking a step back. "I didn't mean to."

"Of course you did." The luminescent man began to pace, circling Caeden. His body language gave nothing away, but his eyes held an intense curiosity. "You have come for Licanius, as you always do. The question is, how did you get in this time? Did the Traveler bring you? Did the Keeper take pity on you? Or perhaps you finally plucked up the courage to return to the Plains of Decay and use one of the Columns?" He kept moving, never taking his gaze from Caeden's face. "Another body again, I see. Which poor soul did you take it from this time? Did you really think it would fool us? Fool *me*? No. No, such a poor deception is beyond you, I think. You have a plan. You always have a plan."

He stopped, this time a little closer to Caeden, who had been gaping at him in silence. "Well? Am I to be kept waiting, or shall I just expel you now?"

Caeden coughed. "I'm sorry, but truly...I'm not sure why I am here. I don't even know where here *is*." He ran his hands through his hair. "Who are you? Do you know me?"

The man's eyes flickered with puzzlement. "We have danced this dance for near five hundred years," he said. "I am Garadis ru Dagen, and I know you, Tal'kamar, no matter what you do to your face. Of all of them, you are the only one who ever gets this close. And yet none of you can take her. That law is immutable."

Caeden swallowed, not sure whether to be excited or nervous.

Then what Garadis had said struck home.

"Five hundred *years*?" Caeden laughed. "So you're saying I'm a little older than I look."

Garadis gazed at him impassively, silent, and Caeden's laughter died under the stare.

Suddenly the burning man's eyes widened in understanding. He moved forward at a blinding speed, grasping Caeden's head in his hands before it was possible to react.

Caeden gasped; Garadis's hands were warm, but not searing hot as he'd expected them to be. He could feel something inside his mind for the briefest of moments, a fraction of a second. Then Garadis was stepping back again, his expression this time thoughtful.

"You should not have come back here," he murmured.

Caeden gave him an uneasy look. "But I don't remember being here. I have no memories past a few months ago," he protested.

"That is because you had them removed," said Garadis quietly. "You had them removed so that you could come here, now, to try once again. You don't even remember Andrael, let alone why he bound us to this agreement." The words were musing, more to himself than to Caeden. He shook his head. "Even so—his Law is clear. *He who comes to take Licanius shall be refused her.* And you are not here to take Licanius. You are here to find out who you are, and how you might help your friends." He stared at Caeden with what appeared to be fascination.

Caeden's brow furrowed as he tried to sort through the information. Garadis was right; he didn't recognize the name Andrael.

The sword atop the pillar, on the other hand . . .

"That's Licanius, isn't it?" he said.

"Yes."

"Will my having it make a difference? Will I be able to help my friends?"

"Of course," said Garadis softly. The glowing man stared into Caeden's eyes, then stepped to one side, allowing him a straight path to the sword. "For the first time in five hundred years, you have passed the Tests. As Guardian, I have read your mind and find no thoughts or memories that should cause me to deny you Licanius. She is yours."

Caeden looked hesitantly at the sword, then back at Garadis. "Can you restore my memories?"

"No," replied Garadis. "Though I am sure one who can will find you soon enough."

"Then can you at least tell me who I am?"

Garadis stared at him, expressionless. "Where to begin? You are Tal'kamar, though precious few know you as such. You destroyed Saran'geth for an ideal. You butchered the Arathi for revenge. You created the Plains of Decay for the love of a woman long dead." He paused. "You saved Jala Terr knowing it would cost you a century alone. You hid Wereth from the Shadows because you believed a good man was worth more than a good name. You destroyed us—and then, when we hated you most, you saved us at the expense of everything you ever wanted." There was sadness in those blue eyes as he said the last. Sadness, and bright pain. "You have lived for over four thousand years, and done so much evil and so much good. You are a legend here amongst the Lyth, despised and beloved, famous and infamous both. You are Tal'kamar," he finished softly.

Caeden felt a chill run down his spine.

It was inconceivable—all of it—and yet something in Garadis's voice told him it was the truth.

Numbly, he nodded.

"Now," said Garadis. "Take the sword."

Caeden took a deep breath, then picked his way across the lava-lined floor until he stood in front of the pillar. He frowned at the inscription on it.

"What do these symbols say?"

"Nothing of importance," replied Garadis.

Caeden paused, glancing back at the towering, pulsating being. Garadis's stance and expression were still blank, but now his eyes were ... eager.

A flash of suspicion ran through Caeden.

"What does Licanius do?" he asked slowly. "Can I safely assume that this is no ordinary sword?"

"You can," replied Garadis. "But Andrael's Law binds me. Your friend ensured we could never speak of her specific properties. To anyone."

"My friend?"

"A story longer than we have time for, I am afraid."

Caeden frowned, unconvinced. "Is taking it—her—going to hurt me, somehow?"

Garadis stared at him impassively. "If you are asking whether Licanius has wards to prevent her from being taken—then no, she does not."

656     Caeden gazed at the blade. From up close, even the glow he'd

noticed earlier was muted. It looked like a well-made sword . . . but that was all.

He leaned down, peering closer. Etched into the steel in tiny lettering were more symbols—these ones familiar.

" 'For those who need me most.' What does that mean?"

"Another question I cannot answer." Garadis sounded irritated, but Caeden was still hesitant to touch the sword. Something was holding him back.

"What does Licanius mean? It sounds Darecian. You could at least tell me that much."

There was silence from Garadis. " 'Fate,' " he said eventually. "The translation is more specific, but in your language, it means 'fate.' "

Caeden nodded. Taking a deep breath, he reached down and grasped the hilt, then lifted the sword from its stone cradle.

He screamed.

Pain racked his entire body; he wanted to let the sword drop but his muscles had convulsed, making his grip on it viselike. Tears trickled down his cheeks as wave after wave of agony washed through him.

Then, just as he thought he could stand no more, it was over.

He was lying on the stone floor—blessedly not touching any of the lava rivulets—and still holding the sword. With a gasp he dropped it, letting it clatter against the warm stone. On his left forearm glowed a symbol, something he didn't recognize, which faded away even as he saw it. Not a wolf, but a different animal— a bear, perhaps?

Garadis was still standing in the corner, a satisfied look in his eyes.

Caeden scrambled to his feet and glared at him. "What have you done?" he growled. "You said there would be no traps."

"I said there were no wards that would harm you," corrected Garadis.

"Then what in fates was that?" Caeden demanded.

"A binding," replied Garadis. "The final consummation of the trade between my people and Andrael. The Lyth guard Licanius until one who passes the Tests wields her. In exchange, the one who takes her up must then free us. It is the pact that you have been trying so very hard to avoid these past centuries." He sighed, a contented sound. "You must have been desperate."

Caeden stared at his now-bare forearm worriedly. "Free you from what?"

Garadis leaned forward. "From *here*, Tal'kamar. From *this*. We cannot survive without the raw Essence Res Kartha produces. You need to find a way for us to leave, and not perish."

Caeden gave him a blank look. "But...I know nothing about any of that. It's impossible."

"And yet you have agreed to it." Garadis's blue eyes looked at Caeden greedily. "You have a year and a day. Should the pact be broken, the binding will compel you to return to us. Licanius will become the property of the Lyth, to do with as we see fit. And once she is truly at our command, we will see fit to use her for that which she was designed."

Caeden paled; the last sounded distinctly like a threat. "A year?"

"And a day," said Garadis. "She is yours until then, to do with as you wish. But if we cannot leave Res Kartha after that, she will be yours no longer. So choose your priorities wisely."

Caeden nodded, still stunned. He took a deep breath, then thought for a few moments.

"If you want my help, you'll also want me to survive the next few days," he observed. "I am going to return to Ilin Illan, to fight alongside my friends. If there is any way you can help me..."

Garadis laughed. "You always were a canny negotiator."

He stepped forward and laid his hand against Caeden's forehead again.

A flood of warmth passed through Caeden's mind, sudden but not unpleasant, causing his knees to buckle. The sensation passed quickly, though.

"You are already equipped to fight," said Garadis. "This knowledge will let you use Licanius for your purpose—but know this, too, Tal'kamar. What you are about to face is only the first strike, the first few drops of a torrent. A storm." He bent down slightly, so that his face was level with Caeden's. "The ilshara—what you call the Boundary—is waning, and when it fails entirely, your friends will lose. You cannot protect them forever."

Then he straightened, gesturing behind Caeden. The tunnel door ground open again. "Now it is time for you to go."

Caeden hesitated. "How do I go back?"

Garadis sighed. "To return to a question I asked before. How did you get here?"

Caeden dug around in his pocket and produced the small bronze box, then handed it to Garadis.

Garadis just stared at it for a long moment, stunned.

"You have audacity, Tal'kamar," he said softly. "I will grant you that."

"You know how it works?"

Garadis gave a slow nod. "Considering you stole it from me? Yes, I know how it works," he said, smoldering lip curling slightly. "To think, I didn't even know it was gone."

Caeden found himself reddening. "I *don't* know how it works," he admitted in an embarrassed tone. "I...just touched it, and it took me here."

"That explains much," said Garadis, his tone dry. He sighed. "It is a Portal Box. *The* Portal Box. It will take you to any destination you impart to it." He turned it over in his hands. "Each face has a destination; you need only direct Essence into this character"—he pointed to a small symbol, which Caeden had previously noted as appearing on every side—"and depending on which face you activate, you will be transported to its destination. It seems all six are already set; your touching it triggered only one. Assuming you entered them in sequence, this would then be the next." He indicated one of the faces.

Caeden's heart sank. "Can it get me back to Ilin Illan?"

"No," said Garadis. He gave Caeden a thoughtful look, then handed the Portal Box back with obvious reluctance. "But it is of no advantage to me if I delay you."

He made a sweeping motion with his hands, and suddenly everything...*twisted.*

Caeden gaped as a darkened city street appeared through a hole in the air. It was just as with the stones Taeris had used—except Garadis had done it unaided, as easily as breathing.

"Go," said Garadis. "Do what you must. But return within a year and a day with your solution, else you will lose Licanius forever."

Caeden nodded. "I will."

Without hesitation he stepped through the shimmering portal and back onto the streets of Ilin Illan.

# Chapter 54

Ilin Illan burned.

The night was at its deepest now, and the city below was lit only by naked, furious flames. Davian stared despairingly at the scene from where he'd collapsed in exhaustion, a little way behind the now dangerously thin front line of Andarran soldiers. Every street, every building visible from his vantage point at the palace gates either glowed a hot, angry red, or sat in equally ominous darkness.

He gasped for air and shook his head, trying to clear it, trying to get his bearings. He, Wirr, and Taeris had made it back to the Shields from the Tol, but their time there had been painfully short. Most of the city had been lost in that first disastrous hour after the Blind had found their way inside through Tol Athian; by the time someone had figured out exactly where the breach was, the Lower and Middle Districts were already ablaze.

After the Shields... a desperate retreat, their only option to avoid being trapped in Fedris Idri. Chaos as the Blind hit them from in front and behind, cutting through their lines, the invaders' unnaturally fast blades slashing everywhere. Struggling onward to the palace, the only defensible position left in the city, through a maelstrom of panic and screaming and running and blood.

And then this current, ominous, near-unbearable silence that hung over the city like a shroud as the Blind prepared their next assault. Probably their final one, Davian realized dully. The

Andarrans who had made it back to the palace had managed to regroup, to form a defensible line, but the damage had been done.

They were going to lose.

The Blind had been clever, he realized numbly. They'd known from the start that throwing more soldiers against the Shields would be a futile gesture; the narrow pass had meant that the three hundred men they'd sent had been no less effective than ten times that number. But it had been enough to keep the Andarran defenses focused around Fedris Idri, enough to be a threat. And combined with the Echoes, more than enough to not seem like simply a diversion.

Davian shifted, trying not to let his muscles get too stiff as he watched the ragged Andarran line, its members peering nervously along the steadily darkening street. Red-cloaked Gifted stood shoulder to shoulder with Shadows, Administrators, and battered-looking soldiers—a surreal sight even now, and one that only reinforced how desperate their situation had become.

"Strange, isn't it?" came a familiar voice from behind him.

Davian twisted to see Wirr, his friend's gaze also on the odd mixture of defenders.

"Yes," said Davian softly. "It really is."

There was silence for a few moments, then Wirr gingerly lowered himself to the ground beside his friend. "How are you holding up?"

Davian gave a soft laugh. "About as well as you'd expect. Against that El-cursed armor, I've been about as much use as the Gifted."

"That's not nothing, Dav," said Wirr. "You've made a real difference, as have Tol Athian's people. We'd have been overrun long ago if we hadn't changed the Tenets."

Davian nodded reluctantly, trying not to show his frustration. Though Essence itself was useless against the Blind's armor, the Gifted had adapted, wielding swords, spears, even stones from a distance to deadly effect. The Blind's unnatural strength and speed had minimized actual casualties, though. The presence of the Gifted had made the invaders more cautious, made their losses heavier. But it had come too late.

"You're right...though I'm not going to be able to even use

Essence for much longer," he admitted eventually. "I'm running out of sources." He gestured through the gates to the palace gardens behind him; where a few hours earlier there had been lush green grass and flowering plants of all kinds, now there was only a wasteland of black, crumbling dust.

Wirr just inclined his head, looking more sad than worried. "Between healing and fighting, my Reserve's almost dry, too. I think nearly everyone is about empty, to be honest." He glanced down the darkened street, toward the far end. "It won't be long now," he concluded softly.

Davian followed his friend's gaze. Ordered divisions of black-clad soldiers were lined up no more than five hundred yards away—just out of range of the Andarran archers, and far enough away that neither the Gifted nor the Shadows could attack with any efficacy.

Then, to the side, he spotted another black-clad figure staring toward them. A deep hood concealed its face.

"So the sha'teth finally showed up. Come to finish us off, I imagine," he muttered. They hadn't seen the creatures in battle so far, but it looked as if that was about to change. Davian took a few deep, calming breaths, ignoring the acrid taste of smoke at the back of his throat.

Without warning a violent red gash of light ripped the air between the opposing forces.

Davian leaned back, shielding his eyes from the blazing illumination. It faded almost as suddenly as it had appeared; when his vision cleared, a lone figure stood in the gloom, halfway between the Andarrans and the Blind.

Davian stared in shock.

"It's Caeden," he said in disbelief, pushing himself to his feet.

The street had fallen deathly silent, neither side seeming to know what to make of this turn of events. Caeden glanced around as if getting his bearings, his gaze sweeping across the Andarran ranks. Then he turned calmly toward the Blind.

"What's he doing?" muttered Davian, trying not to sound panicked. Caeden had touched the box...and now here he was at the end, appearing as they teetered at the edge of defeat. Ilseth's memory flashed through his thoughts. *It will ensure our victory.*

"Just wait, Dav," breathed Wirr, his tone suddenly hopeful.

Caeden stared at the Blind in silence, and with every passing moment Davian found himself more unsure of their former companion's motives.

Finally Caeden took a deep breath.

"I give you this one chance," he shouted toward the black-armored men, his words carrying clearly to the Andarran line, too, echoing through the street. "Leave now. Go back beyond the Boundary."

There was movement along the front line of Blind soldiers, and a helmetless man stepped into view. Davian's eyes widened; he recognized the figure despite the distance.

"I am Andan Mash'aan, Slayer of Lih'khaag, Second Sword of Danaris," the man shouted back in a loud, confident voice. His smile was mocking as he examined Caeden. "My people have waited two thousand years for this moment. Who are you, boy, to dare ask them to give it up—and with us on the cusp of a victory more complete than even the Protector had hoped, no less? Understand this, child. We will drink your blood. We will grind your bones to dust. We will carve our names—"

The man's words were cut off, and his eyes widened. Caeden hadn't moved, but the commander was sinking to his knees, his look of confusion quickly replaced by one of sheer terror. After a moment Davian could see exactly what Caeden was doing—though how, while Mash'aan was wearing that armor, he had no idea.

It was precisely what Davian himself had done to Ionis earlier that day.

The Blind commander's face began to wither, his eyes becoming hollow, his skin creasing and then stripping away. Suddenly Mash'aan's armor burst into a thousand pieces, tiny black discs skittering across the cobbled stone street, barely discernible in the murk. The stark white of a skeleton was visible for a few moments before it too disintegrated, crumbling to the ground in a fine white powder.

"I give you this one chance," repeated Caeden into the hush that followed.

Not a single Blind soldier moved. Caeden watched them for a few seconds more, then his shoulders slumped.

"So be it," he said, this time only just loudly enough for it to carry.

The sha'teth that Davian had spotted earlier glided forward, its sinuous movements making it hard to follow in the darkness. It said something that Davian could not hear, but Caeden didn't acknowledge the words. Instead he drew the sword that was hanging at his side.

Davian gaped. The blade drank in what little light was in the street, bending shadows so that they swirled around it, cloaking the steel from view. He felt the hairs on the back of his neck stand up as primal energies around him began to shift and flicker.

The sha'teth faltered, then fled as screams filled the air.

The first of the enemy troops began to fall.

Some clutched their heads as they slumped to the ground; others tore off their helmets or other parts of their armor as if they were being burned by them. The smell of smoke was suddenly mixed with something else, a pungent, sickly sweet rotting odor that momentarily threatened to relieve Davian of the contents of his stomach.

Davian's stunned gaze made its way back to Caeden, but the young man didn't seem to be doing anything. He just held the sword at his side, watching sadly as men continued to collapse. To die. For the first time, the ranks of the Blind shuddered, men out of formation, taking stuttering steps away from the horror before them.

A ragged cheer went up from the Andarran line, but it soon died out. It felt wrong to celebrate in the face of what they were watching. The multitude of Blind soldiers who had moments before been standing down the street now lay motionless, surrounded by thousands of small black plates, the debris of their armor. Inky red blood pooled around their heads as it poured from their noses and mouths. Davian didn't need to be any closer to know that they were dead.

Wirr ran his hands through his hair as he stared at the scene. "We need to talk to Caeden. That may be all of the Blind, but it's just as likely there are still others left in the city," he said eventually.

Davian inclined his head; he was already watching Caeden walking toward the Andarran lines, silhouetted against the flames of the burning buildings beyond. The dazed Andarran forces parted nervously as the young man approached, and a few of the soldiers pointed in Wirr's direction when Caeden spoke to them.

Caeden gave a tired smile when he spotted the two boys.

"I can't tell you how good it is to see you both. You especially, Davian," he added with genuine warmth as he walked up to them. He looked around, taking in the extent of the devastation, and his tone sobered. "What of Aelric, Dezia, and Taeris? And... the princess?" he added after a moment, a little awkwardly.

"All alive—and that's mostly thanks to you, Caeden," said Wirr. "We were moments from defeat when you showed up."

Davian nodded his silent agreement. He still wanted answers from Caeden, but Wirr wasn't wrong.

Caeden looked relieved. "I'm just sorry I couldn't get here sooner... and that I cannot stay longer." He shook his head. "If what I've learned is true, this is merely the beginning. The first strike. Devaed is gathering his forces, and you need to prepare. All of you." He drew something out of his pocket, staring at it grimly. "As do I."

Davian took an involuntary step back as the detailed inscriptions on the bronze cube glittered red against the distant light of still-raging fires. The box no longer glowed with the wolf symbol, but that made Davian no less nervous.

"Wait, Caeden," he said quickly. "I Read Ilseth Tenvar earlier today, and... that Vessel is dangerous. It was sent to you by the same man who ordered the deaths of everyone at my school; from what he said, your using it is going to play straight into Devaed's hands. If it hasn't already."

Caeden stared at him for a long moment, puzzled, then slowly shook his head. "No. I don't know what you saw, but this took me exactly where I needed to go. I wouldn't have been able to help you here, to stop the Blind, if I hadn't used it." He unconsciously touched the sword at his hip. "Maybe I fooled whoever it was you saw into sending it to me, somehow. But I do know that I *planned* to get this box—and that I need to go wherever it takes me next. I *know* that's what I'm supposed to do now, Davian. You have to trust me on this."

Davian scowled. "It's not a case of trust, Caeden. You cannot just leave without giving us more reassurance than that," he insisted. "Please. At least tell us where you've been, where you got that sword. Help us to understand what's going on."

Caeden shook his head. "Even if *I* fully understood, there's no time." He cast a nervous glance over toward a group of red-cloaked Gifted who were heading in their direction. "I can't afford to be delayed here, either by the Athian Council or Administration. I've been given a schedule, and I suspect the consequences of not keeping it would be dire. For all of us." He looked Davian in the eye. "I *am* sorry, Davian. This is just how it has to be."

Davian gritted his teeth. Caeden was telling the truth... but in that moment, it didn't matter. All of the frustration, the gut-wrenching fear of the battle, the pain of the last few months hit Davian as a raw wave of emotion. He couldn't just let Caeden go again and hope for the best, not when he knew what the consequences might be.

He focused. Drawing enough Essence to weaken Caeden without harming him would be difficult, but after what he'd already done over the past few hours, Davian was confident he had enough control. He didn't want to cause any harm—just keep Caeden immobile, keep him here until he'd better explained himself.

As he reached out, though, he almost faltered.

Caeden's Reserve was more than just a pool. It was something...immense. An unending ocean of energy and light.

For a second he hesitated, wondering if it was wise to proceed. He wasn't even sure he *could* empty a Reserve that large.

Then he thought again about Caladel, about all his unanswered questions, about the months of not understanding what part he was supposed to be playing in these events.

He closed his eyes and hardened the kan bridge between himself and Caeden.

A sudden torrent of Essence slammed into him, causing him to physically stumble from the shock. There was so much. *So* much. It just kept coming, a river of white energy, until Davian wasn't sure he could hold it any longer. He forced his gaze to meet Caeden's, wondering if the drain was taking effect yet.

Caeden just smiled sadly back at Davian.

Suddenly the Essence Davian had been drawing into himself reversed direction, inexorably flowing back to Caeden. It gathered in a glowing nimbus around the young man's hands, then along his forearms, his torso, his head. Davian struggled against the current, tried to stop the flow, but Caeden was too strong. The other man's expression had barely changed, as if what he was doing took only a minimal effort. As if Davian's attack had been little more than a nuisance, a buzzing insect in need of swatting.

Within moments everything Davian had taken was gone again. He dropped to his knees, still shaking from the effort, and looked up at Caeden in stunned, disbelieving silence.

Caeden stared back at him for a long moment. Then his eyes flicked up for a few seconds, toward the Andarran lines. Davian got the distinct impression he was examining people's faces, scanning the crowd for someone.

Whoever Caeden was looking for, he evidently didn't find them. The young man's eyes flickered with disappointment as he closed them, pouring the Essence he'd retaken from Davian into the box in his hand.

There was a roar, and a tunnel made of pure fire exploded into existence.

Caeden turned to Wirr, unperturbed by the raging vortex.

"He's coming, Wirr," he shouted over the thunder. "Tell Taeris to make sure everyone is ready, because I don't know how long it will be before I can return."

Before anyone could move he turned. Leaped forward, into the swirling flames.

He vanished.

Wirr stared as the tunnel of fire faded and darkness reclaimed the street.

He turned dazedly to Davian, ignoring the stares of those around them and helping his friend to his feet. "Are you all right?"

Davian didn't respond for a few moments, his eyes fixed upon the spot where the vortex had been. Then he shook his head.

"I did everything I could, and it didn't even bother him," he said softly. "He's *so* strong, Wirr. It's terrifying."

Wirr followed his friend's gaze. "Given what he just did for us, we should probably be glad about that."

"Maybe." Davian turned to look at his friend, and Wirr could see the frustration on his face. "I know he said he was only able to save us because of where that box took him, but after what I saw in Tenvar's memory...it just doesn't make sense." He rubbed his forehead, expression worried. "I feel like there's something we're missing. Something important."

Wirr sighed. "I don't disagree, Dav, but there's not a lot we can do about it now. Let's just hope that Caeden knows what he's doing." He glanced back at the Andarran lines; a few of the men were still gaping in their general direction after Caeden's spectacular exit, but everyone else had evidently gone back to worrying about more immediate things. "I need to find Karaliene, start organizing the recovery effort. We can sit down and figure out what to do about Caeden later."

Davian grabbed Wirr's arm before he could walk off. "Can we? People saw me fighting, Wirr. *Administrators* saw me fighting. If they haven't already figured out what I am, they soon will."

Wirr paused, then grimaced.

He hated to admit it, but Davian was right; despite everything else that had just happened, it wouldn't take long for Administration to come after his friend. And though Wirr was now technically the Northwarden, the ban on Augurs was a part of the Treaty—which superseded the authority of any one man.

Besides which, if he was being honest, Wirr didn't even know whether his authority as Northwarden was going to be recognized now that everyone knew he was Gifted.

"You may have to lie low for a while," he conceded, trying to evaluate what was likely to happen over the next few weeks. "But once everything's settled down, people are going to realize that we need the Augurs to strengthen the Boundary again. And when we get to that point..."

"The Assembly will have to amend the Treaty. Remove the ban," finished Davian, looking suddenly thoughtful.

Wirr blinked; Davian had come to that conclusion faster than he'd expected. "Yes," he said slowly. "There's a good chance they will."

Davian hesitated, then shook his head. "I hope that happens, Wirr—I really do. But I can't stay. I can't risk getting caught just for a possibility."

Wirr stared at his friend in open surprise. "Where else would you go?"

"Prythe. Tol Shen." He held up his hand as Wirr made to protest. "I'm not joining them permanently. I've agreed to help them find a way to fix the Boundary—and they already have another Augur with them, so it seems like the place I can do the most good for now. But once the Boundary is secure, if things really are different here in the city, I'll come back." He gave Wirr a tired, rueful smile. "Besides, from what I've seen, you're going to have your hands full enough without having to worry about protecting me, too."

Wirr stared at Davian for a few moments in silence, heart sinking. There was no refuting his friend's logic, but that made it no less painful to lose him again so soon after getting him back.

He nodded slowly and clasped Davian by the shoulder, swallowing a sudden lump in his throat. "Fates. I understand. I hate it, but...I understand." He glanced around again, this time realizing just how many blue cloaks were among the crowd. "Does Asha know?"

"Not yet." Davian looked at the ground, pain flashing across his face.

"Then you should go and find her, before it's too late. You've probably got an hour, maybe two until anyone recovers enough to worry about you. I'll keep the Administrators occupied with other things for as long as I can."

Davian hesitated, then inclined his head. "Thank you," he said sincerely.

Wirr just nodded back, the lump in his throat returning. "Just...fates be with you, Dav. Stay safe."

"You, too, Wirr. I'll see you around," said Davian, his voice catching. He gave Wirr a tight smile, then spun, heading in the direction of the palace.

Wirr watched him go for a few seconds, then took a deep breath and refocused, scanning the crowd for any of the people he needed to talk to. The battle was over, but his jubilation at the victory was already fading.

The real challenges were about to begin.

∞

Davian sat on the palace steps, doing his best to fend off exhaustion.

Asha sat shoulder to shoulder with him, occasionally shifting her weight but always touching, as if to reassure herself he was really there. He understood the sentiment. The past few hours—the past few *days*—had gone by in one stunning blur, and it was only now that events were slowing, allowing him time to process everything properly, that it was beginning to set in. Asha was alive. She was *alive*. It was a miracle.

Davian knew he should already have left, but he once again pushed that uncomfortable thought to the back of his mind. Despite their emotional and physical tiredness, he and Asha had spent the last couple of hours exchanging their stories, determined to spend some time in each other's company. For a short time, the horrors they had just witnessed faded into the background as they smiled and laughed together; even after the months apart they had fallen back into an easy, comfortable rhythm in their conversation, allaying Davian's fears that things might have changed between them.

Eventually, though, the trials of the day had taken their toll, and the conversation had died out. Now they just looked out over the broken city in contemplative silence.

It was an absorbing scene. The hellish red of the fires in the Lower and Middle Districts still illuminated the city, some of the taller buildings below silhouetted against the flames. Soldiers were hard at work bringing the various blazes under control, though; as little as a half hour earlier the entire Lower District had appeared to be ablaze, but now only a few smaller sections by the docks were alight.

Though it was mostly invisible against the night sky, Davian knew that black smoke was billowing overhead, blotting out any stars that might have been showing through the clouds. Fortunately a gentle breeze was pushing most of it away from the Upper District, but the smell had still managed to saturate everything. He'd grown almost accustomed to it by now, but sometimes still winced at the acrid taste at the back of his throat when he inhaled, the slight burning in his lungs.

Soldiers and civilians alike still dotted the blackened palace grounds in front of them. The last of the wounded were being treated by a combination of Gifted and physicians, and those who had some lesser medicinal knowledge were also helping where they could.

Despite everything, the mood was noticeably upbeat. Even attitudes toward the Gifted appeared to have shifted a little; passersby would often smile at red-cloaked men and women, some even stopping for an apparently genial conversation. The friendliest smiles were reserved for the Gifted from Tol Shen, though. The soldiers all knew who had been there from the start, and though everyone still acknowledged Athian's contribution, it was Shen that was receiving the accolades.

Best of all, no one appeared to be overly concerned that the Tenets had been changed—in fact, from what Davian could glean, it was a matter of some relief for a lot of people. It seemed that there would be at least one positive to come out of tonight.

"So what are you going to do now, Asha?" he asked.

Asha bit her lip. "I'm not sure yet. I'll have to talk to Michal... assuming he's all right. I saw him on the Shields a while back, but not since." She stared into space worriedly at the realization. "Other than that, there's probably going to be an investigation into how the Shadows ended up with all those Vessels. The Tenets may have changed, but the Treaty certainly hasn't. Administration is going to want answers."

"They're going to want blood, you mean," said Davian quietly. He glanced over to where Wirr was talking with a group of noblemen in the distance. "I'm sure knowing the new head of Administration will help."

Asha followed his gaze. "Maybe," she said. "But everyone knows he's Gifted now. Administration is going to resist every decision he makes." She turned to look at him. "What about you?"

Davian hesitated, but he'd been avoiding this moment for too long already. "I have to leave. Soon."

Asha's expression was suddenly sad, but she inclined her head. "I wondered about that," she admitted. "So you're going to take the Shen Gifted up on their offer?" Concern made her tone heavy.

"Just until the Boundary is strengthened," said Davian quickly. "Then I'm coming back. I promise."

Asha gave a slow nod. "Just make sure you do," she said. "Those stories the Elders used to tell us about Shen...I've heard some of the same things here, and I've got no reason to doubt they're true. Power really is all they care about, Dav. Once they have someone like you working for them, they're going to do everything they can to keep you. You'll be too valuable for them to just let you walk away."

Davian grimaced. "Maybe," he said. "But the Boundary's weakening and from what Caeden said, stopping it from failing entirely might be the most important thing I can do. Fates, it might be the most important thing *anyone* can do, right now." He sighed. "If things were different, I'd choose to stay here with you and Wirr in a heartbeat. But Caeden says there's something else coming— something worse than what we saw tonight. If that's really the case, then I have to go where I'm going to be of most use."

Asha bit her lip, but eventually gave a reluctant nod. "Have you told Wirr?"

"Yes—we've said our good-byes." Davian glanced around nervously as he caught another flash of blue from the corner of his eye. He was tempting fate by staying this long. "I know you don't approve of Shen, but...you could come with me. From what you've been saying, it might be safer for you away from Administration, away from this Scyner and the Shadraehin."

Asha shook her head. "And be what—a servant of some kind?" She sighed. "You're right, Dav. We need to be where we're going to have the most impact, and my place is here."

Davian's heart sank, but he nodded. He'd known that would be Asha's answer, knew that they were both making the right choices. It didn't stop him from desperately wishing that things were different, though.

"I understand," he said.

Suddenly he spotted someone in a red cloak waving to him; he blinked in surprise as the figure came closer.

"Ishelle?" He stood, helping Asha to her feet too before giving the other Augur a confused smile as she approached. "What are you doing here?"

Ishelle raised an eyebrow. "You said you'd give me my answer if I came," she said, expression serious.

Davian stared at her for a moment, then laughed as he realized what she was talking about.

Ishelle grinned back, then turned her gaze to Asha. "I'm Ishelle," she said, her tone cheerful. "Davian and I met on the road a few days ago."

"Dav told me all about it," said Asha easily, giving Ishelle a polite nod. "I'm Asha."

Ishelle nodded in return, though for a moment Davian thought he saw a flash of irritation in her eyes. Then she turned back to him. "I didn't want to interrupt, but one of my friends over there"—she nodded toward where a group of red-cloaked Gifted were gathered—"overheard a couple of Administrators talking about you. They were becoming a little...agitated, apparently. I thought you might want to know."

Davian grimaced. "Wonderful." He rubbed his forehead.

Ishelle watched him closely. "Are you still coming to Tol Shen?"

Davian paused for a moment, then nodded.

"Then you should join us. It's a long trip to Prythe; I'm sure you'd prefer not to do it alone." Ishelle tugged at her cloak. "We have a spare one of these, and we're leaving straight away. We'll be out of the city before anyone thinks to look too closely at who is in the group."

Davian hesitated, but Asha laid her hand gently on his arm. "Go," she said, giving him a small smile. "We both know you've already stayed longer than you should have. I don't want you getting caught because of me."

She wrapped him in a sudden, affectionate embrace. Davian returned it, and they stood like that for several seconds, neither wanting to be the first one to let go.

Eventually there was a polite cough from Ishelle, and Davian and Asha reluctantly separated.

Asha gave him a final parting smile, and was about to turn away when she hesitated.

"Wait. There's one more thing." She reached into a pocket in her dress, then drew out something that glittered in the flickering torchlight. She grabbed Davian's hand and pressed the object into his palm. "They're eventually going to take this away from me if I hang on to it. Just…keep it for me." It might have been Davian's imagination, but he thought her eyes were glistening. "You can give it back to me when we see each other next."

She gave him another tight, brief hug, then spun and walked off before he could say anything.

He opened his hand slowly.

The ring was silver, three bands twisted together in a distinctive pattern. Davian stared at it, dazed.

The last time he'd seen this ring, Malshash had been destroying it in Deilannis.

He hesitated for a long moment.

Then he slipped the ring onto his finger, shaking his head slightly at the familiar weight. Taking a deep breath, he nodded to Ishelle, and they made their way toward the cluster of red-cloaked Gifted.

It was time to move on.

# Epilogue

Asha leaned against the wall of the Great Hall, tired eyes squinting against the light as the first rays of dawn found their way through a nearby window.

She stared around dully at the gathered nobility, everyone talking in hushed tones as the aftermath of the battle continued to be assessed. Tol Athian's input into the proceedings hadn't been needed for a while now; she knew she should go back to her rooms, try to sleep, but her grief was still too sharp. It had been only a few hours since the Andarran victory, yet the elation of that moment had already worn off, rapidly replaced by the heavy knowledge of what had been lost.

She had only just returned from identifying Michal's body. Her mentor had evidently been slain in the chaotic flight from the Shields to the palace; her only comfort was that it had been with a single blow, dealt from behind and straight through the chest. He had probably never even felt the blade go in.

An hour before that, Kol's body had been moved under her watchful gaze and placed into the heartrendingly long line of those who needed burial. It had been hard to see her friend's lifeless form again—and even harder to see it alone. Erran and Fessi had been true to their word; Asha had visited their rooms, but they were gone, having left no sign that they had ever been in Ilin Illan. Davian had left hours earlier. Wirr was still busy trying to deal with an angry and confused Administration, and probably would be for days to come.

She knew she'd done the right thing by staying, knew that this was where she needed to be. It didn't make it feel any less lonely.

Even as she had the thought, though, she summoned a small smile as a weary-looking Wirr hurried toward her.

"Representative Chaedris." He stopped in front of her, and though he smiled back, she could see the worry in his eyes.

"What's wrong?" she asked him quietly, heart sinking even lower. She wasn't sure she could handle more bad news. Not now.

Wirr glanced around, making sure that there was nobody nearby to overhear. "Administration has asked to go through my father's office. They phrased it as a courtesy to me, of course—to ease my workload—but they've started to realize that he must have known something about my being Gifted. They're suspicious, and I couldn't refuse them without looking like I had something to hide."

Asha paled. "I don't know if there's anything in there, but…"

"I know." Wirr clasped Asha's hands in his; he made the gesture seem like a condolence, but Asha felt the hard, uneven iron of a key slip into her palm. "I can hold them off for maybe an hour. Make sure you're done by then."

Asha nodded, and Wirr turned to go. Then he hesitated.

"Be careful, Ash. Try to stay out of sight if you can," he said in a low voice. "I'm trying to keep things in Administration under control, but there's more than a little hysteria about the Shadows right now. It's not official policy, but if an Administrator sees you and they don't know who you are, I wouldn't be surprised if they try to detain you. Especially since you're an obvious target at the moment."

Asha gave a short, rueful nod. Most of the Shadows had melted away, unnoticed, within the first hour of the victory—along with their Vessels. By the time it had been brought to anyone's attention, Asha had been one of only a handful of Shadows left in the city.

She watched Wirr hurry away, then took a deep breath, moving out into a deserted corridor and heading for her rooms. Once there she quickly retrieved the Veil she'd hidden earlier, slipping it onto her wrist and watching pensively as it molded to her skin. Everything shimmered for a moment, and when she moved over to look in the mirror, only an empty room stared back at her.

She nodded in satisfaction and then left again. The palace hallways were still mostly empty, and she had no trouble avoiding collisions with the few people she came across. Once at Elocien's office she made sure the passageway was clear in both directions, then used the key Wirr had given her, slipping inside and locking the door behind her.

She just stood there for a moment, looking around the room sadly. It felt...odd, to be in here without the reassuring presence of the duke. Her stomach twisted as she thought of him—wondered again how many of her conversations had been with him, and how many with Erran. Or if there was ultimately any difference.

She sighed, then moved over to Elocien's desk, methodically checking through his drawers and scanning each piece of paper on his desk. There didn't appear to be anything incriminating, much to her relief. It seemed that Elocien—or Erran—had thought to be careful, even in here.

Ten minutes had passed when a key turned in the lock.

Asha's heart leaped to her throat and she quietly shut the drawer she'd been searching, then moved back into the corner of the room. Wirr had said an hour, but it couldn't have been more than half of that since they'd spoken.

She gave a silent sigh of relief as the door swung open to reveal Laiman Kardai standing in the hallway. The king's adviser had known about the Augurs, was trustworthy. Was probably there for the same reasons as she, in fact.

She was just about to remove her Veil when someone called Laiman's name. Laiman's head turned, and he smiled as another man came into view.

"Taeris!" Laiman glanced around to make sure no one else was in the vicinity, then beckoned the heavily scarred man inside. "They decided not to keep you locked away, I see," he said with some amusement.

Asha studied the newcomer's crisscrossed features as he entered. This was clearly Taeris Sarr—the man Davian said had orchestrated the attack on him three years earlier. She frowned as she watched Laiman's and Taeris's body language. The two men appeared relaxed around one other, like old acquaintances.

Taeris smiled back, though his eyes were tired. "They're still not entirely happy that I deceived them with the Travel Stones, broke into the Tol, or showed them up as fools. Particularly the latter. But Caeden's little performance has changed a few minds, convinced them that there might at least be some merit to what I've been saying." He sank into a nearby chair. "Enough for a reprieve from my cell, anyway."

There was silence for a few moments as Laiman walked over to the desk, rifling through papers just as Asha had been doing. Asha stretched her muscles cautiously, unsure now whether to reveal herself.

"I hear the king has recovered," said Taeris.

"He has," said Laiman absently as he scanned a document, though his tone held a note of reservation.

"You don't sound happy."

Laiman grimaced, looking up from what he was reading. "He remembers very little from the past two months."

Taeris frowned. "Control, then," he concluded. "We're fortunate they didn't try to take things further."

"That's what has me worried." Laiman resumed his search. "If the Blind were really Controlling him, it doesn't makes sense. I mean, I can see why they wouldn't want him changing the Tenets. But they could have done *so* much more damage." He scratched his head. "And the timing of his being released, too—straight after the Tenets were changed..."

Taeris shrugged. "Maybe the Blind realized what had happened, and decided he wasn't worth the effort anymore?"

Laiman shook his head in frustration. "I thought that too at first, but he's the *king*. He could have ordered the surrender—fates knows what would have happened, exactly, but I guarantee it wouldn't have been pleasant." He hesitated. "Just think, for a moment. Given the way things turned out. Who benefited most from having the king act the way he did?"

"Aside from the Blind?" Taeris tapped his fingers together as he considered. "Well, the king looks a fool now, stubborn for not changing the Tenets. There's no proof he was Controlled, and most people don't even believe that power exists, so it's not exactly something the palace can claim. So I suppose..." He trailed off, staring at Laiman in mild disbelief. "*Us?* The Gifted?"

"Tol Shen, to be more precise," said Laiman, opening another drawer. "It's no secret that Athian decided to hide in the Tol until the Tenets were changed. Shen, on the other hand, had people on the Shields healing the wounded from the start." He paused, rubbing his forehead. "And the only memories the king has that are recent are of when Karaliene was away. When I insisted that Lothlar and some of his people accompany her, despite his protests."

Asha stared at the king's adviser as he flicked through more papers, stunned that he would even hint at such an accusation. Taeris's skeptical expression, however, wavered. "You think they have an Augur?"

"No. If it was an Augur, the distance wouldn't have mattered—and Kevran wouldn't have had any physical symptoms, either. But we both know there are Vessels out there that can simulate Control, and it's my belief that Lothlar has one."

Taeris was silent for a moment, looking troubled at the thought. "Even if he does, there still has to be an Augur involved for your theory to make any sense," he pointed out. "If this all started two months ago, then it was well before the invasion—which means that Shen knew about the attack before it started. And power hungry though they can be, they won't have aligned themselves with the likes of the Blind. Fates, if they really did plan this, they'd have needed an Augur to tell them ahead of time that we *won*!"

Laiman flicked the last drawer in the desk shut. "There is another possibility."

Taeris frowned for a few seconds in puzzlement, then grunted as he realized what Laiman was hinting at. "You still think they have the Journal pages."

Laiman gave a grim nod and walked over to sit opposite Taeris, apparently satisfied with the results of his search. "You know I've always had my suspicions as to who took them. And we both know that Seeing twenty years ahead wasn't a stretch for the likes of Jakarris, Eleran, or Siks." He sighed. "There's no proof, of course—Shen could equally have an Augur working for them.

But if they did know this attack was coming since the war, their political maneuvering over the past ten years suddenly has more logic behind it. The Houses they chose to ally with never really made sense to me until today."

Taeris sat in silence for a few moments, then nodded reluctantly. "So the king looks like a bigoted fool, everyone sees how valuable the Gifted truly are, and Shen takes the most difficult step back toward power. They gain the trust of the people again, while simultaneously undermining the Loyalists." He sighed. "I can see what you're saying. It's unlikely Shen got into a position like that by coincidence."

"Exactly," said Laiman quietly.

Still standing motionless in the corner, Asha stared at the two men in horror. Could it be true? The Journal Erran had shown her had pages missing; that must be what the king's adviser was referring to. Though how he thought Tol Shen could rely on those visions, when the others in the book had been so clearly wrong, she had no idea.

Regardless—she hadn't even considered, hadn't *imagined* that anyone except the Blind could be Controlling the king. The very thought made her nauseous.

Taeris, though, just looked annoyed. "Fates. Shen was playing a dangerous game, even by their standards."

"And now it's paying off—they're going to be more powerful than they have been for a very long time. When I raised the possibility of the king being Controlled, they went so far as to suggest that the palace was trying to invent a story to cover up its own incompetence." Laiman's lip curled in disgust. "This success has made them bolder."

Asha shook her head in disbelief, almost forgetting for a moment that she was invisible. Tol Shen had used foreknowledge of the invasion, the deaths of thousands, to play *politics*? And Davian had left only hours earlier to work with them...

"And now Davian, of all people, has thrown in his lot with them," Taeris noted, echoing Asha's thoughts. He scowled, rubbing his forehead. "I tried to find him after the battle, but the lad had already left. He doesn't trust me anymore—which is my fault, I suppose, but it makes it no less of a problem. I still think he's the key, Thell. We've both read Alchesh. He's as important as Caeden, maybe more so."

"I agree," said Laiman, making a calming motion. "Shen has pursued him more aggressively than I would have expected; if they really do have the missing Journal pages, that could be significant in and of itself. All we can do for now, though, is try to find their purpose for him. Once we know that, we can figure out our next move." He paused. "And Taeris? It's Laiman now. Always Laiman, even in here."

*Thell.* Asha's brow furrowed, and she made a mental note of the name. If the king's adviser wasn't using his real name, it was worth finding out why.

Taeris acknowledged the rebuke with a nod. "Sorry." He frowned contemplatively, then exhaled. "At least I still know where he is, I suppose."

Laiman looked at his friend, expression worried. "He could break the connection now. I think he would if you asked, no matter how he feels about you."

"No. It's too important to be able to find him," said Taeris, his tone firm. "Besides, the lad has problems enough right now—there's no benefit to burdening him with the knowledge of what he did. It's been three years, and I don't think he even remembers anything about the attack. As long as Torin or Karaliene don't bring it up, I think it's best to leave it alone."

"Karaliene knows, too?"

"It was the only way she'd let me into the palace. Torin told her—before he realized Davian was still alive, of course."

Asha frowned. When she'd spoken to him after the battle, Davian had been convinced that Taeris was responsible for the attack on him three years earlier. This, though...this made it sound as if there was more to the story than he'd realized. And Wirr knew? She'd have to find out more from her friend when she next had the opportunity.

Laiman leaned forward. "Still—it's too dangerous. You only need to lose control once, and you'll be dead. Don't think I can't tell that scar is fresh," he added accusingly.

Taeris made a dismissive gesture. "I've managed for three years. A while longer won't make a difference."

Laiman frowned. "Fine. Just...be careful."

"I will." Taeris shifted in his seat, clearly wanting to change the subject. "Have you heard anything more about the remaining Blind in the city?"

"All dead, as far as we can tell. Caeden was effective, I'll give him that," said Laiman. "I've had a closer look at the Blind's armor, by the way. It was made up of these." He dug into a pocket and held up a black disc, careful not to let the edges touch his skin.

Taeris shivered, and behind him Asha felt herself doing the same at the sight. "Dar'gaithin scales?"

Laiman nodded grimly. "Melded together into plates somehow."

"So that's our confirmation, then, if we needed any. Devaed was behind the invasion."

"It would appear so." Laiman shook his head, a hint of frustration in the motion. "But as to the why—the reason for this focused attack, before the Boundary has weakened enough for him to send his real forces through...I have no idea." He sighed. "Your theory about Caeden is probably our best guess; this entire thing seems to revolve around him. Did you get to speak with him after the battle, before he disappeared again?"

"No...but Torin did. Caeden told him that this was only Devaed's first strike—and said that we were to prepare for worse." Taeris hesitated. "Much worse."

The sick feeling in Asha's stomach stirred again. Davian had already told her about Caeden's warning, but this was the first time it had really struck home. The city had barely survived the attack the night before. She didn't care to think about what anything worse would mean.

Laiman was silent for a moment. "Did he at least suggest how we were to prepare?"

"Nothing so specific, I'm afraid. But...he *did* have a sword, Laiman. A blade that made the sha'teth turn tail as soon as he drew it."

Laiman raised an eyebrow. "Did he now," he breathed, and Asha could see a spark of intense interest in his eyes. "I hadn't heard that little piece of information. You think...?"

Taeris sighed. "Maybe. I didn't get a good look at it, so I don't know," he admitted. "And Caeden is not around to ask."

There was silence for a few seconds as Laiman stared into the fire. Then he drew a deep, reluctant breath.

"Speaking of the sha'teth."

Taeris nodded. "I know. All three got away."

Laiman's expression twisted, and this time Asha could see real pain there. "They showed the Blind how to get access to Tol Athian, Taeris," he said, the burden evident in his tone. "We were responsible for many deaths today."

Taeris nodded bitterly. "Just one of our many mistakes, I fear."

They sat in silence for some time, Asha barely daring to breathe. She didn't know what to make of that last exchange... but if there had been any doubt before, she was certain now that there would be unpleasant consequences should she be discovered eavesdropping.

Finally Laiman straightened and shook himself back into the present, glancing across at Taeris.

"I *do* have some good news. I wasn't going to tell you until it was official, but..."

Taeris raised an eyebrow at him. "I'm listening."

"I spoke to both Torin and Karaliene earlier, and I mentioned that Representative Alac had fallen in battle. They thought that young Ashalia should stay on, but agreed that she will still need someone with more experience to guide her. When I put forward your name, they both seemed amenable to the idea." He shrugged. "Torin was going to speak to Ashalia once everything had died down, but assuming neither she nor the king have any objections..."

Taeris stared at him in disbelief. "Ah...have you forgotten I'm still a wanted criminal?"

"A matter I believe our young Northwarden is clearing up as we speak," said Laiman cheerfully. "Nothing is set in stone yet, but he has the power to reverse his father's verdict. And despite Administration's protests it looks like both the king and Karaliene want him to keep his new position, so I don't foresee any problems on that front, either." He gave Taeris a slight smile. "Welcome back, old friend."

Taeris was silent for several seconds, stunned. "And...and Athian?"

Laiman chuckled. "I assume that when you are named their Representative, they will have to take you back, like it or not. It might just force them to give what you've been saying a little more consideration, too."

Taeris barked a disbelieving laugh, then leaned back in his chair. "You've been busy." He shook his head incredulously. "I truly don't know how to thank you."

Laiman inclined his head, smiling. "No need." He gestured to the door. "All the same, we should find somewhere out of the way for you to stay tonight. We don't want some overzealous Administrator recognizing you before everything's sorted out."

Taeris rose, a renewed vigor in the way he bore himself. "Lead the way."

They moved into the passageway and paused just outside the doorway, blocking it. Asha took a hesitant half step forward, but there was no gap for her to slip through. She clenched a fist in silent frustration. If she couldn't get out now, she'd have to wait until they were long gone.

Laiman grinned at his friend as they stood in the hallway, unaware of Asha's dilemma. "So. After all these years you're finally going to have some resources at your disposal, a bit of freedom to move around again. What's your first order of business?"

Taeris thought for a few moments, tapping a finger absently against the side of the door. Then he leaned forward, eyes glinting.

"Laiman," he said quietly, "I think it's time we organized a trip back to Deilannis."

He flicked the door shut, cutting off Laiman's response.

Asha was alone once again.

Caeden crept forward, parting the darkness ahead with a small sphere of pulsing white Essence.

He was underground again, though his surroundings were markedly different from Res Kartha. This place was silent, dead: just a long, narrow, gritty shaft that seemed intent on going nowhere but deeper into the damp, musty earth. He'd been walking for at least an hour now, and in all that time there had been no side tunnels, no rooms, no change in slope or direction. No sound except the soft pad of his own footsteps, either. Veins of quartz and metals occasionally sparkled in the wall as he trudged forward, but otherwise he had neither seen nor heard anything of note.

Just as he was beginning to wonder if he'd somehow arrived at the wrong place, the tunnel began to level out.

Abruptly he realized that the walls ahead were widening into a small room, an antechamber of sorts, from which there were several exits. He came to a stuttering stop, hesitating. There were four passageways, each looking as menacing as the next. His light did not penetrate far into the tunnels, but he could see from the sloping floors that one led up, one continued down, and two appeared to keep on level. Which way was correct? *Was* there a correct choice? He didn't even know why he was here, so whatever decision he made would inevitably be a guess.

Suddenly there was a stirring in the darkness from the leftmost passageway, just beyond his light—a scratching of movement against stone, slight, but comparatively loud after the heavy silence of the past hour. Flinching toward it, Caeden instinctively drew Essence from his Reserve, then extinguished his sphere and directed a blast of energy at the tunnel. Enough to stun, but not kill.

The afterimage of the flash quickly faded, leaving only complete darkness and a sullen, tense silence. Nerves stretched taut, Caeden stood motionless for a few seconds, listening. There was nothing.

Then an unseen force gripped him like a great hand, raising him a full foot into the air and slamming him back hard against the stone wall. Dazed and not a little disoriented, he drew in Essence again—as much as he could, this time—and threw it wildly at whatever was holding him. To his dismay the pressure on his chest and arms did not relent even a little.

Suddenly the room was lit; the illumination had no source he could pinpoint, as if darkness had simply been transformed into light. A man was standing in front of him, arms crossed and expression thoughtful as he studied his prisoner. He was older, nearly bald, with a lined face and a small beard of startling white. Still, his blue eyes glittered with a keen, strangely energetic intelligence.

"Tal'kamar. I'd begun to wonder if something had gone wrong," said the old man. "But I see that all has gone as planned after all." He indicated the sword hanging from Caeden's belt.

Caeden struggled in vain against his invisible bonds. "Who are you? Where am I, and why am I here?" he demanded. He tried to reach for Licanius, but it was no use. His arms might as well have been encased in stone, for all he could move them.

His attacker smiled. "Good to see you too, old friend," he said. "To answer each of your questions: I am Tae'shadon, the Keeper—Asar Shenelac to my friends. These are the Wells of Mor Aruil. And you, Tal'kamar, are here to remember."

Caeden was silent for a moment as he processed the response, then forced himself to relax his tensed muscles. He appeared to be in no immediate danger. "The last part might be difficult," he said in a dry tone. "My memories have been erased."

"Not erased," chided Asar gently. "Just hidden."

Caeden scowled. "Then let me down and show them to me!" he snapped.

To his surprise the pressure on his body vanished. He dropped to the floor awkwardly and stumbled forward, falling to his knees; he scrambled up again, wary, but Asar just watched him with an unperturbed expression.

"You know me?" asked Caeden once he had recovered, irritably trying to dust off his already ragged attire.

"We are acquainted," said Asar. "You asked me to restore your memories, once you arrived here."

Caeden stared at Asar for a moment, then just shrugged. He refused to be surprised, or concerned, by his own plans anymore. "Very well. No point in wasting time."

Asar shook his head. "There is more," he said. "You have asked me to only restore *specific* memories—the ones that will help you fight in the coming war. No others." He hesitated. "Against my advice."

Caeden frowned. "Only some? Why would I want that?"

Asar sighed. "I think...I think you wanted to change who you were." He leaned forward. "The problem, Tal'kamar, is that if you do not know who you were, you cannot know to change."

A chill slid down Caeden's spine. Who had he been, that he was so willing to leave parts of his past erased? "I will have to take your word on that," he said slowly, "but there is at least one extra memory I wish to have returned to me."

Asar blinked, for the first time looking as if he hadn't anticipated something. "Which is?"

"The hours before I awoke in that forest. The most recent memory I do not have," said Caeden softly. He knew he'd arranged all of this to fight Devaed, *knew* which side he was on—but the faces of those villagers, their accusations and their unbridled, unthinking hatred, still haunted him. He needed to know, with certainty, that it had been undeserved.

Asar hesitated, then nodded. "Then we shall do that first."

Before Caeden could react, the old man stepped forward and placed two fingers against Caeden's forehead.

*Caeden's heart pounded as he walked into the village.*

*It had worked; he'd appeared only a few hundred meters into the forest, exactly where he'd planned. No one would think to look for him here in Desriel—at least not unless Tenvar talked, and he was fairly certain that taking the man's finger had ensured against that.*

*The Waters of Renewal had quickly begun to take effect; his days as a youth in the Shining Lands were already barely more than a fog. He'd estimated that it could take as little as an hour for all the memories to go—but they should at least fade in sequence, according to his experiments. That was fortunate. He needed only to remember the last few years to know what he had to do, and why.*

*He found he was clutching the hilt of his sword tightly, nervously; he took a deep breath, forcing the hand to his side again and trying his utmost to appear casual. He had no wish to do what came next, but he'd carefully considered the alternatives and had accepted that this was the only way. The Venerate between them knew each of his faces. If he was identified too soon, this would all be for naught.*

*A few people gave him a second glance as he walked by, but travelers were not uncommon, even this far from a major town. It didn't really matter if they remembered what he looked like,* 689 anyway. He'd thought about choosing a more isolated spot—a farm, perhaps—but the risk had been too high. In that scenario, if no one had been home, his memories could have been gone before he found a replacement.

After a minute or two of aimless wandering, he spotted a young man strolling up to a quaint, thatch-roofed house that was set a little apart from the other buildings. Caeden checked to see that no one was looking his way, then hurried up to the stranger. He was little more than a boy, Caeden realized with a slight pang of regret—reddish-brown hair, blue eyes, and an easy smile. A farmer, probably. They almost all would be around here.

"Excuse me," Caeden said in a polite tone. "I'm a little lost. I was wondering if you had a map of the area?" He knew it was unlikely, but any excuse would do.

The young man shook his head, then nodded to the door. "Sorry, friend," he said. "No maps, but if you'd like to come inside, I'll see if I can help you out with some directions."

"I'd appreciate that," said Caeden. He kept his face carefully neutral, even as his stomach twisted. The poor lad was so trusting.

They were soon inside, and the door shut. "Now," said the boy, turning toward the simple hewn table. "If I can just—"

Caeden's long, thin blade caught him in the side of the throat, stabbing upward into his brain. He was dead before he hit the floor.

Caeden checked his memories. Nothing before the Siege of Al'gast; that was worryingly recent, not too long before he'd realized the Darecians had escaped. He got to work, taking note of the boy's features and then cutting into his face. It was horrible, stomach-turning work, but the body had to be unrecognizable. Even as he went about the grisly task, he concentrated, picturing the features of the young man he had just killed. Pain abruptly snapped through him, his bones breaking and reforming, muscles tearing, contorting, and stretching. Caeden gritted his teeth, but kept working as best he could. He was well accustomed to these transformations.

It was over in the space of a minute. Now all he had to do was dispose of the body and—

"Caeden?" a cheerful female voice called from the front door.
"Where are you, Son?"

Caeden's heart sank. There was no time, no way he could get the body out. He froze, keeping quiet, praying that the woman would not walk into this room.

An ear-piercing scream shattered that hope.

"Caeden!" the woman shrieked. She was looking wildly between Caeden and the disfigured body on the floor. "What are you doing?"

Caeden stood, his blade whipping out, slicing smoothly through the woman's throat before she could say anything more. She gurgled as she stared at what she thought was her son, uncomprehending horror in her eyes. Caeden looked away. She'd seen him in this form, seen what he'd done. He couldn't risk leaving her alive.

Before he could move, though, shouts from outside were followed by the sound of the front door crashing open. He closed his eyes for a second, breathing deeply.

Pretending it hadn't gone so wrong.

There were thirty-one dead by the end—seventeen men, nine women, and five children who had been drawn by the screams. Most of the village, he suspected.

He stared at the bodies morosely. It had all happened so fast, and it was getting harder to focus as more and more memories drained away. Could he have avoided this? Using Control hadn't been an option—Alaris would have located him within minutes. Fleeing would have meant leaving witnesses, which would have led to his inevitable capture, a quick trial, and a failed execution. Though the flow of information from Desriel to Talan Gol was still limited, word of something like that would have doubtless found its way back across the ilshara.

No. This way he'd probably be detained, suspected of what had happened here, but they wouldn't have the evidence to execute him. It was still a risk, but it left him hidden from the people who mattered. He hardened his heart against the guilt, as he'd done so many times before. It had been the best course of action in a bad situation. The practical, necessary choice.

He put his hand against the still-warm skin of each corpse in turn, then carefully disfigured them. Their deaths would not be for nothing. Even though he wouldn't remember them directly, their Imprints would remain with him; each one would eventually give him a new, untraceable identity, a body in which 691 *he could move freely outside Talan Gol. He'd not wanted it to come to this, but now that it had, there was no point wasting the opportunity.*

*He checked his memories, startled to find that his oldest one was of speaking to the Ath. That had been only a hundred years ago—not long before he'd finally rejected the name Aarkein Devaed, realized his mistakes, and started along the path that had ultimately led here. He knew he'd hated what he'd done, hated what he'd become as Devaed, but he couldn't remember the details anymore. Odd, but he supposed it didn't really matter now. He would be free of it all for good soon enough.*

*He finally turned away from the corpses, knowing he had only minutes left—nowhere near enough time to hide the bodies. He needed to flee, to get as far from here as he possibly could.*

*He ran.*

*He dashed into the forest heedlessly, ignoring how the twigs and branches scraped at his arms and legs, tugged and tore at his bloodied clothing. He had to survive a few weeks, just until Davian arrived with the Portal Box. He had to get far enough away to give the Gil'shar reason to doubt his guilt. If they tried to execute him, the Venerate would get word. It would jeopardize everything. It would jeopardize...*

*He frowned in confusion. Why was he running? Where was he? He glanced down, horrified to see blood all over his hands. He quickly checked himself, but aside from minor cuts, he did not seem to be wounded.*

*He took a deep breath, tried to concentrate. Why was he here? Panic began to set in. Where was he from? What was his name? He stood for a long few minutes, heart pounding, trying to recall something. Anything. But it was of no use.*

*He started forward. Evening was coming, and whatever had happened to him, he needed help.*


Caeden gasped as he came awake again.

He was on his knees, he realized numbly. Vomit spattered on the cold stone before him; his hands shook, and his entire body spasmed with heaving sobs.

"It's not true," he choked, staring up at Asar, who was watching him impassively.

"It is," he replied.

"But it can't be!" Caeden shook his head desperately, tears streaming down his face. The images of the people he'd killed flashed in a grisly parade before him. "No. I can't be him. I can't be Aarkein Devaed. *No.* I'm supposed to *fight* Devaed, to help *save* Andarra." His voice broke. "I *can't* be him."

Asar just stared at him. For a moment his expression was... pitying.

"You are who you are, Tal'kamar," he said softly. "When you're ready to know more, come and find me."

Without another word he turned and vanished back into the darkened passageway, leaving Caeden—Tal'kamar—alone to his grief.

# Acknowledgments

A big thank-you, first, is owed to all my alpha and beta readers—Ross, Nicki, Chiara, Aiden, Brett, Jeremy, Dean, David, Rex, Callum, Tim, Stuart, and (of course) Sonja. It's no small commitment to test-read a book of this size, and their feedback proved invaluable in honing *The Shadow of What Was Lost*.

Thanks also go to Pat, who read what was a very rough first draft and still managed to spot the promise in among its many flaws. To this day it amazes me that despite how much more work the story needed, he somehow delivered his critique with enough encouragement and tact that I ended up being inspired rather than deflated.

Finally I'd like to thank my family for all their encouragement over the past couple of years—and in particular my wife, Sonja, whose love, constant optimism, and ability to soothe my fragile ego kept me sane as I worked through each draft. This book is dedicated to her, as it could not possibly have existed if it were not for her enduring support.